I0650773

The Cosmos

The Runup

Book II

by

Professor Gamer

Edge Interactive Publishing
New York

Edge Interactive Publishing Inc.
15 China Circle Court
Carmel, NY 10512
212-581-3000

The Cosmos: The Runup: Book II

Copyright 2017 Edge Interactive Publishing Inc.
All rights reserved
Including the right of reproduction
In whole or in part in any media form. V1.0

This is a work of fiction.

Book designed by Fantasmo.

Created in the United States of America

Library of Congress Control Number: 2016961024

ISBN 978-0-9977487-4-1

First Edition

To Porn Stars and their Masturbators everywhere

Inspiration

Caliph Harun al-Rashid & Three Slave Girls: Compete for Prize

Caliph Harun al-Rashid, the subject of this tale told by Shahrazad in *The Thousand and One Nights*, was born in either 763 or 766 and ruled the fifth Abbasid Caliph in Baghdad from 786 until his death in 809, at the peak of the Islamic Golden Age. He was born in Rey, in what is now Iran, the son of al-Mahdi, the third Abbasid Caliph, and al-Khayzuran, a former slave girl from Yemen.

Whether or not Shahrazad recounts the facts correctly matters little to the Cosmos. Competition between and among the seven Pledge occurs in many ways. Some Cosmos do aspire to be concubines and slaves, some want to walk the middle path, and some of them will obtain influence whether they aspire to or not. The moral of Shahrazad's recounting however remains as true today as when the story evolved, and is relevant to all Gamers, and not just the Cosmos:

"The Caliph Harun al-Rashid once slept with three slave-girls, a Meccan, a Medinite and an Iraqi. The slave from Medina put her hand to his yard and handled it, whereupon it rose and the slave from Mecca sprang up and drew it to herself. The Medinite quoth to the Meccan, 'What is this unjust aggression? A tradition was related to me by Málik, after Al-Zuhri, after Abdallah ibn Sálim, after Sa'íd bin Zayd, that the Apostle of Allah (whom Allah bless and keep!) said: "Whoso enquickens a dead land, it is his."' And the Meccan answered, 'It is related to us by Sufyán, from Abu Zanád, from Al-A'araj, from Abu Horayrah, that the Apostle of Allah said: "The quarry is his who catches it, not his who starts it."' But the Iraqi girl pushed them both away and taking it to herself, said, 'This is mine, till your contention be decided.'" —And Shahrazad perceived the dawn of day and ceased to say her permitted say. —*The Thousand and One Nights*.

Table of Contents

Chant & Dialog

Game Mistress & Slavesex China Doll: Chant & Dialog

§ Slavesex: A Chant

Chant solo or in unison: "Please chastise your Slavesex and all its holes, bind it, beat it, piss it, fuck all its holes, and enslave it to cum."
Short version: "Please secure and force-cum Slavesex!"

§ Game Mistress & Slavesex: The Duality of Up & Down

It is Slavesex China Doll whom we hear speak first.
"So why are we here and why do we play the Game?"
Game Mistress (GM for shot) responds. "Stop. You're not allowed to be asking me questions!"
Slavesex persists. She is stark naked, of course, and has at least one hole opened for use. "Maybe the purpose of the Game is playing each moment."
"There you go. Just because you are Slavesex doesn't mean you are stupid."
"You're too kind. But Slavesex who ask questions need their mouths washed out with soap."
"Now you are telling me what to do again!" GM demurs while wagging a warning finger.
"But winning and losing—promotion vs. demotion—these are indeed arbitrary; each of these are their own opposite. We can't exist independently of the other!"
GM purses her lips. "So you're a philosopher now?"
"Maybe it's just chemical balance. Take the Cosmos. Half will Opt Up and become Monitors next Term, and half will Opt Down and go Strip."
GM wrinkles her brow, "Among other possible outcomes. So do you suggest that winning and losing are arbitrary?"
Slavesex must approach with delicacy now. *Arguing with GM has been known to be painful, like getting one's lips sewn shut with one's tongue sutured in place.* Slavesex pushes slowly forward, "Mistress, may it please you, Monitors have responsibilities to command and to mentor Pledge; whereas Strippers have responsibilities to undress, dance naked, and masturbate for the Crowd. Masturbate for the whole Prefecture."
"Some of them even want to compete with you for your position, Slavesex." Game Mistress says.

Slavesex rotates her finger insider her fuckhole and makes sure her clit is out and cream coated (one of her standing orders) while she composes her response, "Mistress, I beg you that there is no obvious truth as to which outcome is a 'better' position, for the Cosmos that is. Each outcome has advantages and disadvantages!"

"Just like with you and me," Game Mistress states.

"Mistress, please, Mistress keep me your total Slavesex. I am your bondage fuck, I am your Whore, your Strip Dancer, stealth Pledge, Monitor, MomCap, Madam, or even you, Mistress. I belong to you, inside and out. Feed me, fuck me, tie me down, rent me out. I am your Slavesex."

Game Mistress waves her arms to silence the outburst. "I guess the Cosmos Pledge will come to appreciate that winning and loosing are easy to mix up."

Slavesex offers, "Or they will get what they want. Look at us, Mistress, we're opposites and we're both happy."

"They're coming after you, kid, some already beg to be Strippers, one begs to Whore and re-acquire Porn Star status." GM pauses and considers. "Some will be drawn to the challenge, the excitement of the rise, the taken captive. Some will get pushed."

"You can tattoo and pierce me without limit. My entire skin counts as one tattoo. And all my piercings constitute one set. And I have multiple sets!"

GM says, "Gotta love the Game. Four ranks up, four ranks down: net change zero. No value judgment."

Slavesex agrees, "See, just because you are a GM doesn't mean you are stupid, Mistress."

It is a complement no matter how twisted one takes it. They laugh together. Then Slavesex once again tops from the bottom, "Now will you punish your Slavesex for asking a question?"

And GM is compassionate in her reply, "Asking two questions. So fetch me some soap...and a needle and thread."

And they speak together in unison: " I love you."

Plans and Elevations

The Cosmos House and Yard

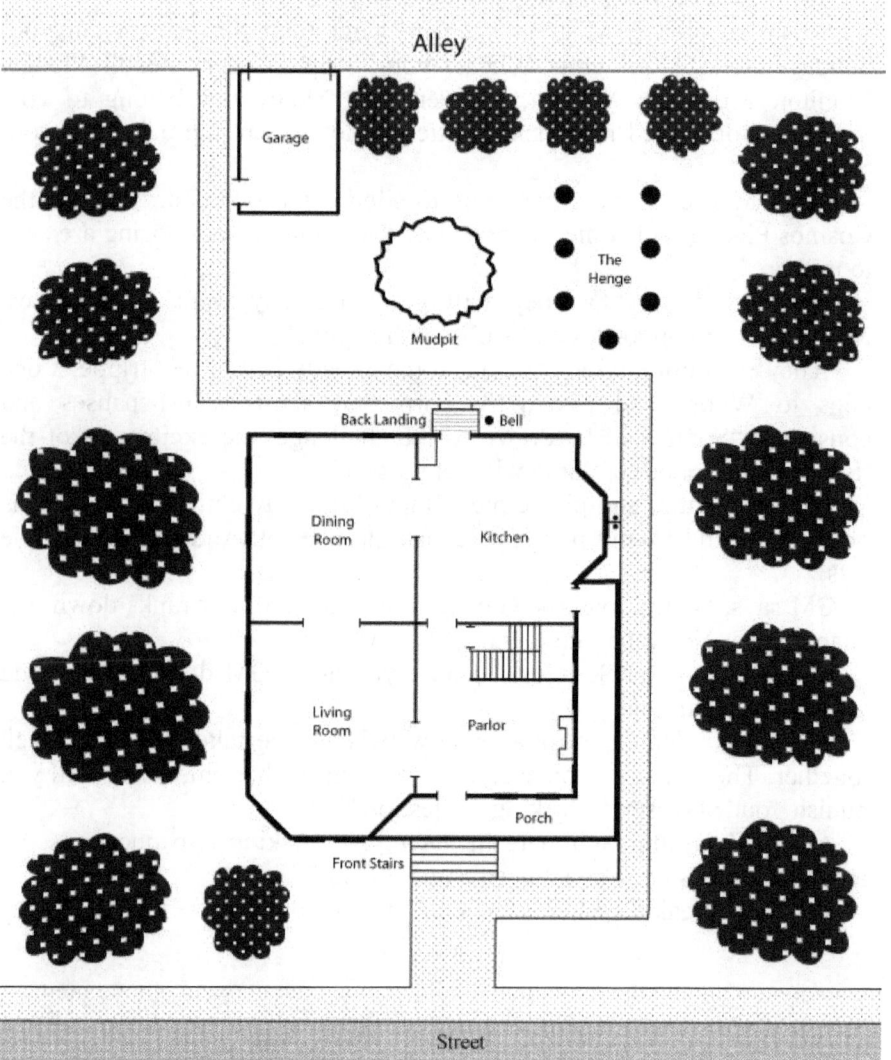

The Cosmos House First Floor Plan

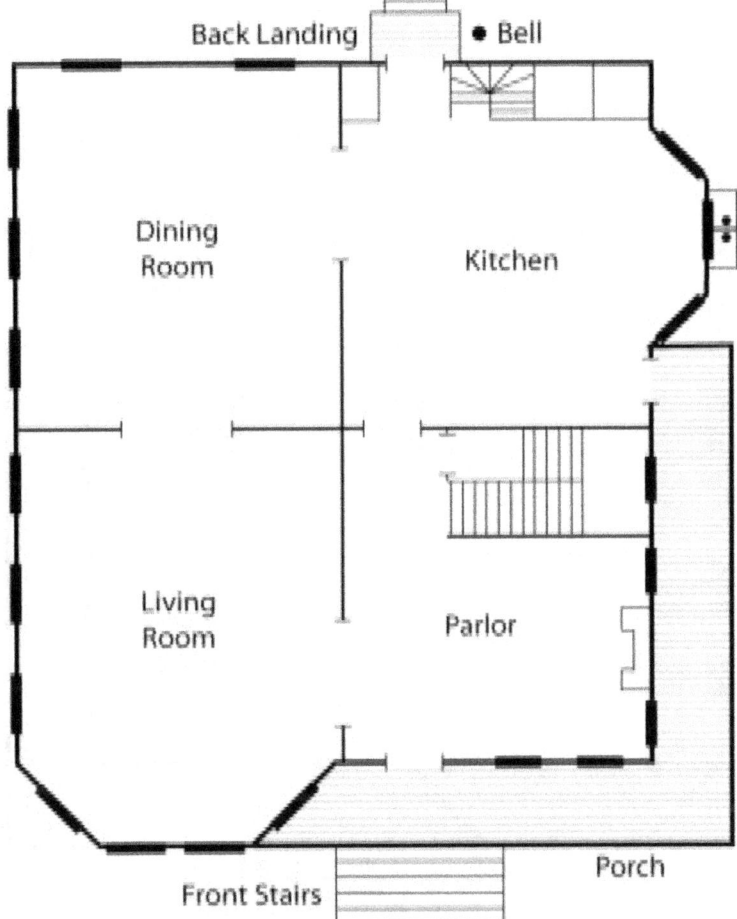

Back Landing   • Bell

Dining Room

Kitchen

Living Room

Parlor

Front Stairs

Porch

The Cosmos House Second Floor Plan

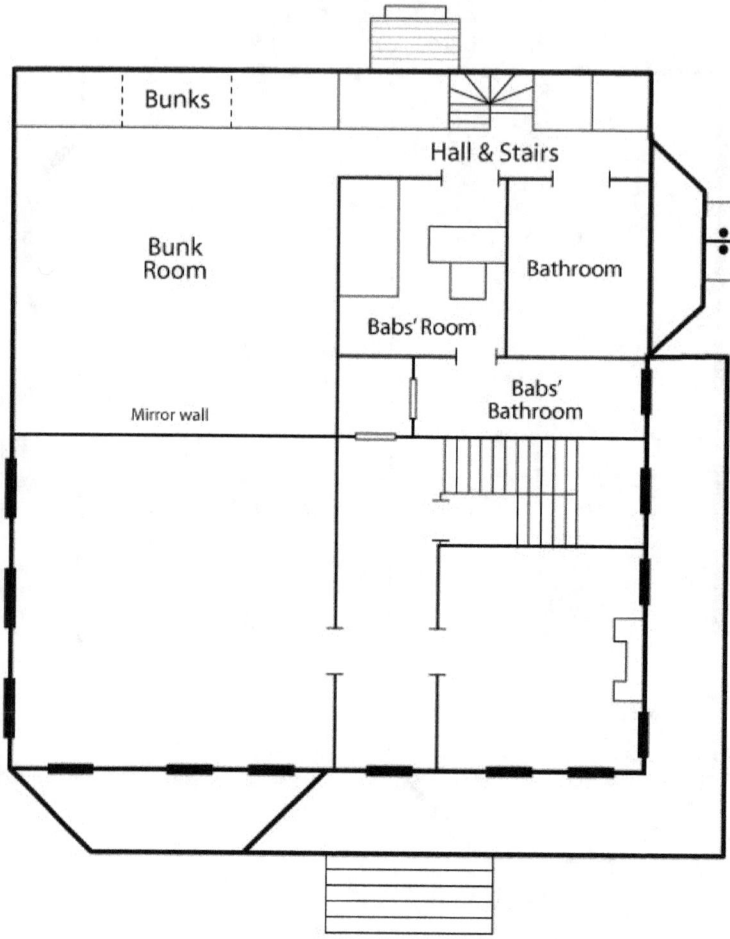

The Plan of the Nugget

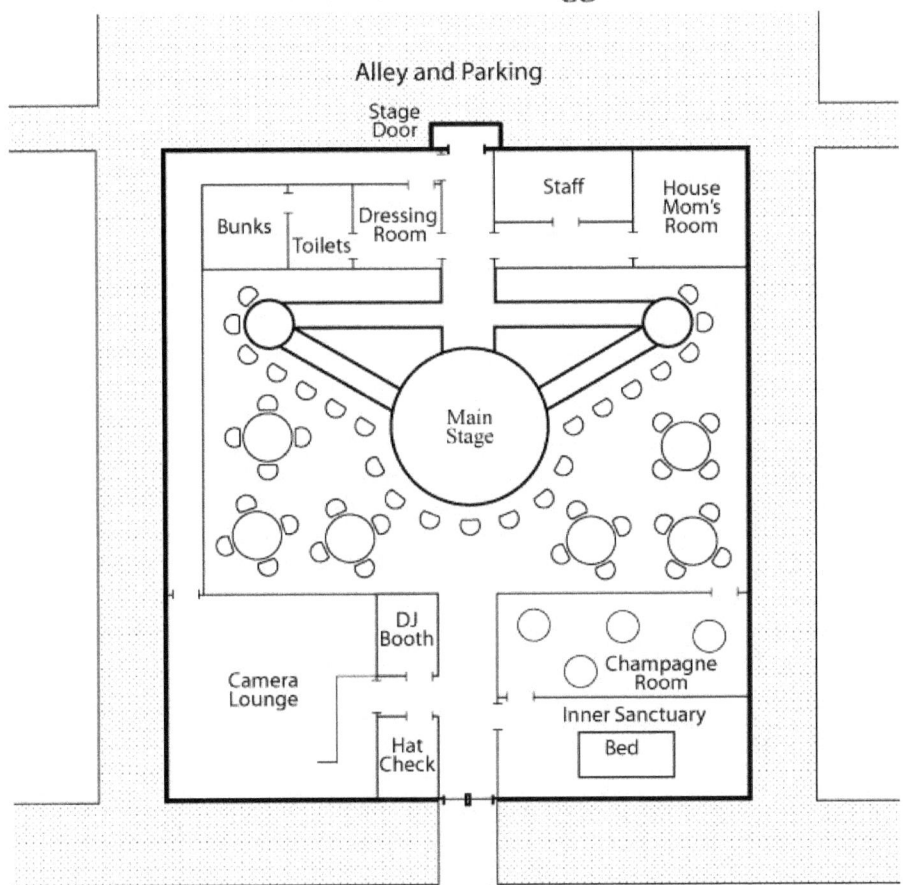

The Cosmos

Book II

The Runup

The Runup Begins: The Past of Current Events (D15)

II-1 Babs & Cosmos: Reveille & Costume Evaluation (D15)

§ Babs & Seven Cosmos Pledge: BB Examines Her Lineup

On the first morning of *The Runup* the stately and statuesque Monitor Babs examines her Cosmos Pledge, Lined up in the Backyard. *My Pledge,* Babs says to herself. *And I am their Boss Babe, a.k.a. BB.*

BB also means Bikini Babe, and in the mouths of some Cosmos, the "Bling Broad," the "Boss Bitch," and other concoctions.

BB lines up her brood of Cosmos Pledge for Reveille every morning, and today, the first Day of *The Runup* and Day Fifteen (D15) in the Term, is no exception. *The Arrivals* are over; *The Runup* has begun.

The Seven Pledge stand side-by-side in stand spread surrender position: legs spaced wide, postures erect, hands clasped behind their heads with fingers interwoven, elbows thrown back, armpits concave, bellies draw in, eyes straight ahead, mouths ovaled. All Cosmos show their belly buttons all of the time; Monitor Babs, in her Black Bikini, included. Navelage 24x7 is the first Cosmos Rule.

All of them, even Babs, are barefoot.

BB paces in front of them, tall, erect, and seemingly confident. She addresses her Pledge. "Now that you all have arrived the next part of the Term shall commence. According to School tradition, we call this *The Runup.* You will all compete to determine winners and losers, that is, who shall Opt Up and become Monitors next Term, and who shall Opt Down and become Strippers next Term. That may not be why you are here, but it is a way of the Game."

The Seven Cosmos Pledge digest this; some desire to Opt Monitor, some desire to Opt Strip.

"In the Game stay the Game," BB reminds her Pledge. "Perhaps some of you wish to learn how to handle power, perhaps some of you are pleasure junkies, perhaps some of you enjoy the dangers of challenges, others the pleasures of cheating, and perhaps some of you desire prison.

"Your Options and thus your Caste next Term relate to the acquisition and/or loss of power, and here at School this includes sexual power. Come next Term some of you may Opt Monitor and some of you may Opt Strip, but all of you will Option one way or the other. It is true some Castes—like mine—may Hover and stay the same Caste next Term, but your Caste, the Pledge, is required to Opt. One way or another."

The Game can be very binary… except when it is not.

Two of the seven Pledge who eye the prickly hedge along the side of the Backyard wonder who in the house next door might surveil them topless and bare-assed. They are Kimju and Molly, ex-Nugget Strippers, now Cosmos Pledge. Kimju continues to wear only a tanga; its waistband rides an inch or two below Kimju's belly button, the legline rides inside her pelvis and the backside totally bares Kimju's butt. Molly wears worn pale rose panties, only with the panties pulled into her moonshadow (her posterior rugage) so that both moons of her hairy fat magnus supply plump backsides to any paparazzi behind. Molly's accommodation allows her to equal Kimju's buttage exposure. *Kimju is always knockers and kabedis,* Molly knows. *And with my panties gathered backside I'm equal to her. I'm mammies and moons.*

The two topless tanga Pledge game for opposite Opts. Molly willingly begs to gather the front of her panties tight into her sex meat and bunch her muff out. She considers, *Kimju most reluctantly bares her boobs and butt and outlines her tanga with pussy hairage. Especially out here in quasi-public view, with the Cam and paparazzi loose. But so what if anybody can look or whole Prefecture sees me. I'm safe. And if I can tighten my panties all the way in Kimju won't beg to follow. Leaving me a better change of Opt Stripping next Term.*

Kimju holds topless tanga. *Boobage buttage or whatever you call it.* Kimju holds her tongue in her back teeth to help her not forget to close her oval-mouth. *I need to Opt Up next Term,* she confirms silently as she keeps her eyes forward. I don't like standing here with my knockers exposed. But that's trivial. *I had to pullaside, pink, cream, and climax during* The Arrivals, *and I still don't have a clear path toward a second Garment.* Kimju blinks slowly. *Molly's begging to yank her panties into her mooe, and if she does, Gamers will want to see what I do. Right now I'm not begging anything. But I do need to acquire a second piece somehow, if I expect to Opt Up.*

Molly, who stands next to Kimju in the Lineup, has also gotten to pink, cream, and climax. *Except she wants to,* Kimju frets, *she's also gotten herself a Pee-Cam and Piss Mouth; and these are particularly hazardous.* Kimju's knockers are smaller that Molly's massive mams, and she is taller and weighs less than her squat companion. The Back Door Cam, which has detached itself from its post near the Back Door, hovers in front of the twosome and collects every detail of Kimju's knurled knobs and Molly's minarets.

Babs takes a deep breath and walks around behind the Lineup and goes out of view (although not out of mind) to the Lineup. BB paces herself. *My time to think.* She crisscrosses her hands across her low-cut underwire bra and her deep, formidable cleavage between widely-spaced shoulder straps. But more significantly, Babs covers her bling, the two crescents d'areolage where her bra barely encases the bullets centered in that deep maroon disc topping each bosom.

Panic attack. Look at me: I'm covering myself up. Hiding my bling. Am I so insecure I can't stand the paparazzi and Cam? No, they've already collected me over and over. I'm good.

Babs looks at the backs of her two topless and bare-butted Pledge and lowers her hands so she can finger her areolage. *Bling! Except Kimju and Molly being topless all the time really isn't areolage or even titter. The first thing anyone who looks at me sees is my areolage, my bling; I'm BB, Bikini Babe, Bling Babe, and everyone knows it.* Babs takes a deep breath. *All my Pledge know it too. But they also know I can influence Options. Some of them think I can order them to build a fire in the Parlor, toss every Garment in, and they'll all be Strippers next Term. Ha! Maybe I'm still Bikini Babe, but I am the Boss Babe now!*

Babs braces herself. Shall I order Kimju and Molly to handbra and tease areolage? Draw attention away from my own bling? I know the answer: I'll do what's best for me. Boss Babe is good to go. Monitor Babs rolls her shoulders and moves her hands to her hips. Bling!

Babs steps backward from the row of backs, buttocks, and legs. Barefoot all, bare-belly all. The two ex-Strippers present the only bare butts; several more Cosmos are cheeking. She scans down the Lineup, and settles upon the newbies. On the end, Elle's back, a bare back except for halter neck and back straps and very cheeky shorts. Boss Babe ruminates. *I was a newbie Pledge last Term but never what Gamers call Low Girl on the Lineup. And the other newbie next to her, Beka, she wants to go wild.* BB tightens her thoughts. *Yes, I'm now playing my second Term, and I have to admit that my commitment to Bikini Babe facilitated my promotion from Pledge last Term. My crescents d'areolage get a permanent tan and I presented my Black Bikini body to every Gamer in the Prefecture. Now I'm BB the Boss Babe. Like today the Cam collects me; this has been my only way Up.*

BB scans her eyes to the opposite end of the Lineup and observes Tiffany, the lithe redhead and first Girl on the Lineup. Tiffany wears a clear vinyl, front-button, longsleeve croptop and low-rise stretch slacks. From the back the slacks ride so low across Tiffany's tush that the top of her tail trough rises out. *Her posterior rugage,* Babs knows. *My bikini nombril was so low that I had to do that last Term.* BB fingers her own bikini's waistline, *a daring, but not obscene, four inches below my belly button. Maybe I had to crack butt last Term, but I don't any more!*

Babs also knows that from the front side Tiffany's slacks ride so low that her red thatch erupts above her waistline. *Hairage,* Babs knows. *My bikini nombril was so low that I had to do that last Term. Not any more!*

Tiffany's stretch slacks fit so tightly that they part her tush whenever she moves, and so tight in her crotch that her cameltoe can't avoid stain marks. *I never did anything like that,* Babs assesses.

Babs considers her place. *A few blocks away from where I am now the School buildings face onto a Quad. I did well in School when I was a Pledge last Term. I know that Tiffany's tits in see-through don't qualify as a topless Pledge, even though everyone can see everything through her clear vinyl shirt. The Game can be particular like that; after all, the shirt matters, transparent or not.*

Topless is when you don't wear anything at all up top. *I remember last Term during the Mudwrestling Contest when my own babambas got spilled out. When Janet and I defeated Penny and Coco. We achieved Monitor Caste, and Penny and Coco were forced to Opt Strip.*

BB casts an eye at the Pledge in a maillot and the Pledge wearing a minidress. *Robyn and Steph—one refereed the Mudwrestling Contest and doesn't remember, and the other wasn't there.*

Boss Babe squares her shoulders and bounces her busty bazoombas. *Will I be making any quick moves and popping nipples today?* Babs knows. *Won't be any of that!*

Tiffany is in on that secret. Babs lets Tiffany use the Makeup Case and apply all the Cosmos' makeup.

Babs' olive-colored bare belly glistens in the morning sunlight; her bikini nombril still grips her curvy hips and she fingers her belly button, *the cratered remains of a center-knot.* May Bikini Babe be diligent her bikini waistline stays above her full bush and keeps it hidden... just barely. She checks behind to ensure that her bikini bottom exposes neither rugage nor butt cheeks. *It's a balancing act.* BB rests her hands on her hips. *I'm learning. The Black Bikini is symbolic yet also malleable. And I know I have much to learn.*

Babs does consider her bling. *Areolage. Yes, I know that sometimes the crescents bubble up and Kundalini endeavors to seek my favor.*

Probably true. Kundalini is a sexual Sprit that drives Nature forward and is thus a component of the Universe. Energy force resides in all living things on planet Earth, humans and Gamers included.

Some say the spirit of Kundalini may also be found in inanimate objects including physical Props and fetishes, in shapes and forms (e.g., a cross, a vesica piscis), and ideas shaped and recognized by humans, especially ideas about power, including sexual powers, where the Kundalini specializes.

Sometimes Kundalini emerges as a coiled snake wrapped around a Gamer's spinal cord or food track. Sometimes Kundalini constructs around an erection or vagina, bites nipples, or loosens itself into kissing lips. Permitting Kundalini to emerge entails surrender as well as controlling aggression. The art of making Love.

I know Kundalini is loose, BB admits to herself. *And I know the vocabulary of Kundalini entails every possible kind of contact among life forms: mind body and soul. Wildness as well as control.*

With Seven Pledge and Kundalini loose, Babs, as well as her Monitor alter ego Boss Babe, knows *I must devote my own mind, body, and soul to not just to myself, but the entire Cosmos House. I must sacrifice for my Caste power.*

"You must absolve yourself of any and all guilt of making Pledge wait for you," her superior, House Mom el Capitan—MomCap—had warned her; and so Babs practices... and allows her Pledge to wait. *Learning persistence is a good thing for all of us.*

"But you are also responsible for their faults," MomCap had added.

BB positions herself behind Steph and Beka and Elle. Steph and Beka were last seen yesterday in the Dining Room as *The Arrivals* concluded, face down on spread knees, worshiping the Baseboard Strippers, the naked and pinking pictures showing ex-Cosmos and now-Strippers Penny and Coco.

Yesterday both Steph and Beka wore a minidress and miniskirt and availed their pubes the world. They still wear skirts today, more correctly, Steph wears a strapless minidress with a cutout hole around her navel, and Beka sports a croptop and low-rise miniskirt. Standing as they do with their legs spread and their bodies stretched, and their hands clasped behind their heads, neither the short minidress nor the short miniskirt entirely cover their crease of their buttocks.

No problem. Boss Babe reaches around from behind to lift Steph's minidress just enough to reveal soft blonde wavy hairs for any paparazzi out ahead, then lifts Beka's miniskirt to reveal a bare box with a racing stripe upstairs. Babs steps backward and watches the minidress and skirt slowly slide back down the buttocks, come to rest on the hips so that the hemlines neither quite cover the standing spread crotches.

Babs takes a breath. She looks around and watches the Cam collect butt shots, then buzz around to the front of the Lineup to collect scruff and a shaven box. *I would never have done that at the beginning of the Term,* BB admits to herself. *But Steph deserves it, and Beka's a wannabe Stripper then Whore. I'm sure Gamers want them to continue to titter and vagflash—solo and together. Too bad they have opposite goals and each has the wrong number of pieces.*

BB contemplates. *Steph I know from last Term; she was my Monitor, now she's my Pledge. And Beka, the newbie? She's already earned her name Beka Broda because she is so horny she creams all the time.*

Well, not *all* the time.

Kimju and Molly might cream and climax, and Steph and Beka might titter and vagflash together, and but neither couple are Roommates.

Indeed, it is Molly and Steph who are Roommates. Beka's Roommate is
Elle, next to her and on the end of the Lineup. Kimju's Roommate is the
one Cosmos Pledge Boss Babe has saved for last, Robyn. Robyn stands
second on the Lineup, between Tiffany on the head end, and Kimju.

Babs walks around to the front of the Lineup and audits the seven
pairs of eyes and seven oval mouths. Only Robyn, alone among the
Cosmos, permits herself to follow Babs with her eyes. *Yes, I know
Robyn; she sneaks her eyes around. Later.* The rest of the Cosmos
Lineup remains unaware of Robyn's transgression and keep their heads
held high, and their eyes stoically forward and their mouths ovaled; not
even Robyn dares pivot a head, just her eyes.

"Pay attention," Babs coaches them, "Hold position. Don't speak
unless you are spoken to."

Babs quietly considers MomCap's advise. *I am learning I need not to
rush. My Cosmos will wait for me. Wait all day if it is convenient for me,
if only because I have taken charge.*

Babs formalizes to her Pledge. "During *The Runup,* Gamers and I will
hear your pleas and assess your prospects for Options. I'm sure you know
Roommates may exchange and share Garments and shall first compete in
Roommate Games. And all of you shall beg forfeits. You shall please
me."

BB explains a tactical detail, "During *The Runup* we shall determine
our first pair of outcomes; one Opt Monitor and one Opt Strip shall
precipitate out." BB raises an arm while wiggling fingers. She provides
another factoid, *"The Runup* will end on the eve of *The Beach Day*, but
that's a couple weeks away, and a lot will happen between now and then.
Besides trading Garments, and some of you may also exchange Props and
Obeisance."

Boss Babe pauses and allows the Cosmos to fret. Newbies Beka and
Elle think that a lot has happened already. They have never experienced a
Beach Day. Tiffany, Kimju and Molly all have, although at different
points in the Game. Who knows what Robyn Redacted remembers?

Former Monitor Steph furrows her brow; like the current Monitor
Babs, Steph was once a Pledge, she was a Monitor once (last Term), and
now I'm a Pledge again. Except I expect to gain a Garment, end the
Beach Day with two, and Opt Monitor next Term.

Monitor Babs and all the Pledge know that the Term will end at
Midnight on *The Beach Day,* two weeks from now, when the Fates of
each Cosmos will be finalized. Any Pledge with two Garments will Opt
Up and become a Monitor next Term. Any Pledge with one or no
Garments will Opt Down and Strip. It's very simple.

§ Babs & Seven Cosmos: Evaluates Whose Clothes to Take

Babs knows she and all of the Cosmos Pledge in the Backyard present themselves not only a live capture by the hovering Back Door Cam, but also expose themselves to the telephotos of paparazzi who can't trespass but can spy from afar. Babs uses the big Desktop in her Bedroom to control what Cosmos House Cams feed to the Prefecture and get digested in Automatron, but she can't control who watches from the back alley or next door. So the paparazzi points-of-view get collected without the Cosmos'—including Boss Babe's—interference.

I can't stop the Gamers who look in and purview me, let alone my Pledge, but I shall not let them impede with my *evaluations and plans.*

BB mulls. *Have I become more comfortable with being exposed? Perhaps. But if I have then why do I avoid confrontation with my earlier, hairaged, self-displays atop the Dining Room Pictures?* Babs grits. *I am not going to reveal any signs of weakness!* She scans the Lineup quickly, tilts her head back in the sunlight, and makes a decision. *I will take clothes as soon as it pleases me. Make no mistake about it.*

Boss Babe considers the crescents of areola that remain exposed in the wide-strapped underwire bra. *Areolage sill soon lie behind me. My exposure is already in Automatron. And do I like exposing myself? Hummm. I do want to cover up, but I shall do it on my terms and my pace. Because now I have Kundalini power now.*

I might have had to become a Bikini Babe to become the Cosmos Monitor, but now that I am, I shan't be Bikini Babe much longer. BB purses her lips.

So does BB consider wardrobe candidates as she walks up and down the Lineup? She does. And does her Lineup wonder about how BB might advance her coverage? That part with a brain does.

§ Babs & Tiffany: Is Tiffany Transparent Too Toxic?

The tall House Monitor pauses in front of her Roommate and signs Tiffany to step forward thrice so Babs may speak to Tiffany in confidence.

Tiffany's stretched stomach glistens with sweat, and Babs drags a fingernail up the side of her belly below the clear croptop. It tickles, Tiffany jiggles, and Babs drolly remarks, "You act like you are begging for electricity." She wipes the electrolytic sweat across Tiffany's lips.

Tiffany kisses Babs' fingertips and replies coyly, "Oh, no Ma'am, I'm a Pee-Cam Piss Mouth Cosmos Pledge begging to Strip. Only Slavesex get shocked!"

Babs sighs in mock resignation, "And I though all along you were a Porn Star."

They laugh together carefully, knowing that Tiffany's Porn Star past carries momentum and that Tiffany possesses a boomeranging desire to reunite with her previous Caste. Make new Suck Fuck Facial Videos. Tiffany keeps her fingers interlocked behind her head and her armpits cupped.

"I guess Opt Striping next Term gets you halfway to Porn Star," Babs says.

Astute Gamers already know BB will not be trading her bikini for Tiffany's see-through shirt or vulgar hip-huggers. One reason Tiffany and Babs get along well is because Babs finds Tiffany's costume toxic. Another reason is that *although Tiffany's former Whore's experience gives her an advantage and makes her dangerous, it also renders her useful. Informatic. Roommates working together, albeit different Castes and with different Opt goals.*

Babs takes her time to consider her Roommate and most experienced Cosmos Pledge. *I don't think Tiffany has a lethal personality, but I must remain leery and respectful.* Babs flashes on a question she had asked Corvette Monitor Janet, "How does a Whore Double Opt Up, acquire two pieces, and become my Cosmos Pledge? In a Game where even Strippers promote topless or nude." Babs had playfully poked Janet. "Hello, Janet, any more secrets you want to share with me?"

Janet had twisted her lips to one side and said, "No. I mean, Tiffany took on a Piss Mouth to avoid Slavesex, but she could have just as well have promoted to Stripper. Piss Mouth didn't earn her a Double Opt Up. But hey, ask her, she's your Pledge."

Babs appreciates that Tiffany stands spread surrender and waits for her, oval-mouth, eyes forward. BB makes a decision. Now is not the time to go deep with Tiffany.

Babs teases Tiffany. "You can beg me for a more opaque shirt you know, so Gamers can't see your titties through clear vinyl anymore."

Tiffany cants, "Ma'am, please let me wear an opaque shirt, Ma'am. Go ahead, frustrate me and force me to cover up. But Ma'am, my Eraser Head always stand up and make headlights, and I keep my cameltoe tacky. Gamers will demand I take any opaque shirt off and beg you to burn it, Ma'am."

"Enough out of you," BB retorts, "I'm not into destruction."

Tiffany begs, "Ma'am, please let me pledge topless, bottomless, full-frontal naked. I'll shave bare and bald and stay naked. I'll pink and cream for you. I'll rub and finger-fuck myself to climax. I'll cum on a dildo, I'll cum on a plug up my tailpipe, I'll cum on your finger down my throat.

I'll cum if you allow me to Double Dong. Please let me Pledge naked and cum be a Stripper next Term!"

Babs startles. "That's quite a mouthful!" She exclaims.

"I mean every word," Tiffany asserts. "I'm a wannabe Stripper wannabe Porn Star. I'll do anything to get to the Nugget next Term. You can sit your bush on my face. I'll drink your pee."

"You'll do nothing of the sort." BB laughs. "You'll just be my friend and help me navigate the Game. I'll make sure you get to the Strip. You make sure I make House Mom el Capitan."

"Ma'am, thank you, Ma'am," Tiffany says.

"You can take on some of my Karma," Boss Babe suggests.

"Ma'am." Tiffany expounds.

"You can take on any new bad Karma I accrue." BB dictates.

Tiffany hesistates and warily advances, "Ma'am punish me for your sins, Ma'am."

"Better perhaps you can satisfy any favors I owe," Boss Babe suggests.

Tiffany hesitates. "Ma'am that would be an honor for me," she accepts.

Babs purses her lips. "Janet sat twice for the Figure Drawing Class last Term; I never went. She danced naked at least two Bachelor Parties. I never did. She climaxed naked in the Mudpit, once for each of us. Finally she auditioned the Nugget."

Babs pauses and looks at Tiffany, "Wait, you were there that night, yes?"

"Ma'am yes I was!" Tiffany formalizes. "But maybe she didn't do that for you, Ma'am. After all, Janet had been a Stripper before, and it was her Alumni Reprise. You might recall that she and I climaxed the Dong together and she gave me Piss Mouth."

Babs says, "Any other pearls of history I should know about?"

Tiffany shrugs, "Janet and I shared the Shaving Kit when we were Stripper Roommates two Terms ago; that's when she transferred her Pee-Cam to me. But the Piss Mouth is much harder core."

Babs rolls her shoulders. "So if I owe Janet some Karma you'll work if off for me, right?" she asks.

Tiffany pauses, and focuses, "Ma'am giving Janet power over me wasn't exactly what I had in mind, you know, she has ground me before and she doesn't need to grind me any more."

BB remains silent.

Tiffany expounds, "Ma'am, I can do all of those things. I've done Figure Drawing Classes just like Molly did and I've done Bachelor Parties except I danced naked, popped ping pong balls outta my twat, and blew every cock. I'm there. I worked Flesh Ranch. I'll Audition the

Nugget. I can pretty much do anything Janet can do, has done, I mean, hello, I was a Porn Star." Tiffany tilts her head and looks Babs in the eyes, "Some people think I'm still a Porn Star."

"You were a Whore." Boss Babe states.

"You make me insist I'm a wannabe Porn Star," Tiffany retorts, "so that's what I am. If you want me to be a wannabe Whore, I am a wannabe Whore. Janet was never a Whore. We were both Strippers, yes, but I outrank her in depth of the Game. Right now she's a Caste above me, but overall, I've been deeper into the Game than she has ever been. I've not just danced and solo Cam sex, I've shot porn and I've performed live sex shows at conferences. I've gangbanged an entire Bachelor Party."

"Janet streaked to get to and from the Nugget," Babs recalls. "How did you get there?"

"Me?" Tiffany startles, "Flesh Ranch dressed me however they wanted, and then they sent me out. Maybe I street-walked a Wild Patch. Or maybe a nice hotel with a dress over lingerie and hose. But I never had to streak to get anywhere, including the Nugget. Streaking is against the Rules. So if you owe Janet streaking Karma, I'm not sure that's transferable."

"Interesting." Babs fingers her bling, distends two fingers into the top of her bra and pinches her bullets. She says, "Molly streaked to the Bachelor Party. Maybe she has more commitment to becoming a Stripper than you do?"

"Ma'am may it please you to streak me I'll do it." Tiffany stumbles and looks down at her body. Eraser Heads in see-through, red thatch above the waistline below the button, tangy cameltoe. She must elaborate, "Ma'am, you must understand that I'm not like some other streaker who gets caught and ends up in the Stocks or cuffed around the Flagpole. I do have a lot of Porn Star clips out there. Gamers will claim I'm a Runaway and secure me in Lockdown. They'll strap me down naked, three hole me, clamp my nipples and clit, drench me with splooge and gangbang me for hours. Days even. I'm worth their maintenance; they'll rent me out and Cam me. I won't even get sentenced until the end of the Term, and when that happens I'm Slavesex. You'll never get me back. Not this Term, not ever."

Babs scratches her head, "Really now. Molly isn't valuable enough for them to keep after they sex her, but you'd be a prize? Interesting."

"Ma'am, excuse me. I'm a Porn Star who avoided Slavesex with a Piss Mouth and Double Opted Up. Gamers want me gangbanged again. They want me dunked in a tank of semen. They want me secured in a cage, three-hole plugged, gas-masked, and machine fucked. They want me totally helpless, Mind, Body and Soul. I am cool with the gangbang and even dunking me in a tank of semen or even machine fucked. It's the cage and blindfold and gag and earpods that scare me."

Babs accepts, "You just keep staying valuable to me."

"Ma'am may I please you, Ma'am," Tiffany respects, "And perhaps you should have Steph streak, after all, 'Roommates share,' and she's Molly's Roommate."

"Your thoughts are always productive!" BB complements. Any other favorites?" Babs smiles.

Tiffany softens, "Well, you know I hate Robyn. Well, I don't *hate* her, I just despise her, but no, I take that back, I don't even despise her, she's just who she is. And I so want her to Opt Strip. But for all the wrong reasons." Tiffany grabs her chin. "She's not like a Molly, or even a Beka, who covet the Stripper Caste. It because it's the only way to put Robyn toward Slavesex, and they will love her there, because she will be one of the rare Slavesex who don't want to be there."

"You're cruel," Babs laughs. "She's completely dangerous. She remembers everything differently and any action she takes damages those nearby. She needs to be locked in a cell so she can't hurt the Pledge around her, especially her Roommate Kimju."

"Well, before your order Robyn to streak to the Stocks and lock herself in, may I suggest you order that she and Kimju Flip-Flop. She will go bananas having to go topless." Tiffany grins. "And Kimju would appreciate the gesture. She'd still only have one piece, but she wouldn't be topless any more.

"I worry Robyn might flee!" BB says. "And that can't happen. If she 'wanders off' I could get in trouble for that."

"Maybe you'd get into trouble if I streaked and got caught," Tiffany adds.

BB smiles. The two look at each other and laugh together.

§ Babs Considers Beka & Elle: Newbies Begging to Strip

Babs turns her consideration to the two newbie Pledge, Beka and Elle. Each wear two garments, just like herself and Tiffany. "And what do my favorite titty teasers have to say today?" Babs inquires.

The Roommates stiffen. They stand spread surrender position and operate their mouths in unison, "Please let me Pledge naked and become a Stripper next Term."

Boss Babe appreciates their proper response. "And a wish worthy of granting!" she exalts.

BB hangs faux-curious thought, "You vagflashers too?"

And "Ma'am yes Ma'am, I'll do anything to go Strip next Term." Beka replies, but Elle is silent.

"Don't worry Pledge," Boss Babe disses them, "It's no secret *I* am looking to cover up more. But unfortunately I find no component of your costumes worthy of impoundment."

BB addresses Beka, "You can keep your open armhole croptop and low-slung miniskirt."

BB circumrotates her head toward Elle, "You can keep your too-loose halter and notched belly-button and ripped shorts. You keep right on leaning over and tittering, and pull your seam into your crotch."

BB steps back and nods to the both of them, "What you wear might be excellent for advancing *your* Caste, but titters and vagflash do not advance me. I'm a Hover or a MomCap next Term. Don't ever forget that."

Elle feels her jean shorts tighten themselves up into her crotch and cue her curlies to sneak out the sides of the legholes. She flinches, but keeps her legs spaced wide, her hands behind her head. Smooth armpits.

Boss Babe catches Elle's unease, points, speaks, "Don't worry, you can beg a Flip-Flop with Beka and eliminate that seam in your nookie."

Elle furrows her brow and discovers her body has gone into a soft shake. "Ma'am," Elle protests, "Gamers already look at me." Elle breaks a rule when she asks a question, "They don't need to look up a miniskirt."

BB consoles, "You're gonna tease however much Gamers demand that you tease. You're going to share the parts of you that don't belong to you any more."

Elle tries to steal a glance at Beka but gets caught. Elle's recall leads her mind; just yesterday Elle confided to Beka, "You know, I'm finding out that our status is a lot less certain than what we had assumed it would be when we arrived."

Beka had shrugged her shoulders but didn't argue, "Babs is not our only threat, Elle," Beka had insisted, "especially now that we're into *The Runup.* Now things start to get real."

"You're meat," Robyn had spit at them shortly thereafter, "You have no control over who might play what Game with you and with what Rules."

"Rules?" both newbies asked together.

The viper had forked her tongue out, "Boss Bitch might let you both promote unfettered… in your sexy office outfits, or she might make you compete against each other, she might make you compete against another pair of the Roommates, or she just might strip you both naked and throw your clothes in the fire."

Beka and Elle had considered this threat. Elle had pushed both lips out together, pouting while she thought about it.

Robyn had kept dishing it out, "Hey, here's some gossip, Kimju and Steph view you two newbies as *costume resources*. Steph's only wearing a minidress and all Kimju's got is a thong. So they both need an extra piece if they wanna Opt Up. And they do. They're gonna strip you naked, shave you bare and bald, and send you to pink, cream, and cum at the Nugget."

Robyn had given it a beat to sink in and had added a slammer, "Besides, you're both already begging to Opt Strip! It's over for you."

Elle had cringed at this but Beka had made wet.

"Enjoy, losers," Robyn pranced out, "Thank me sometime."

Elle gathers her thoughts back to the moment. *I am standing spread surrender in the Lineup, eyes forward, oval mouth. This is not the time to glance at Beka. Once before when Beka looked when she wasn't supposed to I ended up in the Doghouse. I don't want to do that to her. Or give Boss Babe a reason to blindfold us.*

Elle twitches her pelvis, and realizes that her bladder speaks to her. Robyn's prophesy confirms a vibe Elle feels now and then. Elle double checks she holds her position firmly and allows herself a thought, *Now that The Runup commences begging to "Pledge naked" becomes less of a lark and a more serious consideration. And the destination more real.* Elle stumbles in her thought, corrects herself from moving her lips, and chases the thought, *Destination? Off to the Nugget. And something about staying naked 24x7. And dancing naked too.*

Babs moves to the next Pledge, Roommate Beka. Boss Babe tests to ensure three fingers can lay into this crotch, a shaven vulva now level with the bottom of Beka's miniskirt. Beka's crotch presents spicy béchamel; BB wipes her palm dry on Beka's face.

"Thank me Beka Broda," BB commands, "for cleaning your boneroo off and wiping it all over your face.

Beka answers quickly, "Ma'am thank you Ma'am. Anytime you want I will finger myself, show you a pink butterfly, and climax."

Elle wishes Beka would be less forthcoming.

§ Babs Signs Kimju & Molly: Topless to Handbra & Buttage

Once Babs concludes her analysis of the Cosmos who wear both tops and bottoms; the tall buxom Monitor turns her attention to the four Cosmos who wear only one costume piece, either a maillot or minidress or panties or thong.

The two former Strippers—Kimju and Molly—are both seasoned Gamers but however over-exposed they remain today, neither Kim's topless thong and Molly's topless panties provide solutions to Babs' indecent areolas. Trades or takings? No thank you.

Babs knows what is expected. She locates Molly's Watering Can sitting near the Bell, and the astute Molly hears the water filling it up somewhere behind her. Babs appears in front of her eyes-forward vision, raises the can, and pours. Molly's body twists and her baggy sacks sway at the onset of cold water; goose bumps erupt out of her skin and fat belly, her areolas pucker up like a moonscape, and both nipples erect like minarets. But Molly holds her stand spread surrender position. Her soaked panties become totally transparent, sag, and reveal a thick black minge, not just above the waistband, but also in see-through.

"Thank me." Babs commands, and Molly responds, "Ma'am thank you for my Watering Can. And for watering me. Ma'am."

Alone among the Cosmos only Molly retains all of her body hair. All the Cosmos retain hair on their heads and some of the hair on their pubes and pudenda; all but Molly keep their legs and underarms shaven. Boss Babe graces Molly's long black hair, then feels the inside of Molly's hairy and damp armpit with the back of her hand; Molly is not only completely unshaven, she's also a very hairy person, with thick black growth on her arms and legs, and her belly and butt too.

Babs issues a complement, "Some Gamers get very put off by this, but others find you beautiful."

Ma'am, thank you, Ma'am," Molly speaks at her most formal best, "All my hair belong to you. Please let me forfeit my panties to Steph. Please let me Pledge naked and cum be a Stripper next Term."

Boss Babe collects a breath of fresh air. *I'd always assumed Molly wanted to Opt Strip, but I never heard her beg so directly.* BB responds, "So it's official then. You're the fourth Cosmos begging to Opt Down. You join Tiffany, the first Cosmos to beg and one deeply committed, and the two newbies—Beka and Elle—who pronounce more nuanced begs." Babs looks Molly in the eye, then continues. "But of the four of you, *you're* the only one who qualifies. One Garment. Tiffany and the newbie Roommates each have two pieces."

Boss Babe nods her head, grabs Molly's now-soaked panties with two hands in front, and works them tightly upward, burying them deep into Molly's mooe as well as into the crack of her ass, her moonshadow. Molly rises onto tiptoes to avoid hurt. BB steps back. Molly's thick black muff erupts to both sides of the buried panties.

"Make sure you keep them like that." Boss Babe commands.

"Ma'am, thank you for exposing me, Ma'am," Molly speaks hurriedly. "I'll dance nude, I'll pink and cream and cum for you."

"You're telling me what you've already done, BB affirms. "You're a streaker too, yes?"

"Ma'am," Molly peddles slowly, "Please let my Roommate take on my streaking. Streaking to the Bachelor Party was no picnic. It's time you let my Steph take on this Obeisance, Ma'am."

Boss Babe studies her Pledge, "Excellent, Pledge. Tell us some more of your accomplishments during *The Arrivals* here at the Cosmos House."

Molly gushes, "Ma'am er, ah, I am your second Pee-Cam Pledge."

"Indeed." Babs seeks to raise, "And what did you audition over at the Bachelor Party?'

Molly squirms and the goose bumps flash to life again. "Ma'am, I practiced a Piss Mouth, Ma'am," finally comes out.

"You won't forget that?"

"Er, ah, no Ma'am. You can see a shot of me peeing outdoors on my Pink Page. If you let me I'll pullaside, pink, and finger my holes. I'll twist a dildo and pop anal beads. I'll do double insertions. Put me on a Cam and you can meter me to the Prefecture."

Babs sighs. "Thank goodness that for you life exchanges food and shelter for erotic dance and sexual displays and arousal. You don't need to show off, you just need to obey me."

"No problem." Molly understands, and she raises, "if you let me forfeit my panties to Steph I'll ride the Double Dong with Kimju. I've never done that before!"

Monitor Babs muses, "maybe you two can perform an Alumni Reprise. You wouldn't be the first, you know."

Molly accepts, "Ma'am, I'll dong my Roommate. Ma'am, I'll dong any Cosmos, any hole, center Stage at the Nugget, Ma'am."

This produces gasps in the Lineup; it's an offer that causes Kimju to bite her lip. *And concentrate on remembering to keep oval mouth.*

Babs reigns in Pledge Molly. "Nicely plead, Pledge, but don't expect me to make any deals." BB sets Pledge Molly straight, "You role in the Game is to beg, I have no responsibilities to you, including listening to you."

"Ma'am, I understand, Ma'am. You are the boss. You order I obey." Molly commits. "You decide how I Opt next Term. I beg, maybe you listen."

"Well said, Pledge," Boss Babe appraises, "You must beg Kimju to piss in your mouth. See if she wants to listen." BB smiles.

Molly rushes forward. "Ma'am, thank you, Ma'am." Molly forms an image of herself and her friend, and promises, "Kimju and I will piss into each other's mouths. We are both wannabe Pee-Cams and Piss Mouths. Please let us both Pledge naked and cum be Strippers next Term."

Boss Babe graces Molly's lips. "You're sweet," she says.

BB turns her attention to her least-dressed Cosmos: Kimju wears only a thong, a.k.a. a tanga, a.k.a. "a kunny kover." BB queries, "Confirm what Molly said is all true."

"Ma'am, you know that I'm fully vested in the pink, cream, and cum department. Like Molly, I was the second Cosmos to climax; you watched us both, Ma'am." Kimju answers smartly.

"And like Molly, you also donated your Pink Pages and archives to the Automatron?" Babs knows the answer.

"Ma'am, yes, Ma'am," Kimju answers. "My Pink Pages are also available at the Nugget. Hat Check Girl can print out on very good glossy paper."

"Molly seems committed that you two ex-Strippers want to return to the Nugget," BB dangles.

"Ma'am," Kimju proceeds carefully, "we were Roommates last Term, we were both great Strippers, and Molly wants to get back to that lifestyle. My goal is to Opt Up, become a Monitor like you, and eventually make it to MomCap and run the Club." Kimju squints. "Ma'am, that's no secret to any Cosmos, Ma'am."

"Except your Roommate?" BB inquires.

Again Kimju practices diplomacy. "Ma'am, Molly and I are good buddies, we've danced together, shared Double Penetrators, performed for the Cams. But if we Opt in opposite directions we become separated, and that is hard to accept. Sad for both of us."

Boss Babe turns to Molly, pinches a nipple between fingertips, and rolls it erect. She turns to Kimju, draws the back of her hand across Kimju's beige silver-dollar-sized areolas, watches them pucker up, and observes Kimju's knob-like nipples stand up.

BB can't resist teasing her Pledge. "I hope an aspiring management-type like yourself still has Kundalini in you?"

Kimju stammers, Ma'am, anything that Molly can perform I am better at, Ma'am."

Boss Babe fingers Kimju's tanga. "Maybe it pleases you I yank your tanga into your koot and rub it back and forth until you cream for me?"

Kimju falters. "Ma'am, may I please you, Ma'am."

"Your Roommate suggests you want to join her on the Pee-Cam." BB cavaliers.

Kimju gasps. *I did hear Molly say that.* "Ma'am," Kimju begins, "I'm not Molly's Roommate this Term, we're not Nugget Strippers anymore, and Molly's Roommate is now Steph. Maybe Steph should join her and beg to be the next Pee-Cam Pledge. Steph can streak for Molly, too, they are Roommates, after all."

Boss Babe fingers her bling; she can feel the sunshine tanning them and knows that the crescents d'areolage will become permanently darkened. BB spins, "Molly suggested you two share Piss Mouth." Babs toys a finger. "After all, you did French kiss her during *The Arrivals* when she had a salty taste in her mouth."

Kimju consolidates. "Ma'am, that's not the same. I couldn't even tell she had pee on her breath." Kimju falters, "Ma'am, afterwards when I thought about it, maybe, but Ma'am, Steph is the one who wants Molly's panties. Let Steph and Molly piss on them and see if Steph will beg to stuff them into *her* mouth. You could see how badly she wants two pieces and an Opt Up."

Boss Babe straightens, raises a finger, praises: "Excellent thought!"

Kimju holds position. Bubbles of sweat form in her armpit, under one knock, and where her thigh meets her crotch.

"Molly says you should Pledge naked and cum be a Stripper with her," BB proposes.

Kimju calculates. "Ma'am, Molly should transfer all her allegiance to Steph, make Molly give her panties to Steph, Ma'am."

Bikini Babe teases, "Maybe I should have them Flip-Flop, and let Molly wear the dress and Steph present herself topless and panties. That would qualify the to Opt Strip, Roommates Together."

Kimju feels deflation.

BB brightens. "Maybe then I could give the minidress and panties to you and your Roommate, and that way you and Robyn would each have two Garments and would Opt Up."

Kimju breathes relief. "Ma'am, that would be kind of you, Ma'am. I do know how to striptease and dance; I know how to bump and grind and wiggle. I appreciate you had no choice but to enable Robyn to force Molly and me to cream and climax." Kimju steadies her posture. "Ma'am, you know I'll do what I have to get a second Garment. I know how to cream on my own and can climax for the Gamers again and again if you want. I will beg you to play my *Nugget Stripper Videos*. And like Robyn suggests, I'll masturbate and climax in sync with them. Molly and me both. We'll climax to each other; we'll climax together. Any way you want it, Ma'am."

Babs gives a pause.

Kimju wants BB's nod. "Solo or with any Pledge. Anywhere, anytime in front of anybody!"

Gamers suspect this and know that Kimju's seriousness contrasts to Molly's indifference. But BB also savors Gamer insight. *I suspect that before any of Kimju's aspirations shall be considered that her thong will get reduced to a g-string. Followed by a* long *dose of the nudie.*

Babs is learning to appreciate that the Lineup waits for her; *will wait for me, Monitor Babs.* BB adjusts her position in front of the topless tanga Kimju and wonders out loud, "So how come you and Molly get to arrive here topless whereas Ginny and Lee over at the Corvettes had to promote nude?"

Kimju ponders the question but pregnant silence invites her response, "Ma'am, ah, Molly and I said we would parade topless in public. Ma'am."

"Really. But if you are going to Pledge naked and become a Stripper next Term won't you also parade nude?"

The conditionality of this question confuses Kimju. *I haven't pledged anything—yet! And naked inside is different than public nudity—like streaking.* Kimju stumbles, "Ma'am, er, ah, Molly's already streaked. We might have been Roommates last Term, but this Term it is her current Roommate who should be the one to streak with her, Ma'am. That's Steph."

"Perhaps you and Molly might confine yourselves to the Front Porch, and repeat your pullaside, pink, cream and climax act for the Front Door Cam?" Boss Babe asks.

Visions of paparazzi across the street dance through Kimju's head. "Ma'am may I please you and the Gamers, Ma'am, I will pullaside, pink, cream, and climax whenever and wherever you see fit, Ma'am."

Babs takes a step backward. Kimju sighs and makes eyes with the Boss Babe. *I'm not supposed to do that.* And looks across the hedge to the next house. *Steady yourself.* Kimju says to herself. *Because I know pinking in public will not happen.*

Kimju clenches her teeth. *Except that it might.*

BB assesses the pair of topless buttage ex-Nuggets standing before her. *Yes, during* The *Arrivals I made them cover their knockers and milk sacks and only later did I let them hang out. I have learned to not care about how they feel about exposing themselves. More importantly, I learned to not care about how I feel about it. That's progress!*

Babs makes a gesture and signs both ex-Nuggets to crisscross their hands across their breasts. She signs a second time for them to tease areolage, and third to rub their nipples with their fingertips and arouse them. They both do. And don't stop.

Okay, I made them handbra or not during The Arrivals, *but now I know to make them tease areolage and keep their nipples twisted into erection. I would never have commanded Kimju and Molly like that at the beginning of the Term,* BB realizes, *but now I suspect it's something Gamers desire I do. So I enable them.*

The Cam follows as Babs moves on to Robyn.

§ Babs Studies Robyn: How Does one Reduce the Redacted?

It is bad form for a Pledge in the Lineup to make heaving sighs or otherwise demonstrate impatience, but Babs has a special purpose for allowing Robyn's impudence. Kimju and Molly and Steph should all be experienced enough to sense Boss Babe's machinations, but only Tiffany stays sufficiently steely to separate emotion from Game.

Babs' third "newbie" permits herself to meet eyes with her Monitor when the tall buxom Bikini Babe positions herself in front of her. Babs remembers Robyn as a fellow Cosmos Pledge last Term, but Robyn seems to have no memory of these events. Robyn Redacted. The other Cosmos who keep their eyes straight ahead should not witness this intimate glance. But Robyn knows, *the Rules are special for me. I know I'm a knockout; my 34Cs might not be a big as Boss Bitch's 37Ds, but my rig is plenty big to impress, and* all *of it stays inside* my *swimsuit!*

Robyn holds stand spread surrender position but mentally she runs her hands down the front of her maillot. *My daintily omphalos barely reveals itself, whereas BB ripples her entirely belly around her button. I might be shorter than Bling Broad, but I know blondes have more seduction.*

Robyn also knows, *I am superior to my Roommate Kimju. My costume is the extreme opposite: she is the barest Cosmos and I am the most decent. Her butched kelp—cut right to the edge of her thong—is about the only part of her body that remains covered—except when her thong gets yanked up into her koot! Ha ha ha. I don't show off my knockers, and my crotch doesn't leak any pubic hair.*

Unlike all the other Cosmos Pledge! Robyn asserts to herself.

It is unlike Robyn to check her own facts but she can't really break out of standing with her legs apart and her hands behind her head, even if she whinnies. Three fingers wide in a crotch covered with fabric, and armpits cupped. It is times like these that straps make a difference.

Yes, it is true that I really am the only Pledge not showing hairage! Robyn inventories to herself. *Tiffany spills or'top, Steph and Beka vagflash upskirt, Elle leaks hairage to the sides, Molly has her panties yanked tight, and Kimju is shaven back except that her butched triangle extends slightly outside her thong. And she shows all her butch when she gets yanked. So be it. Even Boss Bitch shows hairage in her Dining Room Picture, and BB isn't even a Pledge. So I really am a special Cosmos.*

Babs affords attention to the most poorly postured Cosmos before her. "Nice swimsuit," Babs affords herself a modest interaction with Robyn. Robyn's one-piece maillot, with its shoulder straps, horizontal legline, and yes, cutout hole round her button, keeps her navel uncovered and decent. "You're a winner," BB adds, "you really do have the smallest buttonhole."

Robyn beams. "While you show off an acre of bellage, belly-up and belly-down, all around your belly button. With me the guys can only see my button, nothing more. You're more exposed. Gamers want to see more of me, but can't."

Babs ignores Robyn's failure to address her properly and runs a finger inside Robyn's shoulder strap. Robyn flinches and Babs advances, "Too bad that your maillot won't fit on my body." BB purrs softly, "even with the straps it would add only the smallest marginal coverage to, you know, my overworked cleavage."

The intimacy of this confession swells Robyn's head and she stands more erect. The Lineup ripples, brows tighten and ears twist to listen. Alert! That Boss Babe passes over Robyn's maillot perks the ears of every listening Cosmos.

"Right!" Robyn can't resist stammering, whipsawed between the dispensation and the unreality that Babs might consider impounding her second skin. And leave her stark naked.

Babs advances, "You know, should there leak files from last Term of me escaping from my bra in the Mudpit, or anything else inappropriate that you might have held secretly, rest assured I will hold *you* responsible. It doesn't matter if you are responsible or not. I've decided to hold someone responsible and I've decided that someone is you! After all, you were there and you promised."

Robyn finds this assault confusing. "Ma'am I wasn't here last Term!"

"Perhaps you think I forgot about you." Boss Babe espouses.

"Oh no, Ma'am," Robyn retorts, "I'd never think that."

"Because you never think."

"Oh no, Ma'am, I'd never think you'd forget about me. I'm memorable!"

"You forgot I remember."

"Ma'am, no, Ma'am. I'd never think you'd forget."

"In the Game stay the Game," Babs says sweetly and pinches Robyn on the cheek.

Robyn wishes she knew what this means.

§ Babs Considers Steph: Role Reversed Implications

Babs pauses in front of the Lineup and considers Steph. Steph chaffs standing spread surrender; Steph wears the last Garment BB will evaluate for impoundment today. Because Steph and Babs are role-reversed from last Term and because Steph is the only Cosmos demoted from a Caste above, Steph presents unique challenges to the Boss Babe.

Steph resents her demotion and is constantly on the alert to test her former Pledge but now Monitor. *I must wait for opportunities. Up until now Bikini Bitch has provided me with a series of variously vulgar minidresses, although I think the Gamers provide them, and Bikini Bimbo is just a pawn.*

Steph controls a twitch in her ovaled lip, but keeps her eyes forward. *Fact of the matter is that Bikini Bimbo doesn't even have what it takes to make me spread my legs. She lets Robyn Redacted force me to titter and vagflash. And then that ragho couples me with Beka Broda and forces both of to spread. Beka always leaks brodeas out her box, but I'm better than that.*

Okay all right, Steph acknowledges silently, *Robyn's been making me vagflash since the day I arrived and every day since. She's not the only one but she is a special case.*

Steph keeps her lips ovaled but sucks them inward. *Robyn betrayed me last Term, and me getting demoted for covering my button seems overly harsh. Unfair. The first thing on my short list is crushing Robyn, although crushing Babs is right up there.*

Today Steph's minidress is strapless. Her buttonhole is designed in the shape of a keyhole, with the round part of the hole centered around Steph's birth crater with its rim of flesh and a rising bulb in the middle. The key part of the cutout descends vertically down Steph's belly, and displays soft body hairs.

But Steph's problem is not her buttonhole; it is that the minidress is too short. Standing with her hands behind her head ensures that the dress doesn't quite cover the crease where the semi-globes of her stern meet her shapely legs. Nor cover her crotch. Steph steels herself for BB's sarcasm.

Boss Babe surveys Steph's body from her bare feet and shapely legs to the top of her head. "Nice armpits," Boss Babe complements, "Too bad you only got one piece."

Steph rationalizes and speaks out loud, "I have been dealt a temporary reversal of fortune at the hands of Gamers envious of me."

Babs can see the glint in Steph's eyes, and she sidesteps Steph's aggression, "I'd already earned my promotion last Term before the Gamers broke you. I had nothing to do with your drop."

"Yeah, and I know how you got your nickname!" Steph retorts.

Babs slaps her face. Hard. "Shut up. Don't speak unless spoken to. And it's 'Ma'am,' slut. Apologize or strip naked and streak to the Nugget right now!" Fire dances out of Boss Babe's eyes.

"Right." Steph stammers. Her cheek stings. Her ear rings. She wonders if her nose bleeds; Boss Babe lacks practice at slapping faces. The former Monitor unhooks the fingers behind her head, then reconnects them and regains composure. "Ma'am, I am sorry if you think I'm disrespecting you, Ma'am."

"You're downwardly mobile!" BB decrees.

"Ma'am, I am a Cosmos Pledge, Ma'am." Steph's ear still rings.

Babs remains well aware that Steph knows much about what transpired last Term. *But I also know some things about you that you don't know I know.* Babs leans forward, babambas testing her bra, then grabs the bottom of Steph's minidress with both hands, and lifts upwards. The dress follows and when Babs steps back she observes that now all of Steph's snatch patch and stern globes display themselves to the Cam... and the paparazzi.

"Nice snatch," Babs observes and commands, "Open mouth," and extends two fingers all the way into Steph's mouth until she tickles Steph's throat and Steph gags. BB retracts her fingers partway but holds her knuckles inside Steph's teeth.

Babs look into Steph's bent-back head. *The origins of my nicknames might reside in places that include Robyn Redacted's memories, and not just Steph. Maybe Robyn remembers referring the Mudwrestling Contest and maybe she doesn't, but Steph wasn't there so maybe neither of them knows where to find that scurrilous tit-mashing ass-baring video.*

Babs twiddles her fingertips. It's just enough that Steph feels the touch on her tongue, yet not deep enough to again provoke the gag reflex. *Steph might know—she does know—secrets known to only a few Gamers. Like the incident at a motor speedway where I was encouraged to participate in a Bikini Contest, or the Bikini Contest at the Hog Ride, and maybe even some secret Cam files that should not even exist.*

Babs presses, "If you know what is good for you, you will not be spreading vicious rumors about things you cannot verify."

Steph gurgles and chooses not to bite the fingers that invade and violate her mouth. *Okay, no Steph tattle!*

Steph continues to feel the heat of the red imprint of Babs' hand smarting her face. *Hold stand spread surrender position!* Steph steels to herself. *The Cam takes this all down and I don't have a chance if I overstep.* Steph inventories her body. *Yes, armpits, navelage, and enough upskirt that my scruff shows out. Fuck Babs. I should have ensured she became a Stripper this Term, because now I want to see her turned into a* Suck Fuck Facial *Porn Whore. I shall bide my moment; I do know how to hold onto information until its revelation will advance me. Janet knows I secretly watched her pour shots for Tiffany at the Nugget last Term, but I also saw Tiffany climax Janet on the Double Dong. Betcha Boss Bitch doesn't know that.*

Or if BB does she keeps it a secret.

For a moment Steph's headlights alight, erect nipples clearly visible in stretch fabric outline. Slowly and carefully Steph closes her mouth so her teeth rest on BB's knuckles; she doesn't bite, so when BB rotates her hand Steph rotates her head with her. She doesn't know that this action wiggles her buttonhole just enough to cover her button up.

"Throat my finger, slut," Boss Babe demands, and Steph obeys, opens her teeth wide again, and thrusts her head forward until she gags the back of her tongue on BB's finger.

Babs extracts her hand. Steph takes a breath of fresh air and again forms oval-mouth. She feels a breath of fresh air on her sluice.

Babs squares her bosom forward, calms down, and her thoughts return to impounding Steph's minidress as her most useful advancement. BB smiles, flicks an eyebrow, and appraises, *Steph's minidress is mine when I want it. Not necessarily* this *minidress; but any minidress. Steph doesn't believe it is I who select the minidress, but I do, well, sort of. And after I take it, I will pick a minidress that flatters* my *figure and* covers *me* up *the way* I *want to be covered: high neckline, short-sleeved, and a hemline down to the knee!* Boss Babe controls the urge to physically float her hands down her body following the contours of this imaginary form-fitting minidress. She smiles at Steph. *I'm not going to act out for you. You need a surprise or two.*

Navelage 24x7? *Of course, a cutout hole I don't have to worry about.*

Babs scans to Steph's navel but doesn't find it, despite a buttonhole bigger than Robyn's. Babs steps forward, says, "Let me fix that for you," and adjusts fabric that has gotten bunched over the keyhole-shaped buttonhole. "It must have gotten covered when you wiggled your skirt up," she surmises.

Steph twitches a nostril, squares her chin, ignores Babs, and stares straight ahead. She keeps her thoughts to herself. *No Bitch, it got covered when you lifted it up, twisted my head back, and mangled my buttonhole. Nice of you to fix it, you stupid bungler.*

Passion grips Babs. She bites her lip and raises her chin as she considers the long blonde beauty before her. "Do you know what everyone called you behind your back when you were Monitor Steph last Term? Everyone called you Steph Sorostitute." BB scratches her chin. She says, "From now on that's what everyone is going to call you to your face. So if anyone asks you your name, that's what you tell them."

Babs watches Steph stare into the Cam, patiently hovering in front of her. Oval mouth, but jaw tensing. Elbows tensing too. Automatron logs Steph's headlights fade, and considers doing analysis of what turns them on and off.

Boss Babe says, "What's you name, Pledge?"

Steph holds position, responds, "Ma'am, "I'm Steph Sorostitute, Ma'am." And returns to oval mouth. *Gonna get you Bitch!*

Babs closes her mouth and considers. *The more I think about the possibility of stripping you stark naked and sending you off to the Strip next Term, the more "the utility of the idea" makes sense. Appeals to me.*

Boss Babe curls a smiles; indeed, rending her former Monitor naked creates pleasure thoughts! On an impulse Babs points to Steph's exposed snatch, "Beg Tiffany to bleach this." Babs twitches her nose like she catches a waif of bad smell. "As a matter of fact, beg her to bleach all your hair. That includes the hair on your head. And shave off your eyebrows."

Steph rolls her upper lip around as if to brush a fly off; there is no fly, of course, and Steph holds her position, unsure if she has been invited to talk, *except that I have nothing to say to this baudetrot.*

Impulses flood Babs' thoughts. *Why not take the minidress right now and let Steph spend the Term naked?* Rational? *The addition of the minidress will cure my areolage problem and position me for an Opt Up to MomCap next Term, if I ever want to.*

May Cosmos Pledge wait patiently while Boss Babe noodles what to do next.

May Boss Babe play a cagey Game? BB mulls about damage control, *I know Steph is dangerous and divisive and may try to resurrect skeletons from my past. Perhaps I might want to acquire the minidress in a roundabout fashion. Avoid direct kickback. Circumspection is in order. I need to develop a plan.*

Babs steps backward, away from the Lineup but still facing it. Robyn's eyes follow her. Beka sneaks a peek. All the others keep their eyes forward.

BB smiles at the Back Door Cam as it follows her backward from the Lineup toward the Bell and the Back Landing leading into the Cosmos House. She pauses with the hanging Bell rope in hand and talks to the Cam, as it delivers her head and shoulders with full underwire bra cleavage to the Prefecture.

"You can't scare me with Tiffany's teats, Kimju's knockers and Molly's mammies, Steph's spouts, or Elle's nobs. You can't can scare me with Beka's beaver and Steph's snatch. I'm immune to all their exposures. As for me, I actually like my cleavage and bellage and leggage. And most important, you can't blush me with my own bling!"

BB gestures over her shoulder to the Lineup. "Take your time with my Cosmos Pledge. I've got work to do. I control their exposures and I'll decide for them what's most convenient for me. I'm not afraid any more."

Babs pulls the rope and rings the Bell, loud. The Cam pans with her as she bounces up the Landing and disappears through the Back Door. The Cam lingers, shudders, and reassigns itself back to canvas the Lineup.

Hey, not such a bad task after all: Seven Cosmos standing spread surrender in a Lineup as the sun climbs into the sky. The one with her golden pussy exposed below her now-bottomless cutout minidress carefully releases a droplet of pee to run down her leg.

Steph seethes silently, *I know I need a second piece and I have no intention of asking Boss Bitch's permission to Game for it!* Steph runs her mind back through *The Arrivals. Molly has already given her panties to me, but Boss Bitch insists Molly wear them even though she doesn't want to wear what is mine. I don't appreciate BB forcing me to titter and vagflash, nor her letting Robyn Ragabash order me around and pretending to not be responsible. Monitor Babs, ha! I wish upon you the most unfortunate of outcomes!*

Steph writhes her body in small contortions. *Bikini Bitch slapped me, lifted my dress, and right now I am exposing my shrubbery.* Steph advances nastier thoughts. *Bikini Bitch should never have been promoted to Monitor in the first place; BB should have been sent to the Strip and it should be Babs' picture hanging on the low baseboard of the Dining Room wall with her bacon strips sizzling a dildo drilling her buttermilk box. Now it will take two Terms to work her way down to the Nugget. No Rule prevents BB from Opting Down and Pledging next Term. What happened to me can happen to her for no fault of her own—although in her case it's deserving. And then I want to see BB wrap her naked bouncing bawagos around the pole, center Stage in the Nugget.*

Steph curls her lips and allows her eyes to wander, then steels them into a virtual Babs. *So why stop at the Nugget, you Baudetrot Bitch, take another turn and make Whore, so that men can devour your big tits, throat you, and fuck your senseless. Then after Gamers are through with you as a* Suck Fuck Facial *Porn Whore, I'm going to turn you into a Slavesex, chained spread eagle in the Mudpit, gangbanged, bukkaked, given soapy enema, pissed on, and force-climaxed into the Zone.*

Steph knows to be careful that her harsher thoughts never get recited back to Babs. Steph watches a paparazzi in the window next door carefully compose her. *Photo me at your peril,* she scowls, *cause I'm gonna get back at you.* She grimaces, *Yes, I am going to zone Boss Bitch. And I'm going to encase Robyn inside a block of plaster.*

II-2 Janet & Babs & Cosmos: Reconsiderations (D15)

§ Babs Gossips with Janet: Spiderweb In Command

After disappearing inside the Back Door Babs passes through the Kitchen and uses one of her Skeleton Keys to go through the door into the Parlor, where Janet, the overweight Monitor of the Corvette House, awaits her in a big easy chair. BB sits in a chair adjacent to her.

Janet continues to wear the Spiderweb Bikini, even though *The Arrivals* are over and *The Runup* has begun. Today's Spider is a different color and different web; Janet has tied the two straps over her shoulders instead of behind her neck, qualifying the Garment as a bra and not a halter. The bra might hoist up Janet's heavy jaboos, but the crochet webbing thins out so that her large brown areolas with their bubbly milk glands are clearly visible, and so her puffy nipples poke out holes in the center.

Below a vast track of plump belly, Janet wears a g-string that today is one size smaller than the mini she wore during *The Arrivals*. Janet's full pubic hair spills out above, to the sides, and through the open mesh, now size micro.

Babs can't resist teasing her former Roommate and now fellow Monitor. "I see you continue to wear the most minimal Spiderweb Bikini, even though you are a Monitor now. You must like sitting on your bare jaxy and having the paparazzi all cam you."

Janet grabs her 40EEs in both hands and shakes them. "Don't forget I Pledged naked last Term, we both made our deals, and this is the most I've ever worn since." Janet jostles, "Hey, this thing got crocheted right on my body. It's the least I can wear and still qualify for two pieces."

"It gets you attention," Babs rudes.

Janet wags her finger, "Don't forget I won all the Bikini Contests last Term and you surfed on my Spiderwebs. You're lucky all you have to do is bling!"

"I had to hairage and crack my butt," Babs chomps.

"Memorialized in your Dining Room Pictures!" Janet reminds. "Here and at my Corvette House. You poor thing, maybe you also showcased your butt cheeks." Janet squeaks her bare butt in the chair. "I've kept my jaxy completely exposed, since before you met me, it's never been covered. I'm only now less-slightly nude."

"I know, Janet, you carried freight for me." BB tugs at the widely-spaced bra straps. "I have Karma with you from last Term, but you did succeed in Opting Monitor this Term. We both did."

"Relax, you can be the Bling Bra Bikini Babe." Janet laughs, "No problem, you know I like the attention."

"I'm surprised you haven't reduced your bra to a necklace and your g-string to a waistband. That's still two pieces!"

Janet laughs, "Watch out, I just might do that."

Babs inquires, "Are you going to get a third piece and Opt Up to MomCap next Term?

"Absolutely," Janet decries, "House Mom el Capitan! I like the idea of running a bunch of Strippers."

"Do you know which Pledge you'll take from yet?" Babs asks.

"No need to rush ahead of Events," Janet declares, and teases, "Besides, maybe it's you who should donate. Don't forget I had to streak last Term. And some Gamers think I also streaked on your behalf."

"Janet! Please!" Babs watches as Janet laughs. "Don't scare me like that. I know I owe you but you got to be reasonable."

"You know what I want," Janet says.

"I know who you want," Babs says, "I know I owe you. You also came in the Mudpit."

"Listen to me." Janet pauses and leans forward to speak in a quieter tone. "When it's time to send Steph over to me at the Corvette House, make sure she streaks and make sure she knows I will be keeping her naked."

Babs sighs, "I know, Janet, I owe her to you. But you're going to have to wait until I find a way so what I am doing is not obvious to her."

Janet accepts this conclusion, shifts gears. "I snuck a peek a while ago." Janet nods her head in the direction of the Backyard. "You're doing okay. But why do you have your two topless Pledge hiding their milk machines?" Janet shakes her own very large jaboos. "You still afraid of tits in your face?"

"Janet, I'm so over with that. Right now they make areolage, like I do. But I've also commanded them to keep their nipples erected. I'm learning what the Gamers want." Babs squints even in the dim Parlor light. She fingers her lower belly, where her nombril waistline crosses four inches below her belly button. "Back to the topless count. I understand Tiffany Transparent doesn't count as a topless, but is she a titter? And tell me about her Eraser Heads."

Janet concedes, "Technically, even though her clear vinyl shirt is completely see-through, she doesn't rate topless. Areolage and titter perhaps, boobage for sure, but if you let me, *I'll* unbutton her shirt so she can display her teats bare to the wind."

"She'd like that," BB agrees, "she'd like you to take her shirt away completely. She can't wait to cock all her holes."

"Let me let Tiffany tease a little, I'll tell you all about her Eraser Head," Janet offers.

"Deal," BB confirms. "You can also tell me about her *Suck Fuck Facial* tapes. Later."

Janet queries, "Has Elle brought in her Measurement Nudes?"

BB relaxes. "Not yet, but she promises to go get them soon. She titters a lot but has yet to go topless. And she's definitely not keen on having to present herself naked.

"She'll just have to get use to it," Janet lacks sympathy, "Besides she's the one who exposed herself."

Babs weakens, "Yes, but I'm the one who's making her fetch."

Janet shrugs, "Okay. I won't argue with you. You're making her do it. Good for you. Now you need to do Elle a good thing and go topless like Kimju and Molly. After all, isn't she begging to Strip?"

Babs lets out a sigh, "Yeah, her and Beka both. Except Beka really means it."

"Well, so do Tiffany and Molly," Janet adds and tilts her head. "And do you think Beka will compromise Elle?"

Babs wrinkles her nose. "We'll find out. There is more to the two of them than Elle simply wanting to save Beka from herself."

"Now that's a goal Elle won't be able to achieve," Janet decrees. "Beka already begs Opt Strip for real."

"And Elle begs but doesn't mean it." BB states.

Janet shrugs, "How's Robyn doing?"

"I'm not sure," Boss Babe pushes her hair back. "I can't decide if she even retains memory of the events so far *this* Term, or if she just observes the present.

"Robyn believes the world revolves around her," Janet pronounces, "yet she gets anxious when shapes shift."

BB nods, "My memories of the past are as solid as hers are convenient. She's communicated clearly to me that she expects a promotion."

Janet chuckles, "I trust you've done nothing to dissuade this perception."

The Monitors laugh. Babs speaks, "Would Robyn ever think to offer something in exchange? Help out? Butter the toast?"

Janet makes a dismissive hand gesture, "Most certainly you don't need to do anything." Janet hefts both jugs, nipples centered in spiderwebs. "Robyn will eat her own tail."

Janet sidles the conversation to the Cosmos she most wants to discuss. "So what about Steph. You keep dressing her like a slut, make Tiffany overdo her makeup, and ensure she titters and vagflashes. You got her standing out in the Backyard with her scruff showing. How long before you take our former Monitor and hang her all out? How about you let me do it."

BB takes a big breath. "For just as long as it is convenient for me. You taught me that, thank you."

"You're welcome," Janet responds. "I understand, you've got a task to perform. A responsibility. But remember, you're not the only Monitor at the School. My Pledge will titter and vagflash too, you know. In fact I'll make them all pink, cream, and climax."

"Except maybe Darleen," Babs teases.

Janet bristles. "I am by no means a sadist, but one must be a strong disciplinarian to survive here. So don't hassle me about my girls." Janet pokes a finger, "You've never been a Monitor before. And you got a big Steph problem. It's more complicated than just you two being role reversed: you were her Pledge when she was a Monitor last Term, and now she's your Pledge now that you are a Monitor this Term."

Babs listens.

Janet continues, "Steph thinks you disrespected her during *The Arrivals.* And you're letting Robyn haze her? Steph hates you for that."

Babs opines, "I think Steph mostly holds Robyn responsible for her Opt Down, and the fact that you and I Opted Up irks her. Fate happens."

Janet says "Steph resents you give her her daily minidress."

Babs tattles, "She calls you 'Janet Jintoe,' and says you took on the name while you and Tiffany were Nugget Strippers, two Terms ago. Before you were my Roommate last Term. I never knew that."

Janet nods to history. "You also never wanted to know how I got to Opt Up."

Babs studies a friend and a rival and wonders, *Who actually controls Janet's collection of Spiderwebs? The same Gamers who control my Black Bikini?* Babs closes her mouth and draws slight suction to draw her cheeks inward. She furrows her brow. *Maybe I showcase my crescents d'areolage, but all of Janet's Spiderweb Bikinis pretty much divulge her as if she appears naked. Like today. Hairage to the sides and through the micro-g-string webbing, a string kissing her asshole, jewels poking out of a crochet bra, a clit trying to worm its way out of the mesh, and something sparkling there to the sides where the lips might lie.*

Janet's gem.

Janet catches Babs stare and shrugs. "Okay, so I've totally exposed myself to the Gamers. And it was for the both of us, last Term. So if Gamers want to keep me exposed in public?" Janet shrugs, "So what. They've already gotten their play out of me. Full-frontal, spread and pink, asshole, finger-fucking, climax. I'm good at this. I was a Stripper before I was your Roommate last Term. I've already revealed my secrets. I've dildoed and proctoed; I've DPed toys. On Stage live at the Nugget."

"You volunteered to masturbated naked to climax at a Bachelor Party," Babs augments.

"You know it was your Karma that I took on!" Janet reminds.

"Yes, thank you," Babs agrees but objects, "But you just keep on giving! You didn't need to let them photograph the string across your jimmy, you didn't need to pullaside your g-string, grab your rings, and pull your jute patch to the sides. You should see yourself!"

Janet doesn't argue, "Hey, right now I have two pieces and Monitor responsibility. I had to do a workout to make Monitor this Term. Unlike you, who let me take on your load."

Babs concedes, "Janet, okay, I know you took on some of my Karma. I really appreciate it. It was bad enough we lost our tops during the Mudwrestling Contest. I know you also streaked for me. I know I owe you. But I also know you like being out there."

Janet shakes her head quickly. "I do. I pinked twice, once for me and once for you. You know that I like ending up more exposed than you. But if someday I need for you to be less exposed than I am I know you'll trade Bikinis with me."

Babs fidgets.

Janet waves her off. "Okay, so I'm big and fat and I like the attention. But you're also my friend and I know that I am also much better equipped to take it—psychologically that is—and I'm better able to dish it out. So watch out!"

The Monitors laugh together. And Babs carefully fingers her bling. *I'm not completely sure I know what "it" is, and I don't want to ask.*

§ Babs & Janet: Discuss Trading Steph for Ginny

Janet returns the conversation to Steph. Yes, Janet, like Babs, was Steph's Pledge last Term; this Term Steph is a Pledge and Janet is a Monitor. "She and I *almost* reverse roles," Janet advances, "except I am not Steph's Monitor. You are. I desire to be. Steph should count herself lucky that it is you, not I, who is her Boss Babe."

BB shakes her head, "I don't think it would matter who she reports to. Steph feels too overcome by injustice to appreciate the fine details."

"Stung by her own deflation is how I would put it," Janet opines. "Look, you don't just have to let me have her for a few days." Janet raises her eyebrows and tilts a chin, "Tell me who you'd like back in exchange."

Janet's overtures to possess Steph are not new, but her escalation weakens Babs' reluctance to commit at this very moment. BB uses her fingernails and combs her long hair, suddenly very aware of herself in her bikini. Her areolage. But nothing compared to Janet.

Janet persists, "and How about you take Lee; she can give Elle lolly lessons. And I'll pop Steph's bubble."

Babs puckers her lips, unimpressed, "Elle Lollydor has gotten quite good at licking up valiva, thank you. So ex-Stripper Lee Lollydor in exchange for broken Monitor Steph? I don't think so."

Janet persists. "Perhaps Louise might interest you. She's a broken Monitor, like your Steph. Except she's got a bandeau and a t-front maillot, two pieces, unlike your Steph." Janet watches BB shift her weight in the chair. "She's got bigger lung cones too," she parries, "Almost like you."

"Thank you, Janet. Tell me about your Roommate, Darleen. She was a Monitor last Term; is she really another broken Monitor, or is she a MomCap in disguise?" Babs demands.

"Ah, so many questions," Janet bounces her jaboos. "So few answers."

Janet escalates, "What about Ginny for Steph? She's a Whore-For-Life. That should send some shivers through your House!"

Babs considers this offer. *A Whore-For-Life, even of Pledge rank is an asset to seriously consider. A money fuck.*

Janet presses, "Steph treated you shabby last Term." Janet shakes her jaboos to underline her determination of this statement. "She made you spit-wash feet with your tongue."

Babs puckers her lips. "That's not entirely correct. She sent me to work for Madam Nurse Beautician. And it was there that I washed feet, and not usually with my mouth."

"Everybody in the Prefecture watched you lick Steph's feet clean."

"Well, sort of. I manicured all the Cosmos. I collected toenail clippings and put them in jars. I polished toenails. Filed and buffed, you know. Painted and lacquered and dusted."

"You sucked Steph's big toe. You sucked each of her toes one by one."

"I did do that and Steph knew she humiliated me that I had to do it for her. In front of everybody. It wouldn't have mattered what the task. She just felt it necessary to crush me."

"I hope you'll remember your happy experience and allow Steph to suck your toes. Suck all of ours." Janet smiles.

"I don't know, Janet, I have it in for her but I really don't want to get her angry with me. She resents Robyn more than me, and I want to keep it that way."

"You are the Monitor," Janet consoles. "You're the Boss Babe."

"Yeah," Babs confesses, "Something like that."

"You needn't wait till the end of the Term to begin training Steph in the crafts of the Strip, silly," Janet lobbies back to Babs, and advances, "I'll make Steph pink and cream and cum so hard that she squirts!"

Babs tends to agree, "Enough of her titter and upskirt in a minidress! Maybe it's time for Steph to learn some of the advanced Hand Signs that Roommates Kimju and Molly have so ably demonstrated." BB clarifies the task, "Maybe it's time for Robyn to practice on Steph and turn her out. That would be the ultimate humiliation!"

Janet laughs and concurs, "So let Robyn sign her to not just spread her legs, but also spread her slash, hollow out some *really* deep pink, and play with herself. Make slosh for the Cams. And *want* to cum for us."

"She deserves to be treated as lovingly as she treated you," Babs wisps. *Yes, Steph did force Janet to pink, masturbate, and cum last Term. And at least once stark naked in the Mudpit, and on my behalf.*

BB augments, "Don't worry, Janet, she get a new minidress every day or so, and Molly begs to give her panties away, so I'm not so sure about what her destination next Term will be."

Janet doesn't give up easily, "Don't be too kind. So let Robyn strip her naked. But then make her streak over to my Corvette House. You owe me. The closer I can get to wringing a climax out of her the happier I'll be. And the more I'll forgive you. So don't wait too long to chop her minidress to nothingness and train her in her birthday suit."

"I'm going to take her minidress," Boss Babe declares, confiding, "but in a round-about way. She's going to be resistive."

Janet furrows her brow, "Resistive, yes; but oh, so compromised!"

Babs decides, "Don't worry. I'll make sure she begs to cum be a Stripper next Term."

"I'll put Steph in the Zone and wring a howl outta her that you'll hear clear across campus. She'll be unable to stop cumming." Janet decrees, and raises the ante again, "Trade her to me and I'll give you Ginny *and* Lee or Louse. Remember, Ginny's a Whore-For-Life and she'd be yours for a stretch. You could sell her without limit!"

Babs takes the offer seriously, "How about I take a look at all of your Pledge, Janet. Because I have to be careful. Ginny would probably love me too much."

And both Monitors laugh.

Babs nods in the direction of the Backyard. "I feel guilty leaving them out there like that."

Janet guides BB's eyes back to her own, "Don't be guilty; it's their privilege to wait for you. Learn perseverance."

"Kimju worries about Robyn's Charm," Babs dangles a thought, "Robyn repeats this Term for a reason, but I am not certain if Robyn Redacted even knows the reason why."

Janet makes quick work, "How could she? She forgot the pact she made to start all over right after she made it."

BB ponders, "I'm not so sure I know what happened… or that you do either… or even Penny and Coco. Steph knows something, but not a lot, because Steph got broken first, before Robyn Redacted."

"Probably Gamers put Steph into Lockdown." Janet shrugs and spanks her weighty bare ass. "Gotta go."

§ Janet & Seven Cosmos: Corvette Monitor Hazes the Reveille

Babs stays behind when Janet exits through the Kitchen and out the Back Door to pay an unexpected visit to the Backyard Lineup. The Cam pivots from the Seven Cosmos Pledge still standing Reveille and settles upon Janet. Fat or not, the Cam augments it's collection of Janet's crochet Spiderwebs. An even smaller size micro today, but still, nothing but open mesh over breasts, nipples, and copious pubic hairage. Jaboos and jute patch, with a bare jaxy backside.

§ Janet Plays with Tiffany: The Past of Current Relationships

Janet settles her 5' 7", 180 pound frame behind the slender and taller redhead at the end of the Lineup: Tiffany stands spread surrender, eyes forward, mouth ovaled, belly-up belly-down, back skin all the way down into posterior rugage where two sweeping curves of tush gather into the tail trough and disappear down into pants which contour the covered tush perfectly, and emerge to split the cameltoe in the front as they rise upward.

Janet walks around the end to position herself in front of Tiffany, and of course the entire Cosmos Lineup, although all eyes should be looking forward. She eyes the Lineup and decides to start where she knows best, Tiffany. *Get her take on her position, her Caste, her momentum, her goals.*

Tiffany considers herself pro. *I know what Janet knows. Two Terms ago Janet and I were Stripper Roommates, with the plump one teasing cocks, and the slender me begging to fuck them. Then last Term I became a Porn Star and Feature Dancer whereas Janet Pledged the Cosmos House. Last Term we only met once, during Janet's Alumni Reprise at the Nugget.*

Janet evaluates Tiffany's Garments: *Eraser Heads visible right through Tiffany's clear vinyl longsleeve front-button croptop, bellage galore from the ribs way down past navelage until finally colliding with red pubic hair erupting up out of skin-tight low-rise stretch pants with an elastic waistband.*

Janet speaks, "Hello Tiffany Transparent! I haven't seen you at all this Term, although I did meet some of your fellow Cosmos during *The Arrivals*. When was the last time we saw each other, Pledge, do you recall?"

Tiffany answers. "Ma'am, on Stage at the Nugget, when you bestowed Piss Mouth upon me, Ma'am." She affords herself a wry smile, "And we climaxed the Dong together."

Janet puts her palms on her wide hips and leans backward. "I believe that Kimju an Molly witnessed our performance when they were Nugget Strippers last Term. Now they join you as Cosmos Pledge. Have you begged they bear witness?" Janet pokes.

Tiffany speaks, "Ma'am yes Ma'am. Not only that, last Term they got to bear witness to my fornications. They saw me get fucked in the Champagne Room, clean myself off the dick with my mouth, and collect a facial. They saw me in the Inner Sanctuary get gangbanged. That's one of my Porn Star Calendar months."

Tiffany squares her thoughts, "Monitor Janet, your pee was the only pee I tasted, until Babs forced me to taste myself during *The Arrivals*."

Janet gentles correction, "You didn't just taste my pee center Stage at the Nugget, you begged to chug shots." Janet opines, "You'd do anything to avoid Slavesex."

"Ma'am!" Tiffany extols. "I took on your Pee-Cam when we were both Strippers; I Opted Porn Star and you Opted Pledge; Slavesex wasn't an Option." Tiffany argues.

"Correct," Janet agrees. "And you took on Piss Mouth when you were a Whore—a Porn Star as you choose to call yourself—and Slavesex *was* an Option."

Tiffany sighs, "Ma'am, yes, Ma'am. First I have to lick up after you and now I'm licking up after myself."

"Maybe it's time to expand your feedstock, Tiffany Tinkle Tongue" Janet cajoles. "Did you beg Babs?"

"Ma'am, I begged her pee on me. I begged her to pee in my mouth. I think I overburdened her. I couldn't tell if she thought I was trying to be funny or was embarrassing."

"No problem. You may beg me to be my toilet," Janet suggests. "I don't want you to feel shut out."

Tiffany rolls her eyes and licks her lips, "Ma'am, please pee in my mouth," Tiffany begs.

"You can beg all the Pledge," Janet suggests.

"Ma'am, thank you, Ma'am." Tiffany squares. "You know I have taken on not just wet work from you but also lots of other Karma. When we were Strippers together you got to Opt and become a Cosmos Pledge last Term."

"And you got rewarded with your dream Caste." Janet extols, tilting her chin upward. "You got to Opt Down and Whore at Flesh Ranch."

"Ma'am, excuse me, I got to be a Porn Star!" Tiffany prides. "I still am a Porn Star, even if Babs insists I'm a 'wannabe Porn Star.' But face it, I've done everything explicit, all holes, all sexes. Gamers still masturbate to me all the time."

Janet curls her lip and squints, "So which are you, Pledge?"

Tiffany clear her throat and clarifies. "Ma'am I am a wannabe Porn Star, Ma'am."

"So besides not valuing you as her toilet, does BB value you for anything?" Janet asks.

"I got in a lot of trouble trying to protect you, Janet," Tiffany says. "She disciplined me for not revealing to her I knew you. I was the first Cosmos to feel the Minxy Mirror. I had to scratch myself up in the bramble hedge, eat soap, affirm my Pee-Cam and, worst, end up affirming my Piss Mouth. That was all because I didn't tell her about you and me at the Alumni Reprise. But she is my Boss Babe and I am her Pledge so I must appease her first. I'll dance and pink, I'll Double Dong. I'll do stuff she's not aware of yet! I just need to Opt Strip next Term."

Janet nods in approval, "Would you like me to share a secret with you?

"Ma'am, I would be honored Ma'am," Tiffany guards.

"Have you heard that when she was a Monitor last Term that it was Steph who escorted me to the Nugget the night of my Alumni Reprise?"

No! Tiffany shakes her head, allows herself to make eyes with Janet, and speaks, "I though you had to streak. Both ways."

"I did. Steph provided me no cover and may have even tipped off a paparazzi or two. She took a Van, and watched from a secret viewing booth up near the Master of Ceremonies' announce booth. She saw it all. She probably took a Cam, but there were lots of cams that night. But Steph's Videos vanished when she vanished into Lockdown."

"Does Babs know this?" Tiffany asks.

"Ah, asking me a question." Janet jaunts. "So what should you be begging me, Pledge?"

"Ma'am, please soap my mouth, Ma'am, for asking a question." Tiffany begs. "But you know it's in your advantage you tell me, Ma'am," Tiffany sasses with a sexy shake of her body.

"Remind me again please the first part of your answer," Janet guides.

"Ma'am, please soap my mouth, Ma'am. My mouth belongs to you, Ma'am. You can fill it with soap, you can fill it with laxative, you can fill it with your urine. Please let me Pledge naked and cum be a Stripper next Term! I'll keep every secret."

"Do you want to know another secret that Steph knows?" Janet dangles.

"Ma'am, I'm not sure, Ma'am," Tiffany quivers. "You make secrets expensive."

Janet grins. " Once when Babs was a Pledge last Term, she crossed her legs when she wasn't supposed to, and I ended up bartered to sit Cravat for this transgression. Babs always knew I did something, but never knew what. We never had a chance to share any secrets. Steph knows, because it was her idea, and because she visited me and cammed me secured and forced climaxed. I lost so much control I pissed myself."

"Steph arranged for you to sit Cravat for Babs?" Tiffany seeks to confirm.

Janet ignores that Tiffany asks still another question. "Right. Now listen to me. Once I became a Monitor this Term I went looking for Steph's video of me. I looked in Automatron but it's not there; it seems to have disappeared when Steph vanished into Lockdown."

Tiffany asks, "I gather you haven't told Babs about this?"

Janet waggles a finger, "Asking questions a third time, Pledge, what does that get you?"

"Begging soap, Ma'am." Tiffany knows the answer. "Please give me a soapy enema then soap my mouth. May it please you to expose me inside and out, Ma'am."

Janet nods. "Besides soap and begging Opt Strip, do you have any other special requests today? After all, it is I who, two Terms ago, helped you acquire your Pee-Cam. And last Term I assisted in your acquisition of your Piss Mouth. Have you any other needs?"

Tiffany smiles yet continues to stand spread surrender. "You could take my shirt away, Ma'am. You could roll my stretch slacks down and off. Please totally expose me, Ma'am."

Janet rests her hands on her wide hips and ponders.

Tiffany gazes. *Janet is wise to deal with me last. Most Cosmos might not know many of Janet's secrets, but I do. I know her measurements: 40EE-34-46. I know she wears three rings on each side of her long inner lips; I know because I've had my mouth in her pussy. I licked her jimmy, center Stage at the Nugget. Check Automatron.*

Janet also understands circuits of information. She gestures toward her own Spiderweb Bikini. "Right now we both might have two pieces but I'm closer to naked than you are. You want to be more like me but with fewer Garments. You must have done something extraordinary to Double Opt Up and become a Pledge this Term."

Tiffany feels her every-erect Eraser Heads brush the inside of her clear vinyl longsleeve croptop. "Ma'am, I'm being tormented by Gamers who want to sexually frustrate me. Drive me crazy with lust. And you,

Ma'am, thank you for letting me pink and cream during *The Arrivals* but make me hold back my climax so I can present it to you upon your commands. Please help me Pledge naked and cum be a Stripper next Term."

Janet shrugs, "You know Strippers can't sex. You're going to stay frustrated even more."

Tiffany begs, "Ma'am, you know I have no other choice. I need to shoot new *Suck Fuck Facial* scenes just as soon as possible. I'm already too horny. If I'm not careful Kundalini might take me over completely and I'll lose all control of myself."

"You could break the Rules," Janet says.

"Ma'am, please don't say that, Ma'am," Tiffany retorts, "I know that if I break the Rules and get caught and put in Lockdown that when the next Term begins I won't be broken to Whore; I will be Slavesex. And that is *not* something I want."

"I hear tell you're a Double Dong aficionado?" Janet drolls.

Tiffany appreciates the tease, "Ma'am, I climaxed you on the Double Dong, center Stage at the Nugget, during your Alumni Reprise last Term! Ma'am!"

Janet remembers. *Well, sort of. I came so hard I lost it. Tiffany really did put me into the Zone. Then she kept me there while she played me for the Crowd, made me drip and squirt, collected my pee in a jigger and tossed a shot.*

And then she kissed me.

Tiffany smiles at an old friend, "Ma'am, I'll dong with anyone any chance that I get. Pledge are allowed to, you know that from experience, Ma'am."

"Sound like you need to locate the Dong," Janet wiles.

"Ma'am if I can find the Dong in a pussy I'll attach myself to it, pull it out, and bring it to the Cosmos House," Tiffany offers.

"Perhaps you'd even accept a handoff," Janet teases.

Tiffany grins, "Ma'am I'll take the Double Dong in my hands, in my mouth, up my tailpipe, but especially in my twat."

"You know I'll do it all. I'll dildo, buttplug, Double Penetrate. I'll shave myself bare and bald and stay naked. I'll pink, cream, and cum. Just please let me Pledge naked and cum be a Stripper next Term. I'm a wannabe Porn Star, Ma'am." Tiffany raises her eyebrows and tilts. She adds, "Babs doesn't understand my passion."

Janet curls, "So do you know where the Double Dong might be?"

Tiffany speculates, "Ah, Ma'am, Robyn says that Penny and Coco climaxed the Double Dong at the end of last Term, after you and Babs held them down and stripped them naked in the Mudpit. Babs confirms that Steph got put in Lockdown before your Mudwrestling Contest and didn't see the Contest or the aftermath, Ma'am. Babs also says that she didn't see Penny and Coco pose for the Dining Room Pictures either, and she wasn't aware of them until she found them, the Baseboard Strippers, hanging on the Dining Room wall, below you and Monitor Babs."

Janet brushes out crust from her jam pot, aligns the rings in her sex lips, leans in, and whispers to Tiffany. "Confidentially I think BB was shocked to discover herself on the wall. Me, I rather like myself. I hang it all out. I am worth masturbating to." Janet leans back.

Tiffany quickens, "Ma'am, most certainly. But Ma'am, if Robyn's story is true then maybe Penny and Coco took the Dong with them to the Nugget, Ma'am."

Janet picks her nose. "Except Strippers are not allowed to share the Double Dong at the Nugget."

Tiffany volunteers, "Ma'am, perhaps you have enough Caste to ask Automatron if it collected Penny and Coco's Double Dong delight at the very end of last Term."

Janet casts an eye toward Robyn, standing next to Tiffany. Janet catches Robyn's eyes looking at her, and in response Robyn draws her eyes back looking straight ahead.

Again Janet whispers to Tiffany, "We shall probe Robyn for more details. Sometimes Robyn knows things she shouldn't" Janet muses, "Redacted or not."

Janet steps back and away and surveys Tiffany carefully.

Tiffany offers, "Ma'am, I'll suck on your jewels, I'll bury my face in your jam pot, I'll service your jimmy, you can pee in my mouth. Please let me Pledge naked and cum be a Stripper next Term."

Janet sighs. "Very well. You may draw your legs together just enough to roll your slacks down so they are tight on your thighs and there is clear space below your twister. Then you may unbutton your croptop and hold it wide open."

"Ma'am, thank you, "Ma'am," Tiffany brightens as she scrambles, before Janet changes her mind or Babs arrives. *Once again I get to show my tits, thatch, and tush outside. The Cosmos House Cams have collected me pinking, peeing, and naked; but I have not been allowed to display myself naked outside where the paparazzi collect for the unauthorized.* Tiffany retains a stand, legs open, hold-shirt-open position. *It's not just the Gamers who want to see my titties and twat. It's everyone, and now everyone can!*

§ Janet and Beka & Elle: Boobage & Vagflash Training

Janet takes a step back from Tiffany, politely nods to Robyn, gazes over the middle part of the Lineup and settles upon Beka and Elle at the end. A croptop and miniskirt, and a halter and shorts.

Janet rears her head back, "So, did you enjoy your visit to my Corvette House during *The Arrivals*? Did you like admiring the Dining Room Pictures in *my* House?"

Beka doesn't know what to say and Elle flusters, "Ma'am thank—"

Janet interrupts, "You must admit that the Baseboard Strippers—Penny and Coco—did a fine job of showcasing a rectal portal and colon. Along with a puddy and coot." Janet tickles Beka under her chin. "But you did pretty good too, didn't you Pledge?" Janet tilts her head. "You leaked brodeas out of your breach."

Beka bumbles, "Elle says you put a thermoprobe into my borehole. And in the Dining Room William inserted a gelatin egg suppository."

Janet pushes her lower teeth forward and opens her mouth. She flares nostrils. Elle stands spread surrender; Janet casts eyes downward across Elle's torso. "I like how the seam of your jeans digs your nappy out, Pledge," she says. "Aren't you curious about what your *Corvette Baseboard Worship Video* look like, when you and your Roommate visited me? Besides tittering, what else do you think happened?"

Elle falters, "Ma'am, I mean, Ma'am, I don't quite know what happened to my rear end. It felt like somebody pulled my seam to the side and Darleen cammed my na-na and nadir way. At first I though you lipsticked my asshole, or gave me an enema, but I had no after effects."

Elle gathers, "Then after I saw Beka get a gelatin egg suppository while worshiping the Dining Room Pictures at our House, I thought that might have been what happened to me. Especially when Steph got thermoprobed like Beka did."

Janet offers advice. "Beg me to screen your pullaside, so that all of your fellow Cosmos, indeed, the entire Prefecture, might see what you revealed. And what got fed into your nadir way."

"Ma'am," Elle stumbles, almost breaks position, "Ma'am, please screen my pullaside while worshiping the Baseboard Strippers at the Corvette House in front of the Cosmos, Ma'am."

Janet considers the reply, "Modify your beg, Pledge, and beg Babs screen them to all the Cosmos *except* you, so they can see what happened and you can hear the facts secondhand."

"Ma'am, please let me be the last person in the Prefecture to see what got fed to asshole," Elle begs.

Janet praises, "Once you know what happened to you you shall determine what you must do to maintain parity with your Roommate in your anal compartments."

Elle opens her mouth. *Beg the thermoprobe?*

But Beka rushes, "You taught us that we're 'Hot hot. Titters and twat. 98.6 in my anus.' Beka turns her head toward her Roommate, proclaims. "Elle and me both!"

Janet doesn't appreciate the interruption but tolerates it. She turns toward Elle and raises an eyebrow? "

And Elle responds, "I'm Hot hot hot. Titters and twat. 98.6 in my anus. You can take my temperature, Ma'am, and sink the thermoprobe into my nadir. I will do what I can to maintain parity with my Roommate, Ma'am, because we desire to Opt Up, Roommates Together."

Janet digests this mouthful, carefully settles her clit inside her g-string and asks Elle, "So remind me about your contributions."

Elle emotes, "Ma'am, I cleaned up after my Roommate, Ma'am. I'm Elle Lollydor now."

Janet observes that Beka dangles out fresh béchamel. She elaborates to Elle, "Seems like Kundalini's stirs."

Elle catches the drift, "Ma'am, I will lick up after her again. I licked up at your Corvette House, and I licked up in the Dining Room.

Janet surveys the Backyard. "You'll lick up here in the dirt," she says.

"Ma'am. I even licked up after Steph," Elle sidetracks.

"One drop!" Janet laughs, and breaks the tension. "Don't worry, Steph will learn to delivery you more than one drop."

Elle isn't sure she should speak.

Janet inhales. "Did BB screen you the part of your visit where Ginny gets throated and fucked in the Cravat?" she inquires.

Elle feints backward, "Ma'am, Monitor Babs hasn't shown us that either, Ma'am."

Beka interrupts, "But we heard it happen so we know it was real."

Janet opens her mouth to apply correction but Elle rescues, "Ma'am we will both beg Babs to screen Ginny Cravat, Ma'am."

Beka rushes, "And we are both begging to Pledge naked and become Strippers next Term."

Janet narrows her eyes upon Elle, "And what about you, Elle Lollydor?"

Elle understand, "Ma'am, please let me Pledge naked and become a Stripper next Term." She casts her eyes downward.

Janet nods ruefully. "Look at you. You've got the two pieces you need to Opt Up yet you are begging to Strip." Janet hefts her belly. "I'd say you are conflicted."

Elle squirms.

Janet calms. "But don't worry. If I don't un-conflict you, Gamers certainly will."

Elle says, "Ma'am, thank you, Ma'am."

"So prove to me you say what you mean. You've got buttons that hold the neck strap of your halter together." Janet sucks her cheeks in and snaps her head down. "Show me you know how to put your fingers to work, Pledge."

Regretfully, ruefully, Elle thinks she understands. Paparazzi and the Cam catch her front and back as she unlocks her fingers behind her head, works them down the back of her neck until she finds the two buttons of her halter strap, works the first of them through its buttonhole, double checks that her armpits are deepened, checks that she looks straight ahead and holds oval-mouth, then pushes the last button all the way through its hole, and lets go.

Elle feels the two triangle patches fall forward, baring both noogies. Pear-shaped 34Bs with a slight hang reveal themselves to *everyone*. Paparazzi watching telephoto see Elle's eyes search for watchers; her face flushes and her nipples crackle up. Uncertainty gathers, but Elle figures it out, interlocks her fingers behind her head again, and double checks she holds full stand spread surrender position. *I can do this,* Elle determines. *Even if I am in a dream. I don't think I'm tittering anymore. I'm hanging boobage, and it's only because I still have my halter hanging down to my waist I'm not technically topless. Except that my nackers completely hang free.*

I don't know what I am anymore.

"You, Pledge," Janet commands, "thank me."

Elle awakens, "Ma'am thank you for letting me expose my noogies completely. Here in the Backyard where everyone can see. Boobage for the first time. On the Cams. Ma'am." Elle's head spins.

Janet purses her lips. "You shall beg Tiffany to gention your nipples and stain them violet."

Elle blinks.

Janet turns to Beka, "How about you?"

And Beka gushes, "You can stain my nipples *and* gention my mouth, just please let me Pledge naked and become a Stripper next Term!"

Janet leans forward, catches the end of Beka's hanging bead of brodeas on her fingertip and lifts upward, letting the thick valiva build on her fingertip until it breaks. She extends her fingertip to Beka's mouth, and lets the newbie Pledge suck it. *No problem.* Janet steps back, Kundalini constructs, and Beka surges to replenish her stalactite.

Elle makes the mistake of looking at Janet, luckily discovers that Janet isn't paying her any attention, and realigns her eyes back gazing forward. *Standing spread surrender is both easy to do and hard at the same time. Easy because there is nothing to do and there is time to think. Hard because I'm hardwired to respond to stimuli.* Elle double checks her position and shakes her bare naturals, concerned about Janet's lack of attention. *But why should Janet hurry to see me? See my nubs?* Elle figures it out. *She's going to leave me standing like this!*

Janet is. Elle discovers Janet's wet fingertips at her mouth. "You should be grateful you don't have to lolly Beka out of the dirt," Janet says; Janet tilts Elle's head, and Elle sees a paparazzo watching her.

Beka rustles. Her stretched posture ensures that her croptop rides up her boobies but not quite enough to reveal nippage. Still, belly-up belly-down bellage galore. Still, Beka begs. "I'll pull my shirt up," she promises. "Both of us will go topless."

Janet applies correction, "Your Roommate still has her top, it just doesn't cover her noogies anymore. Boobage, that's what you both want."

"Boobage please," Beka begs.

Janet considers. Beka's miniskirt has crept up enough so that the very bottom of her racing strip lies out. It's butched stubble, brunette, about an inch wide, with a half inch showing. Above a totally shaven bare boneroo. Automatron logs hairage and the shaven lips. "Beg," Janet commands.

"Please let me Pledge naked and become a Stripper next Term!" Beka exclaims.

Janet considers. "Perhaps you should beg Stripper lessons from Kimju and Molly.'

"Absolutely," Beka vibrates, "Elle and me both."

"Oval mouth, eyes straight ahead" Janet orders, and Beka obeys, although her eyes go wild in their sockets. Her body quivers, she pushes her head against her hands and deepens her armpits, feels Kundalini twist, and transudes more brodeas out. The hanging bead swings and sticks to the inside of her thigh, making a loop.

Elle knows. *More brodeas to come.*

§ Janet signs Kimju & Molly: Handbra to Surrender Position

Janet pauses in front of Kimju and Molly. Both ex-Nuggets stand spread surrender and clasp their breasts in a handbra. Both carefully expose their areolas through parted fingers, and both finger their nipples just enough to keep them upright.

"Hello Kimju and Molly," Janet says. "I've seen you dance—live, on the feeds, on the tubes. You're both pretty good at it, and it's my pleasure to meet you in person. Say 'Hello Monitor Janet.'"

Kimju and Molly do in unison, "Hello Monitor Janet."

Janet nods toward Beka and Elle, standing at the end of the Lineup, while she addresses a question to a what used to be Strippers last Term.

"You heard the newbies begging you to teach them to Strip," Janet looks each in the eye. "You willing to oblige them?"

I heard one newbie beg, Kimju assesses, but details out loud, "Ma'am, yes, Ma'am."

Molly augments, "Ma'am, Robyn's already demanded we do this, but we're not sure what to do."

Janet bemuses, "Maybe you don't want them standing ahead waiting in line at the Stage Door of the Nugget?"

Molly capitulates, "Ma'am, I'll teach them how to climax a Dildo. I'll shoot Ping-Pong balls outta my mooe.

Janet bows. "You may move your hands, so you stand spread surrender."

Molly blinks but obeys easily, letting her heavy mams sag free as she raises her arms and intertwines her fingers behind her head. She joins other Cosmos in the Lineup in this position, but only Molly doesn't present cupped armpits. Overweight, plump, Molly presents armpits that puff convex and outward, and are obscured behind a thicket of black armpit hair.

Janet curls a smile and appraises Molly's topless appearance, then looks downward across a distended belly, also rich with body hair. The wet panties that Babs yanked up into Molly's mooe remain buried and commanding, with minge splayed to both sides of the gathered fabric. It is possibly Molly's clit is rolled out but it is impossible to see what color she is inside, so thick is her pubic hair and so tight the gathering. Janet knows the panties also wrench up the moonshadow so that 100% of Molly's moons shine.

Janet faces Molly square on. "You're perhaps the only Pledge who is more nearly naked than I am. And I don't see why you are so anxious. You've only got one piece so you're sure to Opt Strip next Term."

Molly expounds, "Ma'am if I were naked I'd be less anxious. Right now if I were to acquire a second piece somehow I'd end up a Monitor next Term. Like you."

"I'm a bad place to end up?" Janet queries.

Molly flounders, "Ma'am, I meant it would be a bad place for me. I'd surely fail, and I could end up worse than a Stripper for that. But one piece or zero, please help me Pledge naked and cum be a Stripper next Term. I really mean it. I'll climax the Double Dong with you center Stage at the Nugget."

Janet says, "You mean you'll climax the Double Dong with anyone anyplace anytime this Term.

Molly agrees, "Ma'am, I will, "Ma'am."

Janet reaches forward, grabs a Molly mam, and shakes it. Molly holds her position and Janet lets go.

Janet speaks, "You're the only Cosmos streaker so far this Term. Are you aware that your Roommate Steph made me streak when I was her Pledge last Term. She didn't need to, but she did anyway. Maybe now Roommates should share."

Molly begs, "Ma'am please let Steph take over my streaking, Ma'am."

"You'll share." Janet decrees.

Molly agrees, "Ma'am, I'll share streaking with any Cosmos," Molly begs. "And I'll do whatever you say in order to make sure I don't get caught."

"Beg Monitor Babs," Janet advises.

"Ma'am thank you Ma'am." Molly squares up her body, "Please let me Pledge naked and cum be a Stripper next Term."

"Both of you beg Babs for an Alumni Reprise!" Janet commands.

"Ma'am, thank you, Ma'am," they speak in unison.

Janet curls her nose. "You may climax the Double Dong with your Roommate Steph. That will make her love you." Janet eyes Kimju, "Or perhaps you may climax the Double Dong with your ex-Roommate Kimju." Janet nods toward Kimju. "You two can do your own Alumni Reprise."

Molly baubles, "I'll share the Double Dong with anybody Ma'am. I'll share Pee-Cam. I'll share Piss Mouth. But I don't want to share begging to Opt Strip. I guess I don't care who all goes to the Nugget next Term, as long as I'm one of them."

Janet turns to Kimju and asks, "So what are your goals, Pledge?"

Kimju steadies, "Ma'am, please help me Opt Up and be a Monitor next Term."

"So what do you need?" Janet inquires.

Kimju feels her nipples with her fingertips. She still stands spread handbra, still wears a tanga that covers all but an outline of butched kelp and her kawazoo, but leaves her butt bare. She answers, "Ma'am I need a second Garment. I know I can be as good as Monitor Babs."

"Do you think you can be as good as I am?" Janet asks.

"Ma'am," Kimju hesistates. "That's a long order, Ma'am."

"So you think I'm better than Boss Babe?" Janet likes to box.

"Ma'am I don't think I quite put it that way," Kimju dodges.

"Perhaps each of us is better at some things." Janet provides.

"Ma'am, you are so correct, Ma'am," Kimju agrees.

"Perhaps you're less gracious at respecting Monitor Babs than I am," Janet suggests.

"Ma'am, it is my wish to honor Monitor Babs always," Kimju declares.

"You may beg her to eat soap, for suggesting she's inferior to me." Janet suggests.

Kimju cringes, "Ma'am most certainly, Ma'am. Please let me eat soap for you, Ma'am."

"Your Roommate Molly has already become a Pee-Camer Piss Mouth," Janet observes. "Tell me Pledge, don't Roommates share."

"Ma'am," Kimju studies, "Molly was my Roommate last Term, when we both Stripped at the Nugget. But may I advise you that Robyn is my Roommate now, Ma'am. She has no such Obeisances to share."

Janet accepts, "How could I not have know that, Pledge. Please forgive me and accept an invitation to join me on a Yacht outing on the day after tomorrow!"

Kimju finds herself confused and accidentally removes one hand from her breast. Gamers tag a titter before she recovers again.

Janet laughs, "Go ahead, Kimju, stand spread surrender like your ex-Nugget Roommate. I'll give you every opportunity to prove you love your current Cosmos Roommate as much as your ex. Maybe Molly isn't your Roommate anymore, but I'll still help you share the Dong, obtain Pee-Cam equality, and watch you Game with Robyn!"

Kimju moves her hands behind her head, feels her nipples harden, but keeps her eyes forward. "Ma'am, thank you, Ma'am," she says, confused a bit about the dialog and blurting now. "I'll eat soap if I let me acquire a second Garment."

And regrets it immediately.

No problem. Janet steps backward so she may review the full Lineup again. Heads, armpits, spread legs, bellage. Plus a playful sparkling of topless, hairage, rugage.

Janet smiles as the Back Door Cam, now roaming the Backyard, details her. She smiles, points at it, and laughs. "Ha ha ha." She brings her fingers up to rub the jewels that stand out of the center of her Spiderweb bra, and indulges herself a touch on her gem, irritated by rubbing the micro g-string, and also out standing.

Janet compares herself to the Cosmos exposures. Two Cosmos, *Kimju and Molly present genuine topless; Tiffany in clear vinyl and Elle with her halter hanging tag boobage.* Janet adds herself. *Me too.*

Janet angles an eye toward Steph. There is no question that Steph shows headlights, however the cutout minidress shows hairage *below* the legline, in the crotch.

In her mind Janet rolls Steph's minidress down to her waist. *May Steph provide a fifth pair of spooters lined up and awaiting Bikini Babe!*

Janet addresses the two ex-Nuggets again. "So did you beg Babs to fetch your Pink Pages and hand them out?"

Kimju updates, "They're at the Nugget, Ma'am. The Hat Check Girl prints them out. Or at least she did while we were there."

"Once you make a Pink Page it stays with your forever," Janet reminds, "I ought to know. Now tell me all about your video clips."

"Ma'am," Molly bumbles, "BB let all our pink, cream, and climax Videos flow into the public domain."

Kimju bemoans, "They used to have passwords, but now they are in Automatron. Anybody can watch."

Janet fingers her gem. "Babs tells me you are both begging to masturbate and climax in sync with yourself."

Kimju corrects, "Ma'am, Robyn has advocated that idea, Ma'am."

"Have you begged Babs to screen any of your lapdance clips?" Janet inquires.

Kimju gasps.

Janet presses, "I bet your lapdance videos aren't as legal as they should be. I watched you lapdance the night I performed my Alumni Reprise, and you both let the Patrons paw you."

"House Mom pretends like we don't do it," Kimju complains.

"You let Patrons finger-fuck you." Janet claims.

Kimju backpedals, "It beats Whoring."

"You let Patrons mangle your mams," Janet tells Molly.

Molly seeks to assure, "It's okay, Janet, it's just their hands. Or their face and mouth; they like to bury their heads in between my mammies or suckle me. But it's okay, as long as they don't bite."

Janet graces, "I guess then it gets awkward. I gather you know my Ginny and Lee?"

Kimju acknowledges, "Ma'am yes Ma'am. We were all Strippers last Term."

Janet dismisses the similarity. "Ginny and Lee had to streak to get to my Corvette House. All you two had to do is make a topless dash."

"Ma'am," Molly protests, "I've had to streak too." Molly firms, "You know I had to streak to the Bachelor Party, the Figure Drawing Class and to your Medical Exam."

"You'll streak to the Nugget if that's your only way to get there," Janet proclaims. "You'll streak anytime anywhere you are told to. Don't even think about making any deals."

Molly backtracks. "Ma'am, at the Figure Drawing Class I was only naked on the loading dock. And in the freight elevator. And during the class of course."

Molly watches Janet draw in a breath; she hurries to an affirmation. "You are correct, Ma'am, I don't make deals. I'll streak anytime anywhere. You can pee in the Watering Can and pour it all over me. Just please let me Pledge naked and cum be a Stripper next Term, Ma'am."

Kimju advances, "Ma'am, we know you've had to streak too, Ma'am. You've been a Stripper too; you're one of us."

Janet purses her lips. "You are correct, Pledge, we are all one. Steph made me streak to *and* from the Nugget the night you saw my Alumni Reprise, last Term when I was a Cosmos Pledge."

Janet prides her posture. "Tiffany climaxed me on the Double Dong and I gave her Piss Mouth. Center Stage at the Nugget. Talk about Kundalini and Karma."

Janet tilts her head toward Kimju, "Seems like you still need to prove yourself."

And Kimju begs, "Ma'am, please, Ma'am, I'll streak if my Roommate Robyn does."

Molly interrupts. "Ma'am, we saw Tiffany dong you to climax. She was a Porn Star, Whore Caste, so she could dong anybody, except us Strippers back then and us Pledge currently. Tiffany really took you over the top, Janet, but she could do that to anybody."

Janet considers. "Please Molly, you wannabe Stripper, don't lecture me on climaxing. *Nobody ever Stripped better than I did! Once upon a time.*

Janet carefully adjusts her labial lips, so each lip rides to one side or the other of her crochet g-string. Her thick, dark pubic hair makes it difficult to discern the six rings, three to a side, and definitely there. If during *The Arrivals,* Janet wore a mini g-string, when she exchanged the halter for her bra she also reduced her g-string by one size, to a micro Spiderweb. There is really not much there, except irritation. Janet knows *there are sizes smaller still in this Game.*

Janet addresses a question to both ex-Nuggets. "Besides watching Tiffany and me piss, dong, and climax, Tiffany claims you had the privilege of watching her suck cocks in the Champagne Room? Make *Suck Fuck Facial* Videos in the Inner Sanctuary?" Two questions.

Molly rushes, "She did it all, Janet, not just *Suck Fuck Facials* but also Triple Penetration with cocks. We saw three giant naked Negroes work her twat, tailpipe, and throat at the same time. There's a picture in her Porn Star Calendar!"

Janet looks toward Kimju for confirmation.

Kimju affirms, "Ma'am, all true, "Ma'am. We had to watch. Once upon a time she even triple penetrated, hand-jobbed two more guys, and a line of men kept drenching her in the face."

"Drenching her everywhere," Molly augments. "She got gangbanged."

"She had cum running out of every hole," Kimju sweetens.

Molly tries to be practical, "Tiffany told that once she had been fed a large portion of clam chowder, and then got throated so deep it all came up. Not just the phlegm, all her puke."

Janet professes to be appalled, "What a mess!"

"Game Mistress was there too," Kimju adds, "and Slavesex China Doll got to eat breakfast."

Janet tosses, "Well, at least someone was thankful!"

§ Janet & Robyn: A Braggart Gets Invited to go Yachting

Janet turns to Robyn; Robyn stands between Kimju and Tiffany in the Lineup; Robyn's maillot cutout has no headlights, no hairage. Robyn holds her position. *I needn't actually stand spread surrender but I will play along with the Game for the moment.*

Janet considers Robyn's one piece: The maillot cutout with its spaghetti string shoulder straps insures the neckline stays across the top of Robyn's rig, with only the gentlest suggestion of cleavage.

Nothing obscures Robyn's two beautiful armpits, concave, smoothly shaven… and, Janet recalls, *ticklish.*

The cutout hole around Robyn's button keeps it exposed yet minimal. The nearly horizontal leglines, arching from her crotch, are modest, and help keep the cutout centered on Robyn's birthmark. Navelage 24x7.

"Hello again, Pledge Robyn," Janet flatters. "You never fail to stun me with what must be the smallest buttonhole!"

Robyn offers, "Listen Monitor Janet, I show the least amount of bellage, none at all actually, I'm exactly the opposite of Babs, who is supposed to be the Monitor. In fact, I only show my navelage, that's it. And my cutout hole is always smaller than Steph's cutout minidress. Some of her buttonholes are so large she flashes hairage at the bottom. She's a slut. On the other hand, men desire me, even though they know I'm too good for them."

Janet sounds a line, "I saw some clips you cammed of Monitor Babs. Automatron sorted them out. You got BB leaning over, cleavage galore. You got her standing up, stretching her belly and back."

Robyn accepts the complement. "I've collected more Bikini Babe bling that Automatron knows what to do with. What everyone wants is another bazoombas bust out, like what happened at her Mudwrestling Contest. And I'll be there to cam it. But face it, BB's just like you. She doesn't control her Bikini. You'll wear a 'Spiderweb Bikini' crocheted around your little finger and big toe if Gamers say so."

Janet grins. "I will!" She puckers her lips, "So you're the official Cosmos Camer, you document all the Cosmos, not just Boss Babe?"

Robyn expounds, "I do all the directing, I don't just tell the Cam where to look, I also tell the Cosmos what to do. I directed the Back Door Cam when Kimju and Molly arrived and I wallowed the both of them in the Mudpit. I hope you saw that, if not just ask Automatron."

Janet fingers her jaxy.

Robyn advances. "I'm the one who taught Kimju and Molly Hand Signs and took them up to the Bathroom, made them pullaside, pink themselves, drip kloop and muscovado onto the tiles, and climax." Robyn confides, "I made sure the Cam got every last pore, every last drop of cream, and the air coming out of their mouths when they koekjedoodled and mambo-jamboed!" Robyn chortles.

"Mmmmm," Janet approves.

"I've made Kimju masturbate to Tiffany's Porn Star Calendar and pull her first knittle outta her kennel, I made her climax with Molly in the Bathroom, and I made her slick up the Post Henge and climax naked in public. That was the second time I drove her over the top! Kimju knows to not mess with me. I don't care if she hears me say it or not. It's true. I've said it before, my Roommate's going to cum in sync with her videos before I'm done with her."

"You're good!" Janet praises. "I hear your keeping that other ex-Nugget, Molly also mumping her muff.

"Listen to me. I also cammed Beka and Elle. They've been tittering for me since the moment they arrived."

"They mistook you for BB," Janet augments. "I like that they got slapped around and spent the night in the Doghouse!"

Robyn details. "I cammed Molly and Elle making out with the Minxy Mirror yesterday, the last day of *The Arrivals!*"

Janet pauses, advances. "Maybe you also cammed yourself on the Mirror?"

Robyn brags, "Listen, Janet, I am going to cam Kimju and Molly giving Beka and Elle dance and Stripper lessons. And that will be rich. I've cammed Beka's titter and upskirt every day since she's arrived. Beka and Steph too. They're both tittering vagflashing wannabe Whores."

"May both of them honor your predictions!" Janet curls. "When I saw you at the end of *The Arrivals* you were too busy camming yourself to cam anyone else. Shame on you. My Roommate Darleen and I shall invite you and your Roommate out on the Yacht so you can cam yourself more. Cam your Roommate more. Cam both of you together!"

Robyn twitches her nose, tilts her head, twists her torso, but holds her stand-spread-surrender position. She questions, "And Darleen would be camming for your house?"

Janet dismisses, "Possibly we invite William so that Rodney can collect footage for the Peacock House. You can all cam each other."

Robyn counters, "I don't need to go anywhere."

Janet saddens. "If you don't want to go Yachting with us you could loan your maillot to Kimju, streak over to the Corvette House, and beg Darleen to Cam you there. But I'm afraid you'd never remember your maillot was missing, and you'd forget about how to get back."

Robyn retorts, "You're very funny, Janet, but you're not my Monitor. Maybe you've forgotten that during *The Arrivals* it was *I* who brought Babs over to your House so she could look at her butt crack in your Dining Room Picture."

Janet frowns, uncertain as to the veracity of this claim, and probes, "I remember returning to the Cosmos House with you and Babs and meeting my ex-Monitor Steph," Janet conditions. "I guess Steph really loves you for what you did to her last Term."

"Listen Janet," Robyn advances, "Don't you try to fool me! You know perfectly well I wasn't here last Term! The first time *I* encountered Steph was when she was waiting for us in the Parlor. Day Four during *The Arrivals.* You might recall *I* made her uncross her legs and open them wide. I cammed her upskirted sanpan scuffle. I took her upstairs, made her sit spread surrender admiring herself in a mirror, commanded Tiffany go into the Bathroom, which activated the Cam, and broadcast her spreads to the Prefecture. Pretty good, huh, vagflash within minutes of arriving."

Janet considers Pledge Robyn and observes that headlights have formed.

"One more thing you might have seen in the Videos," Robyn offers, "Tiffany pinked her twat and tinkled right there in front of Steph and the Cam."

"So what," Janet bemuses, "She is a Pee-Camer after all."

Robyn is indifferent to who might overhear her, "Tiffany's a wannabe taco peddler. She makes herself up like a wannabe Porn Star. Out here in the sunlight the ultraviolet light makes her Eraser Heads glow. During *The Arrivals* I decided to put her and Kimju naked on the Post Henge and cam them cumming together. Babs gave Kimju's tanga to Tiffany to wear and forbade Tiffany to climax. They both worked up a slick but only naked Kimju got to solo over the top."

"Cams don't lie!" Janet proclaims as if this were a fact. "Congratulations to you for snagging all that for the Automatron! Tiffany must love you feeding her frustration to her Gamer fans,"

Robyn snarls, "Tiffany will drink cum to prove she's a Porn Star. She's begging Babs to screen all her hardcore. Her *Tiny Tit Fuckers,* her *Suck Fuck Facial* series. Tiffany Tatterdemalion. She brags about how many leading men she's fucked. Like over 60. But so what, some of the leading ladies have worked over 300 cocks."

Janet humors Pledge Robyn, "So does her 60 include her gangbangs?"

Robyn startles. "Certainly not! She's bragged she's in the '100+ Bukkake Club.' So go ask the thumper how many times she's touched, throated, twisted, and tailpiped five cocks at once. You'll be surprised."

Janet raises her eyebrows.

Robyn augments, "And besides always wanting me to cam her, Tiffany always wants to put on my makeup. I don't care that Bikini Babe has decided she's to do all the other Cosmos, but I'm special."

"Good for you," Janet praises. "You should worry less about Tiffany and more that your Roommate Kimju doesn't get sassy about following the Rules," Janet advises.

Robyn nods and Janet inquires. "So are you begging to share eating soap with her?"

Robyn draw air in, rises her shoulders up, looks into Janet's eyes, closes her eyes briefly, and tosses her head. "Don't be silly, Janet, you and I both know it's the ex-Strippers who are all going to eat soap. Tiffany started the trend when she spoke carelessly, now you got Kimju and Molly into it. Any other ex-Strippers around? They're next! They can each roll Dice for how many bars they eat!"

Janet smiles, "It's always so nice to hear your suggestions, Robyn. Maybe I will get an opportunity to teach you some lessons you should not forget. But which you probably will."

And Janet turns to Steph.

§ Janet & Steph: Janet Assures Steph Maintain Navelage

Janet pauses in front of the Lineup, then moves and draws herself up in front of Steph. Janet examines the state of Steph's strapless cutout minidress. "Nice," Janet observes, "I guess it doesn't matter if your minidress rides up because you stand spread surrender and stretch it upward, or because it's simply too short to begin with. But I adore how the scruff over your socket wrench is exposed."

Maybe Boss Babe is responsible; maybe the control of Steph's fashion lines comes from higher ups.

Janet beckons Steph to step forward and signs her to resume her stand spread surrender position. Steph tenses as Janet draws her body close and gracefully kisses the imprint of Babs' hand, still rosy on Steph's face. Janet extends three fingers into Steph's exposed crotch, feels to see if Steph's short and curlies have collected secretions, and presents her fingers to Steph's nostrils so Steph may perform her own analysis.

Steph blanches, twists her head but holds her cool, straightens her position, and cups her armpits. She sniffs warily. "Ma'am, I'm dry, Ma'am." Steph states. "I am not Beka Broda!"

Janet advances. "You and Beka Broda sat spread surrender on the Front Porch of the Cosmos House. Monitor Babs switched on the Front Door Cam and delivered you out to the Prefecture. Your lips were starting to become unstuck."

"I never did that!" Steph insists.

"Don't be silly," Janet pierces, "Automatron spooled you."

"Just a minute," Steph defends, "maybe Beka puddled her brodeas onto the floor but I never did. And neither of us ever pinked."

Janet considers Steph's breach of etiquette and steps back to examine her former Monitor and now Cosmos Pledge. The new relationship pleases Janet and clasps her hands together.

It is a fact that the cutout hole of Steph's strapless minidress is not quite as small as Robyn's, yet despite its size it has little margin for error because the minidress has more play.

Unfortunately either the action of Janet's kiss and vaginal feel, or Steph's reaction, has caused Steph's keyhole cutout to shift just enough so that Steph's navel becomes obscured.

Janet steps back and points to the obscured navel. "Tell me if you want me to fix that," she commands. "Navelage 24x7."

Steph looks down at her body, her shoulders rise and she sasses her former Pledge, "You messed it up, Janet, you fix it," she says, although she holds surrender position.

So Janet nods, takes a step forward, gentles her fingers into the top of Steph's strapless tube minidress, gives it a tug, and bares both sinusoidals with their sundials on top. Obviously the Cam feeds on this. Janet observers, considers, and tugs again, gathering the Garment and folding it downward until it rests upon Steph's hips, below Steph's belly button. Janet now gathers the lower portion upward with her fingers, then twists and rolls to ensure that what used to be a minidress shall become a rolled tube belt surrounding Steph's waist. It rests on Steph's bare hips, hangs below her belly button, and graces the top of her otherwise exposed pubic hair.

Steph bends, but holds her position. She wears a waistband tube, but otherwise she's naked. Automatron adds keyword "full-frontal" into her metadata.

"Thank me for making your navel bare again," Janet demands of her former Monitor.

Steph flaps her lips, and Janet touches Steph's reduced single Garment and teases, "If you can wear this tube belt all the way to the Nugget you won't have to streak to get there."

Steph squirms but holds position. *I am very aware I am full-frontal in public.*

Janet allows herself to touch Steph's nipples. "Here's some free advice: you need to beg for the Nugget with a conviction that equals your Roommate."

Steph shakes her head. "The Nugget is not my goal, it's Molly's goal. Molly and I have opposite goals yet ironically our goals coincide. I'm taking her panties and Opting Up."

Janet agrees, "Unfortunately, Steph Sorostitute, my goal for you is different, so when you come visit me at the Corvette House I shall expedite your Opt Stripper next Term."

"Stop it. You're not my Monitor," Steph firms. "And if during *The Arrivals* you made me beg to visit you at your Corvette House you did it under false pretenses, so it's null and void."

Janet grins, "You made me streak to the Nugget Alumni Reprise last Term, pee center Stage, and then get climaxed on the Double Dong." Janet grimaces. "You made me pink, cream, and climax in the Mudpit." Janet growls. "You made me streak and sit naked in the Cravat. That was even less fun. I might not have been sexed, but I was force-climaxed until I squirted and pissed myself. You know this. You cammed me there."

Steph snaps back, "You put yourself in the Cravat. You cut the deal, and not just as a favor to your Roommate Babs after Bikini Bimbo crossed her legs, but because you love all the attention. All I did was allow you to streak and display yourself helpless spread and splayed."

Janet tries not to argue. "May I find time to correct your world view someday," she says.

Steph advances, "Listen, Boss Bitch still doesn't know you sat Cravat for her. Besides any vids I shot vanished with my Lockdown.

Steph asks, "So did you tell Babs I saw you and Tiffany climax the Dong and perform Watersports? Center Stage at the Nugget. I liked that, but you know that because I told you so last Term."

Janet canvasses Steph's nearly naked body. *Shall I finger her, cup a spout in my palm, grab her stern, or slap her!*

Janet scowls. "Is that a question you're asking? Because if it is you need to be begging soap as part of your diet."

"A statement, Ma'am," Steph corrects herself, "Ma'am I've never told Babs I took you to the Nugget and watched you climax the Dong with Tiffany. Or saw you perform Watersports. I feel bad I should hold anything back from my Monitor, Ma'am, however to do so would violate other confidences, like with you, Ma'am." Steph frames her standing spread surrender full-frontal body. She adds, "Tiffany got herself a Piss Mouth for not being forthcoming about your Alumni Reprise."

"Tiffany begged Piss Mouth when she tossed shots center Stage at the Nugget last Term," Janet advises, "she's a Double Opt Up Whore and will do anything for attention." Janet quiets more still, "As for you and what you saw with your own eyes, I agree, we need to maintain those confidences most completely. Your behavior so far is the correct one."

"Ma'am, thank you, Ma'am." Steph answers and it's decided.

Steph ventures, "Ma'am, I know you like to walk on the edge, like you could have gotten the Spiderweb Bikini anytime last Term, and not stayed naked until just before the Mudwrestling Contest."

Janet preens. "You're right, I love my Spiderweb. It allows me to expose myself nearly completely, yet retain two pieces! And how about you? Do you love your minidress? I'm not sure which of us is more exposed. What do you think, Pledge? And thank me."

Steph speaks, "Ma'am, thank you for exposing me full-frontal. I'd we are pretty equal."

Janet corrects. "We are not equal, Pledge. Tell me what is the difference between us, and it is not how much skin we expose."

Steph knows. "You have two Garments and I have one Garments. But we are still both full-frontal."

Janet agrees, asks a question: "Tell me, Pledge, what does a one piece tube cutout minidress get you at the end of the Term?"

Steph knows, "It gets me something to wear to the Nugget, Ma'am."

Steph wrinkles her nose, "So does it provide you some kind of sadistic satisfaction to strip me nearly naked in public like this, Monitor Janet?"

"It does!" Janet affirms, smiles, "Now five pairs of Cosmos' tits await Monitor Babs! And you look splendid with your spigots and snatch!"

Steph opens and closes her mouth.

"You were never nude during *The Arrivals,* were you Pledge?" Janet queries.

Steph knows the answer, "Ma'am, no, Ma'am. I have tittered and vagflashed. And I kept navelage 24x7."

Janet considers, "You're almost nude right now, aren't you?"

"Ma'am," Steph considers, "I might be full-frontal, except I do wear my minidress, even if it is a tube waistband."

"One piece," Janet observes. "You need two to Opt Up."

"Ma'am, I know that," Steph snaps. "I told you, Molly keeps trying to give me her panties."

"BB interferes?" Janet speculates.

"Ma'am, yes, Ma'am."

"Maybe you need to beg Opting Down before you beg to Opt Up," Janet observes.

"Ma'am, that's really a bad idea, Ma'am," Steph says.

Janet curls. "You could forfeit your minidress to Molly, streak to visit me, and beg me to climax your brains out."

"Ma'am, maybe Babs knows I don't need any forced climax."

Janet smiles, "Confirm you shall visit me at the Corvette House."

Steph rebels, "You don't need me to confirm that."

Janet insists. "Ask me nicely to come visit."

Steph weakens, "Ma'am, please let me visit you at the Corvette House."

"Remind me that you will be streaking naked to visit me," Janet curls.

"Ma'am," Steph guides carefully, "I can't streak as long as I wear this minidress, even if you have it rolled into a tube."

"So true!" Janet declares. "But don't worry, Gamers will fix that. They are looking forward to me climaxing you right out of your body!"

Steph feels an urge to urinate.

Janet continues, "Tell me, Pledge, are you going to seep more than one drop outta that slot of yours? Ask nicely, Pledge."

Steph squares her eyes, looks forward, and says, "Ma'am, I'll beg Babs to secrete more, Ma'am. But I am not Beka Broda."

Janet steps back so the Cam and any paparazzi might feast unobstructed upon Pledge Steph.

Steph feels hot flashes across her body.

Janet asks, "You know to never forget the first Rule of the Cosmos. What might it be, Pledge?"

Steph seethes at Janet, but holds her near naked standing spread surrender position. She grits, "Navelage 24x7, Ma'am."

Janet trades eyes with her former Monitor. "What do you say to me, Pledge?" she inquires.

"Ma'am thank you for helping me retain navelage, Ma'am," Steph recites. And carefully balances on her two spread legs, cups her open armpits, ovals her mouth, casts her eyes straight ahead, and tries to forget, *I'm topless, bottomless and my snizzle shows its finer lines.*

Janet ends the conversation, "You're going to be much more thankful before the Term runs out, Pledge." Janet signs her former Monitor to step back and align herself with the Lineup, and exits the Backyard.

§ Babs & Seven Cosmos: Tickling, Pee, and Shaving Request

Boss Babe detours into the Dining Room before she returns to her Lineup. *Yes, there I am on the wall at the top of the four Dining Room Pictures. Wearing my Black Bikini, with my crescents d'areolage showing, just like now.* Babs purses a lip. *The only difference is that my waistline is rolled down. Thank you, Ms. Interior Decorator, for forcing me to look at my own hairage in the Picture.* Babs curls her nose.

Elle and Beka have reported that over at Janet's Corvette House there exists another four Dining Room Pictures, where again Babs wears her Black Bikini also with the waistline rolled down, only this Picture shows Babs' backside. *If indeed this Picture makes sure I hairage my bush; the one at the Corvettes surely shows me cracking my butt. Posterior rugage.* BB fingers her waistband to assure herself her waistline stays hoisted. *No hairage, no rugage, no cheeking.*

Babs attempts to hikes her bra straps upward, to no avail of course. *Maybe I had to play Dice when I was a Pledge, but now I've got the Dice and my bush and butt crack stay covered.* BB snickers, *I might show bling, but I no longer blush when Gamers look at me or I look at my own pictures!*

"Janet's Picture shows her string up her jaxy," Beka had added, and Babs frames Penny and Coco as naked, and showing their backsides.

Babs exits back through the Kitchen, pauses to consider Tiffany's Porn Star Calendar and confronts a picture of Tiffany with more cocks than just the three inside her. She shudders, exits out the Back Door, paces across the Landing, steps down onto the yard, rings the Bell, and approaches her Lineup. BB's return tenses the Pledge: bodies square up, fingers interleave behind heads, widely-spaced toes face forward, armpits deepen, belly and navelage tuck flat. A few beads of sweat emerge.

Babs twists her lip in wry amusement that Tiffany holds her unbuttoned shirt wide, that Kimju and Molly no longer form handbras and bare their breasts, and that Elle's halter hangs down in front of her, baring both breasts. Steph also sprouts and appears nearly naked. Only Robyn and Beka fail to present bare-breasted. Boss Babe doesn't have to ask her Pledge how or why they advanced their toplessness. *I get the picture. Janet ordered Tiffany to unbutton her shirt and hold it wide open. She ordered Kimju and Molly to return their hands to surrender position. She ordered Elle to unbutton her halter. This is all Janet's good humor at attempting to intimidate me. Well, I'm not intimidated. I'm cured.*

Well, perhaps. Babs gives Steph a once over. Steph stands spread surrender, eyes forward, oval mouth. Babs decides. *I'll deal with you in a moment.*

Boss Babe shuffles her position so she stands directly in front of Elle and looks down her nose at her red-faced Pledge. "Topless but still with two pieces. Nackers with nips erected above a halter hanging down. There's a description you can write down!"

Fear of discovery atop embarrassment of exposure flush Elle from her face to her chest, and both nipples pop up.

Beka interjects and blurts, "I'll give a piece away and go topless."

"You'll beg to eat soap for begging without permission," Babs decrees, then turns to Elle and commands, "Button up."

And Elle scrambles to fasten her halter back up with relief. *Babs cares for me; she makes me important. I feel* The Runup *lift me like a wave. Everything's going to be okay.* Elle gathers her thoughts. *Except it really isn't, is it?*

Boss Babe says not a word to Kimju and Molly, and they do not volunteer unrequested speech. They fret because each assumes they will be punished for changing their handbras into surrenders, fret because they expect Babs to demand an explanation, yet doesn't. BB picks up the

Watering Can and soaks Molly's head, mamazulons, gathered panties, hairage, and full moons. They shall continue to stand spread surrender, topless buttage, for many more hours, and continue to fret.

BB turns to Tiffany, playfully pinches her ear, squeezes her nose, tickles an armpit, and carefully feels an Eraser Head. Babs pinches to see if Tiffany's hard nip senses the squeeze. It does. No problem; BB lets go. She steps back and signs Tiffany to button her shirt, lift her slacks up, and return her hands to surrender.

Of all the Pledge, only Robyn allows her eyes to follow Babs' movements, sometime furtively, sometimes not. BB continues to ignore all such transgressions.

Robyn repositions herself in front of Steph so she may examine Steph's minidress reconfiguration as Steph holds her body stand spread surrender. Steph appraises her situation. *Janet could not resist reducing my minidress into a tube belt hanging on my belly, crossing my stern divide and kissing my shag. This is not to tease me, this is Janet payback for whatever she thinks I did to me last Term.*

Babs closes then opens her eyes. *My problem is I kind of appreciate Janet helping me keep Steph in line, and although I don't really want to trade her away to Janet, I do owe Janet favors.* Babs discerns that the Cam documents that her crescents have bubbled up. She scans the house next door for paparazzi. She puts out of her mind an image of Steph hanging naked by her feet and being dunked in a well. *I can't really complain about Janet, she's offered to let me train Ginny and Lee and Louise. Or some subset thereof. That's more than fair.*

Boss Babe asks Steph a question. "Maybe tomorrow or someday you'll want a different cutout minidress?

Steph hedges her bets, "Ma'am you've said that every day I'm entitled to new minidress."

"Did you beg Janet to visit her at the Corvette House?" Boss Babe inquires.

"Ma'am," Steph stumbles, "She seems to think I'm going to streak over to see her. You need to straighten her out. I've still got one piece and Molly is begging to give me her panties."

"Did you make any other commitments?" Boss Babe asks.

Steph hesitates, and BB adds, "Don't forget that Automatron spools the Cam.

Steph considers the Cam canvassing her near-naked body. "Ma'am, Janet said I need to make Elle Lollydor lick up any seepage I might make." Steph looks Babs in the eye, adds, "Ma'am."

Babs walks around behind the Lineup again and makes sure that her palm can fit into any crotch; one of the two bare slits oozes brodeas, and BB makes sure that the other's satchel flaps are not stuck shut.

Babs puts her hands on Steph's bare shoulders, presses her cleavage against Steph's bare back, and coos, "May it please you to know..." Babs slides her hands down to twist Steph's nipples to erection, "we have received an offer for a Steph shaving video!" Steph's body snaps, her eyes glower, and the Cam lowers to capture Steph's totally exposed thin blonde shrubbery square on.

Babs breaks her hold and moves laterally behind her Lineup. Boss Babe reaches her hands forward and tickles both sides of a belly. Much squirming and air noises emerge. Now BB's mocks the entire Lineup, playfully, "Steph, don't think you're so special! Because we have received requests for shaving videos for *all* Cosmos Pledge!" This produces a gasp, a fluttering of six bare breasts, and a wiggling of intertwined fingers eager to disengage and touch the money. All the Cosmos have pussy hair...even though one of them, Beka, has only a narrow racing stripe. Babs spots one pair of hands in midair, thoughtlessly disengaging before they snap back into standing spread surrender position.

BB tickles another Pledge inside an armpit; more squirming, more air noises, and a uncontrolled urine release. Another Cosmos wants to join Tiffany and Molly on the Pee-Cam! But would any Pledge dare turn a head and look in the direction of the tinkling sound? All but one keep their eyes forward; but by the time Robyn cheats to look, Babs has moved on.

For the rest of today the Cosmos shall audition for what some Gamers call tableau vivant, French for living statues. The Cosmos aren't naked yet, but before Midnight on the last Day of the Term, some of them will beg to become a naked tableau vivant display at an art opening, a cocktail party, or in a nightclub. And may Gamers honor their begs.

Babs Anoints Robyn: Haze Cosmos Pledge (D16-19)

II-3 Robyn Hazes Cosmos: Videos & Deeds to Do (D16)

§ Tiffany Makes Up Six Cosmos: Bathroom Beautification

Six Cosmos spend their first night of *The Runup* in their bunks at the back wall of the windowless Bunkroom, opposite the Minxy Mirror, which sometimes masquerades as a Screen. The Pledge all know the Bunkroom lies to one's right as one comes up the twisting staircase inside the Cosmos House onto the second floor. Across from the top of the stairs one would be well advised to not enter Babs' Bedroom, to the left is the Bathroom, with the only Cam on the second floor—and only activated when any Pee-Cam Pledge enters the Bathroom.

Gamers who mapped out the Cosmos positions during *The Arrivals* will recall that each pair of Roommates sleeps over and under: furthest down the back wall Elle sleeps above Beka, in the middle Steph bunks above Molly, and nearest the stairs Kimju resides above Robyn. Depressions with a hook and a shelf between the bunks provide opportunities for Pledge to hang Garments on hooks; all the shelves are absent of any possessions. There is no place to store secrets.

Tiffany sleeps in Babs' Bedroom, on the floor beneath Babs' bunk. Five of the six in the Bunkroom sleep in their Garments, or wisely decamp them and use them for pillows.

Alone among them Steph always sleeps naked overnight; Steph always folds her minidress and lays it neatly on the shelf adjacent to her bunk. Steph fumes, *I resent I must let go of it during my sleeping hours, even though there are no Cams here in the Bunkroom.* Steph hypothesizes, *I doubt Babs has it in her to make me do this; it's Gamers who supply her with my daily minidress. Or maybe MomCap picks it out. But it's not something Bikini Bitch dials up on her Desktop.*

Last night Steph never bothered to unroll the bundle her dress had been reduced to, and left the rolled tube sitting on her shelf. *Boss Bitch can sort it because she knows to gives me my new dress in the morning, before I use the Bathroom.*

On the new morning (that is the morning of what is now Day Sixteen, the second day into *The Runup*) Steph awakes early, observes that her old proffered minidress no longer lays on her shelf, and find no replacement there. Still naked, she decides to hurry to the Bathroom. She tiptoes past BB's Bedroom door, ascertains that that Bathroom is empty, the Cam asleep. She enters, quickly pees, and rises to leave.

Tiffany's entrance catches Steph by surprise. Tiffany, naked because she only enters the Bathroom naked, activates the Cam.

Steph quickly covers her breasts with one hand and forearm and covers her crotch with the other. She eyes the Cam.

"The Cam likes you," Tiffany observes. They both know Monitor Babs feeds live to the Prefecture, and that the pictures and video streams spin into Automatron's vast archives.

"But it like me more than you. All I have to do is make to pee and it will return its attentions my way. My fans know that my pissing is different every time!"

Steph complains, "I need Babs to give me today's minidress."

"Patience, she'll be back soon." Tiffany surveys. "I hear you're getting something special to wear." Tiffany gestures to the stool in front of the makeup mirror and table. "Sit like you're supposed to," Tiffany instructs. "I'll make you beautiful now. And after you, I've got five more Pledge to makeup, plus myself.

Steph clenches her bare breasts tighter with her hands as she sits and wrinkles her nose. She carefully parts her legs enough so her thighs don't touch, then in a burst of uncertainty, opens them wider. *Enough so the wavy hairs across my crotch aren't constricted. I can see what I look like in the mirror. And I can see that the Bathroom Cam takes me handbra and bottomless. It's not like I haven't had to open my legs to the Cam before. It's just that I've never had to display myself naked before. Even if I do keep by spouts covered with my hands.*

No place better to start than the Cosmos House.

Tiffany is quick with the makeup, but to Steph, *it seems like the Cam takes me in for ages. And that my outer lips are coming apart.*

"I need to get my minidress from Babs," Steph urges.

"Okay, so I'm done with you then. You'll pass." Tiffany empowers.

Steph takes a final look at her naked open-legged position in the mirror and gives the Pee-Cam a glance. *I'm hot.* And she stands up.

Tiffany instructs her: "Babs said you are to stand spread surrender outside her Bedroom. I'm sure whatever she has for you is worth waiting for."

Steph scurries the few feet down the hall and out of view of the Pee-Cam, just as the other the Pledge scurry into the Bathroom: Kimju, topless; Molly, naked and ready to Pee-Cam; Beka in croptop and miniskirt, and Elle in her button halter and ripped jean shorts. All present themselves to naked Tiffany for makeup.

Tiffany is proud of herself. Like Steph, Tiffany sleeps naked, not because she must beg alternate clothing, but of free will. She hangs her shirt and slacks up any time she enters the Bedroom, and has left them there now because she honors her beg to always enter the Bathroom naked, always turn the Cam on, and always pee for the Cam.

Babs returns; she summons Steph into the Bedroom and gestures she stand in front of her Desktop. "You have something really special today," BB announces, "A single-shoulder strap evening dress. It contains foundation, uplift for your graceful sinusoidals, modestly exposes your button, and comes all the way down to your mid-thigh."

Steph zippers herself into the elastic contraption. *Finally, Gamers come to respect me!*

Babs approves, "Go to the far end of the Bunkroom, stand spread surrender, and look at yourself in the Mirror. The rest of the Pledge will Lineup with you for Reveille."

Steph obeys, and in time Kimju and Molly, and Beka and Elle emerge and stand side-by-side spread surrender. Wannabe Strippers all, two of them with colored nipples to boot.

Robyn's exit is delayed. She has chosen to argue with Tiffany about her makeup—in front of the Bathroom Cam no less, and seizes lipstick and eyeliner and rouge to harken herself. Tiffany doesn't stop Robyn's self-applications, nor does she appreciate Robyn's devilish barbs, "When I get in charge of makeup, remind me to make you up like a clown, dye your hair red, and see if the Circus will find a cage for you." Robyn laughs.

Tiffany considers if this is a tease or a threat. *It's not a tease because Robyn doesn't know what tease is. And if it is a threat I don't know whether to pay any attention or not.... Or if it matters what comes out of her mouth. She'll probably forget she said it.*

Robyn gives Tiffany an evil look and Tiffany gives her another large splash of perfume, first across Robyn's shoulders and then into her hands. "Slather yourself," she commands and tilts her head down, "Don't worry about expense. It's our cheapest perfume. Now beat it. Monitor Babs wants to see you."

Tiffany reserves for herself a post-punk decoration: fire tips at the ends of her hair, lightning bolts on her cheeks. Lips double outlined. Eyes lit up. She squares herself within the dressing room mirror and examines her visage. Naked, full-frontal, 32A-23-33. She rolls her lip down and reads the reversed tattoo; it says, "Porn Star," *except only I can read it in the mirror. I need this tattooed inside my upper lip too, by not reversed, but normal, so everyone can read.*

Tiffany gives herself a final power and pinch, emerges from the Bathroom still naked, and positions herself at the head of the Bunkroom Lineup.

§ Babs Assigns Robyn: In Command of Cosmos Pledge

Babs snags Robyn into her Bedroom just after Robyn leaves the Bathroom, and can tell in three heartbeats that Robyn's face differs from that of the others.

Babs exits from her Bedroom with Robyn trailing behind her, she strides into the Bunkroom between the Mirror and the Lineup, and examines six Cosmos Pledge standing spread surrender: Tiffany has chosen to remain naked, Kimju and Molly remain topless, and Beka and Elle and Steph all bare their arms, legs, and navels. Upon hearing Babs' footsteps, all six oval their mouths and each stares into her own image in the Minxy Mirror, only to watch themselves fade as the Mirror becomes a deep silvery black.

Babs places her thumbs behind Robyn's shoulders, grips her, and guides her forward in front of the Lineup. "Relax your eyes and look at me, Pledge," Boss Babe commands her Lineup, "because you shall listen and obey me. From now on it is my will that my surrogate Robyn command you, and under these circumstances, Robyn shall be obeyed as if the orders come from my very mouth!"

That should be clear enough. Robyn flares her nostrils, sucks her cheeks inward, and lifts her bare shoulders up. Bare shoulders because Robyn's maillot cutout has spaghetti shoulder straps; it conforms to her body, breasts, belly, and crotch, except for the "smallest cutout hole."

Robyn may or may not possess trace memories of Babs from last Term, but Robyn knows, *Boss Bitch won't let anything happen to me. And I am positive Babs owes me big time!*

Robyn's presumption of privilege confuse the Cosmos and so they shuffle their weight on their feet. It's not the first time Babs has ordered the Cosmos Pledge to obey Robyn, but it is the most definitive.

Why does Boss Babe do this? Kimju wonders. Kimju is not the only Cosmos Pledge to silently question motives, but for Kimju the issue is particularly tactical. *Robyn is my Roommate, after all, so does this give her leverage in making me play—if not lose—a Roommate Game? What if Robyn really does have Charm? Or if her Charm works on me by working on BB first.*

Babs gives Robyn a little push, "Go."

Robyn struts and zeros in on her Roommate Kimju, "Maybe the time has come for you and Molly to cum in sync with their videos. What about it, ex-Nuggets?"

Dead air, then Molly fills the void, "Robyn, we'll both cum in sync with our clips. We'll match new pink to our old Pink Pages. We'll Pee-Cam. We'll teach Beka and Elle to dance, just like we said we would."

Kimju keeps silent. *Does Babs know she has empowered my Roommate to boss me around? It's not fair, because I need a way to take* her *down. I need another Garment, and by the Rules, my Roommate Robyn must be my first contest. I'm in trouble now.*

§ Robyn Sends Steph: To Fetch Kimju & Molly's Pink Pages

Babs hangs back and carefully considers the two Cosmos in the Lineup not implicated in Robyn's dance machinations: Tiffany and Steph. *Ex-Porn Star Tiffany has managed to stay naked again this morning and the more Robyn tries to humiliate her the more Tiffany will like the attention. Robyn doesn't conceive that promotion is Tiffany's weakness. My former Monitor Steph dazzles in her single shoulder strap party dress. It's the most covered up she's been this Term, and it's button hole is safe. And when Robyn attempts to humiliate her forgotten former Monitor, fireworks result, because Steph blames Robyn for being in this place, being a Cosmos Pledge.*

BB fingers the straps on her bra; areolage haunts and temps her as she evaluates the minidress and Pledge, *Yes, a single-shoulder party dress can tailor to my body perfectly, I'll add a second shoulder strap and I'm home free. I can keep the minidress overtop my bra and nombril bikini and Opt MomCap next Term, or I can forfeit one of the two pieces underneath just before Midnight and Hover as a Monitor again next Term.*

However! I must not be too eager to take Steph's minidress, Babs concludes. I too must learn patience.

Babs retreats to her Bedroom.

Yes, BB is correct, it is former Monitor Steph who takes the greatest offense at Robyn's surrogate authority. Being demoted grates on Steph, but does not dull her assumption. *I can and will control BB. BooBs, bOObs, Bikini Babe, Bling Bitch. I won't forget she's a party to this.*

But I am going to crush Robyn. And not just for double-crossing me last Term. Steph's thoughts flash to a memory of herself during *The Arrivals. Robyn made me sit out on the Front Porch and spread upskirt with Beka. And then in the Dining Room she made me get on my hands and knees, stick my stern up, and display my star and smoo to her Cam. And then leave me there for Janet and Darleen to cam and Rodney and William to watch. She even tried to get me to hang streamers outta my stash, like Beka Broda does.*

Steph twists her lips. *Boss Bitch really lets Robyn Redacted go too far with me, and BB granting Robyn even more power is foolish, stupid, and rude. More fundamentally, Babs owes me for where she is now. Janet too.*

Steph's thoughts become broken when Robyn bares her fangs. "How about you Pledge. You've got an upskirted gash. Maybe you should learn to pink, cream, and climax just like all the other Cosmos."

Steph takes umbrage and the stridency of Robyn's over-statement empowers Steph to address Boss Babe's surrogate harshly. "Maybe you should be stripped naked, tied spread eagle in the Mudpit, and gangbanged." Steph accidentally lets her intertwined fingers come apart, stops herself in time, and re-entangles them behind her head. She squares up, makes sure her armpits are cupped, and firms her lips realizing that today's minidress covers her far enough down her thighs to avoid any upskirt. Steph makes a final evaluation in the Mirror. *Navelage 24x7, no thanks to you, Robyn.*

Kimju squints as she watches Steph's brash reaction. *Is Steph foolish to talk back to Robyn?* She wonders. *Might Robyn really lack Charm?*

"I'm going to make you masturbate with your Pink Page!" Robyn threatens Steph.

Steph doesn't take it, "Listen, Robyn, I don't have any Pink Page. Hello, anybody home? I've never been a Stripper. Get it? Not me, not Babs, not Beka and Elle, not even you!"

Robyn pursues, "Your Roommate Molly is a pinking, creaming, cumming Pee-Camming Piss Mouth. You need to catch up beyond your upskirted gash. Maybe you should, lie on your back, roll you snatch up, and beg to masturbate to climax while you pee into your mouth."

Boss Babe hears words between Robyn and Steph, emerges into the entrance of the Bunkroom, and commands the conversation. She bows ever so gently to Steph, and ices in a casual but officious tone. "Permit me, Steph Sorostitute, to offer you a choice today. I guess it's no secret your Roommate already promises to pull her maw wide open, meringue and mumbo-jumbo a while. You get to make a choice: do you want to hang around and join your Roommate for lessons, or perhaps... perhaps you'd rather run errands?"

"Ma'am, I'll run errands, Ma'am," Steph elects. It's an easy decision, really. *I'm pretty covered up! And Babs is wise to protect me from Robyn.*

"Make her fetch Kimju and Molly's Pink Pages," Robyn urges.

"Excellent suggestion," Boss Babe praises, and orders Kimju, "Give her directions."

Kimju snaps to. "Ma'am, yes, Ma'am." Kimju connects with Steph's eyes via the Mirror and directs her. "Steph, you must go to the Nugget. See the Hat Check Girl at the front. Ask her to make a set of Kimju and Molly Pink Pages. She knows what to do."

Babs nods, turns, and urges, "Move it, Steph. And if the Hat Check Girl tells you to do something, obey her." And she's slips back inside her Bedroom door and goes to examine her Desktop.

Steph doesn't wait for Robyn's discharge. She breaks out of the Lineup, paces toward the hallway and stairs, pauses and turns at the top, and points to Robyn, "You ratty rag mop, Gamers should hang you by your feet and dip you in a vat of warm sperm. Head first." And she's gone.

§ Robyn Torments Tiffany: Go Pee & Masturbate Post Naked

The five Cosmos—Tiffany, ex-Nuggets Kimju and Molly, and newbies Beka and Elle—continue to stand spread surrender.

Tiffany tries to hold onto her composure. *This is not the first time that Babs has empowered Robyn to give orders. But this time she gives Robyn carte blanche... and power over me as well. That's rude. And without even a Cam here to let my fans watch her abuse me! That's double rude. Babs is supposed to be my friend.*

Robyn interrupts Tiffany's contemplations. Robyn seems to have some memories after all, "Tell me Pledge, about your tinkling tricks."

Tiffany rotates and squares her shoulders, "Ma'am, I'm a Pee-Camer, Ma'am."

Robyn tightens her upper lip, "Tell me what that means, you taco tailpipe tramp."

Tiffany straightens her shoulders and ripples her naked torso. "Ma'am, every time I pee, Cams collect me, feed me live to the Prefecture, store me in Automatron, and distributed me to every Gamer who collects me. All my pee is public property, Ma'am. I'll Pee-Cam anywhere, anytime, in front of anybody."

"You'll Pee-Cam naked in the Backyard." Robyn decides. "And masturbate your Henge Post.

"Ma'am, I'll cum for you, Ma'am. In the Backyard, on the Post. I'll pink and cream. I'll slick up the Post, Ma'am.

"You may make yourself pink, wet, and slick up the Post." Robyn states. "Pink-wet-and-ready, but you may not climax! Am I clear on that?"

"Ma'am, Yes, Ma'am," Tiffany acquiesces, augments, "I will beg you for release. I will give you everything I have, both Garments, any Obeisance you desire."

"Don't forget to keep reminding me that," Robyn says smartly. "Be sure to give the Cam a timely announcement before draining your piss."

"Ma'am, may I please you, Ma'am," Tiffany says.

Robyn digs bare heels into the Bunkroom's wooden floor and half-puckers her lips. "Good. Now tell me the other half of your watersports experience, you twat tunneling tenderloin."

I know what the other half is, Tiffany admits to herself; she speaks, "Ma'am, I'm a Piss Mouth, Ma'am."

Robyn augments, "Does that mean Gamers can piss all over your body or only piss in your mouth?"

Tiffany tremors. "Ma'am, you can piss on me anywhere, Ma'am." Tiffany gathers her strength, "It's no secret, Ma'am, Automatron has clips of me from last Term." Tiffany challenges. "Ma'am, you can order me into the Mudpit, piss in my mouth, let me practice keeping up with your stream. I am a Piss Mouth Porn Star, Ma'am."

Robyn steps backward. "Listen, Pledge. Neither you, nor anyone else, will be sharing any of *my* body functions. And you are not a Porn Star. Not any more. You are a wannabe Porn Star, that's what you are. Remind me."

Tiffany obeys, "Ma'am I am a wannabe Porn Star, Ma'am." And smiles.

Robyn escalates, "You're lucky there are no Cams here in the Bunkroom, because if there were, you'd be blowing soap bubbles for claims like that!"

Tiffany hustles, "Ma'am, you can order every other Pledge to pee all over me, pee in my mouth."

Robyn bites. "You're a Whore."

Tiffany charms, "I'm a wannabe Whore. I'm begging to Pledge naked and cum be a Stripper next Term."

Robyn twists her lips and decrees, "Beg me to piss in your mouth, you tinkling tenderloin tramp."

"Ma'am," Tiffany stabilizes, "You can see me in my Kitchen Porn Star Calendar doing just that. Cutout bra, garters, hose, high heels. And if you screen my vids you can see I'm not always on target. But I do pee all over myself. I'll do it again if you want. I'll do it in the Mudpit in the Backyard, live on the Cam. May it please you even the paparazzi will collect me."

Robyn blinks, then squares her shoulders. "Listen, you naked tatterdemalion. You're a Cam tart not worthy of all the attention. You can save your self-matriculation until more Cosmos beg tinkle training. Right now I have more important plans for these two ex-Strippers and two newbies."

Tiffany looks down as Robyn continues, "So take your tits and twat to the Backyard, affix yourself to your Henge Post and rub up a slick of your tapioca. Keep your body and hands affixed to the Post. No touching yourself and *no* cumming! You understand me, you twisting tinkle tramp?"

Tiffany does. "Ma'am thank you Ma'am, for the opportunity to masturbate and pee in public, Ma'am." she replies, and breaks position to head for the curved stairway downward. *Wow!*

"Stop." Robyn orders, and Tiffany pauses at that point where the Bunkroom meets the hallway. "Beg the Cam on your way out to keep an eye on you, and beg Automatron to make sure you don't cum. You can kiss, rub, and slick up the Post as much as you want, you can work up a pant, but I want you to wait until I'm ready for you to let out a howl. So but keep your hands on the Post. I repeat. You are absolutely not allowed to touch yourself anywhere and you are not allowed to climax. You can quiver, shake, and hang out some tacky. Gamers want to see just how important cumming is to you. While you're outside you can tinkle and. empty your tailpipe. I guess there are some things about you that I don't want to see, because let's face it, you're a tawdry, turgescent, taco peddler. Now scram!"

Tiffany scrams: down the stairs, through the Kitchen, out the Back Door, across the Back Landing, down two steps, and onto the ground. She rings the Bell loudly and begs the Back Door Cam, "Please surveil me, send out my alerts, and feed me to the Prefecture!" And heads toward the Post Henge.

The Cam hustles; it hops off its perch, hovers, chases, and catches up with Tiffany as she takes a few strides, then wraps her naked body around the top Post. *My Post.* Tiffany reviews directions. *No touching myself, no climax, but tonus some tapioca and smear my Post.*

And I'm sure Automatron will put my Eraser Heads up for bid.

Tiffany tests out the Post. *Solid.* She rubs her cheek on it, graces her neck, draws each of her Eraser Heads down the Post, torques her belly, then wraps her legs and masturbates her treasure chest against the Post.

Tiffany take in a deep breath and evaluates. *I don't think Robyn is smart enough to do this me. But somebody, beyond even Babs and Janet, seeks to frustrate me sexually, yet at the same time, feed my fans. It's Gamers who want to get me really frustrated, all the while they all cum in their pants for me.*

One more thing. Tiffany looks at the hovering Cam. She begs, "Automatron, please keep me honest, so even if I try to I cum subtle like, and thrash a little or it looks like I'm starting to lose control, please slow me down. Bump me with the Cam, make the Post get too warm, send Robyn out to switch me. You know what I'm like when I climax. I could attract the entire neighborhood."

Tiffany outs her pelvis into a slow grid and considers the high-resolution Cam that examines her. She considers paparazzi. *They will discover me. Steph and Robyn think they can shame a Porn Star? Hah!* It takes but a moment, but Tiffany carefully squeezes her trap door, and the tacamahac starts to transude downward between her opened thighs. *Ha, I'm already making a slick spot! All Robyn does is butter my fans!*

Tiffany lets her timbale grow downward, then carefully swings it so it catches the Post and not her inner thigh. *Long day still.*

§ Robyn Screens Penny & Coco: Double Dongers Last Term

Tiffany's departure leaves four Cosmos Pledge plus Robyn in the Bunkroom.

Robyn draws air into her lungs and smoothes her maillot cutout. "Obviously you must always obey me because Boss Bitch tells you to. But you also need to fear *me!*"

Kimju and Molly, and Beka and Elle, stand spread surrender and converge their eyes upon Robyn. "Try this," Robyn suggests. "All you Cosmos clams have been clamoring for Monitor Babs to screen Penny and Coco's *Double Dong Climax Video."* Robyn smiles is self-satisfaction, but when the gazes back don't reflect presold, Robyn hawks. "We're talking about the *Video* they 'allegedly' made after BB and Janet defeated them in the Mudpit at the end of last Term.

"But BB hasn't been able to screen this for us, has she. Can't deliver."

Robyn pirouettes in front of the Lineup. The Minxy Mirror has metamorphosed from a deep silvery black to a licorice black with slow motion taffy waves of image vestiges fading into the blackness.

"Fear me!" Robyn commands, raises her finger and snaps.

The Minxy Mirror roars to life: the wall-sized Screen shows the two then-Cosmos—Penny and Coco—sitting face-to-face, naked, pussy-hair trimmed to butched hearts, with hands and fingers working the long Double Dong into their facing vaginas. Penny and Coco wiggle forward until the Dong penetrates each so completely that they are able to rub their clits together.

Elle finds herself horrified. *I can't tell if the Dong comes to life and take these two ex-Cosmos for a ride or if they have lost all self-respect and are simply grinding themselves into climax!*

And climax they do. Penny and Coco's climaxes are prolonged, noisy, and totally reveals their sexual selves. There is a moment of afterglow, and the Pledge watch the Minxy returns to a deep black with a Mirror deeply seeped into it.

"That's you next Term," Robyn tells the Lineup, and directs special scorn at a brimming Beka and horrified Elle. "You're already begging to Opt Strip," she advises, and focusing upon Beka, adds, "And you're already hanging brodeas between your naked thighs!"

"You're nectar's next," Robyn advises Elle. "You're gonna beg Roommates Together, so that you and your Roommate can Opt Strip together!"

Kimju shuffles and finds herself looking deep into the Mirror. *My nipples have erected and I have spotted my tanga. But that's the least of my problems. Where is a Cam when I need one? Whatever Robyn does to us right now, it's just her words against ours. No other witnesses.* Kimju rotates her eyeballs and again watches the video of Penny and Coco climaxing the Double Dong. *One made after their defeat but before they streaked to the Nugget. I know, I saw them arrive.*

Kimju shifts gears. *If Robyn really did manage to access the Penny and Coco scene from Automatron somehow, then maybe she really does have Charm.*

In which case she really could reduce me to a Stripper next Term.

Kimju worries. *Somehow Robyn broke Steph last Term when Steph was her Roommate. Now I'm her Roommate and unless I get a second Garment, she's going to break me too.*

§ Robyn Reminds Kimju & Molly: Pee-Cam & Lapdance Videos

Five Cosmos Pledge remain in the Bunkroom, four of them—Kimju and Molly, and Beka and Elle—stand spread surrender in a Lineup admiring themselves in the Minxy Mirror. Hands behind heads, bare feet spaced wide apart, eyes forward, oval mouths. Kimju and Molly present themselves topless buttage, Kimju's thong is outlined with stubble, and Molly's panties are pulled tightly into her mooe. Beka and Elle present themselves with bare arms and bellies and legs. Tiffany should be masturbating a Post in the Backyard. There exists a space where Steph stood; right now Steph should be picking up Kimju and Molly's Pink Pages at the Nugget. And for all, navelage 24x7.

The fifth Cosmos, Robyn Redacted, stands to the side of the Lineup and surveys it. Surveys its reflection in the Mirror. "Be sure your own eyes never stray upon me," Robyn commands. "And make sure you never steel glances of me in Minxy Mirror. It will report to me and the discipline will include blindfolds and hoods. Keep your eyes looking into yourselves in the Mirror. You're gonna go deep."

Kimju considers her Roommate, a case study in what some Gamers call the "ostrich hypothesis." *Robyn has the ability to remain ignorant of Rules she pretends don't apply to her.* For example? *Robyn can't decide if she knows the rules for Roommate Games, especially if Flip-Flop might be one of them. Flip-Flopping with me would leave her topless with her rump visible for all to scrutinize shamelessly. Sweet. 34C-25-34 all out.*

Gamers can even take a commission on the transfer and give Robyn a smaller size tanga, or maybe even a g-string.

Kimju scans down her body in the Mirror and then back up to again meet her own eyes in the Mirror. *It's hard to hold this; Robyn is right about going deep. Maybe before I Opt Up I will have to go deeper still. I might have to wear a smaller size tanga or even a g-string. Mini, micro, nano, right down to a size pico knot.*

Robyn sidles up to Kimju and speaks to her cheek. "I know you're my Roommate, but we are not playing Roommate Games. I did not come to School to expose myself. Or to get exposed, if that is how Gamers want to put it. I came to School to be admired!"

Robyn takes a step backward, "And you are here to obey me. Is that clear?"

Kimju takes it, "Ma'am, yes, Ma'am."

"Pull you waistline down and show yourself your butched pussy hair," Robyn commands.

Kimju lowers her thong down her thighs until she can see the very top of her clithood in the Mirror. Robyn walks behind her and digs into the side of Kimju's belly with two sharp fingernails, below the ribs. Kimju jerks.

Robyn lectures, "You don't just have a bare belly, you're a full-frontal wannabe Stripper. Me? My torso remains covered. And my belly button is bared by the smallest of cutout holes. Men desire me! And I know I control them!"

Kimju compliments, "Ma'am, you are much desired, Ma'am." Thoughts about Flip-Flopping with Robyn bounce.

Robyn leads, "I am, in fact, among the most covered of the Cosmos— Pledge or Monitor—and *quod erat demonstrandum,* this indicates I am the most valuable Cosmos!"

Ma'am, you are beautiful, Ma'am," Kimju says.

"Oval mouth, Roommate," Robyn instructs Kimju.

Kimju obeys. Robyn leans in, and spits into Kimju's open mouth.

Kimju recoils. And Robyn laughs, dances back, and dictates, "Kimju Knock Knock!" Robyn scowls, "Now yank that thong of your up into your koot so that you and Molly are both splitting hairage, then stand spread surrender again."

Again Kimju obeys.

"Kimju Knock Knock Kava Kava," Robyn chortles.

Kimju eyes her near-naked body in the Mirror and asks her visage a question, *What am I supposed to do? Not follow BB's standing orders to obey Robyn? And what if Robyn really does have privilege? What if she really does carry Charm?*

Indeed, Robyn has no shortage of malicious ideas, and her unleashed hazing often incorporates an element of the new and the old. During *The Arrivals* Robyn had screened some of the videos that Kimju and Molly had made last Term. These videos are as benign as Molly popping her top on a public beach nearby a woody with surfboards, to Kimju striking Betty Page poses for a Camera Club. Beka and Elle had watched the clips play on the Screen in the Dining Room.

Another time the Cosmos watched the Minxy Screen and saw a full-size Kimju and Molly dance and masturbate themselves at the Nugget, also from when they were Strippers last Term. Sometimes center Stage, but also on the side stages, on table tops, daises next to tables and chairs. There are lapdance videos, along with highlights from their daily visits to the Camera Lounge.

At times endless loops play on Screens throughout the Cosmos House, high definition captures of every intimacy: painted fingernails, distended clits, peeholes, gapping vag interiors, and plenty of cream. Sometimes the then-Strippers brushed dried crost out of their koot and mooe, sometimes they were slippery with kloop and mung, and again and again they masturbated to wailing climaxes.

In the here and now Elle notes that the Minxy fades from Mirror to black. She tidies up her position. Armpits, belly taut, navel framed in the V-notch of the shorts' waistline, feet wide. Elle considers herself in the Mirror, now, in this moment. *Good position, even if my seam digs into my nook and splays even more hairage and cheekage than usual.*

I worry Robyn will make me unbutton my halter again, like Janet did yesterday. Although here in the Bunkroom there are no Cams, unlike yesterday.

Elle introspects. *I never took it seriously that Robyn promised Kimju and Molly they would masturbate and climax in sync with their own videos. But now Robyn's in charge. But would she do that?*

Elle steels a glance at Robyn. *Yes. You made Beka and me watch Kimju and Molly masturbate to climax in the Bathroom together. You made Kimju masturbate the Henge Post naked, open air in the Backyard. Now you're going to make them masturbate and climax in sync with themselves.*

So are Kimju and Molly apprehensive as to what Robyn might have in store for the present?

They are.

The Minxy becomes Screen again and assaults the newbies with a montage of Kimju and Molly plunging toys of all sizes, shapes and colors into their mouths, vaginas, and rectums. Beka freshens; Elle blanches. The shots quicken and the explicitness escalates. Suddenly two toys get inserted at the same time: Double Penetrators. Kimju slips vibrating ben-wa balls into her kypsey and an electrified procto up her kawazoo. Molly carefully uses a speculum to open her mooe wide, and then penetrates her mawkport with a stainless steel anoscope.

Elle blinks. *Apparently Molly's Medical Exam during the Arrivals was not her first after all.*

Too much to deal with! Elle closes her eyes to block out the Screen before her. She opens them and confronts Kimju urinating at the Nugget last Term. Elle blinks as the a larger-than-life Kimju squats and releases a stream from her pee hole. No secrets for Strippers.

Kimju's anger flashes and she speaks, "These videos violate my privacy. They were made last Term. I peed at the Nugget, I peed in the woods, I peed lots of places. But I am not a Pee-Camer!"

Robyn responds, "Something for you to beg to reinstate to your portfolio! And soon, I trust. So Molly doesn't outclass you. Or Tiffany Transparent. You're the next Cosmos whose gonna join the Pee-Cam brigade. It's something every ex-Stripper can do."

Kimju keeps her cool, "Be sure to insist Janet pees too."

Robyn curls her nose at Kimju. "Don't worry, Pledge," Robyn raises her chin, "I've met Janet and she's a fat slob who will piss into her mouth when I tell her to!"

Too bad the Cam isn't here to record such indignities, Kimju reflects, although deep down inside Kimju knows, *It may not matter what Robyn suggests, or whether Robyn has Charm or not; sometimes one must volunteer to get ahead, if not just stay even. So if I have to Pee-Cam to get a second Garment, well, I'll consider that.*

Kimju scowls; she resists an instinct to grace her exposed knockers with one hand and touch where the tanga bunches into her kootch with the other. Kimju confesses to herself, *Molly and I have both had to pink, cream, and cum this Term, however Molly might be ahead of me in the pee department. Meanwhile, my Roommate Robyn stays unscathed. I need to Flip-Flop with her, or better yet, defeat her in a Winner-Takes-All Game.*

Kimju licks her lips. But if Robyn's got Charm she'll get whatever she wants.

Robyn takes a step back, squares herself, and snarls at Kimju and Molly. "Tiffany told me all about you two lapdancers. She said you let the tippers cop feels, suckle your knocks and mams, grab you keister and moons, and twist their fingers up into your koot and moneybox."

Kimju is unable to resist the urge to defends herself, "Robyn, maybe you should giving Stripping a try, because Molly and I could never stop the fondling if we wanted too. What I resent is all the other Patrons who get to look for free. Freeloaders gawking me on one Patron's tip. They shouldn't haves been ogling me."

"And what about you, Molly Mammoth, you big fat hairy mumbo maduro molliwog?" Robyn demands.

Molly augments, "Robyn, please, I don't care who sees me get my body pawed over. And MomCap let anyone cam the Patrons mauling us and breaking the Rules. Gamers want us to lapdance on them and allow them to take liberties, and then threaten to punish us for breaking the Rules. It's not really a fair Game, and Kimju's right, you should try it sometime."

"You should be grateful House Mom el Capitan let you get away with misbehaving yourselves," Robyn prides. "She apparently didn't consider you important enough to warrant fairness." Robyn breezes. "Lucky you. Because if she did consider you important, your lapdancing vids would have sent the both of you to Flesh Ranch."

Robyn picks a ball our snot out of her nose and flicks it toward the two ex-Strippers. "You both should be Whores this Term."

Kimju proffers, "Ma'am, because Molly and I are no longer Strippers any stills or vids from last Term can't be used against us to demote us to Whores. We are Cosmos Pledge now."

"So no harm then in begging me to screen them?" Robyn tilts her head.

Kimju squirms.

Robyn emphasizes, "Beg me. Now."

And Kimju recites for herself and also for Molly, "Ma'am, please screen any lapdance video of us from last Term."

Robyn snaps her fingers and the Minxy Screen now presents a barrage of Kimju and Molly lapdance scenes. "Tiffany pegged you," Robyn decries, "You lick fingers off after they've been inside you. You're both already Whores and you know it. You deserve cocks in your mouth, cocks in your kootch and mooe, and cocks up your kawazoo and mawk port. You need to make *Suck Fuck Facial* Videos. You're not going to be Porn Stars, you're going to be three-hole gutter Whores getting gangbanged in the Mudpit and living in the Doghouse together!"

Robyn catches her breath. She had raised her voice to a shout.

Kimju also finds herself catching her breath. *I am not a wannabe cocksucker, fucker, nor anal Whore. I am not a wannabe Stripper either, but unless I get one more Garment and Opt Monitor, I will indeed be back at the Nugget, lapdancing naked and getting felt up just like before, and one Caste away from the Whorehouse. Maybe Robyn can snap her fingers and make pictures appear, but I can't; I need a way around Charm.*

§ Robyn Hazes Kimju & Molly: Beg Double Dong Alumni Reprise

Robyn paces and settles affront the two topless buttaged Pledge with their gathered culottes.

"Boss Bitch gave me a message to give to you two," Robyn lies to Kimju and Molly, and continues, "She has given my recommendation that you shall beg to visit your alma mater her whole-hearted approval. You shall be booked as an 'Alumni Reprise!'"

"The Nugget?" Kimju asks.

Robyn gives Kimju the look one gives to someone who asks a stupid question. "You'll perform just like Janet did last Term, except there is a pair of you, and opportunity to build your fan base!"

Robyn walks forward and assures herself she walks amongst angels and will be Opting Up next Term. "I'm sure you're aware that the Nugget isn't my kind of place, but you two could shuck your thong and panties, toss them to the Crowd, and streak back to the Cosmos House. "How about that?"

Molly finds an answer, "Ma'am, how about you let me shuck my panties center Stage at the Nugget, and then just stay there.''

Kimju smolders. *My tanga is Robyn's first opportunity to acquire a second garment and make herself whole! The last thing she needs is for me to toss it away at the Nugget. If I do that, what's to be had for her might she even win a Winner-Takes-All. Nothing.*

Only if she has Charm would she consider this. Or if she is really stupid.

Robyn's attention once again drills into the two ex-Nuggets. "You bitches got to single and Double Penetrate last Term but you never got to share the Double Dong," Robyn snarls. "And I bet you know where it is right now."

Kimju stays mum. *Well, you just screened Penny and Coco climaxing the Double Dong. That was just before they left they Cosmos House at the end of last Term. So they could have taken it with them to the Nugget. But Molly and I didn't actually see them arrive, we heard them arrive, but I certainly don't really know where it is.*

Analytics aside, Kimju finds it hard to control her reaction to Robyn's rollicking behavior. *My distain for her and her privilege has built slowly, a constant slow-burning resentment.* Kimju evaluates. *I have given her every chance; what I must do is control any flash of hatred that gets magnified whenever Robyn aggresses me, like now. I am at a point where I detest her. Robyn Redacted, Robyn Ragho, Robyn Ragabash.*

Kimju mulls, *Steph Sorostitute might be a slinky squeeze, but I don't really care if what Robyn did to her last Term is forgivable or not. Steph got broken and is a Cosmos Pledge this Term. But what happens to Robyn as a result? Robyn gets nepenthe and forgets all about it!*

An oblivion potion?

But what about me? I have no doubt that I can crush her physically or mentally. So why do I let her dominate me, like during The Arrivals, *when she made me grovel in the Mudpit, or made me pullaside and masturbate to Tiffany's Porn Star Calendar, or masturbate on the Henge Post for the Cam and any paparazzi?*

So why did I let Robyn cam Molly and me masturbate to climax in the Bathroom?

I know the answer. It is because Monitor Babs put Robyn in charge. Babs can be stately, but she vacillates about power. Hesistates. Attempts to delegate. But BB also set it up so everyone hates Robyn, and not her.

Kimju calculates, *Basically I have three choices. If I never challenge Robyn to a Roommate Game, I'll stay a topless tanga, one Garment, and I'm a Stripper next Term, done deal. If I game with her and lose I'm naked, which is inconducive to advancement. If I win I can keep what I got and take Robyn's maillot. That leaves Robyn naked, and two Garments for me. Best outcome.*

Kimju pauses to hunt for conclusions. *So I have nothing to lose by Gaming. If I end up naked or with only one Garment, then I could game again with any other Cosmos who has also played their Roommate Game. If I do nothing I be a Stripper for sure.*

Kimju pauses again. *I know, I could always lose again too, and still end up at the Nugget. But there is only one way Up, and to do that I have to try. I have to Game with Robyn, whether I want to or not.*

Kimju concludes, *I'm going to have to shave bare bald and naked, pour shots, and Double Dong center Stage at the Nugget, before I get out of this one.*

Apt predilection.

§ Robyn Syncs Kimju & Molly: Masturbate & Climax to *Video*

Robyn has more goals to accomplish. "You two," she says, indicating Kimju and Molly, "are going to train Beka and Elle how to dance and audition the Nugget next Term."

Elle fidgets. Beka gets wet.

"Sit on the floor," Robyn commands Kimju and Molly as the Minxy becomes a Screen again, two side-by-side Screens actually, wide and tall, highest resolution, *Nugget Stripper Videos* each ex-Stripper watching herself looking out: also stark naked, sitting legs spread, and masturbating.

On the Screen Molly mashes her humungous melons; Kimju uses one hand to alternate nipple twists, and the other to pinch her keystone and finger dip.

"Sync up to your *Video*!" Robyn orders Kimju and Molly, "Cause we know in this scene from last Term you both go over the top. And you're going to go over the top right here too!"

Kimju and Molly look at themselves on the Screens, pullaside, and masturbate. Molly freshens instantly. And Kimju knows, *Right now I'm going to have to get klammy.*

"Pay attention," Robyn commands Beka and Elle, "Kneel, spread, cross your hands behind your back. Watch, because you're going to pull pink, masturbate, and make wet long before you get to dance and strip naked center Stage at the Nugget."

Beka and Elle kneel, cross their hands behind their backs, and watch.

Next to them Kimju and Molly masturbate. In the video on the Screen they sit in a similar position, except both of them are stark naked.

Elle closes her eyes. She opens them again because she knows she can't not watch. Kimju and Molly keep up with their Screens. The heartbeats and breathing of the two ex-Nuggets increase slowly and at a steady pace, both in the video and in the Bunkroom, as the now Cosmos breath steadily, hand vibe, and finger-fuck with aggression. Aroma floods the Bunkroom. *I know there is no doubt they will climax,* Elle predicts. *Robyn—or whomever—picked the Screens for a reason. I saw them climax in the Bathroom during* The Arrivals. *Will I now witness them lose themselves completely, and in sync with their past Stripper selves?*

Correct.

From inside the bubble, Kimju accepts *I must go with the flow.* Molly feels the buoyancy and floats.

Kimju feels a bare foot lift her chin to better align her eyes with the Screen. Kimju dizzies. *The experience of having to watch myself become aroused on the Screen, coupled with the necessity to follow, doubly scandalizes me.*

That is Kimju's last thought. Her breathing gets faster, the rubbing more intense and slippery, and the topless Cosmos synchronizes herself to her media and abandons all control of her mind, body, and soul.

Kundalini sings out. Molly vocalizes first, the approachment of a wail, and with that Kimju palpitates a wavering cry, and the ex-Strippers sing a duet. Real cumming, no fakes, not on the Screen or in the Bunkroom. Half exhausted, they follow themselves from the peak down to a plateau, and insidiously, because they know from the first time that they will rise and peak again, and they do, before finally lying back onto the floor completely exhausted.

Beka and Elle interpret the ecstasy in Kimju and Molly's faces differently.

Beka has wettened the insides of her thighs with brodeas. Beka marvels that Kimju and Molly can synchronize with each other, and with their previous selves, and masturbate to climax in unison. *I'm not sure I could do that,* Beka admits to herself. But the performance so turns her on that she catches herself with her hand up her miniskirt and her fingers sopping wet in her own synchronization. Luckily, Robyn misses the transgression, even after Elle smells Beka release scent into the room and signals her to get her hands crossed behind her back again.

Elle interprets, *Kimju and Molly climax their bodies in shame.*

Robyn decides the time has come to make sure that the two aghast newbies understand the stakes. "This is a goal for you two to aspire to," Robyn preens.

Elle closes her eyes. *I feel sorry for Kimju and Molly that they must watch their own Stripper Videos that they made last Term. And now climax in sync with them. Is this only Robyn's nastiness, or do Babs and other Gamers drive the Game play?*

Elle opens her eyes but blurs out the Screens. She touches the front seam of the jeans where it sinks into her nookie, to see if it's wet. It is, and she smells her fingertips. *Urine.* She shakes her body, tilts to glimpse Beka. *Yes, Kimju and Molly's Videos are causing me anxiety. But I worry that neither fear nor uncertainty has been cast into Beka. Beka just hangs broda outta her bare boneroo.*

Robyn addresses Kimju and Molly. "You two each drink a quart of water. Then head for the Mudpit. Molly, locate your Watering Can, fill it up, and water the Mudpit, and when you feel the urge you can show Kimju how to pee in the open air. But don't worry, if she doesn't make Pee-Cam today she can audition tomorrow. Lie down, kiss and make out, and be passionate. It's where you came from when your arrived, it's where you belong, and it's where you're going to end up. Earth to Earth."

The ex-Nuggets scoot. Down the stairs, out the Back Door, ring the Bell, water the Mudpit, and climb in. The Back Door Cam, up until now devoting itself to Tiffany's nude masturbation on the Post Henge, starts to oscillate as two scenes compete for its computer cycles. Automatron dampens the shake, and enables the Cam to time share.

Kimju processes, *I never thought I'd feel safer with a Cam on me, but with Robyn loose, I do.*

Molly draws her arms around her former Roommate, gives Kimju a kiss, and offers condolences, "Shucks Kimju, Robyn long ago dismissed your thong as trivial… and besides, it's likely to get smaller."

Kimju clenches her knockers, "Right, Robyn doesn't have a plan but she has it all figured out."

§ Robyn Taunts Beka & Elle: Hazing has a Purpose

Babs' reluctance to dolt upon her Pledge and let Robyn haze them receives different interpretations among different Cosmos, especially the newbies, Beka and Elle, who are largely naïve to the wiles of the Game.

Hazing has many purposes: superior hazing arouses, intimidates, embarrasses, and empowers not just newbies but veterans as well. Beka and Elle learn that the hazing is not just physical, like getting muddied up, wearing whorish lipstick, flashing titties, upskirting vag, or getting one's rectum violated with thermoprobes and suppositories. Hazing also involves a psychological component, and Babs via Robyn, makes sure that the newbie Pledge shall get a full treatment.

Perhaps even an overdose.

Gamers know hazing is designed to control and arouse the newbies at the same time, although neither Babs nor Robyn quite see it in those terms. Babs wants ease of control; Robyn wants to hurt.

Robyn signs the two kneeling spread surrender Pledge who remain in the Bunkroom onto their feet, and Beka and Elle rise carefully. "Do you admire how Kimju and Molly demonstrate how to pink, cream, and climax?" Robyn inquires but doesn't wait for an answer. "Kimju Knock Knock Kava Kava and Molly Mammoth got to masturbate and cum in synchronization with their own videos! Tell me that's a goal for you two newbies to aspire to!" Robyn preens.

So Beka and Elle stumble a reply, "Ma'am, yes, Ma'am."

Indeed, Robyn's manipulations of Kimju and Molly—making them masturbate and cum with their videos arouse Beka but remain extremely disturbing to Elle. Elle presumes, *Kimju and Molly are going to Double Dong center Stage at the Nugget. That will be their Alumni Reprise. And there will be more to it than a slippery climax!*

"You like watching a foursome sing a quartet?" Robyn asks Beka and Elle, a direct reference to Kimju and Molly's climax with their clips moments ago. "Maybe you two would like to sing along with Kimju and Molly? Would you prefer to sing with them live, or with one of their replays?"

Elle finds herself speechless; Beka unfolds, "I'll masturbate and cum in sync with their videos, Ma'am.

"You'll masturbate and cum in sync with them live center Stage at the Nugget," Robyn pronounces.

Beka concurs, "I'll masturbate and cum anywhere anytime in front of anybody. Please. Elle and I both will. We're both begging to Opt Strip."

The Mirror has brightened now and Elle steals a glance at Beka, standing spread surrender next to her. Beka looks slightly wild in the eyes, her hair is ruffled, her lower bare belly and hips tremble, and she displays sex lips beneath a miniskirt that has already risen up. Elle considers, *Probably already wet inside, soon leaking, and eventually me lollying up.*

Elle shifts her weight, wiggles her own body around in an attempt to work the seam of her shorts out of her own crotch. It's stuck, wedged, not going anywhere. *I guess we're both making hairage,* Elle confesses, *although at least I have a seam buried in nookie, and my lips aren't starting to open out.*

Robyn questions. "Do you two know how lucky you are that Kimju and Molly have agreed to give you dance lessons and teach you some Stripper skills? Do you appreciate what an honor it is to have them teach you?" Robyn asks.

Elle hesitates but Beka bubbles an answer out, "Ma'am, thank you, Ma'am."

Elle protests, "But I don't need to be a Stripper next Term, I already have two pieces."

Robyn rotates her shoulders. "You want to keep two pieces? Between now and Midnight on the last day of the Term either you will or you won't. But either way you're gonna audition at the Nugget. So best be prepared!"

Beka reaches out, "Elle, it's no problem. All we have to do is show the Crowd we can titter and vagflash."

Elle retorts. "Yeah? And how we gonna do that? I know, you'll just lift your croptop up and spread your legs."

"And you can unbutton your neck strap and walk around with your nurbs flapping," Robyn retorts. "Just like you did in the Lineup yesterday. You did it for Janet, and you'll do it for me when I say."

"Ma'am, yes, Ma'am," Elle concedes, and feels her nipples get hard.

"You," Robyn turns to Beka, "keep your hands behind your head, down and out the Back Door; you can use your teeth to ring the Bell. Then run around the House three times and beg the Front and Back Door Cams every time you pass. Hurry!"

Beka looks at Elle, shrugs, but keeps her hands behind her head as she carefully heads downstairs.

§ Robyn Queries Elle: Where are the Measurement Nudes?

Elle hears the Bell ring in the distance as Beka exits. *Beka's seriously begging to Pledged naked and cum be a Stripper, and she'll lift her croptop or upskirt her miniskirt for anyone. What matters is what I might have to do.*

Robyn asks a personal question, "When are you going to bring in your Measurement Nudes?" Robyn asks.

Elle blanches, lifts her arms from behind her head into midair, and swings a barefoot off the ground. She catches herself, and snaps back into stand spread surrender position. Ma'am!" she exclaims.

Robyn smiles. "Beg me a penitence for moving your hands from behind your head."

Elle begs, "Ma'am, please let me unbutton my halter, Ma'am."

"Anytime, anywhere, in front of anybody," Robyn dictates.

"Ma'am, please let me unbutton my halter. Anytime, anywhere, in front of anybody," Elle recites. Her head spins. *How does Robyn know Monitor Babs ordered me to fetch my Measurement Nudes?* Elle casts her eyes looking for missing Beka. I don't think Beka knows. Elle frowns. *And how come Automatron doesn't have them?*

"You failed to answer my question." Robyn says.

Elle feels a need to urinate again, more seriously this time. She processes, recalls Robyn's question concerned her Measurement Nudes, and utters, "Ma'am, Monitor Babs says I am to fetch them tomorrow, Ma'am. She has authorized me to trek out of the House." She chances a question, "How do you know?"

"Soap and Caster Oil for asking a question, you numskull neophyte nizzy." Robyn glows. "You just disrespected me."

Robyn gives it another thought, walks behind Elle, and unbuttons the neck strap herself.

Elle watches her reflection in the Mirror as her halter falls forward and both noogies fall free. *At least, unlike yesterday, there are no Cams, no paparazzi to collect my boobage here in the Bunkroom. Just me self-examining.*

If you really believed what you beg," Robyn taunts, "you'll beg to keep yourself unbuttoned *all* the time. Then you could unbutton the front, and be done with your halter entirely."

Elle bubbles, "Ma'am, thank you, Ma'am." Her face is red, her chest is flushed, and both nobs pucker up.

Robyn decrees, "Learning how to submit is a principle goal for you, Pledge." Robyn advise. "And learning how to discipline Pledge is a principle goal for the Monitors." Robyn twitches a nostril, "I ought to know. You beg, I discipline. Now beg me, you needy nazy notch girl!"

So Elle begs, "Please let me Pledge naked and become a Stripper next Term."

Robyn admires Elle from the front and nods approval. "Just so you know what a good person I am, I'll answer your question. How do I know about your Measurement Nudes, you titty-stripper, you? I've known since Babs ordered you to go fetch during *The Arrivals*. I know everything. You're a nincompoop begging to Pledge naked and go Strip. Beg Kimju and Molly to teach you some moves. Learn to unzip your jeans shorts, and keep the Crowd poppin' as you wiggle them all the way down to your ankles."

The twosome hear the Bell and Back Door as Beka reenters the House.

"Does she know about your mission yet?" Robyn raises an eyebrow.

Elle hushes. "No!" And besides, it's not about her, it's Babs and me."

Beka bursts into the Room, observes Elle's halter hanging down, and obeys Robyn's sign to stand spread surrender.

"Thank me," Robyn orders.

"Thank you, Robyn, for letting me run around the House and beg the Cams to Pledge naked and Strip." Beka catches her breath. "And I'll pull my croptop up, so I can show my boobs, like Elle. We'll pink, cream, and climax together."

"Oh shut up." Robyn commands. "The only thing Gamers need from you is the size of your big mouth, bangbox, and anal bore."

Robyn paces in front of the Roommates and waggles a finger at Elle. "You're both gonna make cream," she declares. "And lollying up after everybody includes lollying up after yourself."

Robyn laughs. Elle shuffles but holds her position.

§ Robyn Beka & Elle: Screens Penny & Coco *Dong Videos*

Robyn takes the liberty of reaching out and pinching Elle's totally exposed nipple. "After you and Beka Flip-Flop you can be one of the three bellage Cosmos: Tiffany, Beka-soon-to-be-you-Elle, and the Bellage Bitch herself. Belly-up belly-down, all of you."

Elle swallows. *Okay, Robyn has selected videos to hit us newbies hard and give us a jolt. A taste of the stakes in the Game. A taste of what we are up against in Kimju and Molly... let alone Tiffany's experience.*

Robyn examines Beka and Elle. "I'm delighted you two newbies are begging to Strip naked. You like what you see on the Screen... and in real life? Ex-Strippers Kimju and Molly opening their raw kuder and mutton, jerking off, and cumming with a howl? You like watching Penny and Coco wrench the Double Dong and blast off? You got something to look forward to, Pledge, a goal to audition for.

"Penny and Coco are your role models, Pledge. They used to be Cosmos Pledge—just like you—but they are naked Nuggets now. They got to Double Dong while they were Pledge, just like you're going to. They had to streak to get to the Nugget, just like you're going to.

"And you want to know what I know?" Robyn lazes, "I know they still don't have anything to strip off!" Robyn cackles. "But they can still pink, masturbate, and lapdance. Or they can function as footstools, oeuvres tableau, and drink-holders.

"Now there's a future for you to look forward to!"

Beka feels an urge to talk but Elle uses the moment to lick her lips with a wet tongue around her oval mouth.

"There's only one thing keeping you two from sharing the Double Dong." Robyn retorts. "Do you what it is?" she asks.

Beka and Elle look at each other and draw a blank.

"It's the same thing keeping Kimju and Molly from donging," Robyn urges.

A more cautious look this time. Elle answers the question, "Ma'am, we don't know, Ma'am."

"It's very simple and I'll tell you," Robyn confides. "The Double Dong is not here."

Elle blinks. *I think I knew that already.*

Robyn queries Elle directly. "You probably wonder if Penny and Coco took the Dong with them, don't you?"

Elle closes her eyes. *This possibility never occurred to me.* She opens her eyes, blinks twice, and retracts. "I never saw them with the Dong. I've never ever actually seen them. I've only seen their Dining Room Baseboard Stripper Pictures—here and at the Corvette House. Plus the clips you showed of them climaxing the Dong while they were still Cosmos." Elle squares up as she completes her answer.

"You didn't answer my question," Robyn appraises.

"You asked if I wondered, Ma'am—" Elle begins.

"You may beg me to eat soap," Robyn commands.

"Ma'am," Elle gathers her wits. "Please let me eat soap, Ma'am, and remember to answer your questions. Yes or no." ."

"No matter, Pledge," Robyn jaunts, "Your answer is meaningless, because nobody cares what you wonder." Robyn snaps her springy shoulder straps of her maillot cutout. "Besides, *I know* where the Dong is." Robyn asserts. She snaps her fingers and the Mirror becomes Screen again.

Beka and Elle watch a full wall of Screen before them.

At first Beka assumes the feed is live, but Elle quickly determines the tumble of images she watches are replays.

The *Video* captures Penny and Coco stumbling into the Stage Door of the Nugget the night of their arrival. They hold the Double Dong hand-in-hand, and they pass it back in forth between them as they tumble onto the Stage, then pinking, creaming, shaving bare, and masturbating themselves to wild climax.

Quite an arrival. None the less, they remain forbidden to share the Double Doug, and they have not shared it since their arrival.

Elle tries to stabelize herself. She straightens and shakes her shoulders. She looks and observes Beka breathing slowly with a horizontal open mouth.

The Minxy Screen splits to two side-by-side screens, a *Side-by-Side Video. There is Penny, then there is Coco, one of them then the other, walking naked around the Nugget with the free end of the Dong swinging from either a poontang or cooze. Hanging out like a penis, that's what.*

Robyn narrates as the video plays. "They swap back in forth, masturbate to each other's videos, and stay pink-wet-ready all the time."

Beka can't resist. "Please," she begs, "me too!"

Robyn rolls shoulders toward the Screen. "Penny and Coco vs. Babs and Janet at the Mudwrestling Contest spun some Karma into the Game." Robyn snorts, "But I wasn't there. I didn't have anything to do with Penny and Coco's defeat." Robyn curls a nostril. "But if I had been the referee, they'd have been lucky to simply streak off muddy and naked holding the opposite ends of the Dong in their fists. I'd have turned them over to a transport crew. And Babs and Janet would owe me for their Opt Ups."

Elle processes. *Does Robyn really have no memory about Penny and Coco, despite the fact it was she who refereed the Mudwrestling Contest? I for sure wasn't there, but Babs and Janet were there, defeated them, and sent them off streaking naked to Opt Strip at the Nugget this Term. Robyn intimates there is supposed to be video of this, video in which Babs and Janet both lose their tops, but how does she know?*

Babs and Janet are Monitors now. Penny and Coco are Nugget Strippers now, pulling pink in the Dining Room Baseboard Pictures, pulling pink every time, everywhere, in front of everyone.

And Robyn Redacted is here tormenting me. On behalf Monitor Babs.

The Screen becomes wide angle again and a two-shot appears. Penny and Coco sit side by side, naked, nipples erect, legs and pink spread wide; one of them strokes her privates with the Dong while the other furiously masturbates her cootch with her fingers and palm. *Both hands on.* The scene cuts and now the opposite ex-Cosmos strokes the Dong while the other commits invigorating self-arousal. Elle again observes, *both hands on.*

And slippery everywhere. And if they make too much new slippery, they will need a Lollydor to lick it up. Elle feels Kundalini twitch.

Penny and Coco climax in a montage of finger-fucking, Dong fucking, rub-a-dub, panting, and screams. Elle recoils, then relaxes. *They might be life-size in front of me but they are not really here. I can't crawl through the Screen and lollydor them. I—*

Robyn's narration interrupts Elle's thoughts. "As you can see," she details, "Strippers can solo the Dong just like they can solo any dildo or buttplug. They can even Double Penetrate and use the Dong for as one of their Penetrators, or bend it and muscle in both ends."

Robyn snides, "But as much as Penny and Coco want to share the Dong, the Game Rules forbid them!"

Robyn gathers Elle's attention. "Game Rules Forbid Double Dong sharing between Strippers. Only hand-to-hand passes are allowed. MomCap makes sure the two of them never share it together."

Robyn leans in. "Stripper Rules for the Double Dong are different that for you Cosmos Pledge. Or for the Whores."

Elle observes that the Minxy has become a Mirror again, albeit a deep, oily back. *Too dark for me to see my hairage, but not dark enough to shade my noogies.* Elle holds position, hands still behind head, feet wide apart. *It's chilly in here.* Goosebumps. *I can see my napoleons bubbled and my newels erected.*

Elle absorbs. *Strippers can solo the Dong but are not allowed to share it.* The Minxy divides into many Screens now, and Elle scans the flow: *It appears that the Dong has been alive inside in multiple vaginas!* The Screens reprise the Double Dong forcing orgasm of several Cosmos Pledge.

Elle closes her mind to thinking about Dong insertions and theorizes about the Prop itself. *The Double Dong must be wireless, and it is surly connected to Automatron, who monitors a whole slew of body parameters, and cybernetically calculates feedback. Which the Dong uses to stimulate one of us, tip her into the Zone, or ride her to climax.*

Something like that. Besides, Automatron has many appendages, many gauges and sensors, and lots of decision-making algorithms.

Elle catches her breath, keeps her hands behind her head, and cups her shaven armpits.

Elle projects. *Penny and Coco will pass the Double Dong to Kimju and Molly when it becomes their time to visit the Nugget. The two ex-Strippers will climax the Dong together during an Alumni Reprise, because Pledge can share the Dong.*

Elle anticipates the step after. *And then Kimju and Molly will bring the Dong back to the Cosmos House. And all of us Pledge will share. Like an infection.* XE "Double Dong: Kimju & Molly: Alumni Reprise: Elle *will bring from Nugget to Cosmos House, all will share* (Bunkroom D16)"

The images changes. Now two rectums fill the Minxy Screen. One of them is empty, the other swallows most of the Double Dong. The Screen cuts. This time the Dong is in the other rectum. It cuts again, this time a side-by-side of both Penny and Coco solo Dong inserted.

Elle feels a need to urinate and her eyes dart about. She discovers Beka using one hand to touch her bare box, hisses at her, watches Beka discover herself, stop, restore her position, and confirm with eyes.

Robyn fails to catch either transgression. "You're watching Penny and Coco climax on the Double Dong," she breezes. "They might jerk off together but only one of them at a time sinks the Dong." Robyn twitches her nose. "Make sure if you ever see them to tell them you watched their *Double Dong Climax Video*. They got a taste of Dong just after Babs and Janet reduced them in the Mudwrestling Contest when they climaxed the Dong together. Their only moment. As you can see in the *Side-by-Side Video* they can't share it, and so they covet donging together even more."

Robyn twitches her lip and addresses both newbies, "There is only one way for Penny and Coco to share the Dong next Term: they have to beg to take it with them together next Term. And if their beg is honored, they invite themselves to Opt Up and Pledge, or to Op Down and Whore; Gamers' decision."

Robyn brags, "But before I'm done with them they'll both be begging to Opt Whore." Robyn spins away from them.

Yes, Elle knows. *Instead of competing in the Game, the Dong will drive Penny and Coco so horny they will beg the Dong together next Term, even if Gamers Opt them to Whore.*

Beka simmers. Her bead of broda hangs down in between her thighs yet still above the knee line. She begs, "I'll go fetch the Dong from the Nugget, and bring it back in my bronzo."

Elle quivers her head; taut tremors. *No!*

§ Robyn Threatens Beka & Elle: Screen Their *Corvette Video*

"Beg me to screen your Corvette House performance." Robyn commands Beka and Elle.

"Ma'am… " Elle feels unsure. "Please let us watch the scene of Beka and me admiring the Baseboard Strippers at Janet's House."

"Do you think anyone cares to watch you lolly your Roommate up?" Robyn inquires.

Again, Elle swivels her foot and takes her hands off the back of her head. For an instant; she scrambles them back, feels in haste behind her neck for her buttons, and discovers them missing. She examines her nocks in the Mirror.

"Boobage!" Robyn laughs.

Elle retorts, "Babs let you see our videos at the Corvette House?"

Robyn snorts, "Boss Bitch? I don't ask BB. If I want to see something I just go look. More soap for your question, you negligible nincompoop nitwit. Besides, nobody cares about you tittering or pulling your pink. Ginny Cravat got climaxed using a procto, a pogo, and a cock. Now that's serious."

Beka interrupts. "I wanna see, Robyn. I want to see what we heard."

Robyn pinches both pairs of nipples. "Keep begging, both of you. The sooner Gamers let you masturbate the better off you are."

Beka keeps begging. "I'll masturbate on a Cam, Robyn, please I will!"

Robyn considers Beka. "Beka Broda, you're hanging valiva out below your knees. You're going to puddle the floor."

Beka shifts uneasily. For once she knows what comes next.

Robyn shifts her torment to Elle. "You know, Elle, maybe after you and Beka Flip-Flop, then you, instead of Beka, can hang your valiva outta your nectary. You can vagflash together with Steph."

Elle panics, "Ma'am, may it please you, Ma'am!"

It pleases Robyn to be called Ma'am even though she isn't entitled to the salutation. She curls, "Gamers hardly expect you to equal your Roommate's prodigious output, that's a magnificent feat, but Gamers do expect you both transude a lot more than Steph dropped for you in the Dining Room. You're on board for that, Pledge?"

"Ma'am please Ma'am," Elle hurries, "I'll lolly up Beka again. Today. No matter how big a puddle she makes."

"You'll puddle too," Robyn declares.

Elle furrows her brow, compensates. "Ma'am, I'll make a puddle too, no matter what it takes. And I'll lolly up after myself, too."

Robyn squints, "I recall during *The Arrivals* that you also lollyed up after the Peacocks."

Elle objects, "That's not true! It was Tiffany who got them to all pop but I hadn't arrived yet. I've only lollyed up Beka—more than once mind you—and Steph, but only one drop."

"Tell me your name again," Robyn commands.

"Ma'am, I'm Elle Lollydor, Ma'am," Elle recites.

§ Robyn Proposes Beka & Elle: Beg the Double Dong

Robyn gestures toward the Minxy Screen that occupies one wall of the Bunkroom. "Penny and Coco are going to beg to be Whores. Like ex-Porn Star Tiffany. Bikini Bitch wants to humiliate Tiffany by making Tiffany insist she's a '*wannabe* Porn Star' but BB's stupid. Tiffany really is a tawdry tang tart." Robyn snorts. "Once a Porn Star always a Porn Star," she affirms.

Elle tries to remain aloof to the presentation, but the more Beka watches Penny and Coco's clips, the more Beka squeezes out cream. Robyn laughs at her, "You are just gonna have to wait for cock, Beka Broda. First you need to shuck a Garment and Opt Strip, so that next Term you can beg to Whore. How's it go Pledge?"

Beka blurts, "Please let me pledge naked and become a Stripper next Term!"

Robyn lifts her nose. "You can beg for the Dong right now, Pledge, you don't have to wait.."

Beka begs breathlessly, "Ma'am, please let me go get the Double Dong from the Nugget. I'll let them put it in me on Stage and bring it back. Elle and I will climax on it just like Penny and Coco. All the way buried, our bud and nib rubbing."

Elle tries to stay analytical and keeps her eyes forward and her mouth ovaled as Robyn examines her closely. *No time to analyze Beka's outburst.* Robyn affords herself the opportunity of Elle's halter hanging down her midriff, reaches forward, and rolls first one nipple, then Elle's other, up to erection. "Looks like you got a pair of volcanoes there." Robyn taunts. "Perhaps you might perform for us a volcanic eruption?"

"Ma'am, may I please you, "Ma'am." Elle's body wavers but she keeps her feet planted wide and her palms tight against the back of her head.

"Pledge, it will please me for you to beg to roll your own nips," Robyn commands.

Elle stammers, "Ma'am, I can't do—"

Elle rears her head back as Robyn leans forward, gathers her lips together, and spits into Elle face. The glob hits onto and in between her moving lips, splatters her nose and cheeks, and sprays an eyebrow and eye. Plenty gets inside Elle's mouth. "Now what do you say?" Robyn demands.

"Ma'am, please let me touch my nipples, Ma'am," a stunned Elle responds.

"Don't you dare wipe that spit off your face," Robyn says. "You understand?"

"Ma'am, yes, Ma'am."

"Thank me, Pledge."

Elle obeys. "Ma'am, thank you, Ma'am."

"Beg like your Roommate," Robyn commands.

Elle stammers. "Ma'am, please let me Pledge naked and become a Stripper next Term." She catches her breath.

"Anything else?" Robyn wants to know.

"Ma'am." Elle processes quickly. *It was Robyn who unbuttoned my neck strap and unless I am careful she will use her fingers to unbutton my front buttons as well. My halter will fall to the floor, leaving me totally topless. And maybe only wearing one Garment.*

Elle begs, "Ma'am please let me keep my halter hanging down, 24x7. I'm boobage Pledge now. Me and Beka both. We'll stay that way."

"I'm tittering but I'm not actually boobage!" Beka interjects. "But I am vagflashing! Whereas Elle only hairages."

Robyn considers, "Remind me to Flip-Flop you two so Elle can vagflash and you can boobage. And I like that you want to be Roommates Together, because that means you can both Opt Down."

Robyn turns to question Elle, "Any final commitments you want to match with your Roommate?"

Elle tries hard to remember, "If Beka gets the Dong we get to keep our two Garments, and share Roommates Opt Up Together."

Really?

Robyn comes around front and steps back to survey Pledge Elle. Elle keeps her eyes focused upon her visage in the Minxy and watches her nimbi bubble up and her nips arise. Her bladder reminds her of its presence. Armpits cupped. Oval mouth.

Robyn observes Elle's erections and waggles a finger horizontally at her. "No, I will not touch them again for you. And you will not touch them either. You will beg. You want to be a Stripper so much, you can beg the other Cosmos to play with them."

Elle applies uncertainty, "Ma'am, thank you, Ma'am." *I'm exposing my noogies now, but at least I'm not on a Cam. Or technically topless.*

Robyn seems to have forgotten about the last buttons on the front of Elle's hanging halter. Instead Robyn chooses to lecture Pledge Elle: "It's not going to be easy to get your wish and become a Nugget next Term! If you think it's just you and Beka with Tiffany and Molly next Term, well, think again, Pledge, because you're going to get more Nugget competition soon. And it is not just *my* Roommate Kimju who's itching to beg Stripper, Steph's gonna beg the Strip too. All six of you Cosmos Pledge are gonna beg."

No! Elle reacts. *This is not supposed to be the outcome! Kimju wants to Opt Up; she doesn't want to pink, cream, and climax the Club anymore, this or next Term. And Steph? Steph just assumes privilege and promotion. But better she than me at the Nugget next Term.*

"Look at each other in the Mirror," Robyn commands, and the Roommates obey her. They let their ears echolocate Robyn's fading footsteps, their eyes sink into each other, and they finally canvas each other's not-yet naked bodies. Elle watches Beka heave a large breath of air, and watch the stalactite of brodeas thicken and distend longer. *I don't trust that the Minxy Mirror can't also witness, but I know if I looked at myself that my nimbus boils and my nipples show hard.*

§ Steph & Hat Check Girl: Fetches Pink Pages

Steph's errands earlier today take her first to the Nugget. She enters via the front door, dressed in a lavish single-shoulder strapped cutout minidress, and confronts the Hat Check Girl standing behind a counter gracefully inside the front door. Hat Check Girl wears a corset that uplifts a pair of breasts with double pierced nipples: two stainless steel barbells through each nipple at right angles to each other. She wears her hair in a bun and sports a ring in her nose. *Good sized one, too,* Steph realizes, but fails to gauge.

"May I help you," Hat Check Girl asks and smiles.

Steph finds herself unable to determine Hat Check Girl's Caste. She plows forward, "Robyn Redacted from the Cosmos House sent me to pick up Pink Pages of Kimju and Molly. I'm told you're the one who will give them to me."

The coat counter blocks the lower half of Hat Check Girl's body. "Come around," she invites, and brings Steph into her small room. The coat rack is mostly empty, with what looks like a full mail sack next to it on the floor. Hat Check focuses upon a small terminal and printer. Steph watches from behind and observes: *All she wears is a corset... and boots. Bare behind, and with something hanging down from her pussy lips.*

Hat Check Girl turns and hands two pages to Steph. "They are not ordinary printouts, mind you," she advises. "They are laminated plastic, fireproof, and contain GPS trackers. Who's gonna jerk off to them anyway?"

Steph gathers more of her wits. A glance reveals, *Hat Check Girl is shaven bare, and whatever metal sphere hangs down between her thighs hangs from piercings in the lips of her vagina.*

Hat Check catches the glance. "Sometimes the hanging ball is electric and shocks me if it touches my inner thighs, sometimes it's like a ball of sandpaper and roughens me up, or maybe it's diamond studded and cuts me. Right now I can move carefully, but if the coats start to pile up, I'll need to beg something."

"Hot jizz," Steph remarks, and considers opportunity. "Janet claims that she and Babs sent Penny and Coco over to dance. They climaxed the Double Donged naked and then they streaked here."

"They climax here still, center Stage at the Nugget!" Hat Check appraises, "They are allowed to solo the Dong, nothing more." Hat Check waves fingers back into air. "MomCap keeps them pink-wet-and-ready. She saves their climaxes for lapdances. Before MomCap is done with them they will be wannabe Whores. She'll have them begging to share the Dong instead of it hanging out like a dick from one of them or the other." Hat Check Girl twist a lip and squeezes her chin between her thumb and her fingers. "Would you also like me to output Penny and Coco's Pink Pages? They're brand new."

Steph hesistates.

"I'm sure they wouldn't mind and Boss Babe would be delighted," Hat Girl cajoles.

Steph sees advantages, "Sure. Absolutely!"

Hat Check Girl again turns her bare ass toward Steph. The boots rise above her knees, they have only a small heel, and match the corset color scheme. Steph tests, "Maybe you also have Janet? She was a Stripper once. And how about Babs?"

Hat Check turns around to appraise Steph, feeling somewhat put upon. She touches a nipple ring. "Babs? Babs was never a Stripper! But maybe if you take Janet, you should also take Tiffany. They were Stripper Roommates after all, even though it was two Terms ago."

"You got Tiffany sucking cock or fucking or taking it up the ass?" Step quickens.

Hat Check turns, hands the additional sheets to Steph, and wags a finger, "Nugget Pink Pages document Nugget show-and-tell. If you want Tiffany hard core, you'll need to visit Flesh Ranch."

"Flesh Ranch?" Steph repeats.

"Where Whores work," Hat Check glides, "You should visit. You might like it there. But another time. Today, on your way back to the Cosmos House, Gamers have decided you're to stop by the Snot House. Present yourself at the front steps, strip naked, fold your dress neatly, lay your dress on the porch behind your head, and sit spread surrender on the steps. Somebody will emerge, take away your dress, and leave you a Garment in exchange. Don't turn around. After they exit, you may break out of position, and put your new Garment on, and return to the Cosmos House."

"And what if there is a Cam at the Front Door of the Snot House? Or paparazzi?" Steph worries.

"If they want to cam you naked, they may cam you for as long as they want. It's their porch, so you don't have to worry you're streaking. Now, out of my booth."

Steph shakes her body and backs out and around so she can consider Hat Check Girl across her counter.

"What about paparazzi?" Steph frets.

"Perhaps the Snots will even monetize your position," Hat Check appraises. "But if you want some free advice: don't take your hands from behind your head and don't close your legs."

Steph seeks assurance. "So why am I doing this?"

Hat Check provides a cordial response. "My understanding is that one of their Pledge guys is being feminized and needs a dress."

Steph double checks. "And I'm to put on whatever they leave me?"

"Sounds like a plan!" Hat Check retorts. "But whatever you do, I'd make sure your button stays lit. Else you'll be in naked Lockdown… until you either get spit out on Stage at the Nugget next Term, or moved into a stall at Flesh Ranch. Lockdown won't be for just a day or two, like last Term."

Steph blinks again. Gamers could hand me a g-string and leave my sputs showing out. Or just a tee shirt so I have to run back bottomless. But whatever it is I must keep my navel bare!

The Hat Check Girl senses delay. "Perhaps they will give you a string to tie around your little finger and you won't have to think so much. Now scram. I've given you more Pink Pages that you deserve," she scoulds. "And when *you* come back to Audition, be sure to use the Stage Door!"

Hat Check makes a vague wave and Steph finds herself escorted to the outside. Six Pink Pages under her arm. Steph checks her buttonhole. *Open season.* She shakes her shoulders, one bare, one strapped. *No titter today!* She wiggles with the elastic single shoulder strap party dress. *No vagflash today either!*

Steph wonders while she travels just who directs her movement. *Certainly not Monitor Babs; even Bikini Bimbo doesn't have this kind of power.* What about MomCap? *She was my superior last Term and she is Babs' superior this Term. She is two Castes superior to all of us Cosmos, and she directly superior to all of the Strippers at the Nugget. So MomCap does have the power.*

§ Steph Visits the Snots: Exchanges Minidress for Undershirt

The Snot house sits back from the street. The front yard is un-mowed, the paint is peeling, and when Steph examines the front steps she observes boards are broken and cracked. She works her arm out of the single shoulder strap, lifts the hemline up above her stern, places the Pink Pages on the bottom step between widely spread feet, and peels the lavish minidress off overhead. She folds it neatly in her lap, pivots and places it on the porch behind her, draws her hands up behind her head, and spreads her legs.

I am aware of what I am doing, Steph analyzes, *I am sitting spread surrender stark naked on the Snot House front steps. I am completely open to the world. To paparazzi across the street, to anyone walking by, to anyone who ventures up the sidewalk.*

Steph hears a whirring and discovers that a Cam now hovers in front of her. *It takes in all my nakedness: face, spigots and torso, spread legs, even my scruff and vertical vulva slit.* Steph eyes what she correctly identifies as the Snot Houses Front Door Cam. *Okay, enough already, how much of me like this could you want after all?*

It depends on how much Gamers want to deepen Steph's humiliation.

Or maybe I'm worth a lot of surveillance, Steph considers.

Steph hears the Front Door open above and behind her, hears footsteps approach the folded minidress laid behind her head, hears the cloth get removed an the footsteps retreat and the Door close.

Steph's eyes dart; she decides to count to 60 but by 30 decides to turn around and....

Nothing there. She thinks she hears a door creak and so she snaps back into sit spread surrender position, looks deep ahead, sure of Cams out there, paparazzi even, and that I have no retreat. No fallback. I am sitting spread surrender naked to the Game, nowhere to run, and for as long as Gamers want to look at me.

Steph gets wet inside.

Steph comes out of a trance as footsteps retract from behind her head and the Front Door closes. Again she decides to count to 60 but by 30 she turns around to possesses whatever Garment awaits her.

Steph unfolds a man's undershirt out in front of her. *Very funny,* Steph snides. *So Gamers think this is just a different minidress. Not funny at all. Unacceptable!*

Unacceptable? In terms of the size of the armhole, the hemline, and the tightness factor the undershirt is not much different than the daily minidress Babs has been assigning Steph. Same number of tan lines, of edges.

But there is one difference. Steph calculates, pulls the undershirt overhead and down, sits, and then lifts it back above her waist again. Above her navel, actually.

The one difference is that the undershirt-dress possesses no buttonhole. Steph considers if she should just pull the shirt down and march right back to the Cosmos House. *After all, I have more Pink Pages that I was sent out for!* But Steph also recalls the parting admonitions of the Hat Check Girl. *Last time Robyn ratted on me and I went into Lockdown. This time she will rat on me again, only now Lockdown won't occur just before the end of the Term. Midnight is days away.*

Steph scans to see if a scissors might lie about. Or a razor. *Tiffany has both in the Makeup Kit. I'm just not sure I want to test Robyn or Babs on getting to the Cosmos House with my button covered up.* Steph considers, *I suppose I could just run back holding the undershirt up above my belly button.* Steph snorts. *No way I am going to let paparazzi collect me bottomless.*

Steph scans again, identifies a sharp end on the side of the stairs, aligns the undershirt in front of her, gets on her knees to sidle and rips a hole in the fabric. Does the Snot House Front Door Cam collect an exclusive? Steph knows it does; she stands and consents partially, digs the hole bigger with her fingers, but finally expands it by lifting the undershirt to her teeth and chewing the buttonhole out. *More unintended showmanship.*

She smoothes the undershirt down her body, assures herself that her freshly-formed buttonhole will present no problems, observes that *the armholes are too big,* and observes *the bottom of this bedraggled "minidress" squares level with my crotch.*

Steph scratches her ear, picks up the Pink Pages, and finds the Cam still hovering a-front her, and snaps at it, "You're gonna pay for this! All of you!"

§ Steph & Cosmos: Review Pink Pages on the Kitchen Table

During her return to the Cosmos House Steph stays too seared by her latest Garment to think much about the images and statistics on the Pink Pages. After ringing the Bell, Steph gains entry into the Kitchen.

All the Cosmos are there: Bikini Babe with her bling, Tiffany nude, Robyn with the smallest buttonhole, Kimju and Molly still topless and crusted with stinking dried mud (having been fried from the Mudpit earlier), and Beka and Elle with their boobs and nubbies covered. Babs' orders.

Bikini Babe and all her stupid Cosmos, Steph assesses.

Steph has planned the presentation. She sits delicately in her ripped-buttonhole undershirt, and then carefully lays Kimju and Molly's Pink Pages side-by-side on the Kitchen table, so that the two additional pairs of Pages hide underneath.

Seven Cosmos gather around to examine. Kimju and Molly expect to see what they do: The front side of each Pink Page features a large, full-color glossy 8x10 inch image of each former Stripper. Each presents herself naked, sitting spread-legged, and holding open her gynecological assets.

"Naked and spread," Robyn details. "And they're still at it today. Pink, wet, and cumming in sync with themselves." Robyn laughs.

Kimju feels properly humiliated, yet Molly feels pride.

"What's on the backside?" Elle innocently asks.

Robyn reaches and turns. And confusion erupts amongst the Cosmos. "Hey, there's another Pink Page underneath!" And "Get your finger out of the way!"

Boss Babe adjudicates. "Lay them on top of the next ones."

And Steph obeys.

"Seems like you brought a surprise for us," Babs appraises. "But first permit Kimju and Molly the honor of completing our examination of their inverse."

Steph bows to Kimju and Molly. The backsides of both Pink Pages speak for themselves. One smaller pictures on each depicts an insertion, another depicts each taking a pee. One of the insertions is in the anus, one is in the vagina; one of the pees is made over a tile floor, the other over the side of a motorboat. Kimju feels a flush coming on: her cheeks and chest redden, her nipples erect, and hairs stand up on her forearms and belly.

The rest of the Pink Page backsides contain credits and statistics: first, all of the basics: their hair and eye colors, heights, weights, and measurements. And not just their normal vital statistics, also the circumference of their necks, wrists and ankles, thighs, and even the distance from their belly button to their clits and assholes. It doesn't stop there.

The Pink Pages continues with a series of intimate, internal measurements, including their blood type, erected nipple and clit dimensions, butt plug size, vaginal depth and diameter, and renal capacity. No hiding the past for Kimju and Molly! Even a list of dance steps there is!

"Enough," Boss Babs says, and signals Steph to move Kimju and Molly's Pink Pages and reveal the Roommates beneath. The Pink Pages are so toxic that Steph attempts to handle them by only touching the edges. Her hands freeze in mid-air as Penny and Coco Pink Pages are revealed and show the two ex-Cosmos revealing themselves, naked, spread, and in the midst of a finger-fucking climax.

Hotter than what hangs on Baseboard in the Dining Room next door, Elle calculates. *Or at the Corvette's.*

Babs takes a step backwards, but only Steph notices her surprise. Steph squints at Babs. *I've already seen all the Pink Pages, so no surprises for me! Babs and I both know these two, Ms. Punt and Cunt. They were my Pledge last Term. And they are exactly fine where they are. Even if their Opt Down wasn't my Karma.*

Steph turns Penny and Coco's Pink Pages over so the Cosmos—Pledge and Monitor—may view more intimate facts and pictures.

Somehow or another, Robyn volunteers commentary. "Both of them have a spot that embarrasses them more than any other. A flaw. And so of course the Patrons want to see that spot more than any other."

Steph listens and trades eyes with Babs, a rare event. *We know what those spots are, we were here for real last Term, only Caste reversed. But how does Robyn know this if she has amnesia?*

Robyn points to a picture of Penny. "Read what the pretty purdah admits on her page, 'I'm more afraid of the freckles on my inner lips than any other spot on my body. I'm afraid if anyone who sees them won't desire me, unless maybe it's dark. What fears me the most is the idea of having to pull pink, and watch myself masturbate in a mirror!'"

Robyn looks at Steph. "The Patrons at the Nugget like that Penny likes for anybody to look."

Robyn points to a picture on Coco's Pink Page, and reads a caption, 'My most humiliating spot is a little keloid adjacent to my colon exit. It reminds me that even my imperfections have no secrets.' Isn't that sweet?"

Robyn shakes her shoulders and speaks to the Pledge, "The Patrons at the Nugget like that Coco doesn't want anyone to look."

Steph purses her lips during Robyn's elocution, and uses the pause to reach and slide Penny and Coco to the side, revealing Tiffany and Janet's Pink Pages. The Cosmos gawk.

Steph curls her nose at her former Pledge Janet's Pink Page, a full-frontal with eyes into the camera and oval mouth, detailing everything intimate. "Look at her!" Steph laughs, "Jugs, jelly belly, jungle patch, jaxy. Pink-wet-and-ready to jockum."

"Turn it over," Robyn commands, and Steph does. One picture captures Janet naked and streaming into a cup center stage at the Nugget, the other feasts upon her Double Penetrating Climax, with a vibrator sunk in her jam jar and a butt procto snaked into her junk chute.

Babs feels embarrassed for her former Roommate. She blushes and touches her bling. Catches herself. That's the first blush in a long time. *But it isn't about my own bling, I'm embarrassed to be this exposed to Janet's revelations.*

Tiffany, delighting in her own unexpected revelation, reserves expression of judgment and watches as hands turn her naked spread Pink Page over as well. *More tame than my Porn Star Calendar.* At the moment the Calendar presents Tiffany naked, and with her mouth overflowing with ejaculate.

Robyn calls attention to something that might disturb the newbies. "Look at Kimju and Molly," Robyn fans the glossy spreads side-by-side, "They are not just pinking, they're also sloshing their wet." Robyn tilts toward the newbies, Beka and Elle, and adds, "Something else for you to aspire to!"

Elle clamps her jaw tight.

Beka feels a twitch, discovers herself wet just like the pink and wet Kimju ad Molly, and blurts out, "Please Robyn, I want my own Pink Page. Elle and I both!"

Elle startles. *No!*

Beka accelerates. "And I'm not like Steph. I want to pass out my own Pink Page, and not somebody else's."

See, hazing helps Kundalini emerge!

II-4 Tiffany & Robyn & Kimju: Yachting with Others (D17)

§ Tiffany & Robyn & Kimju: Depart for Yacht Outing

On the following morning, the morning of Day Seventeen, Babs empowers Robyn to escort Tiffany and Kimju on a Yachting excursion. The threesome exit the Back Door, ring the Bell thrice, and are transported in a Van with blackout windows and a blackout partition between them and the driver. The remotely controlled side door of the Van permits them to exit onto a public dock somewhere.

Kimju, angry about being subjugated to her Roommate once again, doesn't bother to clench her breasts as she prepares to board the Yacht. *Some Gamers think it sexy for strangers to gawk at me in my topless tanga in public? Hey you! You want to see me embarrassed like this? Go ahead, look at me. Don't look away.* Kimju digs her tanga out of her crotch in full view of astonished dockhands and covers what she can of her hairage. *Perverts!* The gangplank extends, Kimju crosses her arms to form a handbra, and boards the Yacht.

Tiffany stretches her bellage and lets a stranger cam her erupting pubic hair. Robyn steps onto the Yacht wearing her maillot cutout with its narrow shoulder straps. And soon the three Cosmos, plus five others, are all-aboard and the Yacht casts off.

§ Molly & Steph and Beka & Elle: Sit for Bathroom Cam

Back at the Cosmos House Babs does seem to have allowed Robyn to confine the remaining four Pledge to the Bathroom. Molly takes her panties off before she goes into the Bathroom. She washes them out, showers, and leaves them hanging over on the side of the sink. *Good,* she appraises, *they no longer threaten my health.*

Molly's presence assures that the Bathroom Pee-Cam says lit. Her Roommate Steph still wears her undershirt; it titters, and Steph finds it easier to just sit on her bare stern than try to sit on the hem. And as far as her scruff goes, it goes without saying that upskirt is a misnomer, spread crotch with the snizzle showing beneath the soft wavy hairs is what Steph displays to the Bathroom Cam. She scowls at the Cam as it samples her. *Haven't you got enough of me?*

Molly queries, "What's with you, didn't Babs swap your undershirt for a new minidress today?"

Steph retorts. "No. Last night Babs told me I would be keeping this. She said that 'an undershirt is not a minidress' so she could not exchange it."

"Babs told me," Molly offers, "that since you want my panties you should stay with the undershirt. 'Underwear attracts,' she said."

"BB said that?" Steph double checks.

"She did," Molly affirms.

Elle worries. *I might be here all day. Will Steph and Beka and I be able to hold out, or will some of us audition Pee-Cam today?*

Beka just relaxes and lets the Cam collect titter and upskirt.

Molly also doesn't worry about the Pee-Cam. Molly knows, *Of course I will pee for it.* She touches both hands to her mooe and examines it for cleanness. *No dried valiva, no panty lint, no urine crystals, no yeast. Good.* Molly observes that now she has attracted the Cam, gives it the eye, then drops her eyes to coordinate opening her inner lips to reveal purple deep down her vaginal canal.

Ah ha! Molly laughs to herself. *Robyn is gone and I am not forbidden from masturbating and cumming today!* Molly rolls her body so that her large hanging mams flop around. She tilts her head and presents the Cam with a smile that is almost laughing. Then for a moment, her eyes command it with the power of the Stripper Caste. *You are under my Spell!*

Molly lifts her hands from her mooe to her mams, cups them underneath, shakes them, rubs her big medallions, and pinches her minarets. *But I'm not going to say out loud I'm going to pink, cream, and cum for you because if I do, you might just be programmed to stop me somehow.* Molly brushes her long black hair. Hairy armpits. Hairy arms and legs, hairy all the way from the belly through the crotch, growing in her moonshadow, and hairy down her inner thigh.

Robyn had told all four them all to "sit and spread," but there had been no other restrictions on movement, except 'no talking.' Molly surmises, *Babs always feeds this Cam to the Prefecture, and Automatron will report any talking, if not transcribe it.*

Molly ponders. *But Babs has not stopped me from climaxing before. I was the first Cosmos to climax this Term—in front of everybody at the Bachelor Party. And then I climaxed in the Bathroom with Kimju. Kimju might not like she's the second Pledge to knockadoodle, but she is. After I give my panties to Steph I want to climax on the Double Dong with Beka.*

Molly relaxes her smile, shifts her weight, and frames her hands behind her body, rests backwards still with legs spread, and masturbates. *Please I want to get to the Nugget, but I will not be performing Piss Mouth. Unless I have to.*

§ Janet Greets Tiffany & Robyn & Kimju: And Takes Control

The Yacht is a boat large enough to walk around on, with a spacious deck and a cabin below deck. Out on the Yacht, away from shore, Janet organizes all hands on deck and welcomes eight Gamers aboard: three Cosmos, three Corvettes, and two Peacocks.

Once again Janet wears a different Spiderweb Bikini, different color, size, and crochet pattern. Today's Spiderweb features a tiny opaque web with an area smaller than her areolas; likewise although what is now a smaller, size nano crochet g-string, it too has become opaque. In fact, the tiny triangle so small that it ensures that Janet's jute patch spills to all sides of the g-string, and her three pairs of stainless steel rings escape to the sides. Might she be proper the triangle cover her clit.

Janet turns to Tiffany and welcomes an old friend. Tiffany reminds herself, *Janet doesn't just have rings in her jepoot, Janet has a tattoo as well, albeit well hidden.*

"Tiffany," Janet opens, "I thought you'd be bringing me Roommates Molly and Steph. Instead you bring me Roommates Robyn and Kimju. What gives?"

Robyn interrupts, "Listen Janet, it is I who have brought Pledge, not Tiffany. Monitor Babs has put me in charge. Tiffany is a slutty ex-Whore and isn't in charge of anybody. And Kimju is my Roommate, and whether she keeps her topless tanga or gets naked, she shall Opt Strip next Term."

Janet eyes Tiffany for confirmation. Their contact two days ago during the Lineup had been playful yet stern, and today could provide them with more private opportunities. Tiffany still wears her clear vinyl shirt and low-riding slacks, with Eraser Heads in see-through, red hairage erupting above waistline, and her trough trailing backside.

Tiffany squints, "Ma'am you know the last thing I want is to be in charge of anybody. Please feel free to strip me naked and throw my clothes overboard. I will—"

Robyn interrupts, "Janet, I'm quite certain that Babs wants Tiffany's clothes first."

Janet turns upon Robyn, "Pledge, do not interrupt me. I don't need your help in this matter."

"Janet, I thought—" Robyn begins.

"Shutup," Janet snaps. "First off all, if I want your thoughts I will ask for them. Do you understand me?"

"Ah, yeah," Robyn responds unsurely, "I'll approve that."

"Listen carefully, Pledge," Janet glowers, "I am not 'Janet' to you. I am 'Ma'am.' Is that clear to you?" Janet queries.

Robyn stumbles, "Ah, yes, Ma'am."

"Beg me to feed you caster oil for addressing me improperly," Janet orders.

Robyn looks around. Outnumbered, strange faces. "Ma'am, maybe you should give caster oil to my Roommate instead."

Janet startles. "You approve of feeding caster oil to your Roommate in lieu of yourself?" Janet queries.

Robyn flusters, "Ah, yes, Ma'am, I approve of whatever you do to Kimju." Robyn scans as the small group focuses upon her. Besides her Cosmos Cam hovering nearby, two other Cams record the proceedings, one of them controlled by one of the Corvettes, the other by a Peacock.

Janet laughs, turns to Robyn, and asks, "How about you approve of Kimju prostrating herself on the deck, pulling her thong to the side and begging for a thermoprobe up her kawazoo?

Robyn nods, "Ma'am, I approve, Ma'am."

Janet signs Kimju, and Kimju reluctantly kneels and then flattens her bare knockers and belly on the deck. She reaches around behind her with both hands, and with one of them pulls her tanga to the side and with the other she parts her keelson. She tries to hide her face on the deck. *This is the first time I've had to openly display my kawazoo this Term,* Kimju frets, *and not just for the Cosmos House, but for* three *Cams.*

Kimju expects Janet to put her "at ease," but this doesn't happen.

Perseverance matters when it comes to offering up assholes.

Janet runs a finger inside her nano g-string and asks Robyn, "How about you approve of yourself spotting your maillot with cream today?"

Robyn seems confused. "Ma'am, I—"

"Don't approve," Janet aids.

"I don't approve," Robyn asserts.

"You don't approve anything," Janet provides.

"Ma'am—" says Robyn.

"Thank me, Pledge," Janet commands.

And Robyn acknowledges, "Ma'am, yes, Ma'am," Robyn looks down. "I don't approve anything, Ma'am."

"Very well," Janet accepts. "Now tell your Cam to keep a watch over your Roommate."

"Ma'am, thank you, Ma'am," says Robyn. "I already cammed her during *The Arrivals:* pink, wet, and cumming out of her gourd." Robyn signs the hovering Cam to point at Kimju's puckered kawazoo. Then Robyn sits and rests her back.

Kimju closes her eyes. *I know what happened to Beka and Steph during The Arrivals. I'm going to be the next Cosmos to get thermoprobed.*

§ Tiffany Meets Darleen: Another Cam Opportunity

Once again Janet and Tiffany trade looks. Janet says, "Your task today is to assist me and my Roommate. Permit me to introduce you to Darleen."

Darleen moves forward, with her arms swinging, and stops in front of Tiffany. She wears a longsleeve pullover that kisses the waistline of skin-tight slacks. Flat-chested, slim-waisted, 33A-25-32 hips, long-legged. Tanned face arms, and bare feet.

Darleen is not a Cosmos and not mandated to navelage, but she is a belly flasher.

Darleen nods to Tiffany. "I'm sure that sometime today you'll want to show off your twat and tube tunnel, if not flash your tailpipe tattoo. I've already collected Steph and Beka and Elle's titter and anus and vag in the Dining Rooms and I look forward to adding you, Tiffany Transparent, to our Corvette Video collection."

Tiffany perts, "Darleen I will strip naked, pink, pee, masturbate, and climax for you and your Corvette Cam." And although part of Tiffany enjoys the exposure, a part of her resents the hubris. She studies the lanky Corvette. *If indeed Janet wears two Garments that mostly expose her, Darleen wears two Garments that mostly cover her up. A longsleeve high-collared pullover that kisses waist-level slacks.* When Darleen rises onto the balls of her bare feet and lifts her arms she flashes bellage and the occasional belly button, but that's her only exposure.

Tiffany understands the difference. *A Cosmos dares not engage in one of those teases where she flashes her belly button every time her shirt rides up or she thumbs her waistline down. Maybe Darleen is a belly flasher, but I am not a belly flasher at all, I'm belly-up belly down all the time. I'm tits transparent, I hairage, and my slacks have stained creamy cameltoe. And as for flashing my navel, all us Cosmos are button bare all the time. Navelage 24x7.*

Tiffany listens to Darleen speak, "During *The Arrivals* I even cammed your Bling Bitch's areolage when Janet and I visited on the last day of *The Arrivals*."

Tiffany frowns at this insult to her Roommate, the not-present Monitor Babs. She shuffles and provides Darleen's Corvette House Cam her best smile, best eyes, best head twist. "You can take all of me!" Tiffany proposes, "If you let me strip naked I bet there's enough ultraviolet to make my Eraser Heads light up!" Tiffany brightens, "Maybe my ultraviolet ink tramp stamp descending down into my tail trough will become visible. Please share your vids, Darleen, and feed me to the Prefecture."

"Stop that," Janet scolds, "you're upstaging me!"

Tiffany pays respect, "Ma'am, "I've done everything explicit, all holes, all sexes. Don't forget that now that I'm a Pledge I'm allowed to Double Dong, Ma'am."

"Double stop it!" Janet commands laughingly. "You need to stay frustrated."

Darleen injects a creative thought, "You'll pee for my Cam."

Tiffany circumspects this order. *Should I obey order from a Pledge at a different House?* "I will!" she beats, collecting the opportunity. "I'll pee for all the Cams here."

"You'll pee in your own mouth." Darleen states. "You don't fool me. You begged Piss Mouth to avoid Slavesex. You'll let anyone pee on you, you'll even drink man piss. You just don't want to be tied up first."

Tiffany closes her eyes. *True.* She opens them and retorts, "And you're a broken Monitor and now a Corvette Pledge."

Darleen huffs, "I'm Janet's Roommate and consigliore. Don't you ever forget that. Maybe Steph thinks she got Janet her promotion. I know better. I did. So watch out, you wannabe Whore."

"Don't try to diss me," Tiffany wrings, "I'm the one with a Porn Star Calendar hanging on the wall. I don't see you hanging anywhere, not with a dick in your dugout, or without.

Janet puts an arm on Darleen's shoulder. "Tiffany will pee when we need her to. Right now I want to continue her introductions."

§ Tiffany Reacquaints with William & Rodney: Peacock Pomp

Janet gestures toward the only two males in the group, and teases them both, "Tiffany, you need to help me keep these two Peacocks under control: Peacock House Monitor William and his Roommate, Pledge Rodney. You've met them before?"

Tiffany catches the twinkle in Janet's eye. She had recognized both Peacocks when she boarded, but had not said a word nor traded eye contact, despite knowing that their eyes sought her out. She squares herself and speaks, "Ma'am, indeed I have! I changed my shirt in front of the entire Peacock Lineup there on the first day of *The Arrivals.* They all popped, including this one." Tiffany points to the bare-chested lad wearing only a jockstrap.

Janet demeans, "Did you know that Rodney is a former cock-wagger and perpetually hard? Perhaps you over credit yourself in your ability to encourage him to soak his jock with his semen."

Tiffany draws her lips tight and narrow in front. *Rodney cammed me that day and he cams me again,* Tiffany observes, and turns to explore the eyes of Monitor William, dark brown hair and eyes, 5' 10", 160 pounds, politely attired in a black shortsleeve t-shirt and slacks. They trade eyes and hostile sparks fly; Tiffany knows, *William is equal in rank to Janet, and for that matter, to Babs (who isn't aboard). All of them outrank me.*

Janet details, "William and I are the co-captains for this sunny day on the water."

Tiffany reads William's eyes exactly. *The cocky Monitor has not forgotten that I declined to suck him when I traded shirts* and *popped his Lineup at the start of the Term. Now he relishes another opportunity to get some private time with a star of the* Suck Fuck Facials *series.*

True, and it's not like Tiffany hasn't sucked countless dicks before. Tiffany's see-through titter and hairage above her slacks excite William, and he joculars, "Tiffany Transparent! Welcome aboard, Porn Star! Can't wait to see me again. You gonna fuck me today?"

Tiffany lifts her chin but Janet rescues her. "Oh, behave yourself, William. Tiffany might be a Porn Star but she's retired! Ever since she pledged the Cosmos sexing is no longer allowed! You know that."

Tiffany confirms out of the corner of her eye that Rodney cams her. Without breaking momentum or looking away from William, she tugs her waistband upward and works the cameltoe deeper into her treasury. She glances again, and assures herself Rodney collects the close-up. *My own wet spot.*

William demands Tiffany's attention and mocks her, "You're a natural-born tail peddler, and it frustrates you that having sex is strictly forbidden. Your frustration is your torment."

"Touché," Tiffany admits and counterpunches, "William, too bad you'll need to wait until I Whore again. Then you can pay to fuck me." Tiffany rubs her fingers on the outside of her shirt over her nipples, "And don't think you're so special that my titty-tips stand up just for you. My Eraser Heads stand up all the time."

William flinches but recovers, "You're gonna pink, cream, and cum for me, Pledge! Today on this boat! And Rodney's gonna cam you, a Peacock exclusive. Our second dip, only this time, you won't have cloth between your legs."

"Mister, yes," Tiffany responds, using the proper form of address for a male Monitor but in a tone of voice that William can't tell is serious or mocking. "Please I'll cum on a toy for you. I'll cum on my fingers. I'll cum rubbing the mast. I'll cum on the Double Dong center Stage at the Nugget. Anywhere, anytime, in front of anybody. I am a Porn Star!"

Tiffany suddenly remembers Janet stands behind her. "Mister, I am a *wannabe* Porn Star. Cam me, feed me to the Prefecture, and please let me Pledge naked and cum be a Stripper next Term."

§ Tiffany Reacquaints with Ginny: A Whore-for-Life

There remains one Corvette Pledge to be introduced; it is a Pledge Tiffany knows, a medium-built stark naked Corvette with curly hair and a racing stripe, and who up until now has always stood with her eyes cast down. *Ginny.*

Janet queries, "Certainly you remember Ginny?"

"Ma'am yes Ma'am," Tiffany recalls. "Ginny Stripped at the Nugget last Term whenever I was a Feature Dancer."

William interrupts. "Clarify yourself!"

Tiffany tilts her head, graces William with her eyes, and lets Rodney's Cam score. "A Feature Dancer means I was a Guest Whore; whereas Ginny was the House Whore."

She turns to Ginny, "Hello again!"

"Hello to you, Tiffany," Ginny lifts her eyes and grins, "But let me clarify, I was a Nugget Stripper last Term and I was a Whore-for-Life. This Term I'm a Corvette Pledge and I am still a Whore-for-Life. Right now I can have sex but you can't."

True, Tiffany accepts. *Last Term we both could have sex. Even sucked cocks together, as one can see in my Porn Star Calendar.* Tiffany twists her lips and considers Ginny with envy and wary affection. "I guess you left your costume behind?" she says.

Ginny bows, "Tiffany, you know full well I've worn nothing since before I was a Stripper, and I've worn nothing ever since. Actually I've been naked since the first day of my first Term."

Ginny more carefully considers Tiffany's two Garments. "Seems like instead of making Stripper this Term, you Double Opted Up and became a Pledge. Seems like you're headed in the wrong direction. How'd that happen?"

"I am a victim of overshoot," Tiffany protests, "I committed to taste piss to ensure I did not Opt Slavesex. But instead of letting me Opt Strip so I could return to Porn Star next Term, Gamers parked me here: a Cosmos Pledge. *And* with two pieces!"

Ginny jests, "You're special. You're a Porn Star chastised. Gamers say you're the perfect Porn Star because you love to fuck and you *want* people to watch."

Tiffany jives Ginny back, "You're pretty special too. You never care if they want affection or want to be rough, you just love the ride. That's why you're a perfect Whore-For-Life!"

Old rivals laugh together.

William interjects, and sticks his jaw toward Ginny, "How come I never met you before? You danced the Nugget last Term?"

"Every day. 8x5: eight hours by five days. Stripper hours, even though I was a Whore-For-Life. You're loss you missed me because I would have done you in the Champagne Room." Ginny laughs.

William ponders this and Janet augments, "Ginny is still a Whore-For-Life; her past, present, and future are unified, no matter what her current or future Caste. Corvette Pledge Ginny performs all whorish acts, always and forever. But right now I manage Ginny's holes. Get it?"

Ginny seizes the moment and advances to William, "Maybe Tiffany can't fuck you. But if Janet lets me, I will."

Tiffany feels a need to compete and challenges Ginny. "I climaxed your Monitor center Stage at the Nugget last Term. Maybe you watched us Double Dong that night, and watched Janet lose it completely?"

"Maybe I watched Janet pour shots for you center Stage at the Nugget and watched you toss them down," Ginny retorts. "Maybe I'm a Pee-Camer by virtue of being a Whore-for-Life, but you're Piss Mouth! And you want to know why? Because you were not ready to become a Slavesex. You might like to climax for real and let go completely. You might like to get roughhoused and drink cum that was shot into your tailpipe, but you are not ready to be possessed completely: mind, body, and soul."

Ginny casts a dubious look in Tiffany's direction. Tiffany breathes in through her mouth, *okay, thank goodness I'm not a Slavesex,* and then speaks out loud, "Okay, so I am a Porn Star, or as Babs says, I am a wannabe Porn Star." Tiffany pauses and scratches her bare belly, "I love making guys cum. Hey, gals too. I'm the best, I'm a natural, and anybody who watches me can't help but fall in love with me. But the Slavesex, they can be different. Totally secured, every hole taken, nipple and clit stimmed, and climaxing to a tone pitch. A whole row of them, a human organ, blowing their pipes. Machine Zoned, with ink and steel head to foot."

Tiffany nods her head toward Ginny, "We've all made compromises."

You're the one collecting ink and steel," Ginny responds. "Everyone knows your Eraser Heads count as three piercings. And the ultraviolet ink your nipples and tailpiece tattoo count as two tattoos." Ginny curves, "Rules suggest you should have a third tattoo."

Ginny just might know a fact here. Tiffany deflects, "I know my nipples are very sensitive and stay erect all the time. There are things about them I've never found out, like am I given drugs, or if there is some wireless cyber-circuit inside controlled by Automatron?"

"You and Ginny may stop trying to out Caste each other," Janet ordains to Tiffany, "and instead of begging Darleen to strip, pink, and cam you, you need to beg *me,* and make *me* your first priority."

Tiffany agrees, "Ma'am, of course I will. I'll eat you out, Ma'am."

Janet bolds, "You'll drink my piss. This time you won't be pouring shots, you'll be keeping up with my stream."

Tiffany begs, "Ma'am, please let your Piss Mouth Pledge naked and cum be a Stripper next Term."

§ Robyn Curries Favor with Janet: Sneaky Leaker

Robyn becomes aware of a figure standing above her tickling the bottom of her foot with a big toe. She rustles, looks up from her sitting position, and hears Darleen speak to her, "Janet wants to talk to you. Get up and follow me. We're going to her cabin, below deck. Leave the Cam to surveil Kimju's offered kawazoo."

Yes, Kimju still lies on her belly on the deck, still pulls her tanga to the side with one hand, and still displays her asshole with the other.

Robyn enters a small cabin and encounters Janet sitting at a table. Darleen vanishes.

"Who are you to send your minion to talk to me?" Robyn complains. You're not my Monitor. You can't tell me what to do." Robyn insists. "I don't know you."

Janet firms her posture and makes a mouth like that of a talking bird, "I know who you are. You do not." And changes countenance. "You're correct, Robyn, I am not your Monitor. And so to whatever extent you do have Charm, it has no effect on me; I'm not a part of your House. But it is very simple, I am a Monitor and you are a Pledge. So you shall hear and obey me. Or I'll let all the Pledge here strip you naked and throw your maillot overboard. They will obey me. Then when we get back to the dock you can streak to the Cosmos House."

"Ma'am, I'm here to work with you, Ma'am," Robyn demurs. "I don't approve anything."

"A wise decision," Janet agrees, "because I've decided to take you under my wing and entrust you with a most important task!"

Robyn shifts her feet and smoothes her maillot cutout. She hesitates.

"I'm assigning you to manage Kimju," Janet advises.

Robyn stammers, "I already manage Kimju. Babs orders. And I manage Tiffany too."

"You don't manage anything here, Pledge," Janet reminds.

"I'll strip my Roommate naked, and audition her for the Pee-Cam," Robyn proclaims.

"You do that," Janet agrees. "Be sure to cam it. And make sure Darleen and Rodney get good footage too."

"I'll make Kimju a Piss Mouth," Robyn bubbles. "And I also have a secret to share with you. Something you should know about."

"Really?" Janet scratches her nose. "You remember something?"

"Ma'am," Robyn braves, talking with her hands also, "Did you know that Steph went over to the Nugget yesterday brought your Pink Page back to the Cosmos House?"

"Really?" Janet starts, "Whose idea was that?"

Robyn flusters, "Ah, well, probably Steph's. She volunteered to fetch Kimju and Molly's Pink Pages, so that the ex-Strippers can show Beka and Elle something else they have to look forward to."

"So have Kimju and Molly been reprising all their Stripper clips from last Term?" Janet asks.

Robyn expounds, "Janet, that's nothing. I already made Kimju and Molly masturbate in sync with their *Nugget Stripper Videos* from last Term. And now they are begging to perform an Alumni Reprise at the Nugget!"

"Wow!" Janet exclaims.

"I'm making them teach Beka and Elle to dance!" Robyn declares.

"Interesting," Janet says slyly, "It's really smart of you to tell me this. So did Steph collect any other Pink Pages?"

Robyn remembers, "Penny and Coco. Apparently their Pink Pages just got released. Steph said the Hat Check Girl offered them to her, and she brought them back to the Cosmos House."

"Any other offerings?" Janet queries.

"Apparently Steph asked for your and Babs' Pink Pages, but only got you and Tiffany," Robyn reveals.

"Babs has never Stripped," Janet reminds Robyn. "Tiffany and I made our Pink Pages when we were Stripper Roommates two Terms ago."

"I'm seen them," Robyn distains. "You were both naked and spread."

"Really?" Janet exclaims.

Robyn details Janet's Pink Page to her, "Yours shows you pinking and peeing center Stage at the Nugget. Everyone gathered around the Kitchen Table to look. Steph called you a 'jizzing jamtart' and said she made you ass-fuck a buttplug taped to your Post. Babs and everybody but me were laughing at you. But BB got disturbed when she see saw Penny and Coco's Pink Pages. Apparently they were Cosmos last Term, so maybe you know them.

"You're a real charmer, Robyn," Janet affirms, "Don't you love the old days, last Term, when BB and I were Cosmos Pledge? Did you see my Dining Room Picture that hangs just below Babs? Back then I wore a size mini halter and g-string. And today? Today my Spiderweb Bikini is even smaller. At the start of the Runup I changed into a micro, and now that I'm hear with you on the Yacht I'm wearing a size nano. Explain that, Pledge."

"Maybe you're a pico next," Robyn suggests. She spins her hands. "And then 'poof' your naked and you Opt Down next Term.

Janet pretends laughter. And proclaims, "You know I really value you as my most important back channel!"

"Great!" Robyn accepts, "We're like equals!"

Janet leans forward and confides to Robyn, "I assume that Kimju and Molly will be heading right back to the Strip. After all, they only wear one Garment."

Robyn puffs her chest up and advances her private thoughts. "Kimju knockers with a snatch patch and Molly mamazulons with her panties yanked up tight," Robyn pronounces. And carefully laughs.

Janet chuckles, "You're so smart." She points to the hallway. "Now go turn out that Roommate of yours before I change costumes with you."

"Right," Robyn scrambles up to the deck. Janet watches Robyn climb up through the hatch, and puts a cross hairs next to her name.

§ Robyn Meets Darleen and Rodney: All Camers Today

Up on deck Robyn finds her path blocked by Darleen. The ever-strident Darleen lifts an arm, flashes her belly, and advances to Robyn, "I'm sure you don't remember me," Darleen curls, "I visited your Cosmos House and cammed Steph and Beka admiring the Baseboard Strippers during *The Arrivals.*

Robyn hesistates.

Darleen elucidates, "You were too busy camming yourself. I see you brought a Cam today. No doubt you are going to stay busy camming yourself."

"Wrong." Robyn snides. "I shall be camming my Roommate Kimju peeing today." She considers that Darleen also guides a Cam.

Darleen answers the unasked question, "Excellent. Be sure to strip her naked and pink her so I can add her to our Corvette feeds."

William's Roommate, the wiry blond Pledge Rodney, sidles up to the twosome, also with a Cam in hand, and flatters Darleen, "I hear that you really run the Corvette House, and that first-time Monitor Janet acquiesces to your every suggestion."

Darleen looks at William and replies coyly, "So, believe it."

Robyn takes stock of Rodney. His bare chest is shaven, and his privates are clad in a skin-tight Spandex jockstrap. Suntan oil glistens on his chest and bare ass, and his cock bulges inside the jock. Nobody misses it. Rodney offers Robyn sly praise, "And I hear you're in charge of the Cosmos Pledge."

"Correct," Robyn confirms with an ominous presence, "I am Babs' advisor. And I know all about you." Robyn lifts one side of her nose. "Everyone has watched the clips of you wringing your rod at bridal parties and dancing in leather bars. Everyone knows you were a Stripper last Term. Tiffany took one look at you on Day One, and you spotted yourself. You're unable to takes your eyes off my belly button in my little cutout hole. Everyone can see that Kundalini arises in your jock."

Darleen interjects, "Robyn, don't you have a Pledge who needs to beg a Pee-Cam?"

Robyn takes a step backward on the deck, shifts her eyes from Rodney to Darleen, and attacks. "Tell Janet," Robyn snarls, "That she should swap her Spiderweb Bikini for your shirt and slacks. That way everyone could purview your dittlebuttons and drey, and not be confused about who is the real boss at the Corvette House."

Robyn snorts at the both of them, spins on her heels, and seeks Kimju.

Darleen sucks in the side of one cheek, turns, and decides to seek Janet.

§ Robyn orders Kimju: Strip Naked & Leave Tanga in Sink

Robyn approaches Kimju. Robyn fails to appreciate the stamina it takes for Kimju to keep both hands behind her back all this time, one of them pulling her tanga to one side, and the other parting her butt cheeks. Robyn announces her presence. "Hello, Roommate. You don't know if you're halfway to Monitor land... or halfway back to the Nugget! With your keister parted and your kawazoo offered up. And down below that, your keewee wanting to open up. You're a disgusting, kimshaw kipper klute. Maybe you don't know where you are halfway to, but I do. You are halfway to the Nugget next Term. And you want to know why? Because you need to get to Flesh Ranch just as fast as you can, and once you get to the Nugget you are halfway there. Ha ha ha. Too bad you have to layover and Strip next Term, but after that you can put your kawazoo and kunny to work full time."

Kimju stays silent.

Robyn pokes a toe. "Roll over, Pledge. Keep those legs of your spread and rub that thong of yours back and forth between your legs. Keep it up. Kloop for my Cam!"

Kimju obeys. *Robyn is not the only Cam,* Kimju observes as she looks outward. *The Corvette Cam hovers, the Peacock Cam hovers also. Rodney cams.*

Kimju feels a flush come on. Her face and chest redden. *My pelvis feels hot.* She looks down and sees, *my knobs have risen up.*

Prolonging only gives them more build up, Kimju acknowledges. She rubs the tanga harder and deeper into her kooch, fits it down in between not just the outer but also her inner sex lips, and rubs it up and down and then angles back and forth across her clitoris. *My keystone.* And surrenders to ecstasy as Kundalini unrolls. *No secrets for me this Term.*

"Strip naked," Robyn commands.

Kimju looks around, rolls her tanga down her thighs, knees, calves, ankles, and feet. She considers the soaked tanga she now holds in her fingers. Where do you want me to put this?" she asks.

"Suck your klammy outta your tanga and use your fingers to scoop out your keekelay and eat yourself," Robyn retorts.

Kimju knows the order is disgusting. *At least to an unseasoned Gamer.* She obeys and consumes her own juices.

Robyn orders. "Take that rag down below, wash it out in the sink, and hang it up to dry."

"I can just put it back on," Kimju tries to be helpful.

"You'll throw it in the toilet if I have to tell you again," Robyn firms. "And if I have to tell you a time after that, you'll throw it overboard."

Kimju understands, "Ma'am, I'll wash it out in the sink, Ma'am." And heads for the hatch.

"Hurry back!" Robyn commands.

Kimju scrambles down the short ladder, unrolls and washes out her tanga, and lays it over the edge of the sink. *I really don't want to leave it behind and separate it from myself,* she considers, but obeys. She turns into the passageway down the center of the vessel and finds herself gathered into Janet's tiny space.

"You understand you are to obey Robyn?" Janet queries.

"Ma'am, yes, Ma'am," Kimju resigns.

"She will make a Pee-Camer out of you next," Janet predicts.

"Ma'am, You watched me dance the night you visited the Nugget last Term for your Alumni Reprise. I peed center Stage at the Nugget last Term, just like you did."

"I saw you get your knockers fondled and your koot get finger-fucked." Janet steels, "But since everybody's watched your vids yesterday, everybody knows you bent the Rules. Beg nicely, naked Pledge, and you just might get your tanga back." Janet grins.

"Ma'am, please—" Kimju begins.

"Stow it, Pledge." Janet hefts both jugs. "Save it for up on deck."

"I really need two Garments to Opt Up," Kimju pleads.

"Begging your tanga back would get you to one," Janet breezes.

"Otherwise you'll give it to Robyn?" Kimju queries.

Janet lifts her eyebrows.

Kimju realizes she should not have asked a question. "Ma'am, soap please, Ma'am."

"Upstairs!" Janet commands. "You're holding up the proceedings."

§ Tiffany & Kimju & Ginny: Nugget Tales & Present Positions

Kimju returns to the deck to discover Tiffany and Ginny hobnobbing, and moves to join them. Gamers recall that Kimju and Ginny were both Nugget Strippers last Term and that Tiffany was an occasional visiting Feature Dancer. Kimju compares, *Both Tiffany and Ginny fucked last Term, although Tiffany now wears a transparent vinyl croptop and low-rise stretch slacks, whereas Ginny has no such accouterments; she has remained stark naked since the first day she arrived, many Terms before she accrued her Whore-for-Life status.*

Tiffany and Ginny have already jousted about who made the most explicit *Videos* in the Inner Sanctuary, and they welcome Kimju, although neither Kimju, nor Molly, ever participated in sex while Stripping last Term.

"You both Opted Up this Term," Tiffany romances both ex-Nuggets.

"Except I got Opted Up naked," Ginny proclaims, "whereas Kimju got a thong."

"Had a thong," Kimju admits. "Apparently I'm now naked too." *Possibly because my Roommate has Charm.*

"You're equals!" Tiffany cheers, and presses Kimju, "Beg Janet to let me give you all of my clothes, so I can be naked instead." Tiffany turns and heads down the hatch to below deck. She has seen Robyn approaching.

Kimju sighs. *I am extremely vulnerable now.*

§ Robyn Doms Kimju & Ginny: Sunbathe Naked Spread Eagled

Robyn approaches upon the two ex-Strippers standing on the deck: one naked Cosmos, one naked Corvette. The Cosmos Cam, left unattended by Robyn, the Corvette Cam, left unattended by Darleen, and the Peacock Cam, left unattended by Rodney, hover nearby.

Robyn sticks a chin out toward the two Pledge. "I guess you two know each other. You both pulled pink and peed at the Nugget last Term."

Kimju and Ginny trade looks; Ginny speaks, "True. But never forget I am a Whore-For-Life, so even though I'm a Pledge, my privileges of Caste procure me powers that Kimju does not possess."

Kimju watches silently. *Ginny's presence and contagion at the Nugget provided one impetus for the Patrons to take liberties feeling* me *up, whether I wanted to or not. I thought when I graduated from a 'naked fondle' to a Cosmos Pledge I would avoid Ginny, but now I must confront her again.*

Robyn rises onto the balls of her feet and interjects, "Kimju, pay attention to me. You and your ex-Nugget friend Ginny here can lie down flat on your backs on the deck. Spread eagle and side-by-side. You can sunbathe naked while I, your best friend, will go... I shall find you something to drink!"

Naked Kimju and naked Ginny scramble onto their backs and spread their arms and legs just as wide as possible. Three Cams harvest knockers and milk glands. Kimju's kypsey can't hide beneath butched pussy hair, and Ginny's garage, bare below her racing stripe, parts enough to reveal a pair of lines between her outer lips and center section. Robyn leaves the Cosmos Cam on autopilot, and flounces off to report her success to Janet.

Kimju processes. *Yes, I pinked creamed and climaxed with Ginny last Term, and yes, all Strippers peed on Cam and on Stage, myself included. So if I have to beg the Pee-Cam I can do that, but I can't be caught begging to Pledge naked and cum be a Stripper next Term. I really, really don't want that.*

Ginny studies each Cam and steals looks. The Cams have all observed that her clit has snuck out.

§ William Orders Kimju & Ginny: Spread Pink & Sunburn

William and Rodney return. Rodney points his Cam at Kimju. "Love your knockers and butched kohlrabi. You're going to pull your klammy apart and curl some knittle out. You're going to beg the Nugget."

Rodney rotates toward Ginny, spitting his venom. "As for you, it doesn't matter if you stay stark naked or not. Your holes are for sale no matter what your Caste."

William seizes upon opportunity and directs aggression toward the two naked, spread-eagle Pledge, "Go ahead, both of you, pull your pinks wide open, raise your pelvises upward, point your keyhole and gyno up at the sunshine, and get a little sunburn in there!"

William leans over and snarls toward Ginny, "Maybe Tiffany isn't allowed to fuck me, but you are. I'm gonna make your gash redden up. And then I'm gonna fuck you! Maybe I'll even let Rodney fuck you."

Below deck, Robyn fails to consider that Kimju's discarded thong, draped over the side of the sink, might actually provide her with a needed second Garment. Robyn finds it far more satisfying to gingerly pick up the Garment with a thumb and fingertip, pivot her hand over the toilet, and let go.

Up on deck Kimju and Ginny stay spread and hold their vaginas wide open. Kimju surveys the Cams collecting her. *I'm naked, I'm exposed, and I might not get my tanga back.* Kimju's upside-down butched triangle of pubic hair kisses the top of her clitoris. *I'm shown my hair before,* Kimju admits, *and I've pulled my inner lips apart many times for the Cams.* Once again she pulls her inner lips wide, forms the wings of a butterfly, and pops her clit up as the butterfly's head.

Kimju hears the three Cams jostle for position. All will transmit and collect close-ups of how the ring through her clithood lies forward, allowing the clit to swell up inside it. A smaller round hole sits on the flat space above her deep pink vagina. *My pee hole.* Kimju shudders. *I'm going to be Pee-Camming today, unless something very unusual happens.*

Kimju feels irritation at her situation. *I don't like being paired up with Ginny. We might both be Pledge, and we pink, cream, and climax whenever we're told to. Or in Ginny's case, allowed to. But we are not equals. Maybe I still have one Garment and maybe I don't, but I know Ginny won't be covering herself today or any day soon. The worse that can happen to me is another Term at the Nugget, whereas Ginny is a Whore-for-Life.*

In fact, both former Strippers sparkle clithood rings, rewards for Stripping last Term. Ginny uses two fingers of the same hand to form an inverted V and spread her inner lips apart. She tugs her clithood ring up with her thumb and index finger of the other hand, and uses her other fingers to gyrate her gem, engorging it to full size. Suddenly Ginny's goop flows and aroma erupts. Ginny stretches her middle finger, dips, and gobies her clit.

Kimju squirms, assesses that her tight sex gateway collects sunburn. It is skin that has never seen sunlight, and the pink skin will burn fast. *I feel sorry for myself, but I feel especially sorry for Ginny.*

Ginny's aroma stimulates Kimju to kloop, and as the minutes pass both up-arched pelvises freshen, but the sunlight evaporates the glisten, leaving deposits of white crost behind. Rodney canvases naked Kimju for what should be a tattoo somewhere but finds none, but does glimpse that Whore-For-Life Ginny has words and dollar signs tattooed around her anus.

Kimju sneaks a scan around her but doesn't see William or Rodney's feet nearby.

§ Robyn and Kimju & Ginny: Kimju begs Pee-Cam for Tanga

Robyn returns, oblivious to the fact that William moved Kimju and Ginny's arms from spread-eagle to spread pink. And that both pussies seep. Robyn also has forgotten about managing the Cosmos Cam, but the hovering eye is doing fine on its own at capturing Kimju and Ginny's intimates and sharing them with Gamers throughout the Prefecture.

"We might be Roommates," Robyn advises Kimju, "but whatever I say you have to do. Don't ever forget that. Janet told me you left your tanga downstairs and need to beg it back. Is that true?"

Kimju hesistates. *I haven't made any deals, yet.*

Ginny interjects, "Ma'am, I am naked and I will pee for your Cam. I'll pee for everybody. And I don't want anything back, except please let me fuck William and Rodney."

"Shutup Pledge, I wasn't talking to you." Robyn snorts. "I'm questioning Kimju."

Kimju feels pressure. *My time to beg to donate.* "Ma'am, yes, I'll beg for my tanga back. Please let me pee for your Cam, Ma'am."

The knot of bodies dissipates for a while. Kimju feels the inner skin of her kuder hotten and burn. *It will itch, peal, and keep me horny for days.*

As for Ginny, I know sunburn spells pain ahead. Should she acquire two Garments and Opt Up next Term she'd still be a Whore-for-Life, although with more responsibilities, and more control over her holes.

§ Janet Invites Tiffany: Urinate Below Deck for Two Cams

Unbeknownst to Robyn and while Kimju and Ginny sunburn their privates, Janet summons Tiffany down below decks and shares an intimate moment: "Last Term," Janet begins, "when I danced my Alumni Reprise at the Nugget, I peed, you swallowed, but then you kissed me." Janes smiles, "This Term you can kiss me, then I'll pee, and you can swallow my stream."

Tiffany stands before the seated Janet. "Ma'am, may I please you. You know I am your Piss Mouth, Ma'am." Tiffany gathers, "Ma'am, at the Nugget I climaxed you on the Double Dong; today you can strip me naked and dong me to climax. You know I am your cum machine."

"You keep begging for the Double Dong," Janet curls, "And by now you know where it is."

Tiffany does. "Beka and Elle reported that Robyn screened them *Side-by-Side Video* yesterday showing Penny and Coco each soloing the Dong at Nugget.

Janet preens, "Two losers begging to share it, but forbidden to do so."

Tiffany teases Janet. "Robyn Redacted has conveniently erased you from her memories about last Term, and you feint equal forgetfulness. But I'm not fooled."

Janet laughs, "You're right, I remember Robyn all too well. "We really were both Cosmos Pledge last Term." Janet jiggles her body. "I ended up with the a Spiderweb Bikini headed toward its skimpiest; it's her doin', and she just starts all over again!"

But you also Opted Up. Tiffany purses her lips. "So you think Robyn has Charm?" Tiffany queries.

"She's here and I'm wearing a size smaller Spiderweb today." Janet frowns. "Mini, micro, nano, and a pico next. I don't like her one bit."

"But she was a fellow Pledge last Term," Tiffany affirms.

"I roomed with Babs last Term," Janet reminds, "and Robyn bunked under then-Monitor Steph.

"Steph hates her," Tiffany confirms, "but Robyn remembers not."

"I'm glad I'm not a Cosmos Pledge," Janet affirms. "I get to watch. And you, my Porn Star friend, Pledge, and wannabe Whore, are asking too many questions."

Tiffany defends, "Ma'am, I only asked one, Ma'am."

"One is one too many," Janet breezes, "but instead of begging me to gobble down a bar of soap how about you step backwards out of my door, back yourself into the head, roll your slacks down, hang your tush in the air, and tinkle into the toilet."

Tiffany angles her eyes and obeys, and as she starts her stream she looks out at what becomes a crowded doorway and observes Darleen and Rodney (but not Robyn) cam her release of yellow body fluid. William, never one to pass up a private moment, crowds another head into the doorway. Janet stands back, arms crossed.

Tiffany pinks herself with the fingers of one hand and collects her last drop of pee on the fingertip of the other. She gives Rodney's Cam a hard look, draws her fingertip to her nostril, sniffs, then inserts her finger into her mouth and sucks her finger clean.

Tiffany laughs and points as Rodney spots his stretch jock. The spot spreads, and has bubbles on top. Tiffany lifts her slacks up partway, rotates and provides the Cams a tailpipe and twat opportunity before she lifts her slacks up over her hips to their resting place, not quite covering her tail trough and red tufties.

Tiffany wonders how to flush the toilet and as she turns to look into the toilet bowl she sees what might well be Kimju's tanga!

And not seen before? *No. I backed into the stall, pulled my pants down, squatted over the seat, and emptied my bladder.* The bodies part as Tiffany exits the stall, leaving a thong behind to soak in urine.

§ Robyn Trains Kimju: Practice Peeing so Tiffany can Clean Up

Robyn returns from the galley and rustles Kimju and Ginny out of their reverie while still spreading pink to sunlight. Robyn holds an open brown bottle in each hand. "Sit up," she orders her Roommate, "keep your legs spread and your pussies splayed and scalding. Robyn waves Ginny up and away. "Down the hatch, you guzzling grindhouse grippo," she says to the naked Corvette.

Ginny exits below deck.

Robyn extends one of the brown bottles toward Kimju. "Take this," she commands.

Kimju adjusts her balance; she slides her feet closer and her knees up, adjusting her posture while using two fingers of one hand to maintain her pink. Robyn forces the bottle toward her and Kimju reluctantly takes it with her free hand.

"Drink," Robyn commands.

Kimju hesistates. "Ma'am, I'm not really thirsty."

"Chug it," Robyn insists. "The Cams are my witness. I'm not repeating myself."

Kimju obeys her Roommate. The fluid is light, watery but heavier than water. *It may contain oils or alcohols or flavor to mask diuretics, laxatives, or mind-altering drugs. I can't tell what I am drinking!*

Kimju hands the bottle back to Robyn, empty now, and Robyn hands her the second brown bottle. This one Kimju drinks piecemeal, and is harder to go down. *Tastes different, but what do I know.*

Kimju hands the second empty bottle to Robyn's only to discover that Tiffany has ascended from the gallery with another two brown bottles in her hands. Tiffany gives Kimju's pinked koot a sly look which Kimju interprets as *Tiffany's gonna suggest I squat and pick up the bottle with my vagina.*

No such luck. Robyn exchanges an empty brown bottle for a full from Tiffany, and passes the full to Kimju saying, "pour this down your throat.' Again Kimju drinks, followed by another, *I think. I'm losing count. Four, five?*

Kimju looks up and sees Robyn laughing, but in slow motion, and for the moment, the usually assertive Kimju finds herself unable to challenge her Roommate. *I am going to throw up,* a dizzying Kimju considers. *Robyn is going to make me piss and climax at the same time. Robyn uses her Charm to let Monitor Babs let her control me. And she is beating on me: mind, body, and soul.* Kimju relaxes in stupor, only to discover her bladder bloated and wanting to urinate.

Short uncontrolled driblets of pee wetten the deck and Robyn hazes her. "Look at dirty you!" Robyn taunts.

The Yacht guests swarm around to admire Kimju's torments, Cams a-blazing, Gamers out in the Prefecture deciding which Cam to watch.

"Most of us presume the privacy of the toilet below for all body functions," Robyn chortles. "But I guess you want to pee here up on deck."

Kimju releases another squirt, a bit longer burst before she can regain control. *Help me,* Kimju prays; she pivots and attempts to stream her pee toward the side of the boat. Mistake. The stream catches in the wind and blows it back all over her and the deck.

Robyn howls with laughter as Darleen and Rodney join her in camming the misadventure. "You're gonna beg to join your fellow former Stripper Molly on the Pee-Cam," Robyn decries.

Kimju scowls. *I can smell my piss all over my body and face. The piss will air dry eventually; the problem is Robyn feeds me to Automatron and the media will always stay fresh.*

William sees another opportunity for vengeance and addresses Tiffany, "Clean up the deck, Piss Mouth."

And what's a Porn Star to do? Certainly not argue about command and control. Tiffany drops to her hands and knees and starts licking up Kimju's fresh urine. The low-ride pants ride down her butt crack and the sunlight makes a fringe of her ultraviolet ink tramp stamp dance as it descends down toward the visible ink that surrounds her tail pipe. Rodney cams. Tiffany slyly soaks most of the pee into her hair. Does Tiffany swallow? *Yes, but as little as possible. It can't hurt me but it can be hard to digest. And no streams please.*

Tiffany doesn't look to see whose big toe catches her waistline at the center of her back, then pushes it down until the tattoo around her asshole is completely visible. The Cams also collect the backside pocket of twat.

Kimju hears Robyn demand through a fog, "Get you hand to work and rub your keystone back and forth." Robyn cackles with laughter.

Kimju points her normally hidden clithood ring toward Robyn and commences to masturbate. She lifts her eyelids and sees Tiffany on her hands and knees still licking pee off the deck. They make eyes, Tiffany interprets a plaintive look and responds with a sympathetic neck tremor. Kimju tries to speak but slurs, her bladder is again very full, but this time Kimju finds the wind, unabashedly points her pee hole overboard, and arches a long stream of piss cleanly off into the water beyond. The Gamers aboard admire her performance, record all the details, and applaud her.

Tiffany consumes any last dribbles on the deck, and stands. The taste of Kimju's pee does not leave her mouth. Won't anytime soon.

Kimju flops onto her back again, butterflies with both hands, and rolls the head of the butterfly with her fingertips. *The deck is rolling. My mind is rolling. I'll cum for Robyn again. Nothing matters anymore.*

Robyn relishes, "You really are the very proper Pee-Cam princess." Robyn howls with laughter. Kimju knows, *I need to wait for the world to stop spinning. I'm going to vomit. I'm going to lose control of my bowels.*

"Too bad you're no use to me, knockbox," Robyn says to her Roommate, "You're a dirty naked piss hole begging to join the Pee-Camers. You just auditioned the part!" Robyn cackles again. "The next thing you know you'll be begging to 'Pledge naked and cum be a Stripper next Term.' You're just reverting to type."

Kimju diddles her keystone harder, transudes more kloop from her keyway, and moans. *I can't control outcomes anymore, I've lost,* she realizes, and succumbs to a gentle, rolling climax.

Tiffany curls a lip at Robyn's behavior. *When thoughts tumble out of her mouth, rude suggestions frequently emerge.*

Royalty often fails to be careful using words.

§ William Privately Fucks Ginny: Cums in Her Mouth

All day Kimju has worried. *Should I expect to get my thong back at all? If Robyn claims the tanga then Robyn will have her two pieces and I will stay naked. Would Janet or Tiffany arbitrate?*

No. I will be a Stripper next Term.

More correctly, I'd be a naked Cosmos Pledge who just played the mandatory Roommate Game, and who is ready to Game again.

But who would have nothing to game with except skin. Kimju touches her sticky clithood ring. *I might be at ease but I'm still naked.*

But Kimju needn't panic; now, toward the end of the Day and heading back toward shore, she finally decides to ask Robyn, "So before we dock should I go below and get my tanga to put back on?"

Robyn makes a small lift of her head. "Asking a question again."

Janet interjects and directs that Ginny, always naked and with her gyno sunburned, make the trip below decks.

"Step and fetch it," Janet commands.

And Ginny responds, "I hear and obey," as if she recites a secret Corvette routine. William follows her down the hatch. And Rodney, with the Peacock Cam, trails after.

Kimju's spirits sink. *Perhaps Janet wants naked Ginny more dressed? And will leave me to stay naked?*

Or maybe William wants Ginny.

Down below deck William blocks her passage.

"Okay," Ginny concedes to William, "So help me find them."

"Help starts with pussy," William demands and unbuttons his fly.

Ginny knows the routine. She wears nothing so nothing is in the way. She brings her body forward, leans against the passageway wall, lifts a leg, works her pussy apart, and displays a sunburned gyno.

William insults. "Listen, you Whore-for-Life, you're not even a Porn Star, you're just a suck, fuck, anal grunt. So I'll groove you however I want. We all will.

Correct. Ginny allows William to force his dick inside her sunburned and painful insides. He pumps her a few times, withdraws, opens the head door and backs her inside; Kim's thong lies soaking in yellow urine in the toilet bowl. Ginny doesn't know what to do.

William does. "Sit. Make a contribution. Suck me."

Ginny sits on the toilet seat, bends her naked body forward, observes Rodney camming her and irritates to William, "You gonna let him cam me blowing you?"

"Pee and suck me," William repeats, and Ginny does, cleaning William's cock with her lips while draining her pee into the toilet, she slides him into her throat, backs him up so his rim rides just inside her lips, and curls her tongue across the cock's head.

William discharges his cum onto her lips and into her mouth just as she finishes urinating.

"Swallow," he instructs, and Rodney captures her swallowing on this gonzo-style video. It doesn't mater if Ginny likes swallowing semen or not, if that is what Williams demands, she will oblige him.

In fact, Ginny considers, *I don't know if I should be doing William or not; it doesn't matter, a Whore-For-Life does them all, even the Williams… and Rodneys.*

Last Term Ginny Stripped at the Nugget, but was always available to fuck and suck cock or eat pussy in the Champagne Room. That had made her a very valuable dancer. And at the Corvettes it means Ginny is the one Pledge always available for sexing.

Ginny might like to fuck but that doesn't mean she likes to suck or fuck William. She stands, and William points to the piss-sopping-wet thong in the toilet bowl, "Fetch that, Pledge, wring it out, and thank me for not making you suck the piss out with your mouth."

Ginny obeys, tightly wrings the urine out of the thong, turns the faucet but no water comes out, and humors William, "Mister, thank you for shooting a vid of me sucking your cock."

William points toward the ladder, "Upstairs, Lifer."

§ Kimju: Begs Third Pee-Camer & Gets Her Thong Back

Back up on deck, a relieved Ginny returns a pee-soaked tanga to a relieved Kimju, who carefully untangles it with her fingers.

"Apparently you left your thong in the toilet, and it got peed on," Robyn cheers.

Kimju scowls, "I did not toss my thong in the toilet. I left it drying on the sink, like you told me to. Did you cam yourself peeing on it so you could prove you soaked it, you rapacious ragamuffin." Kimju snaps.

Robyn stops short. She tightens her lips, tilts her head, and speaks, "You should be careful about what comes out of your mouth, Roommate, because you'll be wearing your thong in your mouth if you ever watch me pee on it. Which you never will."

"I'm not a Piss Mouth," Kimju declares.

"Shush, both of you," Janet intercedes, "Kimju, you can beg to stuff a piss rag into your mouth another time. Like Molly."

Like Molly, Kimju recalls. *I know Molly took pee-soaked panties into her mouth during the Bachelor Party. Okay, I wasn't there, but Molly and Steph both tell the same story, and whoever's seen the videos knows for sure. I don't have to match that part of Molly's scene; all I have to do is put the tanga on.*

Robyn disobeys orders. "My Roommate Kimju needs to prove she's better than her ex-Stripper Roommate, Molly Mammoth. She should shove her tanga into her mouth now!"

Kimju disobeys orders. "Molly volunteered and it was her own pee. This is different, it's somebody else's pee!"

"Maybe even more than one!" Robyn rises cheerfully.

Janet has no time for fights. "Kimju, put your tanga on or put it in your mouth. Make your decision or I will make it for you!"

And so Kimju climbs into her piss-soaked tanga with gratitude. *The stretch fabric of the tanga maintains opacity when wet; the pee should be sterile, and it will dry out eventually. Although all the contributing odors will stay on my skin and waft up to my nose. Until I shower again. I might not be a puritan in terms of what touches my body, but I don't need Robyn piling on the haze.*

Perhaps Robyn reads Kimju's mind. "I'll make sure Babs doesn't let you shower any time soon," Robyn deprecates, as if this is within her power. "You will not be showering at all until you beg to use the Bathroom naked." Robyn curls her nose, "You've just another ex-Stripper begging the Pee-Cam. You got that?"

Kimju stumbles but gets it out. "Sure, Robyn. I'll remember that. I'll become a Cosmos Pee-Camer." Kimju sweats. Her sunburned privates feel fire-kissed, and she suppresses an urge to touch and check herself. *If I'm not already Cosmos Pee-Camer number three, then I'm about to be.*

§ Tiffany & Ginny: Pee-Camers Discuss Games of the Idiom

Robyn might be eager to deliver her Roommate Kimju onto the Pee-Cam, but she doesn't fathom the depth of the idiom. Or that the cadre of Cosmos begging the Pee-Cam might grow beyond the current Tiffany, Molly, and auditioning Kimju.

Tiffany and Ginny trade looks. Last Term the Porn Star and the Whore-For-Life actually competed at watersports, and this is a rare opportunity to share memories together. Both know that all Strippers, and certainly all Whores, pose for the Pee-Cam.

So does Ginny, a Whore-for-Life yet also a Pledge, still volunteer for the Pee-Cam?

"Of course I do!"

"So did you pee on Kimju's tanga?" Tiffany curves a question in.

Ginny, always stark naked, dances a two step, "I wasn't the only one, but I bet I was the only one who sucked cock at the same time."

"You swallowed?" Tiffany asks.

"I did the whole push-it-around-in-my-mouth, swallow, then open my mouth and stick my tongue out to prove it. Rodney cammed. Maybe Darleen too. Not Robyn. Sorry. Next time I'll try to save some for you and we can snowball together."

They laugh quietly. Tiffany romances, "Remember when they made us both drink a lot to see who could pee more? First they made us each drink the same amount of water and collect, and then they let us drink as much as we wanted."

Ginny remembers, "The freestyle."

"Every time I Feature Danced at the Nugget last Term," Tiffany recalls, "I had to pee on Stage. I've gotten pretty good at it too. Not just targeting a stream, pouring shots too."

"Peeing is one thing," Ginny observes, "once I played for an entire weekend with a whole bevy of Gamers, and all the collected pee was used to motivate the less prolific providers!"

"Oh that's harsh," Tiffany responds, and they both laugh. But it's not really funny; Tiffany doesn't really enjoy the tang from Kimju's urine that remains in her mouth after licking the deck clean. *And my hair smells sharp.*

Ginny puts it succinctly, "You and I might both be Pee-Camers, but I am not a Piss Mouth. I might be a Whore-for-Life, but there are some things I won't do. Besides, the consumption of golden nectar is supposed to be a privilege reserved for Slavesex." Ginny grins, "What's your excuse?"

Tiffany sighs, "It's very simple, I could either become a Slavesex, and ergo a Piss Mouth, or volunteer a Piss Mouth, and Opt Up. I choose the latter. Seems like you volunteered to become a Whore-for-Life."

Ginny shrugs, "We each made our compromises to avoid Slavesex. I worry that Janet gives me diuretics to drink because I pretty much can't control my bladder anymore. I drip pee all the time. And I'm really not all that sure what the Rules are."

Tiffany lays a hand to the side of her mouth and speaks quietly, "Don't forget Janet and I were Roommates two Terms ago at the Nugget. Maybe you should ask her if she made some tinkle vids. And what some of her acts were. For sure she knows all the Watersports basics: pouring shots, putting out candle flames, long and short squirts sending Morse code."

Ginny laughs, "Right. The first thing I won't be asking, Janet." And they both laugh again, because they don't know if it is funny or not.

§ Janet & Kimju: Kimju Begs to Flip-Flop Robyn not Piss Mouth

Janet was a Stripper a Term before Kimju was, which was last Term, when Janet was a Pledge and Kimju stripped. Both have advanced to this Term, Janet and Monitor now and Kimju a Pledge. Rank has privileges, and so Janet enjoys a discourse with Kimju, topless and with her pee-soaked tanga drying in the air. Janet rolls her shoulders and sounds: "So, Pledge, are you having a good voyage? You got to pee into the wind! And you got pee onto yourself!! Have you any other requests?"

Kimju does. "Ma'am, thank you, Ma'am," she says and suggests, "If you let me to Flip-Flop with Robyn, then after I put her maillot on, I will roll it into a tanga that's even smaller than the tanga that I'm wearing right now. I'll roll the neckline down below my belly button and the leglines into my keelson. I'll even yank it up into my kooch if you want me to. Please let me Flip-Flop with Robyn. Then she and I can both be topless tanga Pledge. Gamers want that."

"You really don't wish to serve her very much, do you," Janet states. "Maybe you're volunteering to rolldown the maillot to keep yourself topless, but Robyn won't have any choice, will she?"

"I don't have any choice either, and I haven't since the Term began," Kimju snorts. "And not just topless tanga 24x7. During *The Arrivals* I got my knobs stained and made up, I had to pullaside and pink, and I had to climax, and on Cam, too. During *The Runup* only yesterday, Robyn made me cum in sync with my own Masturbation and Climax Videos. Today she makes me audition the Pee-Cam."

"Save a climax for if I ever see you again," Janet advises. Janet snorts and smiles, "I know your latent agenda. Once you've played your first Roommate Game you can game with any other Cosmos who is similarly unconstrained."

"Tell me, Pledge," Janet jiggles. "Have you begged to Pledge naked and cum be a Stripper next Term?"

Kimju falters, "Ah, er, ah, Ma'am, no, Ma'am."

"Make that a goal you shall aspire to, Pledge," Janet crowns. "Until then you may wear your tanga gashed in the front. 24x7."

Kimju accepts, looks down, and uses her fingers to tug her thong into her koot.

Kimju advances carefully, "Ma'am, you know I will pullaside and pink and cream and climax for you whenever you want. Just please let me Flip-Flop with Robyn. I'll visit your House, rub spit on my keystone, and masturbate to climax. Exclusive for your House Cams. Ma'am.

"Maybe you should streak to visit me," Janet proposes.

Kimju hiccups, "I'll three-hole Double Dong with Robyn center Stage at the Nugget, every hole, every combination. If I make her cum, I Opt Up and she Ops Down. If I fail then just the opposite."

Janet bemuses, "Dong with Robyn? I thought that you and Molly were already begging a Double Dong climax at your upcoming Alumni Reprise."

Kimju cringes. "Ma'am, I'll dong with any Cosmos, but the fact is that Robyn is my Roommate, and if there is anybody I should get naked or pink or dong with, it's her."

Janet says, "If you game with Robyn Roommates Apart and she is Charmed, you risk losing and being naked 24x7, but a Flip-Flop leaves you still topless yet better positioned."

Janet snides, "Maybe you should beg Babs to pee in your mouth. That would make you equal to Molly."

Kimju deflects, "Ma'am, Molly and I aren't Roommates anymore! That was last Term. This Term her Roommate is Steph, so maybe Steph should share Molly's Pee-Cam and Piss Mouth. Or maybe Robyn should share my Pee-Cam, or does she have too much Charm?"

"So many questions, Kimju Knock Knock Kava Kava," Janet prances and tosses her long black hair behind her wide bare shoulders. Janet snides. "Kimju Knock Knock Kava Kava? That is what Robyn calls you. As if you are worth so many syllables."

Kimju fingers her waistband, the hem inside her inguinal, and the skin of her bare kabedis.

Janet bounces, "You want me to persuade your Bikini Boss to favor you. May you should beg *me* to pee in your mouth."

"Ma'am!" Kimju exclaims.

Janet rears back, tugs on her crochet Spiderweb g-string so that the rings on the two sides of her lips jingle out. "Beg me to pee on your feet. Then after they get good and soaked you can beg Tiffany and Molly to lick you clean. Are they not both qualified Piss Mouths?"

"Ma'am, yes, Ma'am," Kimju acknowledges, but defends, "Not every ex-Stripper or Whore is a Piss Mouth. Ginny's not a Piss Mouth." Kimju casts her eyes back to Janet, adds, "You aren't either."

Janet wags a finger at Kimju, "You could have become fuck meat this Term, instead of becoming a Cosmos Pledge. Lucky you, you even got to pledge with one Garment, whereas Ginny and Lee pledged naked. Last Term when I got promoted I pledged naked, too. So you are halfway to making your coveted Opt Monitor.

Kimju begs, "Ma'am, I don't want to suck cock, eat pussy, and get fucked in my kuder and kawazoo. Not on top, not on the bottom, not doggy style. Please."

Janet smiles. "Well, now that you've auditioned the Pee-Cam, I would advise you to start begging to Pledge naked and Strip next Term, just like all the other Cosmos Pledge. And be sincere about it. You can start by begging a smaller tanga, if not a see-through one."

Kimju closes her eyes for a moment. *No, all the other Pledge are not begging to Strip.* She seeks safety. "Ma'am, I'm always in search of a size smaller," Kimju reasons. "Like you. Nano technology.

Janet laughs, "My Spiderweb g-string is a goal for you to aspire to, Pledge. And when it pleases me to turn you into a Piss Mouth, I will accommodate your begging."

Things could be worse, Kimju accepts. *Who knows if Janet has influence on BB to let me Flip-Flop with Robyn. Janet doesn't know me very well but she's knows when I'm forced to expose myself I get wet. That's just how I am. But I don't want to be controlled that way. I want to be controlling. That's just what I want.*

§ Cosmos & Corvettes & Peacocks: Back at the Dock

At the end of today's voyage Janet gives Robyn copies of the videos Darleen and Rodney shot of Kimju, but no other Corvette or Peacock Video is shared. Janet directs Robyn. "Deliver to Babs, along with your own Videos so everyone can see your Roommate Kimju's audition for the Pee-Cam,"

Robyn nods. Kimju doesn't say much about what's happening, but her worried look communicates a reticence that somehow or another, Robyn snookers her with Charm. Kimju curls her nose; her knockers bounce, and her wet thong smells pungent.

Tiffany and Ginny get to French kiss goodbye.

II-5 Elle & Cosmos: Measurement Nudes & Old Videos (D17)

§ Babs Inspects Four Cosmos: Molly & Steph and Beka & Elle

Back at the Cosmos House four Cosmos Pledge continue to "sit spread hands-free." Molly and Steph, and Beka and Elle scratch, touch, or play with themselves with their free hands. While on the Yacht power is in play, here in the Bathroom boredom sets it. Some minds go into a trance; some minds race.

Elle looks around and scrutinizes her Roommate. Beka appears in a trance, her tugged-up croptop rides above her boobs so she can easily play with her nipples, and she sits in her miniskirt with her legs spread, masturbating, with brodeas hanging down from her bare brim to puddle on the tile floor.

Elle blinks. *I lolled my Roommate twice during* The Arrivals, *and I licked her brodeas off of Janet's fingers.*

Elle hears a cough, looks up and sees Monitor Babs standing before her. BB signs her onto her feet, defraying her from lollying Beka's broda pool, at least for now.

Elle stands, smoothes her halter, and wonders, *Should I beg Babs to unbutton my neck strap so my noogies hang free?* She wiggles her seam from her ganged-up crotch, expunges the bulk of her hairage, and assures herself her button sits in the notch of her tattered jeans shorts.

"Come with me," BB commands.

Elle scans Molly and Steph, then follows Babs out the door. *Molly is like Beka, hanging her mung outta her mooe. And Steph glowers at Beka for pulling pink and brimming. Steph knows she's had to sit and spread with Beka in the past, and that if they are pitted against each other for another round that this time Steph might have to match not just Beka's spread, but also Beka's pink and cream.*

And Beka's inevitable climax.

Elle catches her breath in the hallway. *Babs will make me lolly up after Molly, just like I lollyed up Steph the last day of* The Arrivals. *Then Babs and Robyn will make Steph surge again; payback from doing Babs wrong, or in Robyn's case, heaping more wrong upon her.*

Elle concludes. *Steph climaxing will be her ultimate humiliation.*

Ultimate humiliation?

And I'll be the one to lolly more of Steph up, Elle presumes.

May Elle insist.

§ Babs Orders Elle: Procure Old Nude Pictures & *Gonzo Videos*

Elle follows Babs into her Bedroom. Babs goes around her desk and settles herself into the Room's only chair, behind the Desktop. Elle stands herself at attention in front of Babs' desk, just inside of the door: hands crossed behind her back, legs open, head erect.

"You have never had the pleasure of standing where you stand now," Boss Babe advises her Pledge. "At ease."

Elle relaxes and shuffles her shoulders; she has no choice but to remain standing, to let her hands fall to her sides, and draw her legs closer together, although she makes sure to keep them enough apart so her thighs don't touch. She scans her eyes around the Bedroom. Small and tight, bunk bed to the right for Babs, floor box below to house Tiffany, currently in the Bathroom. The back wall contains a locker, a hook, and a door.

Looking down at the Desktop, Elle sees a picture of herself getting out of a car before entering a nightclub: a genuine sanpan vagflash. *No panties, open crotch upskirt, shaven lips and a double centerline niche. It was taken before I enrolled in School.* There is another picture also from her past, this one from a fashion show: topless. Elle draws her eyes upward and squints. *I have seen these before, when Babs showed them to me during* The Arrivals.

Boss Babe taps a finger on the Desktop surface. This is proof that Beka is not the only Cosmos pre-qualified vagflasher."

Elle isn't so sure. "Er, ah, Ma'am…."

"Your Game is very simple," Boss Babe leans back in her chair and explains to Elle, standing at easy attention. "You desire that you and Beka want to retain two Garments, declare Roommates Together, and Opt Monitor next Term?

"Ma'am, yes, Ma'am," Elle says.

Boss Babe purses her lips. "A minor problem exists. Gamers accept that both of you have tittered and hung boobage once or twice. Maintained navelage 24x7. But only one of you has vagflashed."

BB leans in. "So tell me, Elle Lollydor, do you feel it is fair that Beka has to expose herself more than you do?"

Elle answers, "Ma'am, it is not fair, Ma'am."

BB probes. "So, do you feel guilty?"

Elle stammers, "Ma'am, I don't know but I'll do whatever is needed to play fairly."

"Excellent decision," BB coos, "Time for you to start begging a Flip-Flop. It will cure your disposition and enable you to vagflash 24x7."

"Right," Elle stills. *Like my Roommate is now. I won't have any choice in the matter. I'm not even sure I have any choice any more. And Beka? Beka likes to let them look upskirt. She really is begging the Strip.*

Elle looks down at the Desktop again. Feeds from the Front Door and Back Door Cams show only gray, but the Bathroom Cam contains action, albeit upside down from Elle's point of view. Elle deduces, *Molly keeps the Cam live. Molly and Beka have synchronized their masturbation. Steph is out of the shot.* Elle scans more of the Desktop: trip alarms for the doors and the inside stairs, buttons for what Screens get what feeds, where AIs reside....

Boss Babe looks up at her and demands attention. "You shall use this opportunity, while three Cosmos Pledge enjoy the Yacht and three others enjoy the Bathroom, to track down your three Measurement Nudes. You did make this commitment to me, did you not?"

"I did," Elle agrees. She gestures down to the Desktop. "Ma'am, when you showed me my nightclub pictures during *The Arrivals* you never said how you obtained them." Elle shifts her weight, "But I fail to understand why Automatron doesn't have my Measurement Nudes, after all I did submit them with my application."

"You told me you knew where you could find them," BB reminds.

"Ma'am, yes, Ma'am. I told you I know who I can get them from. But I don't know what I'll have to do to get them."

Boss Babe tucks a chin.

Elle concludes, "But if you want me to go get them now, I will."

Babs studies, pushes a button on her Desktop, and commands, "Go!"

And Elle scurries, down the spiral stairs, out the Back Door, and a-ringin' the Bell.

§ Babs & Seven Cosmos: Evening Gathering Watching the Screen

The Cosmos gather that evening in the Dining Room, at ease around the table and the large Screen between the two out-facing windows on the side of the House. Three have returned from the Yacht, three from spending the day in the Bathroom, and Elle after running her solo errand. Babs, seated at the head of the table, need not account for her whereabouts earlier, least of all to her Pledge.

All seven seated Cosmos Pledge sit with their legs apart—no thighs touching, no ankles crossed.

Movies tonight.

It is dark outside, and any voyeurs who might look in from the side of the House or the Backyard would see the Cosmos in their minimalist attire:

The Bikini Babe relaxes in her bling bra and navelage nombril. *I am the Boss Babe!*

Gamers debate if Tiffany chose to wear clothes on the Yacht or was forced to. Her Eraser Heads continue to rub color onto the inside of her transparent croptop, and her skin-tight stretch slack dig cameltoe, erupt hairage, separate her buttocks, and crack her tail trough. Experts argue if Tiffany is a titter or boobage or topless, but Elle logs Tiffany as boobage in her secret mental Manifest.

Robyn wears her spaghetti-strap maillot with "the smallest cutout buttonhole."

Kimju and Molly sit topless with their tanga and panties tightly gashed, although Molly seems to be carefully keeping herself wet using her Watering Can, a response to Robyn's discovery about her germ phobia.

Steph romances the men's undershirt as best she can, knowing that her latest "miniskirt" ensures it is impossible to avoid titter and vagflashing snatch.

Beka, unsure of herself, resists the temptation to lift her croptop up above her boobies, yet she relaxes her legs more apart than necessary, inviting miniskirt inspection.

Elle wonders, *Do I need to beg to unbutton my halter neck strap? And have I really committed to a Flip-Flop?* Elle looks at her jeans shorts. *At least I still have a seam between my legs. At least for a little while.*

Voyeurs who might look in from the Backyard might see the Screen, although highly oblique. And why bother? What feeds the Screen feeds the Prefecture. It's what's inside the Room that's unique.

§ Robyn tells Elle: Watch Tiffany *Ride Glass Bull Video*

Babs hangs back and lets Robyn program. Robyn's psychological twisting, never spent despite making Tiffany lick up Kimju's Pee-Cam on the Yacht earlier, now turns upon the newbies. "Your role models are by no means limited or confined to the antics of current and former Strippers, of which you saw in abundance yesterday. *Elle figures, the current Strippers are Penny and Coco and the former Strippers are Kimju and Molly.*

Robyn arcs her pitch to the newbies, but leans toward Elle, "The former Whore amongst you Pledge also provides a role model of future outcomes."

The lights dim and the Screen fades up and displays a naked Tiffany riding what looks to be a mechanical Glass Bull.

"That's Tiffany when she was a Pledge three Terms ago," Robyn explains. "Performing in the outdoor Amphitheater."

Outdoor Amphitheater? Beka and Elle wonder.

The Bull gyrates on a support in the ground, and suddenly Beka and Elle can see that, in addition to the gyrations, a vibrating plunger in the center of the Bull's back impales Tiffany's twister, and oscillates. Elle blanches; Beka constricts and springs wet.

On the Screen, Tiffany climaxes. In the Dining Room, Tiffany touches her cameltoe. *Tacky.*

Elle discovers herself pushing her bottom teeth forward with her tongue; her discovery occurs as she starts to lock her jaw into place, hurting herself.

Robyn charms the newbies, "Rules say that only one Cosmos gets to ride the Glass Bull each Term, and whoever does is a Stripper for sure! You're both begging to Strip, so it could be either of you."

Robyn bows to Elle, "I'd recommend you Flip-Flop first, so that after you get Beka's miniskirt, you don't have any cloth between your legs to get in the way. Ha ha ha!"

Elle purses her lips and focuses upon her own Options. *I know that after any Flip-Flip with Beka that the croptop won't protect me and the miniskirt has nothing underneath.*

Robyn seems to read Elle's mind, "As soon as you get sanpan, you will beg me to ride the Glass Bull, won't you Pledge?" Robyn seeks to affirm.

Elle steals a glance at Beka. Eyes glazed, breathing through an open mouth. Croptop revealing underboob. An unmistakable bubble of brodeas pushes out between inner lips.

Elle alarms, Okay, so only Babs has my Measurement Nudes... and everything else I gave her. *But if Robyn knows Beka and I got cammed at the Corvette House will she Screen these images of us?*

Patience please.

§ Tiffany & Ginny: Video Showcases Cocksucking Together

The next video answers a question the newbies have debated: is Tiffany's Porn Star Calendar is real or not?

The Screen dances a three-way to life; running action of Tiffany and Ginny double orating a long and thick back dick, a moment of which is frozen on one of the Calendar months.

The newbies watch as the Cam slowly pulls back from the cocksuckers to reveal that another pair of cocks penetrate Tiffany and Ginny from their backsides, fucking them hard, until they are able to make the cock they share with their mouths ejaculate.

"From the Inner Sanctuary at the Nugget," Robyn glides. "It is a part of the Nugget that is off limits to Strippers, but you can get there once you beg Whore work."

Elle can't quite believe what she sees, especially Tiffany and Ginny sharing the cum, kissing, swallowing afterwards.

The presence of Ginny in the *Videos* fuels Elle's unease. *Yes, during The Arrivals I saw Whore-for-Life Ginny in the flash, hole-gagged and locked in the Cravat. Gamers know I was there, saw someone push a gelatin egg into my uplifted nachas. Right now Gamers are trying to condition me.*

Excellent analysis.

More cocks appear in the *Video*, quick cuts of Tiffany getting facial on top of facial.

Beka dangles an even longer bead of brodeas. Tiffany stains an even larger patch of cameltoe.

Robyn patters as Tiffany's *Video* concludes. "You may rest assured that Porn Star Tiffany Tailpeddler Tinkle Twat didn't get any shower after that performance!"

Robyn chortles, "I bet Flesh Ranch put her in a box for a day or two for the semen to dry out, get absorbed, and become dust." Robyn snides toward the real Tiffany in the Room. "You got Whore in your blood."

Tiffany acclaims herself, "I've done everything explicit, all holes, all sexes!"

§ Beka & Elle: *Ginny Cravat Video* Reveals What they Heard

Sound leads the next picture, and as if to compound the brainwashing, both newbies strain to identify what they had heard live with their ears but did not see with their eyes during their visit to the Corvette House Dining Room, Day Eleven of *The Arrivals.*

Now the image emerges out of the gray and Beka and Elle can verify what actually happened: Ginny sits on her butt and heels with her knees up. She remains immobilized in the iron inverse-V Cravat, wrists secured, ankles spread and secured at the bottom of the V, neck collared at the top, wrists secured halfway down the irons. Hole gagged. Pink held open with clamps. Elle watches Ginny get mouth fucked, then throated, then helplessly facialed. For the first time Elle understands that *Ginny also sits on a buttplug!* Elle watches the buttplug extract, watches Ginny get rolled onto her back, and watches Ginny's clamped-open and pulled-wide gyno get pogoed, touched, finger-fucked, and then penetrated by cock. Cocks. She watches Ginny climax out of control... and not be able to stop.

Elle's unease heightens, justifiably so, as she stares at the Screen. *A lot happened the day that Beka and I visited the Corvette House, and what was real and what I imagined gets more unclear in my mind.*

The Dining Room Screen assists in knowledge recall. It cuts to Beka and Elle on their hands and knees, admiring the Baseboard Strippers. *Okay, so I'm going to get answers whether I want them or not.*

The *Corvette Baseboard Worship Video* of their two raised asses resolves uncertainties.

Yes, Elle confirms, *somebody did sink a foot-long thick stainless steel thermoprobe sound into Beka borehole, and someone put a gelatin egg into my nadir. It's the same thermoprobe that Steph collected in this very Dining Room, the last day of* The Arrivals *(three days ago); and it's the same kind of gelatin egg Beka collected posing with Steph.* Elle suddenly feels very embarrassed and flushes. *Beka's egg melted inside her, just like mine did.*

Beka watches the *Video* of herself struggling as the foot-long thick stainless steel thermoprobe sounding rod slowly sinks its way down into her raised borehole. More brodeas spins, on Screen and here in the Dining Room. Beka looks and sees Molly quietly masturbating herself, and so Beka, pulls pink, follows her lead, and begins to masturbate too. Soon her hanging brodeas puddles onto the chair seat.

Elle feels jealous. *I need to control myself!*

Elle looks back at the Screen just in time to see herself, still on hands and knees, about to lolly Beka's broda off the Corvette House floor. She turns her eyes away from the Screen but Roby snaps, "Watch yourself, Lollydor!" And so Elle watches herself lick Beka's cream up off the floor.

Elle takes in a very deep breath of air, fills her lungs, and catches the scent of Beka's fresh puddle, here in this very Room, right now. *Yes, I have volunteered to lolly, however I still have two Garments. If I have to Flip-Flop I shall end up wearing Beka's croptop and miniskirt, and vagflashing if I want to or not. But I will still have two pieces.*

Hello? Elle considers, *Must I arrive as well prepared as Beka for the Nugget next Term?* The *Video* changes, and shots of Steph and Beka up-assed, thermoprobed and jelly-egged, flash by on the screen, the *Corvette Baseboard Worship Video.*

Elle knows. *I was here; I witnessed them in this very Dining Room.*

Elle ponders. *So am I going to beg a thermoprobe up my own nadir way?* Elle shakes her head and touches her forehead, *No way! No thermoprobe, no Double Dong. No going to the Nugget next Term!*

The Screen returns to the newbies visit and showcases them to *'Pledge naked become a Stripper next Term.'* Elle squirms and checks that the buttons of her neck and front straps are intact. *I can unbutton my neck strap, hang boobage and straps, and still retain two Garments.*

If I have to.

§ Babs Presents Elle & Beka: Measurement Nudes on Screen

Babs and Seven Pledge continue to sit around the Dining Room table and watch the Screen. Now a freeze frame appears on the Screen: a naked woman holds a tape measure around her waist. Beka does a double take as the Screen zooms out on the image and reveals her. "That's a selfie I sent I sent when I applied to the School. It's one of my three Measurement Nudes." Beka turns away from the Screen and her selfie, and casts her eyes for Elle, but now Elle appears on the screen, a different selfie, this one with Elle also stark naked, and holding a tape measure around her waist. Shot in a mirror, which is why the numbers read backwards.

The Cosmos murmur with approval and watch as the image on the Screen changes. Yes, the second pair of Measurement Nudes appear: Beka holds the Cam away from her body while she holds the tape measure around her boobs with the other, Elle again selfies her mirror while taping her naturals. And then finally the selfies of Beka then Elle measure their hips.

Boss Babe smiles at the newbies nude revelations. "Gamers welcome your contributions, Pledge Elle. I am sure that because you re-submit your Measurement Nudes to the Game a second time, Automatron will ensure there are no access restrictions to them. I predict your selfies will be in every collection in the Prefecture. Three Measurement Nudes of Beka 33B-25-33; three Measurement Nudes of Elle 34B-24-34. Boobs, button, and bush."

and Beka's   and those of your Roommate

BB considers her Pledge Elle. "You will beg for an opportunity to present yourself full-frontal, and since you were so kind as to re-submit your Roommate's Measurement Nudes along with your own, Automatron kindly permissions both of your Nudes to the Prefecture."

"We will both go full-frontal any time you want," Beka asserts. "But Nudes I sent when I applied were supposed to be kept secret."

Boss Babe purses her lips. "Correct, Pledge. Those are still secret. What Elle has done is fetched and presented Nudes afresh, so they are not the same Nudes.

Elle knows *they are not the same Nudes. Same content, same file size, but not the same because they came into the Game two different ways.*

She feels the eyes of the Cosmos around the table settle upon her and she can't stop a red face from coming on. *I feel my chest getting warm.* She casts a glance at a somewhat fearful Beka, looks to a cocky Robyn, and blurts to Monitor Babs, "Ma'am, please let me unbutton my halter neck strap." She tries to tighten her grip on herself. *I didn't mean that!* Elle adds, "Ma'am."

"For what you did to Beka," BB states.

"Ma'am, yes, Ma'am," Elle says.

Beka senses her Roommate's sense of betrayal yet penitence. "Don't worry Elle," Beka rushes and consoles her, "It's okay, we already had to give them Measurement Nudes to Pledge the Game, and they will find a way to release them whether you brought them again or not. So what. We're probably going to have to strip naked before we Opt anything. More of the same. It's okay. We can handle it."

Boss Babe gestures toward Elle's neck strap and pronounces a finger action. Beg granted; Elle unbuttons. *Boobage again.* Elle grits. *I still have my two Garments and I am not going to become a Stripper next Term!* Elle observes that her bare nipples are erect. *Cold air,* she blames, and considers, *I had not envisioned that Stripper avoidance could be so extreme.* Elle clenches her teeth, *I have to learn how to Strip in order to avoid Stripping next Term. Am I in over my head? Also, Beka doesn't comprehend she's getting trapped in her own horniness. She more and more wants to just pink, cream, and climax. And Opt Stripper next Term.*

True. The evolving possibilities contribute to keeping Beka wet and Elle leery.

Elle keeps her mouth shut. *Not more of the same. Beka may not care I outted her Measurement Nudes, but I feel I had no choice in the matter.* Elle finds it difficult to look at her naked selfies as they rotate on the Screen. *Beka and I shot selfies on the same day. There is nothing particularly provocative about my Measurement Nudes, except that I am naked.*

Beka's stills flash by again and Elle looks away. *I'm guilty, for I am their procuress, even if Beka takes no offense.*

No offense so far.

I'm atoning with very proper boobage. Elle nods her head. She scowls. *Beka might have much different thoughts might she discover I also gave Babs our Gonzo Videos.* Elle scans the Dining Room. *I might not have had a choice doing this either. So Babs has something heavy hanging over me, and not just me but hanging over Beka too. Deeper than Measurement Nudes.*

So if Babs, or her surrogate Robyn, demands that I Flip-Flop with Beka, I probably will.

I might have to do a lot of stuff. Kimju and Molly are making me dance, teaching Beka and I how to bump and grind. Elle's eyes dart; six other Cosmos Pledge sit and watch the Screen, all legs apart, except Robyn, who has her legs crossed. Elle blinks and tightens her body. *What if Robyn demands I secrete nectar? She can try to train me to squeeze my insides, but I'll need a cattle prod up my nadir_before I'll be able to squirt. Let alone climax.*

Elle's eyes drift toward Babs and connect with her. Babs smiles at her Pledge. Elle looks to the floor, sees BB's bare feet. *I'm beholden to her. I told her about the Gonzo Video and then I went and got it and gave it to her.*

"Ma'am, please let me wash your feet with my tongue, Ma'am," Elle begs.

"Lolly instead," Boss Babe commands, and lolly she does: Elle drops to her hands and knees: she lollys up Beka's chair seat, and lollys up Molly too. Tiffany's cameltoe is sopping, and when Elle hesistates not knowing what to do, Tiffany digs her fingers into her cameltoe and lets Elle lick her fingers clean.

"Now beg like you mean it," Boss Babe commands.

And Elle does, "Please let me Pledge naked and become a Stripper next Term." She feels alone, adds, "Beka and I both."

§ Elle & Beka: Elle Recalls Shooting the Two *Gonzo Videos*

Procuring the three Measurement Nudes had been easier than Elle had thought, although it did involve two compromises. The first compromise had been that Elle also procured Roommate Beka's three Measurement Nudes. *That was not a decision I was able to consult with Beka about.*

Nor was I able to consult with her about my second compromise, a much more personal and humiliating secret.

This secret involves a boyfriend they had shared a year or two ago. There had been a camping trip—Beka and Elle, the boyfriend plus two other guys—and the boyfriend had a cam, and somehow or another an orgy ensured, in which Beka and Elle had managed to suck and fuck most of the equally naked and horny young men.

Correction: all of them.

Afterwards Beka and Elle had watched the *Video* together with the boyfriend, begged to be given it considering its incriminating nature, and agreed to suck his cock together, gonzo style, before being induced to go down upon each other, and indeed, it was the only time in their lives that either of them has ever eaten pussy. They left sated, forgetting about the latest as well as the first recording, and in the tumble of life they had moved along, found new men to seduce, and left their sexual evidence behind.

Elle kicks herself. *Oh why oh why, with something so forgotten about, would I confess to Babs that this checkered depiction of my past exists? Well, Beka too.* Elle doesn't know why, *except that when Babs demanded if I had ever been photographed nude—other than the Measurement Nudes—I just spilled the beans, and told her everything.*

The Gamer able to provide a copy of Elle's Measurement Nudes had been genteel in helping send Elle to locate a copy of her and Beka's

Gonzo Videos; and these two small personal sacrifices enabled Elle to return to the Cosmos House and to present the selfies and videos to Babs.

Earlier today, when Elle had presented her data retrieval to Babs, she had confessed, "I know that should they get screened I will be deeply humiliated. And damning to my Roommate as well; she didn't beg to go get them. She doesn't deserve to get outted in a *Gonzo Sex Video*."

"You'll make a sacrifice to protect her?" Boss Babs asks.

"Ma'am, may I please you, Ma'am. I know I must give you power over myself." Elle spins.

"Beg me to screen your *Gonzo Sex Videos*," Boss Babe commands.

Elle falters, "Ma'am, even if I provides extraordinary service to you I realize that you might still choose to screen me."

"You may beg me to screen Beka and not you," BB offers.

"Oh, Ma'am," Elle pines. "Let me beg you to screen me first."

"You just want all the attention, is that it, Pledge?" Boss Babe challenges.

"Ma'am, please, Ma'am," Elle begs. "My Roommate did not run the errand. I'll do whatever you want."

"I want you to beg that I screen the both of you," Boss Babe orders.

"Ma'am, please. Ma'am." Elle pauses before continuing carefully, "Ma'am, please screen both of our *Gonzo Sex Videos*. Beka and me both."

"Chant correctly," BB ordains, pats Elle's head, and promises, "Don't worry Pledge, Kundalini shall inspire you to desire Obeisance."

Elle had bitten into the sonics and became lost in the trance: "Please let me Pledge naked and become a Stripper next Term." Over and over again.

Now, sitting in the Dining Room with her halter hanging down and her nackers out, Elle trades eyes with her Monitor. The look says it all and Elle accepts, *Boss Babe has my* Gonzo Videos, *but she's held back giving them to Robyn to screen. And Babs knows I know it, and that she will use this to control me.*

Elle doesn't just keep her legs ajar so her thighs aren't touching, she keeps her legs open, and so her hairage in the crotch seam stays visible.

But about Beka? Beka thinks the Measurement Nudes are the end of the line. And besides, what does Beka care? She'll be happy to be a bobbing Stripper next Term. After I'd Flip-Flop with Beka, we'd still have two Garments, but she will get gamed and let herself get stripped naked in four blinks of an eyelash. She'll Opt Strip next Term, but I'll Opt Monitor, like I came here to do. So maybe we end up Roommates Apart.

§ Elle: Secret Notes & Worries About a Pink & Wet Climax

That night, out of sight in her far-most upper bunk, Elle addresses a concern that has been haunting her. *I may be loosing track of the status of all the Cosmos—myself included.* Earlier in the day she had located and secreted a single sheet of paper into a jeans pocket, along with the stub of a pencil, so that now she is able to unfold the sheet and handwrite. *A record of each Cosmos' costume description and the exposures from the beginning of the Term to the present, any Props put into play, and the various begs and Obeisances the Cosmos perform.*

Elle attends to details. *Costumes. like my own halter and shorts. Begs, I'm already begging to Pledge naked and Strip. My exposures include that I already titter and whenever my halter hangs down I'm boobage. I also hairage, I'm cheeky, and my navelage stays 24x7.*

As for Props? Elle considers, *Well, I don't have any props, but Molly does have the Watering Can. Beka and some of the other Pledge also beg Obeisances that include upskirt, vagflash, pink, masturbate, cream, and climaxing. Two Cosmos commit to Pee-Cam and Piss Mouth.* Elle takes a breath. *Kimju is at risk of becoming the third Pee-Camer.*

Elle worries, *Beka and I though we could necessarily hold onto our two pieces. I should be able to, but Beka? Beka's in over her heads. Maybe we both are.*

Elle hears Tiffany down the hall exit the Bedroom and enter the Bathroom. She instinctively folds the paper tightly, and slips it back into her pocket, and listens to her own thinking comes alive. *Why did I just hide my notes?* The tightly folded secret sheet of paper she keeps in her jeans pocket feels radioactive. *Should I be doing this? And why does Tiffany have to leave the Bedroom to go pee?*

Elle hears footsteps again and hears Tiffany return to her Bedroom.

Elle's thoughts return to her notes. *I have no reason to believe my notes are against the Rules, but I don't want my secret discovered either. I intend to Opt Monitor next Term, even if I have to titter and vagflash between now and then. Or even beg to get naked and Strip, even if that won't happen.*

Elle debates with herself. *My notes consolidate each Cosmos' Game status, and this frame table of information gives me an advantage. However. Okay, I understand that notes aren't cheating, but maybe they bend the Rules? I've played bridge and blackjack and rummy before. Card counting marks the superior Gamer, but it is not normally something one writes down.*

In a moment of insight Elle learns. *I keep records not merely for the obsession of it, but to allow me to project into the future.* And so she makes a decision, *The predictive ability of keeping my notes compensates for the risk of possession. .*

Serious Gamers, including Monitor Babs, would most certainly know how to decipher Elle's Manifests, should someday Elle's possession no longer remained secret and her jeans pockets are cut off.

And what does Elle's analysis reveal? In the dusky light she extracts the paper and pencil stub from her pocket, unfolds it, and constructs a cross-reference table for each Cosmos vs. a number of factors:

Navelage. Elle inventories that *all the Cosmos, including me and even Babs, maintain navelage 24x7. Steph and Robyn do wear the only cutouts, although Robyn always remains the smallest and Steph has sometimes displayed a buttonhole that ranges from her underboob to her scruff, although it never encircles her body. All the rest of us bellage fully, although Babs and Tiffany and Beka have extensive belly-up belly-down.* Elle considers herself. *Me too in the future, assuming Beka and I Flip-Flop.*

Elle scans down the list of Cosmos names as she considers factors: *All of us, except Robyn and Babs, titter one way or another and hairage some of the time. Two Cosmos, ex-Strippers Kimju and Molly, stay topless 24x7. Tiffany and Beka rugage, and Kimju and Molly stay buttage all the time. Beka and Steph both upskirt and vagflash. And Tiffany and Molly both claim to be Pee-Camers and Piss Mouths.*

Elle ponders and creates a distinction: *"Pinking" is an axis independent from "cream", in my notes. One can pull pink or pink for a cam; pink is an action, a visual, and a "come fuck me" pose. Cream is valiva, vaginal secretions; cream presents that aroma of freshness that announces arousal. You can see valiva* and *you can smell it.*

Two axis, Elle concludes, *one can cream without spreading pink. One can pink but not cream. And of course one can do both.*

Elle logs the two Cosmos pinkers, *the two former Strippers, ex-Nuggets Kimju and Molly. And now my Roommate Beka feels like she's allowed to pink and play with herself. That's unhealthy.* Elle considers adding Steph to her pink list; Steph presents a tougher call. *Clearly Steph showcases her open skuddy upskirt, but nobody has chattered about Steph pulling her pink.* Elle also knows, *There is no way Tiffany can pull pink with her slacks on, and that Robyn's maillot and Babs bikini are equally preventative.*

The Cosmos creamer constituency includes both former Strippers and again Elle's Roommate. *Especially my Roommate! Beka Broda is the most creamy of all.*

Elle halts. *And I'm her lollydor!* Elle noodles, *I feel that my proximity to her increases my own chance of Opt Stripping next Term; Kundalini lies too close to her surface.*

Once again Elle details Steph. *Steph keeps her thighs always apart— well we all do—yet remains determined to neither pink nor cream, even though you can see the line of her slit underneath her short hairs all the time.*

But Elle's observation lacks perfection; she remains sufficiently inexperienced to not look for spots in Tiffany's cameltoe... or even Robyn's maillot.

And climaxed? *I've witnessed Kimju and Molly climax twice. Topless, bare butt, gathering ones tanga and panties into the crotch, pullasides, pinking, and creaming seem preludes to climaxing.* Elle considers. *So why haven't the Gamers let Beka cum too? She's already begging.*

My worry, Elle confides to herself, *is that after a Flip-Flop with Beka that I will no longer just be flashing my nippies and nookie; I will be upskirt, spread, and begging to open my niche up.* Elle pauses and looks down the bunk at her body. *I wonder how my body will react if I really were to be called upon to butterfly my nectary, secrete noble fluids, and lose control of myself? I don't think I can do that.*

Elle furrows her brow and considers any necessity to climax. *Climaxing is* not *a Pledge requirement. Except I'm already begging to Pledge naked and Strip. Four of us Cosmos are, Beka and I, also Tiffany and Molly. Robyn says more beggars soon. Good. If I were to become a Stripper I wouldn't need to* volunteer *to pink, wet, and climax; Strippers masturbate to climax, that's all part of their Caste. Cum in front of a Crowd, cum in front of a Cam crew, cum dancing a lap*

Elle feels herself caught in a whirlwind. *There is what I am wearing, and there is what is happening around me. I know Beka will cum just as soon as she's allowed to; but I don't know what I will do. It's like I'm in a dream.*

I understand that when Janet made me unbutton my halter and let it hang down my chest that I wasn't topless. Or when Robyn unbuttoned me and I had to stare at my noogies in the Mirror. Or when I unbuttoned it myself today out of guilt. I am definitely exposing my breasts, but I am not topless, because I still wear my halter, albeit it hanging down. Boobage, that's what I am, I'm neither covered or topless, I'm something in-between. A half state, and in a way my half-state conveys momentum and directionality.

Elle winces. *Showing my noogies with my halter hanging down in front of me is more severe than just being topless. It shows Gamers that I'm willing to let myself be exposed. It's not just a titter and flashing my noogies. And its not that I've lost the top.* Elle breathes out slowly. *I'm begging to unbutton my own halter, let it go, and expose myself. Gamers know that's the sizzle. It's part of me losing control of myself.*

Elle folds the paper, puts it in her pocket, and carefully re-buttons her halter neck strap. *I might not be on the Yacht, but I am headed overboard.*

II-6 Robyn Hazes Tiffany: Sass & Piss Mouth Prospects (D18)

§The Beginning of a New Day

Tiffany crawls out of her cubbyhole underneath Babs' bunk the following morning, Day Eighteen, the fourth day of *The Runup*. She has remained naked since last night, when she had unbuttoned her see-through croptop and wiggled her low-rise stretch slacks down her hips, thighs, ankles and toes, and hung both Garments on the hook at the back of the Bedroom.

She draws her knees up under herself, rolls her Eraser Heads with the fingers of both hands, then descends her fingertips to her twitchet, parts her sex lips, and brushes any crost out of her burgundy-colored vagina.

Tiffany's thinnish red pubic hair grows naturally, and lies above her shaven legs.

Babs sits in her bunk, dangles her bare feet over the edge, and Tiffany takes it upon herself to gently massages Babs' swinging feet, and speaks her first words of the morning, "Ma'am, please let me Pledge naked and cum be a Stripper next Term." She checks to see if BB's toenail polish needs any touch-up.

"I really mean it," Tiffany says. "I don't need to put anything on unless I go out."

"Unless you go outside past the Backyard," BB corrects.

Tiffany licks her lips carefully. "Ma'am, may I please you I will go outside to the Backyard and masturbate my Henge Post stark naked. I'll slick it up with my tapioca, and thrash on it until I'm exhausted. I put on a show your Cosmos House will be proud of. You can feed the Back Door Cam to the Prefecture and Automatron will archive me for posterity. And any paparazzi will get, well, you know, unauthorized content."

Babs blanches. Boss Babe finds a way through. "Remind me why you don't want to streak."

Tiffany looks up at Babs from the floor, "Ma'am, Gamers want me in Lockdown. So if they tell you I need be sent on an errand, and I 'volunteer' you'll never see me again. At least not this Term. I'll vanish while I'm out streaking. I'm not an ex-Stripper like Molly Mammoth; you won't find me chained around the flagpole or in the stocks the next morning either, I'm an ex-Porn Star and in Lockdown until the clock runs out at Midnight at the end of the Term. They'll pump me full of hornyness drugs and deny me, and I'll beg anything they want for next Term."

"You're seem rather choosy. You don't want to Opt Monitor either," BB remembers.

"Thank you," Tiffany responds. "I need to Opt Strip, dance for a Term, and Opt Whore the Term after that. Then I can be a Porn Star again. You know my goals."

"Somehow you Double Opted Up," Babs reminds. "If you did that, why can't you Double Opt Down?"

"Because, Ma'am." Tiffany tosses back long red hair and decides to continue. "You don't understand what it's like. Gamers denying me sex. They deliberately make me starved for sex. I itch between my legs all the time. You've forbidden me to touch myself without permission, and I have no chance of cock."

Boss Babe shrugs her shoulders, "It's nothing personal."

"Ma'am, please let me stay naked and I'll trigger some tapioca outta my twat and puddle the floor like Beka does."

"No doubt you seek complements for advancing Elle's lolly practice?" BB tests.

Tiffany touches the balls of two fingers to the ends of two Eraser Heads. "Hadn't thought about it that way. Although yesterday she collected me off my fingertips."

"You're a bad Pledge sometimes," BB scolds.

"I'm training her," Tiffany defends.

"Very sweet of you to propose Elle collect you off the floor... or will it be her chair seat, like Molly and Beka?" BB eyes twinkle.

Tiffany draws her hands through the air and stretches. "I was thinking it would be sweet to let Elle collect my transductions from the end of the Double Dong. First we Double Dong pussy to pussy, then my twat to her mouth, and visa versa, and we can hug and throat the dong together, and climax."

"I confess," Babs states, "I don't know if you're crazy or not."

"It's okay, Babs," Tiffany explains. "There are lots of ways to Double Dong. I'll show you sometimes."

§ Tiffany Recounts to Babs: Yesterday's Yachting Watersports

Babs shifts. "I saw all the videos from the Yacht. Seems like Kimju is pretty primed for the Pee-Cam. I saw you lick her piss off the deck." Babs rolls a fingertip inside her belly button. "So how did her tanga get soaked with urine? And don't tell me it didn't, because I could smell it, even dry."

"It got peed on, I guess," Tiffany acknowledges.

"By you?" BB asks.

"Well, yes," Tiffany admits. "But it was already soaking in the head before I got to it." Tiffany hastens to volunteer. "Darleen and Rodney both cammed me, and Janet and William watched. Robyn never knew. She was too busy making sure Kimju and Ginny sunburned their pink parts."

Babs cleans her teeth with her tongue in response to this answer. "So you Pee-Cammed for everyone but Robyn, did you give them any other exclusives I should know about?"

Tiffany squares her body up. "Ma'am, I assumed it was Janet's prerogative to share the details with you first."

"Don't let me contaminate your memories," BB wiles. "Tell me from your perspective."

Tiffany feels Babs' leg for traces of stubble. She confesses, "Ma'am, Janet let me practice keeping up with her stream, something I've never done before. She stopped when I spilled, and after I cleaned up the floor it was all over. Darleen cammed it and said it was 'Corvette Exclusive' and 'wouldn't be found on Automatron.'"

"Big disappointment to you," BB drolls.

"No problem," Tiffany breezes, "when my fans want me they'll get me from Janet."

"So did William and Rodney get to watch?" BB inquires.

Tiffany has to recall. "Ah, no. They watched and cammed me when I peed on Kimju's thong in the toilet, but only Darleen captured me capturing Janet's stream."

"Janet peed on the Cam," Babs fingers her bling and evaluates.

Tiffany isn't surprised, "Trust me, Ma'am, you and I have each spent a Term with Janet, so you should know by now that she isn't a shy Gamer."

"You knew her before her Alumni Reprise last Term," BB summarizes.

"I took on her Pee-Cam when we were Strippers, two Terms ago, and I expected her to confirm a Pee-Cam during the Alumni Reprise, which she did. Only I didn't not expect to be handed the glass," Tiffany recounts.

"You said it was that or Slavesex," Boss Babe reviews.

Tiffany pauses, takes one of Babs' feet in her hands again. "Ma'am, I tasted more than just Janet on the Yacht. I tasted man piss. Janet presented me two shot glasses and I had to determine which was William and which was Rodney. I got it wrong the first time, had to practice twice, and got it right the second time. I never saw their dicks nor saw them pour the shots. It was just me and Janet there, no Cams."

Monitor Babs greets this news with silence. *Maybe hidden Cam.*

Tiffany interprets, "Hey, Babs, don't feel slighted. You can cam yourself peeing into my mouth. I bet I can keep up with your stream better than Janet's. Give our House some clips instead of me being exclusive elsewhere."

Boss Babe holds her quietude. "No secret suck and fuck videos you want to tell me about?" she asks.

"Ma'am, no, Ma'am. But I suspect Janet let Ginny have sex with William, especially because the sunburn would make it hurt a lot. But I didn't see anything."

"Maybe Rodney got to wack off." Boss Babe suggests.

"Ma'am, he spotted himself just looking at me!" Tiffany claims.

She laughs. "Ginny said to tell you that she'll service you. But you don't need that, Ma'am, because you know I'll eat you out anytime!"

Babs laughs. "I know you won't be doing that Pledge. But I won't rule out your begging to pink, cream, and cum. Begging to bury a dildo and buttplug if not Double Penetrate. Begging to climax the Double Dong with each and every Cosmos Pledge."

Tiffany switches her attention to Babs' other foot. "Ma'am, thank you, Ma'am. You know that anytime you want to take me into the Bathroom and use me as your toilet that I am your Piss Mouth."

"Silly you," BB admonishes, and pushes her toes into Tiffany's face. "You're just trying to trick me into making Pee-Cam."

True, and they laugh together.

§ Babs & Tiffany: Goals & Garments and Begging to Streak

Tiffany opens, "You find it ironic that you and I are different in Caste but identical in Garment count, even though you let me stay naked sometimes." Tiffany teases, "I think Bikini Babe seeks to cover up more."

BB defends, "I will cover up when the moment is ripe. I'm playing the Game to learn how to exert authority."

"You haven't done anything about covering your bling up." Tiffany probes.

Bling! Babs draws both hands under her bra cups, just above the underwire, and tugs upward and inward. The breasts kiss all the way down the cleavage. Gum Arabic (eyelash glue in the Makeup Case) helps keep both breasts affixed inside the bra, but the crescents d'areolage are always 24x7.

Babs pushes a big toe into Tiffany's mouth. "I'm over trying to hike up my bra straps," she provides, "I have learned to dominate my bling and not let my bling dominate me. That kind of confidence is central to learning how to exert authority." She retracts her toe.

Tiffany grins. "Good you're learning to hone steel."

Babs leans back on her elbows; Tiffany takes her foot into her hands and mouth, sucks toes, and cleans out in between them. Babs says, "Sometimes I don't know why I enrolled in School. Officially, what I tell myself, is that I'm here to learn to manage. To overcome self-doubt about leading people. I know men look at me a lot, that's okay, but I'm not really interested in attracting them into sex. Except sex is a big part of the world, especially here at the Cosmos House, where it is forbidden."

Babs relaxes. "What about you?"

Tiffany completes one foot. She ripples, "I'm here to expand how to surrender myself to Kundalini. I've never had any guilt about sex in the first place, so I don't have your kind of hurdles. I know that the more the build-up the bigger the surrender, and I like letting go completely, even if I do get played like a musical instrument."

"So maybe Gamers Double Opted you Up to put you far away from being a Porn Star," BB suggests.

"Certainly part of it," Tiffany confesses, "The bigger a wet spot in my cameltoe and a bigger the trill will be."

"You've got two Garments, and unless something happens you will Opt Monitor next Term." Babs considers as Tiffany cleans her other foot, toes, ankle, soles. BB frets, "I worry about Karma. Karma alters the future because it alters the physical forces acting of the forward momentum of the Universe. Throw a rock and you change things because witnesses anticipate a direction and landing point."

"Yeah, and sometimes chance happens. Chaos." Tiffany shrugs, "Sometimes you just have to feel your way forward."

"I feel myself acquiring another Garment." Babs muses.

"Ma'am, please may I beg you," Tiffany agrees, "please take one of mine, Ma'am, you could Opt MomCap next Term."

Babs frowns. "I thought you were begging naked."

Tiffany is. "Ma'am, please let me Pledge naked and cum be a Stripper next Term, Ma'am. You know I mean it. You know I'll pink, cream, and cum. You've watched me Pee-Cam, and I've begged you to become your toilet."

"You begged me to Piss Mouth you in the Bathroom," BB waggles a finger. "Did you really think I am so stupid I would consent to what is effectively a Pee-Cam for me?"

Tiffany bristles, "Ma'am, you'd be a great Pee-Camer. But I'll be your toilet anywhere, anytime, in front of anybody or not, on or off Cam. Just us. I belong to you, Ma'am, please let me Pledge naked and cum be a Stripper next Term."

"Beg me to streak," Boss Babe commands.

"Ma'am, after you strip me naked, please keep me naked for the rest of the Term. When it's over, I'll streak to the Nugget, just like Penny and Coco did."

"You'll streak whenever it please me," Boss Babe firms.

Tiffany agrees, "Ma'am, please let me Pledge naked and cum be a Stripper next Term. Please streak me anytime, anywhere it pleases you, Ma'am." Tiffany pleads. "I know you know that if I get caught out past the Yard, you won't have a Roommate the rest of this Term because I'll be in Lockdown from then on. Don't ask me to predict what happens next, but it can't be a good thing."

§ Tiffany Teases Babs: About Her Deployment of Robyn

Babs pushes her curvy body forward, stands erect with her feet on the floor, and pivots to sit in her chair. She takes the Makeup Case out of her drawer, hands it to Tiffany, and Tiffany, on hands and knees before standing, gets to work. She touches up finger and toe nails, wipes Babs' body with a cloth, prepares her face and hair, kneels and shaves her legs.

Tiffany converses, "Ma'am, I know you're using Robyn as a 'second-in-command' to make your life easier, but I'm not fooled, I know you're making a devious calculation."

"You're onto my intentions?" BB queries with one raised eyebrow.

Tiffany says, "I know how the Game works. I've scrubbed floors in a Glory Hole, twisted for Pimp Cowboy at Flesh Ranch. I've trained Strippers, and I've changed straw for helpless Slavesex—guys and gals.

"I appreciate you're using Robyn to irritate the Pledge, and all of them are starting to hate her, even me."

Babs raises her eyes, "And you're supposed to be the professional."

"Maybe there is damage she can cause other Cosmos," Tiffany admits, "but there no way she can impair me. I'm immune, yet I still hate her."

Tiffany elaborates, "Ma'am, I understand you're not just shifting the burden of your own work, you want to probe your Cosmos. And irritate and swelter the whole pack of us. But, Ma'am, forgive me, you are also demonstrating weakness. *You* need to be the one to swelter all of us."

BB looks down Tiffany out the bottom of her eye. *True.* Still, BB responds, "I'm letting Robyn run out her own rope, and as long as it is convenient, I will politely ignore this activity."

"You still have ownership of the Karma," Tiffany argues, "even if you didn't create it."

BB shrugs. "Maybe, maybe not."

"You're testing if Pledge take offense to following orders from what some might consider a lower being," Tiffany teases. "Of course they do! Kimju and Molly take it in stride and even understand the pragmatics, and the newbies—Beka and Elle—they're simply eager to follow instructions. But Steph Sorostitute? Your undershirt tittering sanpan ex-Monitor? She feels especially put off and taken aback. She got extremely shamed when you screened her thermoprobe clips last night, because they remind her she got broken last Term."

"Steph got broken for no fault of mine!" Babs exclaims. "Her Opt Down happened through her own actions. And besides I didn't screen her, Robyn did."

"There you go again. You make your former Monitor take orders from her former Pledge! The one who turned her in and is responsible for her Fate! Robyn Redacted! Ouch! Double indemnity."

BB agrees. "Okay, I'm aware that Robyn relishes dishing out insult and humiliation delivered as only Robyn can." BB tugs on the shoulder straps of her underwire bra.

Tiffany suggests, "She has forgotten that her duty is to act as your mouthpiece. It's bad enough that whenever a Cosmos steps out of line the more she tattles on them the happier she becomes. She exhibits sadistic glee in grinding us Pledge, totally indifferent to her own heavy-footed rudeness, and beyond your command."

BB concedes, "All right all ready. But I have no problem being the Boss Babe! Understand that! Even you!"

"Ma'am, take it easy, Ma'am," Tiffany lifts her hand, "Take a complement. You're becoming a smooth operator and you don't need Pledge backfiring on you for Robyn's misdeeds. Resentment can flow upstream."

Babs relents. "Thank you Tiffany Transparent for helping make me wise. Tell me, Pledge, what might I do for you as a reward for your wisdom?"

Tiffany startles. "Oh, that's easy. Please let me Pledge naked and cum be a Stripper next Term. Help me rid myself of my shirt or my slacks as a minimum. You can take them, then I can Opt Strip next Term."

"Robyn only has one piece," Babs chides, "maybe she'd like your outfit."

"Over my bound and beaten body!" Tiffany exclaims, but pauses and reconsiders. "I take that back. And if that's what I have to do to get to the Nugget, I'll do it. But listen, if you love me, you'll let me teach that rum doxy how to piss into her own mouth."

"You just want to transfer your Piss Mouth Obeisance to Robyn," Babs philosophizes with a teasing grin.

"Fair enough, I don't mind being a Pee-Camer but really don't need to be a Piss Mouth." Tiffany concedes kindly.

"You love being a Pee-Camer," Boss Babe reminds.

"I do," Tiffany agrees. "Please let me lavish Robyn. I'll charm the ripeness out of her and snowball her mouth-to-mouth. And then you can give her my clothes. Shirt or slacks, or all together. Just please let me Pledge naked and cum be a Stripper next Term!"

Boss Babe muses. "I like you begging to stay naked 24x7. And not inside and the Backyard. Begging to streak, too."

Tiffany kneels, leans forward, and kisses Babs' feet. "Ma'am, if you streak me and I get caught you know I'm instant Lockdown and you'll never see me again. Well, not this Term for sure. And I know you don't want that to happen."

Babs listens but does not deny Tiffany's allegations. "I have only one problem giving Robyn your Garments," Babs confesses and grits her teeth. "I wish to distance myself from Robyn. This Term, next Term, forever. Robyn is toxic. Toxic because she has the potential to cause collateral damage."

Babs signs Tiffany to stand up, Tiffany must roll, sit up, and rise her body upward. She brushes dirt out from under her thicket, brushes dirt off her taffrail, and considers BB's passion.

Boss Babe waggles a finger, "I intend to put the scorch on Robyn! As far as I am concerned, Robyn shall become a Stripper next Term, Charm or no Charm. I want her to collapse like an ember squeezed."

§ Tiffany with Kimju, Molly, Steph, Beka, Elle: Bathroom Makeup
   3

In the Bedroom, Babs shifts gears and instructs Tiffany, "Go to the Bunkroom and tell the Six Cosmos Pledge bunking there that five of them are to follow you to the Bathroom for makeup, and that Robyn, apparently because she's objected to your treatments of her, has been selected for a special makeover at the Beauty Salon."

Tiffany rises, leaves her clothes behind and exits the Bedroom naked. She rousts the Six Pledge out of their bunks, lines them up feet spread, wrists crossed behind backs, and announces Babs' directive. "Now move, all of you, Babs' orders!"

Robyn pauses at the top of the circular stairs for an opportunity to hurl love back to the Cosmos Pledge, "Happy Pee-Camming," she sails, and disappears down the circular stairs. Five Pledge follow what seems to be a perpetually naked Pledge Tiffany into the Bathroom. Her presence, as well as Molly's, ensures that the Bathroom Pee-Cam lights up.

"Sit somewhere," Tiffany commands, and Kimju, Molly, Steph, Beka, and Elle sit, either on a stool, or the edge of the bath, or the floor. All make sure their thighs don't touch.

Tiffany addresses the five Cosmos, "You shall remain in the Bathroom with me until we are relieved. Possibly Robyn will prance in with her 'superior' makeup. You can move your arms and torsos and heads around as long as you keep your legs apart. So make yourself comfortable. You shall be made into Cleopatra's Wannabe Strippers par excellence. You shall have curled hair, outlandish faces, rouged nipples, colored navels and clits swabbed with chili powder. I shall take my time with you. No rush, this could be a long wait. And you will all look extraordinary!"

Of course the Bathroom Cam—not preoccupied with collecting pee at this moment—gathers them all in. No hiding, no secrets; everybody knows that this is a Cam that Boss Babe always leaves turned on, live to the Prefecture, with its streams archived by Automatron.

Steph catches Tiffany looking at her and discovers that she has attracted the Cam's attention. She still wears the undershirt she fetched from the Snots two morning ago. Dirtier now, the ripped buttonhole more ripped still, titter without stop, and it barely comes down to her crotch where she sits but it doesn't matter, the legs apart ensure this qualifies as a extended vagflash. *This might even qualify as an upskirt if the undershirt completely covered my crotch.*

It doesn't matter, Steph doesn't take chances. *I recall that during* The Arrivals *all the Cosmos Pledge begged to keep our legs apart and not our thighs touch. Me too.* Steph can't stop the Cam hovering before her and she adjusts her legs to a more open position. *Can't take any chances right now. I dare not provide any reason to spread my legs and pink myself.*

Kimju, Molly, Beka, and Elle follow Steph's action and all advance their legs to open position as well. Elle knows, *only one more position wider.*

Kimju and Elle display hairage to the sides of cloth yanked into their crotches. Tiffany signs Elle to unbutton the neck strap of her halter top, she does, and lets it fall free. Elle grimaces, accepts she's being cammed, realizes she has no restrictions on where to place her hands, and forms a handbra. Tiffany laughs and signs topless tanga Kimju to handbra. "Good for the both of you," she cheers, "you can practice Striptease together!"

Elle will learn that holding handbra for long periods of time has its disadvantages. *And what difference does it make? The Back Door Cam already collected my boobage. So it hardly matters if I cover myself with a handbra or not.* Elle trades a look with Kimju, and catches a smile. *It matters,* Elle festers. *Kimju wants me to Opt Strip. She intends to prepare me, grab my halter at the last minute, and Opt Monitor next Term.*

Elle knows that outcome. *That leaves me topless with shorts to Opt Strip next Term. That won't do, except that's what I am begging. Well, me and Beka both.*

Time goes on. And after a while Elle doesn't want to keep her nipples covered any more.

Molly, a naked Pee-Camer like Tiffany, knew to leave her panties behind before she entered the Bathroom, and were the Pee-Cam not already illuminated it would turn on at her entrance. Molly assumes, *I will for sure Pee-Cam this morning. So will Tiffany.*

But what about Kimju?

Molly plops her maximus down onto the tile floor and rolls it around until she can rest her back up against the side of the bath and view her naked and open-legged posture in a mirror ahead of her. It is the same spot that Steph and Robyn sat and spread the day Steph arrived. Back then Steph did not have cloth between her legs, and she still doesn't.

Molly looks in the mirror and obligingly parts her legs outward to full spread position, more than is required of her. Molly has a thick muff that extends upward toward a swirl of fur about her navel, outwards down her upper thighs, and of course, overgrows her asshole and moonshadow. And of course she has hair everywhere: center back, arms and legs, belly, armpits, long on her head.

The Cam displays a nervous attentive; it scans the Bathroom for alternate options of focus. Molly wiggles her minge to the sides and opens her mooe up: brown, with purple deep inside, thick inner lips, and a thick clit that Gamers call Molly's maraschino. Molly looks into the mirror and can see the ring imbedded in the hood above. *If I Opt Strip again I know that my piercing hole will be stretched and the ring gauge enlarged.*

The Cam hangs with Molly as she commences to play with herself. *Good,* Molly deduces, *at least the Bathroom Cam will surveil me beyond me just passing urine. Might as well enjoy myself. Nobody to stop me. I might as well whip up some meringue pie, and if I can get away with it I can lose my pee and koekjedoodle at the same time. Might as well do something to make the Crowd want me at the Nugget every day.*

Tiffany repositions Beka next to Molly and waggles a finger at Molly. "Teach her how to pink, wet, and stay ready, but *no* cumming either of you!" Tiffany humors Molly, "You can practice cream-dancing together!"

They shall. Among all the Pledge, Beka displays the most uncovered genitals. Unlike Steph, whose wispy blonde strands flow across her center line, Beka's sex lips are completely shaven, and only above where her bolus tops her bourse does Beka display any bristles, a butched rectangle an inch or two wide which runs upward toward her navel: her landing strip.

The Cam gives Beka a close-up. Gamers watching the live feed expect that soon Beka's center line will become two if not three lines, and for brodeas to brim. The bets placed by the Crowd at the Nugget, who watch the feed on the Screens, aren't about whether this will happen or not, because it always does. The bets are about when.

And how long before Beka forgets to hold handbra, and follows Molly's action to touch herself.

§ Robyn Visits Madam Nurse Beautician: Trip to Beauty Salon

Robyn finds the Beauty Salon near the Village town square. The front door is open, she enters, and comes face-to-face with Madam Nurse Beautician, a woman she has never met in her memory, and whom she doesn't bother to evaluate as to Caste.

"Monitor Babs sent me," Robyn dictates. "She said you're suppose to give me the full works: hair, face, lips and eyes, nails, shave my legs and armpits."

Beautician gestures toward a chair complete with stirrups. "So nice I can serve you," she says.

Do the Cosmos back in the Bathroom sit and wait for all this? They do. Do they get made up like Cleopatra's Strippers? They do. Do they keep their legs open? Absolutely. Do Kimju and Elle maintain their handbra positions? At least for a while. And do Molly and Beka pull pink and masturbate? In synchronization! And what does Steph do? Steph sits with her hands in front of hers exposed slash. No one corrects her.

Tiffany surveys her makeup. *Job done.* She considers the Bathroom Cam. *Gamers like to watch me here in the Bathroom. They like to watch me make up myself. They watch me makeup all the other Cosmos Pledge too, only BB gets private service.*

Most of all they like that I have no secrets. They want to watch me pee? No problem, I've been a Pee-Camer since the first day I Pledged the Game. I was a Pee-Camer when I was a Stripper, before I ever made it to Flesh Ranch. And then to here.

But Gamers doesn't want to just watch me pee, they want to watch me masturbate, whip up some tapioca, and trill. I can do that for them whenever I get permission. I know Gamers are winding me up. I know they aren't going to let me go anytime soon.

Or maybe BB will let me run out a little bit, work up some sweat, and then wind me back even tighter than the first time. I know in the end I will lose all control for as long as it pleases the Game. Minutes, hours, days.

What the Gamers really want is they want their Porn Star back: Tiffany Transparent, swallowing new cocks in all holes.

Tiffany sighs, *The Gamers want me back for live hardcore, but in the meantime they will continue to jerk off at my archive, watch whatever I can get out now, and may they beg Babs to let me climax the Double Dong.*

§ Robyn Aggresses Tiffany & Molly: Pee-Camers Log Pee Stats

Robyn returns with three objects in her hands: a Measuring Cup, a Logging Chart, and a bottle of hair bleach. She calls the six Bathroom Cosmos to Lineup. "Stand up, legs apart, hands crossed behind backs."

Six Pledge fall in. Hands crossed at the wrist to be particular, thighs never touching (all bare except for Tiffany), and feet flat on the floor. They sort themselves into a Lineup, with Tiffany next to Kimju given Robyn's lack of participation in the Lineup.

The Cam is live and Monitor Babs is not here.

Robyn preens before this Lineup. "Never forget, when I speak, it is as if Monitor Babs speaks with her own voice. All of you must accommodate me."

There is accommodation and then there is what a Pledge must do when Robyn adds malice into the power equation. Like now, when she chooses to focus upon Tiffany. "As you can see, Madam Nurse Beautician outclasses you in the makeup department. She's Castes above you, Pledge Tiffany Transparent, even if right now you are wearing the Gamer's new clothes! She's higher Caste than Monitors and higher Caste still than MomCaps. She begged me to let her give me a manicure and permanent, and although I demurely resisted the lavish praise she bestowed up me, I finally felt that she really did need to make me beautiful. And so she did!"

Robyn considers the three objects she holds in her hands. "Oh yes," she adds, "Beautician asked me nicely if I would consider bringing these things to you, and of course I honored her humble request!"

Robyn rotates one shoulder and then the other while she rotates her head around as if to drive creaks out of the top of her spine. She addresses Tiffany and Molly directly, "Every time you void your urine you shall pee into this Measuring Cup." And hands the cup to naked Tiffany. "Fill the Cup up, empty the Cup, and then fill it up, until your bladder is empty." Robyn bows and hands the Logging Chart to Molly. "Hang this Logging Chart on the wall. So every time you pee you shall write the your name, the day, and the number of cups on the Chart. It's not very complicated, really, even for someone like you."

Robyn senses she encounters blank faces. She scowls or orders Tiffany, "You're holding the cup. How about you be the first to squat for the Cams and practice collected release!"

"My pee is your pleasure Ma'am," Tiffany bows, squats, fingers her inner lips to the sides, touches spittle to a peehole presented on the flat plain, and carefully fills up one cup. "No secrets for a naked Pee-Cam

Pledge begging to Opt Strip next Term!" She laughs to the Cam, rises, and writes "Tiffany, D18, 1 cup" on Logging Chart.

"You're a tinkling twat wannabe Porn Star who will piss in her own mouth!" Robyn slices.

"I am a Pee-Camming Pledge!" Tiffany chimes, finds her way to a basin, and dumps the Cup. *Out of sight, out of play,* old Cosmos saying. "You know, Robyn, if you had access to Automatron you could screen my *Clear Glass Toilet* clips from when Janet and I were both Strippers, two Terms ago. And that was nothing, when I was an active Porn Star I did two cocks every which way. I even did a shoot where I got analed, climaxed, and arched pee at the same time. Let me assure you I am not your ordinary DP Whore, I qualify as a triple penetration Porn Star!"

"You're crazy," Robyn advises,. "How about you pee in a flask, pump your pee up your tailpipe, pee a second time, and *then* you lick your pee up? How about that, you'd be a tinkling tailpipe! Ha, ha, ha, ha."

"You're a Whore," Robyn snorts.

Tiffany controls herself carefully, "Ma'am, I am Porn Star. Just tell me what I need to do to procure a flask and ass pump."

Robyn snorts, "Don't play fancy with me. I know exactly what you are, "You're a *wannabe* Porn Star, and if you don't obey me, I'm going to tell Boss Bitch you are bragging again. You need piss and castor oil poured down your throat and a soapy yellow enema up your tailpipe.

"Ma'am, that's harsh, Ma'am." Tiffany wonders. *Would BB let Robyn do that to me? Robyn called her 'Boss Bitch' on the Cam; does BB even understand what's happening?*

Robyn continues. "Maybe yesterday your ex-Stripper Roommate Janet took pity on you and let you off easy. That was yesterday. You're both showoffs, ready to get off dancing a lap. Maybe Janet wants to Opt MomCap, but you're not just a wannabe Stripper, you're a wannabe Whore!"

Tiffany begs, "Ma'am, please let me Pledge naked and cum be Stripper next Term. And cautiously adds, "And Robyn, if you really do have Charm, please let me Double Opt Down and break to Whore Caste next Term. That is my biggest wish! Ma'am."

Robyn closes her eyes. Opens them and speaks, "I can't understand what you're saying and furthermore anything you say doesn't matter. You're a sick piece of tail-hook trailer trash; today I'm in charge. I'm superior to any Porn Star, wannabe or residual. *My* lady parts were never for sale. And let's get this straight: You were not just some Whore who fucked in private; you fucked in front of people. In front of Cams, live audiences too. You're a public fuck and you're lower than a Whore. You're not just a cheap piece of fuck meat, you let people watch you and let them take pictures of you having sex!"

"Ma'am!" Tiffany astounds, "I am a Porn Star!" Tiffany hesistates at uttering forbidden language, twists, "Ma'am, I am trained courtesan Caste, versed from the love bites of the Kama Sutra to the stories of Shahrazad. Even when I lapdanced at the Nugget, I knew how to make the lap and me get off together."

"You're no Porn Star any more, you tawdry thumping turbulator," Robyn snaps. "You're an ex-Whore wannabe Whore."

Tiffany takes umbrage, "Ma'am, I love to fuck and my fans love to watch me. I am *very* good at it."

Robyn flares her nostrils. "So how come your so-valuable tenderloin resides at this Cosmos House?" Robyn asks. "How come your trap door and tail tube aren't being leased out to a bunch of gangbangers? How come you don't have jizz all over your face?"

Tiffany understands, *I am a Double Op Up and I have been awarded two pieces. But what is behind my upward mobility? And how do I stay dignified when I must deal with this empty-headed haughty blonde stuffed into a golden maillot cutout?*

But Tiffany does use her own head. Not all Cosmos plan ahead, but those who do often go to significant lengths to strategize opportunities. To scheme. To be cagy. To make plans. Tiffany tells Robyn, "It's very simple really: Gamers Opted me to Pledge to frustrate me sexually and to make my fans crave me even more. After I make Stripper next Term, then in the Term after that I will be a Porn Star, again. And I'll be an even bigger Star than I was the last time. Even more than I am now." Tiffany hedges.

"You're a three hole fuck wannabe Whore," Robyn states. "Your biggest claim to fame is eating pussy while getting fucked with a strapon, memorialized on your Tiffany Porn Star Calendar. What, did you run out of guys to fuck?"

Tiffany irks, "You know Robyn, Gamers will make me into whatever Caste they want me to be, and they will frustrate or fuck me. I can't do anything about it. And that goes for you too! You should be asking me for my help. You're the one stuck with one Garment who might not be getting another. I can teach you how to strip better than Kimju and Molly can train Beka and Elle. You are better off getting help, sooner than later."

"Oh shut up, Tiffany," Robyn pooh-poohs. "I'm the most covered Cosmos. I don't titter or flash. I've never been topless or rumped out, not even cheekage like Boss Bitch is sometimes."

Tiffany considers that the Cam is live. "Don't say I didn't offer to help you," she braces. "I bet once you Opt Down you'll take off your maillot *before* you ever get to the Nugget."

Robyn sputters, chides, "You're the naked Pledge lighting up the Cam. Best you can offer your fans is Pee-Camming your Piss Mouth. Maybe that's fresh but if Gamers want to satisfy themselves watching you fuck, then they'll just have to satisfy themselves masturbating to your old Videos." Robyn strikes a beauty pose. "Or maybe you can find something to entertain Gamers with besides your pee and your tapioca.

"How about you and I climax the Double Dong together?" Tiffany offers.

"How about you Double Dong with every Cosmos except me," Robyn snaps back. "I'm going to be a Monitor next Term. You're the one begging to Pledge naked and cum Strip."

Tiffany considers her Bathroom Cam nudity. "Robyn, may it please you, I'll go to the Bedroom, fetch my shirt and slacks off the hook, and bring them to you, Ma'am. You keep everything. Then let me masturbate and climax naked in the Mudpit, Ma'am, for you Ma'am, total Backyard exposure."

Robyn tilts her head and considers this serious offer. "Listen, you tizzy twist twit," Robyn states. "You head directly to the Mudpit. Stay naked and wet it down good. Be sure to ring the Bell and beg the Cam to get on you. And by the way, drink a lot of water first, and don't forget to announce to the Prefecture before you tinkle. And before I see you next, every square inch of your skin better be covered in mud. Now scram."

§ Robyn Confirms Kimju: Pee-Cam Status

With Tiffany gone Robyn returns her attention to the five Cosmos who continue to stand, legs apart, hands behind back, in the Bathroom: Kimju, Molly, Steph, Beka, and Elle.

Kimju suddenly draws Robyn's full attention. Robyn points at the tanga Kimju wears. "Molly's a Pee-Camer and she knows to take her panties off before she comes into the Bathroom."

Kimju blanches.

Robyn clicks her front teeth together then rolls her lips. The tight stretch fabric of Robyn's maillot cutout reveals to observant Gamers that Robyn's headlights have erected. She queries Kimju, "What don't you know?"

"I know Pee-Camers may only enter the Bathroom naked," Kimju parries with her Roommate.

"Did you tell all your fellow Pledge you arched piss over the side of the Yacht yesterday?" Robyn asks.

Kimju interjects, "But Ma'am—"

Robyn cuts her short. "Did you not beg to pee for my Cosmos Cam yesterday on the Yacht? Did you beg to pee for Darleen's Corvette Cam?

Did you pee in front of Rodney's Peacock Cam? So have you not, in fact, peed in front of the entire Prefecture?"

Kimju back peddles, "Ma'am, that was yesterday, Ma'am."

"You begged the Pee-Cam." Robyn firms, "And you failed to enter the Bathroom naked."

Kimju scans the Bathroom for assistance. Babs is nowhere around, Tiffany is gone, and neither Molly nor Steph, nor the newbies quite know how to offer support. *I know I must capitulate.* Kimju determines. *Impossible to argue with the video.* She says, "I made a mistake, Ma'am. Tell me how to correct myself."

Robyn hesistates only a moment. "Drop that tanga of yours to the floor."

Kimju startles, and obeys. She hooks her thumbs into the waistband, pushes down and wiggles the garment out of and down her kootch and keister, then down her thighs and knees, stepping feet out of ankles, and leaving the thong on the floor. Kimju is naked now.

"I put you on the Post Henge twice during *The Arrivals,* and the second time I climaxed you naked. You haven't forgotten that, have you?"

Kimju doesn't argue about facts. "Ma'am, I'll climax naked for you center stage at the Nugget, I know I have to do that."

"Squat, beg the Pee-Cam, and pee on your thong. Then, since you want to wear it so much, pull it back up, remove yourself from this Room, and go spend the rest of today in the Doghouse. And don't ever appear in this Bathroom again unless you are naked, or you will be practicing how to pee into your own mouth sooner than expected."

Kimju assesses that the Cam, the Pee-Cam, *observes me with curiosity.* She does as she's told and begs to the Prefecture, "Please let me be a naked Pee-Cam Pledge." She squats, and the Bathroom Cam faithfully documents 27 seconds of yellow stream, soaking the thong. Kimju debates what to log on the Pee Chart, and Gamers watch her try not to drip as she pulls the soaking mess back up and over her pubis. She hustles down the stairs to the Kitchen and bursts out through the Back Door. She spots the Back Door Cam looking at her, looks down toward the Doghouse, and realizes, *now I'm really in for it.*

Robyn's lips slyly grin. She gives Molly a nod, and Steph and Beka and Elle watch Molly Piss Mouth clean up Kimju' spill, including the drips that lead to the door.

§ Robyn Hazes Beka & Elle: Pee-Cam Futures & Breastplay

The events in the Bathroom, both before and after Kimju's Pee-Cam, send Elle into a dizzy. Now only two pairs of Roommates remain. Molly and Steph, and Beka and Elle.

Kimju's Doghouse presses in on Elle's psyche. *I worry about becoming a Pee-Camer. I remember pulling aside to pee in the Doghouse under the Back Landing the day I arrived, but I have kept this early morning contribution secret. But should Babs ask about it, I know I'd confess.*

Elle deepens her worry. *But what if Babs already knows, and demands that I repeat my performance, and because I didn't tell her* I'll *end up having to pee naked in the Mudpit? I don't know what I would do. Is escape even a possibility?* But Elle has read the Rules, she knows, *Attempted escape bestows Slavesex.*

Elle doesn't share her concern of becoming a Pee-Cam Pledge with her Roommate; Beka now stands between her and Steph in the shortened Lineup. Nor does Elle share a creeping fear that Beka might be starting to believe her own begs. *Her begging to 'Pledge naked and become Stripper next Term' is becoming increasing genuine.*

Robyn sidles over to both newbies and tilts her head toward them, "You two are the only Pledge begging to Opt Strip who aren't begging to Pee-Cam. Competition is emerging to see who gets to Opt Strip next Term! And all the rest of the beggars are begging to pee-pee."

Elle breathes in carefully.

Robyn laughs and pinches Beka on the cheek. "What you worried about? You already got a miniskirt. All you gotta do is squat for the Cam."

Elle feels an urge to speak, but Beka begs first, "Please Ma'am—" but Robyn gets in the way.

"You," Robyn instructs Beka, "pull your croptop up to your chin. Now both of you go to the Bunkroom, rub your tits up against each other and start kissing until you freshen. Now scram."

And they do. Elle's halter already dangles down with the neck straps flowing below her waist. Beka lifts her croptop, wraps Elle in a hug, and presses her boobies flat against Elle's bare nugs.

Elle hesitates at kissing a girl but Beka places her lips on her lips with passion; Kundalini assists, and Elle kisses back. Beka grinds her boobs against Elle's and Elle's nipples arise. Elle opens her eyes, looks into Beka's eyes, and Beka draws her hands around Elle's hips. Beka draws her tighter, and this time Elle parts her mouth, touches the tip of Beka's tongue with her own,, and puts passion into her kiss and body rub. May Beka and Elle forget about Robyn with Molly and Steph in the Bathroom.

II-7 Robyn: Molly & Steph Negotiate Roommate Game (D18)

§ Robyn Strips Steph: And Molly Bleaches Steph's Hair

Robyn struts in front of the two remaining Pledge in the Bathroom. "I am, as you are well aware, Babs' agent and in command." She hands Steph the final item she has brought back from Madam Nurse Beautician's Beauty Salon. A bottle of hair bleach.

"You can assist Steph," Robyn grins at Molly, "You make sure every hair on her head and her snatch gets bleached out completely. All of it."

"Pull your undershirt off over your head," Robyn commands Steph.

Steph obeys. She gathers upward: Hips and short curlies, belly, smurfs, armpits.... The Garment separates from her long blonde hair, and Steph gathers it into her hands.

"Gimme," Robyn commands.

And Steph does. She presents naked to the Bathroom Cam. To the Prefecture. She freshens at this moment, but only on the inside.

"You can both stay naked now," Robyn decrees, tosses the undershirt into the toilet.

Steph blanches, and Robyn twists a lip as she addresses the now naked Pledge. "You can beg the Cam to shoot you peeing on that rag if you want to claim it back. Sort of like Kimju did, except Kimju didn't pee on her own Garment, everyone else peed on it for her."

Robyn addresses Molly, "Wring it out and use it to clean up the floor. Don't worry if bleach stains it or it gets more ripped and tattered, it befits you, you fat hairy molliwog."

Molly teeters uneasily and volunteers, "Ma'am, please let me go fetch my panties, toss them in the toilet, and pee on them too."

"Stupid you," Robyn snarls, "You just don't want to get bypassed. Don't worry, we will find out just how desperate you are to get to the Nugget, and it won't be just how fast you can pink, cream, and climax.

"Right now, you need to give your Roommate a bleach job. Every last hair. Get to work. I'll be back later."

Yes, Robyn will return; in the meantime Molly keeps the Cam lit up. She and Steph both break position, trade eyes, and Molly signs Steph into one of the makeup stools, facing the makeup mirror, with her legs spread and her feet on the counter, hands behind head.

Steph grimaces, balances herself, and *well aware I display open crotch. I am naked now. Soft curlies over my slot. The Cam collects me full-figure, naked from the top of my head down to the tip of my toes. And close-ups of my spouts and opened legs.*

Molly taps Steph inside her knees. And Steph spreads as wide as possible. *Close-ups of my spouts and spread legs.*

Steph watches in the makeup mirror as Molly rubs the bleach mixture into the sweeping hairs breezing across her vagina. Molly uses rubber gloves found with the bleach. Steph blanches as she feels Molly's fingers swab her squeeze box. She steels a glance at the Cam, *Molly's hand blocks my snatch, but the Cam watches me. Watching Molly too, but what does Molly care? She'll pink and pee anywhere, anytime, in front of anybody. If she's careless she'll pink me.*

Molly goes to work rubbing the bleach into the hair on Steph's head. This is a longer task; Steph watches in the mirror as Molly is careful to keep bleach away from Steph's eyes and ears. *Well, you should care for me, and not just because I will be taking your panties off of you.*

§ Steph: Contemplates About Who Admires Her Naked

Perseverance comes in many forms and the Roommates wait while the bleach reacts with Steph's hair. Molly sits down on the makeup chair adjacent to Steph, tucks her feet in under herself and proceeds to slowly masturbate. Steph keeps her legs stoically spread, balancing her body with her arms behind her. Molly scoops mung out of her mutton, drips on the chair, and lubricates her moonscapes and minarets.

Meanwhile Steph's long bleached hair hanging down from her head feels increasingly stringy, while her satchel flaps hide behind increasing brittle short and wavy pubic hair.

Eyebrows bleached too.

Steph discovers that the Cam has lost interest in Molly's masturbations and has positioned itself level with her crotch. Steph licks her lips. *It wants to reports my snapdragon to the Prefecture. Good luck, Gamers, it's a little foamy with bleach down there.* She rests her arms on the chair and relaxes.

But unease prevails and Steph wiggles in the makeup chair. Prefecture aside, Steph wonders *exactly who might be looking at my snizzaroo.* The weighted hair irritates Steph's bare shoulders. She resists the urge to touch it with her hands *least I discolor my fingers.* She looks down at her body and sees that *my spigots stand up.* She constricts her vagina, but in the event she bequeaths a line of liquid silver between her innermost lips, *the bleaching strands still protect me from any prying eyes.*

Steph returns to her question. *Who's watching me now?* She shifts her weight around but the chair back ensures she holds her legs apart. *Certainly Boss Bitch watches me, even though I have BB under control. And Janet Jintoe watches me; Janet acts like she has designs on my soul, even though I made her the Monitor she is today.* Steph clenches both breasts in her hands, rolls her palms on her spigots, and returns her hands to her sides.

I think Janet's Roommate Darleen provides a bad influence upon her. I haven't figured out if Darleen is a MomCap, a hovering Monitor, or a Pledge; she might be superior to Janet, equal to her, or a Caste beneath. I just know I never liked her and I still don't.

And then there is William. Steph looks toward the Cam and feels the presence of William, the Monitor of the Peacock House, *looking into my eyes and surveying my bleached and spread crotch. Laughing at my predicament. Laughing at me.*

And I'm not going to stop you from looking.

Now Steph looks at herself in the mirror; this more careful look discerns that two lines now show through underneath the stiffening, colorless bleached scruff. The double lines are the troughs between her inner and outer lips, and Steph can see that her inner lips are stuck shut.

Steph squints. "Go ahead," she silently mouths to William via the Cam. "Admire my spigots and snooch. And jerk off. I'm coming to get you next Term!"

Such hostility! Indeed were not William and Steph fellow Monitors last Term? And during a brief encounter during *The Arrivals* did not William represented he was a Hover this Term? Didn't they agree to hook up sometime?

All true. But then, Steph recounts, *William and his camming sidekick Rodney turn up at the Cosmos House Dining Room the day Beka worshiped the Baseboard Strippers. William provided the thermoprobe that sounded my rectum. And I bet he wanked off later at the thought of me!*

As for Rodney, he doesn't know that I once got to watch him last Term stroke his rod and see how far he could shoot. He lost that contest. He probably leaks lube all the time. And Tiffany claims to have made him spot himself, twice.

Steph drifts. *This Term Rodney cammed my sizzle and stern star. Like the Cam does now,* Steph observes. She looks to the Cam and mouths words, "Hot hot hot. Titters and twat. 98.6 in my anus." She blinks and comes to her senses, purses her lips, and observes the Cam still watching. She mouths a wish directed to William and Rodney, "May the both of you cocksuck and bumfuck each other."

And feels her snapper go slippery again. This time she looks in the mirror and *I'm not sure I can see this or not.* She feels Williams eyes drill into her. *Maybe you collected me spotting one drop in the Dining Room during* The Arrivals. *Okay,* Steph body twitches, *I can't stop you from looking at my smoo right now, but I am not going to spot for you!*

Or any other Gamer! Like who? Like MomCap, that's who! *I bet even Madam Nurse Beautician, whoever she is, watches me. All the Peacocks watch me, even the Corvettes envy me!*

Steph considers the origins of her currently absent undershirt/minidress. *The Snot House. I wonder if the Snots looks at me?"* Steph sours, *Uuugg, because I would never have anything to do with cross-dressing transsexuals, however they parse out. Maybe they were the first to Cam me naked spread surrender, and maybe they kept the videos exclusive.*

This, my second naked spread surrender, is anything but exclusive, albeit my first for a Cosmos Cam. I know Babs lets the Bathroom Cam— the Pee-Cam—feed the Prefecture whenever it's active. I know I did last Term. And it's active now, so I'm in Automatron forever.. Steph gathers air into her body and glares at the Cam. *You're all going to pay for looking at me once I'm back in control!*

§ Molly & Steph: Molly Pisses on Undershirt & Masturbates

As the time approaches to rinse the bleach out of Steph's hair, Molly disengages from her chair and lazy masturbations and Steph watches in the mirror as Molly performs behind her. She watches Molly procure the Measuring Cup, carefully urinate into it, pour the Cup into the toilet, fill another Cup, and repeat her actions. Bladder emptied, Molly logs her name and date and Cups on the Logging Chart on the wall.

Steph fears what happens next.

Molly collects Steph's undershirt out of the toilet bowl, wrings it out, and sends Steph for a hair rinse and shower. Possibly Steph sneaks a stream while the water washes over her still-naked body. But the Cam lingers on Molly.

Molly now uses Steph's undershirt dress as a rag to clean up any traces of bleach and to clean up the floor. She rings the rag out again, rolls it up, and when Steph returns, she bides her to lift her arms again, and sweeps the rolled tube downward around Steph's body until the rolled up undershirt hangs from her hips. It drapes across her posterior rugage and hangs between her navel and pubic hair.

Steph passes a hand through what used to be long blonde hair on her head and feels the deadness of bleached hair. The Cam examining her can't stop her from feeling the strands protecting her slit, and these also feel brittle. *I'm a topless bottomless tube-belt, just like what Janet reduced my minidress to during the Lineup in the Backyard, three days ago. Except now I've got bleached-out pubic hair. Bleached out hair on my head too. And with my undershirt dirty and wet.*

Once again Steph looks in the mirror and considers the Cam surveying her. She checks her snooch. *Don't worry, no slippery for you!*

"You owe me big time," Steph says to Molly.

It doesn't matter for what. "Don't worry," Molly promises, "You can take my panties anytime, except here in the Bathroom, because here I'm a naked Pee-Camer."

Molly indicates for Steph to unroll her undershirt and work her arms through the armholes. Steph hustles to struggle back into the damp Garment, and position the undershirt to make sure her button shows out. Steph grimaces. *It feels wet and clammy. Makes my spires hard and my sand dollars bumpy.*

"Sit," Molly suggests, indicating one of the makeup chairs, and positions herself in the chair adjacent. "The only thing you have to do is keep your legs spread. You do whatever you want. Me, I've got nothing better to do than play with myself." Molly draws the Cam away from Steph, opens her merrymaker, diddles her maraschino, and spills fresh meringue out onto the chair seat.

Steph curls her nose. "Maybe Elle will visit and lolly up after you. Too bad you're allowed to collect piss but not mung in your mouth."

Molly defends. "Steph, I'm allowed to eat pussy and swallow the Dong in my mouth. You and me both. So take my panties please and you won't have to share with me. Please let me Pledge naked and cum be a Stripper next Term!"

§ Robyn Threatens Molly & Steph: Equal Roommate Obeisance

Robyn breezes into the Bathroom. The Roommates see her first behind them in the mirror before she comes around in front of them to evaluate Steph's bleach job. Steph shifts her weight ever so slightly, naked Molly lazily fingers her own clit.

Robyn seems to have forgotten that the undershirt is not where she had commanded it be but smells it anyway. She purses her lips as a symbol of power, runs her hand down her maillot and tilts her head toward Steph. "Oooh, Steph sitting with her legs apart… and nothing in between them. I like how your undershirt doesn't quite cover your butt cheeks. And your nipples make headlights."

Robyn gathers steam. "I gather that buttonholeless is not something you want to repeat?"

Steph bites her lips. "Ma'am, no, Ma'am." And trades eyes with the Cam surveying her open satchel flaps. Gamers know Steph's back story: last Term then-Monitor Steph got cocky, covered her button, and is lucky to be a Pledge this Term. Gamers also know Robyn helped seal Steph's Fate.

Robyn laughs and gestures dismissively to the Cam. "The Cam is the least of your problems. You are naïve in your self-appraisal; you are about to get twisted. Wrung out."

Robyn rolls her shoulders. "Now that you have been deprived of your natural color and you spread yourself for the Cam, the time has come to surge splurt like all the other Cosmos. Like Molly here. You're gonna pink and Pee-Cam!"

Enough! Steph snaps at her fellow Pledge, "Listen to me, you pretty little rum doxy. You're gonna pay for treating me like this! I am not your Roommate. It's too bad it will take you two Terms before you can rim, ream and runt full time. And I hope it gets really painful when you make Slavesex."

Robyn digests this insult, and counter-taunts Steph about the always-keep-thighs-apart Rule. "However, right now you're an upskirting vagflasher." Robyn pulls her head back like a bird, "One Garment and a spread snatch!"

Steph scowls and talks back, "Yeah? And my naked masturbating Roommate Molly keeps begging to give her panties to me."

"But they are not here to give you!" Robyn says, correctly; Pee-Camer Molly, sitting in the makeup chair adjacent to Steph, may only enter the Bathroom naked.

Robyn snides, "Besides Steph, you already got to try them on." Robyn leans forward. "Remember? Figure Drawing Class, Photoshoot, and that wild, wild Bachelor Party!" Robyn waggles a finger toward Molly. "Molly volunteered to suck pee out of them to get them back."

"Molly will do anything so she doesn't have to streak to the Nugget next Term," Steph retorts.

"Listen to me, you skeezy shag skank!" Robyn angles her head forward. "You got to see Molly lick up after Kimju today; she's pink, creamed, and climaxed. And what have you contributed to the Game? All you've done is flash your flat rosy spigots and slot machine. Steph Sanpan. That's you. You want to know something? After you dye your scrag white you can shave yourself a racing stripe and advance your slitage." Robyn tosses her head back. "Ha ha ha!"

Like Beka's racing strip, bare lips though. Steph grits her teeth. *I didn't appreciate vagflashing before I took the panties from Molly the first time, and I especially don't like it that I'm flashing again. It is an ominous sign when winnings get reversed.*

"Beg me to off-shoulder one of your shoulder straps," Robyn commands. "Maybe you can even let your spout show out."

"Maybe you and I should Flip-Flop," Steph projects a nasty to Robyn.

"Listen, you stinking screw socket, I'm not your Roommate," Robyn snaps.

Steph escalates a taunt to Robyn, "Then maybe you should Flip-Flop with your Roommate Kimju. You'd look cute in a thong. Show off your rack and your rear end. Maybe you can beg Monitor Babs to just order a swap, and use all that Charm that you got."

Robyn closes her eyes and shakes her head slightly, unfazed, "Boss Bitch knows better than to confuse me with that excuse for a Roommate: some topless tanga kloop kuder knockabout ex-Stripper. Kimju. Need I remind you that Kimju has moved into the Doghouse?"

Steph shifts her position in the chair. She discovers that her undershirt-minidress has rolled up into a bunch directly beneath her stern and begins to hurt, and she ever so carefully wiggles the undershirt up so that she is able to sit on her completely bare semiglobes. Legs completely spread wide, thin bleached blonde hair above and to the sides. *If I lean forward the Cam collects armhole titter when the wet fabric falls away. If I lean back the wet fabric hangs on my ribs and outlines my sand dollars and spires perfectly.*

"I shall let you in on a secret," Robyn prides. "I'm about to Flip-Flop Beka and Elle; the time has come for Elle to showcase her nookie."

Robyn scowls at Steph, "The time has come for you beg to dig down inside your scruffy socket and pull your satchel flaps apart."

Steph stiffens. "You know, Robyn, you're just BB's mouthpiece retread. Every time you fill up a Kotex with blood you drain your brains out."

Robyn glowers, "Maybe *you* should beg to dip Molly's panties into urine, stuff them into *your* mouth, and suck panty pee. Since you want panties so much. You'd look pretty cute streaming urine out the sides of your mouth."

Steph recalls a scene, *Molly streaming urine out of her mouth at the Bachelor Party.*

Steph process Robyn chortling over her. "Ha ha ha. Your Roommate made Piss Mouth; now it's your turn to match Game! No Winner-Takes-All for you, you're going to Flip-Flop and end up running around wearing just panties with your flat shimmies out."

Steph does not believe Robyn possesses Charm. "Listen to me, Pledge, I am going to acquire a second Garment. And once I get a chance I'm going to come after you, raghole," Steph admonishes Robyn. She shifts her weight, waves her arms, but maintains her spread crotch, "Don't think I'm going to keep running around titter and v-flash. I need a second Garment, so I do not to run around topless... or naked. I'm not about to pink my snapper or hold it wide open. Hear what I say: When the time comes for me to grab another garment Monitor Babs won't stop me. So watch out Miss Maillot. Because if you Redact yourself again I'm going to be your Monitor next Term again!"

Robyn falters before this assault and Steph expresses even more self-confidence, "Never forget that I am the most popular Cosmos! I'm premium."

Robyn knows best, "Premium?" She laughs, leans backward and points a finger forward, "You're delusional. "You're a titter and vagflash Pledge who gets passed out for free. You need to pink, cream, and climax then eat pussy and Double Dong center Stage at the Nugget." Robyn retorts. "Maybe then Gamers will let you Opt Strip." Robyn crows, "Beg me, skank."

Steph flusters, "Ma'am, please dye all my hair white, Ma'am."

Molly, sitting adjacent, rushes to interject. "Ma'am, please let me stay naked and cum be a Stripper next Term. Please let Steph take my panties. For good, Ma'am."

Robyn Redacted draws air into her lungs and then exhales; she ignores Molly and addresses her former (forgotten) Monitor. "May your Roommate Molly provide a role model for you. Beg Molly to teach you how to make pink-wet-and-ready. You shall audition the Nugget, just like her. But no climax until I decide you're ready to blast off a salvo or two." Robyn forcefully snorts at Steph. "Everybody has it in for you: Boss Bitch, Janet, all the other House Monitors, all the MomCaps and Dads, the Madams and Pimps, and even the Game Masters and Mistresses."

"And that's the good news." Robyn picks snot out of her nose and flicks it at Steph. "You're even gonna have to kowtow to the downtrodden. You're gonna get drafted to tip Strippers, kiss Whores, and piss on Slavesex." Robyn wrinkles her nose, " And trust me, you're not playing any Winner-Takes-All. I've decided you and Molly are going to Flip-Flop."

Molly glances at Robyn and glances at the Cam, rubs both nipples up, and spittles her mainspring.

Robyn snarls. "Now both of you get out of here. Go prostrate yourself at the Post Henge. Wraps your arms around your Posts. Move it. Now!"

Robyn chortles as Molly and Steph scramble out the Bathroom door. And with bleached out Steph begging white hair.

§ Molly & Steph: Negotiate A Winner-Takes-All Contest

Passing through the Bunkroom, Molly and Steph observe Beka and Elle remain deeply engrained in making out, but Molly does not detour to collect her panties.

Kimju, still in the Doghouse beneath the Back Landing hears their bare footsteps pass overhead, hears them ring the Bell. Molly and Steph trade eyes with Tiffany, naked and filthy in the Mudpit and masturbating herself for the Back Door Cam. The Cam, sated with Tiffany, pivots and follow them as they lie themselves down in the dirt and hug their arms around the two middle Henge Posts.

Molly, still naked, plops her fat and hairy body into the earth: mammies splayed to the sides, moons up, thick thighs not touching, mutton fresh. Steph, still wearing her dirty long undershirt with its ripped-out button hole, pulls it down as best she can over her cheeking semi-globes and she stretches prone onto her belly. Vagflash? Unavoidable.

No directive prohibits them from talking; their only mission is to hold onto their Posts; and yes, keep their legs apart. Molly, never wanting to be caught short on a Rule, widens her things until her legs qualify as open position. Steph, unsure at first, follows her.

"I hate Robyn Redacted." Steph seethes. "I hate BB too, but I hate Robyn the most. When the time comes, I'm going to crush her."

"In Robyn's past you were her protector," Molly observes, "but you also let her be sadistic, just like Babs does."

"I gave her every opportunity. I let her pick her own maillot. Then I discovered that she was hazing the Cosmos Pledge on her own, and when I tried to stop her, she framed me." Steph sputters. "She's a dangerous, lying, rag mop. I haven't forgotten what she did to me. I'll get her. You'll see."

Molly philosophizes, "Seems like Robyn's memories have dissolved, no matter how or why."

"Right!" Steph rubs a fist into the dirt. "And now Boss Bitch uses her as a sycophant and overzealous hatchet girl to haze me, and that's personal and deliberate. BB knows what she's doing, she thinks I was rude to her last Term, when in fact she owes her promotion to me! Bikini Baldober is stupid, and Robyn Ragabash is a cheat."

Molly ventures, "Somehow at the end of last Term Robyn never really acquired the necessary two pieces to Opt Up, yet she somehow didn't Opt Down either?"

Steph snaps, "Now there is an exception to House Rules!"

"I hear she was allowed to Redact the Term in exchange for outing you," Molly ventures.

"Outing me? What does that mean?" Steph lets go of the Post with one hand, but contains her temper. "It means she covered my buttonhole while I wasn't looking and took snapshots." Steph tucks the side of her head aside the pole and worms her neck against it. "Listen, Stripper wannabe, I should not be your Roommate or sharing the Cosmos House with Robyn; Robyn should be pinking at the Nugget, and I should be the House Mom el Capitan in charge of it all!"

Molly offers a superstition, "Kimju thinks Robyn is blessed with Charm. Robyn really does act like she's an invaluable personality."

Steph snaps, "And that her suggestive maillot with its tiny buttonhole empowers her."

Molly considers, "Robyn treats all of us nasty, Steph, and not just you. She has already made some of us pink, cream, and climax this Term. Kimju and I have had to masturbate to our old clips. I guess I didn't mind, but Kimju thought it was unfair and humiliating and that she should be past that. Besides, I'll dong with anyone, but Kimju needs persuasion to go over the top."

Steph considers, "If you say so. Kimju is Robyn's Roommate so I will let them sort themselves out. Absent a Game they will both become Strippers next Term."

Steph defends. "Maybe last Term I got stuck with Robyn as my Roommate, but she was never anything other than a burden to me. She betrayed me. I hate her… and consider her a ripe costume prospect. After all, her maillot, worn under my minidress, would provide the necessary two pieces for me to Opt Up." Steph considers her body as she lies on the earth on top of her undershirt. *And solve my flashing problems.*

Molly objects to Steph's strategy. "Wait a minute, Steph, I've already promised to give you *my* panties! I'm easy pickings." Molly massive mammies rub into the dirt, she lifts her head, and brushes her round ass, only to cover it with earth.

"I appreciate your panties, Molly," Steph steels, "Really I do. And I will take them from you. After I take them I shall trade them for Robyn's maillot. You would still get to stay naked, but that leaves Robyn topless tanga. Too bad she can't be my initial target."

"Be careful Steph," Molly warns, "Kimju's holding off on her because if Robyn really is Charmed Kimju could lose. Kimju's already logging her Pee-Cam, just like Tiffany and me. You could lose too, if you got in a situation with her." Molly shuffles and rolls her melons in moist dirt. "Any of us could lose to her; you got to admit, she does lack fear."

Steph ponders, "Lacking fear doesn't equal being brave."

Molly begs, "Please Steph, take my panties! And you got all you need to Opt Up. No more skuddy upskirt."

Steph speculates, "Kimju has no choice but to Game with Robyn because if she doesn't, her one Garment commits her to Opt Strip next Term. She can't get a second Garment if she doesn't play a Roommate Game with Robyn first. Sooner or later Kimju knows she must fight. And I can't think of a better Fate for Robyn than popping ping pong balls out her rent at the Nugget."

Molly stays silent. Then speaks, "Please take my panties Steph. They're on the shelf next to my bunk. They're yours."

Steph considers and advances, "And in the Term after next, I want to see Robyn become a scrunched-down Whore getting fucked up the ass at

Flesh Ranch. I'd like to see her naked, covered in sticky goo, tossed into a splooge pit where she can flail and cry tears, and get three-hole gangbanged. And then another Term to see her turned into Slavesex and flogged in the Cravat and get a cock shoved down her throat and phlegm spilling out the mouth! I want to see marks on her! I want her bukkaked and branded!"

Molly cautions, "Easy does it Steph! Maybe there's reasons why she's repeating. I mean, she's the only Cosmos whose vital assets have never been uncovered, aside from her bare shoulders and legs, the subtlest of cleavage and her little buttonhole. She gets what she wants; it's like she does have Charm."

Steph's eyes narrow "Listen, Molly, you can convince me to take your panties—and I will—but you can't convince me there is any such thing as Charm. That ragabash double crossed me."

"Monitor Babs says you let Robyn get away with it Last Term," Molly advances.

Steph brisks, " And BB lets her get away with it now."

Steph brushes dirt on her cheek. Her undershirt rides up enough so that her pelvis and crotch grind in the dirt, and her backside hemi-spheres now display most of themselves to the daylight. Paparazzi harvest, the Cam feeds the Prefecture, and Automatron's spools the shots into its archives.

Steph grovels forward onto her undershirt and works up onto her elbows, hands and head still hugging the pole. The undershirt falls away and she titters. The Cam collects from one then the other side. Steph ignores the intrusions, she expounds, "You want to know what I think? I suspect Babs and Janet are setting Robyn up, giving her a big confidence boost." Steph asserts, "I know a few things about Robyn, she was my Pledge last Term after all, and 'naïve' and 'careless' are two words that come to mind, be she Redacted or not. She's a vicious, confused hot mess, with no sense of who she is, what, when, or where she is, or why she exists. She is dangerous to be around. Not that I really care about Kimju, but she has more risk than any other Cosmos."

Molly makes a final pleading, "Please Steph, when you go upstairs put my panties on! I do whatever you want. I'll beg Tiffany for hair softeners and I'll wash your hair for you. I'll scratch your back. I'll wash your undershirt. Groom you. You can shave me bare bald and naked. I'll service your smoo. I'll Double Dong. Just take my panties, please!"

"Listen," Steph tells Molly, "Forget about you and I doing a Flip-Flop. Maybe that's what Robyn wants, but that's not going to happen."

Steph flattens herself on her belly and uses the time to evaluate.

Molly provides. "Some Gamers argue that a Flip-Flop isn't a fair Game, because the more covered Pledge always has more to lose and less to win."

Steph snaps, "Some Gamers say fairness isn't essential for fun."

Molly, still naked, brushes dirt out of armpit hair. She irritates, "Maybe it would be fair for you to runaround with your shimming flat out. How would you like to go to the Mermaid Parade wearing just wet-see-through panties?"

The Watering Can isn't a part of any Flip-Flop," Steph insists. "And besides, you'd never fit in my dirty undershirt incarnation of a minidress," she reinforces.

"I need to Pledge naked and cum be a Stripper next Term," Molly repeats.

"You need to lose a Winner-Takes-All," Steph reminds. "I'll Opt Up and you'll Opt Down. Deal."

Molly concurs. "It would put a stop to all your titter and vagflash. And my odds of getting to the Nugget increase. My only problem is I would be naked 24x7. Being naked inside the House or even here in the Backyard is one thing, but I had to streak during *The Arrivals* and I don't want to have to streak again. Because if I get caught streaking I could be in Lockdown for the rest of this Term. And next Term, I could be like, who knows?"

"You need to demand a Winner-Takes-All Game, so that I can pick the contest," Steph provides.

Molly sighs, "I will do that, but please, no rush, Steph, the longer we wait the less chance I get caught in a streak."

Steph draws in a deep breath. The undershirt rides completely above her stern division, baring the base of her spine and threatening to reveal her lozenge of Michaelis and sacral dimples. Right now, Steph cares about other things. *There's a vibe from Robyn to Flip-Flop me and my Roommate. And Boss Bitch will let Robyn do this, and I'm going to end up nearly naked with wet panties yanked up my snatch and stern crack. I have no choice but to move now.*

Steph adjusts her undershirt mostly down over her dual semiglobes and sets conditions. "Fine, Molly, but understand me, that if Robyn is about to force us to Flip-Flop and you're slow on the call, then I'm going to go ahead and demand we Game a Winner-Takes-All."

Molly nods, "No problem, Steph, you do whatever you want. And once you challenge me, I'll pick a Game I'm sure to lose."

Molly recoils and points toward a small spider that has walked onto the back of Steph's hand as it clenches the Post. Steph looks at the focus of Molly's horror, draws her hand to her mouth, sucks the spider in, and swallows.

"Don't you dare double cross me," Steph advises her Roommate.

Molly looks at Steph's hand, "I was afraid it might bite you, sting you, poison you to death."

"Probably weaves a web like Janet's Spiderweb Bikini." Steph her Roommate. "Beg me to take on any bad Karma put upon me," she declares.

"Ma'am," Molly begs, "I'll take on all your begs, all your Obeisance, and all your exposures. I'll even keep the Watering Can. Just please help me Pledge naked and cum be a Stripper next Term! I belong to you, Ma'am."

II-8 Babs Pinks Molly & Steph: For Visitors & the Cams (D18)

§ Babs Surveys Tiffany & Kimju: Mudpit & Doghouse

The sound of the Back Door slamming followed by the Bell draws Tiffany and Molly and Steph's eyes toward the Bikini Beauty descending from the landing.

Tiffany watches from the Mudpit. She qualifies as naked, even though she is covered with urine and mud. Head to toe, hair soaked. *If you make me a Porn Star again, I'll come back and fuck my brains out right here.*

Molly and Steph watch from the Post Henge. They have remained prostrate and clenching their Posts. Molly presents a naked body lying in the dirt; Steph wears a minidress disguised as an undershirt. It has ridden up sufficently so that Steph's entire stern exposes itself to full view.

And with the Back Door Cam darting about he Backyard, "full view" means every last pimple high resolution out to the Prefecture. And no chance to reach around and tug the undershirt downward. Both keep their legs spread; Molly will cream before being asked to, Steph has some learning to do.

Inside the Doghouse, a place of confined inconvenience, Kimju wonders, *Robyn put me here, so does BB even know I am in here? She can't even see me here.*

Kimju tinkled a long time ago. *It doesn't matter if there is a secret infrared Cam watching me here or not, there will be a Cam watching me tinkle from now on.* Kimju had pulled her thong down to her knees and tried to pee in the corner of the box, *but I ended in lying in my own puddle of wet soil anyway. My hair is a mess too. And my peehole and insides are itchy with sunburn.*

Kimju hears Boss Babe's bare feet move away from the Landing and Doghouse beneath. The footsteps stop at the edge of the Mudpit. Bikini Babe stands tall: underwire bra with extreme cleavage and areolage and a culotte nombril with a horizontal waistline four inches below navel. Leglines only slightly arching up from the crotch. Leglines not unlike those of Robyn's maillot cutout, although Robyn isn't here in the Backyard.

Babs considers her naked, covered-in-mud from head to toe, Roommate.

"I came," Tiffany admits.

"I bet you did!" BB exclaims. "What are you doing here? I run an errand and—"

"Robyn ordered me," Tiffany states. "That's what you get for letting her train your Cosmos Pledge."

Babs closes and opens her eyes.

Tiffany waits. White eyeballs in an face otherwise covered in mud. Hair full of mud. She augments, "Later she came by with the hose and gave me more to drink."

Boss Babe amuses herself. "Perhaps you should thank Robyn for letting your fans watch you sneak a climax." BB smiles. "Hose yourself down, go inside and shower, and after you dry off, clean up your tracks."

"If you let me stay naked, Ma'am, I'll sit spread in the Kitchen and masturbate to my Porn Star Calendar," Tiffany suggests.

BB groans. "Sounds like a plan."

Tiffany reaches. "Ma'am can I let the Back Door Cam follow me in? Please, Ma'am. I know I can climax again."

"Oh, listen to you, my wannabe Porn Star who begs to be naked." Babs laughs, "Of course you can't. Molly and Steph need get their turn."

The hose water bubbles up Tiffany's skin, and she rings the Bell before she drips across the landing and through the Back Door.

Inside the Doghouse, Kimju knows Tiffany was wet because she feels the drips later on.

§ Babs visits Molly & Steph: Post Henge Game Proposals

Yes, Molly and Steph remain on their bellies. Each grasps opposite Posts, both are basically naked from their waists down; Molly is naked completely. Both keep their legs open. Or spread. Or apart. Never closed. Never crossed. Never their decision.

Sometime during the afternoon Robyn had returned, struggling with a full Watering Can, and wet the both of them down. Them and the earth they lay in.

Babs purses her lips. The negative air pressure in her mouth draws her inner cheeks together, and slightly concaves her cheeks. Now the Cam devotes its full attention to the stately House Monitor. Boss Babe laughs inwardly. *Go ahead, Cam, observe my bling. I'm so over that now.* BB tucks to make sure her legline keeps all her butt in, and touches her bra straps. *A bad habit.* She tucks thumbs inside her waistband.

"I see on the feeds that you're begging a Flip-Flop with Molly?" Babs proposes.

Steph quickens, "Ma'am, that was Robyn's suggestion, and way premature."

Molly straight-talks, "Ma'am, please, Steph and I have different needs. I'll stay naked and Opt Strip. Steph can take my panties and Opt Up next Term."

"It appears Steph and you both are preoccupied hugging your Henge Posts," BB observes. "No way for Steph to take anything at the moment."

Molly, lying on her belly naked in the dirt, details, "My panties lie on my shelf. If you let her she can go take them now."

Steph, also lies in the dirt and holds onto her Post. She is not naked but her undershirt has risen to well above her stern. "It was Robyn's suggestion that Molly and I should Flip-Flop, that's not even a Game, we'd still both end up Strippers," she explains. "Robyn's haughtiness is a provocation directed toward me, and she's not even my Roommate."

Steph hurries her words. "What Molly and I really need is a Winner-Takes-All Game."

Boss Babe purses her lower lip forward, raises her black eyebrows, and looks at a Molly nod. "I like that," BB agrees. "May the Winner-Take-All!"

Babs irritates Steph, "Maybe Molly should challenge you to a dance-off at the Nugget?"

Steph blinks. *Ouch! This is not a place where I would ever consider performing! And not an competition I care to relish.*

Molly misses the point. "Ma'am, please, I'll spread and lose my pee while orgasming center Stage at the Nugget. I'll climax the Double Dong every hole with every Pledge. I'll do whatever I need to do so give Steph a Winner-Takes-All."

Steph tells Babs, "You should make Molly pee into her own mouth, prove she's serious, and grant her wish to Opt Down."

Molly begs Babs, "Ma'am, please let me stay a naked Pledge and cum be a Stripper next Term.

Steph wipes her fingers across her brow and addresses Monitor Babs. "You should believe Molly, Ma'am. She wants to lose. She'll go as dark as she needs to."

"As dark as I'm allowed," Molly corrects. "Plus new things you haven't seen before."

"Maybe you should both audition the Nugget," Boss Babe proposes. "Winner-Takes-All, including the Pee-Cam!"

Molly bursts, "Including the Piss Mouth!"

Steph's worries darken. *No, I don't think so. No way I'm about to abandon myself sexually in front of a Nugget Crowd. And at the Nugget, Molly may be unable to perform badly and lose.*

Boss Babe adds a flourish: "Loser can streak back to the Cosmos House."

Naked, obviously, and Steph allows, "Molly, under cover of darkness."

Molly interjects, "I had to streak to the Bachelor Party in daylight! Steph, just please take my panties!" Molly whines, "Please Steph. I know I'll have to streak some more, and take on all your Obeisance. I don't need panties anymore, especially wet. I'm better off naked."

Steph instructs Molly, "Tell Monitor Babs that a Winner-Takes-All at the Nugget is not Game you want to play."

Molly rubs her mams in the dirt, looks up, "Ma'am, must I repeat all that?"

Boss Babe presents a foot for Molly to kiss. "You may select a different Game then."

Steph shivers. *I don't like where this might lead.* She constricts her vagina and feels the inside of her pussy make wet. *Damn,* Steph says to herself, *This place is getting to me.*

Boss Babe advances the Roommates. "Roll over, both of you, then scooch up and rest your backs on your Posts, sitting and facing each other."

Molly and Steph obey; they discover they must bend their knees and press the soles of their feet together to keep their legs open. Steph finds it easiest to rest a bare stern on the earth; Molly has no choice in the matter. Molly moves her hands to the Post behind her back, and Steph, cautious, follows form. The Roommates look each other in the eye, look over each other's crotch. Steph has bleached short and waives; Molly has a thick black muff.

Steph discovers that one of her undershirt sleeves has fallen off-shoulder, and in an attempt to stabelize it one nipple squirms loose and escapes the top of Steph's excuse for a minidress. *Should I fix it?* she wonders. And looks at Molly. *Molly sits naked and spread.* Steph casts her eyes at BB and understands to leave her one nipple exposed.

Boss Babe addresses Steph. "Let me tell you what you can do. First, get out of your undershirt straps completely and roll that excuse for a minidress down into a tube belt, up above your belly button. That's your look from now on. Unless you'd rather share your undershirt with Molly?"

"Ma'am, I'll keep it, thank you, "Ma'am. Steph scrambles and rolls the undershirt-dress into a tight bundle. *Been there done that, you stupid Bling Boob Bikini Babe!* Steph needles, "I already had to do this for Janet, then Molly, now I'll do it for you too."

"Much obliged," Boss Babe praises. "And keep it that way from now on."

Steph's undershirt tube belt hangs from the crests of her ilium, sweeps across her belly below her navel, and graces the top of her stern crack. Otherwise, *I might as well be as naked as Molly, except I am full-frontal. Like I was upstairs on that Cam.*

What's next? Pinching my nipples and lolling my tongue like a cheap skank?

§ Babs Ensures Molly & Steph: Get Pinking Equality

Upstairs it had been Robyn's hand that guided Molly to render Steph naked and open her legs for the bleach job. Now at the Post Henge, here in the Backyard, Boss Babe commands. She addresses Steph directly. "I've heard you've said that Robyn is running me, and she is unjust with you."

Steph grips the Post tighter. *I feel my whole body displayed. The Back Cam, the paparazzi. Near naked and open-legs.*

Boss Babe walks behind her former Monitor, catches Molly silently in the eye, and signs her to spread, pink, and masturbate.

Molly shuffles her mammoth weight, and obeys. Molly might have a thick bush but she reaches around in front and pulls her lips wide with opposing hands. Steph looks and can see all of her deep brown insides. She startles as she watches light sparkle on the stainless steel clithood ring, a painful accoutrement of Opt Stripping that Steph finds thrust into her vision. *Not for me!* Steph asserts.

Steph looks down at her own opened crotch. *Bleached short and waives with some of them breaking off at the roots. And I suspect the Cam can see my slit through my brittle hair.*

It can. Single line.

Steph rests her hands behind her. She reaches behind her and grasps her Post. *Safety there.*

Molly lazily fingers her clit, relaxes, steadies her breathing, and settles in for a long wait. *The next play in the Game will happen when it happens,* she says to herself. *I still have one piece in the Game until Steph takes it from me, even though I left it back in the Bunkroom and am staying naked now.*

Boss Babe advances the duo. "Gaze upon each other's pussies, and admire each other. Don't look anywhere else. You're quite lovely you know!"

Both obey but Steph declares, "I never made you do this."

"Maybe not this," Bikini Babe retorts, "but you made me humiliate myself in public."

"This is different," Steph defends, keeping her eyes on Molly fingering her maraschino and showing a hole inside her inner lips.

"This is different because you are different. This is humiliation for you."

"You lie." Steph argues. "You humiliate all your Pledge in Public."

"Fine, so I do." BB concedes, "And so you're not special. You're just one of the pack. Now you see that meatlocker staring you in the face? With the big mange around miche that gets purple down inside. Anything about that not to like? You can even see Molly's little peehole, her clithood, and her puckered mawk pipe. I guess the Cam has already collected your tailpipe, but the time has come for you to match Molly and open your inner lips up."

Steph hesistates. "Ma'am, I never treated you like this. You don't need to do this to me to prove to me you're superior Caste. Just tell me what to do and I'll obey you, Ma'am."

"Thank you, Pledge" Boss Babe affirms. "I need to convince you that Robyn isn't running me." BB smiles. "Let me remind you that the Cam is my witness. Now obey me or my commands will be obeyed for you. Janet won't be the last Cosmos to sit Cravat."

Steph keeps her eyes on Molly's mooe and yields. She draws her fingers around and onto her sex lips, wiggles the fingertips through the thin brittle bleached hair, and separates her outers. The Cam collects the details, so too do any gyro-stabilized paparazzi telephoto overlooking the Cosmos House Backyard. Steph knows that her inners are slippery on the inside but still stuck together at the rim, but her stamen stands clear of her hood, and her peehole shows out. Her face flushes and her spouts erect.

"Stay like this," Boss Babe commands them, "Don't take your eyes off the other's pink and keep your clits stood up.

And they do. They hear the Bell ring and Babs disappear inside the Back Door, but both know not to take their eyes off the other's spread pink. Perseverance matters.

§ Steph & Molly: Steph Reacts to Her First Pink Performance

Steph finds the world spinning. She knows in her mind that *I deserve to win any pending Winner-Takes-All. Even Molly wants me to win! My Roommate and I are not equals; we never were. And our outcome is decided. I am going to Opt Monitor and Molly's an Opt Pee-Camming Piss Mouth Stripper next Term. She'll be carrying a bigger portfolio than ever before.*

Steph tries to put out of her mind that the Cam surveys her innermost regions. *I can't get more naked than this.* She focuses on Molly for a moment. *Yes I can.*

Steph squints and calculates ahead of the Game, *Okay, so right now both Molly and I pink our vages. That's the easy part. Because beyond naked, Molly's also keeps masturbating, she even hangs mung for Elle to lolly up.* Steph steels herself. *And I'm glad Bling Bitch made me roll my undershirt tighter; I wrung more urine out and the tube doesn't keep me damp all over.*

Steph circumspects as she watches her Roommate lazily finger her very ripe maraschino, dig fingers of her opposite hand deep into her purple, rotate, and scoop a palm full of thick white creamy meringue out.

Steph scowls at this uninhibited display of self-pleasure. *We all saw Molly's masturbation and toy videos from last Term, her explicit magazine layouts, website climaxes, and this Term's Pee-Cams. In fact, I saw Molly suck her own piss out of her panties at the Bachelor Party!*

Steph clenches her teeth and flushes, she feels her spigots tighten, and worries that her inner lips might seep. *Me pinking is different. And right now Molly and I aren't just pinking, we are pinking together; our eyes and gynos are connected!*

Steph feels a deep stirring of Kundalini deep inside, awakening. She furrows her brow as she looks into Molly's muliebre. *Careful now! I've not only watched Molly climaxed, I've watched her kiss girls, she says she'll eat snapper and lap slop, and she's begging to Double Dong any Pledge. She believes all that, but I know I'm better than that!*

Steph feels herself drifting now, a panic attack? *Am I going to leak splurt out of my slit too?* Steph gathers her breath. *I know the answer. When it comes to any secretions, Molly goes first. She's already presenting.*

Well, I've presented too, albeit only one drop.

No rush. Right now two Roommates stare into each other's opened sexual organs. Steph's eyes keep getting drawn to Molly's stainless, but after a while Steph realizes *that Molly continues to slowly erupts a thick white* meringue from her mound.

Steph's body makes a very soft series of shakes, and constricts. *I must be careful holding myself open, least I too ooze wetness.* Steph continues to stare at Molly's clithood ring and the muscovado oozing downward toward her mawkeye. No rush to shake.

Steph dares not turn her head to explore her own wetness but when she hears the Cam behind her she does tilt her eyes up toward Molly's face. Molly, with her eyes focused upon Steph's sex cavity, never sees Steph lift her head.

Steph recalls. *Yes, I secretly got to see Molly dance live at the Nugget, the night of Tiffany and Janet's Alumni Reprise. That molliwog let lapdance clients fondle her mammies and finger her holes.*

Earlier, Steph had assumed she had a monopoly on this secret. *Except so far during* The Runup, *Robyn seems to have access to Kimju and Molly's lapdance archive. Still, I bet Robyn doesn't know I watched Janet turn Tiffany into a Piss Mouth, or see Tiffany climax Janet on the Double Dong.*

Only Janet knows I was there that night, and Janet would never share this secret, because Janet will hold it over me when she wants something from me. And she can't do that if the Cosmos know.

Steph struggles to keep her mind on the task. *My task is to gaze at Molly's vagina.* And she returns her eyes to it at this moment. Shadows deepen as the afternoon wanes into evening, but even in the warmer air, Steph can not just see but also smell Molly now, small distance across the bent knees and touching soles.

I do not deserve to be put in this position, the broken Monitor asserts to herself. *And I especially do not deserve to be pulling pink in opposition to* this *Pledge. Molly absolutely does not deserves to be a Pledge; Molly should have been notched from the Strippers and turned into a Whore this Term.*

And I should have been promoted; I should be a House Mom el Capitan now. Molly and I should be three Castes apart, not both Pledge at this place.

Steph positions. *I need to get Molly's panties from upstairs and get this over with! After all, I am the most valuable Cosmos,* Steph reminds herself. *Premium.*

And as for Molly, Steph bites her lip. *If Molly has to streak, well, that's her problem. Molly better beg right, or I'll have to put steel in the moil.*

§ Janet & William let Molly & Steph: Play Greatest House Roar

Janet and William loom. Steph did not see them coming.
"Surprise!"
Surprise indeed. Were it not for the fact the Molly holds Steph's feet wide with her own, Steph would have clenched her thighs together.

Yes, these two Monitors from two other Houses enter the Backyard unannounced. Janet still wears a size nano Spiderweb Bikini, only today Janet choses a different color and style, one which is both boobless and crotchless as well: two open triangles frame the breasts, while the g-string adopts more of a thong silhouette, except with a hole in the crotch. William wears his trademark black t-shirt and slacks. Janet's lips flare out and her rings jangle. Monitor Janet commands the Cam.

Steph closes her eyes. *Oooh, why are they here?*
Molly processes Janet. *Jiggle jugs and Jell-O with crochet around.*
Steph feels gross, her skin crawls, she sweats, she slipperies her inside. *I feel exposed. They should not be here! Especially with BB thinking that Molly gets to pick a Winner-Takes-All Game.*

But what makes a Cosmos Pledge think they have any privacy? Especially here in the Backyard on a live Cam already feeding the Prefecture.

Janet speaks before Molly and Steph have time to blink twice. "Everyone's been following you two and is excited about your Winner-Take-All Game!"

William taunts Steph, "Gamers love your naked pinking debut."

Janet tweaks Steph's ribs with her big toe. "So why are you still wearing that filthy, stinking rag. You're disgusting. Isn't Boss Babe supposed to give you a new minidress every day?"

"Very funny, Janet," Steph retorts, "BB says it's a men's undershirt, and although it might have the same silhouette as a minidress that it isn't, and therefore she can't change it."

"So she's right in the matter, then," Janet presumes.

"Well, maybe the undershirt part," Steph hedges.

Janet breezes, "I love how you keep it rolled up in a tube. Do you keep it that way all the time so you can prance around naked?"

Steph takes no chances, "Ma'am, I do now, Ma'am. Except I'm not naked.

"At least you couldn't be busted for streaking," William acknowledges

"No way I'm wearing this anywhere!" Steph informs her former Pledge. "And the Backyard here is way past my limits."

Janet smiles, "Silly Pledge, don't you know that School is all about exercising limits?"

"You owe me," Steph asserts. "If it weren't for me you wouldn't be where you are now."

"You forced me to stay on the Pee-Cam last Term," Janet phases.

"You loved it!" Steph snaps. "You love that Gamers consider a Jell-O bag like you worth watching."

"Perhaps I also loved sitting Cravat?" Janet queries.

"You volunteered that for your Bikini Babe buddy. You always covered for her. Uncovered is more like it. Was it because you have a soft spot in your heart or because…." Steph draws in air, exhales. Twitches a lip. "Naw, it wasn't because you had a soft spot, because you don't have a soft spot in your heart for anybody. You just want to gather Garments yet at the same time expose yourself. Good luck, Monitor Janet, but never forget you must honor me, your ex-Monitor, who has done more for you than everyone else together."

"Probably more than I'll ever realize," Janet condescends. "Maybe my ex-Monitor should give her undershirt to Molly," Janet suggests. "I hear underwear attracts."

Molly interjects, "Ma'am, no please, Steph needs to go upstairs and get my panties from their shelf, and put them on."

"Nonsense," Janet decrees. "William's volunteering to host you both over at the Peacock House! More private than the Nugget. You can do a Greatest House Roar! You'll need your panties so you don't have to streak there."

William augments, "Freestyle. Each of you get to pick and do your own Game; you can't watch the other, but you can hear the guests roar!"

Janet grabs her chest with both hands and hefts her jaboos, "Greatest House Roar wins!"

Steph objects. "Wait a minute, Janet, it's not your Game to choose. Molly gets to pick."

BB nudges Molly with a bare foot, "Speak."

Molly tabulates. *Greatest House Roar. Been there done that. Will do.* She keeps her eyes glued on Steph's developing wetness and says, "Ma'am, please may we play Greatest House Roar, Ma'am."

Steph dares not look up but she knows both her former Pledge Janet and the former fellow Monitor William look down upon her predicament. A flush comes into her body, especially her face, and her spouts toughen up. Her slit quivers and Steph feels the inside of her inner lips become slippery.

Janet parlays, "Whose idea was it to show off your sex innards, Pledge?"

Steph answers, "Monitor Babs ordered me to do it, Ma'am."

"Did you thank her?" Janet inquires.

"Ma'am, I don't recall, Ma'am," Steph fidgets her fingers. *But the Cam knows.*

"If you begged me to let you touch your strophoid and cream yourself, do you think you would remember to thank me?" Janet questions.

Steph lets out a series of pants and squeezes her vagina. Kundalini constructs. "Ma'am, I'd thank you, Ma'am," Steph assures.

William interjects. "So what might you beg from your friend Janet? You're both pinking, but Molly's already transuding muscovado."

Steph hedges, "Ma'am, Molly has made cream since—"

"And climaxed as well," Janet completes. "Don't worry, you'll get your opportunity. But right now, my near-naked former Monitor Steph, you beg to cream for me."

"Ma'am!" Steph expounds. She stops, scans the limited edge of the Backyard and the houses beyond. She looks William in the eye and William cocks his head. She looks at Molly; Molly's eyes stayed glued on Steph's smoo, and Molly's minge and mutton are sopped with thick meringue. Steph looks down to her own showcase. *Full flower.* "Ma'am, please," she begs, looks at Janet, and touches her fingertip to her clit. That's all it takes to surge the slush out the inner lips, no longer hidden beneath the bleached short and curlies outside the parted outer lips. Steph feels her inner lips part. *Now I'm totally on display. I can even smell myself now, faintly.*

Not so faintly, they all can. Molly starts to twitch with excitement, and this time both of them squeeze cream together.

Steph takes a deep breath and recovers her composure. She remembers, "Ma'am, thank you, for letting me cream, Ma'am."

Augments, "So you happy now, Monitor Janet, now that you make me pink and cream on the Cam, like you did last Term,?"

Janet tosses her head back and throws her hair behind her. William lifts his eyebrows.

"I'm happy now," Janet says. "But if you want me to be as happy as you were last Term, you can beg me to cream naked and cum be a Stripper next Term. Or lock yourself into the Cravat, like I did for you."

"Like you did for Babs," Steph argues. Kundalini synchronizes both Roommates, constricts and they both surge and saturate their innards.

"Everyone got to watch Janet Cravat," William purrs, "I hear you cammed her, or did you send Robyn as your surrogate and she's forgotten she was there."

"Stop it!" Steph complains. "William, you used to be nice to me."

"I can be nice to you again." William smiles, and salutes both Roommates, "See you both at the Greatest House Roar!"

And Janet and William are gone.

Quiet returns.

Molly worries that William brought no thermoprobe today. *He brought it for Beka and then for my Roommate Steph, but he doesn't bring it to sink into me.* Molly observes that Steph has become lax at holding her inner lips open. Molly rotates a finger around the opening into her vaginal canal, tips a fingertip inside, feels the constrictor, lets muscovado flow, and zones out. Steph shivers then dries up.

It is not until after dark that Tiffany pokes her head out the Back Door and hollers them in. Tiffany makes a prediction as they ring the Bell and pass inside. "Don't give up, you two, next time you Roommates sit down together I bet that both of you will get to climax."

Nobody rescues Kimju from the Doghouse, although late at night and so silently that the Cam doesn't wake up, somebody pees on the Landing above. Kimju wakes up, well sort of, *although I'm not really getting much sleep.*

II-9 Kimju & Molly: Teach Beka & Elle to Dance (D19)

§ Babs & Tiffany & Cosmos: The Dawn of Day Nineteen

It is the morning of Day Nineteen. There are no windows on the second floor of the Cosmos House, no way for the Cosmos to tell if it is light or dark outside, and there is no Clock. Were any Cosmos to consider the House from the outside they would realize that an attic also lies above the upper floor, thus no sounds of rain on a roof would be heard in the Bunkroom. Five of six bunks here have been occupied overnight.

Steph slides the undershirt worn in the Backyard over her head to use for a pillow tonight. *Boss Babe has made it clear to me that I won't be swapping my undershirt for something more decent, so I have no reason to offer it on my shelf or hang it from the hook overnight.* Steph spirits herself to the Bathroom before anyone else rises, pees while the Cam sleeps, hesistates to wash or shower, and returns to her bunk with her skin still a blend of dust, dried urine and sweat, and no other Cosmos any wiser.

Babs arises in her Bedroom, avails herself of the privileges of her private bathroom in her Black Bikini, and returns to sit in her chair and permit Tiffany to use the Makeup Case to comb her long black hair, makeup her face, and touch up her nails.

Tiffany, still naked since yesterday, heads to the Bathroom, where her entrance lights up the Cam. She carefully empties her bladder into the Measuring Cup, squatting about the floor drain, and carefully pours each Cup down the drain after its filled. The Cam drinks it in; Tiffany wrinkles her lips with a proud satisfaction, *pleasing my fans.* She rises, and the Cam hovers with her as she logs "Tiffany, Day 19," and her number of Cups on the Logging Chart on the wall.

Tiffany observes that the Cam hovers affront her and collects a head shot. No problem. She draws the Measuring Cup to her mouth, extends her tongue, swivels around the inside, and cleans the Cup. She addresses the Cam square on, "Gamers, I'm Tiffany Transparent. I'll pink, cream, and climax. I'm a Pee-Camer and Piss Mouth, and if you let me, I'll pee into my own mouth. Just please let me Pledge naked and cum be a Stripper next Term. Because in my past, I've done everything explicit, all holes, all sexes."

§ Tiffany Makes Up Beka & Elle: Face & Nipple Preparations

Beka and Elle enter the Bathroom. Elle continues to let her halter hang down with her neck strap unfastened and her noogies dangling free;

Beka, never to be outdone, keeps her croptop rolled up into a bundle so that her boobs are also displayed. The Cam shifts its attention as Tiffany glides them into adjacent makeup chairs, "Great, you're first today! Consider yourselves in the mirror, and spread your legs."

The newbies obey. Elle silently logs: *Beka and I, boobage.* Elle assesses more carefully. *Boobage on Cam. Again. Seems like persistence every day now.* Elle looks down; hairage spills to both sides of her jeans crotch seam. She glances to Beka. *Nothing covers Beka's bare boneroo. Two lines already, and in no time her brodeas will push her inner breach apart. And I can already see the bottom of her racing stripe above her bolus pop out.*

Tiffany takes the liberty of rotating Elle's nipples into erection. Elle parts her mouth. *She doesn't even ask my permission.* Elle watches in the mirror as Tiffany swabs makeup around her areolas, and then tops off the erect nips with a metallic color. She winces. *I know that Kimju and Molly and even Steph have gotten nipple makeup before. I know it's a stain and doesn't wash off. But why me, now?*

Tiffany turns to Beka and adorns Beka's berries with equal aplomb, except Tiffany doesn't have to finger them to harden them first. Elle glances and detects that Beka's inner breach has opened. *Three lines now.*

As the paste and stain saturates into their nipples, Tiffany signs Elle to lift her halter up and re-button her neck strap, and for Beka to wiggle her croptop back down. "Now you can give your titter fans something special to hunt for!" Tiffany praises.

Indeed! Elle feels her nipple makeup soak into the inside of her halter. She adjusts her posture, but her nipples stay up. She quiets while Tiffany turns her face into a "wannabe Stripper." I *fail to share Tiffany's enthusiasm for the role.* Elle slowly releases air from her lungs, studies her face in the mirror. *What I see and what I'm begging isn't what I aspire to be.*

So it's not just a stain that fixes itself into Elle's body. *There is a certain inevitability unfolding ahead. More and more my Roommate wants to rush forward. Believes her begging. Maybe she really can pink, cream, and climax, even Double Dong center Stage at the Nugget. But that's not something I am capable of.*

Once again Elle's nips feel a nipple makeup texture inside her halter. *I know, not just stain, thick dye. Like when Steph had to wear her minidress inside out during* The Arrivals, *and show off her spots. So that my nipples stay on my mind constantly, so that when I titter today Gamers will see my painted nipples standing up. Like Tiffany's Eraser Heads, except that Tiffany's teats stand up all the time.*

Maybe mine too.

Elle looks at Beka. *Like Beka too. Her nipples indent when they're aroused, but if her thick dye stains through her croptop she will present her best attempt at headlights.*

Elle fears. *We're both gonna go topless.*

§ Robyn Sends Tiffany: Off to the Doghouse to Replace Kimju

Robyn flitters into the Bathroom, maillot-clad of course. She confronts both newbies just as Tiffany signs them out of the makeup chairs.

Robyn turns to Tiffany, "I'll take over from here. I apply my own makeup. You're not needed. You can move into the Doghouse."

Tiffany hesistates for a moment, trades eyes with the Cam, and flees, staying naked. The Cam shuts off.

Tiffany exits the Back Door, rings the Bell, and drops to hands and kneels to open the shallow Doghouse door underneath the Landing.

A filthy and forlorn Kimju looks out.

"Robyn wants you in the Bathroom for morning makeup," Tiffany explains.

Kimju awakens, considers her topless tanga, piss-muddied body. "I can't wear these there," she accepts. "That's what got me here yesterday."

Tiffany shrugs. "So leave them behind. Stuff them in a crack in the wall. You know I don't want them."

"Yeah, right." Kimju says. She wiggles the dusty, dank tanga down her hips and legs, and pokes it into a crack on the back of the door. "They're pretty dank," Kimju admits as she crawls out of the Doghouse naked. "No one would want them." She moves on all fours now.

"You'll be back for them," Tiffany breezes.

"I will." Kimju nods, and vanishes toward the Bell and Back Door and Tiffany crawls into the Doghouse.

Inside the Doghouse Tiffany suppresses an urge to throw up. *Don't need to add punk to what's already in here.* The Doghouse is dank, dirty, smelly, and cramped Tiffany frets. *These are accommodations befit for a Slavesex, not a Cosmos Pledge, not even a Whore. It's one thing getting naked and filthy when the paparazzi and Cam can collect every intimate detail. It's something else in this hole, where my naked body is out of sight.*

I felt sorry for Elle. I felt sorry for Kimju. Now I feel sorry for myself. Tiffany locates Kimju's mud crusted tanga, and alternates using it between a pillow and rag. *Could be a long day and a long overnight.*

§ Robyn Hazes Beka & Elle: Get Ready to Flip-Flop

Robyn hazes love upon the newbies, the only Cosmos Pledge still in the Bathroom, standing side-by-side with their hands behind their backs and their legs apart. "Oooh, look at you two, Cleopatra's Wanna Strippers. Beg for me!"

Beka leads, "Please let us Pledge naked and become Strippers next Term." Elle catches up at the end and adds, "Ma'am."

"You wish." Robyn curls a lips. "Besides Tiffany and Molly, you can bet that Kimju and Steph will start begging soon. That makes six of you begging for four Nugget slots. Seems like you're gonna get some competition for this prize."

Elle furrows her brow. *Ah! A way out. Dilution of the number of Pledge beggin means somebody else will Opt Strip, I really will be able to Opt Up, after all. Like had I assumed in the first place.*

Robyn snarls, "Don't get your hopes up, Beka Broda and Elle Lollydor. Tiffany here is ex-Whore, 'all holes, all sexes.' She and Kimju and Molly all possess dancing, modeling, and Striptease experience. They've already pinked, creamed, and cum. Toyed their holes. So if you want a bunk in the Nugget, you're just gonna have to beg harder."

Beka begs, "Ma'am please let us Pledge—"

Elle interrupts, "—Ma'am please let us Flip-Flop."

Beka is hopeful. "Then afterwards any Pledge can Game with us."

Elle darts her eyes.

Robyn snorts at both newbies. "You don't fool me, Pledge. Need I remind you that you *begged* to attend School?" Robyn chides. "You arrived barefoot and bellaged in your own slutty clothes. Clothes *you* wore before you ever applied here. Clothes *you* selected! Maybe before you were able to control your own hairage and titty tease, but do you think you control your own hairage and titty tease now? Tell me 'no,' Pledge!"

Elle answers, "Ma'am, no, Ma'am."

Robyn firms, "You're outta your league."

Robyn snorts and points at Elle, "You better remain conscious that your belly button always sits in your v-notch, and you," Robyn points at Beka adjacent, "better make sure that you keep sharing your bristles and breech à la your upskirt. For you vagflashing is no longer an option; vagflashing just is."

Beka rushes, "Robyn, please, let me keep my waistline tugged down so I can show hairage, and also rugage my butt. I'll pink, cream, and climax too, you know that I will. I'll Pee-Cam. After I Flip-Flop with Elle I'll give her a Garment back so she can Opt Monitor next Term. She can pick. I just want to Pledge naked and Strip next Term. I really mean it."

"You really mean it, Ma'am," Robyn corrects, lifts her nose as if she reacts to a bad smell. "Say it."

"I really mean it, Ma'am, *you* can pick whatever Garment *you* want to give Elle, Ma'am."

"And I will turn whatever is left on your body into a string tied around your neck," Robyn promises.

Robyn holds up her hand and focuses upon *both* newbies. "Don't worry, I know both your futures. Both of you will get a chance to pink, cream, and climax, and both of you will beg the Pee-Cam. Right now you can stand spread surrender."

"Remind me why you are here," Robyn commands.

Elle gets the answer first, "Ma'am please let me," Beka joins in, "Pledge naked and cum be a Stripper next Term."

Elle adds, "Ma'am."

Beka and Elle hold their position and yes, they do get spooled inside Automatron. Beka presents a thin croptop stained through from nipples within, coupled with a low-rise and too-short miniskirt. Elle presents in a halter with two pairs of buttons, coupled with notched and ripped shorts. Both titter and hairage, both beg boobage, and Beka vagflashes.

Elle knows, *after boobage Beka and I are both going to be topless, no getting any top back, and with only one Garment our beg will come true.*

Elle bites her lip and feels the seam through her crotch bite into her nether lips. Elle has another urge. *I need to pee soon.*

§ Babs & Steph: Boss Babe Orders Steph to go Strip in Mudpit

Babs intercepts Steph on her sojourn to the Bathroom and signals her to step inside the Bedroom. BB positions herself behind the Desktop, sits, and eyes her Pledge and former Monitor.

Steph stands at ease in front of the Desktop and inside the door. On here way from her bunk Steph has taken the liberty to unroll her dirty, ripped belly-hole undershirt dress, slip back into both armholes, and smooth is as far down her hips as possible. Steph stands uneasily. *The undershirt kinda hides my spigots and crinkly bleached shrubbery. It smells from getting pissed on, used as a bleach rag, and from the sweat and dirt ground into it while hugging the Post in the Backyard yesterday. I've got dirt in my long bleached hair. If I'm not careful I'll be begging to shave in order to get one more Garment, or else I will be a Stripper next Term.*

Steph directs her glance toward the door on the back wall of the Bedroom and announces, "I need a way to clean up without Tiffany's

Bathroom Cam getting all over me." Steph knows what the door on the back wall of the Bedroom leads to: Monitor Babs' private bathroom. Steph ought to know; she was Monitor last Term and this was her private Bedroom.

Boss Babe ignores Steph's gaze. She touches the Desktop and conjures up the feed of Robyn hazing Beka and Elle, from the Bathroom Cam, next door.

Steph's eyeballs redirect to the Desktop.

"You have to see this," Bikini Babe lightens, "Beka's begging to light up the Cam."

Steph cocks her head.

Boss Babe lightens up, "I'm afraid to let you go into the Bathroom. Robyn's got a particularly wicked tooth this morning and she's gunning for you."

Steph lifts her eyes up to look at BB directly while she waggles a finger toward the Desktop. "That ragazze framed me last Term and I'm paying for it now. She knows I'm coming to get her, but has conveniently forgotten why."

"Nice of Robyn to have run you out to the Backyard and allow you to spread your legs," BB proffers.

"She tried to hitch me to Molly," Steph storms. "Lookit, I'm onto you using Robyn as your surrogate, because you're basically afraid to do anything. Word is out that she's running you."

"Really now?" BB bristles. "Tell me, Pledge, who was it that commanded you and your Roommate to pink themselves?"

"Ma'am…." Steph hammers.

"Answer me nicely," Babs warns.

"Ma'am, yes, Ma'am," Steph smarts. "It was you, Monitor Babs, who commanded that Molly and I pink ourselves."

"Thank me," BB orders.

"Ma'am, thank you for letting me audition pink in the Backyard." Steph hesistates.

"Any other secrets to share?" Boss Babe queries.

Steph shakes her head. "No. Ma'am thank you for making me roll my undershirt into a belt, sit foot-a-foot, legs open and knees up with Molly, pull pink, and gaze into her mutton."

"As she gazed into your snatch," BB concludes, then asks, "Did you forget that Janet and William forced you to seep surge outta your slit?"

Steph jumps. "Ma'am, I didn't realize that part of it was what you were thinking about, Ma'am."

Babs smiles. *Apparently Robyn isn't the only Cosmos with selective amnesia. Steph, you seem to have also conveniently forgotten about secretly witnessing the Alumni Reprise last Term.*

Steph does consider the tactical. *If Janet has told Babs I secretly watched her Alumni Reprise and I don't reveal it to Babs—like now is a good opportunity—then what am I guilty of?*

"You may stand spread surrender," Boss Babe commands.

Steph frowns but forms the position. The undershirt rises enough so there is sunshine through bleached scratchy crotch scruff.

BB palms and hefts both breasts and casts her eyes over her former Monitor. "Kimju thinks Robyn's got Charm, so maybe the words coming out of her mouth do matter," BB suggests. "And she told me that you and Molly are going to Flip-Flop."

Steph tightens her hands behind her head and deepens her armpits. She leans forward, keeping her legs wide, and her outer lips parting. "No way!" she asserts. "First of all, Charm is a fantasy, it doesn't exist. Robyn has always tried to inject sadistic Karma into the Game. Ma'am, you know Molly and I have not agreed to any Flip-Flop. *You* authorized us gaming for a Winner-Takes-All, yesterday, at the Post Henge."

Now Babs feigns selective amnesia.

Steph augments, "Janet and William let Molly pick a Greatest House Roar, to be held at the Peacock House. Surely you know this."

"I do," BB accepts.

Steph clarifies, "Molly's going to capitulate to me."

"You're sure of that?" BB queries.

"Ma'am, yes, Ma'am," Steph formalizes, stretches up on spread tiptoes, and settles. "Molly's a fat, overweight, lazy sloth. Or to put it in her words, a mammoth mumping molliwog. She can't beat me at anything even if she'd try to, which she won't. She wants to lose."

"Very well," Boss Babe enlightens, "we shall test your hypothesis! Go find Molly, borrow her Watering Can, and soak the Mudpit. Fill the can up as many times as you need to work up a thick slop."

"Molly can't do this for herself?" Steph asks a question.

BB ignores the mistake. "Molly's already performed twice in the Mudpit, now you get a chance to prove equal."

Steph feels confused. She rocks on her feet. *Steady as she goes.*

BB continues, "You climb into the Mudpit and make a mess out of yourself. I thought I told you to keep that undershirt rolled up, so maybe this will help you remember going forward."

"Ma'am, this is so unnecessary," Steph protests, "but if it pleases you I'll roll it up into a belt again, although it will get more saturated with mud."

"It pleases me," Babs says and tilts her chin.

Steph breaks position and scrambles out of first one shoulder strap then the other, folding and rolling down the chest topless, bottomless until the undershirt was again a tube belt hanging on Steph's crests of the ilium, swooping below navel but above totally exposed pubic hair, across the stern kissing the top of the split and around to the side of the hip where it began. Steph stands with her legs closer together now, but apart just so the thighs aren't kissing.

"Go," BB commands. "Be sure to keep your legs apart. Beg any passersby to fill up the Watering Can and give you a sprinkle. And don't expect a shower anytime soon. "

Steph turns to exit.

"Boss Babs address her back, "Aren't you forgetting something."

Steph has. She turns and sasses, "Ma'am, thank you for reducing me to full-frontal, and letting me perform in the Mudpit, Ma'am." Steph turns and this time exits completely, but then swings her near-naked body around on the door frame. "I was good to you last Term. You owe me for letting Janet take on your Obeisance and Exposures. You owe me for letting you and her Mudwrestle with Penny and Coco, even if I wasn't there to referee the Contest."

"I owe you to respect me and my commands," Babs says. "The time has come for you experience what mud feels like. So after you saturate your belt in the mud you strip it off completely and lay it next you as an offering to Molly. I hear tell that underwear attracts." BB twitches her nose.

Steph's confidence surges, "That's not going to happen, she'll never take them from me. She really is begging to give me her panties." Anger surges, "You're the one who is attempting to humiliate me."

Boss Babe smiles. "Remind me the next time you think you needn't obey me, or obey my surrogate. Babs touches a button on the Desktop, looks up, and says, "Later, Pledge, I'll make sure the entire Prefecture can watch your reactions.

§ Robyn Welcomes Kimju & Molly: Naked Pee-Cam Pledge

Beka and Elle continue to stand spread surrender in the Bathroom. The Cam is off, and they hear the sound of Robyn showering behind them. Robyn returns to view with her golden maillot stretched firm, and they watch her appropriate the Makeup Case, abandoned when Tiffany got banished to the Doghouse, and apply her own makeup this morning. Robyn boofs herself up with a little too much curl, and a little too much perfume.

Kimju and Molly walk into the Bathroom; both are filthy and naked. Kimju is filthy because she has spent the night in that damp, mud-floored cubicle underneath the Back Landing, also know as the Doghouse. And she is naked because she left her thong behind in the Doghouse, knowing that her destination, the Bathroom, mandates she enter naked. *I am a Pee-Camer now, no escaping it.*

Molly has been naked ever since she had been hustled out of the Bathroom yesterday with Steph, then pinked and creamed on the Post Henge. Molly stayed naked when she and Steph returned to their bunks that night, and slept in the dust and dirt she carried in on her hairy body. Molly continued to leave her panties on her shelf in the hope Steph might appropriate them, and they remain there at this moment, Molly knowing that her Pee-Cam commitment demands she only enter the Bathroom naked.

The Bathroom Cam comes to life again.

Robyn chortles at Kimju's reduction to naked here in the Bathroom.

Molly advances. "Ma'am, please let me pee in the Cup and log my Cups on the Pee Log Chart.

Robyn laughs and turns to Kimju, "You first. Time has come for you to start logging your pee!" Kimju looks around for an escape, sees none, and resigns to the inevitable. She squats, parts her butched kootch, looks the Pee-Cam in the eye, and debuts: Total contribution, almost one Cup. *What's left over from my contribution to the mud floor of the Doghouse a while ago.* Kimju logs her name, date, and amount on the Logging Chart on the wall. *I always peed on cam last Term at the Nugget, but I though I'd get away from that at the Cosmos House.*

Wrong.

Molly empties a full bladder, carefully filling one Cup after another before logging her output. "Ma'am," Molly begs, "Please let me shower. Dirty is not healthy for us, Ma'am. Please. I will stay naked and cum be a Stripper next Term."

The beg falls on deaf ears. "Stand spread surrender," Robyn commands. "Face Beka and Elle. And get used to staying dirty."

§ Robyn Orders Kimju & Molly: Train Beka & Elle for Audition

Robyn rests her hands on her hips and realigns the four Cosmos so that still filthy side-by-side Kimju and Molly face Beka and Elle, all standing spread surrender on the Bathroom tile floor. Kimju and Molly remain naked and filthy, Beka and Elle wear a croptop and miniskirt, and halter and shorts, respectively. Two paces separate the opposing Roommates, and Robyn uses the ample space between to pace between them and preen. She has taken possession of Tiffany's Makeup Case in her hands.

Robyn addresses Beka and Elle. "Listen up Pledge. We've all had to watch you wannabes titter and vagflash, hang boobage, and volunteer your butt holes for proctocation. What you got to say for yourselves?"

And Elle gurgles and Beka solidifies the beat, "Please let me Pledge naked and become a Stripper next Term."

Elle adds, "Ma'am."

"Gamers hear you!" Robyn announces. She raises her voice and lifts a wrist. "So, starting today, I have determined you two titty strippers shall commence dancing lessons!"

Elle shuffles on her feet. *All the makeup on my nipples rubbing the inside of my halter keep my nipples alert. I'm going to unbutton both my neck* and *front halter buttons. I'm going to take my halter off completely before I exchange with Beka. We both will have to do that.*

Robyn shrills, "And do not both of you newbies *desire* to dance? Learn what is needed to perform on the Strip? Of course you do. Tell me the beg Janet taught you."

And they stumble, ""Hot hot hot, titters and twat, 98.6 in my anus."

Robyn bows to them, "May it please Gamers you shall learn some useful skills," Robyn circumscribes an arm full length until her fingertips graces toward the naked Pee-Camers, Kimju and Molly, who face the newbies.

Robyn reaches into the Makeup Case, withdraws bright lipstick, and makes a cartoon out of Molly's lips. Beka and Elle open their mouths in astonishment. Kimju conforms also an oval mouth but to no avail, her mouth also gets turned into bright color caricature.

Robyn bows apology to Beka and Elle, "Don't worry, newbies, you already look like Stripper wannabe Whores.

"And these two," Robyn tosses a gesture over her shoulder to Kimju and Molly behind, her "have faces already dirty. Or as they say at the Cosmos House, "When a Cosmos gets dirty, pile more dirt on!" Robyn cackles.

Robyn spins and speaks to Kimju and Molly with mock deference, "Maybe you two could teach these newbies a wiggle or two?"

And Kimju and Molly respond in unison to Robyn's raised eyebrows, "Ma'am, yes, Ma'am!" Both lick their clownish lips and form oval mouth. They itch.

Robyn details to the newbies, "Lucky you. Kimju and Molly volunteer to train you how to dance and strip; you shall learn the ways to pullaside, pink, and cream; manage insertables; and they shall strategize your climax." Robyn raises her arms. "Who better to teach you neophyte Pledge than our always-topless and willing-to-cum Nugget Alumni. They will give you personalized instruction."

Robyn addresses Kimju and Molly, "You can practice them in the Bunkroom or Kitchen or Dining Room or Backyard or Front Porch. Make sure that when they audition the Nugget that they know how to Strip. Every last stich. If they fail to impress, be forewarned I shall assume that to be *your* failure also, and *you two* will suffer harsh consequences. Don't worry, the Doghouse or Mudpit can be vacated to enable your joint tenancy."

Elle flinches; the idea of dance lessons dampens Elle's thoughts, Okay, *I understand that Kimju really does want to Opt Up, although she really isn't limited by shame of her body. And Molly's somewhere between a shrug and an all-for-it. I've seen them both do pullasides and pink.*

Well be fair. *I've seen them cream and climax in sync with their own videos.*

Robyn turns to Beka and Elle and smiles, "Obviously Kimju and Molly contribute to your outcomes! Some Gamers will tell you that the key to your success involves unleashing Kundalini inside you and unifying with your mind, body, and soul. But that's not true; there is not such thing as Kundalini. What you need to do is obey me. There's a reason Babs assigns you to me, and that reason stands before you."

Robyn prides herself at the expense of both ex-Nuggets. "You newbies got to watch me force the cream and cum outta Kimju and Molly; now it's their reward to teach you to finger pink, cream, and climax!"

Elle rotates her shoulders but holds her hands behind her head. She compares the comfort of her halter to Kimju and Molly's totally exposed breasts. *I'm not sure I believe that Molly actually climaxed and peed at the Bachelor Party. Or that Kimju sunburned her kitty and pissed herself on the Yacht.* Elle rolls thoughts in her mind; she has blanked out watching the video replays; part of her hopes that what she didn't witness didn't happen. *I did seem them climax together in this Bathroom with my own eyes. And that was real.*

And then there's Beka. Elle sneaks a glance sideways. Beka, standing next to her, has become excited by the idea of Kimju and Molly teaching her how to striptease, and dangles a droplet of cream. *I need to get Beka under control,* Elle grits. *Beka Broda. Either I get her under control, or I let her go, but I do not want her to take me down with her!*

"You newbies shall obey our ex-Nuggets," Robyn declares. "Now scram, all four of you."

§ Kimju & Molly Educate Beka & Elle: Chant Correction

The foursome find themselves in the Bunkroom. Robyn's absence is a relief.

Kimju reminds herself that *there are no Cam surveying the Bunkroom,* and that in her naked rush to the Bathroom that *my tanga remains in the Doghouse.*

She considers Elle, "You know the Doghouse. Go fetch my tanga and bring it to me."

Elle scoots.

"How about you?" Kimju queries fellow ex-Nugget Molly. "You got your panties on your shelf. You gonna put them on?"

Molly steadies her frame, "It's okay, Kimju, I'm trying to stay naked as much as I can."

Elle returns with tanga in hand and Kimju steps into its wetness and muddy slime. "Tiffany handed them to me," Elle explains, "she was naked inside." Elle adopts a standing position adjacent to Beka.

Kimju and Molly present formidable role models to Beka and Elle. Maybe Beka wants to masturbate to climax in unison with the Nugget Alumni, but Elle freezes up at any such thought. *Robyn might be a nuisance, but Kimju and Molly both hang a ring of experience to tickle their clits.*

"You two might be new to the Game," Kimju chides the newbies on the obvious, "but you're already titty teasers and hairage honeys. And you know more hand signals than you care to practice. You must discard all your original assumptions and forgone conclusions about next Term. Hello tits. Hello pussies. You're in for a good ride. Enjoy it."

Even Molly, perhaps the most lackadaisical Cosmos, opines about how it will end, "Forget about both of you promoting," Molly predicts, "It's very simple, one of you will Opt Monitor, and the other will Opt Strip. Roommates Apart."

Beka believes her but Elle knows Molly's prediction is not the only possible outcome. Elle now considers *the possibility that Beka and I, despite our two pieces, might Opt in opposite directions. Maybe Molly's prediction should be a possibility. Maybe I can Opt Up and Beka will Opt Strip.*

Elle listens carefully to Kimju's next words, "Maybe you two hadn't expected to be flashing your tits and ass, but believe me, the one who is less forthcoming won't be flashing anything next Term!"

Molly elaborates with lackadaisical wit, "That's right, naked Strippers have nothing to flash!"

Elle opens her mouth to question but Kimju cuts her off. "Pay attention to me," Kimju states, "Tiffany and Molly beg 'Please let me Pledge naked and *cum* be a Stripper next Term.' Not 'and *become* a Stripper.' You've been chanting wrong, you need to chant like them from now on. You will get naked and you will cum! And be Strippers next Term! Yes?"

Beka seems bewildered, "I guess so. I'm wet all the time. I'm ready to cum right now."

Molly helps steer. "You've been begging this wrong and you've got a bunch of Gamers about to turn blue. Problem is you're not as blue as you should be."

"So beg correctly now," Kimju instructs.

Molly leads both newbies in unison, "Please let me Pledge naked and cum be a Stripper next Term."

Molly augments, "However if there's a line, I have seniority, I go in front of you."

Elle seeks assurance, "Ah, sure, Molly, of course." And catches Kimju's smile.

Elle shuffles her feet. *No matter what words come out of my mouth, I don't want to Strip and get naked or masturbate. Or cream and cum. Not this Term, not next Term, not ever.* Elle looks at herself in the Bathroom mirror in an attempt to see the anxieties that gnaw on her soul. *I look like a Stripper now. What I'm begging is not what I want to be.*

I know something has changed, Elle accepts. *It appears there are outcomes I haven't anticipated; even today, I am no longer just begging to Pledge naked, I'm begging to Pledge naked and cum! I have raised the stakes on myself and detailed my commitment. And with each passing day I find myself slipping deeper into a morass I can no longer control. I am being tried and tribulated by many Gamers to insure I feel less sure about outcomes.*

Kimju breaks position, offers advice, "You two are going to love to be Strippers next Term. And Molly and I will make the best of you! Right Molly?"

Molly breaks position also, and hefts her mammaries. "Just don't get better than me. Remember, I'm first in line to the Nugget."

"Except for Tiffany, perhaps," Kimju chirps. "Now off to the Dining Room, both of you. Have a seat, make your legs open, and wait for us."

§ Kimju & Molly Brief Beka & Elle: Nugget Stripper Lore

The Dinning Room might not have a Cam, but it does have windows looking out to the Backyard, as well as into the bushes that brush up against the side of the House. Panes but no curtains.

Kimju and Molly trail their trainees downstairs. Kimju pulls her tanga tight up into her koot, hairage both sides, and tries to wipe lipstick off of her mouth. Molly shrugs and continues to stay naked, and moves a bit of lipstick from her over-drafted mouth to her mammilla. The ex-Nuggets consider the two uneasy newbies sitting and holding onto their chairs, legs open.

Kimju and Molly sit, thighs not touching.

Kimju tests learning, "Beg."

And newbies beg. "Please let me Pledge naked and cum be a Stripper next Term."

"Don't worry, Molly assures, "We will make great dancers of you."

"Ecdysiasts too!" Kimju assures; she is a schooled Gamer.

Elle tucks her ankles behind the front legs of her chair. "Ma'am, we've seen your clips from the Nugget, so we know what you did."

Kimju provides, "Or what you're begging to do. The feeds from the Nugget aren't the same as being there. You watched vids of us pinking, masturbating, and climaxing fully nude."

Beka brims brodeas. "We saw you cum live in sync with your videos. You're pretty amazing."

Elle raises alarm, "You pinked and peed on Stage, you masturbated with dildos and buttplugs. You—"

"We also Double Penetrated!" Molly prides. Like my mutton and my mawkport at the same time."

"Sometimes the DP was the Shaving Kit," Kimju details, "But we never shared the Double Dong, never shared any Prop.

Elle challenges, "We've seen your *Nugget Stripper Videos*. You lapdanced. You both got fondled!"

"Right," Molly agrees, "I got my maraschino squeezed and my mammies sucked all the time."

Elle looks at Kimju and Kimju shrugs, "Once a Patron dipped a finger inside me and then let me taste myself."

Elle frets, "So the Patrons touch you during lapdances? That's not allowed, is it?"

"That depends," Molly replies. "I mean, you touch someone when you shake their hand. And the more you let them touch you the more friendly they get. If you let them touch you too much, you're inviting the Gamers to decide you're a Whore. If you don't let them touch you enough, the Gamers decide you need Whore training, which means getting fondled everywhere."

"Whores get fondled," Elle affirms.

"Whores get fucked," Molly states. "And that's not my cup of pleasure."

"I though you liked sex?" Elle questions.

"I do," Molly agrees, "but I don't want to be a sex worker. It's a great Caste for many—take Tiffany for example—but not for me."

Kimju adds, "Not me either. And remember, newbies, fondling isn't sex."

Elle considers. "How come MomCap never punished you?"

Kimju details, "Well, put it this way, at the Nugget, MomCap left it up to the Strippers if they let the lapdance clients feel them up or not. Fondling was against the Rules, but it wasn't punished either."

"Is against the Rules, still," Molly augments. "Although neither of us slapped many hands. I've always assume that letting the Patrons become familiar with our bodies contributed to our promotions. And as far as I'm concerned, pledging beats turning tricks."

"Some Nuggets wouldn't let the Patrons touch them, and some of those Nuggets are now Whores." Kimju augments, "And they have a whole lot more to deal with than just hands-on."

"I've heard about the Champagne Room," Elle advances, "So did MomCap ever require you suck cock, or, you know—"

"Never." Molly shakes her head. "MomCap knows that's no gray area. Any Stripper getting caught fucking, or even sucking cock, will find herself in Lockdown before she can get the cock out of her mouth. Lockdown for the rest of this Term, then Whoring at Flesh Ranch next."

"That's how Tiffany got to Flesh Ranch last Term," Kimju explains. "She sucked cock toward the end of her Stripper Term to ensure Gamers didn't have any choice."

Beka diverts, "I bet if Tiffany gets a chance to suck cock she do it."

"Naw, I don't think so," Molly retorts. "She Feature Danced the Nugget a lot last Term and we talked a lot. If she were to get caught sexing while she's a Pledge, Gamers wouldn't demote her to Whore like the last time. She'd be Slavesex. And she knows that."

"Tiffany will have to settle for being a Stripper next Term." Kimju projects.

Elle personalizes. "*I* don't want to be a Stripper." She confesses, "I don't know why I'm begging to be one? I thought this was just a Game, but now I'm not sure anymore."

Kimju surveys both newbie Pledge. "It's a Game until it's real, and then it's still a Game. You'll do fine. Strippers aren't allowed to possess Garments and you're already begging to pledge naked. House Mom will give you whatever Gamers want you to wear, and out front on Stage you will take it all off before the Crowd."

"I don't want to be naked in front of a Crowd," Elle confesses.

"You'll do fine," Kimju suggests, "Stripping requires one knows oneself. You came to School for a reason."

Elle grits. *I've never been in a strip club. I don't want to go there. Not even to visit. Stripping is an Option in the wrong direction! Even if I am forced to say I want to.*

Curiosity interludes. "There's Cams at the Nugget?" Elle asks. *As if I don't know.*

"Ah!" Molly praises. "The Nugget provides a multi-Cam full Prefecture feed! You'll get some fans! There are Cams on Stage, Backstage, even the Dressing Room. The shower stalls have no protection, and the toilets are made of clear glass.

"I don't want to be on a Pee-Cam," Elle says.

Kimju pitches. "You've seen Molly and me: we get to pee into the Measuring Cup and fill in the Logging Chart. Maybe you and Beka should take on this task, given your propensity for Measurement Nudes."

Elle furrows her brow.

Molly cheers, "And you got to see our Pink Pages. You'll get yours, don't worry. I'll help make sure you get measured completely. Not just your weight and height, your bra and cup size, and pee shot. Everything. How far your mouth can open, the circumference of your collar, your ben-wa ball size."

"Robyn says after I Flip-Flop she's going to make me pink together with Steph," Elle worries.

Molly shrugs this off, "Don't worry about posing with Steph, you'll get your own chance to pink solo.

Elle closes her eyes. *I really don't want to Flip-Flop with Beka, no vagflash, and no pink.*

"Don't worry, I'll help you get over it." Molly assures. "And I'll pink and cream with you too, if that makes you feel any better about it."

"You've seen us," Kimju smoothes. "We are your role models."

"Pink-wet-and-ready!" Molly lifts a hand high in the air.

Kimju concludes, "And you will climax on a finger snap."

Beka commits, "I'll let them finger-fuck and fondle my boobs if you let me be a naked Stripper next Term."

Elle senses panic. *I don't think I could ever learn to do this!*

Molly tries to be kind to the newbies, "Don't worry, Beka and Elle. Kimju and I will prepare you for your Nugget audition. You'll do fine."

"You don't want to be cumming ahead of time." Kimju smiles.

§ Kimju & Molly Teach Beka & Elle: Dance & Stripper Moves

Kimju gestures, "Moves your chairs back from the table and stand on them.

Beka and Elle look at each other dumbfounded.

"Your chair is your table dance dais and the table is your stage," Molly explains. "Trust us, we know how to dance."

Elle curls the toes of her bare feet against the seat of a Dining Room table chair. She glances at her Roommate. *Beka Broda. Even standing, legs more open than necessary. Wanting to go there.*

Indeed, Kimju and Molly are excellent dancers, they possess a repertoire, and their knowledge involves not just following dance steps and undressing methods, but also following a routine in life, even through their life goals, behaviors, and phobias vary widely.

Kimju instructs, "Molly and I will show you a whole lot of dances."

Show 'em, Molly."

Molly stands in plain view and animates. "We'll teach you how to belly dance, do the shimmy shawabble, how to jitterbug, do the twist."

Kimju adds claims. "We'll teach you some burlesque steps, like how to bump and grind, even how to slab dance."

Elle expresses bewilderment, "Slab dance?"

Molly elaborates, "It's also called the horizontal, because it's a dance you perform horizontally."

"Maybe someday Molly will show you the bottle dance," Kimju wises.

Two looks of bewilderment look down from two newbies standing on two chairs.

"It's a striptease specialty consisting of gripping a bottle with your vaginal constrictor muscles," Molly explains.

"That's one of your acts?" Beka asks.

"Molly will teach you," Kimju offers.

"Maybe I won't," Molly spirits, "I need at least one dance to maintain my edge. But don't worry, we'll teach you all the dances we know: the hootchy-kootchy, the Nancy Prance, the Charleston, even the notorious black bottom."

Kimju pitches science to Elle. "You'll learn to dance using the sensory part of your brain. Muscle and movement memory. That way Kundalini may rise in both sides of your brain: your mental stimulation, and your orgasmic, ecstatic self."

Kimju instructs Beka, "And may you learn to think and be analytical, and not just dance for spiritual pleasure, although I realize that's a long shot."

Beka volunteers, "I can feel Kundalini take hold. I get sexually aroused when I dance.

Kimju nods, "We shall make choreophiliacs out of both of you.

Choreohiliacs? Elle fears she might figure out what that means.

"Dance with me," Molly commands, as she climbs on a chair, and commences to gyrate and grind.

And Beka and Elle follow.

Molly stops dancing and settles her mammoth naked body back down in her chair. Beka and Elle keep dancing. Croptop and miniskirt; halter and notched shorts. Bare arms, bare bellies, beg legs.

Beka's croptop has two stains where the dye and paste has bled through the fabric, marking her bibble-tips. Elle shimmies and feels her nipples squish against the inside of her halter cup. *Nips getting hard now.*

Kimju stands before them, commands their attention. "Molly's begging to Strip, and it's your turn to match Molly so that your begs are serious! Let's test your Sign aptitude."

She signs Beka a shirt lift and Beka lifts the shirt up above two boobs, baring them completely. Elle looks and silently logs. *Boobage.* And with the dye and paste smeared all over her boobies.

"Roll it tight and bite down on it with your teeth," Kimju commands.

Beka obeys.

Elle analyzes her Roommate. *Silenced with a voluntary shirt gag. I wonder how long that will last.*

Kimju directs Beka, "Now tighten your miniskirt into a belt—so you can display your bare boneroo and racing strip all the time."

Beka obeys; brodeas slaps her inner thigh.

"Keep dancing," Kimju tells Beka, and turns to examine Elle.

"I trust you understand that besides wiggling your naka-nake that a Stripper must also know how to remove their Garments?" Kimju asks.

"Ma'am," Elle respects, suddenly sensitive to dried nipple makeup inside her halter. "Ma'am, I've unbuttoned my halter every day so far during *The Runup,* Ma'am. Elle introspects, *I'm boobage and I don't want to be topless. Or Pledge naked and cum be a Stripper next Term.*

"Do you know this sign?" Kimju makes a gesture.

Elle does. "Ma'am, yes, Ma'am, but I've never done that before."

"Do I need to repeat myself?" Kimju inquires.

"Ma'am, no, Ma'am," Elle answers, takes the seam of her jeans in her fingers, and performs a pullaside."

"Next time you see a Cam, you beg it collect you like that," Kimju decrees.

Elle flusters. She looks at Beka and sees Beka dancing and dangling brodeas. So Elle answers Kimju, "Ma'am, yes, Ma'am. I'll show myself off to every Cam."

Kimju makes another Sign. This one Elle knows also and practices as best she can: she tugs the front of her jeans up into her nook, so that virtually all of her nappy splays to one side or the other, even her outer sex lips get pinched. Tugging the jeans shorts deeper into the naka-nake trench confronts physical limits.

Kimju rescues. "Unzip your jeans. That way you can crib more of your naches out. Instead of just cheeking, you can approach full buttage."

Elle wiggles the shorts vulgar and tight. *Now I'm showing hairage in the zipper v-notch.*

Kimju now addresses Elle's halter top. "It's not enough you're just unbuttoning your halter and letting your noogies flop around. You shall master different sequences to unbutton and take your halter off. Seems like you're pretty good at unbuttoning your neck strap. why don't you unbutton the front for a change."

Elle snaps, "I'd rather take my halter off completely and go topless than continue to engage in these kind of shenanigans."

Molly moves her body mass into the conversation and injects calm. "First," she addresses Elle, "you need to learn from Kimju. If Kimju suggests you unbutton the front of your halter, then follow her advice."

"But, but, but—" Elle hurries.

"Now," Kimju and Molly say in unison.

Elle obeys. The halter falls to the side, titters, still hangs from the neck strap, slides into a valley, and boobage.

Molly waves a finger. "Now unbutton your neck strap and let your halter fall to the floor. Your wish is granted. And we will teach you every which way to tease your noogies out."

Beka sidewinds, "Hey, Elle, it's not like you haven't tittered before. Or presented boobage."

Elle tightens her jaw and lets go of her Garment. *This is not tittering. Or about the multiple ways to take off my halter off. This is about not wearing a halter at all. I'm a topless now.*

Kimju leads again. "Now you wiggle your jeans shorts down your legs while turning a circle on the chair seat."

"You gotta go slow," Molly coaxes, "First you slowly push your shorts down your butt, then you pull your nates to both sides and flash your nadir gate. Then you can reach forward and show them your niche, straighten up and keep turning and open your nookie from the front side."

Elle follows carefully stepping out of her shorts at her ankles, and lets them fall off the chair seat onto the floor.

Elle has six tan lines and they all show, although the one at her leghole is fuzzy from loosing threads.

Kimju seems to not mind. "You can increase your tip if you secrete some of your noble proteins at this point."

Elle casts wild eyes, "Cream in front of everybody? I didn't sign up for that. And cumming? I definitely can't do that on my own."

Beka rescues her Roommate, "Elle's telling the truth. She's never been able to masturbate herself to climax, she—"

"Beka!" Elle interrupts, "we don't need to talk about what happened before we ever enrolled in School."

Beka gallants, "Elle's only able to climax fucking a cock. Trust me, I've seen her. And we know that's not allowed and can't happen here."

Molly nods nervously, "Can't happen with Strippers, either."

Beka has followed Elle's action and gathered brodeas onto her fingertips. "Please let me Pledge naked and cum be a Stripper next Term, I'll let the Patrons taste me."

Molly waves a warning finger. "You're not supposed to let the Patrons finger your bolus or rotate around inside your boneroo," Molly forewarns, "but if they are gentle about it I never care."

Kimju addresses both newbies, "Molly leans more toward becoming a Whore than I do."

Molly takes exception. "I do not!" She hefts both mammies together and also addresses the newbies. "Kimju got fingered and fondled just as much as I did."

Kimju retorts, "The only difference is that you liked it a lot more. You let Patrons climax you right in the Club."

"Yeah, well, don't complain," Molly defends. "We both got what we want; we're both here."

"One of us is begging to go back next Term," Kimju appraises. "And one of us not. Me." She turns her focus upon the newbies, Beka and Elle. "Don't you two worry. Besides Tiffany and Molly, the Nugget still has two slots open next Term, so there's space for *both* of you."

§ Kimju & Molly and Beka & Elle: Politics & the Better Dancer

Elle learns the Hand Signs with reluctance. *They grind on me. I'm forced to learn a Signs that allows the House to handicap its own Pledge, me. Unbutton or button my top, pullaside and expose myself.*

Kimju provides insight, "Your success lies in mastering two skills: knowing and following the Hand Signs, that's the easy part, and paying attention while holding your position, that the hard part. You two witnessed Ginny bracketed in the Cravat, that was after her Roommate Trixi Tubes failed at 'paying attention.' That sort of thing could happen to you too."

"Janet sat Cravat last Term in lieu of BB," Molly gossips, "or so the story goes."

Yes indeed. Beka and Elle exchange glances, and the extremity of that corrective discipline sends shivers into newbie psyche. Elle catches herself shaking and quiets herself, wonders, *so does Babs owe Janet Karma?*

Beka leaks brodeas onto her inner thigh. Ginny's perseverance sitting Cravat arouses her. So does denial.

Elle steadies herself in this whirlwind of education. *Following Hand Signs is straightforward, furthermore any wayward performance is easy to document. But dancing—who might be judged a better dancer—invites a more subjective evaluation.* Elle, being the more cerebral of the two, grapples internally about her best strategy. *Is the Pledge who is the "better" dancer more like to Opt Monitor, or to Opt Strip?*

Elle considers Beka again. *We are both great dancers and if I hold back she will be the better dancer and qualify for a Stripper slot. Maybe I should even demonstrate ineptitude at dance, cobble my steps, and flail my arms. So half-trying to dance might actually contribute to an Opt Monitor slot.*

Instructor Kimju reads Elle's mind and advances another outcome, "Sometimes Gamers desire the poorer dancer to Opt Down, for the fun of drumming correction into her at the Nugget. Or if that fails, at some really down-and-dirty roadhouse dive where nobody bothers to wash dried crost off the pole. You'll be banishing your nookie and nadir in front of a club full of greasy jerkoffs waiting to paw your naked body and encourage you to become a Bar Whore."

Yes, Elle understands, *better dancing could cut either way. I'm just not sure how to play it.*

Beka does not overanalyze the situation. She just does the watusi, throws herself into the frug, and curves her arms in the swim. She grasps the croptop by it's opposite sides, pulls it off overhead, and tosses it away. The tubed miniskirt drops easily; Beka kicks it off the chair seat. She chants, "Please let me Pledge naked and cum be a Stripper next Term!"

Elle follows and tries not to lead. *I'm not tittering or hairage anymore. I'm completely naked right now.* Still, Beka's movements imbue Elle with a sense of rhythm, and she quickly learns that the issue of strategically holding back slips out of her control. Kundalini hiding inside the dance infects her and she yields to the fever. She tosses her body about with abandon, and transmogrifies herself into a suggestive wanton erotic animal.

It not that much of a transformation for her actually. Elle's always been able to tease a dance partner into seduction, but what happens now takes her to a new level and into the realm of performance. Lewd performance, copulatory movement, touching her hands to her body, and shaking her nubbies around.

But Elle knows the worst of it, *I know I am good at dancing! My only salvation is that Beka is even more lewd, vulgar, wanton, suggestive, and animalistic than I am. Maybe Kundalini possesses me when I dance, but Kundalini possesses Beka whenever someone looks at her. She's wet all the time"*

§ Kimju & Molly and Beka & Elle: Roommate Game Goals

Dance Lessons have concluded. "Enough," Kimju declares. "Upstairs, shower, and hurry back down."

Elle casts her eyes down on her halter and shorts, lying on the floor.

"Don't worry," Molly reassures, "we'll pick up after both of you."

Beka pauses in the doorway to the Kitchen. "You're gonna come upstairs and turn the Cam on while we're in the Bathroom, aren't you."

She bounces eyeballs back between Kimju and Molly. "Either one of you can do it," she adds.

Elle discovers herself covering her nobs with one arm and hand, and her nest with the other hand. *No escape. So get in and out fast, including any toilet duties.*

"Beg, both of you," Kimju commands.

And they do, "Please let me Pledge naked and cum be a Stripper next Term."

"Thank us," Kimju orders.

Elle leads, "Kimju and Molly, thank you for giving us dancing and striptease instruction."

Beka follows, "I'll stay naked 24x7. I really am a wannabe Stripper. I'll stay pink-wet-and-ready. I'll masturbate and climax anytime anywhere in front of anybody. I'll dildo, I'll buttplug, I'll DP. I'll streak naked to the Nugget, fetch the Double Dong, bring it to the Cosmos House and dong with Elle on Cam. With everybody."

"You'll go upstairs and shower, like I told you," Kimju reminds. "Both of you."

A naked Molly finishes picking up the two pairs of Garments and drapes them over her arm. "Don't worry if you don't get Cammed naked immediately," she advises, "if you can stay naked 24x7 you'll get Pee-Cammed eventually."

Elle pushes Beka through the Kitchen, guides her left, and gooses her naked behind up the spiral stairs.

Kimju and Molly drift into the Kitchen and look out the Back Door. Steph, lying naked in the Mudpit, has managed to get herself even more covered with mud than she intended—she has so much mud covering her body that may not even be naked anymore. Except that she is, because her excuse for a minidress, her rolled up undershirt, lies in a muddy pile next to her.

Kimju advises Molly. "Steph's offering you a muddy rag as a concession. It's yours for the taking. If I could take it I would, but she's your Roommate, not mine."

"I don't want it." Molly affirms. "No second Garment. I want to keep my panties, that's it."

There is a hush in the Kitchen. The two ex-Nuggets presume Tiffany remains in the Doghouse underneath the Back Landing, but neither goes out the Back Door to explore, least they feel compelled to pee on the Landing for the Back Door Cam.

Beka and Elle return back down the spiral staircase, still naked of course, and the two former Strippers and two newbies settle into four chairs at the Kitchen table. Elle finds her nakedness unnerving and eyes the four Garments that are neatly stacked on the tabletop. *I know Gamers watch me from the darkness outside.*

Beka rolls a bare behind on her chair. Elle checks to see that her thighs aren't touching, *however much my legs are under the table.* And not just Beka and Elle, *all* four Pledge remain aware that one of their few requirements is to keep their thigh apart, and they all do. Kimju, the only one of them wearing anything, makes sure her topless tanga stays yanked tight in front, spilling kava-kava hairage.

Molly, naked, keeps her legs more widely open than the others, and occasionally touches herself. And why not. *I left my panties upstairs where I bunk, where Steph could take them again, except Steph is groveling in the Mudpit and can't get to them now.*

Molly finger dips. *But if Gamers insist that I streak to the Nugget, I'm game, although they have to make sure I get there. Safely and without getting caught.*

Naked Elle eyes her folded halter and shorts, and opens the subject of Roommate Games to topless Kimju, "What are you going to do about a Game with Robyn?" she asks. "You can't Opt Monitor with only one Garment, and you can't game with anyone else until after you game with her first." Elle hesistates. "Like you can't game with me now and take my halter top, right?"

Kimju nods, "Right, we're all Pledge here even through three of us here are begging to Pledge naked and Strip. And one of us is not: Me."

Elle brushes imaginary sand off her naked body; she speculates, "You suspect Robyn won't Flip-Flop with you unless she has to. She's not about to exhibit herself topless tanga. But you and she both have to Game or neither of you will have two pieces. But if you play a Winner-Takes-All with her and she does have Charm, you'll lose and be a naked Cosmos Pledge, 24x7. Then Robyn will streak you."

"Can't say that sounds like a positive option," Kimju admits.

Beka turns to Molly. "Maybe Robyn will streak you too," Beka suggests.

"She already has; I had to streak to the Bachelor Party during *The Arrivals.*" Molly worries. "I realize that may be the only way to get back to the Nugget, and although I do see the value of staying topless, I think wet panties are as dangerous as streaking. Streaking is really dangerous, especially long runs. If you get caught you are lucky to get fucked and then left cuffed to the flagpole. You are just as likely to end up in Lockdown. But with wet panties I could catch disease."

"So why give your panties to Steph and risk streaking when you can get to the Nugget with a Flip-Flop?" Elle asks.

"Steph would never agree to a Flip-Flop," Molly explains, "because she would have nothing to gain and much to lose. She needs to game me with a Winner-Takes-All so she can take my panties and wear two pieces. And yesterday she got her wish. Somehow or another I was supposed to pick the Game, and when Janet and William demanded I beg *The Greatest House Roar,* I did."

"Over at the Peacock House." Elle confirms.

"It doesn't matter what the Game is," Molly explains, "I'll do badly and lose."

"But what would be wrong with winning?" Elle inquires. "You would take her undershirt away. You'd have two Garments and could Opt Monitor next Term.

"I'd be a horrible Monitor," Molly declares, "I'd lose control, my Pledge would rebel, and I'd end up worse than a Stripper."

"You'd end up a Whore," Kimju observes.

Molly nods, "In short order. If not a Slavesex. It's very simple for me: Pledge or Stripper, that's all. It's a narrow band, and all I have to do is whatever I need to do so I can go back and forth."

"Oscillating Gamer," says topless Kimju. She tilts a shoulder toward naked Molly. "All you got to do is make sure you lose your panties in the Greatest House Roar."

Molly scratches an eyebrow. "Steph doesn't think Robyn has Charm, even though, well, you know, she made us masturbate this Term."

"She made me masturbate a lot more than you!" Kimju snaps, regretting she reveals herself.

Naked Beka chirps in, unaware she touches herself. "I know. You had to masturbate to Tiffany's Porn Star Calendar in the Kitchen, and then Robyn took you outdoors and made you rub your Henge Post. You made it slick, Kimju, remember?

Molly eases the fall, "the best was when Kimju and I came together up in the Bathroom."

"Live for the entire Prefecture." Kimju snorts and curls her nose.

"Relax, Kimju," Molly comforts, "I don't dispute you'll make a great Monitor, but just because we Opted Up this Term doesn't mean you're out of the woods. You've already had to pink, cream, and climax. Now you're a Pee-Camer too. You think you're going to get a second piece first? You'll be lucky you don't become a naked Piss Mouth before you have a chance of gaining.

Kimju mulls this though. "We could both end up naked Strippers next Term," she snorts, "you'd like that!"

Molly augments, "It's better that we both get what we want and if I have to streak to the Nugget I'll do that for you. But between now and then we can help each other accomplish our goals. We know that Penny and Coco took the Double Dong to the Nugget."

Kimju snorts. "As far as I'm concerned they can beg to share it." ."

Molly hefts her mams in her hands and twists her minarets with her fingertips. "Well, you know who's going to share it, Kimju. We are. We're gonna climax the Double Dong center Stage at the Nugget for our Alumni Reprise, just like Janet did. Only there are two of us."

Kimju grits her teeth, "And a Dong waiting."

"What about your Watering Can?" Beka eagerly asks.

Molly shrugs, "I told Steph if she wanted it she could keep it, and it's out there with her now. But if she wants me to keep it, I will. So I know I'll get stuck with it sooner or later. But I'm better off with the Watering Can without the panties than with them. Wet panties invite germs."

Kimju teases Molly. "Did you ask Steph if she wins if she also wins your Pee-Cam and Piss Mouth?"

Molly rolls her eyes and engages the newbies, "What about you two, seems like you're getting pressured to Flip-Flop."

Elle attempts logic. "Lookit, right now between us we possess four Garments—the right amount for both of us to promote."

Beka appeals to both dance instructors, "Elle and I want to stick together next Term, even if we have to Flip-Flop. We'd still have two pieces."

"I'm not even sure we need to Flip-Flop," Elle says.

Kimju rubs her knockers in her palms. "Molly is jealous. Both of you already got your assholes probed, one way or another. But William never slipped Molly a thermoprobe or gelatin egg."

Naked Elle blushes. The blush fills her cheeks then her face, it runs down her neck and toward chest, heats her nipples, it flushes her sex. Elle feels the heat, glances to ensure her thighs are not touching, that the Room is absent a Cam.

Beka Broda scent strikes her nostrils.

Molly confesses. "I am jealous. Even Steph got her stern tube thermoprobed. I don't want her getting ahead of me."

Kimju leans toward Elle, "Roommates share. So if one of you gets thermoprobed, be sure the other of you begs equal treatment! "

Elle grimaces.

Molly laughs at both newbies, "You need to get fond of Stripping. I was a Stripper before and I want to be a Stripper again. But listen carefully to me: I'll teach you my secrets, and you can even join me at the Nugget next Term, but you can't get in front of me in the line. I have seniority."

Kimju pushes, "Until you and Beka Flip-Flop you won't be able to Game with all the rest of us Cosmos."

Beka concurs, "Yeah, Elle, we need to Flip-Flop. That way anybody can Game us."

Yikes. Elle worries. *It's not just Kimju and Molly urging me to Flip-Flip, my own Roommate loves the idea.*

Kimju nudges Elle. "Maybe it's time to get your nookie exposed.

Beka encourages Elle. "You can do it, Elle. I do it. I'm Beka Broda, remember?

Elle remembers, *You're even making the chair wet.*

Beka points to the pile of four folded Garments on the table, "If you want to keep our clothes, they're yours."

"Stop!" Elle commands. She turns to face Kimju. "you can't Game with Beka and me unless we Flip-Flop first. And if you lose to Robyn and end up naked, and Beka and I have Flip-Flopped, then you will plunder us."

Beka nods, "We can both be streakers then."

Molly calms, "Beka, even if you don't Flip-Flop, you can still pink and cream with me... or with Steph.

Beka agrees. "Ma'am, let me pink, cream and cum please." Beka looks to Molly. "I want to masturbate with you, again and again."

Molly worms a finger into her magenta, fiddles her maraschino and draws musk to her nostril to sniff. "I'll teach you how to control yourself before you let go," she advises "I'll make a Stripper out of you."

Beka rushes, "Ma'am, thank you Ma'am." She scans around the table, looks at Elle, "Elle too, Ma'am, we're both beggars."

Elle feels a bead of sweat pop on her forehead and her shock deepens into a tightening feeling somewhere down where her belly button lies bare. She tries to stabelize. *I must get Beka under control.*

Beka volunteers, "We'll take on the Pee-Cam too."

Molly wrinkles her brow. "Maybe you can even take on my Piss Mouth."

Elle intersects, "Molly, I'm sorry, but I am not begging a Pee-Cam or Piss Mouth!"

Kimju jumps in, "So remind me, newbies, what do you beg?" She steels, "All together now!"

And both newbies recite, "Please let me Pledge naked and cum be a Stripper next Term!"

Beka really means it. Elle looks at her folded clothes and again brushes imaginary sand off her naked body as another liability strangles her thoughts. *Boss Babe will decide whether to screen my Gonzo Video or not.* Elle leaks a drop of pee onto her chair, and silently surrenders, *Kimju and Molly, you can Flip-Flop us anytime.*

Ah, the pleasures of dance instruction.

Kimju & Molly and Beka & Elle: Nugget I (D20)

II-10 Kimju & Molly and Beka & Elle: Alumni Reprise (D20)

§ The Cosmos: Morning in the Bunkroom & Backyard

On the morning of Day Twenty Babs empowers Robyn to Lineup the Four Pledge who arise in the Bunkroom. Kimju and Molly, and Beka and Elle, fall into stand spread surrender Reveille. "Look into your eyes in the Mirror!" Robyn snaps.

And they do. Elle finds it impossible to look herself in the eye and glances furtively. *There is no Cam in the Bunkroom, but could the Minxy be one giant window?* She scans the Lineup. *Steph is not here. Could she have spent the night in the Mudpit?*

Steph has. Steph slept only fitfully overnight and she casts eyes around the Backyard as the dawn gathers. *I'm naked, I filthy, I stink. My undershirt is a muddy rag pillow. My long beautiful hair is brittle and bleached... and saturated with mud.*

Steph looks toward the Doghouse and sees a closed door. *I never saw Tiffany go in but I've never seen her come out either. I thought Bikini Bimbo was her friend.*

Steph catches the Cam colleting her mud-packed open legs. She sits up in the mud and stares into the lens. *She darts thoughts to the Gamers, don't expect me to climax, just be grateful that you get to watch me beg pink and cream. Well, sometimes.* Steph blinks. And admits to herself, *I'm grateful, Cam, that you're here to watch over me. Maybe I'm a naked spread Cosmos Pledge, but at least you're keeping me safe. From some goalie plundering my stern star with his hockey stick.*

Steph knows, *I am not the first Cosmos to wallow the Mudpit, but this is my first Mudpit experience. Kimju and Molly waddled into the muck upon their upon their Arrival and they wallowed again three days ago. Both times at Robyn's behest.*

Robyn put Tiffany into the Mudpit two days ago, except Babs freed her and let her shower. But then yesterday Robyn repossessed her again and sent her to the Doghouse overnight.

Steph studies the closed door of the wood box with its sunken earth floor beneath the Back Landing. *I've seen the videos of Elle crawling in. And I'm sure the Cam collected Kimju and Tiffany bellying in. And I suspect Tiffany remains inside.*

Steph trades eyes with the Cam, gathers her muddy undershirt into her hand, and places it next to her body. *Maybe Tiffany had to crawl naked into the Doghouse, but me here outside in the Mudpit with only me for the Cam to harve*st, that's far more severe treatment. Steph wipes mud off her forehead, and from around her eyes. *Maybe Robyn put Tiffany in the Doghouse, but Bikini Bitch put me here.*

Inside the Doghouse, Tiffany curls up in dust and wetness. *I much prefer a glory hole to this Doghouse. And I definitely don't want to live in a cage.*

Inside the Bunkroom, Robyn issues an order. "Outside, all of you. Find you place on the Post Henge, get on your hands and knees, legs wide apart, and press your face to where your Post meets Earth, and lift your asses up. Let Tiffany out of the Doghouse and tell her and Steph to join you. Now scram."

§ Robyn Decrees Kimju & Molly: Alumni Reprise at Nugget

Morning passes to afternoon and Six Cosmos adorning the Post Henge grow restless. Some of them water the earth. Perseverance matters.

It is not until the afternoon wanes that Robyn goes outside to review their postures. She takes over direction of the Back Door Cam and makes sure the Prefecture gets fed every intimacy. Tiffany remains naked with face in the dirt; she keeps her legs widely spread and her tailpipe and twat raised highest. Kimju and Molly remain topless and buttage; Robyn advises Kimju "make sure you keep your thong buried in your keyway" and advises Molly "keep your panties buried in your meatlocker and moonshadow." Robyn laughs at them, "Hairage is not an option for you two; hairage just is."

Steph, freed of the Mudpit, elected to slip back into her undershirt, but has been careful to fold it over and into a tight roll; the tube rides between her serpentine button and mud-crusted, bleached-out pubic hair. Steph shows stern slit above and below. Sunshine slowly dries the mud to caked earth to dust during the day. Dusty she'll stay.

Beka and Elle first titter but then boobage, as Elle unbuttons her neck strap and Beka rolls up her croptop and bites it with her teeth.

Robyn cams every available intimacy: every nipple, every hairage, every clit and vagina, every raised butt, every asshole. She steps back and signs the hovering Cam to move away and follow her. She ripples her figure.

She reaches out her foot, rakes Kimju's ribs with her toenails, and kicks a knocker. Molly is next with a kick on the side of her ribs. "On your feet, Stripper wannabes. I've decided to grant your wish for an Alumni Reprise at the Nugget! You shall perform tonight! Now stand up and grab the Post behind your head."

Kimju and Molly obey and watch Robyn position herself between them. "Don't you two dim-wits get to full of yourselves," Robyn warns, "You're just a pair of stupid, topless bare-assed Pledge."

Robyn draws the back of her fingers across Kimju's curvy 35Cs, and then fingers one of Kimju's beige areolas. Robyn addresses the Cam. "This wannabe kipper koekje kickshaw has got nose cones for nipples." Robyn pinches and Kimju winces.

Robyn laughs and turns. Now she uses her hands to heft Molly's saggy 38DDs. Again Robyn presents breasts to the Cam, "These milk bags got big sepia areolas with dark pearls atop. Not bad for a lard bag." Robyn digs into Molly's nipples with her sharp fingernails until Molly flinches. She legs go and Molly's mammary glands fall back onto her chest.

Robyn steps back to examine the Alumni together, and mocks the single Garment each wears yanked tight into their pubic hair and vaginas. "One Kunny Kover and Muff Muzzle," Robyn laughs. "And you're both gonna beg me to strip it off before the Day's end."

Robyn turns her attention to Tiffany. She wiggles her big toe into Tiffany's tailpipe and presents the toe for Tiffany to kiss. Tiffany kisses the toe and cleans it while Robyn rants, "Listen, you tamtart taco peddling toilet," she begins, "get up. On your feet. Take this klute and molliwog upstairs to the Bathroom, clean 'em up, and make them look cheap and fuckable. Makeup on the side of excess."

Tiffany scrambles, "I'll make them better than Cleopatra's Strippers. Dancing their Alumni Reprise at the Nugget tonight! Faces, hair, nails, nips, navels, clits, everything. Even pretty on the inside."

The three remaining Cosmos still clench the bases of their posts, cheeks on the ground, and their butts held high. Steph, Beka, and Elle hear the Bell ring trice and the Back Door open and then eventually close.

Robyn walks behind each of the threesome. Behind Beka, Robyn observes that a bead of brodeas swings free below her bare box, so Robyn lifts her foot up and spools the thread onto the top of her foot, and allows Elle to lolly her foot clean.

Yes, there is something about the Game that sure does drive Beka to produce the pollen! Elle admits as she cleans Robyn's foot. It doesn't take much; Beka Broda's compliance draws Elle in and deepens a groove into both newbies' brain cells.

"Pull the seam of your jeans to the side," Robyn instructs, "that way one of our own Cosmos Cams can collect your nookie and nadir way."

Elle obeys. Her face and chest flush, her nipples harden, and her clit worms out. Deep in her chest Elle fears, *I don't want to be following Beka. It is all too easy, too natural. Already, right now, I have my noogies and nookie and nadir exposed, just like my Roommate. And Beka is already slipping away.*

Elle confirms that her belly button remain nestled in the open triangle above her zipper where the fastening snap is gone, and that *both of us hairage. I suspect all us Cosmos will be doing pussy and asshole shoots before we Opt, no matter what direction we head. Me included.*

Robyn pauses behind Steph. She kicks Steph's knees wider apart and addresses her. "Seems like Boss Bitch didn't think I was harsh enough on you. So she moves you into the Mudpit to show you she's harder than me. No problem. I can show you I'm harder still. So reach your hands back to your vag and pull your pink apart."

Steph sighs, but obeys. Now she must rest her cheek in the dirt while pressing her face to the post. Stern still high. She reaches in between her legs, finds her sex lips, and butterflies.

Robyn firms, "Stay like that." And heads toward the Back Door.

Steph can't decide. *Which is worse. Me having to stay covered with dust, me having to expose myself, or me needing to pee soon.*

§ Steph Urges Beka & Elle: Pinking & Cream Competition

Steph feels with her thumb to make sure her tube belt doesn't block navelage. She's learning, and she gets tiring holding her stern up and her lips wide. But she holds her position with her cheeks where the Post meets the ground. *I can't tell if I'm wet or dry with the sun and the air, but I know I'm going to get my lips burnt. Just like Kimju did.*

Beka, likewise with her face in the dirt and adjacent to her Post, relishes the Cam's hovering attention. She allows herself to move her hands between her uplifted spread legs, pull her own pink wide, and leisurely masturbate. Nothing in the way when one wears a miniskirt. And nothing to prevent breastplay when one holds one's croptop in one's teeth. Possibly Beka will be able to sneak in a climax were it not a vibe from first Elle, "Stop it! You know we're not allowed to bambo-nambo!"

Elle still holds her seam wide to the side and kneels with her face on the ground, her knees spaced wide, and her nachas risen. The Cam dutifully indexes her entire butt crack, nadir entrance in close-up, her full niche line her beneath curly pubic hair, parted ever enough so Gamers can observe the top the clithood settled inside.

Beka slows up touching herself. "It's okay, Elle, we're allowed whatever. It's not like we have a choice anymore, we're already begging to Pledge naked and cum be Strippers next Term."

"Shut up, both of you," Steph commands. "It's bad enough I have to wear a stinking' undershirt rolled around my waist, stick my stern up high mast, and have my former Pledge order me to pink myself."

Steph gathers her forces, and directs vitriol toward Beka. "Listen, I don't need to be competing with you about who has to pull pink. So either both of you get with the program or neither of you. Understand me?"

Elle says, "Yeah, sure Steph, you can't tell me to pull pink, and I'm sorry Beka's gotten out in front of you."

"Nobody gets out in front of me, Pledge," Steph tells Elle.

Beka takes a deep breath and comes down off her high. A bead of broda disconnects and soaks into Earth. Ah, the advantages of foot-net. Beka slowly fingers her bene and rolls her bolus with a fingertip. She sops.

Elle explains, "Beka's way ahead of you in the cream department. Robyn's gonna make you work up cream with Beka, just like she made you spread with her."

"Robyn's gonna make *you* pink and cream with *your* Roommate!" Steph asserts to Elle. "So tell me, Pledge, are you going to pink right now or are you going to wait until after you Flip-Flop?"

Elle snaps, "Steph Sorostitute, you just don't want any competition pulling your pink! Or hanging a stalactite outta your slot."

Steph opens her mouth to bite back but an interruption occurs.

§ Tiffany & Steph: Shall Masturbate & Cream Together

The Back Door opens and a still-naked Tiffany emerges. Tiffany steps off the Landing, rings the Bell, strides toward the Three Cosmos holding onto their Henge Posts, and stops short of them. She speaks downward to three faces in dirt. "Beka and Elle, you're wanted in the Bathroom."

Tiffany moves down onto her own face and knees, kisses her Post at its base, and speaks to the remaining Cosmos Pledge, "Steph, I shall join you! Sorry, but you will not be able to monopolize pink. And if you masturbate with me, I'll help synchronize some surge outta your slot."

§ Robyn Makes Up Beka & Elle: To Witness Alumni Reprise

Robyn greets the newbies as they arrive in the Bathroom. Kimju and Molly stand spread surrender, and naked as they are required to be in this room. Both faces look like cartoonish Whores. Both reek of perfume.

Robyn holds the Makeup Case in her hands. She rotates her shoulders and signs Beka and Elle into matching positions facing the Nugget Alumni. "Maybe you two newbies should beg to accompany Kimju and Molly to the Nugget and watch their Alumni Reprise." Robyn pronounces. "You could witness the Cosmos at their finest."

Elle flinches, Beka opens her mouth, and Kimju furrows her brow, *Wait a minute. Wait a minute.* Kimju catches herself before she opens her mouth, sneaks a lick on the lips. *Little good can come from any Robyn idea.* She trades a glance with Molly. *This is a more complex mission than an Alumni Reprise at the Nugget. Or teaching the newbies dance steps.*

Elle senses this might be coming. *It's bad enough I've had to let my halter hang down all the time.* Well, much of the time. *Like outside on the Post Henge where all the paparazzi could all harvest me.* Elle considers the Bathroom Cam hovering a-front her. *Like now. Different Cam, same boobage.*

Beka no longer holds her croptop in her teeth; it hangs down, sort of covering her berks, sort of not. Beka advances, "Robyn, please let us go watch Kimju and Molly's Alumni Reprise! Elle and me both. Seeing them in front of a Crowd would be even more super that watching them climax in sync with their *Nugget Stripper Videos.* Please, please, Robyn."

"Beka," Elle advances, "we've already seen more of Kimju and Molly than we need to. We saw their Pink Pages."

Beka insists, "Elle, we've never seen a live show!"

Elle glares at her Roommate. "And you get wet way to easily."

"It sounds like this is great opportunity then!" Robyn curls, "Because tonight will not be your ordinary 'live Stripper show with bunch of Nuggets.' That's because Kimju and Molly are not Strippers. They are Cosmos Pledge."

"So do they have to obey Stripper Rules?" Beka hurries.

Elle comes more to the point, "Yeah, and what about us, Robyn?"

Robyn squares the foursome so the two ex-Strippers face the two newbies, yet far enough apart so she can walk in between the two side-by-side and facing pairs of Cosmos Pledge. She raises her chin, turns to Beka and Elle, and gestures toward Kimju and Molly. "Be sure these two Nugget Alumni demonstrate their skills tonight. May each masturbate whatever cloth lies against their clit, flash koot and mutton, butterfly pink, and fingerball their clits. They may even finger-fuck themselves, pool cream, taste and trade. But their most important mission is locate the Double Dong and ride it to orgasm. Got it?"

Elle responds, "Ma'am, yes, Ma'am. We'll keep our eye on them." Elle provides a glance out of the side of her eye toward Beka.

"Beg." Robyn commands them.

Beka and Elle beg in unison, "Please let me Pledge naked and cum be a Stripper next Term."

"Oval mouth," Robyn commands them, and takes it upon herself to makeup the two newbies. Their makeup is less in the direction of the overdone and whorish Kimju and Molly, but rather a party-night club-kid look. *We could have done this ourselves,* Elle observes as she looks in the mirror. *Better too. So could Tiffany, were she not outside pulling pink on the Post Henge with Steph.*

What disturbs Elle the most is when Robyn hairsprays color into any exposed pubic hair. Kimju, butched and to both sides of her splayed thong, gets dusted orange. Molly catches red hairspray on both sides of the thick black hairage growing outward from her mooe. Beka's racing strip gets a green tint, and Elle's always hairage to both sides of her seam acquire blue sparkle.

Perfume is dashed on. Kimju and Molly get a heavy second coat and are invited to rub perfume onto their breasts. Both appreciate the opportunity to move their hands from behind their heads.

Kimju complains, "Robyn, I don't like smelling like an advertisement."

"I know," Robyn says, "That why you need to do it."

Robyn sprays perfume judiciously upon Beka and Elle. Both get a dot in the armpit, a spot on the neck, a dab behind the ear, a tap on the wrist.

"More please," Beka begs.

Robyn ignores this request. She commands the Four Cosmos, "Palms forward and up."

Beka and Elle follow Kimju and Molly and present their hands forward with their palms turned up. Robyn walks to the center of the Four, and dispenses a thick grease from a tube into the eight palms, and says, "Put that on your nipples. Now."

Kimju and Molly are first to bring the thick substance to their nipples. It is not grease but it is like grease or fat except it lubricates the surface of the nipples, and the areola too. Beka grabs her croptop with her teeth and follows almost instinctively; Elle lingers until she can linger no more. Four Cosmos play with their nipples; they roll the ends with their fingertips, brush them with fingernails, and circumnavigate their areolas.

§ Robyn Orders Kimju & Molly and Beka & Elle: *All* Beg to Strip

Elle catches a glimpse of herself in one of the Bathroom's mirrors. The grease also has color. I have bright blue nipples now. Elle feels her nipples burn. She looks again. *I'm decorated, my nipples erect, and I'm on Cam.*

Elle triple blinks and challenges, "Hey Robyn, why are Beka and I making up *our* nipples. We're not dancing tonight."

"You wish." Robyn snickers and tolls. "Nippleplay is a craft practiced by Strippers, but for you, newbie Pledge, nippleplay is an act of volition."

Robyn detects Elle cast a frown and elaborates. "Kimju and Molly know this. Acts of volition demonstrate your commitment to Strip. Your desire. Your urgency. That you mean what you say. Like you're learning to dance. Your endless titters and hairage and vagflash." Robyn bends toward Beka. "Your all-too-frequent pink and cream."

Beka perks, "I'll strip naked and spread and stay pink-wet-and-ready."

Robyn chuckles, "You will." She turns to Elle, and signs her to abandon hesitancy in rolling her nips, and speaks to both newbies. "The only secret you two have left are your insides, because after you get Flip-Flopped you're going to be turned inside out. And that won't be the end of it. You're gonna wear your Garments inside out, wear them backwards, wear them upside down. You're gonna be physically revealed, sexually released, and deep souled."

Robyn gives pause, then pans her eyes across all Four Cosmos, "So Pledge how does it go? Beg for me." Robyn commands.

Kimju and Molly trade eyes and Three Cosmos recite, "Please let me Pledge naked and cum be a Stripper next Term."

Robyn smiles. "Guest Mistress and Monitor Babs await you in the alley behind the Backyard, so I have the pleasure of making sure you don't embarrass yourselves, your Monitor, or your House." Robyn tilts a nose down toward Kimju, "You need to obey me as if Monitor Babs speaks with her own voice. You heard her instructions, Pledge?"

"Ma'am, yes, Ma'am." Kimju imagines herself without the thong, naked and spread, center Stage at the Nugget.
So recite for me," Robyn commands. "*All* together now."

This time Elle trades eyes with Kimju and this time Four Cosmos recite, "Please let me Pledge naked and cum be a Stripper next Term."

Elle realizes, *Kimju has just become the fifth Cosmos to beg to Strip— all of us except BB and Robyn and Steph now beg to Opt Down.* Elle takes a deep breath and feels release. *Okay.*

Robyn smiles at Kimju and flips her chin with a finger, "Don't worry my Stripper-begging, Pee-Camming Roommate, before the night is over you'll be begging to advance to a Piss Mouth. Like Molly here."

This time Kimju lashes back, "Hey Robyn, maybe you're the one who should be sharing the Pee-Cam with me. I'm not the only one here with only one Garment."

"True, Kimju," Robyn parlays, "you and Molly and Steph all have one piece… and you're all Opting Down."

The combat makes Elle anxious. *Robyn also has only one Garment. Beka and I still have our two pieces, the only problem is that Beka is now begging for real.*

Elle considers her two currently naked dance instructors. *It's no secret Molly wants to dance and begs attendance for real. And I'm sure Kimju doesn't wants to beg but she feels she has to keep up with Molly. Or obey Robyn as per Babs. This will be an interesting and dangerous visit. There's nothing I can do to stop this Alumni Reprise from happening. And there is no reason for me to be there.*

Elle is right about Kimju. Kimju frowns in determination, *I don't want to be dancing at the Nugget again. Not this Term, not next Term, not ever. And even though I'm a Cosmos Pledge, Gamers keep forcing me to pullaside, pink, cream, and climax myself. On the Yacht Robyn made me beg a Pee-Cam Obeisance. And just now she's making me beg to Pledge naked and cum be a Stripper next Term.*

If the Gamers make Steph also beg that means there will be six of us "begging" for four slots. Tiffany, Molly, and Beka really want it, and Elle needs to lose a Garment or two and become convinced.

That said, I must remain vigilant about Roommate Robyn Redacted, especially if she really has Charm. But even if I play a Roommate Game with Robyn, lose and come out naked, I still have the rest of the Term to plunder and rob. Kimju draws a small smile on her face. *I didn't really mean that, of course.*

Elle contemplates about the validity of her own begging. *Steph told me she assumes the begging is only pro forma. Except she's now pulling pink for the Prefecture. She was a Monitor last Term, and I should have asked her if she ever got to see inside the Nugget.*

Robyn addresses them all. "Monitor Babs shall attend with Game Mistress and a Van in the alley awaits you." She leans in to Kimju and Molly. "*Don't* disappoint Boss Babe! Now chant for me, all of you."

So they grease their nipples and beg in unison, "Please let me Pledge naked and cum be a Stripper next Term."

"Beg BB and GM as soon as you see them," Robyn augments, "Now all of you scram!"

And they do. Kimju and Molly slip into their tanga and panties, then Beka and Elle follow them down the angular stairs, out the Back Door, and a-ringing the Bell.

More boobage, different Cam. Elle steadies. *Kimju and Molly don't want an Alumni Reprise. And I don't want to lolly up Beka if she begs to Audition and hangs a bead outta her brim.*

Elle tries not to rest her eyes upon the naked Tiffany and near-naked Steph kneeling with their faces against Henge Posts, with at least one of them dangling tapioca outta her trap. Elle's glance reveals that Steph's spouts have erected and she steals a glance of herself. *I'm puckered up too,* Elle admits. *I am not ready for this. I am not ready for Kundalini.*

Elle scans upward at windows of houses adjacent, scans along the top of the hedge. *Okay, so the paparazzi collected my boobage again.* Elle gathers the ends of her dangling halter neck strap into her fingertips, smoothes the fabric flat, and considers if she should re-buttons her neck strap.

§ Game Mistress & Babs: Greet Kimju & Molly and Beka & Elle

Game Mistress and Babs stand by the back door of a Van parked in the alley. Babs introduces, "Game Mistress, these are Four Cosmos Pledge. Pledge, Game Mistress grants you permission to look at her, but to never look her in the eye. Kapish?"

"Ma'am, yes, Ma'am," Kimju and Molly and Beka and Elle respond in unison. Furtive glances. Game Mistress wears a black second skin bodysuit, headgear, gloves, and boots. Bikini Babe wears her black bra and nombril. Underwire, wide-side straps, generous cleavage, areolage to top it off.

Game Mistress smiles at the Four Cosmos Pledge. "Don't you love how your Monitor's nombril, waistline at N-4, almost kisses her completely hidden pubic hair?"

The Four Cosmos Pledge are caught speechless by this remark, and wisely remain so. Pledge know N-4 means Babs' waistline lies four inches below her navel and feel GM take power by stating the obvious.

The side of the alley is within the domain of the Back Door Cam, and the alley and beyond is within reach of the paparazzi. Elle flushes, and once again, her nipples erect, visible even amidst the colored grease. Walking has made Beka's croptop fall back down into place, but Kimju and Molly remain topless."

Molly begs, "Ma'am please let me Pledge naked and cum be a Stripper next Term."

Beka bursts, "Me too, please. All of us."

Guest Mistress raises her chin. Elle assays that the bodysuit that covers GM covers her completely. Still, it has a lots of zippers, including a circular zipper around a open-spot navelage. *Navelage 24x7? For a GM?* Elle wonders.

Babs does her duty, "All together now."

And so Kimju and Molly and Beka and Elle chant, "Please let me Pledge naked and cum be a Stripper next Term."

A pause. Kimju moves uneasily. *I've already had to pink, pee, cream, and climax this Term. Now Gamers got me begging to go to the Nugget to make an Alumni Reprise. I'll have to Double Dong with Molly center Stage. It will be a full Club and halfway to Opt Strip next Term.*

Molly touches herself.

Beka freshens.

And Elle presses a finger into one of her nips. *There is like chilly pepper in the grease paint. It makes my nipples hot.* And I'm going to have to watch Kimju and Molly double dong at the Nugget.

Game Mistress speaks. "At ease, Pledge. House Mom el Capitan invited me to visit the Nugget tonight and your Monitor has been so kind as to pick me up and drive me there." GM pauses, tucks her head. "I trust you'll forgive her for the time away from catering to your needs, and a promise you that I will personally make up for any lack of attention on her part."

GM bows to Beka and Elle, "I shall join with you that we might witness Kimju and Molly's Alumni Reprise."

The Pledge tense.

GM continues, "You," she points to Elle, "Pull that halter back up over your nugs and button it properly. Don't worry, you can always unbutton it again in the Club. Buttons are a big fetish there."

Elle scrambles her halter up. The grease gets smudged on the inside.

"Now kiss my boots one after another and then crawl into the back of the Van," GM orders.

Pledge obey.

§ Kimju & Molly and Beka & Elle: Anticipate Nugget in the Van

The Four Cosmos Pledge—Kimju and Molly, and Beka and Elle—sit on the floor in the back of the Van. Up front, separated by a partition, Babs drives, and Game Mistress rides shotgun. Molly finds the ride similar to the one she took with Steph to the Figure Drawing Class during *The Arrivals*, except it is dark outside and the lights that slash through the back comes from signs, storefronts, gas stations.

The car ride provides an opportunity for each Cosmos to anticipate the Nugget.

Beka asks first. "What's being a Stripper at the Nugget really like?" The question directs to Kimju and Molly, ex-Nuggets who stripped there last Term."

Elle irritates, "Beka, don't be rude, we've already seen Kimju and Molly's *Nugget Stripper Videos*. We know what the Nugget is like."

Beka counters, "And we've seen Penny and Coco's *Shave & Climax Video* and their *Side-by-Side Video*." Beka turns to Kimju and Molly, "So are we going to get to see Penny and Coco dance naked? Live?"

"Beka!" Elle interjects. "We don't need to see them live, we're already seen their *Double Dong Climax Video.*"

Kimju stabilizes. "It's okay, neither of you can be rude to Molly and me. We're your instructors. We get you ready for your own Audition." Kimju smiles, "It's not like your not begging to Strip at the Nugget."

Beka wants to know, "Is an Audition something special, Kimju?"

Kimju smiles. "It's a capital letter Event, just like an Alumni Reprise."

Elle checks to make sure her thighs are not touching.

Beka rushes, "Kimju, I heard about the bottle dance. I'm not keen about picking up beer bottles from tables by squeezing my breech. If I get really slippery I might not be able to hold tight enough. What happens if I drop one?"

Elle choughs. *Especially a bottle half full.* Elle steadies herself, speaks, "Wouldn't bottle dancing be Whore work?"

"Good question," Kimju perks, "Except Game Rules allow all Strippers to insert: dildos, buttplugs, both at once. It doesn't matter what it is. Eating a banana, hollow ben-wa balls, a procto with an AI inside."

"No cocks." Elle attempts to confirm.

"Only Whores get cocks," Kimju advises.

Elle extracts the crotch of her shorts from hiding in her nookie. "Tell us what to expect tonight, Kimju." Elle considers. "And how we should be."

Kimju appreciates Elle's concern about begging to Strip next while fearing its commitment. She speaks about more benign experience. "Ah, the things Strippers do!" Kimju aligns the outside of a tanga that almost covers all of her butched pubic hair. *My little outline hairage.*

Kimju also dirties her bare keister on the Van floor; she continues, "You might think it is easy pulling pink for a bunch of Patrons sitting in a circle around the center Stage. Okay, so that's simple. And any Gamer who isn't in the Club can watch live or download from Automatron. But Nuggets also work outside the confines of the Club: Bachelor Parties, Adult Entertainment Expos, photoshoots."

"One thing a Stripper learns quickly is to follow the Rules, or one won't stay a Stripper for long," Molly advises.

Elle guesses, "It's the Gamers watching who catch you."

"And demand retribution." Kimju posits. "Some would say punishment and degradation, others suggest correction. I mean face it, Robyn didn't need to make me beg to Opt Down next Term.

Molly passes hearsay. "Tiffany says last time she stripped—two Terms ago—she broke the rules and sucked cock when she wasn't supposed to, so as 'punishment' for that she Opted Whore last Term. Which she immediately turned into Porn Stardom."

"Why doesn't she just break the Rules again this Term?" Beka asks. "She could have sucked cock at the Peacock House the day she arrived."

Kimju explains, "Because if she sucks cock as a Pledge, she will discover herself in Lockdown for the rest of this Term, however she will not get broken to Whore next Term, she will be Slavesex."

Molly details. "If either of you get caught sucked cock, you will most likely get broken to Whore, but because Tiffany was a Whore once before, she'd get broken to one Caste lower, and become Slavesex." Molly squishes her palms onto her breasts and rubs the grease over a wider area.

Kimju details. "Don't worry, this is not about you two newbies tonight. This is about Molly and me. Whether we like it or not."

Molly details. "The Crowd wants another shot of us, and they're going to get it."

"Whether we like it or not," Kimju caps.

"Maybe you two can Flip-Flop!" Beka suggests.

Kimju catches the toss, "Sorry, Beka, but Molly and I aren't Roommates. So no Roommate Games for us.

Beka blurts, "Elle and I are Roommates, so we can Flip-Flop!"

Molly states, "Don't get in my way, either of you, I need to make the cut. I'm begging to Strip next Term. For real. So don't forget I'm ahead of you in line to the Nugget. Don't upstage me, don't try to cut in the line; I begged before you did.

Elle assures, "Yeah, sure, Molly. I guess only Tiffany is in front of you." *And maybe either Beka or I are next in line.*

There is silence for a moment as the Four Cosmos consider the plight of Tiffany and Steph, cheeks and spread knees on the ground, pinking in the Backyard.

Elle queries the Alumni, "Tiffany said that some of the images on your Pink Pages were where taken in the Camera Lounge, while you were Strippers last Term.

Beka brightens, "And that you posed for anybody for tips!"

Kimju nods, "You two pretty much got that right."

Molly agrees, "We got fondled for tips."

Kimju rubs her bare kaboose on the gritty van floor. "When Tiffany visited and Feature Danced, she also shot in the Inner Sanctuary. In the Camera Lounge all you're allowed to do is pink and carry on. In the Champaign Room you can fool around but no sex is allowed. In the Sanctuary a Porn Star can shoot a *Suck Fuck Anal DP A2M Facial Gangbang Video.*"

Molly augments, "Lesbian, too. Eating, Every kind of sex stimulant.

Elle, astonished. "You had to do all that?"

"Not us, silly," Molly provides, "We were Strippers and Strippers aren't allowed to do that kind of play! But Tiffany wasn't a Stripper, she wasn't a Nugget last Term. She was a visiting Feature Dancer.

"A Whore stabled at Flesh Ranch," Kimju augments.

"A Porn Star," Elle places. "So did Tiffany trick at the Nugget?" she asks. "Did she shoot *Videos* there?"

"Whores suck and fuck cock, Pledge Elle." Kimju stretches her bellage and dances her keister on the floor of the Van. "Maybe Molly and I pinked, dildoed and climaxed center Stage. Maybe we both let the Patrons take liberties when we lapdanced. But Tiffany sucked dick and took facials on her hands and knees in the Champagne Room."

"And we saw her shoot *Suck Fuck Anal Videos* in the Inner Sanctuary," Kimju states.

"We had to watch," Molly adds. "Everything, DP, facials, lesbian, creampies. House Mom el Capitan insisted."

"MomCap." Elle seeks clarification.

"One and the same," Kimju rings. "Be respectful to her if you meet. She might be two Castes below Game Mistress, but she's still a Caste above Monitor Babs."

"Two castes above us," Molly reminds. "Besides, you've seen Tiffany's *Tiny Tit Suck Fuck Facial Videos*. Remember?"

"I kinda didn't pay attention," Elle looks across the Van floor at her Roommate Beka's upskirted bare box, racing strip in the clear, miniskirt upped just enough so that Beka doesn't have to sit on the hem. Like Kimju and Molly, *Beka also bounces butt flesh on the Van floor*. Elle considers her own frayed jeans shorts. *Even I am sitting with my nachas a natural on the floor .*

"Don't worry, Elle," Molly assures, "Maybe sometimes Strippers get fondled during lapdances even if they're not supposed to, but there is no way that the Patrons can take their dicks out and put them inside you. You're safe."

"I'm not lapdancing!" Elle proclaims.

"And you're not allowed in the Champagne Room or Inner Sanctuary," Molly warns.

Elle's head spins.

Kimju guides, "Your best hope is that you and Beka get to pose in the Camera Lounge. Nothing stopping either of you from pulling pink."

Elle quiets. *Okay, so I've already pullaside and vagflash, but that's a world of difference from spreading, and then opening up my insides.*

No so for Beka. "I'll spread my legs and pull pink. I'll masturbate solo or with anyone. And you've seem me hang broda." She gathers momentum. "If they let me climax they can all cam me."

Beka lifts her butt off the Van floor and points her rectum toward the ex-Nugget Strippers. "I've already shown off my brownie before. Taken the thermoprobe, also a gelatin egg. Elle too."

Elle cringes at getting drawn in; Molly rescues. "Beka, stick with me and we'll both get to Strip next Term."

Elle breathes deeply. *I know Beka and I know I can't stop her. Maybe I have to let her go in order to Opt Up. Still, I know Gamers will want to thermoprobe* my *nadir_way and make me beg to pull my nymphae apart. Maybe it's something I have to do if I expect to Monitor next Term.*

Kimju consoles Elle, "Don't worry about having a seam through your crotch. You should know by now how to pullaside and vagflash. But unlike your Roommate you have yet to pull pink, freshen and make wet, and get your body ready to climax." Kimju tilts her head. "Don't think you're the only one who keeps track of the Game."

Elle opens her mouth; closes it. *Well, no, not entirely.* She rolls her eyeballs to their upper left limit, stretches the muscles, blinks, and restores eyes-forward vision. *We are headed to an Alumni Reprise, not a Stripper Audition.*

Molly provides equal opportunity assurance, "Don't worry, sooner or later both you newbies will get to pink and cream for the Nugget Crowd. They're gonna love you."

Kimju pushes her shoulders forward and tells it like she thinks it is, "Gamers got you two newbies figured out. The one of you that's wet all the time gonna wait, and the one of you that's dry… well Gamers got ways to freshen you up. And then you will both get your brains climaxed out!"

§ Kimju & Molly and Beka & Elle: Penny & Coco & Double Dong

Beka jumps a question, "So will we get to watch Penny and Coco dance?"

Kimju mulls, "You might get to watch them walking around with the Dong stuffed."

"We saw that on the Video," Beka hurries, "Robyn also screened them climaxing the Dong, but they were solo.

Kimju escalates her response, "I'm sure Monitor Babs will get to watch Penny and Coco perform whether BB wants to or not. Nice of MomCap to invite Game Mistress.

Elle queries, carefully, "So Strippers can climax on the Dong solo, just like they would on any other toy. Furthermore Strippers aren't allowed to share the Double Dong. But are they required to beg the Dong? And what does that mean?"

Kimju and Molly trade glances and shrug. "Strippers aren't required to beg the Double Dong, Elle," Kimju advances. "But if they do beg to ride that means they must be prepared to Opt Up *or* Opt Down. Opt Pledge or Opt Strip. A Stripper who doesn't beg the Dong can beg to only Opt Up or only Opt Down."

"Why would Penny and Coco do that, Kimju?" Elle asks. "It's a risky position."

"Maybe they liked their taste of sharing the Dong at the end of last Term, and now they are frustrated at soloing it." Kimju shrugs.

"They want to deepen their commitment with Kundalini," Molly suggests. Besides, what's a Stripper to do; come Midnight the Gamers will Opt each of them one way or the other."

"I can't speak for Babs," Kimju says, 'but I know Janet prefers Penny and Coco Opt more Castes away from her. She's probably right that they harbor vengeance, whether or not Babs wants to believe it. I suspect Penny and Coco also harbor vengeance against Babs and Robyn and Steph, for disrupting what had been an agreed upon command and control."

Elle listens. "It's a lot to keep track of, Kimju. You're a good teacher, even if I don't intend to become a Stripper next Term."

"You're the one begging to Pledge naked and Strip," Kimju reminds, and reconsiders her latest begging. "Well, I guess all four of us are."

Elle considers. "Except right now Beka and I got two pieces. You and Molly really do only have one Garment. Even Tiffany has two pieces. So it's really you two who are at the head of the line."

"That's a good thing," Molly speaks.

"Speak for yourself," Kimju snaps.

Elle considers. "Robyn says Steph is going to beg Stripper too. That will make three of you begging with only one piece."

Kimju scowls, "That will make all of us except Babs and Robyn begging to Opt Down."

"I'll forfeit a piece so I can qualify for Opt Stripper," Beka decrees.

"I'll be keeping my two pieces," Elle insists.

"That's your plan." Kimju states.

Elle stirs. "That's my goal."

"May you succeed!" Molly congratulates. "Good you know what your goal is. If I can keep only one piece I won't have to streak to the Nugget next Term, although I expect I will give my panties to Steph at the Greatest House Roar Winner-Take-All. And maybe get a piece elsewhere."

Kimju blazons, "Molly thinks she can Strip next Term, then Pledge the Term after that, you know, oscillate. I do intend to acquire a second Garment and Opt Up. Although pretty much anything I'd have to do as a Stripper I might as well do now. Showing them I'm willing is about the only way to not Strip next Term."

"Plus you can get over on Robyn," Elle observes.

"You will get to watch Kimju and I perform tonight," Molly declares. "I expect we will climax on the Double Dong. Don't upstage us. You will get your own chances to dance."

Elle's head quivers, a terse, high frequency oscillation. "That is not what I though would be happening when I got into this."

"So?" Kimju encourages, "What's the rush to Opt Up? Play the Game. See where it takes you. Yes, you can push and shove and yes you have two Garments, but trust me, before the Term is out you will be buck naked, masturbating yourself to climax, and begging to Strip for real."

"You're both adorable," Molly insists, "the Crowd will love you. But don't upstage us. I need this."

Elle looks at her Roommate. "I wouldn't be here except for trying to protect Beka. I know from before that she can't keep control of herself. I though I could save her."

"You can't!" Beka excites to Elle. "I'm Stripping at the Nugget next Term. And you're coming with me."

"Patience please," Kimju holds out her hands toward Beka. "You're going to make a great Stripper and you will be tremendously popular. And you do need to carry Elle along."

Elle grouses, "I couldn't make myself cum in front of anybody. Maybe while having great sex with a great guy, but sitting in front of a group of men or a Cam and actually climaxing? That's impossible."

"Cheer up," Molly consoles, "You sound just like I did before I began Stripping. And listen to me: It's very important you Double Dong with Beka before the Term is out, because next Term, once you both become Strippers, you won't be allowed to."

Elle purses her lips, "Gee, thanks, Molly."

§ Beka & Elle: Arrive at the Nugget & Visit the Camera Lounge

Beka and Elle are presentable enough to make the journey from the Van to the Nugget front door. Game Mistress opens the back door of the Van, and photographers capture them flashing their way out. Beka delivers the full upskirt monte; Elle isn't able to do this but provides leanover titter in her halter top. Both have yet to discover their fans. The bravest of the paparazzi reach into the door and flash the sitting topless Kimju and Molly, their legs kept wide like they should be, but with their tanga and panties covering them as best possible. No Watering Can. The Van door closes with Kimju and Molly still inside.

Game Mistress accompanies Beka and Elle toward the front door of the Club. Elle identifies the Nugget sign, but a disorientated Beka misses the flashing neon. Double doors part for their entrance.

The darker entrance way is punctuated with Screens and neon. Elle's eyes adjust to the Screen: A giant birthday cake sits in front of a man of giant girth, with dozens of candles. Two naked and shaven women that Beka and Elle recognize as Penny and Coco enter the frame, stand on the table on each side of the cake, release urine, and proceed to put out the candles. The roly-poly man peals with laughter, and the scene jumps back to the beginning and loops again.

The Hat Check Girl catches their eyes. She wears a corset and thigh-high boots, and nothing else. Two Garments. The ring in her nose, double pierced nipples, and a spike ball dangling from a ring above her clit and shaven vulva don't count as Garments. Elle can't begin to inventory her tattoos.

Commotion erupts; the protection of Game Mistress is augmented by the outstretched left wing of the Maître d', a vampirish goth figure, complete with colored contacts, fangs, and a cape. The Maître d' simultaneously comforts and alarms.

"Ladies," the bat bows deeply, lifts one wing of the cape, and directs Beka and Elle, now inside a narrow foyer, to twist left through an opening and then through darkness and a right turn and they find themselves thrust into the Camera Lounge, their first stop. Game Mistress has vanished. VIPs huddle about; the vampire encourages Beka and Elle pose with and for guests who have cameras. Everything from cell phones to pro formats. Elle feels battered by the din; Beka feels elevated.

Deeper into the Lounge the Maître d' allows them to pose standing side-by-side on a small dais. Hold hands. The bat encourages the Roommates to acknowledge requests for kissing, and then French kissing. Beka draws Elle in—she's strong this way—and soon kissing musses up their over-heavy makeup and leaves behind smeared lipstick, even lip imprints on checks, foreheads, and necks. The packed, intimate space ripples as flashes illuminate skin.

The vampire encourages them to sit down on a couch and make themselves comfortable. Will the Maître d' let the defenseless Beka spread her legs and show off what's in-between? Of course the bat will. Is Beka oozing wetness? Absolutely, and the flashes go pop. Will Beka object to suggestions that she flap her own wings wide apart? She hesitates for two heartbeats, then butterflies her full creamy bourse. It's Beka's first wide-open public pinking performance, and the Cams document pronounced inner lips tinted a dark brown. Beka catches juice on a fingertip and daps her clit to verify its hardness. She looks about for guidance and finds the vampire. It signs her to hold her position. Good work!

Elle cringes. *If Beka pulls up her croptop and exposes both of her breasts will I have to unbutton my neck strap and let my halter fall down?* Sure. *Or rub my crotch seam against my clit or cinch it down into my nappy?* Elle feels the space in her peripheral vision close down and she joins arms with Beka.

The bat flaps to their rescue. "Don't be jealous, the vampire advises Elle, completely misunderstanding her fear, MomCap will make sure that you also get to Audition your pink!" The Maître d' swoops into action, sweeps up the two Pledge from their entrapment, and scurries them out into the main room amongst scattered applause.

As the newbies advance the applause thickens and the photo perverts spill out into the main Club behind them. The bat herds Beka and Elle forward side-by-side, wings partly open, toward a table and four chairs at the Stage's edge. Game Mistress has already been seated. Beka and Elle gather their bearings, permit themselves to be shooed forward, smooth out their costumes, and allow the Maître d' to seat them. Leather chairs, and the feel of leather on the backs of thighs.

"At ease, Game Mistress tells them, "except you must still remember to keep your thighs apart."

Elle hears laughter ripple as she discovers her ripped shorts provide no alternative but to feel her nates pressing on leather.

"I'm not quite sure what all happened in there," she admits out loud.

§ MomCap Greets Babs and Kimju & Molly: Nugget Backstage

BB drives the Van around to an alley adjacent to the back entrance of the Nugget. Everyone calls it the Stage Door.

Kimju and Molly know all about the Stage Door but have never had to bolt topless to get there. When they had been Strippers last Term they were kept naked when off-duty, which was half of one's waking hours. They were usually naked on-duty as well. But being naked off-duty meant they couldn't venture outside—back or front door—unless they could borrow a costume.

The Nugget Shooter appears as the topless twosome—the Alumni—crawl on hands and knees out of the back of the Van, pivot themselves around, legs always agape, and rise onto bare feet. The parking area has an asphalt and gravel surface, not pleasant, and the Shooter—a gaunt figure of indeterminate sexuality—captures the "ouch" in their faces with the best quality high-resolution video. "Hold hands," Babs advises them as they dart, the stones painful on the soles of their feet, BB's included. Nor does Boss Babe escape the Nugget Shooter's Cam surveillance. Bling! And navelage 24x7.

The Nugget Shooter documents the dash of tits and asses to the Stage Door; their exterior venerability makes not only the two Pledge but also their Monitor crave the insides of the Club. It offers a place of safety and security. Will the Stage Door guard let them in?

Sprinting topless isn't illegal like streaking—and hey, haven't the Alumni begged to Parade topless? No worry; both scurry smoothly tonight. The Back Door Man, the guard at the Stage Door, welcomes them graciously. Kimju and Molly both know this monster—and ignore him—if only because once inside both Alumni must present themselves to House Mom el Capitan. She who is not to be ignored.

MomCap greets them inside the Stage Door. She wears a front button shirt tied just above the waistline, jeans, and shoes of the sneaker type.

She's got a little roll of belly sticking out with an outie. Babs doesn't have the stupidity to ask her commander if she too must also navelage.

MomCap welcomes and nods to Kimju and Molly. "So nice to see you again. It's proper for your Monitor Babs to address me as 'el Capitan' or simply 'MomCap.'" MomCap rubs her nostrils with the back of one hand. "Strippers, as I am sure you recall, always address me as 'House Mom.'" MomCap firms. "Certain the Cosmos Pledge may call me 'MomCap' as well, but as a sign of respect to me that you are begging to cum Strip naked next Term, then perhaps you should practice your future role and address me as 'House Mom,' and attempt to endear yourself to me."

Kimju and Molly know House Mom; she's a Hover from last Term, and they know she expects no nonsense from them. Kimju and Molly get it right the first time, "House Mom, thank you House Mom. Please let me Pledge naked and cum be a Stripper next Term."

House Mom shoos Kimju and Molly into the Dressing Room, just down the hall from the Stage Door, and sits them down side-by-side on a table, feet wide and knees up, hands behind head: sitting spread surrender. "Stay," MomCap tells them, and they obey, crotches open, tits hanging, eyes ahead, and mouths ovaled. One pair of armpits is deeply concave and smooth, the other is puffy and engrossed with black hair. Kimju and Molly have nowhere to go and are not privy to the agenda tonight, except, as MomCap puts it, "Not only are you two going to exhibit yourself, but you're getting an opportunity to debut your trainees. But don't worry, their Audition won't upstage you, you're the Alumni Reprise and the main Event tonight!"

Molly stretches and the fat rolls across her body, she suggestively shakes her milk cans for a Cam that canvasses her near-naked body, and wiggles in an attempt to worm her panties into her thick muliebre so that unshaven muff spills out both sides.

Kimju tenses up, and grimaces as her cloth tanga cameltoes itself into her keyway, threatening to reveal her clit and the triangle of pussy hair above it.

House Mom lavishes encouragement, "Maybe once you beg your thong and panties off you can show off your rings. Everybody wants to admire your progress!" And exits.

Molly licks her lips and spots her panties with fresh mucilage, and Kimju has a sudden urge to urinate. *Am I expected to Pee here tonight? Molly and me on Stage. Now that would be an Alumni Reprise!*

Babs finds herself awkwardly standing in the backstage hallway. She scans the hallway and hears the noise of the Crowd out front. *I have never been in a place like this before,* BB considers. *And I don't like it. I had assumed I would be borrowing Steph's minidress to wear overtop my bikini tonight but Game Mistress had not enabled any such opportunity.* Now Babs crosses her arms in front of herself, trying to comport herself with dignity and hide her areolage. She remains somewhat dumbfounded—rare for her—when House Mom el Capitan exits the Dressing Room. Babs draws herself tall; she does not say anything but her eyes dart wildly. Babs might stand taller, her figure might be more statuesque than el Capitan's more stout and lumpy figure, but *between my bikini and this place, I'm outranked,* Babs admits to herself. *And I'm overexposed.*

"Hello my Bikini Babe," House Mom el Capitan effuses to BB. "Stop crossing your arms," House Mom orders. Babs might have olive tone, nonetheless her body flushes, goose bumps form, and her areolas shrivel up.

"Lean over and smile for the Back Door Man," el Capitan instructs Babs.

She does, and as he eyes her the Back Door Man speaks, "Too bad Steph never brought you over when you were a Pledge. You're wearing a bigger bikini that we saw in your photos. Crowd's gonna miss your leaky muff and butt crack, but they still gonna love your boobs with your crescents there, all puckered up."

Babs turns even more red, raises an arm and runs it through her hair, plucks on her bra straps, and runs two thumbs inside the waistband of her culotte. The culotte might no longer be rolled down, but BB can do nothing to hide her areolage. MomCap claps her hands and effuses, "You look splendid! You're not overdressed but you're still a stand-out. Congratulations. Let me help you find your table."

They leave Back Door Man behind, and Babs feels his eyes follow her dimples, just above her waistline in back.

§ Game Mistress Greats Beka & Elle: Nugget Stage & Screen

Beka finds inside the Nugget transcendent. *I've found home. This is the most natural place I have ever been in my life. Nirvana.* Elle finds it terrifying, she closes in on herself, develops an urge to urinate, and controls panic. Game Mistress indicate they both sit at the small round table and they do, careful not to kick a tight sack mostly out of the way on the floor that serves as a footrest for GM.

Elle scans high and discovers the many Screens in the Club. Everywhere pink, cream and climax are demanded. A Screen in her small round table—deep beneath hardened glass might a Stripper gyrate on top—depicts such a dancer double penetrating and shaving at the same time. Elle blinks and looks up again.

The blare of the Club would obscure any sound from the Screens, but suddenly a pair of Screens in the mix catches Elle's eyes for a double-take, and yes, *there are Cams under the table that look up Beka's skirt... and at my own only slightly less bare crotch!* Elle catches many eyes in the Club watch her watch the Screen, sees Beka follow her eyes, and, recognizing her own upskirt, jump with glee and open her legs wider. There is a mummer of approval throughout the Club, and Beka looks across and sees many eyes.

Game Mistress leans forward to ask, "Did you get to perform in the Camera Lounge?"

Elle stumbles, "Ah, er, Ma'am, no. But Beka pinked."

GM issues a correction, "Pledge, you may address me as 'Mistress.'"

"Mistress, no disrespect intended, Mistress." Elle bows.

"No disrespect taken." Game Mistress bows back. "Maybe you can pink in the Camera Lounge after you Flip-Flop."

"Ma'am, I mean, Mistress, that would be an honor for me, Mistress." Elle amends. She squirms and opens her legs wider. Everyone in the Club catches Elle sneak a glance at the Screen. *Yes, my ripped jeans show nappy hairage to the sides.*

GM squints at Beka. "Do you know, Pledge, that your endless pink-wet-and-ready videos already populate the Nugget? Everyone already knows you seem to like things up your borehole, don't you Pledge?"

Beka falters and Elle steers, "Ma'am!" she says. "Beka's miniskirt always enables a full unobstructed view, and we both keep legs-apart, too, like Steph, 24x7.

Game Mistress considers the two newbies, purviews the Screen. "Wise of you to keep your legs more open than necessary," she says.

"We'll spread anywhere anyplace anytime." Beka declares.

"I understand that Steph now practices pulling pink and hanging streamers?" GM suggests. She knows.

Beka hustles, "Ma'am, I can hang a lot more broda than Steph. She couldn't keep up with me at the end of *The Arrivals* and she can't keep up with me now. Ask Elle, she's got to lolly up after the both of us!"

GM looks at Elle and raises her eyebrows.

Beka points upward, "We'll strip naked, pull pink, cream and climax right up there, center Stage. Elle and I both."

Yes, center Stage sits at eye level, wooden, with a brass pole in the middle. It forms most of a big circle, with an exit ramp at the rear that connects to a runway and two side stages near the back corners of the Club. A narrow rim around the circumference provides a place to rest drinks and display Tips.

"After we Flip-Flop, Elle can pink, cream, and climax like Kimju and Molly," Beka promises, "We both can!"

Game Mistress takes a big breath of air, speaks, "You two keep begging your Flip-Flop and your wish will be granted. Now, both of you," GM turns to Beka directly, "and you especially, shut up. Don't speak without being spoken to."

Beka looks at Elle and Elle forces a closed-lip smile and shrugs.

§ Babs & M/C introduce Beka & Elle: To the Nugget Patrons

Babs emerges from backstage and walks around the side stage on the floor to join Beka and Elle and Game Mistress, and as she breaks into view a soft scattering of applause and a follow spotlight welcome her. Boss Babe enjoys special merit. She's not a customer, she's not a Stripper, and she's not a Pledge.

The Master of Ceremonies identifies her, "Patrons, welcome Monitor Babs, Boss Babe of the Cosmos House!"

Babs nods and Gamers marvel at her poise and dignity. She walks carefully so that her lifted boobs don't unduly bounce, but she is still a barefoot Bikini Babe. And areolage just is. Applause follows her walk. The wiser among the Gamers know BB reports to MomCap, and that Guest Mistress, seated at the table with the two newbies, invited her. Babs pauses by her chair, makes a shallow bow yet enough to swing her bosom, and allows a sea of faces to purview of her full-bikini body. *Can't fight it, and I know I'd better not take chances. My waistline rides just above my pubic hair and although I might expose my dimples and rhombus, but at least I don't show the base of my spine or crack my posterior rugage.*

A whistle from the Crowd causes Babs to blush.

Game Mistress signs Babs to a seat; she then signs Beka and Elle to their feet and smiles approvingly as a flustered Beka and Elle rise. GM remains seated with her hands folded in front of her mouth. Caste has privileges.

"Ladies and Gentlemen," the MC booms, "welcome Cosmos Pledge Beka and Elle. They are auditioning in the Camera Lounge tonight because they are *begging* to become Nuggets!" Hoots. Beka makes a little wave with her hand and feels her precious fluid run down her inner thigh. There are whistles in the Club and scattered applause and Beka realizes her wetness is visible to all. She giggles.

The applause builds as several Screens in the Club come alive and feature Beka Broda from earlier tonight in the Camera Lounge. The Video shows Beka lying back holding her croptop up with her teeth so both boobies are exposed, then spreading her legs while pulling her beaver wide open with both hands. A white pond fills her inside. Pink-wet-and-ready doesn't get better than this.

Both newbies look to Monitor Babs for guidance and Babs, now seated, signs them both to titter. Elle looks to Beka, watches Beka dance her croptop up and down, and pulls her first one halter cup to the side then the other to flash first one nipple then the other. The Crowd cheers, and Babs signs them both to sit down. Both do, both carefully smooth their tops, and revert their legs to open position on sticky leather seats.

"Nugget wannabes Beka and Elle," the M/C wraps them up, more applause, "and make sure to catch them when they return to the Camera Lounge after tonight's feature act!" Another whoop, they newbies look at each other. Elle looks at the Club video Screens again and this time sees herself from the Camera Lounge earlier this evening. One noogie hangs out of her halter as she pulls the seam in her crotch to the side. Laughter trickles the Club.

I'm trapped, Elle realizes and looks at her Roommate, but Beka beams with glory and pride and Elle can smell Beka's wet. *What will I do if the M/C demands I beg to dance and get naked? I know Beka's reaction.*

A waitress—a topless transvestite with rouged nipples wearing a g-string, hose and high heels—brings hors d'oeuvres and watery liquids to them.

Game Mistress leans forward. "Have you been begging the Nugget?" she inquires.

"Absolutely!" Beka beams.

"And you?" Game Mistress looks toward Elle.

Elle practices diplomacy. "Mistress, we have begged to Pledge naked and cum be a Stripper next Term."

Beka hurries, "Elle and I already know how to dance, even though Kimju and Molly insist on giving us dancing lessons."

Elle looks GM in the eye, "Mistress, please, Mistress. We are by no means prepared to Audition the Nugget. Kimju says we first need to learn the 16 ways to take a bra off. And a whole lot of other stuff. Before the end of the Term."

"Maybe tonight you can demonstrate halter doff sequences!" Game Mistress thrills. "It's so much more suitable for a newbie, yes? And how many are there, Pledge Elle?"

Elle figures buttons at neck plus either front or back. "Six," if you also figure buttons in back. I either have to unbutton my neck first or the front, or unbutton the front first then the neck. So I only have two sequences."

Elle quiets. Praise comes in the form of a smile from Game Mistress. Followed by an order to both Beka and Elle: "Both of you together now, how does it go?"

No rapprochement. Beka and Elle recite in unison, "Please let me Pledge naked and cum be a Stripper next Term."

BB smiles across the table and watches Elle squirm, *Ouch! Way too close for comfort.*

"Praise Kundalini!" Game Mistress exclaims. "May Kundalini come forth and let you reveal yourselves—physically and emotionally and sexually. Mind, body, and soul. No secrets." Game Mistress gives each newbie a kiss on the forehead and examines their makeup. "You're both beautiful," she says as she wags a finger, "but you're going to have to wait to climax your brains out. Tonight is Kimju and Molly's Alumni Reprise!"

Beka squeezes her thighs, realizes she has just gushed onto her chair, and wiggles her thighs open again. She doesn't think anyone notices. Silly Pledge! She is about to open her mouth when Elle catches her eye and stops her. This time.

Beka quiets.

§ Beka & Elle: Watch Nugget Strippers Pink & Beckon

Elle tries to make sense out of her environment. If for Beka this first time in a Strip Club represents a discovery of home, then for Elle this first time feels threatening. *And it is not even like I'm here to Audition, Elle considers, because if that were the case I'd come in the Stage Door. I'm here as Game Mistress and Monitor Babs' guest. I'm safe tonight. And besides, I have two pieces. Beka and I both do. And even if we Flip-Flop, we will both still have two pieces.*

Everything is going to be alright.

Elle tunes into the routine of the Club. A Master of Ceremonies introduces each act. "Ladies and Gentlemen! Put your hands together and welcome Stripper Odee to the center Stage!"

A curvy Stripper bounces forward wearing a halter and miniskirt overtop a g-string. She lewdly dances to a song, swings around the pole, bumps and grinds. The miniskirt slides down the legs until it comes off the ankles and feet. Now the Patrons get to look square-on to a spread but g-string-covered crotch.

Elle licks her lips carefully. She sees Beka watch with mouth agape. Odee's halter comes off during the second song and Beka and Elle watch the Stripper tongue her lips, look directly to them, and erect her nipples with wetted fingertips.

The act is pretty shocking in and of itself but it is the direct eye contact for the nipple masturbation that disturbs Elle. *I feel intimidated that this Stripper arouses herself for me.* But Beka likes it, reaches into her croptop and arouses herself back.

Applause. The Patrons endorse the nuance, and appreciate Beka's torment and frustration. The hovering Cam below the table ensures Beka can't keep her wet secret, and when Beka sees her puddle on the Screens she gushes more brodeas.

The third garment comes off at the beginning of the third song. Minus her g-string, Stripper Odee displays the narrowest of racing stripes just above her shaven lips, and presents a wet butterfly into Beka and Elle's newbie eyes.

Beka reaches under the table and touches herself, fingers pink, and balls her clit out. More applause.

Odee walks to the back of the stage naked, wiggling a delightful ass. She's on the Screens too. If she's lucky the Prefecture will find her, and as her hits accrue Automaton will come to remember her.

Elle looks up toward the Screens again. This time she confronts footage of herself and Beka getting out of the Van moments ago. Elle shifts restlessly and double checks she keeps her legs open. The video freezes on Beka's upskirt and then steps frame-by-frame forward with close-ups documenting Beka's trimmed bush above a slick dividing line down middle. Applause. A shot unbeknownst to Elle from the Camera Lounge with Beka pulling butt cheeks aside and flashing her brown exit star.

And then Beka's live upskirt appears: a bigger patch of slick, and more applause. Elle watches in horror. *I feel slighted, although that's irrational. But I worry that if Beka gets too far in front of me that Game Mistress will make me play catch-up.*

Beka whispers, "I want to see Penny and Coco dance!"

The MC bombs, "You just saw Odee dance, now put your hands together Patrons, and welcome her Roommate, Hanna Hottentot! Cause one of these gals— Odee or Hottie—is going to be a Pledge next Term, and one of them is going to be sucking dicks at Flesh Ranch!"

Elle discovers herself running the center of her tongue up inside her lower lip.

Stripper Hottie plays an alt-exercise theme. The hair on her head has been dyed purple ultraviolet and been shaven back above her ears, her eyebrows are gone, and her armpits and legs are shaven. She wears an exercise tank bra, high-waist briefs (of the montante species), and leggings. Hottie rolls her briefs down below her crotch yet above her knees, kneels and pivots her hindquarters toward Beka and Elle. She reaches around with her hands and pulls both butt cheeks to the side. "Fuck me like you hate me," is tattooed therein.

Elle blanches. She clenches her own thighs together for only a moment, opens again, and sneaks a glance toward a Screen *to see if my pee shows on my seam.* It doesn't. *And it wouldn't matter anyway except that it might.* Elle breathes air out her mouth.

Most of the Screens devote to Cam views of Hottie as she pulls her top up and rubs hooters on the Stage floor. Sometime during the second song, absent bra and briefs, Hanna wraps her legs around the pole and squeaks a shaven honeybox while peeling the leggings off one-by-one in mid-air.

Deserved applause.

Stripper Hottie pivots, squats and full-bore pinks the newbies. Stripper Hanna Hottentot utters, "There's always a way to get to the Nugget, you wannabes." And masturbates.

Elle reels. *Stripping three pieces in three songs flashing her pink and her sphincter. Why do I need to witness this?*

The Stripper crawls on hands and knees toward Beka and Elle, curls a finger at them, and beckons them onstage. Her beguilement amuses the Crowd of seasoned Gamers and they increases the din; Elle sees lips move but can't hear the words. *I feel caught in a spell. Especially if Beka goes over the top. Tries to climb up onto Stage, that is.*

But the spotlight highlights the Stripper posturing them. Hanna Hottentot pivots into a squat and a spread and demonstrates a finger speculum—she buries two fingers of each hand deeply into the opposite sides of her hole and pulls herself wide. The vagina radiates deep pink from the inside. Hottie extracts her fingers, and with her fingers dripping cream she beckons to Beka and Elle to come on Stage for it.

The Crowd tenses.

Elle scowls. *It's bad enough this wannabe Whore up on Stage makes a vulgar display of herself. What makes her truly filthy is that she has the gall to beckon us directly. She's a witch, that's what she is.*

Beka appears immobile and Elle can tell she remains transfixed. *I have an urge to stop her if she tries to go over the top. But another part of me to not going to stop her at all.*

And besides, Game Mistress said no talking.

Elle looks to see Game Mistress rests her elbows on the table, her chin in her hand, and her eyes watching the naked Stripper Hottie.

Hottie now begs to Game Mistress directly, "Please let me Double Penetrate with the Shaving Kit. I'll keep my honey hole bare, shave all my head bald, and stay naked."

The Patrons mummer as the partly-shaven Stripper stands and retreats: another naked back and buttocks receding toward the backstage.

Babs tugs on her bra straps. *I find Hottie and Odee disgusting. They both behave like wannabe Whores. Pity any Patron they lapdance.*

BB shuffles her bra straps. *But Hottie and Odee are not the Strippers I'm concerned about. I'm concerned about Penny and Coco. I'm quite sure neither have forgotten Janet and me. And I doubt they have forgotten about Robyn either, although she professes no memory about her role as the referee of the Mudwrestling Contest. I wonder if Penny* and Coco know that Robyn has been screening their Videos. Screened their Double Dong from end of last Term, screened them naked, spread, pink, and climaxing, screened them soloing the Dong this Term and begging to share it again. .

Babs wrinkles her nose. It's okay Penny and Coco became Strippers. It's natural for them. Well, for Coco for sure.

Beka nudges Elle, and speaks even though she is not supposed to. "Did you see her, Elle, did you see how she shaved some of her hair? We could do that too Elle, on our head and on our pussies. Maybe we can get a hold of that Shaving Kit."

Elle blanches. Maybe you want lose your racing stripe and bare your bourse completely, but I'll keep all my nappy, thank you.

Elle looks at Beka again. I know there is no way I can dance, pink, or masturbate on Stage here at the Nugget. Not tonight, not ever. But Beka will. Elle scans the Club, avoids the faces and eyes of the Patrons, and discovers herself next to her Roommate on a double-wide Screen, side by side, legs open under the table. Yes, Elle accepts, Beka and my box and nookie are being cammed from under the table. No secrets for Beka Broda puddling out.

And for me? At least a seam through my crotch protects my nookie. Elle sighs. Well, sort of. At least my nappy mostly hides my nymphae. Elle rotates and squeezes her na-nas together and accepts, I'm sitting my bare buttage on leather.

Looking down at the table Elle discovers the Screen therein. Hard glass with the feed riding the top surface. A montage cycles Elle's titter and boobage so far this Term. Leanovers and titter from Day One right through The Arrivals. Boobage dominates The Runup. Elle blinks. Seems like I've had my neck strap unbuttoned and my halter hanging down ever since the first day of the Runup.

Something about the sound of the Club causes Elle to look up. I am on all the Screens. They are all watching me watch myself. And now they know me. Elle flushes. And the Crowd murmurs with appreciation. They approve of me!

Elle glances at Babs, makes eyes, Boss Babe smiles, and Elle follows her eyes to a Screen. Measurement Nudes appear on the Screen. Elle can't parse if the scattered applause is appreciation for my naked, tape-measured body, or approves the backstory. Laughter trickles through the Club and Elle's nipples harden. Babs exposed my Measurement Nudes and if I don't obey her completely she will play my Gonzo Videos on the Screens.

Elle understands. May it please Monitor Babs I'll be unbuttoning my halter again here tonight. Elle draws in a breath. May it please Monitor Babs I will take it off completely!

§ Babs Considers Louise: Shall Louise Opt Strip next Term?

The next introduction is different. "From the Corvette House!" the Master of Ceremonies blares over the speakers, "welcome former Monitor, now Corvette Pledge, and Roommate of ex-Nugget Lee Lollydor! Put your hands together and welcome Louise! Pledge Louise from the Corvette House, here to Audition the Nugget for the first time!"

The applause builds. A former Monitor shall audition the Nugget.

Janet had been clear to Louise what to do before Louise ever left the Corvette House, "You will strip naked, spread, and display your pink to Babs. Then you shall make her demand that you beg to Strip next Term.

Louise purses her lips, "I'm going to beg naked center Stage of the Nugget to Strip next Term."

Janet agrees. "You shall." Janet underscores, "Should you fail at this task you will find yourself walking, sitting, and sleeping on thumbtacks. Am I clear?"

"Ma'am, yes, Ma'am." Louise bows. She has worn a t-front maillot and a bandeau since the beginning of the Term. Two Garments. T-front because the neck strap ascends above the waist between the breasts, leaving it to the bandeau the task of covering the breasts. Sometimes the bandeau is atop the t-front, sometimes the t-front lies atop the bandeau.

Louise expounds, "Once on Stage, I will discard my swimsuit, intimidate your ex-Bikini Babe Roommate, and convince her to Opt Strip *me* so as to seal *your* Steph-Ginny trade. Steph for Ginny hour-for-hour, provided Babs demands I beg to Opt Strip next Term.

"May it please you to think that Babs seeks to pay me back Karma from last Term," Janet replies, "feel free to so believe. Just be sure you beg Babs to stay naked and Strip next Term."

Louise snots, "So you can get to rough up Steph, and Babs gets to haze Ginny. Some deal."

"Almost." Janet declares, "Steph shall be taking some of her Karma back. As for Ginny, I suspect that MomCap will borrow Ginny and put her out to Whore. She's far too valuable to be left in Babs' hands."

"Is MomCap at the Nugget going to replenish me with another Bikini?" Louise asks.

"Ah, a question asked!" Janet smiles, and raises a finger. "And a question answered, 'no.' You deserve to streak back if only for asking a question."

Janet lifts a finger. "And listen to me. You make sure that Bikini Babe understands that when she demands you beg naked and Strip, that means for sure you will streak back here afterward."

"Streak back to the Corvette House," Louise mumbles. She offers forfeits. "Ma'am, you know I'm prepared to trade Garments with you, I'll give you any Garment I've got, I'll give them all to you." Louise commits. "You just want to break me, Ma'am, just for the sport of it. And you're making Monitor Babs feel guilty. Especially if I got caught."

"Out," Janet proclaims, "you're disgusting you think you're important enough for the Game to be about you or Babs and me." Janet snorts. Then jovials, "Except it is, isn't it, because the Game is about all of us."

Louise exits. She grits her teeth during the hike to the Nugget. Moving quickly now she must constantly adjust a maillot backside inclined to slip into tanga. *I know what I'm going to have to do. Pull the maillot into my butt crack, peel the tube top off and throw it away, free my neck and roll my maillot down my hips and legs, step out of it with my feet, hold it up, and toss it away. Then face off to Babs, squat in front of her, spread my legs wide, pull my pink in her face, and beg to Opt Strip.*

Louise accepts. *It's not about me even. It's about the Gamers. I'm just a toy for them to play with. At least that's what I am right now. A training exercise for Monitor Babs courtesy Janet.*

But enough of Louise's thoughts. She comes out onto the Stage as anticipated, bandeau atop t-front maillot, and before the second song ends she is naked, a 36D-28-36 figure with horseshoe-shaped breasts hanging down and a full bush. So much for three songs and three Garments. Louise feels the hundreds of eyes, but most of all she feels the eyes of Game Mistress, and, seated next to her, Monitor Babs. Boss Babe. Bikini Bitch.

BB and Louise have never met. Babs eyes the now naked Corvette Pledge. *Louise was a Monitor last Term when I was a Pledge, but we served in different Houses.* Babs mulls and scans the Screens in the club, looking for something she glimpsed before. Steph pulling pink and spinning silk in the Backyard. *Steph might know Louise because she was also a Monitor last Term, except Steph isn't here, except on one of the Screens here. Her and Tiffany both.*

Babs watches Louise come to the end of her dance. By any measure Louise is a bad dancer. The fallen Monitor doesn't want to be here tonight, doesn't want to humiliate herself at Janet's behest as coin in a Steph trade. Or be a teaching vehicle for Babs in the Game.

Babs hesistates, Beka reaches a hand under the table to touch herself, and Elle leaks another droplet of urine into her seam. Babs looks at Game Mistress. *I can't believe I am sitting here and deciding that Louise will Opt Strip and spend next Term here at the Nugget. I am doing this to her. And then I will trade Steph for Ginny. Except I have no choice in the matter. I owe Janet.*

GM smiles and deliberately signs Boss Babe onto her feet. Applause. Babs looks to Game Mistress as the applause builds, and GM signs her to bow.

She does, first to the Crowd, toward Louise, and is about to speak when Louise greets her. "Hello Bikini Babe. Are you planning on dancing tonight?" Louise shifts her weight and crosses her thighs in front of her. "And if you want to trade Steph to Janet for Ginny, you can leave me out of it. You should Opt Down my Roommate, Lee Lollydor, instead. You don't need to break her, she's already broken. She's already been a Stripper, and she's eager to Strip again."

Babs crosses her arm in front of her bra, blocking her cleavage and areolage. She commands Louise. "Spread, Pledge, show your pink out, masturbate."

The Crowd mummers approval for Monitor Babs. Louise hesistates, tilts her head slightly, overcomes the unexpected, digs her fingers into her pubic hair, parts her sex lips, and finger balls her clit. She gasps. And threatens Babs, "If you know what's good for you, you know not to Opt me Down. You can still trade Steph for Ginny. You hold the hole card, she's Janet's obsession. You don't need me."

Monitor Babs feels GM's eyes upon her. No escape. "Rub that lightning rod of yours hard and hang some liquid out of your lair," she orders. "Do it now, lizard Pledge."

Louise tilts her head, seethes, but obeys. Another gasp, and Louise adds a drop of liquidity to the Stage floor. The Patrons rustle in their seats. Again Louise protests, "You're just Janet's lackey insisting I reveal myself here at the Nugget."

"Beg, Stripper wannabe!" Boss Babe commands.

Louise begs, "Ma'am, please let me Pledge naked and cum be a Stripper next Term."

"Masturbate, you licentious loser," BB commands.

Louise tries to maintain defenses, "You're forcing me, bitch, just because Janet wants to wring Steph. So what are you going to do with Ginny, anyway? Whore her in front of your Pledge?"

"And torment Tiffany with sex," Babs tosses her head back and laughs, and the Patrons laugh with her.

Boss Babe hardens. "Now finger-fuck yourself, Pledge, and beg some more!"

Louise growls as Kundalini begins to possess her. She rubs harder, spills more sweet liqueur, begs a more intelligent offer, "Ma'am, please let me stay naked here at Nugget, because you don't want to make me streak back to the Corvette House."

"Climax, you Stripper wannabe!" Boss Babe commands.

And Louise leans back, reluctantly, and hits a high note, and go into vibrating buzz, as the Crowd becomes like a hive of pulsating bees as Louise vibrates in climax.

Babs sits down, collects a nod of approval from Game Mistress, and watches Louise play her lyre. *I feel horrible doing this,* Babs admits to herself.

The Crowd watches a total abandonment Audition. As Louise comes out of her reverie Game Mistress stands, and signs her to crawl forward toward the Stage-side table. The standing eyes meet the crawling eyes up on the Stage for a instant GM and Louise's eyes sparkle, that silently painful kind from looking directly into the soul of another.

Babs considers that her beggar has disheveled hair, a mussed face, a gritty butt, and cream swinging and stuck to her inner thigh. Cream on her hands too and tracking it on the Stage. Louise drops her eyes and focuses her attention on her bandeau and maillot that have been gathered onto the Stage-side table, amidst Babs and Beka and Elle.

Louise's attention reverts to Game Mistress's rising hands. And dissects what they hold. *Janet's last excuse for a Spiderweb Bikini, except not exactly.*

GM holds the halter in one hand. It consists of a torso string-tie with a neck string-tie. Nothing more, not even strings to delineate what would be the sides of any missing cups. Three edges, nothing more, nothing less.

GM holds the g-string in the other hand. A knot with three strings attached, also three edges when tied. Experience in forming ties valued.

GM holds both arms forward in front of naked Pledge Louise. "Prove you commit to your beg to return to the Nugget next Term."

Louise very carefully reaches forward until she grasps the g-string by a thumb and forefinger directly above GM's finger and thumb. "Mistress," Louise advances, "please let me keep only one piece until the end of the Term. That way I never have to streak. And you know with only one piece, I must come back to Strip next Term."

The Patrons mummer approval. Once GM releases her finger and thumb Louise will possess one Garment, one size pico g-string.

Louise feels a need to raise stakes. "Mistress, I'll not even wear the g-string. I'll carry it in my hand. I'll carry it in my mouth."

Game Mistress lets go. Louise now holds the g-string betwixt thumb and finger. She crawls backward a half step. And again her eyes cast toward what *was until recently my bandeau and t-front maillot.*

GM draws Louise's eyes up from the glance. "Don't worry, I'll give the bandeau and maillot to Janet."

Louise snides, "I guess there's a reason Janet's not here tonight."

The Patrons murmur.

Babs opens her mouth but GM speaks first, "Thank you, Monitor Babs, for letting Louise show off her lapland and lagway!"

Louise, still naked, stumbles but rises to her knees as she addresses Babs. "Ma'am, thank you for letting me Pledge naked and cum be a Stripper next Term, Ma'am."

"Thank me for letting you climax," Boss Babe commands.

Louise cups both lactoids in her hands and forms handbra. "Ma'am," she raises her eyes, "Thank you for forcing me to pink, cream, and climax, Ma'am. And turning me into a Stripper pawn in your dealings with Janet.

Babs considers this comment but Game Mistress leads, "May you acquire humility, Pledge Louise. Your Roommate, Lee Lollydor has already Stripped at the Nugget, now it's your turn to turn your inner lips inside out and show your holes to the Club."

A moment of silence inside the Club and then Game Mistress reaches forward and hands Louise the pico halter top.

Louise flusters yet rises onto tiptoes. GM waves her toward the backstage. "Stuff your halter and g-string into your mouth, strike vulgar poses for the Shooter, pink and gape, and after House Mom thinks the Shooter has enough footage of you to announce your next Term, you may depart by the Stage Door."

Louise digests for a moment, turns, and her bare buttocks disappear toward the Dressing Room.

Babs assembles factions. *It will seem like Louise is streaking, except she is not. But if she gets wrassled down and has to spit her costume out, then she will have disobeyed Game Mistress. And all because I own Janet some Karma, and this is what Janet wants.*

§ Game Mistress & Babs and Beka & Elle: The Steph Influence

Game Mistress addresses newbies Beka and Elle as Babs relaxes. "I see that Robyn keeps making Steph vagflash and then cam it.

Beka interrupts, "Robyn cams me too!"

Game Mistress targets Elle. "And what about you? You'll make a much better vagflasher after a Flip-Flop, yes?"

"Mistress, please, Mistress," Elle says.

Boss Babe provides assistance to Elle, "Didn't I hear you begging a Flip-Flop yesterday in the Bathroom?"

Elle reacts, "Ma'am, ah, yes, Ma'am." Elle shifts her eyes sideways then down, "Ah, Mistress, please let me Flip-Flop with Beka, Mistress."

Game Mistress applauds. "Excellent. After you Flip-Flop your next Cosmos task shall be to share pinking with Steph."

"Ah, Game Mistress," Elle protests, "Steph doesn't want to spread and pink and share that with anybody. Especially me. Only Molly wants to share with her."

Game Mistress opines, "Steph needs to be normalized to a commonality, understand she's just another Pledge, which is what she is after all. Sanpan, no secrets. So pink with her, bright sunlight, live Cam."

Elle draws in a big breath.

GM anticipates, "Thank me, Pledge."

Elle confirms, "Mistress, thank you for goodness, Mistress."

Beka doesn't think before rushing a question to Babs. "So why did Steph cover her belly button last Term?"

Elle, recovering, adds, "She had to know the Rules, she's not stupid."

Babs chooses to answer. "Steph thought she could flaunt the Rules; show Gamers she really was superior. Not bound by the Rules of the Game."

Game Mistress curls, "Maybe the dark side of Kundalini got a hold on her and made her feel invincible. Or maybe she craved to Opt Down." GM scans a Screen in the Club to review the under-table Cam's view up Elle's crotch: thighs clear all the way to the flat of her pubis, hairage and with a seam dancing down her nautch line. GM smiles to Elle, "Maybe you crave to Opt Down too."

Elle hustles, "Mistress, *my* belly button is *always* uncovered, *always* on display, *always* navelage 24x7. Beka and I both."

"I like how you and your Roommate keep your legs open," GM complements.

"Mistress, thank you, Mistress," Elle stumbles.

Beka comes to life, "Mistress, Elle and I will spread our legs anytime. We'll pink and cream and cum for you."

"Excellent," Game Mistress praises, again scans the Screens, and directs a question to Elle. "Shall we be looking for you to be spreading and pinking, like your Roommate did on the Front Porch?"

Elle rushes, "Mistress, I'll spread my legs anytime, Mistress. Anywhere, in front of anybody, and keep spread as long as you want. I spread my legs and pulled aside in the Camera Lounge, and I'll even spread after I Flip-Flop. Like Beka did. Like Beka does, Mistress."

"Your Roommate's brodeas leaks out of control." GM accuses.

"Mistress, I lick it up after her. I've licked up after Molly and Steph too." Elle hurries. "Mistress, I'll lick up after you too!"

Game Mistress laughs. "Maybe you'll need to lick up after yourself."

II-11 Kimju & Molly: Nugget Lesbo Dong Climax (D20)

§ Kimju & Molly: Masturbate Together in the Dressing Room

Another flow of images on the screens catch Elle's eyes—Gamers recognize a feed from the Dressing Room backstage—and the Screens depict Kimju and Molly, still topless of course, and still patiently sitting surrender with their hands behind their heads and the legs spread. Strippers come and go in between dancing out front, Strippers might acknowledge them, but their oval-mouths don't talk back. Babs might have abandoned the Alumni to House Mom, but they have been here before. At least they know some of her habits.

Suddenly the Nugget Shooter invades the Dressing Room. Gamers know that anyone in the Crowd can photo Strippers on stage, pose them in the Camera Lounge, or take away a memorial of a lapdance. Fans far away in the Prefecture subscribe to the Club feeds—from Cams out front *and* in the Dressing Room. But the Nugget Shooter is chartered with special privileges: Nugget Shooter can shoot anywhere in the Club—not only the stages and the Camera Lounge, but all of the backstage areas as well, and that includes the Dressing Room with its showers and toilets.

Nugget Strippers possess no privacy. Unlike the Cosmos House where a Pee-Camer must enter the Bathroom naked to light up the Cams, at the Nugget the Cams in the Dressing Room are illuminated all of the time. There are no stalls and the toilets are clear glass. It is not a requirement that Strippers pee naked, except that Strippers don't have clothes to begin with. At the Nugget, all the Strippers Pee-Cam.

And another thing: The Nugget Shooter is not a paparazzi who records voyeuristically. The Shooter is a participant observer; the Shooter both poses and directs Strippers. On any given day the Nugget Shooter might be a man or a woman or something in between; sometimes their Cams are live to the Prefecture, sometimes they record "private stock." Tonight the Shooter person with a hawk-face, short hair, who could be a man or a woman, or something in between.

"Chant and masturbate," utters the Shooter upon entering the Dressing Room, "You know the drill, after all, you're about to perform your Alumni Reprise out front! So play with your tits, masturbate and get juicy, taste yourself, but hold onto your climax for now."

Kimju and Molly look at each other, it has been a while but they know this Chant by heart. They tighten their hands from behind their heads and commence with a Stripper beg, "Please let me Pledge naked and cum be a Stripper next Term," but now continues as both draw their hands to their nipples and recite, "titty titty," lower their hands and work the tanga and panties out of their gashes, pullaside and part their gates, tug out their clitty rings, and recite, "clitty clitty," finger dip, recite "hole mouth," and raise their fingers to their lips to taste themselves.

Hands behind heads and they run more smoothly now, "Please let me Pledge naked and cum be a Stripper next Term, titty titty, clitty clitty, hole mouth."

Fresh cream erupts and two scents fill the Dressing Room, and the two pinking Cosmos hear applause from out front in the Club. The Shooter lines up a hovering camera with the two freshly opened gashes and exits, leaving Kimju and Molly chanting, pinching their nipples, pulling their pink, finger-dipping, and tasting their love juice. The Alumni know the drill: keep themselves ready, right on the edge of climax, but don't succumb to the mounting pleasure.

Kimju scowls into the eye of the Cam monitoring her. *I can accept revealing myself in climax—I'm long past that hurdle—even if my knockers and kunny are not live just on the Club Screens out front, but live on Screens everywhere. I just don't want to return here, to the Nugget.*

Molly's cream overflows into her thick black pussy hair, she shrugs and fantasizes. *Maybe Elle will show up and lolly my meringue up. Maybe she's eat me to climax. I just want to Strip here again.*

Molly steels a glance at Kimju. *Maybe Kimju will eat me tonight. MomCap knows me, and she's going to pop me tonight. Her way, that's the price of my readmission. MomCap's gonna pop Kimju too. Deep down inside Kimju knows this, but her practical side assumes this won't happen. But when she does go knackers she won't be able to hold back.*

§ Robyn Demands Tiffany & Steph: Lick Her Feet & Suck Toes

Elle suddenly realizes she recognizes one of the images on the Nugget Screens. It's Tiffany and Steph on the Post Henge. Still with their faces on earth and their foreheads touching the Post, still with their knees drawn forward and their buttocks raised up. Dirty faces, dirty hands and knees, dirty hair.

The video shifts and Robyn appears in the scene, maillot-clad as always. Elle can't hear the sound but watches as Robyn presents a foot to Tiffany Transparent. "Lick off the bottoms of my feet, you tail peddler," Robyn commands, "And don't tickle!"

Robyn turns to Steph Sorostitute, wipes the bottom of one foot across her cheek, and orders her, "suck my toes one by one, you slithering, spreading, slime slut. I don't care if Tiffany, Kimju and Molly, and Beka and Elle makes it to the Nugget or not, because sooner or later you are going to make it there, and you're going to stay for next Term."

Steph audits that the hovering Cam watches her, and with reluctance, commences to suck Robyn's feet with her tongue. Steph feels humiliated sucking dirt and toe jam. *Robyn Redacted double-crossed me last Term, pretends she wasn't present, and now steps on me. Robyn Ragazze needs her rack manhandled, her rigare plundered, and her rectum reamed.*

Steph considers Tiffany. *Tiffany just wants me to be pink-wet-and-ready, like she is. I don't hold it against Tiffany. She wants everyone to be as enthusiastic about being a Porn Star as she is.* Steph considers her plight. *I'm not all that different right now. Tiffany's Eraser Heads never retract and somehow I can't stop the fresh air from keeping my nipples hard. I'm not totally naked but my undershirt belt leave me full-frontal. I'm bleached, we're both pulling pink, although only Tiffany hangs tortoni outta her twat.*

The Cam hovers around to examine the uplifted stern and tailraff, but the feed to the Nugget suggests Steph's self-assessment is incorrect because she also hangs a streamer out of her snatch.

Steph shuffles her weight to better accommodate Robyn's toes in her mouth. *I should not have to take this. Although if I balk I could end up, will end up, in Lockdown again. I could just walk away, except there is nowhere to go.*

Inside the Nugget, Game Mistress leans toward Elle and acknowledges the Screen. "Perseverance and humiliation contribute to arousal," she says.

§ Beka & Elle: Kimju & Molly's Alumni Reprise Introduction

The drummer hits a beat now, and the Master of Ceremonies raises the pitch: "Ladies and Gentlemen! Welcome our special attraction tonight! Ladies and Gentlemen, welcome two of our Alumni from last Term! Two breakouts from the Nugget who are Pledge right now! Cosmos just like our newbies!" The spotlight brightens and anticipates the center stage. A saxophone chimes in, playing a repetitive rising note riff.

"Ladies and Gentlemen, both of these Alumni Pledge have only one piece, which means that unless one or the other gets another, both of them will be back *here* next Term!" A yelp, and applause starts to build. "Ladies and Gentlemen, welcome Kimju and Molly, our Nugget Alumni Reprise!"

Whatever excitements and horrors Beka and Elle have experienced so far this evening—*the paparazzi, the Hat Check Girl, kissing and boobage in the Camera Lounge, Strippers lolling their lips and pinking to us, Louise begging Boss Babe*—Elle shuffles in her chair and comprehends. *Even though it is not Beka and I on stage we are trapped and we can't leave. We are in the hands of this unruly Crowd. And we must now confront our fellow Cosmos in their ex-environment, and watch our "role models and teachers" perform.*

Elle bites her teeth together and figures. *Big uncertainty. Kimju and Molly might be the nearest to naked, but Beka and I might be wearing the most. But no matter what calculus, Beka and I have the most to lose. Both of us could end up topless tonight.*

Oh silly Cosmos, Beka understands! She leans across the table, titters a nearby Cam, and gleefully whispers to Elle, "Maybe we will all get to dance naked and pink!"

Game Mistress smiles. Boss Babe also logs the infraction; BB wonders if she should intercede to discipline Beka's talking. *Except the orders came from Game Mistress, so they are hers to enforce, nor mine. Except that Beka is my Pledge.*

Elle stays silent.

§ Kimju & Molly: Dressing Room & Watch Come On Stage

Back in the Dressing Room the Alumni hear each successive Stripper announced over the loudspeakers, and hear the noisy Crowd react. Strippers Hottie and Odee fade into the reverie self-arousal.

Topless Kimju and Molly continue to sit side-by-side and Chant: one tanga and one panties pulled to the side so that one trimmed kleave and one randy muff lie exposed. Klunky keekelay and molten myrrh transude from sex lips—this, plus the scent they release into the room, validate genuine arousal.

The cream oozes out amidst thighs and it seeks out assholes—one kawazoo and mawkeye. Pledge Kimju and Molly avoid this conclusion if only because their hand movements during the Chant ensures both collect excess valiva, sticky their mouths and tacky fingers-wipe the back of their neck.

All while the Alumni hold their arms surrender, they display armpits, erected and bruised nipples, and recite the first part of the chant, "Please let me Pledge naked and cum be a Stripper next Term...."

Repetition helps Kimju and Molly build toward a climax, especially as they put their hands into motion for the rest of the Chant, "titty titty, clitty clitty, hole mouth!"

The Nugget Shooter returns and interrupts their Chant. The Shooter hustles them off the Dressing Room Cam into the Hallway so they might perform a particular privatization, one the Shooter records but does not transmit out to the feeds.

The Alumni hear the noise from the Stage of the Patrons applauding Louise's striptease, and as it fades MomCap positions Kimju and Molly side-by-side and holding hands, and propels them down the short catwalk and onto the Stage.

Kimju and Molly discover themselves alone on the Stage, still holding hands, still topless, and still bare-assed. Both still wear what they have worn since the beginning of the Term: one tanga and one panties, except....

Applause greets them. Hesitation. And laughter in the Club. Beka and Elle recognize instantly: Molly's panties are again unrolled and cover her fully in the front, except they are soaking wet and dripping. And so too has Kimju's tanga been dung out of her koot, and laid atop her butched pubes as wide as possible, although now so wide as to allow Kimju to outline hairage along her legline. Molly's panties remain gathered into her moonshadow, so that both Alumni can fully bare butt.

Besides from being now wet, the only visual difference is that Molly's panties are see-through-when-wet whereas Kimju's stretch fabric tanga retains its opacity.

Beka leans forward to Elle, "Molly's got wet panties again, but I don't remember her panties being wet in the Van. Or Kimju's."

And Elle, who also observes the change, nods and remains silent. *Yes, both the tanga and panties were dry in the Van. And the Watering Can got left back at the House.*

Beka talks to Elle's ear above the din, "And their lipstick is smeared."

"Yours too," Beka observes, "They probably got rotated through the Camera Lounge and got mussed up Frenching."

Elle is wrong about that. But how would Beka and Elle know that Kimju and Molly had stripped naked for the Nugget Shooter, dropped their thong and panties into a bowl, and....

The applause builds as the Alumni break hands and grasp the pole at the center of the circular Stage. "You owe me for this," Kimju growls to Molly, "you started a piss trend at the Bachelor Party with Steph."

For once Molly exhibits spine, "Hey Kimju, time for you to own up to reality. You got one piece and a Roommate named Robyn."

Kimju raises her eyes, looks toward the spotlight ahead, and worries what she might have to do to keep the Shooter's clip secret. Kimju firms, *Right now I must deal with the present. I'm not exactly sure about what is going to happen tonight. But I know that that I want nothing more than to strip my soaked tanga off. And with Molly's attitude toward germs, I sure she shares this goal.*

At Stage-side, Game Mistress interprets Babs' quizzical look. GM leans forward, smiles, holds a hand near BB's ear, and speaks. "You've got to love our Alumni. Their sharing intense sensations will help forge their relationship."

§ Kimju & Molly: Strip Naked & Masturbate Each Other

The drummer kicks off first, then the sax takes up a melody, and the rhythm establishes: this is bump and grind music. The twosome sidle center forward, swirl around the pole together, and do a one minute contest of nipple and breast play, pullasides, and finger dip movement. The Crowd welcomes them, ignorant of their backstage secret, as are Gamers watching in the Prefecture, or Automatron with its spools.

Beka and Elle have seen both Kimju and Molly pull pink, but this will be the first time Beka and Elle witness anything like what happens next.

The Master of Ceremonies raises the pitch, "Ladies and Gentlemen. Put your hands together for Kimju in a bare minimum wet Spandex thong and Molly in those see-through-when-soaked panties!" Catcalls and applause ripple through the Club. The snare drum rolls and the sax brings pitch to a height, and a voice in the Crowd yells, "Flip-Flop" and this produces a scattered, not entirely endorsing applause.

Beka and Elle find themselves among the not entirely sure. Elle feels a sudden urge to go to the bathroom and a very real fear that *I could be tossed up onto the stage.* Elle looks at her Roommate. *I certainly don't want to appear overeager.* Elle makes sure her legs stay not just ajar, but clearly open, *ninety degrees or more.*

Beka inadvertently titters an armhole, and Elle tightens the ridge above her nose. *If anybody goes up on stage it should be my Beka; she's already careless with her thighs, she's depositing a big cream drop on her leather seat, and she debuted her pink in the Camera Lounge.*

Elle's body twitches in her seat and she releases another driblet of urine. *I heard the M/C; Beka and I will be returning to the Camera Lounge again tonight.*

Elle glances at the Stage and anticipates. Kimju and Molly are going to pink, cream, and climax tonight. *With what they wear or naked.*

Elle studies Game Mistress and Monitor Babs. *So yes, Gamers are softening me up. Softening both of us up, Beka's just easier.* Elle wonders, *Maybe Beka's eager to showcase pink, but that's not why I'm here tonight.*

"Flip-Flop Flip-Flop Flip-Flop!" The Crowd picks up the Chant again, now with the drummer beating rhythm and the sax wailing in a free style that is a cross between a song and a cat getting its tail twisted. The M/C bounces into the rhythm, "Ladies and Gentlemen. Kimju and Molly! Flip-Flop. Let's see you two dancers swap clothes!" And from all around the room, "Flip-Flop" and the beat running, Kimju and Molly doing a steady bump and grind, the Club lights dim, the clatter of drinks quiets, and after a "yowl" in the room and the coming of a quieter space, a tension builds up.

Many Patrons know that the two Alumni were Roommates last Term and are familiar with their past pink, wet, and climax. Many incorrectly assume that they are contesting Roommates tonight to determine who will Opt Down and return to the Nugget.

A spotlight on the stage tightens focus on the twosome. Kimju and Molly yank the tanga and panties into their kypsey and mooe, masturbate the clithood with the taut fabric, and then pullaside and roll pink out. They hook thumbs into the tops of the tanga and panties, widen the waistline, and begin to "roll 'em down."

The two Alumni pause once the Garments level their pubis and crotch—it is their first totally exposed pubic hair at this Alumni Reprise—and qualifies them a full-frontal tag on the feed. The applause builds they turn around and arch their now-bare butts out, then kneel, reach around behind to pull their butt cheeks apart, and pivot so that every eye in the Crowd can harvest their assholes.

Sustained applause mounts with hoots as the Alumni give the newbies sitting at the side table a direct eyeful, and the applause advances as the kneeling Kimju and Molly's bend further forward, then descend their to tease lips apart, and enable both newbies to gaze upon two clithood rings a-sparkle in the spotlight. This gets a rise out from the Patrons, already schooled on extremes. They know that Kimju and Molly got ringed when they became Strippers last Term, and appreciate that the Nugget Alumni continue to carry the weight.

Elle feels faint and find the room closing in around her and turning gray. She feels wetness in between her thighs. *I just peed myself!* She snaps to, and scans the Screens, *for a feed of my own nookie.* Not there. *But Beka is live and she is oozing brodeas.*

Kimju and Molly rotate around to face the Crowd again. They roll the rolled-up tanga and panties down their calves and stabelize them, stretched out at their ankles, so they can keep their knees apart and the crotches spread. The Crowd anticipates secrets.

The two former Strippers eye the Crowd. They squat then lean back so they can spread their knees, and ergo their thighs apart. Both pull their outer lips apart from the sides: for Kimju this involves pulls against shaven skin or butched stubble, for Molly this involves digging down into her thigh black minge and digging the mutton out. Both separate any stickiness holding the inner lips together, and progress the inner lips forward to butterfly, and roll out their clit heads and pee holes. and pivot so that every eye in the Club gets full bore.

Elle watches with her hands over her mouth. *Their rings stand up, like they invite attachment.* Elle tries to not look. She fails. She trades eyes with Kimju and Molly and watches them each dip a finger, scoop, and taste themselves. The Patrons utter a louder, thirsty roar. The loudest so far tonight.

Elle watches with her hands over her mouth. Elle fears, *What if Gamers demand they taste each other?* She looks at Game Mistress's boots. *I hope you got this under control.*

Beka watches with her fingertips atop her cheeks and her mouth open. Both have forgotten the no touching rules and squeeze their thighs together.

Oops. Beka catches herself again only after her freshness erupts and she feels wetness on the inside of her thighs. She looks down toward her private parts—the short miniskirt really doesn't cover them—and realizes her brodeas also runs down the depression where the crack of her ass meets the leather chair. Beka scans the Club, finds her upskirt on one of the many Screens, and relaxes her squeeze and opens her thighs back apart. Just for good measure she un-sticks her bare booty from the leather chair, lets some of her puddle ease into her bottom depression, and sit again, planting her feet firmly onto the floor to fix her position.

Beka glances at Elle as an image of Ginny in the Cravat flashes through her mind. *I need Elle along. I want Elle along.*

A roar in the Club commands the newbie's attention. A tom-tom drum follows Kimju and Molly at the front of the Stage, ahead of the pole, as they stand and wiggle their feet closer together. The tanga and panties relax their stretch until one leg hole falls to the foot.

Again the Crowd chants, "Flip-Flop Flip-Flop Flip-Flop!" Molly, then Kimju, carefully step out of their Garment with first one foot, then the other. Cautious applause.

But instead of Flip-Flopping Kimju and Molly pick up the discards with their toes, swing a leg forward, and drop them on the tipping ledge just below the center-front stage, and in front of the best VIP table in the Club. The Alumni bow to the waist, and let their hanging breasts swing freely. The Crowd roars and claps as they turn and disappear naked toward backstage and the Dressing Room.

A commotion erupts at the VIP table as the applause recedes. It is an aghast reaction, Patrons standing, and there is laughter as those awarded with the discards discover a latent surprise. Maybe eventually Kimju and Molly's secret will leak out, but until then some incorrect conclusions and partial truths will be theorized.

Elle misinterprets, *they are fighting over spoils.* Beka interprets, *I can be as valuable as Kimju and Molly!* Babs interprets, *the thong and panties weren't wet when I left backstage.* Game Mistress smiles.

§ Elle: Worries about What's About to Happen

Elle looks at Game Mistress and wonders what will happen next. "Kimju and Molly are not Roommates and cannot Flip-Flop," she voices, "I think I just witnessed a discard."

"Enjoy your drink." Game Mistress instructs. Elle nurses it and considers her environs. She realizes that all of the waitresses are topless; some of them might be males and some might be females of the tiny-tit variety. All have shaven bodies and all wear makeup like women—hair and face with pronounced lips, cheeks, and eyes, but also rouged nipples, decorated navels, and tightly-packaged g-strings or thongs.

Elle makes sure her legs stay in position. *Did I shown my nookie earlier tonight in the Camera Lounge?*

It is a question Gamers know the answer to. Elle showed her nookie up to a point. Well, let's be honest, the Screen answers Elle's question. The performance is vivid. Elle had buried the seam into her nook, masturbated her nugogo with it, and then pulled the seam to the side. And she had performed magnificently!

So am I even with Beka? Well, not quite. Beka finger-fucked her burrow and ate her broda off her fingertips. Off her palm. I didn't do anything like that. Elle blinks. *But I have no idea where I am in the pink and cream department. I don't even know what I'm begging anymore.*

Elle reconsiders. *Yes I do! I'm begging to Pledge naked and cum be a Stripper next Term. To come to this Nugget place. Get naked and spread; get pink-wet-and-ready.* Elle scans across the faces of the Patrons. *I'm begging to climax for real in font of all of these people. In front of the Prefecture, get archived into Automatron, so any Gamer anytime anywhere can access me.*

This is not a good thing.

Elle looks across the table at her Roommate, then spots a Screen that shows a remote Cam zoomed in on Beka's wet spot. Beka's wetness runs out of her dark brown inner lips, and Elle can tell the spot on Beka's seat has grown bigger. No secrets for Beka's sopping pussy.

Elle again checks her own thighs and discovers herself squeezing her legs together, *mostly in an attempt to hold in my pee!* Elle relaxes her legs apart, her seat wet from her last burst of urine, and hears the sax blow a high note.

A waitress with ultraviolet hair on one half of her head and a cage on her cock brings Elle another drink. Elle wiggles and wipes her dribble up with what is left of her jeans shorts. *I know my shorts absolutely don't cover the crease where my butt meets my leg; I can feel the bare leather against my nachas.* Elle makes a final wiggle wipe, and squares her legs to open position. *So far the Cam hasn't found any pee, so maybe it won't in the future. .*

Elle worries, *Babs intends to make me beg to go up on stage, strip naked, pull pink, and climax myself.* She grits her teeth at this idea and realizes that *unless I gets excused to use the facilities, I may be pissing myself right where I sit.*

§ Kimju & Molly: The Taste of a Woman is Devine

Two spotlights reveal that Kimju and Molly have silently retreated to the two side-stages in the back corners of the Nugget. They dance quietly and in place, stark naked now.

Kimju enjoys the admiration even though *I don't want to be here. Don't deserve to be here.*

Screens inside the Nugget light up other aspect of Kimju and Molly's histories. Scenes whilst Strippers last Term capture them naked, masturbating, and climaxing their brains out. Shots this Term whilst Cosmos Pledge display Kimju sunburning her pink on the Yacht before piss climaxing, Molly pinking and peeing into a stein at the Bachelor Party, *and the both of us masturbating to climax in sync with our own Videos.* Kimju keeps a bump and grind going, but feels very alone. *Where to next? What happens now?*

The Master of Ceremonies coaxes them both back to center Stage. "Ladies and Gentlemen, "Welcome Kimju and Molly back to Nugget for the next act of their Alumni Reprise."

Molly effuses. Kimju feels like an idiot.

The M/C plays the role of the Nugget fool. "These two ex-Nuggets want to be Nuggets again, don't you?" Scattered applause and the Crowd quiets in anticipation. Kimju and Molly shuffle; make sure their thighs don't touch. Kimju has a butch cut only slightly larger than where her thong used to be. Molly has bushy black pubic hair with overgrowth in all directions. Neither quite know what to do with their arms.

They do actually: they rotate their hips and keeps their elbows nearby.

The Master of Ceremonies challenges, "We've been watching your feeds ever since you graduated the Nugget. So belt it out for me, Pledge."

And so Kimju and Molly let their voices be heard throughout the Nugget, "Please let me Pledge naked and cum be a Stripper next Term"

Firmer, more curious applause. Kimju considers, *that is our third beg since leaving the Cosmos House; Molly might not mind, but I do. Although I can't say I'm surprised Gamers make us come to the Nugget and beg to return whilst we're already stark naked and inside.*

"Patrons want to see you Chant in the flesh!" The M/C declares. A sax and a rimshot kick. Kimju and Molly trade looks. Kimju rationalizes, *I know where we are headed, and this is not a surprise either. Only the doing is different."*

Molly doesn't care. So she works her feet wide, puts her hands behind her head and slowly begins the Chant. "Please let me Pledge naked," and by now Kimju has fallen into position with her and caught her breath, "and cum be a Stripper next Term." The applause ripples yet holds back, there and waiting as Kimju and Molly continue the Chant, "Titty titty, clitty, clitty, hole mouth."

They had together taken a leisurely two finger scoop of their insides, swabbed their cheeks and nostrils, and sucked their fingers clean. The Patrons don't want their applause to get in the way of whatever might happen next.

Kimju begrudges, *Yes, once we chanted in the Dressing Room it was inevitable we would chant on Stage.*

The M/C curls, "You two might be Nugget Alumni, but you are not Nuggets this Term are you?"

"Noooooooo," mummers the Club.

"So you are not bound by Nugget Rules!" The M/C slices, and darker laughter bends the Club.

Kimju understands, *We will beg to climax Double Dong tonight.* She and Molly both hold standing spread surrender position. *We are being proofed to the Nugget. Pinking, cream, finger-fucking, masturbation— our desire is being challenged, and all we got left is our climax.*

Well, perhaps; the M/C surprises them. "You two like to taste yourselves so much, now's your chance to discover what *each other* taste like!" The cymbal crashes and the sax blows lollypop music.

Kimju and Molly look at each other and know that the stakes have just risen. Molly doesn't much strategize but Kimju does. *Okay, so the Master of Ceremonies knows about what we did back in the Dressing Room. Probably the Patrons watched Molly and me live on the Screens. Probably fed to the Prefecture.*

Kimju casts an eye toward the VIP table adjacent to the stage, and checks on Molly again. *Somebody must have gotten their hands damp and smelled our secret.* Kimju casts a glance and catches knowing eyes looking back. Caught but no harm. *So, I'm guilty.* She darts eyes about, spots the Nugget Shooter admiring her. And catching her scanning the Screens. No, your *Private Pictures haven't been screened here.*

But the Crowd doesn't figure what the VIP table knows; the Crowd anticipates that the M/C leads the Alumni toward a tasting of the divine kind, and indeed he is.

Soft lights play on the bodies of the two naked Alumni as they sway and embrace and start kissing in time with the music. Beka and Elle watch transfixed as the M/C flabbergasts, "Ladies and Gentlemen, look at Kimju and Molly rub their knockers and majonkers_together!" The

Alumn step back, squeeze opposite breasts, and finger each other's nipples into erection!"

A "whoosh" as the Patrons settle cautious applause into the room.

Kimju and Molly bend at the waist and suckle each other's nipples. The appreciative applause rises yet communicates it does not want to get in the way, and the Crowd quiets as the ex-Nuggets pull each other's pink open, masturbate their opposite's clitoris, finger-fuck, and then deeply suck their opposite's copious juice off of their finger.

The Crowd accepts the tasting and approves with rising applause.

Molly breaths in the smell and tastes the texture of Kimju's klammy, and Kimju mouth and nostrils gather in Molly mungus. The nearer VIP seats around the stage sniff the erupting blend of scents. For Kimju and Molly the texture and smell of each other's cream augments the tang of their other flavors, already blended into their palettes and then left behind on their pelvis and mons.

Molly finds tasting Kimju's klammy a mildly amusing task, *harmless enough health-wise, and something I've done before. In a way Kimju's klammy belongs to me. I turned it out.*

Kimju finds Molly's taste repulsive but cleans her finger anyway. *Done it before and will do it again. But I don't like being forced.*

Kimju also considers: *Maybe Molly is a Piss Mouth, but that is not something I wish to audition for. Nor am I sure that Molly and I should be playing with each other. Lesbian congress is against the Rules for Nugget Strippers. Except that she and I are not a Nugget Strippers and not subject to Nugget Rules.*

Molly takes action over scholarship. She guides Kimju down to the Stage floor, intertwines ankles, pinks her, and Kimju reciprocates. Together they roll and pivot into a mutual tongue-to-clit licking oral 69.

The Crowd emits a soft "awe." The Patrons includes Gamers of many Castes who are sophisticated in the Rules of the Game. Gamers who know that cunnilingus is forbidden to Strippers on Stage. Whores, of course oral men as well as women, and of course invaginate men. But then Whores do lots of things, even Feature Dance.

Kimju considers the hairy pussy that confronts her mouth. *I never did a woman when I Stripped here last Term, and so the Nugget gets a bonus tonight: me doing lezzy.* Kimju opens Molly's meatlocker and reveals a pool of cream in a deep brown muliebre. *This is where my tongue goes,* Kimju encourages herself, and eats.

Kimju feels Molly part her own deeply pigmented inner lips and play a tongue into her rosy pink kypsey. Molly flickers Kimju's keystone. Kimju thinks quickly. *Molly's coming back next Term so lezzing with me will give her good credentials. Good media. Cause once she's back here she can't lez any more. Sweet.*

Kimju has one final thought. *I hope the Nugget only gets this one shot of me, cause I need to Opt Up next Term.* And rises toward climax.

Kimju might be cerebral but Molly goes with the flow. Both can see faces beyond the spotlight, and the Crowd quiets in anticipation of what the Alumni do next. The applause subdues, appreciative, and watches the duo reverse who's on top. A shuffle in the Crowd and anticipation, then rising applause as the Alumni smother their nostrils, tug on their opposite's clithood rings with their teeth, and pull streamers out of each other with tongues.

The applause builds, Kundalini stirs, both Pledge build toward unashamed cum....

A naked female attendant appears on stage and disrupts them from coming to climax! The naked attendant holds a package and uses a foot to encourage Kimju and Molly onto their feet. The attendant signs Kimju and Molly to cross their hands behind their backs, and invites them to take a bow for their near climax. Solid applause for two deeply-breathing and liquid pussy Pledge.

§ Kimju & Molly: Penny Gives them a Present & Pinks Babs

Beka and Elle watch from Stage-side; they recognize the attendant from her pictures and videos, although they have never seen her in the flesh before: Penny.

Elle twists her head ever so slightly as she contemplates the naked and shaven Stripper with a package in her hand. *We've had to worship your Dining Room Baseboard Pictures front and back, fixate our eyes upon you full-frontal, witness your pink and cream, study your asshole, and look into your eyes.*

I feel like I know you. Elle considers, *you were a Cosmos Pledge last Term, with an unfortunate outcomes. I saw the* Double Dong Climax Video *you made with Coco at the end of last Term, after Babs and Janet defeated you. I saw your* Shave & Climax Video *the night you arrived at the Nugget. I saw the* Side-by-Side Videos *of you and Coco masturbating together, soloing the Dong, and begging to share it again. I've seen your Pink Page showing the freckled lip you are so embarrassed about. And only moments ago, the Screen in the Lobby featured you and Coco in a* Birthday Cake Firefighters Video *that got pretty wet.*

Elle takes in how the real-life Penny is different than her images and videos. *She is more continuous, more three-dimensional. Her breasts appear larger, and a pair of very long inner sex lips distend a good inch or more down from her totally shaven pudenda.*

Up on stage Stripper Penny hands the naked Alumni the gift-wrapped box, bows to the Patrons as they approve with applause, walks toward where Game Mistress, Babs, Beka and Elle sit, squats, snarls, and displays freckled inner lips in Bab's face. She rises, flashes an asshole to Babs, and walks backward toward backstage. Applause follows, not because Penny desires it, but because she's been commanded to perform.

Babs squirms and sits up straighter in her chair. *I have not only witnessed Penny's photos, I was instrumental in helping Penny move to this place. But this is the first time I have seen Stripper Penny bare and naked. I might be very exposed in my underwire bra and nombril Bikini, but I'm not some naked, shaven, pinking, pogoing Stripper.*

Up on stage Kimju and Molly hold the gift box. They too have seen Penny's photos and videos; they also recognize Penny from actually watching her (and Coco) get shaven and climaxed the night they arrived at the Nugget at the very start of this Term, just as Kimju and Molly were departing for the Cosmos House. That was during *The Arrivals,* and back then the observed were not aware of their observers. Even now naked Penny fails to consider that the two naked Cosmos on Stage might have witnessed her back then, or that the Cosmos Pledge might have seen her Videos, either from before or after she and Coco arrived at the Nugget.

Elle blinks and scans the Screens and finds what she thinks is herself, although when she wiggles her open legs to the Cam under the table the Screen doesn't follow. *Confusing.* Elle looks toward Beka's exposed box, sees that Beka touches her swollen bolus, snaps her eyes to the Screens, finds Beka, and compares: Beka is real time. Elle looks at her own screen again, and thinks she sees a replay during which she squeezed her thighs together. The faux paux is but an instant, and afterwards Elle opens her legs wider. *Okay,* Elle confesses, *the Patrons know I touched my thighs. So maybe I'll have to pink to make up for it. Or touch myself like Beka.*

§ Robyn Trains Tiffany & Steph: And Watches Penny on Screen

Back at the Cosmos House Robyn ordains that the naked Tiffany and near-naked Steph crawl back to the Kitchen. Tiffany leads; both tiny-titters pull the long Bell rope at ground level, and they let Robyn proceed ahead to open the Back Door for them.

"Position yourself like you were outside," Robyn orders. "Kneel, keep your assholes up, spread, your knees wide, and pull pink. May you can dangle your tapioca and splurt so that Elle has something to lolly, might she ever return from the Nugget."

Robyn sits in a chair in the Kitchen, crosses her legs, and extends a foot. "Now get your heads together so you can both worship me. My feet got dirty when I had to bring you inside."

Tiffany and Steph commence to mouth-wash Robyn's foot, cheek-to-cheek and mouths near each other on the topside of he foot. "Use your tongues between my toes, you tamtart and scum bucket," Robyn growls, "Lick all the dirt off the bottom of my foot. And suck and lick out anything from under my toenails."

Robyn sits back in the chair. Ahead of her on the wall, and behind the two foot washers, the Kitchen Screen displays a live feed from the Nugget. Kimju and Molly stand naked on Stage while a naked Penny, presents them with a gift. Robyn may not recall her role in the Mudwrestling Contest last Term, but she does recall Penny and Coco's explicit Baseboard Stripper Pictures, which comprise the bottom two of the four Dining Room Pictures in the next room. And Robyn does recall watching their *Double Dong Climax Video* made at end last Term, and their solo *Side-by-Side Video made this Term.*

Robyn looks down at her nearly naked pair of foot worshipers and orders, "Kiss each other. On the mouth, with your lips and tongues, on the cheek, and then lick and suck my other foot clean."

Steph looks upward with eyes that connote hatred. Robyn leans in, "Do it right, Stripper wannabe, or I'm going to strip you naked and heave your minidress into the Parlor fireplace. Like, finger-snap; followed by nothing to put back on. Ever."

§ Kimju & Molly: Climax on the Double Dong

The package is a gift-wrapped rectilinear box, well over a foot long, and about four inches square. Kimju and Molly stand side-by-side and hold the package, each with one hand. Kimju has butched pubic hair trimmed to a size slightly larger than the tanga she used to possess; the butch is suffcently short that Kimju's sex kleave shows out. Like Kimju, Molly stands full fontal, her big black bush hiding her miche. Molly gets special whistles when she cradles and then swings her mammaries.

They look forward and up into the spotlight. The drum beats a quiet rhythm; and two naked dancers slowly rotate their pelvises. Cries of "open it!" emit from the room, laughter; this builds into cheers and rim-shots as the Alumni grin and rip off the paper.

And inside the box? From inside the box Kimju and Molly extract a long dildo; a double header: the famed Double Dong. There is a hush in the Club, then a murmuring, pensive applause; the music is quieter now, still with a slow easy beat as Kimju and Molly contemplate their gift, and share a look of hesitation and confusion. Each holds one end in a hand.

Strippers perform with dildos, most certainly; Strippers are expected to also master buttplugs, and to use a dildo and buttplug together—Double Penetrators—the art of penetrating the vagina and rectum at the same time. Strippers might solo the Double Dong, but sharing the Double

Dong is a girl-girl ride and one of those lezzy action stunts forbidden to Strippers. Just like cunnilingus, or its double, 69.

Kimju grinds her teeth and inhales Molly's pussy scent, now smeared all over her face. *Am I supposed to do what Strippers are not allowed to?*

Molly knows the answer. "Come on Kimju, let's go for a ride."

Well why not? The Alumni grasp the Double Dong by its opposite ends, then sit themselves onto the Stage floor facing each other, and spread their legs apart. The Crowd hushes in anticipation of a pleasure forbidden the Nugget Strippers. Kimju and Molly lube the dong with their own cream and then inch closer together, closing up the space between their pelvises. The Cams collecting best angles, applause rises, and again the M/C erupts, "Ladies and Gentlemen, I think Kimju and Molly are gonna swallow that Dong all the way into their kunny and miche! Go Cosmos Pledge and wannabe Nuggets! Bury it deep! Rub those sex lips together!"

Laughter and applause follow as Kimju and Molly achieve this goal. Their legs intertwine, they wring the Dong together, yet still have their hands free. The drummer and sax blowout and silence. The Crowd quiets so it can hear them breathing harder, watch them pull each other's knockers and mams, grab each other's shoulders, pull hair, French kiss, rub breasts, and bring themselves toward orgasm.

This time there is no interruption. They squeeze, they thrust, they rub clits together, and break through into a shared, but still controlled orgasm. A steady, "huh, huh, huh, hum, hum...."

Now the drummer and Crowd lock into their rhythm by clapping in time, but then they start to drum and clap faster, just a touch, and a hoot and a holler as the Alumni break free into a writhing rolling climax that rocks the Club.

As Kimju and Molly descend from their high, they arrest themselves far above bottom of the excitement, and they connect with a slower breathing, second wind, this one with a slower but committed rhythm. They are still firing with climax, still wringing the Dong, and as they settle themselves down for some more koekje-mumbo they discover the Club and the sax settles in with them and lets them savor their ecstasy. Eventually they catch their breath.

The M/c chimes, "Let's give a hand to the Alumni Dong Show. Kimju and Molly, you took it over the top! A big hand, everyone!"

Beka and Elle, even Babs, suffer a frontal assault watching the Dong show. Game Mistress, sitting with them Stage-side, beams approval. GM leans forward, taps the center of the table to draw Beka and Elle's heads into the middle, and speaks loud enough for them to hear, "Let these Nugget Alumni provide a role model for you newbies to aspire to!" GM nods her head and leans back, satisfied.

Elle appreciates the power of the Game, *I have indeed witnessed a full view of the intimate privates of two fellow Cosmos, but also a view into their emotional insides; how they respond to forces. I've viewed both their physical as well as their spirit selves.* Elle ponders, *I know that I am way out of my league and I suspect that this is true for Beka as well. It's like Kundalini got loose.*

Beka taps Elle's shoulder and talks into her ear, "Looks like the Dong is coming to the Cosmos House."

Elle feels the Nugget leather chair underneath her thighs and naches and realizes she keeps wiggling her thighs because *I need to pee!* She squeezes her legs together again in an attempt to control her bladder. She corrects her position and hooks her ankles around the outside of the chair's front legs *so I can't misbehave.* When she sneaks a glance at Beka she witnesses Beka touching herself with her fingers. Elle clenches her teeth. *If that isn't against the Rules it should be.*

Kimju and Molly exit the stage holding the wet opposite ends of the Dong in their hands.

The Double Dong, slippery with cream, demands a firm grip, but before the Alumni can decide what to do with it, Penny intercepts them as they reenter the Dressing Room. "Gimme it back," Penny responds to the quizzical look from Kimju. "You should know that Coco and I take turns with the Dong."

Molly protests, "But I thought—"

"—you were going to take it to the Cosmos House. Hah." Penny pouts. "House Mom wants me to bury this into my polished poontang." Penny qualifies, "But don't worry, Coco and I aren't like you two. Because we're Strippers only one or the other of us can keep the Dong stuffed inside at any one time."

"Fear not," Kimju suggests, "taking turns will in short order feed your desires, and you will beg to share it. That way you can both become Whores. Or Pledge, if you're lucky."

Out front an approving Crowd demands an encore. Kimju's head spins and she senses MomCap approaching from somewhere. *I need to think now. But I can't think and stay wet at the same time, maintain the physical rhythm, the up-tempo heartbeat, the craving to climax. Climaxing. Molly and I already did that.*

Kimju looks at her fellow Alumni and sees a big smile on Molly's face, "Come on," Molly says, "They need us back out front. Encore!"

Elle muses during the house din, *A Flip but no Flop.* Elle thinks ahead, *Kimju and Molly both left the stage naked. Their wet thong and panties still sit on the edge of the stage in front of a VIP table. The VIP table. .*

Kimju and Molly's Alumni Reprise night isn't over

II-12 Beka & Elle: Dance the Nugget & Flip-Flop (D20)

§ Kimju & Molly Bring Beka & Elle: Onstage to Dance

House Mom dashes Kimju and Molly out front before the demands for an encore lose energy. They waddle forward holding their pussies wide, diddling their clits and reciting, "Please let me Pledge naked, stay pink-wet-and-ready, eat pussy and juice the Dong, and cum be a Stripper next Term!"

Applause rises.

It had taken Elle by surprise earlier this evening when *Kimju joined Molly and Beka and me to "Pledge naked and cum be a Stripper next Term." And even more shocking to watch Kimju eat pussy and climax the Double Dong with Molly.*

Elle steals a glance at Game Mistress and observes her smiling as she watches the two naked Cosmos do a vulgar walk. *Kimju doesn't want to be here at all,* Elle bemuses, *Kimju wants to Opt Monitor next Term, but now she begs Opting Down.* Elle checks to make sure her legs stay open. *Maybe Kimju doesn't have any choice. Maybe I don't either; I've been begging to Strip since Day One.* Elle feels the leather under her thighs and the bottom of her nates. *Except that's not real either. I still intend to keep my two pieces and Opt Up.* Elle considers. *Except maybe we all have to expose ourselves first.*

The drummer rattles snares as the Alumni bow, still naked of course, still pulling their pink wide and still diddling their clits. And then….

A rim shot and the Alumni lean back, let go of their sex lips, and raise their arms into the air as the applause crescendos. As they bring their arms downward they cast their upturned palms toward the Stage-side table seating Game Mistress, Babs, and Pledge Beka and Elle. The spotlight follows and to pans as GM stands for a bow. Babs bows and gestures Beka and Elle to rise to their feet.

Elle feels a stab of fear, freezes; she looks up at the Screen, looks at Boss Babe, and watches as Game Mistress mouths words, "You lucky Pledge shall get a opportunity to demonstrate some of your dance steps!"

Elle interprets. *Either I Strip naked and pink tonight or BB will put my Gonzo Videos up.*

The Maître d' alights, flaps wings, and herds the two tittering bare-belly and leggy newbies around the outer stage, and shoos them up steps to the Stage level.

Elle feels helplessly propelled. *I am moving far faster than I desire! Also, what happened to the Double Dong?* Naked Kimju and Molly position them side-by-side as they arise onto Stage, and guide them forward to center Stage.

The spotlight follows, applause ripples, music begins, and the M/C announces, "Ladies and Gentlemen, the newbie Cosmos will show off skills they have learned from their dance teachers!" Naked Kimju and Molly wave in acknowledgement to welcoming applause, and sashay back out of the spotlight. The announcer rises in pitch, "The Nugget welcomes a work-in-progress, Cosmos Pledge Beka and Elle!"

The drummer and sax man kick up a quiet rhythm. The M/C proclaims, "These wannabes are wearing what they wore when they arrived at School."

Hoots.

Elle's thoughts fill with daunting apprehensions. *Things are happening too quickly! Oh what has gone wrong? What if Beka and I have to Flip-Flop? What if swapping costumes here on Stage at the Nugget involve stripping naked?*

Elle feels goosebumps rise on her body. She remembers, *Beka has been begging to Pledge naked and cum Strip, only she believes it more than I do.* Elle brushes her hair back and the Patrons approve. Elle looks out. *Might Fate be catching up with me? Beka can roll with the flow; she has already tittered and pinked. But I'm not at all sure I can.*

Elle steals a look at her Roommate and sees that Beka already moves with the groove of the music. Elle licks dry lips, and finds and outer rhythm, and slowly isometrics her body.

"Ladies and Gentlemen," booms the M/C, "That's Beka in the croptop and miniskirt and Elle in the halter... and them's some shorts ain't they!" Elle winces as catcalls and howls emerge from the Crowd. *I can never escape hairage.*

A huge roar from the Crowd stuns Elle back to her senses and she looks toward her Roommate; Beka has lifted her croptop and flashes both her boobies. *Show-off!*

No, worse than show-off. And I must respond, I must do something! Elle throws herself into a frug, looks again, and sees Beka dancing the jerk, throwing her arms in the air while holding her shirt up in her teeth. Elle looks past the spotlights and sees eyes—many pairs of eyes— watching her. The Crowd roars again and Elle watches Beka lift her miniskirt up.

Elle looks away, back across the stage into the Club, panics, the situation tilting dangerously out of hand. Her eyes search for exits ahead of her, *Back to however I got in. The front door.* And another roar, this time for herself, and Elle discovers she must once again put a nubbie away. A coffee-colored cone on top of the pear-sized nodules. *Back into your halter, you!* Elle says to herself. She feels applause appreciate her and cheer her on.

But to strip or not? Will this determine which Roommate returns to the Nugget next Term and which one does not? Like Molly has predicted. Beka drops her shirt back down again, looks to Elle, but neither knows what to do next.

While they linger upon this uncertainty their eyes drift to Babs, who plucks them from oblivion, takes control, and signs them to sit down.

Okay. Elle breathes relief. Both newbies diminish the vigor of their dancing and relinquish to BB's control. *Predictability has value right now.*

Beka breaks form but a second away from pulling her shirt off overhead. Beka might not know why she is here intellectually, but blurts to Elle as they get on their knees, "Can't you feel the Club, Elle, and don't you love the Game here!"

The drummer reduces to snares and the Club quiets as Beka and Elle sit on the Stage; look again to BB who now signs their legs spread. Polite applause builds as Beka upskirts her full juicy monte.

Signs work very well in noisy environments; now Babs signs her Pledge onto their hands and knees so that each can hang downblouse. Elle leans forward over the edge of the stage so her halter can fall away from her natural 34Bs.

Beka crawls around the outer edge of the circular Stage, so all the tippers can look into her armhole and detail the unusual dark brown outline around both her beige areolas, and study her indented-when-aroused nipples. More applause. Elle wonders, *What will I do if Monitor Babs signs me to unbutton my neck strap?* Elle knows the answer. *Silly moi. BB's made me do that before. But never in front of strangers. And then not just my neck buttons, my front buttons too. Babs will make me beg to raffle it off to the Crowd. I'm going to be topless after tonight. If only for a little while.*

Elle looks at Beka. Beka has her face cheek on the edge of the stage next to the VIP table, butt high and miniskirt completely ridden up, shaking her torso so her croptop keeps riding up. Beka suddenly finds her nose in contact with the wet wadded remains of Kimju and Molly's tanga and panties, and the smell gives her a start that snaps her head up, indeed she's halfway up and looks toward Boss Babe stage-side. BB lifts a finger in her direction, and warns her away from lifting her shirt up again...or letting it ride up. A very clear "no no," so Beka obeys, even with the smell of tang on her face.

"The newbie Cosmos Pledge!" the Master of Ceremonies declares, as the naked Kimju and Molly reappear from behind and organize all four Cosmos into a row. The four take a bow; Elle knows, *Even though Beka and I still have all our clothes, Beka has out-flashed and out-danced me.*

"Flip-Flop!" It is a new voice in the Crowd, then another, "Flip-Flop," followed by laughter and then a cheer. Beka and Elle exchange uneasy looks, and laughter ripples through the Club. Kimju and Molly turn to face Beka and Elle, laugh, and wag fingers at them.

The Chant builds in the Club, "Flip-Flop! Flip-Flop! Flip-Flop!" Now Kimju and Molly take up the Chant, windmill their arms toward Beka and Elle, so that the newbies, trapped and in desperation, join and pick up the chant, "Flip-Flop. Flip-Flop. Flip-Flop" until the entire Crows reaches a crescendo and quiets with satisfying applause that ripples out.

Elle computes. *Will Beka and I trade tops and then trade bottoms, or will we both strip completely naked before we exchange, or...,* Elle flashes on naked Kimju and Molly, *will we give our costumes to Kimju and Molly, or will we toss our clothes to the Crowd? Like they did.*

Kimju and Molly hesitate, unsure of the verdict. And Elle pounces. "We're off to the Dressing Room!" she announces to the Crowd, grabs Beka by her hand, and rushes her toward backstage. There is a huge commotion in the Club, as Kimju and Molly, left naked on stage to contain the crowd, throw up their arms in mock exaggeration.

Beka and Elle flee across the narrow ramp and into the arms of House Mom.

"So nice to make your acquaintance," House Mom blocks the way with her short stout body. "I'm House Mom. I run the joint."

Neither Beka nor Elle have ever been backstage before and before they can gather their thoughts House Mom speaks again, almost with humor, "I suppose you two want to use the Dressing Room?"

"Yes, please," Elle speaks for both of them, and adds, "and I desperately need to use the bathroom."

Beka accommodates, albeit inappropriately, "Ma'am yes Ma'am. We came backstage to Flip-Flop."

"Excellent, Pledge, except you must address me as MomCap. You may also address me as House Mom, since you aspire to be one of my Nuggets next Term.

"House Mom, thank you, House Mom," Beka acknowledges.

"Apologize," MomCap reminds.

"House Mom, I apologize for mis-addressing you." Beka gives, "Please let me Pledge naked and cum be a Stripper next Term. I only want to be your Nugget, please take me, House Mom."

Elle stiffens. *I shall not make the same mistake.*

§ Kimju & Molly: Coco Presents Smaller G-string & Panties

Up front on the circular Stage a different naked attendant appears, this time holding two small packages, two little cubes in gift wrap.

Kimju and Molly recognize Coco. They have never spoken to her, but they have admired her naked pinking Baseboard Picture in the Dining Room. They've been shown her *Double Dong Climax Video* made at the end of last Term. They witnessed her *Shave & Climax Video* performance, made the night she and the other fallen Cosmos, Penny, arrived at the Nugget, just as Kimju and Molly departed, Gamers passing in the night.

Like Babs and Janet and Penny, Coco shares their propensity for big boobs. House Mom iced Coco's nipples and clit just before sending her onstage with her deliveries.

Coco has already become a Nugget favorite. Neither she nor Penny have ever worn a stitch of clothing since they arrived. Persistence. Both lather up and do a shaving routine every day, and both have been lowball priced and relegated to lapdancing. The Hat Check Girl passes out their Pink Pages for free, and if the big Screen in the lobby isn't showcasing them pissing on a birthday cake, it showcases them soloing the Dong in their clean-shaven pussy and cooze. Or, absent this persuasion, masturbating with their fingers or rubbing the pole.

Coco never saw all of her watchers the night she and Penny streaked to the Nugget, an then pinked, shaved, and climaxed center Stage. So she wouldn't recognize the naked Kimju and Molly, except, as she announces to the Patrons, "Penny and I checked out your Pink Pages once we found out who you were," Coco circles the Alumni, smiles at the Crowd, twists her nipples and flashes pink. Hoots.

Coco lifts each small box above her head as she dances. "The Nuggets salute your Reprise, and your seizing opportunity to share climaxing the Dong together."

Coco curls to Kimju and Molly, "Penny and I apologize for not letting you keep the Dong and take it back to the Cosmos House." She casts her eyes across the semicircle of Patrons. "Wanna know why? Because MomCap expects us to beg to share it, along with potential outcomes." The Patrons murmur approval.

Kimju can't resist, "If you can make Whore next Term you could become a Porn Star. Then you can handle not only the Double Dong but also real cocks."

Coco rises onto tiptoe. "Every time I come on Stage, I pink the Patrons. Every time I take a bow, I pink the Patrons. So both of you, spread your legs and pink the Patrons. And beg to be here next Term!"

Once again, Kimju and Molly beg. "Please let us Pledge naked and cum be a Stripper next Term." They are unsure if more is demanded, and if so, what that might be. Laugher beyond the lights. It doesn't matter.

Coco hands each of the Alumni their box and they abandon their pink to take the box into hand. The box is made from folded fortune cookie dough; a shake and weight suggest fabric inside. Coco lectures. "You arrived with one Garment and you shall leave with one Garment. As a reward for your outstanding climaxes today your Garments have been reduced and are being returned to you."

Coco gestures to the boxes in Kimju and Molly's hands. You may break open and eat your box cookie and put on what's inside." She nods at them smartly. "May you both be improved by these reductions and may they help enable Kundalini to stay connected."

Coco turns to exit and casts a glance at Babs, sitting side stage, as she moves. Coco locks eyes, throws daggers into Babs' eyes, and the sparks fly. Coco pinks BB directly, squirts a short arc of urine, spins and is gone. But the message lingers. *If I ever get in charge I will crush you!*

BB understands. *Maybe my areolage gets cammed, but Penny and Coco pink, cream, and cum for the Cams. Naked lapdance any Nugget Patron.*

Also this: Penny and Coco haven't forgotten that Janet and I defeated them last Term and placed them here. Babs grits. *I just need to keep my wits about myself.*

A hush descends in the Club as Kimju and Molly look at each other, boo-bop for the Crowd, break off and eat the gift wrap, and hold up their presents. The M/C booms, "Ladies and Gentlemen! For Kimju, a solid Spandex size micro g-string! And for Molly, an extremely low-riding pair of panties! See-through panties. What's this? No more see-through-when-wet, just see-through all the time!"

The Crowd roars approval. "Come-on Cosmos!" The M/C commands, and Kimju and Molly wiggle their bottoms up.

Kimju instantly realizes, *this g-string is two sizes smaller than my previous thong,* and casts a glance at the soaking discard still at the edge of the stage. *If my thong before was two inches below my belly button, then this g-string rides seven inches below. And I'm still topless.*

Kimju levels the front from the inside and evokes applause. She smiles. *I know how to do this. But no matter how I wear this g-string, from now on I hairage top and sides. Can't avoid it. And if this upside-down triangle slides down a half inch, I slitage.*

Kimju pivots to give every Patron a full keister, pulls her butt cheeks and flashes Game Mistress and Monitor Babs her puckered kawazoo. She stands, and spins around to face the Crowd as the micro g-string sinks into her kypsey.

Kimju licks her lips, thinks, and masturbates the g-string to and fro on her karat to engorge it to full size. Applause and cheers. Kimju scans out across many faces. *I don't want to be doing this anymore.* Yet something inside her rises to the challenge of bringing the Crowd to a roar.

She does. She dips double fingers of both hands around the g-string, extracts dripping kloop, draws her fingers upward to arouse both nipples to erection, and cleans her fingers off with her mouth. She listens to the cheers and bows. *I'm essentially full-frontal 24x7 now. I'm a slitage, hairage, pinking, creaming, cumming Cosmos Pledge.* Kimju flashes a thank-you as the applause diminishes. *I can't predict if arousing the Crowd brings me closer to the Nugget next Term, or sates the Patrons.*

Topless Molly's new panties ride sufficiently lower than her last pair; six inches below her deep-set belly button, and sufficently low that Molly no longer contain her hairage, and with all the hair beneath her panties remaining visible in see-through. Rugage dominates Molly's ample gluteus maximus; the panties stretch across Molly's rump so low that she shows moonshadow between her two fat mounds.

And once again Molly matches Kimju's exposure and vulgarity; Molly gathers the backside of her panties into her deep moonshadow, and tugs the front side deep into her meat, taunting the Crowd with her very full black muff, massive mammary glands, and moons magnus.

More applause and cat-whistles. Molly restores her panties to hairage, rugage, and see-through.

The Alumni bow, turn toward Boss Babe at the Stage-side table, and chant together, "Please let me pullaside, pink, and finger my holes."

BB, still sharing the table with Game Mistress, digests if she's being toyed with. No matter, she rises as the Club becomes completely silent. Not a glass clicks.

BB bends a knee and rests her palms on her waist. "Beg the Nugget."

Kimju and Molly look from Babs to the sea of faces. The Patrons, the Crowd. They make eyes with a hovering Cam. They beg together, "Please let me Pledge naked and cum be a Stripper next Term!"

And applause, but not a lot of applause. And Kimju and Molly retreat to the two side stages. No Flip-Flop.

§ Robyn Trains Tiffany & Steph: And Watches Coco on Screen

Robyn continues to sit at the Kitchen table with her legs crossed. She keeps an easy eye on the Screen and views the naked Coco there with curiosity. Naked Tiffany and full-frontal Steph continue to kneel with their butts high, knees wide on the floor, faces and lips cleaning and kissing one of Robyn's feet or the other, or both at the same time. Robyn is making sure that neither sneaks glances of the Nugget feed.

Robyn might not think much about Coco, but Robyn does makes the connection between Pledge Tiffany and Tiffany's Porn Star Calendar hanging on the Kitchen wall. The image being displayed shows Tiffany sharing the Double Dong with another woman (*Janet?*) while embracing a second woman with a kiss.

Steph, who can't see the Screen but would recognize Coco as one of her Pledge from last Term, oscillates between naked Tiffany drawing her into kisses, and Tiffany concentrating her onto a particular foot task, like counting piggies and mouthing them up and down the foot. Might Steph's attention wane, Tiffany again draws her into a kiss, or sometimes touches her nearly-naked body with her fingertips.

Steph resists the urge to bite Robyn's foot. She seethes, *I'm going to tattoo a swastika onto your forehead someday and send you to the Slavesex. Just for your part in this.*

Tiffany drops a spot of tacky onto the floor. She removes her lips for a moment, makes eyes with Robyn, collects a sign, and gathers Steph's mouth for a kiss. One that leaves a bit mark on Steph's lip. Steph recoils, but Tiffany plants on Steph's whole mouth, draws her tongue in, and Steph kisses back and reaches out with her hands.

Tiffany loves the challenge. *Time for Steph to add another spot to the floor.*

§ Beka & Elle: Dressing Room Flip-Flop & Dance on Stage

A roar erupts. Beka and Elle return to the stage wearing each other's clothes. The music starts.

"Go Beka and Elle!" the M/C encourages, "dance for us! But remember, just because you Audition doesn't mean you get awarded the role!"

This is not an Audition! Elle firms, and processes that the Nugget Shooter recorded their Dressing Room exchange. Elle turns toward Beka and discovers Beka is into a frug.

Elle freezes but Beka helps her dance to the music. The Flip-Flop enables Beka and Elle to flash their tits and pussies in different ways, and the Roommates quickly find their grove as the drummer and sax set their pace. One look over to Boss Babe reminds them to kick out the jams.

Upskirts in Elle's case now involve dancing without any seam in her nookie, and her dancing reveals even more of what is between her legs—everything in fact. But her larger breasts make the croptop's armholes an insufficient nippage portal.

"Looks like Elle need some scissors," chortles the M/C. More cheers.

Beka dances wildly. She gets no titter relief wearing what was Elle's halter; she cannot hide her smaller boobies from inquiring eyes during any leanover. She unbuttons the front button so the triangle cups can fall to the sides and let her shallow 33B bobbers dance out. No longer any question about areolage and nipple details, and her uplifted nipples indent, forming a crater atop.

On Beka the jeans shorts' waistline rides lower than on Elle, so whereas Elle had to constantly make sure her navel sat in the missing-button notch just above the zipper, Beka's belly button remains safely exposed below the waistline. At the other extreme, however, the jean shorts dig directly into Beka's crotch and force her butt cheeks out the bottom: cheekage rising toward buttage as the leglines fray. In front the crotch seam nestles between two shaven lips, before rising to obscure Beka's racing stripe, further above.

On Elle the miniskirt hangs even lower than on Beka, romancing inches of bellage below Elle's navel that wasn't visible before. Elle senses that *once again Beka has advanced to boobage without waiting,* but when she looks toward Babs (sitting with GM Stage-side) for help, Boss Babe signs her to lift up *what has now become my croptop.*

Elle obeys and absolves her tittering for boobage. She lifts the croptop all the way up under her armpits so that her noogies jiggle in full pubic view. Elle feels the flush come into her face and spread down her chest, looks out and sees not just hovering Nugget Cams but also a sea of handheld. *I'm being memorialized not only on-the-record, but privately.*

Elle turns to see Beka on her hands and knees, pullaside and spreading, pinking and fingering herself. Beka offers, "I'll share my broda just like Kimju and Molly. I'll pullaside and pink for the Nugget."

Beka sees the sea of handheld Cams differently. "You can all post me up and trade me," she declares to the Crowd.

Elle turns to Boss Babe to see if she should keeps her croptop hoisted. Boss Babe ignores this request, but the interaction draws the Crowd's attention back to Elle. Again her face and chest glow rouge, and everyone records her deeply colored areola and erect nipples. Elle pouts and draws cross eyes; the Crowd first laughs, then cheers, and then applauds her.

The M/C blares, "Elle, hold onto that croptop in your teeth and pull that miniskirt up!"

Elle struggles. She adjusts the croptop to wedge it into her mouth. And then lifts the skirt just enough to reveal her crotch and pubic hair.

"All the way up!" a voice in the Crowd yells, and again Elle looks to Boss Babe for guidance. BB nods and raises her hands, and makes a rotary wiggle. The Crowd approves. And so Elle tucks the miniskirt all the way up to its waistline and slowly pivots 360. *Every eye in the Club gets me full-frontal. Full backside too. Nugs, nappy, and nates. Every Nugget Cam, streams, downloads from Automatron. All of that.*

Well perhaps, Automatron must decide if it can spawn storage fast enough to digest her.

Beka is on her feet again, berks still loose and halter flapping; she assesses her new jean shorts and discovers she can bend over, pull the seam enough to the side, pull her booty apart, and showcase her puckered bogey sphincter to the Patrons. Competitive applause and jostling for Cam positions.

Elle doesn't mind getting upstaged. *Gamers throughout the Prefecture are collecting the both of us, Beka more so.* Elle clamps down on the croptop harder with her teeth, cognizant now, *I am soaking a spot in the middle with spittle and drool.* Elle looks out into the sea of eyes. *And I am displaying my nugs to the Club. To the Nugget House Cams. To Automatron. To the entire Prefecture.*

She tucks the miniskirt tighter about her waist and checks that *my navel and my nappy stay unfettered. I'm not nude. I still have two Garments! But I'm full-frontal for now.*

Elle thinks twice about looking toward Boss Babe again. *I guess I'm staying full-frontal now. I'm exposing myself like this until someone changes my status, even if it takes forever.* She takes in a big breath and let it out in a series of pulses. *I'm not just full-frontal, I'm begging to Strip naked, here, all next Term. But that can't be real. I might be bump and grinding here full-frontal, but I still have two Garments! At the end of the Term, only Garments count, not what you're begging.*

Elle has a premonition. *I don't think Beka and I are going to be stripping naked tonight. And not just because I won't or don't want to, and Beka does. Sometimes, it's hard to put a finger on Gamers' intentions. But I think they're gonna take their time in "learning" me to Strip. I'm too valuable for them to not play the Game with.*

Learning me, like making me dance full-frontal now. Gamers are going to make me want to strip faster than I am allowed to.

Elle breaks her rhythm; another bolt of worry flashes across the lobes behind her face. *Yikes!* She looks at Beka dancing, jeans unzipped, boobies bounding. *I wonder if our Flip-Flop in the Dressing Room got cammed?* Elle closes her eyes for a moment. *Did the Nugget Crowd watch on the Screens inside the Club? Did it get fed to the Prefecture? Did Automatron pick it up?*

Maybe it's even a Nugget exclusive.

Or never got cammed in the first place.

Elle reasons, *The odds suggest that either my Roommate or I will be invited to dance here next Term. And we will arrive here wearing either one Garment or we'll have to streak here naked. Like Penny and Coco had to streak.* Elle catches a glimpse of a Screen overhead; she sees Beka then sees herself.

Okay, I'm dancing full-frontal tonight, Elle accepts. *But which of us really wants to Strip.* Elle looks at Beka and sees her Roommate touching her nipples, *Beka already wants to Strip,* Elle concedes, *tonight and the next night, and next Term. She's it.*

The music stops, Boss Babe gestures them to take a shallow bow and recover themselves. The Club quiets as the Master of Ceremonies booms, "Beka and Elle! Newbies from the Cosmos House!" Applause, and then, "Pledge, what are you wishing for?!"

Surprise! Beka and Elle must respond, haltingly and out of sync at first, but falling into sync as they chant, "Please let me Pledge naked and cum be a Stripper next Term!"

§ Beka & Elle: Reprise the Camera Lounge so Elle May Pink

Warm applause follows Beka and Elle off stage, but before they can find their way to their table the Maître d' intercepts them and sweeps them past their table with GM and Babs, and parades them through the Club, back to their first stop, the Camera Lounge.

Once again Beka and Elle will pose solo, pose together rubbing and kissing, and pose with Patrons who believe they have the right to wrap their arms behind their shoulders and backs.

And of course Beka and Elle will deliver all the downblouses and upskirts desired. Beka tangles her arms in her unbuttoned halter, rebuttons the front, then unbuttons her neck strap so her halter can hang down. Elle lifts her croptop up to unpack her nips for the Camera Lounge Patrons packed inside. Elle feels Cams take down her uncertain exhibitionism. *This isn't me they're recording,* Elle affirms to herself, *its some alter-ego of me. Like when a snake sheds its skin and leaves the old one behind. They're collecting my old skin; even if it is rawhide.*

The discriminating voyeurs appreciate Elle's newest upskirts and her gynecological debut. Elle finds herself leaning back on the couch, feels her legs opening wider.

"Spread and pink for your fans, wannabe Stripper" a voice orders.

Elle looks up to see MomCap supervising. She blinks and obeys, too fearful to not honor the shooters with a pink butterfly, round up her clit ball, and pull *wide wide wide for the Patrons! Tonight I'm joining Beka and committing to pink and gyno work.* Elle looks out into the Lounge. *Everybody here touches me directly with their eyes, and I expose myself to them, directly, no media in between.* Elle considers. *Except for our shared energy-space-time.*

Elle closes her eyes while she reveals a dark brown circular vaginal opening flowing into a violet canal tube deeper interior. "Open your eyes, Pledge," MomCap commands, "we don't want to post pictures of you with your eyes closed."

Right. Elle obeys. *The Gamers don't just look at my nackers and notch, they take down my nackers and notch so that they can look at me over and over. Trade my files. Upload me to Automatron.*

Still, Elle defends. *Gamers are making me flash in exchange for keeping two Garments and ensuring I promote. So if Beka has to pink, cream, and climax, or I have to bring in our Measurement Nudes, or titter and upskirt sanpan, well so be it. Graven images aren't the real me.*

"You fail to add your own cream to your list of achievements," MomCap observes. Elle winces, but her potential House Mom soothes, "No problem, Pledge, you will learn to make wetness before Midnight!"

Shutters click and phones hum. BB twists her head toward Beka.

Beka Broda creams freely; she rubs the seam of her freshly acquired shorts back and forth on her crotch until the fabric is thick with béchamel. Beka verges on cumming when MomCap smiles and advises her, "Slow down. You must bottle up Kundalini; you shall wait to climax until you can bring your Roommate with you!"

Beka talks behind half-mast eyelids, "I understand, I will do what you say so I can cum be a Stripper next Term. I know the entire Prefecture craves my release. I want my place in Automatron too."

Elle struggles, her face as flush as her insides. *I'm exposed. I'm exposing myself.* Elle repeats, she holds her nookie wide open, and feels an urge to masturbate. *I still wear two Garments, for how long? And what's so great about being a Monitor like Babs? Or like Steph was?*

Elle tests a final reconciliation. *Must I be humiliated in order to succeed? Is that why I am here?*

Am I willing to reveal myself in climax to ensure that Babs doesn't screen my Gonzo Videos?

§ Game Mistress & Babs & Four Cosmos: Depart the Nugget

Game Mistress greets the topless Kimju and Molly outside the Stage Door, just as the Back Door Man closes the Door behind "The Alumni." The two ex-Strippers feels the crunch of gravel on their bare feet as they walk to the Van parked at the end of the alley in this deserted industrial area. A hovering Nugget Cam trails along, and the mysterious Game Mistress encourages a few liberties before unlocking the door of the Van so the two former Strippers can climb in.

GM takes the wheel, and the Van pulls around front just as Babs escorts Beka and Elle out the front door. Boss Babe opens the door of the Van and provide the paparazzi with Elle's commando, ensuring that Elle gets equal opportunity exposure to Beka's flashing upon arrival. Elle must let the shooters linger on her upskirt and considers, *at least I don't have to pee anymore.*

The door closes, Babs climbs into the passenger seat, and the Van lurches into motion. Four Pledge on the floor in the back begin to jabber.

"Looks like your Garments got reduced in size, but you didn't get to keep the Double Dong," Beka observes to Kimju and Molly.

"Your loss," Molly yarns, "because I really do I want to ride it with you. I'll show you how. I won't hurt you."

"Looks like you two have Flip-Flopped," Kimju observes. "Now anybody can Game with you."

Elle corrects, "Anyone who has already played a Roommate Game is allowed to Game with Beka and me. Except that so far, Beka and I are the only Roommates who've Gamed."

"I'm next," Molly prides, "I'm committed to a Greatest House Roar with Steph. I'm gonna lose and be naked. Steph will have two Garments and Opt Up. After that either of you can give me one piece so I don't have to streak to the Nugget next Term."

"We both will!" Beka volunteers, "that way Elle and I can both Strip next Term!"

Kimju suppresses a laugh and Elle looks at her. Now Elle furrows her brow. "Wait a minute—" she begins.

Molly rarely interrupts, but she does now, "I don't need two pieces because I don't want to Opt Up. One piece will do please."

Elle butts in, "Beka just volunteered to give to you."

Kimju recounts. "So it's very simple. After Steph takes Molly's panties, Molly will need one Garment so she doesn't have to streak to the Nugget. So you, Beka, give her your top—"

Beka interrupts, "And Elle will give *you* her top, so she and I can both Opt Down and be topless Strippers next Term."

"And you would have two Garments and Opt Monitor next Term," Elle observes.

"I approve," Kimju asserts. "Once you become Nuggets you'll be naked 24x7 of course, but getting yourselves there topless, so you don't have to streak, is a wise move on your part."

Much later tonight, long after the Van has returned to the Cosmos House, Elle secretly updates her notes, "Five Cosmos now beg to Strip, Four Cosmos pinked and fingered tonight, one way or another. Three made themselves wet, and Kimju and Molly 69ed and rode the Double Dong to a climax on Stage."

Elle is honest enough but doesn't write down her final thoughts. *I know I must now include myself among the gyno gals, although I am too scared to freshen and cum.*

A final awful though strikes Elle. *So when I peed in the Dressing Room did I make a debut on a Pee-Cam?*

Molly & Steph: The Greatest House Roar (D21-D23)

II-13 Robyn & Cosmos: Greatest House Roar Morning (D21)

§ Robyn Hazes Tiffany & Steph: Stay Pink-Wet-and-Ready

Six Cosmos answer Reveille of Day Twenty-one and Lineup in front of their bunks facing the Minxy Mirror. Robyn paces between them and their visages, except the Minxy doesn't reflect her. Robyn still wears her skin-tight stretch maillot with its spaghetti straps and miniscule cutout hole. It would appear that Babs remains in her Bedroom, "with administration to tend to."

Robyn reviews Tiffany. Since yesterday, Tiffany has managed to leave both her Garments hanging up in the Bedroom. She stands spread pinking at one end of the Lineup. All the other Pledge stand spread surrender, Tiffany is the only Pledge who stands naked.

Robyn locates Steph in the Lineup and says to her, "I see Pledge Steph is learning some lessons. Getting ready for the Greatest House Roar, I bet."

Yes, I am learning. Nearly-naked Steph tightens her face. *My undershirt, (and what should be a minidress) remains in belt roll that hangs on crests of my ilium; sweeps across my stunning pelvis and hips. It resides below my backside dimples, play with my stern crack, and never covers my bleached short-and-wavies a-front.*

Okay, so I tested unrolling my undershirt once before and I ended up worse off. This time I'll go along and leave it rolled into a tube belt. So what if I can't stop Gamers from seeing goosebumps and the fine hairs on my spooters. So what, if I can't stop them from seeing my slit right through my bleached scruff.

Steph twitches a nostril. *Watch out, Gamers. Watch me shim-me-sha-wabble in my tube belt. Watch me play the Greatest House Roar with Molly, take my second Garment, and get back to Monitor again!*

Robyn pauses in front of Steph. "Tell me what you and Tiffany achieved yesterday, Pledge," she orders.

Steph picks words carefully, "Ma'am, we got on our hands and knees spread our legs and pinked, Ma'am. In the Backyard, in full public view."

"Did you drip cream on the dirt?" Robyn asks.

"Ma'am!" Steph flusters, recovers. "Ma'am, I know Tiffany did. But neither of us got to look behind when we got herded upstairs. You were there, Ma'am."

Robyn darts a glance down the Lineup. "How come Tiffany stands spread pink and you stand spread surrender?"

"Ma'am, maybe we pinked and creamed together but that was yesterday, Ma'am." Steph retorts. "And besides, Tiffany always has to be out front."

"Don't want that, Pledge." Robyn says. "Match her."

Steph grimaces, moves her hands from behind her head and pulls her outer lips apart, and looks at her double lines in the Mirror. Hair out of the way to both sides, clithood still protected, and inner lips stuck together.

"Thank me for letting you show yourself off," Robyn commands.

Again Steph falters, "Ma'am. Ma'am, thank you for keeping me nearly naked and letting me stand with my legs spread. And pink, Ma'am, like Tiffany."

Robyn finger snaps at the Minxy and two side-by-side Screens appear, Back Door Cam Video from the Post Henge yesterday documenting both Tiffany and Steph hanging valiva.

Steph flushes and the hairs in her goosebumps stand straight up.

The Video cuts and Robyn narrates, "Apparently you're both also toe-sucking foot worshipers."

They are.

Tiffany allows herself a diddle upon her trigger button.

Steph draws her stomach in; the pinking rolls Steph's short hairs back, and her inner lips, up until this moment stuck together, pop apart. She sneaks a glance at Tiffany in the Mirror, and concedes to Robyn, "I'll clean your feet anytime, anywhere, in front of anybody."

"You'll clean pee off my feet for not addressing me properly, Pledge."

"Ma'am, please, Ma'am," Steph stammers.

"You can surge some sop outta your satchel," Robyn advises, just like Tiffany transudes tapioca outta her twat. You follow her, just like you once followed Beka opening your legs."

"Go," Robyn orders Tiffany and Steph.

Tiffany chants and Steph falls into the recitation, "Please let me stay pink-wet-and-ready to cum be a Stripper next Term." Steph touches a finger to the top of her now-exposed clit and looks at her near-naked full-frontal nude in the mirror. Spouts solid, stamen distended. Eyes on fire.

"I'm not like you two wannabe Whores," Robyn curls her lips and snarls. "I'm special."

§ Robyn Hazes Kimju & Molly: Smaller Garments Bigger Climax

Robyn strikes another sign to the Minxy and it becomes a grid of Screens of different sizes and speeds depicting Kimju and Molly's antics at last night's Alumni Reprise. The Screens present the escapades in intimate detail, in all sizes and replay speeds, especially Kimju and Molly's mutual oral sex and Double Dong climax. Older pink-wet-and-climax reportage latch themes between and among Screens to deepen the imprint.

Kimju and Molly remain topless as they stand spread surrender. Robyn places a fingertip of her own spit into her Roommate Kimju's nostrils. "Your micro g-string wants to worm its way even deeper into her kypsey, and I hope it irritates your keystone, you knock knock kava kava keekelay. If you didn't do pocket jobs the last time you Stripped at the Nugget, you will next time.

Kimju takes it. *I can do this. There is no part of my knockers that the World and Prefecture hasn't seen before. No part of my keister, kawazoo, or kootch Gamers haven't seen before. They just desire me over and over. They want my hairage overwrought, my karat full up, and me clammy on the inside of pink. Gamers already do that to me. Climax me too, already with Molly. And they want more of me now.*

Robyn squints at Molly, leans forward, and spits into Molly's face. Molly holds stand spread surrender position. Robyn points toward Molly's extremely low-cut and totally transparent panties. "Your fans all agree that the muff you display above your waistline constitutes hairage." Robyn spits. "What they don't agree upon is whether the muff they see squished against your see-through constitutes hairage also?

Molly knows the answer, "Ma'am, see-through counts as hairage, just like with Tiffany Transparent's croptop. She's titters and boobage, but not topless."

Robyn pokes fun at Kimju and Molly's reduced costumes. "A small tax for being allowed to perform at the Nugget! An Alumni Reprise and an Audition no doubt? And here you are, knockers and kohlrabi, mammies and muff, already pink wet and cumming just as rude as can be, two Pee-Camers begging to Strip next Term!"

Molly welcomes the exposure; Kimju sucks her cheeks inward at the attention.

Robyn hones in on her Roommate. "Hello Kimju Knock Knock Kava Kava. I guess from now on you'll *always* have your knockers and kohlrabi out. You are my knock knock kava kava kunstwerk." Robyn cackles.

She turns to Molly, "So, maggot, which do I like more? Your black mangy hairage or your rude moonshadow crack? Answer me, you miserable mumping menses-machine."

Molly startles. "The same rule applies," she says without thinking. She thinks and continues, "The bare skin above my panties qualifies as a rugage exposure, but the rest of my moonshadow and magnus is buttage in see-through."

Robyn does not choose to parse this reply. She says, "So, Pledge, do you like your advancements?"

Molly nods, "Ma'am, thank you, Ma'am, for advancing my exposures." Molly shakes her body. "I'm much better off wearing see-through panties all the time because Gamers no longer have any incentive to wet me down and make me see-through-when-wet. Maybe I no longer need the Watering Can. And Gamers know I'll show them everything. Like at the Alumni Reprise." Molly nods.

"You're going to give your panties to Steph." Robyn states.

Molly falters, "Yeah, well, sure. I'm supposed to do that at the Greatest House Roar."

"You'll streak back," Robyn glees.

"Ma'am, please," Molly begs uncertainly.

Robyn adds a caveat. "Steph shall take over the Watering Can, you don't need it any more."

Bad news and good news. Molly sees herself on the Screen and watches herself climax. She closes her eyes and freshens, right here in the Bunkroom, creaming the inside of her transparent panties. *No secrets. Not that there ever were or will be. Things are not settled yet. The Alumni Reunion was successful, and I earned a reduced Garment. Getting rid of the Watering Can to Steph means fewer germs, but getting rid of my panties to her and having to streak again is downright dangerous: Marauding Rachmaninoffs, Jail, Lockdown. I've had to streak before, and I shouldn't have to streak again.*

And I know that no matter how plump I am, the Patrons love me.

Kimju averts Robyn's gaze and tries to drive pounding sound out of her ears as she watches the Screen and sees herself climax with Molly on the Double Dong. *I don't even know if the sound is from the Screen or in my head. What difference. I look like a wanton Whore, climaxing out of control. Gamers double down my humiliation: first they make me reveal more of myself reducing my tanga to string, then they make me climax myself in front of a Crowd. I thought I was done with Patrons.*

Maybe not.

§ Steph: Considers Kimju & Molly Double Dong Ramifications

Steph feels particularly seared at what she sees on the Alumni Reunion Video—*especially Kimju and Molly's pink and Double Dong action. All the kissing too. Molly is my Roommate, after all.*

Steph would fret even more should Molly recount the backstage Private Video that she and Kimju made for the Nugget Shooter last night.

But it's not Molly's panties that concerns Steph, be they wet, lower, or see-through. *Now that Molly has shared the Dong with Kimju, do Gamers expect Molly to share it with me, her Roommate?*

Steph parses her thoughts. *Double-donging isn't a Pledge requirement, but it isn't forbidden either. Kimju and Molly volunteered the Double Dong. And if Roommates are expected to share, am I expected to ride the Double Dong with Molly in order to take her panties away?* Steph curls her nose as she watches Molly climax on the Screen. *Nah, no way!*

§ Robyn Hazes Beka & Elle: Video Secrets & Secret Video

Robyn waves a hand and the Minxy forms two high-resolution side-by-side Screens, this time documenting Beka and Elle's strip and pink Audition at the Nugget last night, both before and after their Flip-Flop, both on Stage and in the Camera Lounge.

Elle allows her eyes to lose focus on the Screens. *Okay, so not just my titter but also full-frontal and pink are up. But it appears that our costume exchange in the Nugget Dressing Room does not appear in this mix. So does Automatron have those scenes? Or are they a different Nugget Shooter exclusive.*

Post Flip-Flop, this morning Beka now wears what used to be Elle's front-button halter and shorts, while Elle wears Beka's croptop and miniskirt.

Robyn bows, "Congratulations to our first pair of Roommates to play the Roommate Game!"

Stills punctuate some of yesterday's witness points on the Screen as Elle consolidates her thoughts. *Yes, Beka and I have witnessed Kimju and Molly watch their own Videos before. Even masturbate and climax with themselves. Now it is our turn.* High resolution video of Beka scooping pink wetness and Elle pulling a butterfly and putting spit on her clit romance the Screens in slow motion. Elle silently absorbs Beka's and her own Camera Lounge and Stage vulgarities; seeing herself crushes her. *I have no memory of some of my actions. I can't believe I did that. That's not me.*

Elle sneaks a look at her Roommate, first on the Screen then next to her. *Beka's smaller boobies fail to fill what used to be my front-button halter, although the jeans shorts she now wears do provide a newfound protection yet irritation to her bare breach. Whereas I have nothing between my legs. It didn't matter before, even though we all had to keep our thighs apart; it's different now, because I'm always flashing my crotch. No panties, no crotch seam. Vagflashing.*

And I'm not just titter and vagflashing, I've auditioned to Strip. Or at least pretended to. Beka believes that's what happened.

I'm in over my head.

And I need to pee.

Again, Elle's dancing boobage and vagflash and pink blink through the Screen. Again, before and after the Flip-Flop, but no Dressing Room footage. Elle ponders harder. *I suspect I also left behind a Pee-Cam clip; but I'm not about to remind anyone about splashing yellow onto the inside of a clear glass toilet! And that's not my only video secret. It's bad enough if my Camera Lounge visit goes viral. Well, maybe Beka doesn't care, but I do.*

Maybe I really am begging to Pledge naked and cum Strip. Except I never would believe that. And besides, I still have two Garments.

Beka watches herself on the replays and squirms her pelvis around. It doesn't matter if the seam rubs the clit or crotch or asshole or not, the Lineup isn't rushed, and Beka saturates the seam of the jeans with fresh brodeas.

§ Robyn Orders Tiffany: Make Up Steph, also Kimju & Molly

Robyn sends Tiffany and Steph to the Bathroom for makeup.

She addresses the remaining Four Pledge Lineup: Kimju and Molly, and Beka and Elle standing spread surrender. Robyn addresses Molly directly, "After you give your panties to Steph," Robyn claims, "Bikini Bitch intends to give *me* Steph's undershirt *and* panties. Ergo, Steph naked, me three Garments and an Opt MomCap next Term."

Molly speaks, "That would leave me naked, Robyn. Maybe you can let Tiffany give me a Garment so I won't have to streak to the Nugget."

Robyn pouts. "You I don't care about, Molly. Just watch me make that bleached scum skank beg to Pledge naked and cum Strip next Term. She doesn't need any rolled up tube belt anymore. Time for naked."

Elle shudders. *Steph might have been a Monitor last Term,* Elle understands, *and maybe Robyn ratted her out, but now Robyn keeps revealing Steph more and more totally. Robyn keeps demanding that Steph completely lose control of her body—climax, Pee-Cam, beg Opt Strip—except none of that's happened.*

Steph returns to the Bunkroom looking like one of Cleopatra's most stunning wannabe Strippers, except she reeks of cheap Whore perfume. Steph's shoulder-length hair and pubic scruff are crinkly with bleach. Her lips are overdone, her navel is splashed with white grease paint. Robyn signs her to stand, spread, and pink herself. Steph obeys and looks at herself in the mirror. Aside from her tightly rolled undershirt-belt, Steph appears naked. Full-frontal.

The Minxy Screen goes live with Tiffany, not far away in the Bathroom. Tiffany squats, collects pee into the Measuring Cup, spills the Cup into a drain, collects another, until done and updating the Logging Chart.

Elle knows *Babs shares the Pee-Cam beyond the Screens of this House, the Screens of all the Houses at School, indeed to the Prefecture, and to Gamers who are Tiffany fans, now or forever, anywhere anytime, via Automatron.*

Robyn sends Kimju and Molly into the Bathroom for toilet and makeup; now Robyn supervises Steph and Beka and Elle watch a live feed, as both ex-Nuggets log Measuring Cups for the Pee-Cam. Tiffany returns them looking like Cleopatra's finest.

§ Tiffany Makes Up Beka & Elle: Stripping & Oversubscription

Robyn sends the two newbies into the Bathroom last. Both pass up an opportunity to pee on cam and resign themselves to the stools facing the makeup table and mirror. Legs apart, thighs not touching, with the Bathroom Cam harvesting Elle's fresh upskirt.

"Open," Tiffany commands, and they both do. The seam of Beka's shorts digs into her bravado and Elle eliminates all shadows.

"Unbutton," Tiffany commands Beka, and Beka unbuttons her halter's neck strap. Boobage attracts the Cam away from Elle's narrows.

"Pink and masturbate the seam of your shorts against your stand-up bolus," Tiffany commands. "Soak the seam good, Beka Broda, keep yourself pink-wet-and-ready. You can pant, but don't climax."

Beka recedes into ready bliss.

Tiffany turns her attention to Elle. Tiffany decides that formerly Beka's croptop fits Elle poorly; the Makeup Case contains scissors, and so Tiffany attacks the Garment with them. In moments Elle's neckline is lowered, her armholes are cut bigger and her rib line raised. "Much better," Tiffany proclaims as the Bathroom Cam surveys the playful downblouse and side-cleavage, "I'll make a Stripper out of you yet."

Elle grimaces and considers the Cam collecting her exposures. *Right,* she admits to herself, *now I shall flash my pear-shaped naturals whether I want to or not. And if I lift my arms I can't avoid showing off my underboob, and if I leanover and downblouse I might as well be topless, and if I stand up straight my armholes reveal me.*

Now, try as she might, Elle cannot stop her nipples from erecting.

But it is not more titter that demarks Elle's new status, *it is the upskirt nookie I must share with the Bathroom Cam all the while Tiffany applies makeup.* Elle grimaces. *Maybe I don't need to pull pink right this moment, but my new normal includes gynecology work even though I retain my two pieces.*

"Butterfly for me so I can check you don't have any crost in your nook." Tiffany commands the Cosmos' newest vagflasher. "And hold still while I comb your nest and make sure your nib salutes.

Elle tries to control a ripple of shakes through her body. *I'm providing a feast for the Bathroom Cam. Pinking vagcam.* Elle worries. *What if I get wet inside?*

What if?

Aside from the ears of the hovering Bathroom Cam, Elle has no restrictions on speech. Roommate Beka plays her seam on her bongo button and plays rhythms with her panting breath, but conversation from the real world remains filtered out.

"Tiffany, tell me, please, now that five of us are begging to Opt Down, isn't Opt Stripping oversubscribed?"

Tiffany firms. "That's one way to look at it. Please don't forget I'm first in line, although I still need to shed at least one Garment." Tiffany scratches her long expanse of bellage, above the tan line of her missing low-slung slacks and below the rib line of a missing croptop. "Babs knows I am disparate and if I have to streak to the Nugget at the end of the Term I will attempt it."

"It's very simple," Tiffany explains. "My croptop and pants hang on a hook in the Bedroom. Babs can take my shirt or my pants. I realize that being transparent that my shirt wouldn't hide her areolage unless she can render it opaque. And if she wears my pants without her bikini bottoms, she will hairage, just like I do. But she is my Roommate, so I can't Game with anyone else first. I need to lose a Garment."

"Maybe she'll take both your shirt and your pants," Elle reminds. "After all, you are begging to Pledge naked. Maybe you could strip naked at the Nugget, then stay there so you don't have to streak back," Elle observes.

"May I be so lucky," Tiffany bemuses. "Because you know I don't have a choice as to the and where. Don't forget that you're also begging to Pledge naked and Strip," Tiffany wises. "However, if *you* get caught streaking to the Nugget all they will do is gangbang you, drench you with bukkake, chain you naked to the front door of the Nugget, and make you swallow the key. I'm different. I wouldn't get off so easy. I'm too valuable. If I get caught streaking I'll be in Lockdown and could end up Slavesex."

Elle feels a tad bewildered. "Yeah, okay, Tiffany. No problem. In the end my croptop and miniskirt secures my Opt Up. Maybe now that Kimju is begging and has only one piece she'll move up in line, and can join you and Molly and Beka.

"Well, Kimju does have a problem." Tiffany reaches behind and fingers her tail trough. "If she does nothing she's a Stripper next Term. And if she calls for a Roommate Game? Robyn will not Flip-Flop, Robyn will declare a Winner-Takes-All, and afterwards Kimju will be naked and Robyn will have two pieces."

"And Steph will take Molly's panties leaving Molly naked," Elle states a forgone conclusion.

"Kimju will be on the hunt," Tiffany bounces.

Elle blurts out a question, "Are Beka and I going to have to climax on the Double Dong at the Nugget?"

Tiffany brightens, "Ah! My free advice is to never pass up an opportunity to Audition! Listen, you should not worry. You're smart and adorable. After you do Beka, let me eat you out and dong with you, while we're both still Pledge. All I ask is that you don't get in the way of me making Stripper next Term, but aside from that, I'll make a Stripper out of you too."

Elle sighs, "I wish you wouldn't give me so much encouragement Tiffany, I'm not a wannabe Stripper. And I'm not a wannabe Porn Star!"

"I think that everyone in the world should want to be a Porn Star," Tiffany rises onto tiptoes. "And when that happens, perfection is achieved!"

Elle opens her mouth but Tiffany knifes in. "Lookit, I'm not the only Gamer trying to be a Porn Star. It's a crowded space after all. I just want to be there. That's important to me."

Tiffany graces Elle with her hand, "Don't worry, I'll be your friend whatever your Caste—this Term or next Term. And once you're a Stripper, I'll help get you ready to be a Porn Star. That's the next step!"

Elle objects. "Tiffany! Please, no!"

Tiffany fusses, "Don't worry, Elle, desire will grow with you. School will help you let Kundalini loose. And then you will be tremendous!"

§ Robyn Chides Beka & Elle: Join Kimju on Minxy Mirror

The newbies return to the Bunkroom. Beka continues to let her halter hang down and Elle wears a much reduced croptop. They encounter a preening and confident Robyn, daintily attired in her string strapped maillot cutout, who halts both of them. Robyn points toward the Minxy Mirror, where a topless g-stringed Kimju already seems lost in a kissing and rubbing embrace. Molly and Steph are no longer in the Bunkroom. Neither see Tiffany quietly return to the Bedroom, don her see-through croptop and low-slung slacks, and exit down the circular stairs with the Bikini Babe.

Robyn waves at the Minxy where her topless Roommate affixes her body; she addresses the newbies, "Witness a Stripper masturbating with her mirage, lost in ecstasy. In a pleasure trance. Zoned."

"Stripper?" Elle asks. "Aren't we all Pledge?"

Robyn ignores she was asked a question. "Okay, so Kimju's begging to be a Stripper, just like Molly. Just like you and Beka. You've been begging to Strip since the day you arrived, it's your natural selves, only you don't know that. You'll learn." Robyn nods toward Kimju. Kimju moans, kisses and tongues a visage in the Mirror. The avatar looks like her, with lips like fire, sparkling eyes, nipples erect, and belly electric.

Robyn raises a shoulder. "Seems to me the Opt Downs for next Term are all settled. Kimju and Molly will return to the Nugget." Robyn smiles. "You two will join them."

Elle complicates, "Wait. You neglect Tiffany. In fact the Opt Downs are oversubscribed."

Robyn ignores this claim and talks down to the newbies, "You two titty strippers want to know why you Flip-Flopped last night and Kimju and Molly didn't?"

Elle rushes an answer. "Gamers wanted to turn me into a vagflasher," she says.

"Duh." Robyn snorts. You think it's all about you. So you shall beg me to cam your upskirt from now on? Pay attention to me, Elle Lollydor, you worthless newbie Pledge. You Flip-Flopped because you and Beka are Roommates but Kimju and Molly are not. That's why, retard."

Beka looks confused and Elle stays silent. Robyn advances, "Molly and Steph are the Roommates. And do you want to know where they are right now, Pledge? They are on their way to the Peacock House and the Greatest House Roar!"

Well, some new data, Elle accepts as she straightens.

Robyn continues, "When that's over you can be sure that Steph will be wearing Molly's panties, like she did after the Figure Drawing Class, and that Molly will be streaking to the Nugget next Term. And taking her Obeisances with her."

Beka looks more confused and Elle listens. *Take Obeisances between Castes?*

Robyn snides Elle, "Yes, of course Molly will take her Pee-Cam with her, but it's worthless at the Nugget, because *all* Strippers Pee-Cam. But with Molly, her Piss Mouth is special! In fact, this Obeisance may be the only thing that ensures she streak safely, because MomCap and the Nugget really do want her to arrive, and not get chained up and gangbanged along the way, or maybe not show up at all."

Beka pipes up, "Robyn, I've told Molly that after she gets naked she can take my halter so she doesn't have to streak. I want to go topless. One piece."

Robyn considers Beka. White crost coats the seam of Beka's jeans shorts where they dig into her boneroo, bejangle her bongo, and tease fresh brodeas out. Robyn deprecates, "You're just a horny piece of fuck meat."

Beka blurts, "I'll toss my halter and shorts away center Stage at the Nugget."

Elle startles. *Wait! My secret notes are still in the jeans shorts' pocket, and I need to recover them sooner rather than later.*

Elle touches her low-rise waistline of her short miniskirt. *And no pockets, either.*

Robyn turns her attention to Elle, "You might be a pinker now, but you still need the nectar teased out of your notch."

Elle draws in a breath and flinches.

Robyn takes a step backward, laughs, but doesn't let up. "Maybe you two are going to get what you beg for after all." Robyn leans into Elle, "How's it go, nimwit?"

Elle stumbles but Beka leads and they both syncopate it out somehow, "Please let me pledge naked and cum be a Stripper next Term."

Robyn shifts the attention toward Kimju, affixed to the Minxy Mirror. "My Roommate and future Stripper klute is crusting klammy up on her seam, slathering it all over her butched sex lips, and running it down her thighs."

Robyn turns to Beka. "Just like you are."

Beka opens her mouth but doesn't know what to say.

Robyn does. "You and your Roommate are about to join her on the Mirror."

Yes, Elle figures, *Kimju has even rubbed klammy all over the Minxy Mirror.* Elle feels a draft between her thighs and uncovered crotch. Elle recalls, *only moments ago Tiffany demanded I butterfly for the Cam. That means that all of us Cosmos Pledge except Robyn has pinked the Prefecture.*

Elle eyes Kimju writhing slowly in passion with the Minxy. *Oblivious to Robyn's ministrations toward Beka and me. Zoned. Sound turned off. So lost in bliss she is unaware of the rest of the world.*

Elle blinks. Steadies. *Could Beka be next to lose control? And what about me?*

Elle nods and feels the draft between her legs from her newly acquired miniskirt. *Okay, Beka and I have played our Roommate Game. Molly and Steph are on their way to the Greatest House Roar to play their Game. But Robyn and Kimju haven't played, so neither can Game with us.*

Elle will not stop Robyn from playing footloose with Rules. "Don't forget that I may take any Garment from you at any time," Robyn brags, then admonishes, "Be nice to me, because *I* might have to decide what Garment to take and from whom!"

Beka blurts, "You're taking Kimju's g-string away in a Winner-Takes-All Roommate Game. I can feel it. She'll beg to doff it to you!"

Elle blanches and also blurts, "Beka, stop it!"

Robyn draws herself a-front Elle. "No 'stop it' when that's the right answer! Now you, Pledge, stand spread surrender and tell me what to do."

Elle moves awkwardly as she moves her feet apart and places her hands behind her head. Sees her own titters in the Minxy Mirror. A reflection of Beka, who chooses to follow her positioning, but no reflection of Robyn.

"Ma'am," Elle begins, "may I recommend you declare yourself the winner of a Winner-Takes-All Roommate Game and take Kimju's g-string away." Elle gestures toward Kimju. "Beka's right that if you let the Minxy charm her out of it she probably won't even know."

Beka pipes in. "Then you can take your maillot off, put the g-string on and put the maillot back on over top. You're two Garments and an Opt Monitor next Term."

Robyn scowls. "I don't like the idea of the Minxy reflecting me naked. You never know what it has back there."

Elle notices that her miniskirt has risen just enough that she teases hairage in clear crotch. She wonders if Beka sees Robyn reflected. She bustles, "Ma'am, you could put Kimju's g-string on overtop your maillot. That would looks very stylish. Announce to the Prefecture your status!"

Robyn walks around behind Elle, reaches around her to grasp her nogs in a handbra, draws her lips on Elle's neck, and plants a hickey there. "Good Pledge," Robyn coos, "now both of you go over to the Mirror, rub your boobies and nackers into your reflections, and give the Minxy a kiss."

Beka and Elle trade looks and glance toward Kimju grinding her captured body on the Minxy Mirror. *Zoned.* Elle considers, *does Robyn not remember she put Beka and me on the Mirror once before?* Elle blinks. *And that time I ended up making out with Beka's visage in the Minxy.*

"Move it! Join Kimju. Now!" Robyn snaps, and the newbies scramble to obey. The Minxy comes alive at first contact and sweeps them in.

Beka, now wearing what used to be Elle's front-button halter, fumbles behind her neck to discover she has already unbuttoned the strap and that her conical boobies already hang out. She uses her hands to tug what remains of the broda-soaked jeans shorts' seam up into her breach and across her bolus, so that fresh brodeas erupts and starts to run down her inner thighs. She squishes both boobies against the image of herself in the Minxy Mirror/Screen. She connects button to button, boob to boob, lips to lips, eyes looking into eyes tracking. Body aflame with sensation, and then with a moan, Beka's gone. Lost in sexual rapture. Zoned.

Elle hesistates, stretches to ride her cropped croptop up, and then drags both bare noogies down the Minxy until they come to a rest where she can carefully press them into the Mirror. Elle feels a tingle as the Minxy connects to her, magnifies her passion, and feeds it back. She kisses the mirror and almost instantly feels the Minxy Mirror kiss her back. She startles, pulls back and looks more carefully into the eyes in the Mirror, and realizes she is kissing Beka's image, not her own. *I can feel Beka's body against mine*, Elle observes, *I can feel her boobs, her belly, her legs, her lips.*

The Minxy draws her tighter, and Elle feels the passion, pure sexual Beka. She draws her head forward and kiss lips—Beka's lips. Only this time the Minxy connects but doesn't want to let go. The Minxy magnifies the sensation ever so little; Elle wants to turn and look at Beka for real, she's next to her, no doubt also affixed to the Mirror, but no, that is so unnecessary, for Elle finds herself drawn forward to the Mirror, as she rubs her breasts and belly and kisses Beka's lips with a full open mouth, and feels for her tongue. *I'm in danger of losing control! I'm being possessed not just by Beka, but by the Minxy Mirror itself.*

Those are Elle's last thoughts. Beware! Kundalini is loose!

§ Robyn Visits Elle: Minxy Kundalini & *Gonzo Videos* Secrets

Elle becomes aware of Robyn's presence beside her, between her and Beka actually, as if Robyn appears in a dream. Elle finds Robyn's eyes and then drops her gaze, landing upon Robyn's maillot navel cutout.

Elle tries to shake herself loose, *but the Minxy keeps a grip. Maybe Robyn wants to speak with me.* Elle processes. *Maybe she knows that the Nugget Dressing Room Cam collected me?*

Elle casts her eyes past Robyn onto her Roommate. *Beka isn't listening. She stays in the Zone.* Elle tilts and looks past. *Kimju too.* Elle sniffs. *Both of them fill the air with scent.* Elle sniffs. *Me too?*

Elle doesn't know that, like herself, Kimju (and Molly) also possess a Nugget video secret from earlier this Term, a secret, which if played out, could augment Kimju's Obeisances. Kimju wonders, *what if the Nugget Shooter told Babs, or Robyn finds out?*

Robyn adjusts Elle's head so that one cheek lies on the Minxy. Elle comes up from the spell enough to understand words spoken lazily,

"You're wondering what to do if you and Beka must confront the Double Dong."

"Ma'am yes Ma'am," Elle worries, one nug now free of the Mirror, and with the other she rubs against her Minxy self. She looks toward Beka. *Beka appears to be engaged with Kimju's visage and lost in waves of sensation. Only I have been brought out of the Zone, and only part of the way.*

"Tell me what you'll do might you and Beka confront the Double Dong."

Elle constricts her vagina. "Ma'am, we climax the Double Dong together, Ma'am."

Robyn nods. "Excellent. Now thank me for posting your Camera Lounge Pinking Videos to Automatron. Now all you need to do is find someone to go look at you."

Elle tries to lift away again, and again the Minxy persuades her to press forward with a gasp; she grinds against the gripping reflective surface. "Ma'am," Elle swoons. "Thank you for letting me pink to the Prefecture, Ma'am," Elle regrets.

"Beka made pink during *The Arrivals*," Robyn observes. "So congratulations, but tell me the truth, are you *all* caught up with her now?"

Elle panics, "Ma'am! I still have to produce my 'naughty secretions,' Ma'am. And I'm not pent up and frustrated like she is."

"You've promised to lolly up your own nectar."

Elle startles, Ma'am, I will pull pink and do my best to transude nectar, and lolly myself up.

"You shall finger-fuck and masturbate yourself," Robyn decrees.

"Ma'am, please!" Elle protests.

"Remind me what it is you're begging, after all?" Robyn queries.

Elle begs, "Ma'am, please let me Pledge naked and cum be a Stripper next Term." She fumbles worries out. "You saw my videos from the Camera Lounge. You can see that the Nugget would crush me."

"Kundalini will save you," Robyn breezes, and fingers the neckline of her maillot and the shallowest of cleavage. "So what do you intend to do with your *Gonzo Videos* that you so dutifully presented to the Cosmos House?"

Elle startles and releases a squirt of urine that Robyn fails to notice but the Minxy observes. Robyn purses her lips and speaks, "Elle, you should be pleased. Babs has already shown your camping trip orgy exploits to Janet."

"Ma'am!" Elle exclaims.

Robyn gestures toward Beka, still glued to the Minxy in a purring passion. "Have you told your Roommate about your Gonzos, or does she still not know about them."

"Ma'am, please." Elle begs, "you know I'll do anything Babs wants. Anything legal. Even anything bending the Rules."

"Maybe Beka should get a surprise," Robyn chides, "like you surprised her with the Measurement Nudes."

"Ma'am, please." Elle begs, "you know the Measurement Nudes are sedate. Beka doesn't need me to do this to her. I'll dance at the Nugget, strip naked and pink on Stage, and streak back."

"You make sure that you don't tell Beka what might be coming," Robyn commands.

"But Ma'am," Elle protests, "I could have told her."

"Except you didn't. You had your opportunity and you chose not to take it." Robyn dispatches, "You already decided. Now make sure it stays that way."

"Ah, yes," Elle fumbles, as a doorway leading to a confession to her Roommate gets closed off.

The Mirror is smudged with her lipstick and makeup, grease and sweat from her noogies and the imprints of her bare belly. The Minxy graces Elle's cheek, and she turns her head to discover lips to kiss as circuits reaching up into the Automatron possess her again, sends a tingle through her body, and entrance her completely. Elle feels her fingers open her nates, touch her nacelle and check for nectar, but it is the last thing she remembers.

II-14 Molly & Steph: Greatest House Roar at Peacocks' (D21)

§ Babs & Tiffany: Escort Molly & Steph to Greatest House Roar

The all-male Peacock House and the site of the Greatest House Roar lies on the other side of the Quad on a side street with hedges and trees. Babs and Tiffany drive Molly and Steph the short distance.

Babs, stunning as always in her bling bra and nombril Black Bikini, has ordered Tiffany to "stop advertising yourself" and don her transparent long-sleeve front-button croptop and low-flying skin-tight slacks, boobage in see-through, hairage and rugage of course.

Babs has ordered that Steph unroll and slip her arms into her tattered undershirt dress with its ripped cutout hole and a legline that barely covers her crotch and butt cheek. The undershirt most certainly enables Steph to titter her armholes and turn her headlights on.

Molly remains topless with hairage and rugage both above and through her see-through panties.

Back at the Cosmos House, Robyn "supervises" Kimju and Beka and Elle as they remain kissing and masturbating themselves in the Minxy Mirror, although the Minxy is quite capable of engaging the tittered trio without Robyn's help.

Molly and Steph, sitting on the floor in the back of the Van, can't see outside as they are driven into the Peacock House Garage.

After the door closes, Steph instructs. "Molly this is what should happen. "First, no begging any pink or pee or toys or Double Dong. No enema tracks. You're only mission in life is to surrender your panties to me at the Greatest House Roar!"

Molly shrugs, "Sure, Steph, no problem, they're already yours. Even if I might have to streak to the Nugget and might need protection."

The back of the Van is dirty and contaminates both Molly's magnus and the bottom of Steph's undershirt and the flesh of her stern.

Steph scowls as she considers her Roommate. *Molly, I know who and what you are, you are an ex-Stripper, and you are watersports qualified.*

Steph studies her Roommate across from her in the back of the Van and considers her own Obeisance: *Unlike Molly, I'm not a Pee-Camer or Piss Mouth. Besides both of those obeisances are strictly volunteered; a watersports credential is not a credential I desire. Even if Gamers try to indoctrinate me by pissing into Molly's mouth.*

The Van comes to a stop. "Don't worry, Steph," Molly calms, "whatever they want us to do, I'll do it more down and dirty. Don't worry, I'll prove I'm more worthy to Strip."

The back door opens. Two figures behind bright lights cam them and feed the Prefecture as they extract themselves. Steph titters and vagflashes her way out of the Van, followed by an apparently naked and very hirsute Molly, whose panties are cloudy with mung.

"Down the stairs," Boss Babe orders the Roommates, and they follow one of the Cams down the stairs trailed by the other. Babs follows and Tiffany brings up the rear. Hanging light bulbs provide harsh light.

Peacock Monitor William and his sidekick and Roommate Rodney greet the entourage at the bottom of the stairs. They are in the basement of the garage upstairs.

William wears a black t-shirt and slacks; Rodney wears only a black stretch fabric thong. Rodney's body is shaven and his face has been made up to look like a female goth girl. Steph suppresses a smile.

William bows to Boss Babe, "Monitor Babs, welcome to the Peacock House!"

Babs bows in return and before she is upright Rodney rudely cuts in, "So nice of Bikini Babe to bring her crescents d'areolage to the Greatest House Roar tonight."

Babs blushes. She grits her teeth, darkens her eyes toward Rodney, and sneaks a glance at her bazoombas and bling. *Bubbling up.* BB steels. *I'll get over it,* she tells herself, and eyes Tiffany's see-through, Steph's ripped undershirt and Molly's near nakedness. *I just need to stick to plan, and not respond to insults.* Boss Babe looks at Rodney harder. *At least not initially.*

Rodney keeps going, "Seems like Bling Boobs is the only Cosmos not displaying hairage. Maybe you should roll your culotte down so you can be like your Pledge. Like your Dining Room Picture."

BB sucks her cheeks in.

Rodney turns his advance upon Tiffany. "Looks like the Cosmos sent over their resident Porn Star. Your Calendar qualifies you. I especially like the month where your mouth was overflowing with ejaculate. You're quite the Whore.

Tiffany glides. "Thank you. If I were shooting this Term I would suck and fuck you, but I'm not, so besides my *Porn Star Calendar* you must content yourself with my *Tiffany Tiny Titter Suck Fuck Facial Movies.* And there's more. I did creampies, lesbians, toys. I did it all. "

Rodney opens his mouth but William overrides. He bows to Tiffany, "Hello tail peddler. Seems like my Roommate and I haven't seen you since the Yacht, although I don't think you got to watch Ginny do us. I trust you're been finding plenty of pee to lick up?"

Tiffany gestures. "Molly has qualified and begs to take on the bulk of that task. And besides, she's the one playing the Greatest House Roar with Steph, not me.

Molly straightens herself; she's still squat only more squared up.

William comes to the rescue and signs Rodney to square up. "Rodney has been making a special effort to stay totally shaven." He pitches a curvy bellaged Tiffany, "Ever since Rodney heard that a tamtart like you was coming his riser has remained hard in his thong."

"Hard and bent, daresay," Tiffany firms. "Seems like he always pops off when he sees me. Maybe he can shoot on my foot. Better my face. Is that allowed? And does he lolly up afterwards?"

"Shush!" Boss Babe commands. "You're not the act tonight. You're here to help us put on the show."

Yes, Molly and I are the show tonight, Steph assays, *two naked Peacocks hand-guiding Cams have documented us from the moment of our arrival. Naked and struggling with erections.*

"Rodney is the only Peacock Pledge who wears anything." William gestures to the two Camming Peacocks and a tunnel beyond. "You'll see."

He speaks to the Four Cosmos. "Tiffany's seen these erections before, you popped the whole Lineup, Day One of *The Arrivals.*"

William offers tactical details about the two naked Camming Peacocks. "One of these erections is entirely natural and a product of all the excitement; the other we keep risen using drugs."

Tiffany smiles, runs her thumbs along her waistband, and lets the Cams share a moment of deepened hairage.

Steph affords a look toward both Camer's dicks; both drip lube. She resists an urge to test her own quasi-exposed privates, but belays her disgust in her face.

Steph looks at Tiffany. *I don't like that the Camers linger their documentation on Tiffany's clear vinyl shirt and Eraser Heads, her eruption of red pubic hair above her low-rise stretch slacks, and her posterior rugage. I'm filthy and worn. I need a shower. I need a new dress. I need cammed at my best.*

The two Peacocks hiding behind bright lights cam topless Molly looking glazed and shameless, hairage and rugage above her waistline, and hairage and rugage in see-through below.

But they avoid recording Babs in her bra and nombril bikini, with its deep cleavage and crescents d'areolage. The Bling Bra.

"Stay hand-in-hand now," Boss Babe cheerily commands them, and Steph follows Molly as they thread their way into a long tunnel that apparently leads from the basement of the garage into the Peacock House basement. And then moving faster up a flight of wooden stairs, across a room, down a hallway, and then—they can hear people now—into a front Parlor, and a hemisphere of guests.

§ Cosmos & Corvettes & Peacocks: Guests & Introductions

The Front Parlor of the Peacock House is packed with people.

Steph finds the world spins rapidly during the brief moment Boss Babe and Tiffany herd the two contestants into a circle of Guests. Steph turns to look behind her but BB and Tiffany block any backward retreat.

Molly and Steph first recognize Janet, the Monitor of the Corvette House. Steph lingers her gaze and gives her former Pledge an evil look. *You no longer wear your Spiderweb Bikini, you fat blob of Jell-O.*

Janet rolls her shoulders at the intrusion. Indeed, Janet now wears a scaled up version of what used to be Louise's bandeau overtop a contrasting T-front maillot. *No jaboos, no jepoot, no jaxy.* There is the slightest twitch between Steph's eyebrows as she appraises Janet: *Never forget, you owe me.*

Molly knows how Janet increased her coverage. So does Babs for that matter as she greets Janet with a knowing nod. And both view Janet as confirmation of Game Mistress's power.

Molly juggles her mammies with both hands. *My two experiences with Janet both occurred in the Backyard and involved mindless supplication to her: At the start of* The Runup *she had demanded I uncover a handbra and stand spread surrender, no problem. Then later she somehow convinced me to beg this Greatest House Roar, for the Roommate Game with Steph. Okay, I'm here and I'm ready to give my panties away.*

A panic makes Molly's moonscapes bubble up and her minarets rise. *Naked is okay if we go back in the Van, but what if I have to streak?*

Tiffany shares dancing eyes with Janet. Tiffany shares with Babs the distinction of having once been a Roommate with Janet: Babs and Janet were Cosmos Roommates one Term ago; Tiffany and Janet were Nugget Roommates two Terms ago.

As if this matters; well, everything matters.

Tiffany and Molly also recognize a naked Ginny and Lee Lollydor, Corvette Pledge at the moment, from the Nugget last Term. Tiffany and Ginny share a silent glance acknowledging their recent Yacht outing, and Tiffany observes still naked Ginny still drips urine. *Ginny's a ho Pledging and I'm a Pledge needing to ho.*   .

Babs recognizes Ginny and Lee from their Cam Screens last night at the Nugget, but has never seen either in person before. *Why are they here?* She trades wary eyes with Janet, *now that I've agreed to Opt Louise Down?*

Janet smiles and pricks, "I presume Ginny had to streak here, but they'll be waiting for her knowing she has to streak back."

Babs scans the Peacock Parlor more carefully. *Yes, Louise is here too!* Louise stands spread surrender, facing forward and strictly decoration in front of the back wall of the room. Tan lines belay what Louise used to wear' today she wears last night's reward: what used to be Janet's Spiderweb, only reduced by one size. The size pico halter consists of a single string around her torso and a second string tied behind her neck and connecting to the string around her torso. And with the neck-tie string carefully positioned and balanced so that for both Louise's left and right lactoids, the string crosses the nipple perfectly, settles into it tightly, although everyone in the Parlor knows Louise must hold her position firm if the string is to stay put. The consequences of failure if the string doesn't stay put could certainty begin with the string clamped to the nipple.

The pico g-string consists of three strings connected at a knot. One string circumnavigates her waist, two others forms an inverted triangle in the front that fiddle Louise's lair open and pinch her clit out as they ascent upward.

Louise blushes under Babs' gaze. Louise is cognizant that possessing two Garments is temporary, and that Babs is party to her reduction to a naked Stripper next Term. Louise doesn't dare scan the room. *Everyone knows I full-frontal from now on.* Louise's nipples push up against the taunt string, and she feels the g-string tease her clit.

Babs looks away from Louise and her size pico Spiderweb Bikini and considers Janet. *Maybe Janet got more coverage and Louise got less. Maybe the Game took some vig.*

Babs remembers something Janet had said, "Lee Lollydor and Louise are Roommates. One's a rising Stripper still naked, the other a fallen Monitor with Two Garments that keep getting smaller. Louise hasn't wanted to share with Lee so they could both Opt Strip next Term, but voilà, now that you get to collect Louise begs as part of our Ginny-for-Steph deal, maybe she'll accept that sharing is good Karma."

Hummm. The things the Game judges you upon.

Babs now evaluates two other Corvettes: Ginny and Lee. They are not Roommates, they are both naked, and they present on hands and knees.

Lee has stereoscopic head Cams fastened to the opposite side of her head—up on her temple and above her ears.

Ginny serves as a chair for a silhouette Babs and others recognize as Game Mistress. Recognize despite GM's veiled eyes and black full-body suit and boots, and despite a kneeling naked Asian's mouth firmly placed onto GM's un-zipped crotch slit.

Steph swallows. *Molly's giving me her panties tonight. Here in the Peacock Parlor. Let's get it over with.*

Molly knows that like herself and Kimju, Ginny and Lee both wear rings to tickle their clits; Molly recounts that Janet has rings too—

opposite pussy lips—and Molly looks. Except the gusset of the maillot fully covers Janet's crotch.

Molly looks back to Game Mistress and considers, *I've heard GM also has a ring above her clit.* Molly computes that the naked pussy-eating Asian, with her long black ponytail with a braided loop at the end and conspicuous body art, must be GM's personal Slavesex, the diminutive China Doll. Owned. Mind body and soul.

Molly looks again. Three vicious parallel cane welts decorate China Doll's buttocks. Game Mistress knows China Doll's butt is searingly hot to the touch, but Gamers who ask GM nicely, touch the welts, and elicit a moan or a screech.

Steph feels very awkward standing in the front of the Parlor. *I'm only wearing my ripped undershirt. It titters me, contours my spouts, and barely covers my crotch. Except that Molly, who stands next to me, doesn't wear anything over her mammies.* Steph watches Janet watching her. A covered-up bellage flasher standing next to Janet stares at Steph as if she possesses her. *Creepy drabble-tail,* Steph assesses. *Wait! This is Darleen, one of my fellow Monitors last Term!*

Okay. *Somebody else who owes me.* Steph shifts her mouth just a bit. *Maybe Robyn's report from the Yacht that Darleen really is higher Caste and is Janet's mentor this Term contains truth after all. Now Darleen wants to watch me take Molly, and I will oblige her!*

Tiffany met Darleen on the Yacht, and in her mind it's simple, *Darleen is Janet's Roommate and sidekick. Steph says Darleen was a Monitor last Term and might be a Hover. But in my book any theory that Darleen might boss Janet is nonsense. I know Janet.*

Besides Monitor William and his Roommate Rodney, the remaining six Peacock Pledge also participate in the festivities. They stand to one side, occupying the space in front of a wall with windows behind, facing forward, naked and with erections. All of them, including the two Camers who followed Molly and Steph down the twisting passageway, stand in a Lineup and stroke their erections in rhythm together.

Some of the Peacocks are made up as women, some have their nipples rouged, and some of their erect dicks are lipsticked, or stained with henna or gention violet. All six cocks are thickly greased so the strokers won't go dry.

Tiffany fills in details from her first encounter, *when the Six Peacocks had pumped cum at my command.* Something about their posture makes Tiffany wonder *might some also possess greased buttplugs right now?*

Steph scowls at the Peacock Lineup, dares to make eye contact, and one Peacock ejaculates in her direction.

The Four Cosmos also recognize House Mom el Capitan, clad tonight in her trademark front-tie shirt, baggy cargo pants, and gym shoes;

MomCap bows to them gently when she catches them looking at her; tonight's loser stands a good chance of dancing in her Club next Term. Either Molly or Steph will be the loser; Monitor Babs and Tiffany are chaperones.

The Cosmos scan the Parlor to see who else they might recognize among the ladies and gentlemen who pack into the Parlor. Eyes dart. The Guests probably include other Monitors, Mom and DadCaps, Madams and Sirs, if not Game Masters and Mistresses. And since it obviously includes other Pledge; might it also include Strippers, Whores, in addition to the one obvious Slavesex?

Another figure leans in a doorway and Molly and Steph recognize Madam Nurse Beautician, who performed Molly's Medical Exam during *The Arrivals.* Tiffany recognizes Beautician also, having studied makeup with her, but Babs, ironically, does not, who, despite washing feet and painting toenails at the Beauty Salon last Term, never had the courage to lift her eyes up.

Molly and Steph fail to study two sturdy wooden crates that sit to the sides of the Parlor, each about four feet on a side.

"Speak!" declares William to the Roommates, and Molly and Steph recite, "Please let me play the Greatest House Roar!"

"Winner-Takes-All!" cries William and the House Roars.

§ Molly & Steph: The Winner-Takes-All Dance Contest

The introductions are over. Babs and Tiffany whisk the two Cosmos contestants out of the Parlor to trickling applause and anticipation, and separate them before they have a chance to speak to each other. Tiffany leads a panicky Steph up the main stairs to the second floor followed by Babs leading a calmer Molly. Once upstairs the two contestants get locked into separate rooms at the opposite ends of the House. Neither Molly nor Steph will be allowed to watch the other perform, but they will be able to hear the uproar. Greatest House Roar wins.

Molly and Steph sit and wait. The rooms are Spartan. There is nothing to do. Steph paces and tries the doorknob; Molly reclines. Then, while they wait, they both hear roars from what is apparently a performance beneath. Each assumes it is the other, except it is not. It is unnecessary that either ever find out just who or what they hear.

Babs unlocks Steph's door and speaks, "You're next, come along now."

And so Steph interprets. *I am the second act, I must beat what was before, and I am confident I can do that!*

The guests in the Parlor receive her politely, music kicks in, but Steph fails to dance with abandon, she holds back, and stumbles upon herself.

She hooks her thumbs into the straps of the undershirt and works it off her shoulders and down slowly down until both her spouts are fully exposed. That gets a roar, but Steph doesn't erect her nipples, and works the straps back up her shoulders and recovers her sinusoidals. The guests in the Parlor groan, but in good spirit.

Steph understands. *It is not necessary I overdo this. I'm too good to humble myself. I'm going to win no matter what. It's already decided.*

None the less, Kundalini stirs inside and Steph pushes the envelope; she lifts her undershirt up above her navel—exposing all of her shrubbery and stern—and gets an even bigger roar, but Steph doesn't push her bleached curlies aside and open her satchel up. She feels Kundalini push her to expose herself top and bottom at the same time, but Steph bottles the power, stops it from flowing through her body. *I rolled my undershirt into a tube belt and did enough full-frontal and pink yesterday to last the rest of this Term. Screw this House.*

She bows, turns, and exits. The guests know they give Steph more applause than she deserves and overvalue her futures.

Tiffany Transparent returns Steph to her holding room, and listens to Steph exude confidence, "I am the winner for sure. I got way bigger applause than the other act!" True, even a few hoots. "And I never had to take my dress off and I didn't masturbate!" Tiffany closes the door.

And then another, a third act, commences; this particularly confuses Steph. *What's going one? First Molly dances, then me, then...?* Steph casts around the room, wonders if it harbors a hidden Cam, sits and makes sure her legs stay apart. *I know I beat out the first dancer—well, the first act whoever it was—but now I don't know who I'm competing with. Could this be Molly again?*

It could but it isn't. Molly figured out while Steph was dancing *that more than two acts are performing tonight.* But it is not until Babs actually fetches Molly down from her room that Molly knows she is the fourth act. *And that maybe Steph has danced already. Or maybe not.*

Certainly Steph upstairs can't tell if this is Molly's act or not, *but it is obvious from the cheers that this is the noisiest act.* Downstairs in the Parlor Molly strips her panties off—it is the only garment she wears—she drops to the floor onto her hands and knees, lifts her maximus up, reaches her hands up in between her thighs, pulls her pudgy pink merrymaker wide, tugs on her clit ring, then masturbates while she starts kissing William's bare feet and toes.

"Please let me Pledge naked and cum be a Stripper next Term," Molly begs the Room. Begs the two naked Peacock Camers. Begs naked Lee Lollydor with her dual stereoscopic head Cams.

Only now does Molly wonder, *Stop! Am I going too far? I have to loose to Steph, remember!* Molly lifts her head and watches Kundalini arise in her watchers. The applause lifts her pride and a rolling cheer erupts as she back her thighs around William's pants, and commences to rub her black muff on his calf and produce a wet spot.

The Parlor onlookers quiet as Molly masturbates harder, her whole body shaking, and she begins to cum. She breaks free of Williams leg, rolls around onto her back and shoulders, grabs her mammies, and arches her mooe up. The breaths come shorter now, "huf, huf, huf." Molly touches her clithood ring and brings her climax up to a shriek.

The cheers and applause rise with her and crescendo as Molly catches her breath, rolls her mooe above her, and lets her own love juice slowly drip down into her mouth. Molly's smell erupts into the room, a feature of the Roar that the Cams fail to record. Molly scoops two fingers deep into her maw, advances whatever mung remains inside at this moment to also fall into her opened mouth, and again, fingers her clit. This time Molly rises into climax quickly, a total surrender, lead first by a squirt of genuine female ejaculate, followed by total loss of control of her bladder, a torrent of piss that splashes all over face and hair. Molly sputters as some spills into her open mouth. She closes, catches stream in her nostrils, finger-fucks herself and rollerballs her clit simultaneously, and opens her mouth again and she brings herself up to into a full roaring screaming banshee climax. Nothing else matters. Wild applause, cheering, and stomping on the floor as pandemonium erupts.

As she comes down Molly arches a stream of pee back out between opened lips and all over her chest and body, and as driblets stream out her mouth several guests react "eeeeech" and one Peacock ejaculates, Rodney, judging by a big bubble of foam in the front of his thong.

Molly rolls over onto her knees, glances upward, and discovers Janet ahead. Too late.

Janet commands, "Show us all your panty piss mouth act, like what you did at the Bachelor Party."

Molly closes her eyes, crawls to where her discarded panties lay, grabs them with her teeth, swabs them in her pee on the floor, and chaws them into her mouth. *You didn't need to do that to me,* Molly pains, mouth stuffed. *Yet, I've still got one Garment!* Molly scans other faces in the Peacock Parlor and realizes, *I just won the Greatest House Roar. It seems like I can't resist. Once they tell me to perform I can't not give them my best.*

However. Molly sighs. *If I take Steph's undershirt I can't Strip at the Nugget next Term, no matter how much I want to Opt Down.*

Molly comes out of her thoughts as Peacock Monitor William offers her a hand, helps pull her onto her feet, and stands her up for her final bow and accolades. The Gamers anoint her. Greatest House Roar.

Molly glances toward Boss Babe for direction and BB signs her to exit the Parlor next to her. She does and Babs escorts her upstairs and returns her to her holding room. "Get your panties back on," Boss Babe commands before she closes the door. Molly obeys. *I know I got the most applause of any of the four acts tonight, so it doesn't matter which act Steph was.* Molly frets. *This could be the wrong outcome.* Could be? *This is the wrong outcome!*

Steph, listening, certainly understands that each act was louder than the one before; she rationalizes, *Molly was the first act and that I have defeated her! Losing is not an option. Bikini Bitch tries to haze me. So dumb of her.*

Downstairs Tiffany finds herself a lone Cosmos. Eyes graze her; she pirouettes and lets her fans admire her Eraser Heads in see-through, and how her low-ride slacks showcase her hairage and tail trough. Tiffany starts to unbutton her croptop when Janet intervenes.

"Clean up the floor, Piss Mouth," Janet orders.

Tiffany runs her tongue around the inside of her mouth between her teeth and her gums. No Boss Babe at the moment. She bows to the Guests, drops her knees, gathers her hair, and commences to lick up after Molly. One Peacock pops.

Boss Babe reappears. She considers whether to wait for Tiffany to finish or interrupt, scans the Parlor, and discovers Louise looking at her. BB startles and without thinking signs Louise to pink, oval-mouth, and close her eyes. Louise glances to Janet, but finding no solace there, obeys. *No more looking at me,* Boss Babe determines.

BB glances at Game Mistress and catches a sparkle above her clit as she pulls the naked China Doll away from her un-zippered and bare crotch and shoots urine into her Slave's mouth. Babs startles. *Show off.* And then GM again seals China Doll's mouth to her vagina. And smiles.

Tiffany rises, bows to applause and Babs raises an arm for her. "Come," Boss Babe commands, "we must fetch our contestants back down to hear the decision!" She turns on her heel and Tiffany follows her upstairs.

§ Molly Strips Steph: The Winner-Takes-All is Declared

Babs and Tiffany lead Molly and Steph down the stairs and present them side-by-side in the Parlor. William gestures to Steph who gets polite applause, and then to Molly, who gets wild cheers. The Greatest House Roar is not even close. The applause dies down so Babs may speak.

"Winner-Takes-All," BB says raising Molly's arm into the air. Molly's milk cans sway; her mammoth belly shakes, and her pee-soaked see-through panties saturate that part of her minge not hairaged above the waistline.

Boss Babe extends her open, flat palm to Steph. Steph hesitates and BB speaks more firmly, "Off with it. Strip. Now." And so Steph gathers the hem of the undershirt in her fingertips, pulls upward, and rolls it up and off overhead, arms rising up, body completely uncovered now, skin stretched tight, pelvis, belly, breasts, all taut, and then the one arm holding the rolled-up undershirt lowers, and she extends it to Babs with an expression blending defeat and defiance.

Boss Babe takes a step backward. "Give it to Molly, naked girl," she orders.

Steph's eyes dart wildly. She scans the Parlor, takes in the Cams, evaluates Janet, frowns at Game Mistress. *I have no choice but to obey. I will stay naked now. At least until....*

Steph hands the undershirt to Molly.

Molly considers the undershirt like a pariah. It's soiled and filthy; it has been in the mud, been on Steph's body. *I don't need it, I don't want it, I can't be a Monitor next Term.*

"Put it on," Boss Babe orders. And so Molly carefully unrolls the garment, stretches her furry armpits, and pulls the stretchy undershirt down overhead and overtop her transparent panties. The undershirt is almost too small for Molly—it grips her very tightly and although it covers Molly's mammaries it by no means stops them from sagging, and although it covers her ass it does not make it any smaller. Molly still has hair all over her body.

Steph's mind focuses on her nemesis. *Boss Bitch has just stripped me naked in front of a bunch of jerk-offs.* Steph looks and can tell that all of the masturbating Peacocks present lube if not semen. She looks at the two naked Peacock Camers with hard-ons. She gives Lee Lollydor with her head-mounted Cams a look. The looks vary, but all share in common an embarrassment, a flush, and a wide-eye look that borders on fear.

And not just that. A whole lot of these Guests have handheld devices, and all of them Cam me in the nude. I'm not just full-frontal, I'm stark raving naked.

And knowing Janet, she'll want to make me spread, pink, and cream. Right here and right now.

Babs calls for a final round of appreciation for Molly, "A final Roar for our winner, Cosmos House Pledge Molly Mammoth!"

"Ma'am, thank you ever so much, Ma'am," Molly announces to BB; she bows to the assemblage, adds, "Thank all of you! I couldn't have done it without you."

Molly trades eyes with Steph, averts her gaze to Babs as BB signs Steph to stand spread surrender. Steph obeys and Molly offers a feeble,

"Sorry Steph. At least you are free now to make a Game with the newbies. They did their Roommate Game last night, now we've done ours."

Babs signs Tiffany to sweep Molly out of the Parlor and toward the Peacock House Front Door.

"Congratulations!" Tiffany says quietly. "You won today. You're a star. Don't forget to keep your thighs apart."

"You got my pee all in your hair," Molly pines, "I'm so sorry."

"Hush," Tiffany coos as they exit the Front Door. No doubt a Cam stands guard outside. You were great and you look adorable! Go. Back to the Cosmos House—it's not even a mile —you can do it. Walk or run, waddle, take any path, just don't get lost. Once you get to the Bunkroom, detach Kimju and Beka and Elle from the Minxy Mirror and put them at ease. Take a *long* bath and make sure the Bathroom Cam stay lit up."

Molly smells her own pee when Tiffany gives her a kiss on the cheek, "I know," Tiffany admits, we both have to lose a piece, even if we get to keep our Piss Mouth."

And so Molly heads home.

§ Babs Lets Naked Steph: Beg to Pink Cream and Climax

Tiffany returns. Boss Babe has ordained that Louise turn around, stand spread with her nose touching the wall, pull her butt cheeks apart, and showcase her lagway. Janet approves. Steph, still awkwardly standing spread surrender in the front of the Parlor, feels very self aware of her nakedness in front of the Guests. Flushed. She sees Janet with a small smile on face. *My former Pledge, Janet Jintoe.*

Steph sees Darleen holding her chin in her hand, and she feels herself squeeze her pelvis and rotate her hips. *We were both Monitors last Term,* Steph assesses, *now she's fully dressed, and I'm standing naked with thin bleached pussy hair. Boss Bitch and Janet have it in for me; they know that forcing me to stand naked before a former colleague only increases my debasement.*

Steph spots a naked kneeling Lee camming the six naked Peacocks with her 3D headset; Steph feels all the Peacock eyes fixed on her, and sees all of them stroking themselves *with me as l'objet d'jerk. Disgusting Lineup with their big erections.* Steph lifts one side of her nose and lip like she has just caught scent of a toxic vapor. She looks up and looks back to Lee Lollydor, who now videos her.

China Doll remains glued to Game Mistress's pussy, with the skin on her buttocks painfully stretching her cane marks. Ginny remains GM's chair. Steph's eyes canvas William's covered body, Rodney's full buttage and spotted thong, Janet's bandeau and T-front maillot, the backside of Louise' pico Spiderweb, and BB's bra and nombril bikini.

Steph thinks fast. *William is a Hovering Monitor. I fucked William last Term when both of us were Monitors; that ought to be worth something. And Darleen was a sister Monitor with me last Term. That's worth nothing, actually. Seems so long ago.* Steph feels lost. *I'm in a fix.* She tries to catch William's eye, but can't.

Fear hits her. Steph gathers her breath in and she volunteers to the House. "I'll match Molly's performance! I'll double down! I'll do whatever she did! I'll outdo her! I want my minidress back."

"Your undershirt, you mean?" Boss Babe queries.

Steph panics, "Ma'am, yes, Ma'am. She breathes in through her mouth. "I'll roll it into a belt tube, I'll keep it that way forever. I'll pull pink, I'll masturbate until I cream myself." She twitches her nostrils. She looks at Babs with wild eyes.

Boss Babe lifts her chin and signs her former Monitor. Hand signs naked Steph into to a sitting position. Steph scrambles her bare stern and feet down onto the floor. Babs signs her legs apart, and as Steph obeys the center line of her slit cracks open just enough so that her clithood and part of her lips sneak out. Steph balances her weight with her hands on the floor behind her.

Gamers, including some victimized by Steph last Term, now relish Steph in the act of being broken, and especially being broken by a past subordinate. Right now Steph begs to follow. Steph formalizes her position, raises and squares her shoulders, lifts her chin.

"I hear that Robyn has taught you all the signs to pull your lips apart, perk you clit up, and finger yourself?" Babs asks the question lazily, to murmurs of appreciation in the room, quieter now. "And how do we all know that?"

"Ma'am, you know that's not true. Maybe you cammed me full-frontal, spread and pinking in the Backyard, with Molly. And maybe Robyn cammed me pinking and hanging a streamer, with Tiffany on our Posts yesterday. Something for Elle to lolly up. But Robyn never made me touch myself. She knows better than that."

"Saved yourself for this moment, I see." Boss Babe collects husky sounds from the Guests. "And your aspire to equal your Roommate Molly's abandonment?"

"Ma'am, please," Steph begins and her knees and thighs vibrate as she overcomes the instinct to close her legs. She blinks slowly, grits, and assures herself her legs are spread just as wide as possible. *I don't quite know what is happening right now.*

Steph moves her hands from behind her and leans forward so she can grab her knees with her hands. *Things are increasingly tumbled but right now is not the time to correct the details.* "Ma'am, please, tell me what to do to match Molly, Ma'am...."

A murmur passes through the Parlor.

Steph adjusts. "Ma'am, please let me pink and cream myself. I'll drip surge on the floor and you can get Elle to lick it up."

"Molly climaxed." Boss Babe states fact. She shakes her shoulders, then, in a rare moment, puts both palms under bra and pushes inward and up.

Steph nods. "I will stroke myself and climax stark naked too." Steph commits, and prospects, "and then you can give me my clothes back." .

Laughter ripples through the Parlor, and Steph scans the room and sees Janet. And Janet cocks an eyebrow, which suggests to Steph *maybe you are not quite broken enough yet.* Steph's body twitches at unpleasantness ahead and darts her eyes upward toward Babs, seeking refuge.

Babs' reddened lips curl as she explains, "Clothes back? I'm sorry, begging isn't about making deals." Boss Babe moistens her lips by forcing a rolled tongue through the center front of her mouth. "It's about you wanting to practice Hand Signs." Boss Babe toys with her victim, "Hand signs for what, Pledge?"

"Hand signs for me to pink and play with myself Ma'am." Steph gets it generally right.

"Like this?" Babs signs her to butterfly.

"Please," Steph utters.

Gamers interpret Steph's response two difference ways. "Please" like "Please don't take this any further," and "Please" like "Please more."

But no compromise; Steph Sorostitute must work opposite fingers into her slit to loosen her sticky flaps up. She pulls her wings apart, displays a pink satchel, and rolls the ball of her distended clit out with her finger.

"Please," she offers.

"Nice sizzle," BB commends, admiring the standup.

Boss Babe outlines Steph's past, present, and future, "Gamers all know this isn't your first pink during *The Runup,* but it is your first totally naked pink, and your first pink in front of a group of Gamers. You're gaining on the World: bigger audience and more naked, and a pink-wet-and-ready-to-cum future!"

Steph stammers. *This is much more public venue than when I pulled pink on the Post Henge with Tiffany. Tiffany might be here, but I'm solo now.* "Please." Steph repeats herself, herself no longer certain what she begs for.

Boss Babe keeps it up, "Please? Please what? Out with it!"

I know what Molly begs. Steph gets it all out, "Please let me Pledge naked and cum be a Stripper next Term."

One Peacock pops.

Babs teases the obvious. "But you are already naked, my Dear."

Laughter ripples through the Parlor. Not fun laughter, evil laugher directed at Steph's misfortune.

"Please. I'll stay spread and naked and pink, cream, and climax." Steph volunteers, "You can play the Video of me hanging a stalactite outta my slit. Play the Video of me taking a thermoprobe up my stern hole."

Steph remembers again why she is pleading. "I don't know what Molly did," she exudes, "but I'll match her every which way. I'll outdo her. It's very simple." Steph pauses, finds herself too far out there, uncontrolled; she blurts out, "I'll masturbate naked to climax. I'll kiss a girl, I'll eat pussy, I'll climax on the Double Dong. With anybody. Mouth, snatch, my stern tunnel."

"Remember you said that," BB nods and accepts, knowing full well that Steph's pleas *will need extended, ongoing, and permanent.*

"Please," Steph says.

BB rubs her thumb and fingers together. "Masturbate for us," she commands. "Now!"

Steph suddenly releases her freshness, the aroma bursts into the room like a flower opening, and she makes a moan in the back of her throat, audible in the now-quiet Parlor. *First slippery cream.* Then, quite uninvited, Steph touches a fingertip to her rosy wetness, draws her hand to mouth, and tastes herself with her tongue. The applause starts scattered and builds.

As if in the Chant, Steph draws her hands down her body, lingers her fingers on her sand dollars, passes her belly button, and comes to rest at her sensitive spot. Now she carefully finger balls the head of her clit, looks up, Kundalini stirs, and Steph escalates her pleadings, "I'll shave my bleached pussy. I'll cut all the hair off my head."

Scattered applause coalesces as Steph attacks her strophoid and sex cavity with vigor. The applause becomes a quiet clapping and huffs that synchronizes with Steph's rhythm as she more and more quickly brings herself upward. No Corvette Pledge and no Peacock Pledge participate in the clapping, but they do participate in the huffs, may the Peacocks masturbate, and may the Corvette Pledge assist as a Camer, chair, and position decoration.

Steph catches a glimpse of Six naked jerking Peacock Pledge. Whatever Cams might have been tethered to them have gone free to roam, including camming themselves.

"I'm going to climax," Steph announces; these are her last words. She buries two fingers and thumbs her stamen. Pinches nipples with the other hand.

Out of control. Steph looks around the room and sees only a blur; Her eyes go wild, her body squirms and spasms, and her animal self latches onto the clapping rhythm of the guests. Kundalini expands, and Steph breaks into a rolling cum, a "huh, huh, huh, huh...."

Suddenly the masturbating Peacock Lineup all spill together, at that point of maximum pleasure and pain. But the clapping and applause continues to ride with the Cosmos ex-Monitor. Steph breaks the rhythm, ascends into a howl, and goes on cumming until she slows to a pant and finally exhausts herself.

Babs is surprised to discover that there is applause is for her too. She bows.

And the Peacock House Parlor quiets. Steph has not come close to fainting or gokuraku-ojo. She is the fourth Cosmos to climax.

Patience my love.

Janet watches with bemusement. *Whatever rebellion I witnessed earlier tonight in Pledge Steph has been exorcised. May she remain a naked Pledge wannabe Stripper next Term. And she's nowhere near the Nugget, which she needs to get to in one piece.*

Right now Steph is a naked, climaxing, Stripper wannabe. *Please, Babs, just play fair with me!* Steph feels herself pulled by her hair and turned over onto hands and knees, stern and spread snatch high in the air, with Boss Babe's barefoot pushing her head downwards and toward the floor.

Steph obliges but talks back once her cheek firms the floor. "Babs, I never did anything to you last Term." Babs moves her foot from atop Steph's head to next to her face on the floor. "Ma'am," Steph advances, "you know I let Janet take on all your mistakes. You owe me, Ma'am."

"You owe me for what you did to Janet," Boss Babe states. The Parlor comes to a deeper hush.

"Janet begged for the exposure," Steph asserts. "She begged for your Obeisance too. She got to pink and climax the Dong center stage at the Nugget. You dodged."

Babs discovers all eyes in the Parlor except two are upon her. *Eight Peacocks, Four Corvettes, MomCap, Madam Nurse Beautician, and Game Mistress. And a whole bunch of mystery guests. The pair of eyes not upon her belong to Slavesex China Doll, whose face remains buried in Game Mistress's gamier parts.*

Monitor Babs touches her Bikini Babe self and breaths carefully. *I am being judged by how I dish out payback. Not only payback for me, but payback for Janet and everyone else. Justice.*

"You made Janet sit Cravat for me," BB declares.

Steph snarls, "So? This Term, Janet made Ginny sit Cravat for Trixi Tubes. She's a fast learner."

"Janet's been desiring you for some time," BB nods.

Steph keeps her mouth near BB's foot, yet is able to cast her eyes across the room. And gets Janet's sparkle in her face.

Steph attempts BB correction. "Ma'am, you're my Monitor, Ma'am. You command and I obey you."

Mummers among guests.

BB considers her former Monitor beneath her, hands, knees, and face on the floor. "Kiss my feet, Pledge," she commands, "put some fingers to work on your spooters and slot!, spread some surge on my foot, and eat your cream."

Seven Peacocks masturbate harder, Corvette Pledge Louise breaths in deeply.

Steph orients her wits and obeys. She kisses first one foot, tugs on her nipples, and fingers her spread slippery. She draws her hand forward to smear the other foot, transfer her mouth to it, and lick up her own spirits. Meanwhile Steph drips on the floor. She lifts up her eyes to scans the Parlor while she licks the side of Babs' foot, half again expecting to see Elle Lollydor. Instead she catches Lee Lollydor licking up some Peacock ejaculant.

Ah, so Lee will also be collecting my tracks.

And no doubt Boss Bitch will try to make me cum and lose control of myself again.

Steph feels a hand grab her by the hair on her head and the next thing she knows she is crawling on her hands and knees out the Parlor, then out the Front Door. And hears shouts hurled after her, "Ring the Bell! Pink the Cam! Watch out for the Rachmaninoff Pledge!"

And laughter from behind as the door slams.

Steph bruises herself going down the front steps on all fours, regains her footing, feels the night air on her naked body, and considers what to do.

Easy. I'm streaking back to the Cosmos House.

Steph doesn't even know if Lee licks up after her or not. Or that maybe China Doll's duties go beyond just eating Game Mistress's pussy.

Or that the two crates might have contained the two missing acts.

"You're pleased with the outcome," Tiffany disguises a question to Babs as they walk toward the Van.

"I am," the tall black haired Monitor confesses, "And I am learning to enjoy twisting Steph's tail."

II-15 Babs Demands the Cosmos: Masturbate Steph (D21)

§ Steph: Streaker Thoughts as she Returns to the Cosmos House

It is while streaking back toward the Cosmos House that Steph realizes that *I am streaking now, and absent some radical changes I am headed for a Strip joint next Term. On a Cam 24x7. Everything. Right now I need to get back inside my own House, even if I have to pull the Bell, and pink the Back Door Cam until BB lets me in.*

Steph bruises her feet; she steps more carefully. *Or maybe Boss Bitch will decide Robyn gets to climax me out in the Backyard first.*

May such wishes be granted. Has Steph perhaps already launched her new career? As she moves naked through the dusk she detects paparazzi collecting her, panics, and begs, *please let live in that voyeur dorm called the Cosmos House. I'll stay naked on Cam 24x7, I don't need to wait until next Term. So Gamers, go ahead and let Automatron index my pink, cream, and climax. I'll masturbate and climax whenever you want. I just need in the Back Door.*

Steph suspects an automobile trails her and scratches her way through bushes and hedge. Steph knows. *No matter how naked I am or will continue to be, I know I must not get caught out like this. Physically captured. That's taken to Jail and a bunch of attendant problems. I've seen streakers caught before and know it is not pretty. Like getting locked in a public stocks on the Quad and left overnight, when the snakes and crawlers come out. I fear that.*

Steph considers. *Jail's a whole lot worse than cumming naked in front of everyone at the Peacock House, or having to offer my undershirt to Molly while groveling in the Mudpit naked. Now I'm naked all the time, expect being naked outside premises is against the Rules.*

Steph rests in a position of cover and brushes rocks out of her soles. Steph has never worn shoes during her two previous Term and her feet are tempered, but now the variety of terrain threatens feet: broken glass, nails, metal can scrap.

Gamers knew better than to watch when Babs forced me to pink at the Post Henge and "equalize with my Roommate Molly." Or when Janet made me rub cream onto her feet.

Okay, and then today , after I'm tricked into defeat at the Greatest House Roar, Bikini Babe force-climaxes me in front of all the guests. Now I'm a naked streaker headed for my *Cosmos House. Gamers are having their ways with me, but I'm too important a play for Gamers to capture right now.*

Steph flinches and evaluates. *This is so unfair. I have been at a disadvantage from the start of this Term. I began this Term with my panties taken away and my minidress hacked. And now that's gone.*

Steph shakes her head as thoughts boil. *I don't know who to be angry at the most: Robyn, for putting me out to pink and cream in the Backyard? Janet and William, for suggesting I play the Greatest House Roar with Molly, and then Molly agreeing? How about the Guests, who tricked me into thinking all I had to do was overcome the last Roar? And Bikini Bitch, for making me beg to "Pledge naked and cum be a Stripper," and then freshen me and force me to cum. To lose myself completely. Not good. I know I dripped splurge on the floor. Something for Lee to lolly up.*

Steph takes a moment to consider her location. *I'm far enough away from the Peacock House that I've safely escaped. Now all I have to do is make it into the Backyard and ring the Bell. And see if I really have to pink the Back Door Cam before I get let in.*

Steph pauses for a moment and presses her naked body against a tree. *I don't know what all I begged. I certainly don't want to Double Dong with Molly no matter what I said. It was pretty frantic during the Roar.* Steph brushes light sweat off her arms and watches the windy air stand both spouts up. *Probably not much of what happened back there counts, especially if I begged Stripping next Term. I've never done that before. Tiffany, and Kimju and Molly, and Beka and Elle, they are all begging to Strip, but for me, I got rushed. I just need in the Back Door.*

As a Monitor last Term, Steph sent Pledge to Strip at the Nugget, in particular, Penny and Coco this Term, so Steph understands that *Stripping transcends pink, cream and climax. Stripping involves dishabille and dancing. Cams plus a live audience. Not where I want to go.*

Steph ruminates. *I'd be the sixth Cosmos to beg to Opt Strip.* Steph is, and she views risk: *Robyn now remains only Pledge not begging to Strip, and is she has Charm then she never will. Robyn doesn't matter anyway. There's a line ahead of me and only room for four Cosmos to Opt Stripper next Term.*

Except, I'm naked now, And could that put me at the front of the line?

Steph targets her anger as she moves again. *It's Robyn's fault I'm even Pledging this Term! I should be a Monitor. But no, now Bikini Bimbo—whom I promoted—lets that rancid ragho force me to titter and vagflash.* Steph must suddenly worm through scratchy bushes to avoid a bicyclist. These scratches draw blood. Steph grunts. *But it is not just titter and vagflash, BB let Robyn make me full-frontal and force me to pink and cream.*

But Bikini Bimbo also has it in for me, because she saves the best for herself, even though I did nothing but make it easy for her last Term. BB owes Janet too, and Janet hates me from last Term. BB isn't strong enough force me to beg Stripper next Term, but she does have the gumption to force-cum me naked in front of a roomful of Guests. Because Janet wanted that, for sure, but I could tell Bikini Bitch enjoyed forcing me too. She also enjoyed making me streak, I know, I saw her face when Molly streaked. And for me it was the same in her eyes.

Steph almost lets her thoughts dominate her. *I hope Babs and Robyn both become Slavesex, and get flogged, caned, single-tailed, bound and gagged, gangbanged, tattooed head to toe, pierced without limit, branded, and water-boarded in sperm.*

Once again naked Steph takes her bearings and considers the possibility of some other destination. *But there is none. Only Ruleless Game out there. Out here right now. And right now what I need a safe haven, the Cosmos House.*

Still, Steph vows, *I am not giving up, and I will get even! Maybe Gamers have stripped me naked for a little while, but I'm entitled. I shall take more control of my agenda. Screw Bling Bitch and Robyn Redacted; I shall use my body to tease and manipulate men, and they will fall upon themselves to promote me! Even William owes me!* Steph tightens her jaw and assures herself, *Opting Up won't be a problem. I've played to win before and I'll play to win again, even if I might have to "grant favors."*

Steph pauses furtively to catch her breath and observes a figure dressed in a hockey uniform with a goalie mask watching her. A Rachmaninoff Pledge! Watching me streak naked. *Yes, it's quite simple, I will need to challenge someone for clothes. Luckily the Term remains young and there will be much more play, so I have time to do this. But I need a different next victim than Molly. I know the Rules.*

Correct, Steph's next target can no longer be her Roommate, inoculated for the time being and now wearing what used to be Steph's undershirt along with her see-through panties nombril.

The night air causes Steph's white skin to pucker with goosebumps and she moves with stealth. *Where do I get two Garments now?* Blood congeals, scratches itch; gravel and broken concrete and earth under foot. *There still remain adequate candidates: That rancid raptatorial royster, Robyn Redacted, my Roommate from last Term,. Robyn's only problem is that the traitorous riffraff wears only one piece, her strapped maillot cutout, and one Garment provides an incomplete ticket to Monitor Caste. Besides, I can't game with Robyn right now; her Roommate Kimju gets first shot. But after that...?*

Steph moves and thinks at the same time. *Right now I only have Beka and Elle to consider for Game. Both have two pieces, they've already*

Flip-Flopped, so stripping either of them naked, or collecting a donation from each provide solutions. Open season on bimbo and neophyte!

Steph hides in a shadow to steady her breathing. Pessimism flouts. *This could take a while. Furthermore, any prolonged nakedness will only broaden my exposures.* Now Steph draws in very full lungs of air. *This was supposed to be an easy Opt Up. Molly's panties to go under my undershirt/minidress. Except Molly's panties are still on Molly, as is* my undershirt dress.

And suddenly I'm a naked, spread, pinking, creaming, cumming Pledge begging to Strip next Term.

I need to get Garments before anybody makes me climax again.

Another set of consternations stir deep inside Steph's memory and she reminds herself, *a Pledge who turns Stripper may get rewarded with a piercing and a tattoo.* She moves and considers, *Kimju and Molly both hang rings from their clits and may have hidden tattoos. And* I'm *the one who forced Janet Jintoe to reveal her pussy lip rings last Term!* Steph looks both ways before dashing naked across an intersection. *I certainly don't want any piercing or tattoos; and if I need to demand favors or revert to seduction to reverse my current momentum, I will.*

Steph doesn't quite understand that the women above her—the Monitors, the MomCaps, the Madams, the Mistresses—might be immune to her sexual charms. Or that some men will play with her seduction, but not succumb to it. Or that women or men who might be seduced lie outside the chain of command of her exit pathway.

§ Babs & Tiffany Haze Steph: Back Landing of Cosmos House

Steph arrives back to the Cosmos House, rings the Bell by the landing, and waits for permission to enter the Back Door. *Now is not the moment to test the Rules. Right now I possess nothing.* Steph clears her mind and stands next to the Bell, with her hands to her sides and her thighs not touching, reluctantly accepting that the Back Door Cam canvasses her naked spooters and sallyport. Bleached hair produces a thinly veiled slit, making Steph feel even more naked.

Evening has become nightfall and a chill in the air erects Steph's spigots. She canvasses the Watering Can sitting next to the Back Landing and denies it. *No panties, no watering can.*

Steph remains waiting and thinking when Babs and Tiffany return. Both ring the Bell and pause. Steph steels herself. *Bikini Bimbo has stripped me naked to get back at me for nothing. For helping her and Janet Opt Up. Stupid Bimbo Bitch.*

But there is a problem. Steph grits. *Still, I have to be really careful around the Bimbo Boss, because BB provides me with my only protection.*

Boss Babe queries, "Have you rung the Bell, Pledge?"

Steph falters, knows the answer, "Ah, Ma'am, yes, Ma'am." She looks out of the corner of her eye to see where the Cam is.

Babs trades eyes with Tiffany, pauses, but BB gets it right to Steph, "Sit spread pink. Am I clear?"

"Ma'am, you are clear, Ma'am," Steph echoes and scrambles to sit on the edge of the Landing. Steph must decide quickly. *The Landing beats the Ground.* She eyes the Mudpit, dry at the moment, *but soaked when I had to wallow in it naked two days ago, while offering my undershirt to Molly. Then, after I spending the night, in the morning I got hustled over to my Henge Post to pink and cream with Tiffany. Nobody even washes the mud off of me.*

Janet and William visit and con me into a Winner-Takes-All Roommate Game with Molly. And so earlier today I get duped into forfeiting my undershirt to Molly, begging to Opt Strip, and getting force-climaxed in front of the Peacock Guests at the Greatest House Roar.

Steph comes to her senses. She spots the Cam collecting her spreads and angles her crotch off its centerline. The Cam arcs its hover. *It can keep up with me and will collect me right down to my sex socket.* The Cam can do this. In fact, the Cam can shoot wide-angle and close-up at the same time.

Steph realizes that this cat and mouse game is over. She smiles at the Cam. It is one of those smiles that say, *Now that you've got me I'm going to be pretty. And you can't take that away from me!*

"Here I am," Steph announces, pouts, and pops out the butterfly's head.

"May Gamers jerk off to you," Tiffany praises.

Steph flinches at this suggestion. *I've pulled pink in the Backyard before, Babs forced me and Molly and Robyn made me pink with Tiffany. And Bimbo Bitch just pink creamed and came me solo, inside in the Peacock House Parlor.*

So, is what I think is about to happen to me about to happen?

"Don't worry," Tiffany assures, "I'll practice all the Stripper moves with you. You know I will, we've pinked and creamed together before!"

Steph blanches and Babs takes charge. "Maybe after Tiffany plays a Roommate Game she you can give you one of her pieces, that way neither of you will have to streak your way to the Nugget."

"Ma'am, that would be very thoughtful of you, Ma'am," Steph cages.

"Remind me what you are begging again." Boss Babe commands.

"Ma'am," Steph organizes, "please let me Pledge naked and cum be a Stripper next Term." She keeps her eyes forward. Bikini Babe's golden belly lies forward and within hand reach. It fills her vision. *Navelage 24x7. That's BB. I'm navelage 24x7 too, except I am all-encompassing naked 24x7 also. Naked and spread and pinking, and begging the Prefecture to Opt Strip next Term.*

Boss Babe points at the Cam. "Beg," she says.

Steph begs, "please let me Pledge naked and cum be a Stripper next Term." Then she repeats herself.

Steph hears Boss Babe in a dreamy haze. "I'm sure that if a need arises for you to enter the House, then someone will come to fetch you."

Boss Babe duty cycles a Pledge. "Until then you shall Chant. Do it right. Keep yourself pink-wet-and-ready, but hold off cumming for now."

Steph puts her hands behind her head but freezes. She looks to Tiffany for help and Tiffany obliges with an opportunity to commandeer the Cam.

"You can do it!" Tiffany leads, tosses her hands behind her head and stretches even more red hairage about her low-rise waistline. "And the next time you cum for your fans you can cum harder." Tiffany dances her taffrail trough and gathers the Cam to her backside. "Please let me Pledge naked," Tiffany recites and means it as Steph considers, "and cum be a Stripper next Term." They make eyes, as Tiffany pinches her nipples through her clear vinyl croptop. Steph lets go of her butterfly wings, reaches upward to pinch her nipples twice and recites, "titty titty," reaches down and pinches her exposed clit twice, and (together) recites, "clitty clitty," finger-dips her slush, and tastes herself, "hole mouth."

Steph again forms armpits "Please let me...," and loses herself in the Chant. She wonders, *did Tiffany set the pace of my Chant?* But that is her last wondering. The pace is quick enough that it requires paying attention to recite properly and leaves little room for processing thought. Steph's body does feel the cooler, moister air, and her sensory awareness lets through the sounds of birds and insects and smells. *Including my own.* "Please let me Pledge naked and cum be a Stripper next Term. Titty titty, clitty clitty, hole mouth."

Just sensations now.

§ Molly: Concerns About Undershirt & Panties—Two Pieces

Upon her return earlier Molly had followed orders: she rang the Bell, went through the Back Door, and upstairs she detached Kimju, then Beka and Elle, from the Minxy Mirror. Overseer Robyn had hurried into the Bunkroom fresh out of a leisurely bath, and Molly provided the Four

Pledge with the news and evidence of her victory: one undershirt worn with her see-through low-rise panties.

"My turn to take a bath," Molly announces, tosses her panties and newfound undershirt on her bunk, and flops to the Bathroom naked, where she lights up the Cam.

Molly casts her eyes about, positions herself above the bidet with the Measuring Cup in hand, sighs, and releases a yellow stream. She fills one Cup, then another, spilling them into the bowl before rinsing herself.

Does the Pee-Cam and Monitor Babs' Desktop feed out this most intimate detail of life? *It better.* Might Automatron audit Molly's actions vs. what she writes on the Logging Chart? *Of course it does.* Molly looks the Cam in the eye as the video spools and feeds her floppy mams and hirsute mooe to the Prefecture. She draws water and climbs into a deep bath.

Back in the Bunkroom and now freed of the Mirror, Kimju and Beka and Elle all want to use the Bathroom, but only Kimju resigns to use it now that Molly had illuminated the Cam. For Kimju, Molly's romance with the Cam matters not. *I light it myself from now on.*

Kimju collapses the knot on her g-string. *I know what I am now. A Pee-Camer begging to Strip. With one Garment, but still with enough time, perhaps, to get another.* Garment that is. Kimju heads for the Pee-Cam.

Elle must restrain Beka, still dangling her straps and halter down, from following her in.

Beka and Elle recline in their bunks with mellow exhaustion and watch a feed of Kimju appear in the Minxy Screen; they watch Kimju pee in the Cup, empty the Cup, and write her Cup-count and date on the Logging Chart. Elle understands. *Gamers possess Kimju's every intimacy. And watching this makes me want to pee even more.* Elle looks at herself. *No seam to collect leaky pee anymore.*

Inside the Bathroom the two ex-Nuggets talk briefly.

"Congratulations on winning," Kimju says to equally naked Molly, languishing deep in the bathtub.

"Thank you, but no thank you." Molly sighs. "I guess the newbies are still out there and I bet they want to pee. They spent a long time making out with the Minxy."

"Yeah, well, me too, Molly," Kimju admits. "I've been completely taken away, and not by the Minxy. I've become a pink-wet-and-ready Pee-Camer begging to climax and Strip. But you deserve your bath and should take your time."

Molly splashes water, "I'm just following orders."

Kimju grouses. "Beka and Elle must learn to beg to Pee-Cam like the rest of us." She exists the Bathroom to regain her micro g-string.

Molly sinks lower into the water and wonders. *So what does winning mean for me?*

The buoyancy of the bath water floats Molly's mammaries in the tub and she graces them with soapy water. Molly's psyche frets about the fortune of her acquisition. *I take no particular pleasure in winning the Greatest House Roar. And yes, I am distressed to be burdened with two Garments. This is the first time this Term I have* not *had a clear path to the Nugget.*

Molly gnaws on the implications of a possible Opt Up and frets about the combinational powers of the minidress and the panties. *I do not want Monitor responsibilities! I know that Steph once wore the minidress over the panties, but recently Steph only wore the undershirt dress without panties. Of course now, Steph wears nothing, she's streaking, and she's gonna Opt Strip next Term. Gamers have it in for her, especially Janet. But I need to Opt Down with her, Roommates Together.*

Molly reconsiders her conclusions. *I know that Steph will soon crave to orgasm, and that if she and I can climax together that she will take me with her to the Nugget. If I can give her my undershirt or my panties, then I can get to the Nugget without streaking.*

Molly concludes. *It's my only choice.* I *can't even give a Garment to Beka or Elle; they already have what they need to Opt Up.*

Molly suddenly feels overcome with conflicts. *I am the one who should be naked, I am the one who should be masturbating all waking hours, I am the one who should be in the Zone! I am the one who needs to go Strip next Term!* Molly stands up in the tub so the water can stream off her body and her matted-down body hair. She carefully parts her muff and displays her dark brown inner lips with their deep purple insides to the Pee-Cam. Suddenly she casts a six inch long defiant arc of pee in its direction, backing it off.

The Cam catches her laugh.

Some Gamers say Molly isn't smart, but Molly suspects *my uptick and cover-up won't last very long,* so perhaps Molly is smart in her own ways. Besides, Molly knows, *Babs wants the undershirt too. Even more than I do.*

§ Babs & Tiffany: Discuss the Burden of Steph & Steph Karma

Tiffany teases Babs as they head inside and spiral upstairs to the Bedroom. "Look at you! You are enjoying hazing Steph! You are pleased about what transpires and will do what you can to influence the outcome. Confess!"

Babs confesses. "Okay, I have enjoyed forcing my former Monitor to titter and vagflash. She deserves it. And she deserved you pinking and creaming with her."

"Thank you," Tiffany says and praises, "You made her cum pretty hard at the end of the Greatest House Roar!"

"Thank you," Babs says. "Keeping Steph pink-wet-and-ready is a burden the whole House will have to take on. Steph hates the Cam, especially when Robyn controls it."

Tiffany guffaws, "She's been face stripped, body stripped, pinked, creamed, and climaxed. Now she's about to get soul stripped. My problem is I love to Strip and I'll help her make that her goal."

"Your love is you want to be a Porn Star," Boss Babe reminds, "and the Nugget is a way stop."

"And now I got Steph ahead of me," Tiffany muses.

Babs interjects. "Don't worry, I'll do whatever I can to help you get to the Nugget next Term. So help me figure out how to reduce yourself to one piece without—"

"I know," Tiffany interrupts, "as long as it doesn't involve you taking from me and Opting MomCap next Term. But why don't you take from me—top or bottom—and then you could pass along. You could give Kimju a break, and that way Molly could Opt Strip in her panties."

"They're ahead of you too," Babs observes, "But I know you, you're kind to everybody, may your Karma reflect upon you, especially when it can resonate with your goals."

"Ma'am, thank you, Ma'am," Tiffany begs, "you know I will do anything for you, I groom you, I obey your commands, please let me suckle your breasts and banggo, eat your cream, drink your pee, and lick your asshole."

"I thought you performed admirably when Robyn forced you and Steph to lick her feet clean."

"Ma'am, thank you, Ma'am," Tiffany affirms. "I appreciate the opportunity to train Steph in the subtleties of sucking toes, tonguing under toenails, and not tickling souls. I hope you let my fans watch because I know I dangled tang. Steph flushed for the Cam, because it represented role-reversal demotion."

"She dangled too," Babs affirms, "And yes, you both got fed. You can watch on the Desktop or House Screens; may it please you to know that Automatron serves the replays and counts clicks."

"Okay," Tiffany says. "Giving Steph and me to Robyn is harsh. She sure does know how to inflict pain and humiliation. She is naturally nasty."

"Sorry to you, but not sorry to Steph. She deserves it. I would do it myself, I'm not afraid to do that anymore, but Robyn delivers a much sharper edge that I could ever scratch with my own claws. And it's more painful to Steph coming from Robyn than from me." Babs reflects, "After all, it was Robyn who tattled on her covered button, nobody else."

"I forgive you," Tiffany says. "I hope my fans all watch us. I help everybody, even the newbies."

"You help me too," Babs affirms. "Listen, I mean, we all know that Kimju and Molly saw Janet and you climax the Dong and perform watersports. So do you ever wonder if any other Cosmos might have seen too?"

Tiffany hesistates. "Well, maybe Steph knows, after all, she was the Monitor until near the end."

"Listen," Babs halts, "I'll share a secret with you. One that Steph knows, Janet too, and maybe you too.

So BB shares a pearl, "Janet says Steph secretly visited the Nugget last Term and observed, unseen, her Alumni Reprise with you. Plus she saw the lapdance antics of then-Strippers Kimju and Molly.

"I will say Steph does know how to keep secrets. And how about you? Did Janet share this with you? You're old Stripper pals, aren't you?"

Tiffany's babble belays her deception. "Ma'am, I belong to you, Ma'am. I'll wash and lavish your body. I'll eat you out while you bleed and climax you. I'll drink your pee. I'll lick your asshole."

"I know," BB declares, "you'll eat my vomit if you need to.

"Ma'am, may it please you, put laxative in my food, Ma'am." Tiffany declares.

"Listen to me." Boss Babe firms. "I don't think Steph knows I know she secretly visited the Nugget, so keep this a secret between us. You deserve to know not because you were there, but because I want to empower you."

Tiffany stumbles, "Ma'am, thank you for telling me, Ma'am."

BB shifts, leery-like, "Something happened to Steph after her takedown and before the start of this Term."

"Ma'am, she was in Lockdown, Ma'am!" Tiffany breezes, "where space and time don't exist and where Rules needn't apply. I bet Steph knows that Robyn witnessed her compromised, and even though Robyn appears Redacted, Steph suspects there are secrets inside her that with the right stimulus might escape."

"Robyn uses you to engage Steph in performance," BB observes.

"No problem," Tiffany assures, "Besides, I understand *you* want to play Steph out. I'll not only teach her how to tongue kiss and worship feet, I'll teach her how to stimulate clits, pussies, and assholes. I'll ride the Dong with her at the Nugget."

Babs continues. "Steph didn't have to make me Mudwrestle, but she did it anyway. She did it just to show me how powerful she was. It was like when she decided she didn't need to keep her belly button exposed. The Gamers didn't care when she trod all over me, but once she stepped on them, 'POW' and it was over. I never saw her again the rest of last Term."

"Lockdown!" Tiffany repeats. "You never saw her until she turned up at your Door during *The Arrivals,*" Tiffany recounts.

"At the Front Door to boot!" Babs exclaims. "She knew better than that."

"She was just testing you," Tiffany pines. "She's compromised yet still strong."

"May she stay pink-wet-and-ready from now on," Babs affirms.

§ Babs & Six Cosmos Pledge: Handling Instructions for Steph

Babs and Tiffany arrive upstairs and encounter Molly, exiting the Bathroom and still naked. Boss Babe gives Tiffany a nod and Tiffany gathers Molly, rousts Four Cosmos out of their bunks, and organizes them into a Lineup, facing an Minxy Mirror that looks like still water on a moonless night. Tiffany joins to complete a Six Cosmos Pledge Lineup.

Babs retreats to her Bedroom for the moment where she can check her Desktop, among other things.

Steph remains outside, sitting naked on the Back Landing with her spread pointing toward the alley. Steph appreciates the security of the Back Door Cam's watchful eye. *Of course it takes me down, of course my ex-Pledge and now Boss Bitch controls that switch. But out here there are paparazzi loose, vans with dark windows, Rachmaninoffs.*

But they can't touch me as long as the Cam is vigilant. Steph squeezes and splurge presents.

Upstairs in the Bunkroom Tiffany forms stand-spread-surrender position, and the Lineup aligns to her suggestion.

Tiffany sports her clear vinyl croptop above the stretch slacks' curvy waistline, belly up and down, ensuring hairage and rugage 24x7.

Robyn, standing in the Lineup, sharpens her thoughts. *Wait. What am I doing? I am not supposed to be standing spread surrender with other Pledge! Tiffany has made a mistake and Bikini Babe needs to extract me! And I need to teach Tiffany a lesson! Maybe I should simply step out of line.*

Babs has returned. Robyn catches Babs' eye and BB signs her to hold firm. Robyn knows, *Bikini Bimbo knows I really am in charge and that I'm just playing along with her. So we can mousetrap Tiffany Transparent.* Robyn still wears her strapped maillot with its tiniest cutout hole. The stretch in her body threatens that the cutout hole maintain its position surrounding her navel.

Kimju, forever topless and now reduced to a micro g-string that spills hairage and bares the butt, is the most-nearly-naked Cosmos.

Molly has remained naked since returning from the Bathroom; she has not had a chance to don her recently-acquired undershirt and her see-through panties, both still in her bunk.

Babs comes to the end of the Lineup: Beka, then Elle.

Beka, now attired in the halter and the remains of her jeans shorts qualifies buttage and hairage 24x7; her dangling neck straps ensures boobage.

Elle, holding stand spread surrender position, demonstrates how her cut-down croptop allows her to titter; stretching also ensures Elle must consider vagflashing her miniskirt.

Elle relents. *Okay, so Gamers can look at my nobs. Anytime, anyplace, in front of anybody.* And has the miniskirt ridden up so that
my crotch is exposed? Or my lowest butt cheeks? Or my pussy hair?

Well, yes it has.

Babs walks behind the Lineup and a Screen in the Mirror opens and shows Steph sitting on the Back Landing, chanting and displaying herself to the Back Door Cam.

Boss Babe watches Steph turn the spoils. And answers a question Steph wants the answer to, but can't hear. "Don't worry, Pledge, I set the crossbar on my Desktop to feed out to the Prefecture, and let Automatron spool bits. The Nugget can screen her masturbations in anticipation of her arrival."

BB considers her own areolage and gives her cleavage a wiggle. She furrows her brow with self esteem. *No need to rush power.*

BB paces around to the front of her Lineup and addresses the six Cosmos Pledge, "Steph Sorostitute chants and begs to get in."

Molly feels sweat form in her puffy armpits and her inner thighs. *I need to pay attention to BB.*

BB continues, "Don't brag about the victors getting the spoils, because Steph Sorostitute is a spoiled, slithering serpent who will require constant attention. It is the will of Gamers that, now, in addition to her commitment to stay naked 24x7 and beg to Strip, that Steph shall keep herself pink-wet-and-ready during *all* her waking hours. This will require our constant vigilance. You will work shifts. You shall put Steph in the Zone, and keep her there."

Images of Steph fade from the Minxy and the Mirror now reflects each Pledge, but only to herself. There is no reflection of any other Pledge nor of Monitor Babs.

Elle overcomes the surprise and looks hard at herself: *Yes, my nipples rub on the bottom of my upraised croptop. And yes, the pubic hair in my crotch is visible.*

Elle flushes and opens her mouth.

But Boss Babe saves her by speaking first, directing an order at both Beka and Elle. "Turn around," she tells them. "You newbies go outside, fetch your fellow Cosmos Pledge from the Landing, take her inside and seat her atop the Dining Room table, facing the Screen between the two windows. And if she breaks the Chant while you move her put her right back into it once she settles down."

"I want to chant together with her," Beka provides.

"You will do nothing of the sort!" BB exclaims, "But what you may do, you and Elle both, is once you get Steph settled, you shall spread surrender behind her, so we know you aren't playing with yourself."

"Ma'am!" Beka exclaims.

"Thank you, Ma'am," Elle completes, and shoos Beka toward the spiral stairs

§ Steph: Masturbates & Cums in Sync with *House Roar Video*

Beka and Elle flash tits and hair to the Back Door Cam as they gather the naked and chanting Steph inside and into the Dining Room, then, up onto the table sitting spread and facing the Screen between the windows on the side of the House, and chanting, "Please let me Pledge naked and cum be a Stripper next Term," followed by two beats of Steph playing with her spigots, two beats of her plucking her strophoid, and two beats of her bringing her sweetness to mouth. "Titty titty, clitty clitty, hole mouth."

Robyn marches Kimju and Molly into the Dining Room. Robyn's conviction her place in the Lineup was but a temporary disguise was confirmed when Boss Babe ordered she take the two ex-Nuggets downstairs to "bookend Steph." Babs remains upstairs and takes Tiffany into her Bedroom to groom her.

Robyn's strapped maillot with "the smallest cutout hole" remains the most covered Garment, whereas her Roommate Kimju's topless micro g-string remains the smallest Garment, in fact at the moment Kimju's micro g-string has settled into her slit, so she hairages completely. Molly, the Winner of the Winner-Takes-All, has put on her recently acquired undershirt; it hangs low enough to cover her hairage and rugage and much of her panties, and the ripped cutout hole confirms navelage.

Robyn places Kimju and Molly to the left and right of Beka and Elle, and all four tighten their standing spread surrender postures under Robyn's gaze. Elle knows *there are no Cams in the Dining Room, but there are windows. And if Cams or paparazzi look in they will collect Beka's boobage and my titter, plus Beka's hairage and whatever is below my miniskirt's hemline.*

Steph masturbates naked and spread on the table and Chants. "Please let me cum be a Stripper next Term. Titty titty, clitty, clitty, hole mouth."

Robyn comes around to the side of the table next to the Screen; she gestures, the Screen comes to life, and Steph sees a loop from Kimju and Molly's *Alumni Reprise Video* made at the Nugget last night. The loop zooms its frame until only Molly sits spread naked and chants over and over again. "Please let me Pledge naked and cum be a Stripper next Term. Titty titty, clitty clitty, hole mouth."

Complete with the hand motions.

"Sync up," Robyn advises Steph. "Kimju and Molly got to masturbate in sync with their *Nugget Stripper Videos*, now it's your turn to chant and masturbate with your Roommate." Robyn twitches her nose. "The Roommate who defeated you in the Greatest House Roar."

Steph turns around to scan the Room behind her, discovers Molly's eyes, and Molly looks down, dejected. Flashes spark in Steph's eyes. *You're wearing my undershirt and panties, you fat mangy maggot!*

Steph stumbles the Chant while she plots. *You failed me, Molly Maggot. You betrayed me.*

Molly, watching herself on the Screen, silently picks up the rhythm of the Chant and recites it to herself. *Doesn't Steph know that the last thing I want is an Opt Up? Now I'm overburdened with two Garments. This is very traumatic to me. Makes me sweat and smell.*

Steph casts about the Room for Babs, doesn't find her. *Babs betrays me.* Steph scowls. *And so does Robyn, in fact, Robyn betrays me again.*

Robyn stands directly behind the chanting Steph, and with Steph sitting spread on the table it is easy for her to dig fingernails into Steph's flesh and tighten Steph's synchronization. "Please let me Pledge naked and cum be a Stripper next Term. Titty titty, clitty clitty, hole mouth."

Steph knows, *I can taste my own wetness but I'm still here.*

Steph synchronizes with the Molly chanting on the Screen, equally naked and spread. *She is a fat, repulsive animal.* Steph feels Kundalini stir. *I'll chant with Molly, but I'll be dammed if I climax in sync with her.* Steph struggles. *But what happens if Kundalini gets loose, like what happened at the Peacock House?*

Robyn focuses Steph's attention back to the Screen. "Listen to me, you sloppy snapper slut. I want you pink-wet-and-ready to cum, all waking hours."

Steph's revulsion at kowtowing to her former Pledge Babs pales at her revulsion at kowtowing to former Pledge Robyn. *Robyn Redacted.* Steph shuffles her soiled butt and feet on the Dining Room tabletop, glues her eyes to the Screen, and maintains her synchronization with Molly's *Alumni Reunion Chant Video.* "Please let me Pledge naked and cum be a Stripper next Term," she declares while she holds her hands behind her head, surrender position, before breaking and completing the Chant, "Titty titty, clitty clitty, hole mouth."

Five Cosmos—Robyn, Kimju, Molly, Beka, and Elle—watch Steph scoop out a finger of surge and lick it down, but only Robyn Redacted turns and laughs into her hands.

Steph tries to think in between moments of the Chant. *It doesn't matter if the amnesic Robyn Redacted is a real or a fake. She's nasty and ugly-on-the-inside.*

Steph stumbles the Chant, corrects herself, and chants on. Nipples erect, clit erect, secretions flowing evenly now, "...hole mouth."

A reflection in a window distracts her. *Do strangers look in from the blackness outside?* Steph steadies, keeps chanting, and sneak a look. Blackness. *Blackness hiding faces in the dark outside, eyes looking in!*

All I have to do is just keep playing with myself! If Molly goes faster, I have to go faster too. Molly on the Screen is going to put me into the Zone.

Syncing with Molly's rhythm on the Screen actually holds Steph back, and she abuses her spigots and stamen with more vigor. Another fleeting moment of thought: *The Back Door Cam can also look in from the windows. I'm all lit up. But I'd have to turn to look and I don't dare do that.* Steph pumps her body harder now, breathes faster and deeper, and tips toward the Zone.

Once again, Steph must steady herself to not get ahead of Molly's pacing. She whimpers, but finds a series of fleeting moments. She uses them to plot revenge: *Bikini Bitch and Janet Jintoe tricked me into tossing my undershirt to Molly. But I will be bouncing back, whatever it takes. And those arousing me will be reduced to Strippers, Whores, and Slavesex. Bikini Bitch among them. And Robyn Redacted, and not just as BB's agent.*

I'm not sure who's in charge anymore., but it probably doesn't matter.

Steph pays attention to her chanting again. Prepares herself for a long haul. *I bet Janet and William are watching me right now, either standing outside and looking in through the windows or watching me because the Back Door Cam spies on me. Or maybe the Screen has a Cam, and collects me spread on.* Steph snorts. *Torment me while you can, Gamers. Because I'm going to Opt Monitor next Term and get back at all of you!*

Once again Steph fumbles the Chant, once again she syncs up with Molly's Chant Video, and this time stops thinking and flows. Breathing hard. "Please let me Pledge naked and cum be a Stripper next Term. Titty titty, clitty clitty, hole mouth."

Just as Steph touches her fingertip to her tongue the Screen cuts. Steph has her hands behind her head and continues to chant, "Please let me

Pledged naked—" before she realizes *that is me on the Screen! I am watching Bimbo Bitch climax me at the Peacock House!*

Steph abandons the Chant. She draws her fingers directly to her slippery sex cavity, and joins with herself on the Screen to match to the pitch at the Greatest House Roar. *I lost to Molly. I might never get any Garments back.* Steph rolls a finger as deep as she can into her socket and strives for a climax. She tweaks her stamen into a shake as she thinks her last thoughts. *Now I get to masturbate and climax in sync with my own climax. That's way over the top.*

Steph lets herself go. She locks into the sound of her past climax, and masturbates her climax in real time and in sync with her replay. There is no thinking involved; Kundalini enables Steph to become possessed with her own physical pleasures, her pure animal self arousal. Zoned, if only for a little while.

Five Cosmos present in the Dining Room watch silently, and four of them forget to keep their hands behind their heads. Kimju unconsciously forms her arms into a handbra. Molly worms her mostly covered transparent panties into her moonshadow and mooe. Beka, boobage with her halter hanging down, tucks the seam in her jeans tighter up into her bourse and rubs herself. Elle, equally forgetful, holds both hands over her mouth and watches Steph live, and on-Screen, in disbelief. *They are a lot of ways to climax Steph and keep her Zoned. But force-cumming her in sync with her video climax is like putting her on autopilot.*

Actually there is a great deal of art and craft to keeping a Cosmos Zoned.

Elle calms herself and makes mental notes. *Today Steph becomes the third Cosmos to climax, and joins both topless Nugget Alumni in this respect. She also becomes the sixth Cosmos Pledge to beg to Opt Strip next Term. That means all of us Cosmos except Robyn, and Babs, obviously.* Elle considers. *But including me. Me, myself, Elle. I'm begging to Strip too.*

Steph's trills compete for Elle's attention, but Elle pushes Steph's warbles out of her mind. She glances at Beka and draws her eyes to the hanging pockets. *I need to get my notes back!*

Steph's trills give way to a slower heaving panting. Elle observes. *There's a big difference between ex-Strippers like Kimju and Molly begging to Opt Down, and a fallen Monitor like Steph unable to stop downward momentum.*

Elle startles. *Steph will soon do whatever it takes to Opt Strip.* Elle blinks. *And so will my Roommate.*

Elle digests and considers the Pledge in the strapped maillot cutout driving Steph's action. *Robyn feels proud of herself. It doesn't matter if she's getting back at Steph for last Term or just piling on evil.*

Elle scans the Room looking for Babs. But Babs and Tiffany remain upstairs. Elle wonders *maybe they watch from a Cam somewhere.* She tilts her body forward to look deep into the darkness of the Room's side windows. *The Cam doesn't just feast on Steph, it feeds on my titter and hairage too.*

Elle scowls. *Babs knows how Robyn treats Steph, and Babs just lets her do it. And Babs knows how Robyn treats the rest of us, and just lets her do it. With a few exceptions: it was Monitor Babs who made Steph beg to Opt Strip and cum, and it is Babs who will trade her to Janet.*

Later, after all second wind has been taken out of her, Robyn tasks Beka and Elle to "help Steph off the table, onto her feet, and upstairs into her bunk bed." Robyn pauses affront the trio before they exit the Dining Room; she signs Steph to open her mouth, and spits into it. Robyn signs Steph to close her mouth, and Steph swallows.

II-16 Cosmos Masturbate Steph: Zoned All the Time (D22)

§ Steph: Joins Cosmos Lineup then Sits Spread Pink on Landing

Uncertainty haunts Six Cosmos as they Lineup standing spread surrender on the morning of Day Twenty-Two. They stand in the Backyard, but in full view of the two houses next door, the alley, and of course a hovering Back Door Cam.

Boss Babe eyes her brood from the Back Landing. Robyn stands next to her.

Robyn, clad as always in her strapped maillot cutout, descends and peers into the individual faces.

"At last," Robyn pretends to care, "all six of you beg to Opt Down next Term. How's it go, Pledge?"

Six Cosmos recite in unison, "Please let me Pledge naked and cum be a Stripper next Term."

"Excellent. Since you all want to be Strippers next Term, then all of you will receive Stripper training. So many desire, but so few can serve."

Robyn pauses in front of Steph. "Although you look like you are first in line," she effuses. She steps back to address the Lineup, "Congratulations Cosmos Pledge. Now you have your own Naked Girl, just like the Corvettes do."

Tiffany, frequently naked, but at the moment dressed in her clear vinyl croptop and low-slung stretch slacks, is not the Cosmos Naked Girl. Kimju remains topless, spills hairage, and present a bare butt. Molly compresses herself into Steph's undershirt, which along with her reduced panties, vulgarizes her as much as it provides coverage. Beka has yet to re-buttoned her neck strap so both boobies expose themselves to the hovering Back Door Cam... and any hidden paparazzi or surveillance Cams. Elle's croptop teases areolage as she stretches the rib line upward, and her miniskirt doesn't quite descend to her crotch. Public exposure.

Bleached blonde Steph is the Naked Girl. Solo performance, standing spread surrender. Steph forms beads of sweat in her armpits.

BB watches from the Landing. *Actually,* BB silently corrects Robyn, *the Corvettes have* two *Naked Girls: Ginny and Lee. One of them is a Whore-For-Life and the other a Lollydor. Oh well.* BB glances up and watches Robyn run the back of her hand down Steph's chest and Steph's brown nipples engorge with blood. "Beg," Robyn commands.

And Steph solos, "Please let me Pledge naked and cum be a Stripper next Term."

Steph suddenly seizes an opportunity to niggle. "I'm not the first naked Cosmos," she asserts, as if that were the challenge. "Molly was naked first." Steph keeps her legs spread wide and her hands behind her head. She feels eyes from neighboring houses canvas her perky bare spuds, her bleached cascade of hair and shrubbery, and her smoothly curving stern. She augments, "Molly gave me her panties at the Figure Drawing Class, during *The Arrivals,* and she streaked to the Bachelor Party the next Day."

"Right," Robyn advises. "That counts but doesn't," settling the issue once and for all.

"You're a wannabe Stripper, that's what you are," Robyn provides, "You need to be more aroused, so you doesn't think so much, you skeezy splurt skank."

Robyn cackles. She walks around behind the Lineup and lays three fingers of her palm into Steph's crotch. Robyn doesn't even need to wiggle her fingers to feel Steph's already slippery slit. She leans over Steph's shoulder and promises her outright, "From now on you are going to be wet or cumming *all* of your waking hours."

A combination of fear and anger surges through Steph's body, as Robyn pinches a now distended stamen and Steph transudes even more surge into Robyn's palm. Robyn Redacted has little sympathy for a Pledge she denies was her Monitor last Term, and wipes Steph's secretions onto the sides of her face and under her nostrils.

"Ask nicely, Pledge." Robyn demands.

And a confused Steph blurts, "Ma'am, please keep me pink-wet-and-ready to cum, Ma'am."

"Tell me what happened at the Greatest House Roar yesterday," Robyn demands. The Cam anticipates hearing Steph's tale.

Steph pivots her torso but keeps her hands behind her head. "I   lost," she confesses, and dares a glance to her side. "Babs and Janet tricked me."

Robyn hones in, this time exploring Steph's slot with her finger.

Steph rocks and shakes, yet fully cognizant that the Cam collects all her expressions. *Me getting finger-fucked too.*

"And so you begged Babs to let you Strip and cum, is that it?" Robyn queries. "In front of her and Janet and all the Peacock Guests."

"Ma'am," Steph closes her eyes and rotates her pelvis, "I was forced, Ma'am."

Steph opens and advances, "And then after I got back here last night, you forced me to beg in sync with Molly's Chant Video."

"I did!" Robyn fills with pride, but then tilts her head and leans in, "But then you climaxed with your very own Greatest House Roar Video climax. You did that on your own. You zoned yourself. No stopping you, you sizzling socket slut."

Steph's eyes gather spite, "Listen, Robyn Redacted, you owe me for last Term no matter how much you deny it. I know what you're up to right now: You're trying to make me crave cock because you know Pledge can't have any. I'm not stupid."

Steph turns and discovers Boss Babe standing in front of the Lineup. BB stands erect in her Black Bikini. Steph lifts a nostril and sasses silently. *So Bling Babe graces us with her presence. Wearing her bodacious bra and low-rise culotte nombril. Stay navelage, 24x7, you Bimbo Bitch!*

Babs, even Robyn next to her, will indeed stay navelage 24x7, as will Steph—easy, when you wear nothing at all.

BB orders the Lineup, "Beg all together now."

And so Six Cosmos (Tiffany, Kimju, Molly and Steph, Beka and Elle) once again recite in unison, "Please let me Pledge naked and cum be a Stripper next Term."

"You," Boss Babe points at Steph, "may sit yourself on the Landing, spread your legs facing out, and pink yourself."

"Ma'am, please, Ma'am," Steph begs.

"Now." BB firms. And folds a handbra over her bling.

Steph moves across the Backyard to reposition herself. Robyn hesitates for a moment, then laggardly trails her, pausing midway to observe.

Babs addresses the Five Cosmos remaining in the Lineup.

"I told you last night that keeping Steph's postures and breathing under rigid control during all her waking hours would require ongoing effort.

Babs tilts her head toward the Back Landing, where a naked Steph sits herself down, opens her legs, and pulls her outer sex lips apart. The Back Door Cam can't decide to harvest Steph or stick with Boss Babe and the Lineup. It oscillates, stabilizes, and chooses Monitor Babs for the moment.

BB nods in the direction of Robyn and Steph. "Do not forget that despite Robyn's shameless abuse of our former Monitor, it was *I* who first rolled Steph in the Mudpit, ordered her pink, ensured the Prefecture witnessed her streamers, made her beg to cum and Opt Strip, and then forced her to climax."

Robyn is out of immediate earshot. "Please never forget that Robyn is *my* surrogate. Might she have Charm, I am immune to it."

Babs turns to the topless and micro g-stringed Kimju, "Go help your Roommate keep Steph in the Zone. Maintain a handbra from now on. I don't want you upstaging Steph."

Kimju blinks, then crosses her arms across her knockers. "Ma'am, handbra, Ma'am," she says, and departs.

BB turns to the others, "At ease. Go inside, Pledge. Your time is your own for a while. May you find an unoccupied wall, touch your nose to it, and stay put. No talking. I shall follow you in shortly."

§ Robyn & Kimju Zone Steph: Paparazzi Harvest Back Landing

Robyn watches from mid-ground as her Roommate approaches the sitting spread Steph. Steph looks up and silently watches as Kimju walks forward holding her breasts in her hands. Steph glares but holds her pink with two hands.

Kimju resists the urge to talk with her hands. *The handbra doesn't just provide coverage, it ties up the hands.*

Steph misinterprets. *Kimju Kava Kava thinks she's better than me covering her knock knocks. But she's gonna Strip next Term like it or not, and in the Term after that, she'll be ringing her knock up.*

Steph has found part of her resistive self. *Maybe yesterday I had pull pink for the Prefecture, but I'll never touch myself willingly on my own. And I'm not going to beg Kimju!*

Robyn watches Kimju stand erect, look at Steph, nod to the Watering Can next to the landing, and ask, "Is that yours?"

"Absolutely not!" Steph resists, then rationalizes, "I don't have any Garments to water any more. I don't have anything."

"Tell me then," Kimju sorties, "and answer me nice, what is your purpose in life?"

Steph isn't sure. *But I should know the answer.* She speaks carefully. "My goal is to stay naked and sit spread pinking." Steph glances and sees the Cam collects her open crotch dead on. *No escape.* She snarls. *Gamers don't even have the decency to cam me on the oblique.* Steph dead-eyes the Cam. *You think I'm going to climax for you? Here? Outside? Where anyone can watch?*

Kimju is thoughtful. "I thought I heard Monitor Babs say you are supposed to play with yourself?"

"Kimju," Steph proceeds carefully, knowing that she speaks for the record, "Monitor Babs told me to sit and spread myself. Maybe she wants me to sunburn myself, like you did on the Yacht."

Kimju considers the insult. "Then unstick your inner lips completely, Pledge, hold your butterfly wings wide and lift its head up. That way you can sunburn your insides, just like I did on the Yacht."

Steph glowers but obeys. The lips unstick and slowly part with a sucking noise as Steph presents scarlet insides. The Cam documents sauce gathering at the lower end of Steph's split sex cavity. Steph hesistates, "Kimju, please, Kimju."

"You're welcome," Kimju says. "You shall stay pink-wet-and-ready to cum. You will streak to the Nugget next Term. *I* intend to gather a second Garment."

The threat erects Steph's nipples, her air-cooled areola raise goose bumps, and her stamen lifts out of her clithood. *Pinking I am.* Steph constricts. *Pinking to the World.*

Robyn lances in at Steph. "Listen to me, you sloppy satchel slut! Look at you oozing slop! Smile for the tally light! You're feeding the Prefecture! Everyone can see everything! You're bleached on the outside, scarlet on the inside, and going to get sunburned bright red! Ha ha ha!"

Steph recoils. "Please, Robyn, I'll stay pink-wet-and-ready to cum," she says.

"You'll stick a finger into your swizzle, scoop out some of that slush, and swab your slippery onto that stamen of yours," Robyn commands. "Let's see you hang a stalactite outta your socket! Now!"

Steph obeys; she dips a fingertip between her flying wings, wettens her clithood, and gasps. She controls an urge to pee, stops the release before any urine can escape, constricts her vagina and squeezes a glob of splurt from between her legs. The heavy whitish streamer suspends itself in the air, detaches, and falls the short way to the Landing.

"Look at you!" Robyn points, "you can't stop yourself from squeezing slop outta your satchel."

True.

Robyn gloats, "You'll climax anytime anywhere in front of anybody. Whenever I say. You belong to me: mind, body, and soul. Now beg the Strip."

Steph begs, "Please let me Pledge naked and cum be a Stripper next Term." Steph checks her position, legs spread wide, pink open, wetness developing.

Steph turns to Kimju to augment her answer, but the force of Robyn's aggression toward Steph has caused Kimju to take a step or two backwards to accommodate Robyn. Kimju continues to stand tall, holding her handbra and ignoring the impropriety of her micro g-string, but before Steph can speak Robyn turns toward Kimju and holds her Roommate at bay.

"Don't mess with me, Kimju Kava Kava," Robyn declares. "When I want to teach a Pledge a lesson don't get in my way. Don't forget, when I speak it is as if Monitor Babs speaks to you directly. You should consider yourself lucky that you still have one piece and won't have to streak to the Nugget." Robyn smiles.

Kimju holds tight to her handbra. *BB did not instruct me to fight with Robyn. More like to keep Steph from being torn to pieces by her.*

Robyn likes to fight. "I know all about you, Kimju Knock Knock. Your Pledge House never got the Dong, and once you became a Stripper, the Double Dong was forbidden. But it isn't forbidden now, and you wasted no time to find a way swallow it into your klammy kootch and koekjedoodle with your_ex-Stripper Roommate, Molly Mugweights. No doubt Automatron added your Alumni Reprise to its holdings. I hear that your 69 and Double Dong climax are getting the most hits."

Kimju scowls but prides. "Robyn, apparently Gamers covet my first Dong experience. Did you notice that the now Strippers, Penny and Coco brought the Dong to us. Remember them?"

"Don't be asinine," Robyn snorts. "Beware of alternate histories. You should beg to streak to the Nugget, do whatever is necessary to procure the Dong, and bring it back here, so that Molly and Steph can share it."

Kimju impulses. "Maybe I should bring it back and share it with you. You're my Roommate, after all!"

"Maybe you should beg to collect spit from me," Robyn retorts.

Kimju shifts her eyes to gaze upon Steph. Naked and spread. *Pinking with one hand and smearing sex sauce with her other: around her lips, around her clithood, and onto a standup clit. Zoned?*

Steph self-appraises and stays silent. She ensures she manages her fingers properly and gathers her wits. *I've played my Roommate Game with Molly; and Gamers made me lose. They abducted me. However now I can game with any Cosmos who has also played a Roommate Game, whether they have won or lost. And that includes just about every Cosmos Pledge, except my two minders: Roommates Robyn and Kimju.*

Steph casts her eyes past the not-entirely-private Backyard toward the alley behind. *I sense myself being telephotoed from the houses and backyards left and right.* She interprets shapes in the alley. *Rachmaninoffs, and more than one of them. Hockey uniforms with goalie masks so no one can tell what sex they are.* Steph grimaces. *Men desire me, and I don't need homos or trannies or lezzies watching me pink and fingerbang my slippery slue.*

Steph closes her eyes, opens them and struggles words to Kimju, an appeal to power, "You don't need to let your Roommate humiliate me," she says.

Steph struggles with her torso, and hangs a short streamer.

Robyn answers anyway, "My Roommate Kimju will humiliate you however it pleases me, thank you. May your stalactite grow and eventually pool on the first step." Robyn remembers, "The last time Elle got a chance to lolly after you all you left for her was one drop. Perhaps this time you'll do better for her?"

Steph drifts toward the Zone and values any interaction at this point, "Ma'am, please let me secrete a puddle of sauce for Elle to lolly up."

Robyn graces Steph's foot with a toenail. "I'm looking forward to watching the newbies zone you," she says.

Steph gasps. "Ma'am, surely that would not happen. They're so very inexperienced."

Robyn soothes, "They might be only half as good as Tiffany or Kimju or Molly, but there are two of them, so maybe they can keep you cumming longer."

"I'm not someone they should be practicing on," Steph argues, and casts wild eyes toward Kimju. "I mean listen, I'll obey you. You can be Babs' surrogate; I accept that."

Robyn snaps. "You'll obey me first. Did you like me humiliating you in front of that hairy mammoth Roommate of yours? How about you masturbate together with that inferior for real, instead of jerking off to her Videos? You liked masturbating in front of Babs, your former Pledge? Are you humiliated that you must masturbate in front of me? I hope so. Because I'm gonna be a Monitor next Term, and you're gonna Strip and masturbate center Stage at the Nugget."

"I'm not someone you should be practicing on," Steph argues to Robyn.

"You'll do." Robyn is curt. "So sit up , keep your legs spread, and lets recite a Chant. You know the drill: put your hands behind your head. You know the words, lets hear them. It's your only path to climax."

Steph cups her armpits and begrudges, "Please let me Pledge naked and cum be a Stripper next Term." She hesistates.

It's okay, Robyn provides, "Move your hands down pinch your nipples now."

"Titty titty."

"Harder!"

"Titty titty!"

"Now spread your snatch apart, pinch your swizzle stick."

"Clitty, clitty."

"And scoop some slop out. Look at my Back Door Cam. Lick your finger off, you skeezy slime slut. Eat your own skuddy lunch!"

"Hole mouth." Steph consumes.

Robyn moves the bottom of her big toe to touch Steph's outstanding clit. She continues instruction, "Keep spread surrender and rub your strophoid, or whatever you call it, up against my foot. Faster now. Pant for me. Rub harder."

Steph obeys. The touching of it moments ago left it craving, now, all thoughts aside, Steph grinds the toe, the foot. She bounces.

Robyn obliges, "Now cum for me you worthless scumbucket. Sing out some slut sounds for the Back Door Cam." Robyn glances around. "For the paparazzi too. Now cum. Do as I say. Cum for your fans."

Steph releases. Helpless, spread, she draws her hands from behind her head to her nipples and starts cumming.

Robyn lets the Cam collect the rocking spectacle. Steph grinds the sole, fucks the toe, and when Robyn finally takes her foot away and lets the climax subside, she extends it, wipes her toes on Steph's cheek, and presents them to Steph's mouth.

Steph, coming out a fog, knows what to do with it. She cleans her own secretions off Robyn's foot.

"Start chanting again," Robyn instructs Steph firmly.

She turns to Kimju, "Make sure she doesn't stop and stays pink-wet-and-ready to cum on cue!" Robyn stomps, climbs over Steph on the Landing, and heads inside, leaving Steph and Kimju alone in the Backyard.

Babs, watching the Desktop Screen, observes that Robyn, who must cross past the Bell, doesn't bother to ring it on her way through the Back Door. BB flags a cue on the scene and wonders. *Does Automatron flag a cue as well, and perform* its *own analysis? And will it react if I don't do anything? Or will it be overpowered by Steph's antics.*

BB watches Steph on her Screen. Outside on the Back Landing Steph touches herself, prepares her satchel in an open position, and moves her hands behind her head and commences to chant. "Please let me Pledge naked and cum be a Stripper next Term. Titty titty, clitty clitty, hole mouth."

Steph slows the Chant to where she can think and imagines, *I am in a dream world. I no longer control who arouses me nor for whom nor when nor where. I can't stop them. Worse, Kundalini is loose.*

Correct.

Kimju gently narrows the crack in Steph's fleeting thoughts. "Pinch yourself harder, and pick up the pace," Kimju advises, and guides Steph to that point where she is unable to stop trying to climax, yet not quite to the point where she is unable to stop climaxing. Stabilized. Zoned.

Steph drifts in and out of reality as she stimulates herself. At first Steph wonders how long this will go on, but she soon loses track of whether conversations around her are real or not, or what day this is. *It doesn't matter anymore. Voyeurs cam my naked spread body. I'd better not care if they are Gamers, freeloaders, or something else.*

Steph watches her streamer extend, break and fall and puddle upon the only step up to the Landing, and then extend again until the leading edge of the drip contacts the puddle, spirals yet stays, and as Steph's body shakes an even thicker streamer distends. Steph's body convulses, as she can't stop herself from trying to climax. Craziness intrudes. *Why must I stay connected to my puddle! It is almost impossible to think and keep up the Chant. If I finger my spouts and my stamen wrong Automatron will report me. And if Kimju speeds me up....*

Steph discovers that she is no longer passing her surge to her mouth but grinding her fists into her snatch. She stops, recovers herself, discovers that topless Kimju is not paying attention, and reverts to the Chant softly and more slowly. She casts eyes about. *I know that Janet's trying to cut a deal with Bikini Bitch to have me visit the Corvettes for some "quality time." No thank you.*

Steph considers. *Except Bikini Bimbo already broke Louise to a Stripper at the Nugget next Term. And that take-down is just the icing. BB's going to trade Janet's Ginny for me, hour for hour. Ginny might be a Whore-for-Life but I'm an ex-Monitor. So if Janet gets her hands on me she needs to be reminded that* I'm *the one who made her a Monitor this Term!*

Steph discovers that she has wiped her nipples as well as the back of her neck with her vaginal secretions. *No just my mouth.* She scowls. *This is disgusting.* Her body shudders the next cycle of pinking scarlet insides and collecting puddling sauce. *Babs and Janet both owe me and they both treat me worse than all the other Pledge.* Steph lightens her touch on her nipples and clit. She licks her lips. *Janet told me I'd beg to streak to her Corvette House. Now if Bikini Bimbo decide to trade me I don't have any choice.*

Well I do but I don't. I have to make Bling Boob strong enough to resist letting Janet twist me. Even if I do get traded, which I shouldn't.

Steph gathers last breaths. *Maybe Louise is a broken Monitor just like I am. Maybe she's going to Opt Strip next Term, and maybe Janet and Babs are trying to make me beg to go Strip as well. Good luck. I know I'm worth a lot more than any of them, no matter how unjust my demotion this Term.* Steph fears falling out of the Chant, she pinches her spigots, twiddles her stamen, pulls her deep sloppy snizzle wide, tastes herself, gasps, and balances on the cusp of orgasm.

Kimju snaps a slightly faster beat.

Steph begs harder, "Please let me Pledge naked and cum be a Stripper next Term. Titty titty, clitty clitty, hole mouth." Repeat.

§ Tiffany Zones Steph: Compares their Opt Strip Possibilities

Monitor Babs studies Steph's Cam feed on her Desktop. Boss Babe curls her nose, double checks the crossbar switch, and makes sure Steph feeds the Prefecture. *Makes sure the Prefecture feeds upon Steph.*

Tiffany enters the Bedroom, slips past Monitor Babs at her Desktop, unbuttons her clear vinyl shirt and hangs it on her hook at the back of the Bedroom. She is about to take off her slacks when BB stops her.

"Enough," BB decides, "I want you to head downstairs and help out on the Back Landing. You can add a pro touch. Now fold your hands across your titties. Handbra. And keep it like that for now."

"You just don't want me upstaging Steph," Tiffany grouses.

"Right you are," Boss Babe commends.

Tiffany bows, "Ma'am, thank you, Ma'am," and heads downstairs. *Bikini Babe doesn't irritate me very often but she irritates me today.*

Tiffany appears out the Back Door: Handbra and slacks, hairage and rugage of course, stained cameltoe. She eyes the Cam as it collects her. Normally Eraser Heads would dust the inside of Tiffany's clear vinyl shirt or dust the fresh air; never any secrets for Tiffany's tits.

But now is different; from behind, Tiffany appears topless, however her crossed arms cup both tiny titties in opposite palms. Some Gamers claim this is the first time since the beginning of the Term that Tiffany's tits haven't been exposed, a powerful claim.

Tiffany stands behind the seated Steph and looks down over Steph's shoulder to where Steph serenades herself. Tiffany grimaces. *This should be me there!* Tiffany leans forward and observes between Steph's thighs. *So nice of Steph to hang a streamer down and puddle on the Landing step.* Tiffany squeezes herself and spots her cameltoe with fresh tapioca. She curls her nose. *So I have to cover my tits, but naked Steph gets to pink and cream to the Prefecture.*

Tiffany calculates pragmatics. *Steph is naked and begging to Opt Strip. I am also begging to Opt Strip, but I can't even get topless. Babs has been letting me hang up my croptop and slacks and parade naked, but I've still got two Garments.*

And now that Steph is out naked, BB makes me cover up even more so that Steph takes all the glare. Good for Steph but not so good for me. I can't even give one piece of mine away because Boss Babe and I haven't played a Roommate Game yet. And if that never happens then I end up a Monitor next Term, which is management and the last thing I want.

Steph remains lost in her Chant: Hands behind head and magnificent shaven and cupped armpits while she recites, "please let me Pledge naked and cum be a Stripper next Term." Then "Titty titty, clitty, clitty, hole mouth," with the fingers following the Chant until they touch the back of her head again.

Tiffany observes. *Not only is Steph's sodden sex cavity thick with white sauce, but her fingertips have transported enough secretions so that the spot of hair on the back of the neck where Steph rests her fingers is slick with sexual discharge.*

Tiffany looks downward and follows how Steph's spooters change shape as Steph draws her arms forward and down, and how her *erected spouts and bubbled saucers also shine slick with sex valiva.* Tiffany looks downward further. *Of course, Steph stands her swizzle stick out, rolls her hood back around it, and soaks her entire environs with slippery lubricant.*

The smell of Steph's secretions fill the air.

Ever so carefully Tiffany squeezes her own teats, parts pairs of fingers apart, and flashes nippage to the Cam. Eraser heads, erect always: Left, then right, then both together, a pinch and roll and then back inside palms again.

Tiffany considers the Steph complications. *I admit, I do believe Steph should consider me her role model. She secretly saw me climax the Double Dong at Janet's Alumni Reprise last Term. She saw me acquire a Piss-Mouth. She saw me pink and cream before she ever did, but soon she will be hanging splooge outta her slush machine faster than I can. She's the last Pledge except for Robyn to beg the Nugget; whereas I was the first. She might be a late-comer but she is naked 24x7 now, whereas BB only lets me stay naked in the Bathroom.*

Robyn shimmies and curls a nose toward Steph as she speaks. "Next thing you know Steph will be competing with her Roommate Molly for the Pee-Cam's attention."

Tiffany trades a look with Kimju and shrugs. "Roommates share. I'm a Pee-Camer too, don't forget, and I share all my pee with the Prefecture!"

"You're a Pee-Camer too," Robyn rocks at Kimju.

"Roommates share," Tiffany parrots and retorts to Robyn, "so maybe *you* need to share all your pee with the Prefecture just like your Roommate Kimju.

Robyn turns her attention toward Steph. Steph keeps chanting, zoned just this side of climax.

Tiffany touches her fingers to her damp cameltoe, draws a fingertip to her nose, and swabs a nostril. She takes her time, savoring the continued attention of the Back Door Cam.

Tiffany contemplates. *Besides being more naked and pink than I am, Steph also rushes ahead of me in the climax count. She climaxed first yesterday at the Greatest House Roar, again last night in the Dining Room and in sync with her Video. This morning, Kimju wrung a slow viscous pour out of her in this wonderfully public Backyard. And Robyn Redacted made her former Monitor scream. Now I'm supposed to up her count.*

Tiffany double-checks her handbra. *I haven't climaxed at all. About all I'm able to do is keep my cameltoe moist.*

Tiffany curls her toes against the wood boards of the Landing. *I know what's going on,* Tiffany nerves. *It's not about me. Boss Babe seeks to crack Steph. I might still be teasing rugage and hairage above my cameltoed slacks, but Steph gets to sit spread naked and make pink-wet-and-ready for the paparazzi, if not the entire Prefecture. I have encouraged Steph to embrace Stripping, but maybe I've been too enthusiastic. I should be the one who gets to do this, not her.*

I must, at a minimum, Opt Strip next Term and right now Steph is ahead of me. And BB is letting revenge get in the way of prudent decision making.

Babs watches the Back Door Cam feed on her Desktop and considers Steph, live on the Cam. Babs considers her Roommate, *Tiffany deserves to haze Steph for secretly watching her during the Alumni Reprise last Term, yet not revealing this to her.*

And I deserve to trade Steph Sorostitute for Ginny Whore-for-Life. Except MomCap intents to appropriate her.

"You might think about forgiveness, or reformation, or correction, or payback," Janet had said during a conversation after they sealed the Steph-Ginny trade. "For me none of that matters. Steph plays the Game. So I don't really care if I'm putting revenge on her, or slavishly slathering her with attention."

Tiffany slides her palms into a different handbra position. *After I climax Steph, BB will streak her over to Janet, and Janet will zone all her brains. No brain left, just shaking, breathing, ongoing climax.* Tiffany hypothesizes, obviously. *If and after Steph returns, BB is going to select me to escort her to her Nugget Audition.*

Steph senses a presence behind her and slows the Chant just enough to process Tiffany's stance and breathing. *Tiffany!* Steph swings her eyes left and right and sweeps the Backyard. *It's not right the Cosmos keep me pink-wet-and-ready all the time. Or climaxing.* Tiffany's presence strikes a deep fear into Steph's soul, *because I know that Tiffany knows how to Whore!*

Images of Whoring dance through Steph's head and she stumbles the Chant. Images of cocks for money and Porn Stars circuit around in the cortex. *I do not want to play with any dildos, pee in public, or share any Double Dong! I don't even want to Pledge naked and cum be a Stripper next Term!*

Tiffany pokes Steph's smooth stern with a sharp toenail, "Chant and masturbate faster, rub yourself harder, you're about to get traded and you're thinking too much."

Steph obeys, and as Kundalini swells inside her the last thing Steph remembers is Tiffany's wisdom, "You must learn that surrendering to bliss has positive aspects."

And Steph tips into the Zone once again, and warbles.

§ Robyn orders Tiffany & Molly: Pee-Cam & Piss Mouth Practice

Tiffany retreats inside the Back Door. Upstairs in the Bedroom, Boss Babe ignores her as she abandons her slacks and hustles into the Bathroom where she discovers an equally naked Molly finishing up her Pee-Cam Measuring Cup and Logging task and washing her mooe in the bidet.

Robyn saunters in after her, still dressed in her maillot cutout, prepared to take charge. Babs stays behind in her Bedroom, and lets the one Cam with two Cosmos outside the Back Door and one Cam with three Cosmos inside the Bathroom both feed the Prefecture.

Outside Kimju monitors the pace of Steph's Chant.

Inside the Bathroom, Tiffany follows Molly's performance; Tiffany dutifully demands the Cam follow her when she squats over a drain, leisurely opens her inner pinks for the Cam, and then drain pee into the Measuring Cup. Gamers watching via the Cam assumes Tiffany will carefully pour the cup into the floor drain, but instead she leans back and pours the Cup over her chest and body.

When Robyn demands she pour her last Cup over her head, Tiffany obliges her. She walks to the Logging Chart where she logs her Cups with wet hands, tastes her fingertips, blows a kiss to the Cam, and showers.

Robyn turns her taunts toward Molly, "You're a Piss Mouth too, you mangy molliwog. See that pool of pee that Tiffany left behind? See the drops to the shower? You lick it up, mutton meat, on your hands and knees, now!"

Molly obeys, mams swinging toward the floor, maximus upraised.

Robyn augments," Listen too me, you maduro maladroit, after you're done licking up you go back to your bunk and you move your undershirt from your bunk, where you left it with your panties, and you put it on my bunk. You give it to me, you molliwog moerskont, because that way you can go topless and reacquire your Stripper Option."

Yes, Robyn is correct, my two pieces lie on my bunk the Bunkroom. Molly uses her hair to soak up Tiffany urine. It will not spare her tongue but it will spare her stomach. She speaks. "Ma'am, you can't Game with me because you haven't played a Roommate Game yet."

Robyn places the bottom of her foot in the puddle. Molly hastens, "And Besides, that doesn't even matter, because my undershirt is already in Monitor Babs' hands," Molly informs. "So you'll have to take that up with her. She told me that she is 'taking the undershirt and will transform into a minidress.' I just happen to still be holding on to it."

Robyn scowls. "Listen molliwog, don't believe that Babs can do magic tricks. What you need to do is obey me."

Robyn lifts her foot, and Molly cleans her sole off.

And with this Robyn stomps out of the Bathroom. After her shower Tiffany will join Molly on the floor, not wanting to missing any Obeisance Cam time and to clean up Robyn's tracks. When she leads Molly for the two to share a tangy kiss, Molly follows.

Robyn scurries down the hall past Babs' Bedroom door and the stairway and enters the Bunkroom, where Beka and Elle relax together in a bunk, talking and almost touching noses.

"On your feet," Robyn commands, "Into the Bathroom, face-to-face, tit-to-tit, wrap your arms around each other, and kiss and fondle and make out. Gamers are curious about you!"

Beka and Elle slowly rise to their feet. Robyn snaps, "Move it. Now."

§ Kimju Prepares Steph: Present Stern, Swale and Star to Public

Kimju lets Steph descend from her trance quietly, yet provides buoyancy might Steph lose interest. Kimju understands, *I have a job to do. And Gamers will judge me upon my abilities to manage Steph. If I can handle Steph, then just maybe Gamers will let me acquire a second Garment and handle a House.*

Kimju catches the Cam observing her unobtrusively, and takes the opportunity to move her hands from crisscrossed over her knocks to hands side-by-side. And flashes a titter. The micro g-string irritates her keystone. *I might as well be naked, except that I am wearing something.*

Kimju considers the prospects for her own Roommate Game with Robyn. *What if Robyn really does have Charm? Then if I Game with Robyn, I lose.*

Kimju considers her more immediate task: Steph now more slowly touches the back of her head, her breasts and nipples, her clit and vagina, her mouth. Kimju concludes the obvious: *I'm certainly not going to acquire a second Garment from Steph.*

Steph remains too placid to question Kimju's goodwill and motives. She becomes aware of Kimju standing in the Backyard in front of her, slightly off center of her naked spread legs. The very center mark is occupied by the Cam, and with it, *my followers,* she realizes as she looks through the lens, *my followers who look at me. Look at me naked and spread.* Steph wiggles her bare stern on the Landing. *Look at me masturbating and hanging my surge down to the step.*

Steph casts her eyes past Kimju. The Mudpit, Post Henge, Garage, and alley lie further away. Steph slows her Chant to a stop and considers Kimju in the absence of Robyn. *I would rather obey Kimju than Robyn. I might have been begging to "Pledge naked and cum Strip" since the Greatest House Roar, and now I lack any disguise.*

Steph runs one finger down her arm. She uses the other to runs a finger down her micro g-string in an attempt to work it out of her kleave. No luck.

Kimju smiles. She maintains her handbra with one forearm and hand, and uses the other to introduce a new rarified Hand Sign, a curled open hand. "Pledge," Kimju teaches, "this means get on your face and knees, face your stern toward the Backyard, reach up between your spread thighs, pull your butt cheeks apart, point your asshole toward the alleyway, and keep your satchel opened up."

Steph halts what she is doing, tilts her head to make sure she understands, and then parts her knees somewhat, rolls over with her knees on the single step, lets her face rest on the Landing, lifts her stern skyward, reaches back with her hands, and pulls both butt cheeks apart. Pink comes along.

Steph sighs. *I can feel Kimju look at my furry sphincter. Fuck Kimju, I can feel the Back Door Cam collect me; I'm being fed to the Prefecture!*

Steph spends a fresh pearl. *More for Elle to lolly.*

And another. *I feel eyes from the alley canvas my everything. My moles, my every last bleached hair. Telephotos in cars collect my drip. I know they're out there, paparazzi too.* Steph spends another pearl. This one the Back Door Cam misses; it's busy collecting the flush in her face... and her spigots hanging down.

But what the Cam misses the paparazzi autofocus.

§ Robyn Zones Steph: Finger Asshole, Masturbate, Climax

The Door slams. Steph jolts out of dreamland but holds her stern split. Robyn steps out, feet in front of Steph's face, a toenail gouging Steph's cheek. "Listen to me, you sabulous scum slut, keep one hand reaching around behind you. Now work that finger of yours all the way into your stern tunnel!"

Steph blanches, obeys; she moans as her finger buries itself up to the knuckle into her rectum.

"Now take your other hand and reach up between your legs so you pink and cream for your fans," Robyn wises.

Steph obeys. She rubs surge onto her popped stamen and moans. Is Steph angry, humiliated, embarrassed, distraught? *I had expected I might have to pull pink this Term, but to finger-fuck my stern tube in front of such an aloof and inferior rattlebrain as Robyn? This is an insult.*

Steph considers, *It's one thing I had to pink together with Tiffany, but now I have to pink—and masturbate—solo. Now this.*

"Get used to getting rectally violated slut," Robyn barks and signals the Back Door Cam to canvas her forgotten-about ex-Monitor. "You

creamed one drop when you took the thermoprobe during *The Arrivals.*
Now you get to finger your own asshole."

Steph glowers silently; she knows the Cam makes witness of her
behavior. *I am wet all the time.* Steph's rectum wants to eject her finger,
but Steph knows better, and pushes in harder. *I am pink-wet-and-ready to
cum.*

She flares her nostrils at the proxy camming her. *Robyn Redacted.
Memory leaks, memory expansion, but deeper than that, down in the
reptilian part of her brain, a vicious snake of a woman.*

Steph gains an insight where before had remained doubt. *I now
officially hate Robyn. I won't forgive Robyn even if Robyn acts as Babs'
agent. I hate Robyn for what she did to me last Term. I hate Robyn for
her haughty, condescending, deprecating, and demeaning attitude to me
right now.*

Robyn curls her nose. "Wanna know something Steph Sorostitute?
Your snapper stinks like stale yogurt. You're gonna have to pay Gamers
to lick or screw your socket, you peroxide princess." Robyn laughs as the
Cam pans over Steph's body. "First the Strip joint and then the Whore
House for you. The Nugget then Flesh Ranch. Then after you screw your
brains out at Flesh Ranch you can Opt to the Slavesex Snakepit. Too bad
you can't Whore *next* Term. 'Cause that's what you want, you slop-
oozing slime strumpet, dicks in your holes."

Robyn laughs. Rolls her shoulders back. Thrusts her chest out.

Steph holds her mouth open, draws in her cheeks and vibrates. *Robyn
deceived me last Term and makes fun of me now. Where did she learn to
talk like this? What on earth might drive such vitriol?*

Steph double checks her body to make sure both her stern and snatch
are finger penetrated. They are. *I need to stop Babs letting Robyn haze
me. Babs would never do this to me. She needs to stop exposing me to all
the Gamers, to the Prefecture, and letting Automatron sock me away.*

"Twist your clit and fingerbang yourself!" Robyn snarls. "And rotate
that finger inside your sewer so you feel it and know it is there."

Steph gathers her actions together and drives herself higher. She no
longer needs encouragement: One hand rotates the finger inside her
sternway; the other hand parts her lips, aggressively rubs her clit, and
finger-fucks her slippery snapper.

"Com'on. Faster." Robyn says. "Cum for me. No holding back. Do it,
you stinking spread sallyport. Obey me."

Steph obeys. She rubs herself into the first trills of climax but comes
to her senses panting for air.

And so Robyn raises, "Beg to Pledge naked and cum be a Stripper
next Term."

Steph gazes into the Cam.

"Come on," Robyn cheers her, "You've been begging that ever since you lost the Greatest House Roar! Beg to climax your brains out, you slimy skeeze skank."

Steph obeys, plunges a finger deep into her anus, and begs out to change Caste, "Please let me Pledge naked and cum be a Stripper next Term!"

And tips into uncontrolled climax. Everyone watches Steph howl in a combination of abandonment and ecstasy. To some who anticipate they might be next the spectacle is scary. But grudgingly admirable, monumental that Steph has overcome a mind that tried to impose a puritanical pride on herself.

Especially when she doesn't stop; Steph finds a high groove, finger fucks two holes, and shimmers.

Robyn makes a shallow bow to Kimju and offers firm advice, "I'm the best. Don't even think about challenging me to a Roommate Game. At the end this Term, at Midnight, you get to run to the Nugget topless with your micro g-string, so officially you don't have to streak. Challenge me? I'll pick the Game and you'll loose, and then you *will* streak to the Nugget. Kimju, before you ever ring the Bell on your way out the Back Door, everyone in the Prefecture will know your release time."

"Maybe you should Flip-Flop with me," Kimju snipes, "that way you could harvest any Cosmos Pledge.

"I'm not about to show off my rack to the Prefecture," Robyn determines. "Listen to me, you klammy kuddy keekelay. If you try and streak to the Nugget you'll never make it. You're going to vanish in between Terms, before Lockdown swings into motion and the last chime of Midnight. Some Gamers will suggest you used your streak to escape the Game successfully. Gone. Once they don't have to account for you anymore, they can do, and they will do, anything they want to you. Because you won't exist any more."

"They?" Kimju squints.

"They. Gamers. Not the normal Gamers like here at School. The ones who take over if you get caught breaking Rules."

And with this Robyn exits back inside the Back Door.

§ Kimju Zones Steph: And Examines Her Own Motives

Kimju lets Steph Zone for a while before she finally brings her down... down a little, that is. It pleases Gamers that Kimju paces Steph into a steady state of freshness easily tipped into cumming. Still, Kimju worries, *Might Steph tip over into the Zone, or get tipped over become self-sustaining climax, I must make sure she doesn't faint or cum herself to death. No gokuraku-ojo, no sweet death by exhaustion!*

Will Steph lose her breath, lose all self-control, lose all dignity, and crave cumming? That goes without saying.

Kimju spots a car in the alleyway. The window rolls down and a camera with a long telephoto records the rear-end view of a naked, stern tunnel being fingered, and a masturbating, blissed Steph. *Records me too,* Kimju accepts, now carefully holding her handbra with both hands.

Fact is I'm being judged by Steph's performance. That's the Game now. Kimju studies herself. *I am a teacher now.* Kimju assesses. *I am a good teacher too.* Kimju slides Steph ever so slightly out of the Zone. "I will help you succeed," Kimju promises, "I know how to help you achieve balance on that cusp of ecstasy. I'll make a good Monitor next Term, and I'll help make you a most desired Stripper."

Steph moans, "Ma'am, thank you, Ma'am."

Kimju jabs Steph with a toenail. "Now turn over. Clean your fingers off in your mouth, spread your legs, and pink and diddle yourself. You can hang a streamer out or lean back and let your slop run down to your stern star."

Steph obeys but discovers a different set of wits about her; she declares to Kimju, "This is so not me!"

Kimju responds, "Oh, but you so begged to be here. My job is to keep you at that place where you can no longer control yourself. So Chant for me, even tempo now."

So Steph recites her begging, "Please let me Pledge naked and cum be a Stripper next Term," and touching herself in rhythm augments, "Titty titty, clitty clitty, hole mouth."

What Kimju knows best is how to set the pace of the Chant, that pace of wanting to cum.

Repeat yourself," Kimju commands, "and do it over and over again."

And Steph continues, "Please let me Pledge naked..." the etceteras flowing until the Chant again captivates Steph, draws her into the fear of it being real. The shock of discovery ripples through her body, and fresh secretions erupts onto her fingertips with each successive probe of her scarlet sex chamber. *The Chant and the fear possess and arouse me.* It is Steph's last though for a while. She rubs her nipples and clit harder, and as she breaths deeply and chants, her psyche steadfastly falls under the spell of Kundalini.

And Kundalini gives Steph the Spirit to continue the task.

Kimju evaluates her own motives. *Maybe Steph Sorostitute is a society snob or maybe she's a spoiled slithery slue, but I don't have any beef with her. Except that she has moved to the front of the line headed to Strip next Term. That helps to move me down the queue.*

Well, not entirely. *Gamers know I want to Opt Up, so they are testing me to see if I can handle a scrappy Stripper wannabe who maybe doesn't want to Strip. So Steph is a good exercise for me. I think I'm able to keep her right on that edge of climax, because it is I who control her breathing and pulse rate. I decide if she goes over the top. It's not about training Steph, it's about training me.*

Gamers who look in via the Cam and who think Steph's Chant is no more demanding than rubbing one's stomach and patting ones head at the same time, should test themselves for an hour or two.

Steph learns that concentrating on doing the task right forces a situation that produces arousal, and that once aroused she occasionally feels prone to break the regimen in order to drive herself over the top. Linger her fingers on her vagina, pile more smear on her lips, wetten the hair on the back of the head. Steph catches herself. *I can't abandon the rigor and strive toward a free-form uncontrolled ecstasy on my own. It's evidence I can't control myself and need to be restrained.*

And be driven higher still.

Kimju monitors Steph carefully and ensures Steph adheres to the Chant's regimen: a deep breathing arousal, a slow and constant thrusting of her pelvic muscles, an ongoing discharge of vaginal secretions... but concentrating just enough on the Chant task so as to not quite be able to go over the top. Conflicted and not entirely rational about an irrational situation.

Kimju is not sympathetic to Steph's plight. *I've been a Stripper; I've climaxed and peed for tips... and for free. Been there done that and I am fine to have made my Alumni Reprise my last ever Nugget appearance.*

I need another Garment, pure and simple. Regrettably you, Steph, no longer have anything to contribute to my costume needs. You only have favors to give and Obeisance to take on.

Kimju again considers herself. *I worry that absent another Garment, that my duty of keeping Steph horny might be a prerequisite before I myself will be taken on an internal journey. And not just cumming in sync with my Stripper Videos. Gamers gonna keep me Zoned for days on end.*

Kimju studies Steph. *No problem. I'll make sure Steph stays in a Zone where she is either crazy with desire or crazy with climax. Creamy Cosmos cooze in heat.*

My problem is I can't collect another costume while I'm minding a zombie, Kimju reflects.

Or too afraid that Robyn will strip me and I can't get anything back.

Steph hangs a bead of cream from her snapper. She's learning to purr.

II-17 Babs Takes Molly's Dress & Tiffany Takes Steph (D22)

§ Babs Takes Molly's Dress: Reactivates the Watering Can

Babs sits at the Desktop in her Bedroom and keeps an eye on the Cams. Astute Gamers know Babs has coveted Steph's minidress since before Steph tried to contest for Molly's panties (and failed). BB had watched, but not interfered, as Molly took the undershirt-minidress away from Steph at the Greatest House Roar last night. *It was good that someone else reduced Steph—and her Roommate Molly conveniently obliged. But I admit I relished the moment when Steph forfeited her Garment—in front of women and men—begged to Opt Strip, and then masturbated, revealed herself in climax, and streaked her bleached naked self back to the Cosmos House.*

Steph humiliated me last term, but my former Monitor really made Janet take it for both of us. Babs thinks forward. *Now that Steph is a naked Pledge, many Gamers will vie to torment her. It's not just me; it's all of us who want to teach her a lesson.*

The feed from the Cam hovering around a naked and spread Steph on the Back Landing reveals that Kimju keeps Steph in the Zone.

Babs changes channels and watches a replay from the Nugget, two days ago. Automatron serves up Louise, *naked and displaying herself to me. Louise taunts me, challenges me to demand that she part her labia minora, challenges me to watch her obey me, and challenges me to observe her suffer the consequences of my decision. Okay, I've decided she shall Opt Strip next Term, broken Monitor, broken Pledge. Some Gamers want the momentum on her maintained, and want her to Whore after her next turn. I'm just a part of that Game.*

Boss Babe considers the proposed trade with Janet. *Louise Opt Strips, like it or not, because that's what Janet wants. Then Steph for Ginny hour-for-hour, except I've already allowed MomCap that when Ginny comes over she could "audition" the Nugget. And she will, I suspect.*

The replay on the Desktop cuts from Louise to a replay of Bikini Babe herself. Babs startles, and flushes as she looks at herself and hears the ripple of applause that greets her entrance at the Nugget that night, and she watches a hovering Cam shot crane down her body. *I wasn't aware of that!* Close-ups of her belly and butt, the sweep of her culotte nombril, deep cleavage, *and yes, my areolage.* Babs blinks, and punches the Desktop back to the Back Door Cam. *Why must they do that?*

Steph, now back on Babs' Desktop and feeding the Prefecture, struggles to cum uncontrollably but Kimju restrains her with the pace of the Chant, so that she either flies at a high shake, or aggresses her struggle to climb into high Zone.

BB looks away from the Desktop and fingers her areolage, in real time and real space.

Gamers audit my tan lines because I am a Gamer of Interest. They count seven on me: Two legholes, one waistline, two armholes, one neckline, and the ribline around the bottom of my bra. Gamers know my crescent d'areolage are tanned for life, but they won't get to see any more or me.

Boss Babe reflects, *I don't like being marked, especially marked her life, but if tanned crescents are my initiation for Opting Monitor, then I need to wear them with pride.*

BB furrows her brow. *Perhaps the time has come for me to take what I covet.*

Right. A Monitor needn't contest to take Garments, Monitors needn't negotiate, Boss Babe may just takes what she wants. *None the less....*

Babs rises from her chair.

Molly appears in the doorway and stands at attention.

Molly wears what used to be Steph's undershirt hanging down over the see-through panties acquired at the Nugget. "Ma'am, please let me beg you please, Ma'am," she says.

BB sits down and signals Molly at ease. There is no place to sit, so Molly relaxes and stands. "Ma'am, you know I've already eaten pussy and cum on the Dong. And I've already played my Roommate Game with Steph."

"You won." BB states a fact. "Fair and square. And now you wear two Garments."

"Ma'am, that's the problem, Ma'am," Molly begs. "You know I'll do whatever you want to ensure you take my undershirt, so I may Op Strip next Term."

BB should have seen this coming; she flaps her lips and Molly advances her case, "Ma'am, you'd get to Opt Up and I'd Opt Down. It's a win-win, Ma'am."

Babs withdraws and sits back in her chair. "Pledge, you need me but I don't need you. I can take any Garment from any Pledge any time. Except I don't want to Opt Up; I intend to Hover."

Molly advances a weaker argument. "You promised that Steph and I would get to cum together, like Kimju and I did. I won't need a minidress to do that."

"You don't need panties either," BB bemuses. "Although you managed to get them plenty soaked backstage at the Nugget."

"Ma'am," Molly exclaims; she wonders, *does Babs know about the Nugget Shooter's private stock?*

Molly deflects. "Ma'am may it please you I am a full-fledged Pee-Camer and Piss Mouth. I'll wallow in the Mudpit. I'll piss and wallow in my own mud and beg you to piss on me, Ma'am."

Babs gulps air to delay. "I shall consider your request, Pledge, but do not expect that I shall be relieving myself upon you." BB smiles and bows to Molly, "Perhaps your Roommate deserves to do the honors."

"Ma'am," Molly hesistates, "Ma'am, Steph is not a Pee-Cam Pledge, Ma'am."

Babs smiles. "Perhaps we can fix that, after all Roommates are supposed to share."

Molly nervously fingers her undershirt to make sure the buttonhole aligns with her navel.

"In the meantime, perhaps the Watering Can will do," BB suggests. "So where is it anyway? And how come your panties aren't soaked?"

"Ma'am," Molly retraces the Watering Can. "Robyn gave the Watering Can to Steph yesterday before the Greatest House Roar. And I don't need to be see-through-when-wet any more because my panties are see-through all the time."

Boss Babe purses her lips.

Molly feels compelled to offer penitence,

Molly breaks the silence. "Ma'am, perhaps Steph put it down besides the Landing, when you sat her down and pinked her."

"Collecting unpleasantreis ever since, I trust?" Monitor Babs snides, although she feels proud of her Pledge for such evasive diplomacy.

"Remind me what it's worth to you for me to take your undershirt?" Boss Babe queries.

Molly knows, *I can't take back the Watering Can!*

She blurts, "Ma'am, I'll wallow in the Mudpit and beg all the Cosmos to pee on me. I'll stay pink, wet, and climax myself. Ma'am, you already saw me climax the Double Dong with Kimju. But I'm not like Kimju, I'll Dong and eat out every Cosmos!"

Babs looks down at her Desktop.

Molly doesn't accept rejection. "I'll cum for you anywhere anytime in front of anybody. I'll groom you, just like Tiffany does. I'll eat out your bajingo. I'll lick your bunghole. I'll be your toilet. I'll do whatever you want, Ma'am.

"Good." Boss Babe squints. "What I want is for you to reclaim the Watering Can. Now beg politely and beg to Game."

Molly begs. "Ma'am, may it please you to take my undershirt, and let me take the Watering Can back. I'll collect pee in it, water my panties and stuff them into my mouth."

Boss Babe extends her hand out, palm upward.

Molly understands at once. She says not a word, blinks very slowly, and pulls the long undershirt off over her head, her hairy armpits on full display in the process, and lays the Garment into Boss Babe's palm.

"Ma'am, thank you, Ma'am," Molly gurgles. "For helping me along on my way to the Nugget."

"You're welcome, Pledge," Boss Babe confirms and taps her Desktop. "Gamers will love that your massive mams are back on display, and that your see-through panties reveal not just your hairage and rugage, but also your valiva release."

"Ma'am, thank you, Ma'am, for letting me reveal myself," Molly says. "I'll pullaside, pink, and eat my own mayonnaise."

Boss Babe dictates. "Beg another time. Right now leave your panties behind at your bunk and relieve Kimju zoning Steph on the Back Landing. Presenting naked in public is hardly new for you, and there is no reason to hint to your fellow Pledge that you are back to one Garment.

"Just before you take Steph out of the Zone, put her into sitting spread surrender position, use both hands to pink her for the Cam, scoop her insides, taste her, then scoop her again and let her taste herself. Then bring her out and up to the Bathroom.

"There you shall sit, spread, facing each other still naked, and masturbate. Keep her hot and running because you will have a big surprise for her when you do take her screaming out of her mind."

"Ma'am, thank you, Ma'am, for letting me Pledge naked and cum be a Stripper next Term." Molly bows, turns on her heel, and exits the Bedroom.

For a moment a topless Molly feels euphoric and carefree. She doffs her panties, tosses them on her bunk, and heads downstairs. *What can Gamers do to me anyway? Take away my panties. So I love being naked.*

I just don't want to streak to get to the Nugget next Term.

§ Babs & Tiffany: Minidress Coverage & Steph's Nugget Audition

Gamers sometime wonder to what degree Boss Babe is the custodian of any and all minidresses. What Steph wore; what BB chooses to wear.

Right now I get to exchange the undershirt for a minidress, and most certainly if the minidress is strapped. Equivalents. So now I get to decide what minidress I choose to wear. Minidress and its controller are aligned. Or, as the astronomers put it, we are in conjunction!

Babs conjures up a form-fitting, shortsleeve, scoop-neck minidress with a hemline closer to her knee than her crotch. BB no longer shows her areolas and this pleases her. Her bare belly is reduced to a cutout hole around her navel; BB pays special attention to the cutout and picks one large enough she need not think about it all the time. *I'm not Robyn; I've got more complex tasks than managing the smallest buttonhole. I have to think for the entire House.*

Babs stands to exits her Bedroom when Tiffany enters, arriving naked from the Bathroom.

Tiffany halts inside the doorway and canvasses Babs head to toe. "Wow! Look at you!" Tiffany says, "I love how that stretchy minidress grips your boobs and belly and butt. Streamlines your legs!"

"No more bling, no more bellage." BB states.

"You're curvy in a good way," Tiffany compliments. She squints. "Your bra and nombril Bikini underneath helps form and uplift you.

"I picked this dress because it allows me to tease my bra straps," BB declares. "That's all Gamers get for now."

"You're allowed to change to lingerie underneath," Tiffany advises, "You're looking good! You're very desirable!"

"I'm more covered up," Babs asserts.

"That makes you even more desirable!" Tiffany claims.

"I don't want to be more desirable!"

Tiffany encourages ascent. "You've got three Garments and you're primed to Opt MomCap next Term."

" I'm not at all sure I want to Opt Up!" BB firms. "I'm barely ahead of the Game. Maybe you or the two former Strippers have a clear idea of the responsibilities of a MomCap, but there is a lot I don't know. I'm better off to Hover next Term. Three Garments suit me now, and I can always give one away just before Midnight. I know that's best for me."

Tiffany rubs both Eraser Heads in her palms. "Well, everyone has to make their own right decision. Caste is one thing, but managing Strippers—a MomCap gig without any knowledge of Stripping—that's a most dubious goal."

Babs mulls this consideration. "Right. You and Kimju and Molly have all suggested that even MomCap's past is... well, checkered."

Tiffany knows but holds back, "Well, okay. So ask Kimju and Molly, or for that matter, ask Janet, she danced two Terms ago.

Tiffany provides insight, "Janet complained to me that you're depriving her of an opportunity to crack Steph." A smile. "And by the way, Janet doesn't share your uncertainty about Opting Up."

"Janet's more confident about everything," BB wrinkles her face. "She's more experienced. More exhibitionistic too."

Babs broods. "Next you're gonna try and convince me that Stripping at the Nugget could be good for *me.*"

Tiffany laughs and carefully adjusts her private parts. "I'm the one who needs to get to the Nugget next Term! I'm a Porn Star wannabe, remember. I love you just fine, you're a great Roommate, but before the Runout concludes, please send me to the Nugget, let me Strip naked and cum, and then just stay there and be a Stripper next Term." Tiffany pauses. "I mean it. I really do. I'll even give my costume to Robyn."

Babs laughs, "So many beggars, so few slots at the Club."

Tiffany's eyes dart upwards across the minidress. "I guess Molly is topless again."

"Molly's staying naked for now," BB shares. "And I don't want you spoiling my entrance either."

Tiffany accepts, "I understand. The Nugget is already oversubscribed; everyone who begs can't qualify. Just let me take Steph to the Nugget. Both of us naked. I promise you, whatever Kimju and Molly can do I can do better. I am a natural born Porn Star. And Steph deserves it."

Babs laughs. "You don't fool me at all. Your willingness to take Steph to the Nugget is just a wily way to get there yourself. Confess, Pledge!"

Tiffany controls an urge to pee and deposits a drop onto her fingers. She confesses. "I confess Ma'am, just please let me Pledge naked and cum be a Stripper next Term, Ma'am. I mean it. I really do. You can screen all my Suck Fuck Facial Videos. I'll pee and cum on your command, anytime, anywhere, in front of anybody. I'll wash your feet with my tongue, I'll bathe and groom you, I'll be your toilet. Just tell me what I need to do to please you."

Boss Babe blinks. Orders, "Quiet now."

Tiffany blinks. And obeys.

And Boss Babe punches up the Screen for the Bathroom Cam.

II-18 Molly & Steph: Climax Bathroom Pee-Cam (D22)

§ Molly & Steph: Masturbate & Chant Together in Bathroom

Babs watches the Back Door Cam on the Desktop Screen and sees naked Molly stand naked Steph up, cross Steph's hands behind her back, and then march her through the Back Door. Molly need not ring the Bell because she never leaves the Back Landing, but ringing the Bell is far from Steph's mind as she stands up for the first time since this Morning. Automatron notices Steph forgets to ring the Bell, but the transgression fails to reveal itself to Monitor Babs.

Nonetheless the evil part of BB grins. *Steph is done with Roommate Games. Next stop for her is the Nugget. And if she gets caught streaking to get there? Well, too bad, it's not my Karma.*

Babs can hear directly as the plump, saggy-mammed and heavy-footed Molly guides a slim and sinuous Steph up the spiral staircase, then left past the Bedroom door, then right and into the Bathroom. Molly carries the Watering Can, a Prop whose contents can pose risk.

Molly considers. *Unforeseen turns of events are guiding my life. First I acquire the undershirt in the Greatest House Roar, then I trade it to Babs for the Watering Can.*

Steph wonders how her Roommate Molly became naked. *I've been Zoned out of today's exchanges.*

Molly finds that shedding the dreaded undershirt has brought her comfort. Naked at the moment but *my panties lying on my bunk count as one Garment.* Molly brushes her long black hair. *I really don't want to "to Pledge naked and cum be a Stripper." I need to keep one piece,* Molly decides. *I want to get to the Nugget but I don't want to streak to get there.*

Nor do I believe that if a streaker gets caught and gets gangbanged that's a sign you want *to Whore. That couldn't be further from the truth.*

Steph also steals moments of though during her movement. *I'm in a daze.* Upstairs and passing by Babs' Bedroom she looks into an empty room.

Steph feels an urge to touch her spires and her stamen. She blinks as she is turned into the Bathroom. *It doesn't matter to me anymore. I'm about to chant for the Bathroom Cam, and my fat wallowing Roommate is about to zone me.*

But it's going to be worse than putting me back into the Zone again.

Babs returns from her private bathroom following Steph's passage to the common Bathroom; she continues to watch the Back Door Cam on her Desktop Screen. She sees Robyn take Elle out the Back Door, point to the Landing step, and watches Elle Lollydor get onto her hands and knees.

Ouch! Watch out for wood splinters!

Babs flips to the Bathroom Can, where Molly's entrance lights that Cam up. She watches Molly puts the Watering Can down; it's out of the way but remembered.   Steph growls and thinks about her Monitor. *Bikini Bitch is a manipulating babbeljaz. First she tricks me at the Greatest House Roar. She makes me strip, beg the Nugget, and then force-cums me in front of all the Gamers and Guests, including my former Pledge Janet, who hates me.*

Steph resists an urge to uncross her hands behind her back and uses the moment when she comes to a stop to assure herself that her thighs don't touch. She adjusts her feet to "legs open" position for safety sake as the Bathroom Cam considers her square on.

Hello Babs, Steph talks to the Cam with her eyes. I know you're watching me, *Bikini Bimbo.* Steph raises her chin and adjusts her posture. *You let your sycophant Robyn do your dirty work, like forcing me to cum with my Video last night. And today ordering all of your Pledge to zone and force-climax me outside in public.*

Steph freshens at her own memories. *This morning Kimju and Robyn kept me pink-wet-and-ready on the Chant and then tipped me into climax.*

Tiffany climaxed me when she told me I'm being traded to Janet. It can't be real but Tiffany played me on the fear.

Kimju put me on my hands and knees and Robyn made me bugger myself to climax. Kimju's kept me zoned ever since. Until Molly just brought me inside.

What happens next?

Steph should know the answer. She snarls at the Bathroom Cam. *More free. I hope you're watching, Monitor Bling Bazongas, because before this is over I am going to plunder your every hole with a strapon.*

Steph watches the Bathroom Cam hover in front of her bleached-out shag, and glares at Monitor Babs via the Cam. *I should have ensured that you became a Stripper this turn, so that you could be a fucking Whore next. I'll never make that mistake again, but trust me, I will make sure that sooner or later Ms. BB ends up Bang Box.*

Molly observes the Cam harvest Steph. "Show it your pink, Stripper wannabe," Molly commands. "Show it your pee hole as well."

Steph draws her hands to her satchel, opens the flaps, unsticks her inner lips, and displays her pee hole below the butterfly's head.

Molly matches Steph posture, pulls her own pink and stretches flesh around her own urethral orifice. "Tiffany and Kimju and I all pink while we stream pee out our holes, so maybe you'll join us on the Pee-Cam. We'll teach you how to use the Measuring Cup and Logging Chart."

Molly moves her hands to her hips. "Us Pee-Camers always stay naked in the Bathroom, but since your already naked 24x7, you'll blend right in."

"I don't deserve what's happening to me," Steph asserts. "I figure you're too stupid to put over on me but you're also too weak to resist them."

Molly waves off the rudeness. "Listen Steph, I'm sorry about what happened at the Greatest House Roar, and maybe I am stupid, so you know it wasn't my doing.

"And if I find out who the other two acts were, I'll tell you."

Steph purses her lips. "You'd better be the last Cosmos to force me to cum, because I don't deserve being given to the newbies."

"I'd be more worried about being traded to Janet for Ginny," Molly says.

Steph lets the butterfly go free, raises her fingers, and clasps a handbra over her sinusoidals.

Molly ignores the transgression.

Molly instructs, "Now sit and face me on the floor, spread your legs wide, bend your knees up, touch your toes to my toes." They settle in and Molly progresses. "Now follow my hands with your eyes and your hands," Molly commands, "and Chant with me."

And they are off. "Please let me Pledge naked and cum be a Stripper next Term. Titty titty, clitty clitty, hole mouth."

Steph's eyes migrate from Molly reciting surrender with her hands behind her head, to touching her mammoth mammaries, to swelling her maraschino, and finally to scooping her own sop as she follows Molly digging mung out of her deep purple insides. Both draw their fingers to their lips, and taste themselves.

We can kiss and taste each other is a little while. Molly breathes deeply. *No rush.*

Today is the first time Molly and Steph actually chant together. Steph got to chant with Molly's Video last night in the Dining Room, but that was very regulated. Here in the Bathroom it's more free-form. Molly and Steph might be post-Roommate-Game free agents, but they are still Roommates. True, before the Winner-Takes-All Greatest House Roar at the Peacock House yesterday, Molly had begged Steph to strip her naked. Instead Steph has been stripped naked and Molly will train her to beg.

§ Tiffany & Kimju then Robyn brings Beka & Elle: All Watch

The remaining Cosmos Pledge trickle into the Bathroom to watch the naked Roommates, Molly and Steph, sit spread, feet-touching, and reciting the Chant.

Molly leads. No rush. Steph knows, *I must follow right now.*

Tiffany and fellow Pee-Camer Kimju manifest themselves naked. Tiffany's Eraser Heads point outward, her thinnish pubic hair a natural. Kimju's kava is butched, and shaven on the outside to a shape slightly larger than her first tanga. Before she traded for the micro g-string, which is back on her bunk.

Aside from Molly herself, only Tiffany knows that Babs took Molly's undershirt, but there is nothing in their glance that reveals this shared knowledge. Tiffany, guardian and respectful of Boss Babe's ways, allows assumptions to remain uncorrected. *Molly doesn't need to know I know.*

And since Molly only visits the Bathroom naked, as she is now, neither Kimju nor any other arriving Pledge has reason to suspect that Molly's Garment count has changed. Even Tiffany, acute observer she is, doesn't theorize that the Watering Can was brought up for other than Steph, or that it's provenance has reverted to the germ-phobic Molly.

Molly knows.

Steph worries. *I haven't had an opportunity to pee all day, and I am most definitely never going to pee in public. Molly thinks I'm going to pee into the Watering Can, which is why she brought it. And that I'm going to pee like she does on the Bathroom Cam.* Steph scans the Bathroom. *Molly Pee-Cams like Tiffany and Kimju. I'm better than they are, and I am a bigger prize.*

Robyn arrives wearing her strapped maillot cutout. Shaven legs below the horizontal-with-crotch legline; shaven armpits also. Queenly make-up. She herds Beka and Elle, who have just carefully climbed the stairs with their hands behind their heads.

The trio come to a stop in the Bathroom somewhere amidst the makeup mirror and chairs and lights, the bathtub, and the bidet. Beka hangs boobage in her unfastened halter, and hairage and cheeky buttage in her disintegrating shorts. Elle titters up her hacked croptop. Robyn signs them to stand-spread-surrender, and as Elle opens her legs the miniskirt rides up and she vagflashes. *Or is this displaying hairage?*

The Cam welcomes the newbies; it zips to the floor to examine how the seam in the shorts mauls Beka's bolus and box, and details shaven lips with a landing strip above. The Cam surveys Elle too: nothing hides an unshaven bush that extends down the thighs.

Elle knows. *Right now my nest obscures my naos. But I still have two pieces and I have to make sure I keep them!*

Robyn ignores the naked and chanting Molly and Steph. She signs the equally naked Tiffany and Kimju to stand spread surrender. She hazes the newbies, "Say hello to the Bathroom Cam, Pledge. It's jealous you offered pink to the Nugget Cams, but not to your own House. You'll make it up, won't you?"

The newbies respond, "Ma'am, yes, Ma'am." Then Beka volunteers so Elle must follow, "Please let me Pledge naked and cum be a Stripper next Term."

§ Molly & Steph: Elle Observes Them Chant & Masturbate

Monitor Babs watches the Desktop Screen in her Bedroom; she long ago switched the Bathroom Cam to feed the Prefecture, but only more recently toggled Automatron to steer the Cam. *I shall present myself shortly, and if I need to steer the Cam I can take control of it when I arrive in the Bathroom.*

BB watches the Desktop Screen and straightens her shoulders. *No more bling!*

Molly and Steph continue to sit on the Bathroom floor and Chant. "Please let me Pledge naked and cum be a Stripper next Term. Titty titty, clitty clitty, hole mouth!" Molly leads. *I must set the pace of the Chant. It must engulf Steph but not overwhelm me. At least not until the time comes for both of us to go over the top in unison.*

Steph's eyes follow Molly's fingers dig into her massive black bush. *Purple mutton.* Molly's steel clithood ring sparkles above her thick puffy maraschino and provides another reminder of Opt Down consequences. Steph worries, *Must I match this molliwog_in order to get another opportunity to advance? I'll climax—I'm sure there is more of that to come—but must I Pee-Cam too? Or get filled up with the Double Dong? Before I can go win clothes from somebody else?*

Steph might not yet always believe her own begging, but she more and more succumbs to the thrill. *I might be pink, wet, and cum whenever wherever Gamers want,* Steph assures herself, *but I definitely can't see myself heading to the Nugget next Term.*

Beka assumes both naked and chanting ex-Strippers masturbate equally, but Elle sees the difference. *Of course Molly will expose herself and climax naked in front of everybody. All she needs is food and care. She's climaxed before; she'll climax anytime, anywhere, in front of anybody.* Elle sneaks a look at herself in one of the mirrors. Titter and hairage. She considers Molly. *Molly assumes that climaxing is a prerequisite to returning to the Strip, a demonstration of her willingness. Molly believes the Chant.*

Elle considers naked Steph. *I saw Steph live in the Dining Room last night, and I don't quite know what got done to her today, but I can tell that Molly does know how to pleasure Steph's circuits.* Elle studies the sitting spread, foot-touching Roommates. *Molly has Steph in that part of the Zone where Steph can't stop wanting to cum, but is unable to climax.*

I bet Molly knows how to chant a bit faster and tip Steph, but not tip herself, or to chant a bit faster still and go ballistic together.

Elle considers Steph's begging to Opt Strip next Term. *Steph believes the Chant when she is surfing the Zone, but unlike Molly, Steph doesn't believe it all the time.*

The seven Cosmos in the Bathroom have no reason to suspect that BB has begun moving toward the Bathroom. Robyn conveniently utilizes the moment. "Loser!" she hisses, and rakes Steph's thighs with sharpened toenails. She offers a sarcastic suggestion, "Sometimes, you have to go down to get up."

§ Babs Entertains Molly & Steph: The Alabaster Flask

Boss Babe strides into the Bathroom. She startles the Seven Cosmos with her stunning appearance: one shortsleeve scoop-neck minidress over her Bikini: three pieces, no bling. Babs' much reduced cleavage, bellage, and leggage focuses attention toward the navel cutout.

Robyn opens her mouth to speak but BB signs her to silence. All Cosmos eyes have her, so does the Bathroom Cam.

BB enjoys the respect her reduced exposures entail. *I can be a respectable guest at a party, a lecture, or an art gallery opening—events at which my Cosmos Pledge are un-presentable. Unless they are the act.*

Bab surveys the Bathroom. Naked Tiffany's transparencies hang back in the Bedroom, the first Cosmos Pee-Camer has been anticipating Babs entry.

Naked Kimju evaluates immediately. *Boss Babe took Molly's undershirt, converted it back to a minidress, and wears it overtop her Bikini!*

Kimju glances at naked Molly and Steph, chanting and lost in the Zone together. *I wonder if Molly know BB's seizure reduces my options. I might stand naked here in the Bathroom, but I still have my g-string back at my bunk. Now all Molly back on her bunk are her panties, and if I take her panties away, she'd have to streak to the Nugget.*

Kimju considers her possibilities: *My problem is that I can't game with Molly right now. I have to* first *Game with my Roommate, Robyn Redacted.*

Molly hears Babs' entrance but maintains her Chant with Steph: "Please let me Pledge naked and cum be a Stripper next Term. Titty titty, clitty clitty, hole mouth." Molly reinforces Steph's rhythms in the Chant, and guides her Roommate, keeping the two of them shallow into the Zone—high arousal—but not cumming.

Babs observes that Beka and Elle share the shower stall. "Make out," Robyn had ordered them, Beka lead them into the shower stall, wrapped her arms around Elle, and drew her inward with a kiss. At the moment they remain lost in embrace. BB ignores them.

Only when naked Molly senses BB's presence behind naked Steph does her descend from the Zone and sneaks a glance at her Monitor. She knows in a flash what she sees: *Steph's undershirt—my undershirt—has morphed into a minidress!*

Steph also sneaks a glance in a mirror. She stumbles the Chant, and steadies her eyes upon naked Molly's hands as they move from her mams to her matt. Steph catches up with her in the Chant.

Steph calculates, *Bikini Babs wears my undershirt now! She took it from Molly somehow.* She glances again; this time she scans the mirror with rotating eyeballs, careful not to catch BB's eyes. *More correctly, BB wears my minidress, like what I wore before I traded it for the undershirt.*

Molly has slowed the Chant just enough so Steph can find brain cycles to evaluate the Garment exchanges. She considers her Roommate, sitting spread and facing her at the moment, and gauges Molly's reaction to Babs' minidress: *Molly is naked, but Molly must always be naked here in the Bathroom.*

Steph reads Molly's reaction. *Molly knows already. I don't really care how Bikini Bitch took my undershirt from Molly and exchanged it for a minidress. But assuming she did, it shows that Babs was too weak to take it from me directly!*

Steph and Babs trade eyes, and Molly and Steph continue to chant, pinch their nipples, diddle their clits, finger dip, and taste themselves.

Babs turns to Robyn. "Go fetch a pitcher and a glass. After you fill up the pitcher with water add three drops from the Alabaster Flask sitting on my Desktop, the return to this spot. Scoot."

Robyn scoots. She obeys exactly except that instead of adding three drops from the Alabaster Flask, Robyn doubles the recipe.

Steph uses her slower moving fingers to pump extra brain cycles and attempts to get her former Pledge into perspective. *Bikini Bimbo has caused me to be naked. She hates me for last Term. She won't be giving me anything back. She's gonna streak me.* Steph feels a draft of cold air pass over her body and goosebumps form on her naked skin. *Gonna streak me? BB's already streaked me. And she going to do it again.*

Masturbating in unison with another woman provides a new experience for Steph. Steph has certainly fucked guys before, but ever since Babs first climaxed her at the end of the Greatest House Roar, all of her self-arousal has been solo, no matter what Cosmos directed her excitation. That's changing today; today Steph shares masturbation.

But weak or not, and with Robyn out of the Bathroom, Boss Babe commands the naked pair of chanting Roommates sitting spread on the tile floor. "You solo today only in the sense you touch herself," BB addresses Steph, "but you lesbo in that you and your Roommate masturbate together. It pleases the Gamers you develop harmony of breath and muscle and mind. Synchronize and share Kundalini."

BB turns to Molly, "I promised you you'd get to climax with Steph, and you shall, but right now I want you to **Feel Steph and** take her back with you into the Zone. Softly, yet make her shake. You can shake too. Make her desire you! You can drip cream but you can't climax!"

Molly leads their arousal. *We can get more physical later.* She incites Steph to passion with her deep breathing, then with her smell. Steph attacks her own clit, freshens, and suddenly desires a clithood ring like Molly's. Molly plays with her nipples, Steph follows, and carefully Molly helps Steph find herself and stir Kundalini.

Molly holds Steph at the cusp of climax, touches her face to slow her rubbing herself and losing breath, steadies her on trying to cum. Steph surrenders into her convulsions easier than she—or any of the Cosmos— thought possible. Kundalini tightens its coils. Molly affords herself a wry smile and concentrates on her training responsibilities.

Robyn returns with the pitcher full of water and her loose lips make Molly's encapsulation of Steph more difficult. Robyn leans in, cackles, and demeans Steph, "Look at you! You're a wanton Whore, that's what you are! You just want a cock inside you! Any cock!"

Steph rubs herself harder and surrenders to the temptation, "Fuck me, I wanna fuck cock." Steph begins repeating; but Boss Babe interjects and breaks Steph's spell.

"You insult your Roommate!" Boss Babe reprimands playfully. "Begging for cock? You should be begging to eat out your Roommate's muliebre. Begging to climax with her on the Double Dong."

And Steph moans.

Babs instructs Robyn, "Pour them a glass of water to drink."

Boss Babe turns her attention to Steph while Molly drinks, "You're always selfish, always thinking of yourself first. 'I wanna fuck cock.' Is that how you talk to your Monitor?"

"Ma'am, no, Ma'am," Steph gasps as Robyn pours her a glass of water to drink. Steph confesses, "I am loosing self-control, Ma'am. My words and thoughts flow out of me carelessly." Robyn pours Molly a second glass; Molly wants to stop drinking, but knows that BB, or Robyn, or somebody, won't let that happen.

Steph doesn't consider the implications of drinking her second glass while Babs provides clarity to her, "First you must successfully Opt Strip. *Then* you can beg to Opt Whore. But until then, no cock for you! You understand me?"

Steph does, "Ma'am, yes indeed, Ma'am."

"Chant," Boss Babe commands, "Both of you."

This time Steph initiates the beg, "Ma'am, please let me Pledge naked and cum be a Stripper next Term." And touches herself. "Titty titty, clitty clitty, hole mouth."

Molly interprets Babs' eyes and sets the pace. It takes but for a few cycles for Molly to put Steph back into the near Zone and cleanse her mind from thinking too much.

Correction: from thinking at all.

§ Molly & Steph: Piss Release Climax

Gamers admire Molly's experience in guiding Steph, the former Cosmos Monitor, to shed inhibitions, gradually lose self-discipline, and masturbate in sync with her. Gamers appreciate how Molly convinces Steph to follow her pace whether Molly chants or freestyles. Hearing Molly's panting and noise, being forced to watch Molly's finger her wetness, smell her, and feel her feet against her own, all of these things drive Steph deeper into surrendering to her own sexual cravings.

Suddenly Steph looks directly into Molly's eyes and the Roommates begin cumming together. This caterwauls Steph, she howls, and accelerates into a vibrating high-frequency panting climax.

Ever-full bladders and a double dose of Alabaster Flask magic drive both Roommates, but it is Steph who uncontrollably voids first, arching a stream of yellow urine up and across Molly's hirsute torso and face. Molly takes it; still, the influence of splashing pee overwhelms her, and she voids as well, launching her own urine outward and all over Steph. Steph falters but Molly syncs her immediately, so that the naked Roommates may continue their climax together. Molly catches Babs' eye and permission, and abandons herself and her Roommate and both build to a prolonged climax, one that lasts until they both need to slow down their breathing.

§ Tiffany & Molly: Volunteer Clean Molly & Steph Piss Up

Molly again connects with Babs' eyes and Babs grants her permission to play with Pledge Steph Sorostitute. Molly folds her knees together and tucks her heels against her rear mounds of flesh, and shifts her position so she sits facing Steph, with her legs brushed to her side. As Steph comes down, Molly wraps her arms around her Roommate, hugs and kisses her, and receives a kiss back.

Steph tastes urine on Molly's face. She recoils, Molly kisses her neck, and when Molly looks up Robyn signs her to hickey Steph's neck.

Molly startles. The sign is complex, *one for sure Babs doesn't know*! Molly double-takes, and obeys. As she places a hickey on Steph's neck the sucking and pain snaps Steph's head back down; Molly lets go of the suckered spot and reconnects with Steph's lips. She pushes forward while opening them, and reaches with her tongue.

Steph releases another squirt of pee, this one all in between her bare legs. Steph looks to see if the Cam got her. It did.

Steph is not alone in smelling fresh pee on Molly's body, Molly can also smell her own fresh pee all over Steph's body—in Steph's hair, on her face, dripping from her perky standouts, pooling in her belly button.

Molly accepts, *No matter, there is pee all over the Bathroom, all over both of us.*

Steph sees that control does matter. *It doesn't matter that Molly looses control of her pee because Molly's already a Pee-Camer. That's why she uses the Bathroom naked.* Steph's body convulses in series of aftershocks. *But it matters for me because I'm naked all the time. And I just peed on Cam.*

Steph braces herself. *Except it doesn't matter because this is a trick. Okay, both of us had full bladders, but when Molly lost control I had to follow. But none of this counts, because BB spiked the water and told Molly to make sure I piss-climaxed.*

Steph finds herself drawn deeper in to Molly's kiss. She squeezes slippery and recoils. *Tiffany, Kimju, and Molly are all Pee-Camers, but they are all former Whores or Strippers, whereas I was a Monitor who should be a MomCap who got cheated out of my Caste!*

Molly doesn't read minds; she reads emotions. She guides Steph's hands down in between her own open legs while she graces her own hand down Steph's belly and draws her away from her thoughts to her body. It doesn't take much: Steph parts her thighs and seeps.

Steph breathes Molly's touch into her consciousness and accepts Molly's lovemaking. Once again, Molly stabilizes Steph on a "high base line" of arousal, spigots erected, stamen distended, squeezebox pumping a slow but steady thick sop.

Molly relaxes her throttle just enough to enable Steph to diddle her own. Molly considers, *It was Steph who turned me into a Piss Mouth. She didn't need to, but if whenever it's easy for her to step on somebody, she will.*

And while wearing heels, if she has them.

Molly twists fingers inside Steph's vagina and explores it completely. Steph's rhythmic constrictions crush the two or three fingers inside her sexcupidity. She opens her mouth and moans like an animal in a sexual surrender. Her scent overpowers the Bathroom and Molly again takes her into a vibrating, steady climax.

Elle considers, *should I log Steph as the forth Pee-Camer in the Manifest?* She startles, conscious after a long embrace with Beka, runs her hands down Beka's hips, and feels the pockets hanging there. *Manifest still hiding out!* Elle controls; she slides her hands upward, runs them upward to Beka's waistline, and gently rocks the seam upward. Beka moans.

Monitor Babs surveys the tile floor and cringes. She takes a step and understands *I have just stepped in pee.* She looks down. *I have pee splattered on top of my foot.* She looks up and around her, only Robyn, standing nearby, also has pee on her foot. BB produces a wry smile and a slight shoulder tilt. *I am not the only Cosmos to have gotten her feet wet.* She reverts to an old habit and seeks to insert her thumbs into her waistband. *Minidress in the way!*

Tiffany rescues her Monitor. "Ma'am, please allow me to clean your feet up."

Babs considers this offer, looks at the perpetrators, Molly and Steph. Steph is lost in the Zone, Molly hesitantly volunteers, "Ma'am, please let me help with the foot cleaning. And I'll clean up the floor. I'm a Piss Mouth too, Madam, and I'll take it with me to the Nugget next Term."

"Very well, you shall both demonstrate your Obeisance immediately," Boss Babe permits. "You're free to use the Watering Can and mop up the floor with your hair. And then shower."

"But be sure you lick up all the tight spots," Robyn injects, "and don't forget you're taking Piss Mouths to the Nugget."

Tiffany and Molly kneel to the task, appreciative they may soak their long hair in order to reduce their oral intake.

Beka and Elle press together in the shower stall and make out. If for a while Elle allows herself to possess her Roommate with affection, the effect only rouses Beka to maul Elle's nuggies, finger her notch, taste her, and let Elle taste herself. Elle continues to be drawn into the kiss, and when Beka takes her hands and places them on her breasts, Elle cups both Beka boobies in her palms.

And feels Beka's nipples grow.

And Steph shall be dealt with.

§ Steph: Fourth Cosmos to Beg Pee-Cam

Steph feels Robyn's bare foot lift her chin, so she looks up into her eyes. All Robyn needs to do is raise an eyebrow.

Steph glances at Babs and sees firmness, chin ever so slightly upraised. She returns her eyes to Robyn, and begs carefully.

"Ma'am, please let me Pledge naked and cum be a Stripper next Term. I'll stay naked and spread, keep pink-wet-and-ready, and cum anytime anywhere in front of anybody." Steph pauses and realizes that the smell of urine comes from Babs' foot.

Robyn rolls her shoulders. "You said at the Greatest House Roar that you'd match Molly every which way."

"Monitor Babs forced us to pee," Steph argues, "She spiked the water." Steph hears the sound of Tiffany and Molly mopping the floor with their hair. She smells pee on herself, on Robyn's foot, and doesn't want to distinguish the difference.

Boss Babe interjects. "You are correct, the Alabaster Flask contains diuretic, but you are not correct that I forced you to do anything."

Robyn hustles, "Listen Steph Sorostitute, answer my question, aren't you the one who begged to match Molly at the end of the Greatest House Roar?"

Steph knows. "Ma'am, please, Ma'am," she begs.

Robyn advances, "So tell me, you slippery strettococki, what did Molly achieve tonight?

Steph knows. "Molly piss climaxed, Ma'am."

"And what did you achieve?" Robyn queries.

Steph knows, "I piss climaxed too, Ma'am."

Robyn nods. "Thank me for making you."

Steph does, "Robyn, thank you Ma'am, for making me Pee-Cam."

The sounds of Tiffany and Molly licking the floor echo in the Bathroom until Boss Babe firms. "So, Steph, you can ask Tiffany or Kimju or Molly about how to use the Measuring Cup and commence Logging your feed from now on."

"Ma'am, thank you, Ma'am." Steph mindlessly retorts, dazed by today's loss of control. *I've been publically climaxed, climaxing so out of control I lost my identity. I've been turned into a spasming neural network controlled by Kundalini. I'm being Zoned. Well, maybe not at this instant, but that's really what I want to do most of all now.*

The part of Steph that can reason believes *I am being engulfed in a conspiracy. The Game is rigged against me!*

Steph suddenly finds Robyn in front of her face, "Hey Steph, everyone's heard you say you'd match Molly. Well it doesn't stop with the Pee-Cam. Does it, you stack of slithering stuff? Because you know what comes next, don't you Pledge?"

Steph does. *Piss Mouth.* And Robyn rubs a foot against Steph's clenched mouth, but doesn't allow her time to beg.

"Guess what, you sinusoidal snapdragon," Robyn snaps a shoulder strap, "Molly has already gotten to eat pussy and taken a ride on the Double Dong.... with her ex-Roommate Kimju. Maybe the time has come for Molly to take another ride on the Double Dong... only this time with her current Roommate! You!"

A sudden rush of fear surges through Steph's body and she turns to beg directly to Babs, "Ma'am, let me Audition for the Nugget with Molly, Ma'am. I'll dance naked. I'll pink and cream on Stage."

Robyn interjects, "You'll climax the Dong with her."

"Ma'am, please, Ma'am," Steph pleads, not sure for what.

Boss Babe gentles Steph with kindness. "You'll ride the Dong with whomever and climax it if you beg hard enough." BB twinkles. "But you'd better take every opportunity to ride the Double Dong now, because you aren't allowed to share it once you start Stripping next Term!"

Steph takes in short breaths of air and controls panic. She stews. *First Robyn cheats on me. Then since yesterday Babs, Robyn, Kimju, and Tiffany all climax me. This afternoon I'm forced to piss climax with Molly. Somebody threatened to give me to the newbies, Beka and Elle, to practice upon. That's beneath me.*

Robyn speaks from above. "Do you know whose pee that is on my foot? Yours or Molly's?"

Steph again urinates... and appears to be unable to wrest control of the stream until the very end.

Robyn laughs, "Well, I guess you know whose pee that is. Before I'm done with you you'll be begging to suck pee out of a used tampon!"

Again Steph looks to Babs for hope. But Babs ignores her, signals Tiffany to follow her back to the Bedroom, and leaves the Bathroom and cleanup behind.

§ Babs & Tiffany: Harder Times Still Ahead for Steph

Babs and Tiffany retreat to BB's small Bedroom. Babs sits behind the Desktop; Tiffany, still naked, prostrates herself on the floor and begs, "Ma'am, please let me lick your feet clean. Like I did Robyn."

BB accepts Tiffany's subservience. *It matters not that before Robyn's feet were only dirty from earth and grime, whereas now my feet are splattered with pee. And after all, isn't Tiffany already a Piss Mouth?*

Tiffany is. She begins with a kiss and takes Boss Babe's big toe into her mouth. *Got to start somewhere. She licks clean the topside, also the bottom. Tiffany cleans in between every toe and utilizes her teeth and fingernails to scrape under every nail.*

Tiffany must rise to her knees to fetch the Makeup Case, with its tools to trim and file the nails, then polish and paint.

Tiffany offers Babs an assessment while she performs her oral duties. "More and more, Steph craves her legs apart, craves masturbating herself. Pink-wet-and-ready keeps her into the Zone.

"I know the type," Tiffany continues, "Steph might believe she's privileged, but she's becoming so horny she can't think, and will soon beg anything just to keep her snapper slippery. Cocks, dildos, and certainly one end of the Double Dong."

Tiffany curls her tongue between a big toe and its neighbor. "And whenever you do let her climax," she adds, "whether you do it yourself or via Robyn, if you don't run her out of breath, you can keep her climaxing on and on. Minutes certainly, maybe zoned for hours."

"The Zone is Steph's best reward," Babs says. She grits her teeth. Memories of Steph, *e.g. making me mudwrestle last Term*, linger in BB's cortex.

Boss Babe offers the bottom of her other foot to Tiffany's licks and kisses. "I have to be careful with Steph," she says. "I detect that her resistance has crumpled to a point where hazing her just a little bit excites her, and hazing her more puts her into bliss. Not just puts her into a state of perpetual uncontrolled excitement, but lets her abandon all self, all mind, body, and soul."

"You need to be professional about how you handle her," Tiffany advises. "Letting Robyn have her ways with her isn't pretty."

"May the both of them descend to Slavesex," BB proclaims. "Steph deserves all the pain she gets and I'll be dammed if the slut likes it too much."

Tiffany shrugs, "Ouch! I guess Steph wasn't my nemesis last Term. I never met her before Pledging here. But, trust me, the more you let me twist her the more she will cream."

Tiffany addresses Babs' toenails. "Listen, I'm not supposed to care if you make Steph a Stripper next Term or not," Tiffany advances, "except that I do care, because, as you know, I need to get to the Nugget for sure. I only need to get rid of one piece. You know I'll do whatever you require. I'll pee in my own mouth. I'll shave bare and bald for you, Ma'am! I'll let you expand my tattoos and Eraser Heads. Whatever you want."

Babs frowns, her thoughts instead attuned to what is next—not for Tiffany—but for her former Monitor, Steph. BB checks her Desktop, validates that Steph continues to chant in the Bathroom, and rants to Tiffany. "I like it that Steph's hair has been bleached out, and that she's been promised hair dye." Babs collects her thoughts. "I'm fine with it that the Gamers want to keep her pink, wet, and zoned. I desire to opt her as far away as possible, and create as many degrees of Caste separation as I can. Believe me, after how she treated Janet and me, she's the one who should be shaving bare and bald. And she's already naked."

Tiffany finishes Babs' feet and slides into her compartment and out of Babs' sight. She pauses for a moment to rotate her Eraser Heads, wetten her tadpole, and makes a suggestion. "Ma'am, if you let me take Steph to the Nugget and the Dong is there, I'll ride her into the Zone center Stage and keep her like that as long as the Crowd wants. I promise."

BB emphasizes, "What would please me the most is for you to not just Zone Steph, but also mind-fuck the Sorostitute."

Tiffany blinks, "Ma'am, thank you, Ma'am. I'll keep doing my best to condition her to *want* the Strip. I will wring her out at a Nugget Audition."

"I appreciate your worry she will get there and preclude you," BB teases. "You just can't help yourself from helping others."

"Ma'am, I know, Ma'am," Tiffany admits, "Besides, she also already naked."

"You just want an excuse to perform at the Nugget yourself. You don't fool me." Babs laughs and holds ups both hands to stop any protest, "No problem, you shall take her to the Nugget and dance with her. Assuming there is anything left of her after she pays a visit to Janet."

"Ma'am, thank you, Ma'am," Tiffany replies, "I'll climax and piss her center Stage. We both will." Tiffany bubbles, "You know I'll suckle your blats, bury my mouth inside your barndoors, and wash your backeye with my tongue."

BB considers and nods. "Your commitments are duly noted," she says.

Tiffany digs a finger deep into her trough, collects tapioca out, and wipes it under her nostrils, and twitches at the smell of herself.

II-19 Janet Haze Steph: Out of Body Experience (D22)

§ Babs Orders Steph: Go Visit Janet at Corvette House

Babs returns to the Bathroom, still wearing her minidress over her bikini, with a naked Tiffany trailing behind. Overseer Robyn has placed Kimju and Molly in a standing position so they face each other and embrace each other with their arms around their companion's back. Robyn has commanded that they rub bellies and boobs, kiss and make out, and the two ex-Strippers have given themselves to Kundalini.

Babs assesses this situation, signals Robyn to quiet, and signs Tiffany "attention." Kimju and Molly remain oblivious to Babs and Tiffany's appearance.

The Watering Can sits directly beneath the two naked crotches and between their jointly spread legs. The kissing, straddling Pledge shall embrace the Watering Can. The making out and body rubbing arouses Molly; she hangs streamers of muscovado that drip. Kimju controls her arousal upon sensing wetness inside her kinky; she evaluates her bladder. *I have already counted Cups today,* and worries, *what will happen if Robyn orders Molly and I void while we are hugging together?*

I know what we'll do. Kimju knows. *I'll add any fresh pee I have into the Watering Can. And so will Molly.*

Beka and Elle are to be found in the bathtub, intertwined and also making out. There is no water in the tub; Elle's thigh can't avoid Beka's grinding pelvis, and her crotch is unable to avoid Beka's grinding knee. Beka leads with her kisses, fondles Elle's nipples, and attempts to bring her to cream.

Steph remains seating spread on the floor, with her fingers touching herself in synchronization with a quiet chanting, "Please let me Pledge naked and cum be a Stripper next Term. Titty titty, clitty clitty, hole mouth."

Reverie ends. Boss Babe joists Steph aware with a polite foot kick. "Silence. On your feet, Pledge. Report to Janet at the Corvette House. Ring the front doorbell. Do whatever she says."

The Cam watches Steph slowly get onto her feet. *Janet? I heard rumors about a trade for Ginny but really? Janet!* A trickle of pee runs down Steph's inner thigh toward her ankle. *No control over my pee anymore. Bad enough Robyn brags about doubling the drops from the Alabaster Flask. Now I have to confront my former Pledge, Janet? Who I promoted to the Monitor Caste, which she enjoys today!*

Steph shuffles her feet in a puddle of pee on the floor. *Fresh pee, my pee.* She plays dodge ball. "Ma'am, please, Ma'am," Steph gurgles, "Janet was my Pledge last Term."

"Outstanding!" Boss Babe accepts. "I was also your Pledge last Term, Janet's Roommate in fact. Are you becoming forgetful, like Robyn?"

"Ma'am, no, Ma'am!" Steph shuffles her feet and asks a question, "But how am I supposed to get to the Corvette House?" She considers. "I have nothing to wear."

"Your Roommate Molly," BB bounces, "has always gone naked outside. So if it's good enough for her to streak around it's good enough for you too! You're the one who begged to match your Roommate."

"Ma'am, I don't need to match my Roommate, Ma'am," Steph retorts.

"You're already a streaker," Robyn interjects, "you streaked back here after losing the Greatest House Roar at the Peacock House. You pinked the Back Door Cam to beg consideration for entry. You're just too stupid to realize you're gonna stay naked 24x7. And pink-wet-and-ready most of your waking hours. Especially from now on, you slithering stretta swaggart. You made Janet streak last Term. Now it's your turn."

Steph attempts another oral foray and appeals to Monitor Babs. "Ma'am, what if I get stopped, Ma'am? You just never know who's out there. I'm sure you don't want to lose me. Ma'am."

"Of course not" Boss Babe laughs. "So don't make a wrong turn and end up streaking into the arms of a Jailer. Rest assured you're not worth paying ransom for. You're lucky Janet *wants* you to get to the Corvette House."

"You're trading me for Ginny, aren't you?" Steph stabs. "Minute-for-minute, her for me. She's coming here, isn't she?"

Boss Babe has the power; she smiles. "So many questions and such informality from a Pledge to her Monitor! Remind me to let you taste drops from the Alabaster Flask the next time you speak to me, Pledge Steph Sorostitute."

Robyn butts in. "Listen to me you stinking skeeze skank. "Maybe BB doesn't want to tell you, but I will. Your trade with Ginny is not minute-for-minute thing; it's hour-for-hour or maybe even day-by-day.

Boss Babe tucks a bra strap under the neckline of the elastic minidress. No bling and much reduced cleavage. She considers trumping Robyn but decides to watch some more.

Robyn forges on billowing Steph. "And here's something else for you to know, now that you've become Gamer swag: You might think you're valuable, but you know, you're a fallen Monitor vs. Ginny, who's a Whore-for-Life. Minute-for-minute hardly seems fair and balanced."

Now Babs interrupts and addresses Steph. "Unfortunately the rest of us Cosmos, including me, don't get to handle Ginny. Ginny will not be stopping at our Cosmos House, she shall proceed directly to the Nugget, and report to House Mom el Capitan."

"MomCap," Steph confirms and smarms Babs directly, "MomCap takes Ginny for herself and she doesn't even let you have her, whereas Janet gets a bite out of me. You think you're getting a fair deal?"

"I don't make deals," Boss Babe ices, "but I do participate in them."

"Ginny's gonna turn tricks in the Champagne Room and shoot Gangbang *Videos* in the Inner Sanctuary," Robyn thrusts her chin at Steph. "And you're gonna worship Janet, you stinking shag socket!"

Robyn advances, "Listen Steph Sorostitute, don't forget to beg Janet to take *you* to the Nugget so *you* can watch Ginny 'learn' you a thing or two about Whoring." Robyn cackles. "I hear it's not your first trip to the Nugget and it won't be your last. Ha ha ha!"

Steph looks at Monitor Babs and BB imposes quieter demands, "You shall chant and masturbate while you streak—hands behind your head while chanting, then "titty titty,' pick your nipples, 'clitty clitty" and finger fuck your 'hole,' and taste yourself in your 'mouth. Don't stop."

Steph carefully draws her hands behind her head into surrender position, waits almost too long, and commences to recite, "Please let me Pledge naked...." She wisely scrambles out the Bathroom, down the stairs, and out the Back Door.

She pauses to give the Back Door Cam a full recital, nipples, pink, cream, and tasting, and heads in an unexpected direction.

§ Steph: Streaks to Corvette House while Masturbating to Chant

Steph feels outside air on her full naked body as she steps down to the ground, and a sparkle makes her hickey flush. She rings the Bell, and takes the alley out. The race is on.

It's dusk outside.

Steph double checks that she still chants and masturbates. *I taste myself, smell my splurt on my upper lips. I have to balance getting horny with getting to the Corvette House. My body is fully exposed; I'm being shown off.* XE "Steph: Chants: must chant while streaking (Cosmos to Corvette House D22)"

Steph pauses a moment to consider her position and never sees a paparazzo collect a full-frontal: erect nipples and sugar bush. *Should I worry that opportunities to Opt Up are slipping further and further from my grasp?* Steph pauses underneath a tree to take her bearings. *No. I need to worry about getting caught. I need to bathe.*

Steph spots a paparazzo and dashes into motion again. *I'm streaking now!* Correct. *Yesterday shouldn't count because I was coming back to the Cosmos House from the Greatest House Roar. But this is my first time going out from the Cosmos House. The Game is getting dangerous now.*

Steph approaches a corner, sees a car with headlights go by, and crosses the street. *Nor is this going to be my last streak. I'm a streaker from now on. Boss Bitch is going to parade me naked in the Mermaid Parade. When we get to the Beach Day, BB will make sure I'll be the only naked one, so that I really stand out.*

Steph spots another paparazzi collect her pinking and finger dip bars of the Chant. *They've been tipped off to keep me honest; to make sure I keep stroking myself.* Relief surges; Steph still performs the Chant, but much slower now as she gains confidence. *I am not going to get captured because being exhibited! I'm too important!*

No, Steph is too important to Janet.

Steph's Chant requires semi-attention to maintain, and she discovers a rhythm between reciting the Chant and walking, speeding up or slowing down as necessary. Fox Trot. Kundalini adds a constriction to Steph's rhythm, a squeeze of the sex organ and a pumping of sauce that synchronizes with that beat in the Chant when Steph's fingers collect surge from her socket.

Steph spots another paparazzi, this one is definitely a woman who stalks with video Cam movements; This adds to Steph's arousal from her public nudity. *Right, Molly might have streaked, but she never streaked and chanted at the same time. I'm better than she is.*

The repetition of touching the back of her head, nipples, clit, vaginal insides, and mouth flood fresh surge onto Steph's fingertips. Sop that had dried behind her neck, been dabbed on and around her erected nipples and clit, and around her mouth, now gets a fresh applique. When she wipes a finger thick with cream above her upper lips the action is neither thoughtful nor aware. It does fill her nostrils with a strong whiff of herself, and arouses her to maintain, if not increase, her sex secretions.

Steph's body vibrates. *I want to climax very badly. But if I let go out here I will make a lot of noise and I will get captured. I need to wait until I get to Janet before I can let go and climax.*

Steph slows down as she approaches the Corvette House. *I am on public display. I am the Star.* She arrives at the Corvette House Front Door with measured breath, bruised feet, and a humming pussy. She allows the Corvette House Front Door Cam to canvas her naked body. *Canvas my Chant. Canvas me pinking, then gathering and smearing my splurt all over myself.* She leans forward and uses her nose to push a doorbell button. *Janet is inside the Door. She needs to treat me like a Goddess.*

Steph waits. The fact Steph repeats the Chant—again and again— grinds on her. *Maybe I don't need to Opt Up anymore. I just need in the Door.* She looks at the Front Door and continues her naked performance.

"Please let me Pledge naked and cum be a Stripper next Term. Titty titty, clitty clitty, hole mouth!"

§ Janet Enables Steph: To Masturbate Herself Out of Her Body

Janet opens the Front Door and stands in the frame. She no longer wears the Spiderweb Bikini; she wears what was once Louise's t-front maillot with a bandeau underneath. The bandeau is wide and stretchy and provides coverage, but zero support of what the Manifest reports as 40EEs. The maillot covers her jute patch and jaxy, but hardly hides the fat that's everywhere. The t-front rises up atop the bandeau and between her jaboos, and encircles her neck. It helps the bandeau stabelize Janet's jumboblats.

Steph further slows down her Chant as she feels the eyes of her former Monitor canvas her spread legs, moving arms, and slick spots. "Please let me Pledge naked and cum be a Stripper next Term," Steph begs, now drawing her fingers forward and down, "Titty titty, clitty clitty, hole mouth," as she dabbles her spouts, pinks and scoops cream, and tastes herself.

"Turn around and face outward," Janet commands, and Steph obeys.

Steph pauses with a big sinking feeling as she considers her former Pledge. *Janet hates me because last Term I reduced her to her crochet Spiderweb halter and g-string. That made her jugs and jaxy jingle jangle! And she loved it.*

Steph surveys the space that she faces out into: *Two paces ahead are the steps down the front stairs.* Steph quakes as she realizes *the Front Door Cam feeds my Chant to the Prefecture.* Beyond the Cam, beyond the sidewalk that passes by the front lawn, Steph spots a parked car. She sees the glint of reflections in the windows of houses across the street, and she imagines paparazzi collecting her also.

But no matter how exposed to the public, it is Janet's presence behind her that Steph fears most. *Last Term I let Janet masturbate to explicit pictures of herself that had been ejaculated upon. I let her streak. I let her sit in the Cravat. I even let her climax the Double Dong at her Alumni Reprise.*

Steph looks at Janet's feet. *And you so deserved it. You wanted it even!*

Janet should be grateful to me but right now I am helpless before her. First she watches Bimbo Bitch force-cum me at the Greatest House Roar, and then sees the feed of the Pledge zoning me. Now Janet wants to play with me herself, and make me some of her Corvette House feed.

Steph cocks her head. *Except Janet is different.*

Janet Jintoe smiles.

Steph teeters on climax, scans the yard with her eyes, turns herself around to face Janet, and manages to speak. "Ma'am, I shouldn't be here. I belong to Bikini Babe." She emits a series of short breaths, a very soft "huh huh huh huh huh." Yes, five of them, like a quiet and slowed trill.

Janet holds open the door and signs the naked, pinking, masturbating, creaming Steph to step inside. She holds the door open for the Cam also, so it may follow Steph in.

Janet halts Steph inside the Front Door, and Steph realizes that the Corvette House layout mimics the Cosmos House. *I'm in the Parlor now.* Steph resists an urge to masturbate harder, holds a steady breathing, awaits. *Is it safer now that I'm inside? Or more dangerous because I'm beholden to Janet?*

Janet leans forward a fraction of an inch and speaks. "You know Babs wouldn't share you with me right off. I've been forced to go to extremes to obtain your visit."

Steph doesn't stop chanting. Cream adorns her fingertips, the back of her neck, her nipples and breasts, and her clit and vaginal area.

Janet straightens. "You've had it easy up until now. Now you're about to cum out of your body!"

Steph should feel pretty blessed, but has no idea what this really means. *No, I have not had it easy.*

A large Screen hovers not quite directly in front of her and on it Steph watches a collage from her past, denial shows in her face as she watches herself titter and upskirt. Watches William push a long stainless probe into her raised sewer, watches herself pink and hang stalactites, and for the second time watches herself cum at the Greatest House Roar. Now Steph chants and watch her multiple climaxes from last night and earlier today. *Cumming with myself on the Dining Room Screen, cumming in the Backyard for Kimju and Robyn and Tiffany, cumming and losing control of my urine with Molly in the Bathroom.*

Janet points to a dirty rug in the center of the Parlor. "Stop chanting. Lie on your side, keep one keen up in the air so you can keep yourself spread, and keep yourself pink-wet-and-ready to cum."

Steph obeys.

Janet steps forward and pours oil onto her reclining body. "Slather yourself, Pledge, masturbate harder. Janet drenches her hair and her body, and Steph mixes the oil with her own sop. The oil feels warm and extremely sensitive to her touch, *as if the oil has intelligence.*

Steph gathers confidence. *I've masturbated watching myself in a mirror, I've masturbated in sync with myself on a video screen, and I've masturbated in sync with Molly—both on a screen and for real.*

Time for gears to shift.

Janet joins the fingers of both hands together in front of her, as in an attitude of prayer and smiles. "Your humiliations are about to exceed your expectations," she announces.

A life-size image rises out of blackness on the hovering Screen and Steph discovers she is watching a live feed of herself taken by the Cam, now hovering behind and above her.

Now, as Steph continues to arouse herself, and, horny beyond belief, a strange thing occurs: For she seems to rise up out of her body and become the mind of the voyeur who watches over her shoulder! *Here I am up here floating and calm, observing a wanton naked woman pleasure herself.* This act of voyeurism, intimate voyeurism, overpowers Steph and she teeters, gasps, and the masturbator being watched and the voyeur watching begin climaxing together. They will stay locked together in a state of licentious, transcendental abandonment. Zoned.

At some juncture there exists a fleeting moment and Steph—whoever, wherever she is—wonders, *Will I be able to get back into my body again?* But Kundalini surges forth, and any last vestiges of whole self are forgotten as the split personalities continue to masturbate together into oblivion, bliss, and eventually exhaustion and sleep.

II-20 Babs Tells Tiffany & Elle: Swap Slacks & Skirt (D23)

§ Robyn Lines Up Five Cosmos Pledge: Reveille facing Minxy

Babs assigns Robyn to Lineup Five Cosmos Pledge for Reveille in the Bunkroom on the morning of Day Twenty-three.

Robyn forms Tiffany, Kimju, Molly, Beka, and Elle into standing spread surrender positions facing the Minxy Mirror and looking at what appears to be their reflections. Robyn continues to wear her spaghetti shoulder-strapped maillot cutout with the smallest buttonhole. Navelage 24x7.

Robyn walks between the Lineup and the Mirror and the Minxy plays a trompe l'oeil on the Pledge: it reflects their Lineup, but not Robyn.

Several Pledge reconsider. *Maybe Robyn really does have Charm?*

Babs remains in her Bedroom. She either wears a minidress over her Black Bikini or is nude in her private shower. Steph is nowhere around, last seen streaking toward Janet's Corvette House.

Babs had demanded that Tiffany dress before leaving the Bedroom: one transparent clear vinyl longsleeve front-button croptop, and one low-rise, skin-tight slacks. Eraser Heads rub against the inside of her croptop, ribs below, hairage and rugage above the waistline, and cameltoe spotted from tapioca stains.

Kimju remains topless and g-stringed. She balances herself easily with spread legs, and the two square inches of the micro hide somewhere below where her keystone gets rolled out, with butched kale lying to both sides. Maybe Kimju does want to Opt Up next Term, but it's also a fact that her g-string stays crosty.

Molly, grateful to be topless and wearing only one Garment again, displays underarm hair, hair on her arms, hair between her mams, hair growing out of her areola, hair down her belly and back, hair erupting above her transparent low-rise panties, hair seen through the panties and pressed flat, hair growing down into her exposed moonshadow, hair thick inside her thighs, and hair all the way down her legs, right down to the top of her toes. Molly is hirsute, fat, and smiling right now.

The Five Pledge have left a gap in the Lineup where Steph would appear. Robyn tightens up the gap.

Beka presents herself with her halter neck strap unbuttoned, boobage begging topless, and with her jeans shorts increasingly reduced to a waistband, a crotch seam, and pockets. Beka can't avoid flashing her racing stripe, and besides this hairage she also presents a coat of crost on the seam and around the insides of her thighs.

Elle stretches and titters the cut-down croptop. Normally the miniskirt barely hangs on the crest of her ilium and is prone to hairage the waistline, although now, standing as she does with her hands behind her head and her feet spaced wide, the hemline rides up her thighs just enough to clear her crotch.

Elle knows. *I'm a tittering, upskirting, vagflashing Pledge now. But at least I still have two Garments. Except Gamers are going to insist that I pink, probe, and pee before I get to keep them.*

Or before they are taken away.

§ Babs Orders Tiffany & Elle: Swap Slacks & Miniskirt

Babs enters the Bunkroom. A scoop-neck minidress overtop her Black Bikini graces her curves. "At ease," she commands and the Cosmos lower their arms, and gather their legs closer together, although apart enough so that no thighs touch. Robyn stands to the side, cocks a foot.

Boss Babe points at Tiffany's slacks. "Gimme," she says, and Tiffany wiggles them downward, extracts ankles and feet, makes sure the Garment has not been turned inside-out, and hands it to Monitor Babs. Tiffany Transparent looks at herself in the Mirror. *Transparent croptop bottomless. Too bad I'm not on a Cam right now.*

Boss Babe points to Elle's miniskirt. "Gimme," she says, and in a moment Elle steps out and hands them to her. Elle stands awkwardly. *Hacked croptop bottomless.*

BB hands Elle Tiffany's slacks.

BB hands Tiffany Elle's miniskirt.

The miniskirt is just like Elle was wearing, only it becomes a transparent clear vinyl miniskirt, tailored to Tiffany's body. Does the Game condone slight of hand?

Elle continues to hold the slacks in her hand. *By exchanging our Garments Monitor Babs creates new possibilities in the Game. She also took Molly's undershirt and transmogrified it into the minidress she now wears.*

And she just Flip-Flopped Tiffany and me. So does that mean...?

Boss Babe advises the still bottomless Elle, "Put your next Garment on, Pledge."

Elle follows her directions and dons what used to be Tiffany's slacks. *I'm a croptop reduced and low-rise stretch slacks. Two Garments.*

And Tiffany follows, and dons what used to be Elle's miniskirt, which as become as transparent as her clear vinyl croptop. *Tiffany Transparent, that's me, except the Gamers are giving me away like I'm naked when I'm not. And I need to be. Two Garments is one Garment too many.*

Monitor Babs turns to Kimju and Molly. "This seems like an excellent opportunity for you two Pledge to perform your Pee-Cam duties."

Robyn takes a step backward and watches an opportunity close to use the Bathroom herself, without fear of intrusion. She can't resist a parting jab to the ex-Strippers, "Why don't you hold the Cup for each other and collect your pee in the Watering Can."

Kimju and Molly blanch but keep moving. They shed a g-string and panties at their bunks and scurry to the Bathroom naked.

Babs instructs Robyn, "Take Beka outside and let a Cam gather some solo pink and wet masturbation. But *no* cumming!"

Robyn assumes the challenge, "I'll make sure she finger fucks herself and eats her own brodeas. Beka Broda, she's gonna be a beat dancer before I'm done with her."

Robyn's eyes oscillate between Tiffany and Elle. "Sure you don't want me to take them too?" Robyn suggests to Babs.

"No." The answer is emphatic and is reinforced with a point toward the stairs.

Robyn rolls in her inner lips, positions herself in front of the casually standing Beka, with her halter untied and hanging down, and her jeans shorts reduced a waistband, pockets, and seam. Or as Elle would add to her secret manifest: boobage, hairage, buttage.
the she will be with her leaving behind with Babs, and the casually standing boobage Beka she is chartered to escort outside.

Robyn raises her chin as she gives an order to Beka. "Hands behind your head surrender position. Now walk ahead of me, down the stairs, keep your hands behind your head, don't fall."

Babs leaves Tiffany and Elle alone in the Bunkroom and returns to her Bedroom.

§ Tiffany & Elle: Swap Slacks & Miniskirt and Costume Count

Tiffany and Elle exchange words while they examine their new Garments in the Mirror. Elle perceives that her reflection in the Mirror....

She turns away, and confronts Tiffany. "This Garment exchange between us isn't a Roommate Game, because you and I aren't Roommates." Elle smoothes out her slacks; when she bends over she showcases an acre of back, but doesn't rugage. The sleeveless croptop with its armholes and scoop neckline ensures Elle titters when she bends over or lifts an arm.

"Okay. More Rules." Tiffany brushes fingers through her tussock and sweeps dried crost out of her trap. "Yes, the possibilities of Garment exchanges have just shifted gears. Yes, you and Beka have already played your Roommate Game: you Flip-Flopped. And Molly and Steph played a Winner-Takes-All: Molly won. Apparently Babs has decreed that she and I have played our Roommate Game too: no changes. She is the Boss Babe after all."

Elle concludes, "Okay, so everyone except Robyn and Kimju has play their Roommate Game." She explores. "Babs took from Molly and didn't give anything back, and then she ordered you and I to Flip-Flop. "Everyone else can now Game with everyone else. Roommates or not? Except Robyn and Kimju."

"Right." Tiffany runs a hand through her hair, rubs her clear vinyl top against her Eraser Heads, and sharpens understanding. "And if Robyn & Kimju game, I'm in a position where I can shed a piece to Kimju."

"Maybe Babs will make Robyn and Kimju fight for your discards," Elle ventures.

"Discard, singular," Tiffany corrects and breathes deeply. "Well, never forget, one of Babs' Rules is that she makes the Rules. She can give or take any Garment from any Pledge any time for any or no reason.

Elle changes the subject. "Steph hasn't returned. And Babs doesn't seem concerned about it."

Tiffany nods. "Which means you shouldn't be concerned about it either."

"Robyn says Janet is going to make Steph suck cocks together with Ginny in the Inner Sanctuary at the Nugget," Elle worries.

Tiffany cajoles Elle. "Maybe Janet will let Steph *watch* Ginny suck cock. Or watch her shoot *Suck Fuck Anal DP Facial Gangbang* scenes. But there is no way Steph will be allowed to participate, no matter how much she begs cock. MomCap and Madam Nurse know any transgression would ripple upward."

Tiffany speaks, "I know Janet. Janet is going to wind Steph up, spin her out of her body, climax her watching Ginny suck cock, and spin her back to us." Tiffany wettens a fingertip with her spit and uses it to wetten the tip of her trigger. "She'll stay naked and Strip next Term, and then finally, in the Term thereafter, Steph will become a Porn Star."

"She's ahead of you to the Nugget because she's already naked and you still have two Garments," Elle observes.

"Kimju and Molly are ahead of me too," Tiffany admits, each with their one Garment.

"And what about Robyn?" Elle asks. "She only has one Garment too."

"The way things stand right now," Tiffany admits, "Robyn is ahead of me too."

"But naked Steph is first in line." Elle seeks to affirm.

"Right." Tiffany freshens and wags a finger at Elle. "And the problem with that is that I'm the one who should get to play with Ginny, instead of Steph. I am the one who Ginny sucked cock with last Term! You've seen my *Suck Fuck Facial Videos* and my Porn Star Calendar!"

Elle has. Elle shakes her shoulders. "Okay, so you and Ginny are ex-Whores, Ginny's still a Whore-for-Life, yet you're forbidden to suck cocks." Elle tries to stand straight up enough to dodge titter. She explores. "Tiffany, you and I are both wearing two Garments and should Opt Up next Term. Ginny is naked 24x7 and will streak to the Nugget again. What does all this mean?"

Tiffany tilts her head. "First, a correction. It would be more polite of you to think of me as a temporarily displaced Porn Star, whereas Ginny is, and will always be, a Whore-For-Life. I am larger than life, she's not."

Tiffany surveys the newbie Pledge. "As for yourself, you might be wearing two Garments, but you are begging to Pledge naked and Strip next Term, are you not?"

"Except—" Elle begins.

Tiffany interrupts with a finger lift. "Please remember *I* begged to Pledge naked and cum be a Stripper before *you* ever arrived. I've Pledged, I've Stripped, I've Whored. And now I'm a Pledge again."

Tiffany glances around the Bunkroom. They are alone. She lowers her voice. "Listen Elle, I don't care if you Opt Strip or Opt Monitor next Term, provided you don't get ahead of me in line to the Nugget."

Elle recoils. "Trust me, Tiffany," she proclaims, "I would never do that. I don't want to dance at the Nugget. I don't even want to Pledge naked. Or pink, or cream, or climax."

Tiffany understands. "Your goal is to keep your clothes; mine is to lose them. We are Kundalini in balance."

Elle worries. "You know, Tiffany, we saw Penny and Coco's Dining Room Pictures and then their Videos, but when we saw them live at the Nugget I realized that it was all real. They really are clean shaven and they really do crave the Double Dong."

Tiffany twists her slender body. "Elle, think of Stripping like an entry position. You and your Roommate are great teasers: you've tittered, spread, and even pulled a little pink in the Camera Lounge."

Elle blinks. *I think I put pink out of mind, not in the Manifest.*

Tiffany catches her breath, but doesn't fray her enthusiasm, "Listen, pink-wet-and-ready should be easy for you, especially since you are already begging to Strip. But what you really need to do is beg dildos and buttplugs, even DP and strapons if the Gamers will let you. You should afford yourself this opportunity to eat Beka out and climax the Double Dong together!" Tiffany purses her lips and sees Elle start to quiver.

"I know, I know," Tiffany apologizes. "But trust me, the Nugget is about as far as you're gonna get next Term!"

Elle tugs her slacks upward but they do not come up as far as she desires. "I don't want to go the Nugget. I want to be a Monitor next Term!"

Tiffany waves her off. "Hear me on this, Elle: I will say to you that there is nothing better in life than being a Porn Star, and I welcome you to join me in that Caste. You're a darling, and in the event we are both lucky enough to Strip next Term I will teach you more Stripper moves than Kimju and Molly know together. I was a great Stripper before I became a Porn Star, and I will be a great Stripper and an even greater Porn Star again."

Elle takes a very deep breath and eyes her new configuration, both in her mirror and by looking down at her own body. She scans down her long expanse of bare belly, bare far below her navel, and narrowing between inguinal lines, below even the crest of the hipbone. Belly curving all the way down until her pelvis disappears into her new slacks. *More precisely these tight-fitting slacks grip me just above my slitage, and they unavoidably cameltoe.*

Tight slacks aren't the only problem. Elle grimaces. *And of course I hairage.* True. The slacks' waistline rides so low that there is no way Elle can avoid floating hairage above the elastic. Elle feels air on the top of her butt, reaches around, and traces the top of her waistline. *So low there is no way I can avoid cracking my ass and logging rugage. And so tight between my nachas that the seam tickles my nadir gate.*

Elle watches Tiffany stare at her erupting nappy and confesses, "Okay, now I'm showing hairage like you were."

Tiffany reacts to Elle's angst, "Hey kid, you're now just about the most-covered-up Cosmos. You've made a big advancement, except you're no longer get to show your nappy upskirt!"

True. Elle gives Tiffany a dazed look, and Tiffany expands her complements, admiring the low-riders erupting brunette hairage. "You're giving your fans something new to focus on!" Tiffany impresses. "After all, you've been tittering since Day One, you've spread your legs and vagflashed, and now you make Gamers desire to push your pants down."

Elle eyes the nappy overhanging her waistline. She draws her eyes upward to Tiffany's eyes and Tiffany furthers encouragement, "With pants on there is no way you can pull pink, but your hairage and rugage will drive your fans crazy."

Elle closes her eyes and shakes her head so softly as to be invisible. *Tiffany sees covering up as a vehicle to precede striptease, but as far as I'm concerned, whatever secrets I was revealing, I reveal less of them now. And that's a good thing.*

Okay.

And I don't want fans.

A new fear suddenly strikes Elle and she blurts a question to Tiffany without thinking. "Is Monitor Babs going to make me wear this outside?" Elle considers herself in the full-wall Mirror, takes stock of her appearance, and looks at Tiffany again. "I am barely able to maintain proper public decorum!"

Tiffany smiles, "Excuse me, but you are not really able to maintain proper decorum, inside or out. And nor should you! You're a Cosmos Pledge begging to Strip!"

Elle shakes her chest and considers what used to be Beka's croptop, reduced by Tiffany's scissors so that "titter just is." *The material cut away around the armholes allows sideboob, any leanover might as well be a topless downblouse, and the bottom of the croptop exposes so much of my ribcage, that when I stand spread surrender, I titter.*

Elle bites a lip, less certain, "But by exchanging with you—even BB doing it to us—doesn't change either of our costume counts. My legs and nook are now covered up, but I show more hairage. And I'm tittering my croptop."

"And I'm Tiffany Transparent!" Tiffany casts her hands down her clear vinyl longsleeve croptop, across an expanse of bare belly with a button centered, down across the transparent miniskirt, to bare legs.

Tiffany wiggles. The miniskirt doesn't hang quite as low as it did on Beka or Elle, in fact the waistline rides higher than Tiffany's slacks had in the past, so that hairage and rugage do not appear *above* the miniskirt.

But, like its upstairs companion, the miniskirt is totally transparent so everyone can see Tiffany's pubis and buttocks right through the Garment. *That's all well,* Tiffany calculates, *but the miniskirt is also short enough that I can vagflash.*

No clear vinyl in the way for that one!

Elle momentarily forgets about her own exposures. "Geez, Tiffany, your like wearing the Empresses' New Clothes!" Elle unconsciously clenches her croptop with one arm and covers her hairage with the opposite hand.

Another fear: "Aren't *you* scared to wear that outside?"

Tiffany curves her body and practices poses in the Mirror. "Gamers are hazing me and I know it," Tiffany provides. "For the first time, I'm allowed to bare my legs while wearing something." Tiffany steps back. "Now I can I display my body completely without actually being naked. I've been nude sculpture before, now I'm an art piece. Gamers know this arouses me, makes me horny for total nakedness, and makes me crave cock. Makes Gamers crave me naked and cocked."

Tiffany shimmers with pride and appraises Elle. "Watch me now! I am now the exclusive vagflashing Cosmos Pledge! You're about to watch a Porn Star pink, cream and climax her brains out."

Elle thinks less about the possibilities of Tiffany's unencumbered crotch than Tiffany's total transparency. *Tiffany's transparent top is the same as before: Gamers see Tiffany's flat titties and Eraser Heads right through. But her new clear vinyl miniskirt adds all of Tiffany's tatter and tush to the see-through spectacle.*

Elle quickly compares herself to d ex-Porn Star and her fellow Pledge Tiffany. *We both completely bare our face, arms, and midriffs. The only difference is that Tiffany now bares her legs while I cover mine. I'm showing off much more bellage, and we both boobage in our own ways.*

Elle jerks. *Why am I comparing myself to Tiffany anyway?* Elle scans the Bunkroom for her Roommate, but Beka is not here.

Tiffany senses Elle's reliance on the Beka bond. "Robyn took Beka outside, remember?" she says.

"Yes," Elle affirms, "and Kimju and Molly light up the Bathroom. I need to pee but I'm not ready to audition the Pee-Cam."

Tiffany speaks, "You should beg the Pee-Cam so Babs will go easy on you. Like me. I always pee naked in the Bathroom and light the Cam up."

"I'm not like you," Elle asserts and recites heresy, "You drank Janet shots at your Alumni Reprise last Term."

"I drank Janet's shots at *her* Alumni Reprise," Tiffany corrects.

"You drank shots to avoid Slavesex," Elle recalls hearing.

Tiffany puts a finger to her mouth. "That was then and now is now. Babs didn't have to make me continue any commitment. She pretends I arrived with a Piss Mouth Obeisance, but the truth is she grinds it in, although the grind could be coming from higher Up: MomCap's doing, or Madam Nurse Beautician, or even Game Mistress. Even the Gamers."

"Okay," Elle accepts unconvincingly. "But Tiffany, I don't want to be a Stripper, I don't want to get naked in public, and I don't want to pink and Pee-Cam. That's just me." Elle gathers herself. "Do you think Babs had other motives for switching our bottoms?"

"Good question!" Tiffany watches herself in the Mirror as she preens in the totally transparent croptop and miniskirt: Eraser Heads, tapis, and taffrail all fully visible yet all protected by clear vinyl.

Tiffany answers. "I'm as surprised as you are about our exchange. I'm actually delighted. BB doesn't share all wisdom with me. But one thing I know: it's a win-win. You get to cover your nookie, and Gamers can see me as if I am naked. And on top of that, the miniskirt lets me pink and cream unimpeded by cloth protecting my crotch."

Elle blushes. "Yeah, sure," she says, except now that Gamers can see all of you, they don't need you to lose a Garment or two." The unexpected exchange disorients Elle, she isn't so sure about the outcome. Again she feels an urge to pee and isn't sure she can hold back, *but Kimju and Molly are using the Bathroom.* She squeezes herself, leaks a spot of pee into her cameltoe, and the urge subsides.

§ Tiffany Encourages Elle: Aspire to be a Porn Star!

Tiffany does not miss the fresh wet spot in Elle's tight cameltoe, and doesn't ask before she touches where the stretch fabric contours Elle's sex lips and draws her fingertip to her nose. Tiffany licks her finger clean and states the obvious, "Those are not noble proteins, like I left there."

"Tiffany, please, sometimes my bladder gets nervous. I need to pee, but the two Pee-Cam nudies—Kimju and Molly—got the Bathroom Cam lit up."

Tiffany bristles. "I'm a Pee-Cam nudie as well, don't forget!"

"Tiffany, I'm sorry, please, no offence." Elle bubbles.

Tiffany sympathies, "Seems like you're started to pee yourself."

Elle confesses, "Tiffany, please. I'm getting more and more worried about being required to become a Pee-Cam Pledge. And if Babs brings this up, I know what Beka would do, but I don't know what I would do."

"What a pleasant possibility," Tiffany cavalierly responds. She offers free advice, "It's not the kind of thing you should wait for Babs to suggest. You should get out in front and volunteer."

Elle hesitates, "and... volunteer?"

"Of course." Tiffany drives an oblique caveat into Elle's soul, "Like those homemade Gonzo Sex Videos you gave her."

Elle cringes and soaks more urine into her cameltoe. "Babs showed you my videos?" Elle flusters, "Wait, there's no peeing in them. There's just...." Elle trails off.

"You're gonna make a great Porn Star," Tiffany complements Elle, "it's too bad you can only make it to Stripper next Term!"

Elle stammers, speechless, "Robyn told me Babs showed my *Gonzo Videos* to Janet, but I never imagined that she would show them to you. And if you then who else? Oh jeez!"

"I'm her Roommate and confidant," Tiffany explains. "Besides, she respects my knowledge from playing more Terms in the Game than she has. She might be a first-time Monitor in her second Term, but I've been a Stripper and a Porn Star! You've gotten to watch *Suck Fuck Facial Videos* of me from last Term. You know I'm real."

Elle has. She reaches behind and slides her fingers her down into the crack of her ass above the waistline of the slacks. *Posterior rugage exposed.*

Tiffany asks an honest question, "So do your homemade hardcore *Gonzo Videos* co-star know you're trying to curry favor with Babs?"

Elle gasps; this time the squirt of pee wettens the fabric halfway down the inner thigh. Elle shoots Tiffany a look and tries to explain, "Beka doesn't know anything! And I'm not trying to bribe Babs."

Tiffany assuages Elle's fear. "Don't worry, I'm not going to tell Beka. That's between the two of you to stress out."

Elle tries to push the wet part of her crotch backward toward her nadir gate and succeeds only in erecting her newel. She forms a handbra over her almost-exposed nuggies hiding inside her croptop, and tries to make sense of her situation. "The Game is very different than what Beka and I had imagined," Elle carefully frames, "I hope Babs doesn't expect me to put out."

"That's not allowed." Tiffany shrugs. "You'll have to limit yourself to begging the Pee-Cam. And pissing your pants is a good start."

Elle tries to make things sound simple, "I really don't want to Pledge naked. Okay, so I tittered and vagflashed before I became a Pledge, but pinking in the Camera Lounge was a mistake, and there is no way I can cum, let alone be a Stripper next Term." Elle closes her eyes, "That's not what I want! Not right now. I need...."

Tiffany shrugs, "Hard to run away from what you're begging."

Elle lets out air, tilts her head, and suggests a compromise to Tiffany, "It's the Garments that count and I need to keep both. If Babs wants me to Audition the Pee-Cam I will consider that. Because I really don't want my *Gonzo Videos* shown to anyone else."

"Maybe BB will let the two of us Double Dong together." Tiffany probes, and adds a final suggestion, "Before this is over may you beg Babs to transfer my Piss Mouth Obeisance to yourself, may it strengthen your way to Opting Up."

Elle curls her lips. "You don't know what I had to do to acquire the *Gonzo Videos*."

"Or what you will do to help Boss Babe control its distribution." Tiffany concludes, "One thing for sure, I like the way you fuck and suck cock for real. It appears you're pretty good at eating pussy too. But just remember, I've been there done that. I am a Porn Star. I was the first to beg the Nugget, and provided you don't try to worm in front of me getting there, I'll do everything I can to make a Stripper out of you. But from now on, you'll have to wait your turn."

Elle steadies herself, "Yeah, sure, Tiffany, that means you should help me to Opt Up. You need to lose a piece, so it behooves you to help me keep two Garments. That way I can never get in your way, even by accident."

"Love you, Elle," says Tiffany, and gives her a kiss.

§ Robyn & Beka: Dialog About Kimju & Loving the Post

As Robyn marches Beka out the Back Door motion detectors and sound alerts snap the Back Door Cam to attention and it zips to cover them.

Beka pulls the Bell cord with her teeth twice, one for herself and once for Robyn. As if it matters to Robyn, clad as always in her strapped maillot cutout. Robyn marches Beka to the Post Henge and a Post away from the head end.

"What's going on, Robyn," Beka queries over her shoulder, hands behind head, hanging-halter boobage and ripped shorts in full public view, as the Cam and Gamers in the Prefecture pick up on her. "How come Elle gets to Flip-Flop a second time and I don't? That's not fair."

"You don't know what's fair and what's not, Beka Broda," Robyn advises. "In fact, you don't know very much."

Beka doesn't disagree, "Okay, but you know a lot."

Robyn responds, "I know everything!" She stands Beka with her face toward the Post and elaborates. "I know where you are headed next Term. And so do you. You and your newbie Roommate are gonna get what you're beggin' for, so what are you both begging for, Beka Broda?"

Beka knows, "Ma'am, to Opt Strip, Ma'am!"

Robyn purses her lips, "You'll bring her along, yes?" she queries.

Beka stutters, "Ah, Elle thinks she wants to Opt Up next Term. You know, we'd be Roommates Apart, opposite directions."

"Maybe you need to convince her to Op Strip Roommates Together with you," Robyn proposes.

"I want that," Beka proclaims. "I really mean It, Robyn, I really do," Beka pleads. "Please let me Pledge naked and cum be a Stripper next Term. Both of us." Beka clasps the Post between two hands. "Anything that Elle won't do I do for her. Really, Ma'am."

"Thank me, Pledge, Robyn commands.

"Ma'am, thank you, Ma'am," Kimju responds.

"Kimju and Molly disgust me, Pledge," Robyn states. "Especially the dalliances my Roommate Kimju goes to! Has gone to! Is going to!"

Beka rolls her opposite palms on the opposite sides of the Post. She stands with her feet in the dirt directly in front of it. It is planted deep, anchored, and doesn't wiggle. Beka begs, "I'll do anything Kimju and Molly do in order to Opt Strip next Term."

Robyn pouts, "I saw the feeds the night Kimju and Molly performed at the Nugget. You and Elle sat Stage-side and watched them for real." Robyn twitches one nostril. "Eating each other out and then cumming on the Double Dong together?" Robyn exclaims. "Kimju didn't have to do that! Pledge aren't required to do any such thing! It was strictly voluntary on the part of *my* Roommate! And a very dangerous precedent!"

Robyn forgets that the unobtrusive yet hovering Back Door Cam has followed their footsteps and records conversation as well as picture. Or perhaps Robyn needn't care that she describes her Roommate with harsh words: "I'll tell you about my Roommate: Kimju Knockers and Kunny Kover. I don't care she's unlucky to be *my* Roommate. She might even make a very adept Monitor. Except that's not going to happen. She knows not to challenge me to a Roommate Game, so Game over, and that lucky keekelay can keep her g-string and won't have to streak to get to the Nugget next Term."

Robyn cackles. "Because once Kimju's again a Stripper next Term, she *will* beg to Opt Whore in the Term after."

Beka shifts position and holds the Post with one hand. She swings on her feet. She practices diplomacy. "You're right that Kimju and Molly have few inhibitions and are begging to get naked and Strip. But Elle and I begged before Kimju did. Kimju didn't beg until the day she performed her Alumni Reprise."

"Too bad for you Kimju's got fewer Garments," Robyn sneers and snarls. "She's disgusting. She should get fed a laxative until she shits her entire body away."

Beka fingers her nipples with her free hand.

Robyn doesn't hesitate her blunt evaluations, "How about topless Molly Mudwumper? She's been begging to Opt Strip since the Day she arrived, just wants to get back to the Nugget. You don't know this but Molly's already begging me to inflate her hydration, so she can pee even more. I might even let her pee outdoors. She's like some kind of hairy repulsive animal that should be walking on all fours instead of upright. She should get put in a cage and fed rich food for a month or two, get *really* fattened up, and then put in a zoo."

Beka blurts a question out, "What about you, Robyn?" Don't you have to take away Kimju's g-string to complement your maillot cutout?"

"I don't need to think about things I don't think about," Robyn declares. She snorts. "As for Kimju's g-string? Pugh. Who would want something so déclassé! And besides, I am inoculated from any breast, bush, or butt exposures. I'm not like you or any other Pledge. I don't need to play Roommate Games. I am the favorite Cosmos, and Gamers will bless me and provide for my needs. How they shall provide me with a second Garment and my Opt Monitor is not something I need to worry about!"

"You're a royal princess, Robyn," Beka praises, "Anything you can do to help Elle and me Opt Strip next Term we will repay tenfold."

Robyn beams. "You're gonna want to mold me in plaster and cast idols of me. Gamers all want to worship me, but they'll have to settle for my graven image instead."

Beka opens her mouth but Robyn squares Beka's face with the Post. "Enough with the questions!" Robyn determines. "Time to prove your Obeisance and obey me. Pay attention!"

Beka shakes her exposed begonias and wiggles her booty.

"Grab the Post with both hands. Your turn to match Tiffany and Kimju during *The Arrivals*." Robyn glibly demands. "Count, then recite 'I love you Post,' then hug and kiss the post, rub you bobbers and bibble-tips on the post, masturbate your pelvis, then start over."

Beka objects, "Ma'am, please, that's too hard!"

"If you lose count, all you need to do is spit on your Post and start over." Robyn preens. "Don't worry, the Cam has its ways to keep your mindful of staying honest. It's simple really, just don't lose the count."

"Ma'am, I'll be doing this forever, Ma'am." Beka pays respects.

"Remember you said that, Beka Broda," Robyn sneers. She reaches forward, grabs Beka's jeans' waistband on opposite sides, and jerks upward, burying the seam into her bourse and spilling *all* her shaven lips and racing stripe. "Now count, chant, and masturbate, Pledge. 'I love you Post,' hug and kiss, rotate your boobies, rub your box. Repeat yourself. Don't stop.

"But how far am I counting, Ma'am?" Beka protests. "Kimju had to count to 1000!"

Robyn seems to remember more details. "She counted to 1000 but had the wrong Post. So she practiced counting twice with Tiffany, and finally counted correctly."

"I'm on my right Post!" Beka emphasizes.

"You are." Robyn wags a finger. "But remember, if you lose count, spit on your Post, and start all over again."

Beka's nipples indent when excited and they indent now.

Robyn curls. "You can keep the Post slick with your brodeas," she advises, "but no cumming! Now start!"

Beka counts and chants. "One. I love you Post." She hugs and kisses, rotates her berks side to side, and grinds her bolus. "Two. I love you Post," and hugs and kisses and rubs. "Three...." Beka freshens, and lets Kundalini's voodoo overcome her.

§ Kimju Worries to Molly: About Costume Games with Robyn

Meanwhile, upstairs in the Bathroom, a naked Kimju and Molly have a hushed conversation about whether the Cosmos Roommate Games are over; they talk while they collect their pee in the Measuring Cup and log their production on the wall Chart.

Molly pees first. As per instructions, Kimju holds the Cup for Molly and pours the urine into the Watering Can.

Kimju commences a Game analysis. "Beka and Elle have Flip-Flopped; they changed into each other's garments back in the Nugget Dressing Room."

Molly adds pathos, "They still both continue to titter, frequently boobage, and each has enjoyed an opportunity to vagflash, although Elle blacks it out. Pinking too."

Kimju grins, "And then everybody watched the Winner-Takes-All between you and Steph Sanpan Sorostitute, ending with you taking the aggressive one's minidress and stripping her naked. That wasn't supposed to happen. Too bad for your Roommate she's Zoned."

Molly scratches her muff, sanguine, "It's working out. I can't complain once Babs took my minidress yesterday. I might be naked here in the Bathroom, but I've still got panties waiting in my bunk. I'm gonna go strip but not streak."

Molly qualifies, "I hope."

Kimju seeks a concurrence. "It seems like that as far as Babs and Tiffany are concerned, they have played their Roommate Game. Tiffany got turned with Elle, and then Babs took your undershirt. So they have each done an exchange.

Molly agrees, "Yeah, and after Babs took the undershirt from me she converted it into a minidress. She has real powers."

Kimju agrees, "Bikini Babe covered her bling up. Belly too, all but for her button."

Molly observes, "So the Roommate Games for all the Cosmos, except for you and Robyn, are over." Molly parts her thick minge and drains her last pee into the Cup. She lets the Cam linger upon her. She speaks to Kimju, "You and Robyn are the only Cosmos who haven't played a Roommate Game."

"Okay," Kimju agrees, and pushes her kozongas together with both hands as the Bathroom Cam relishes a close-up of the naked Pledge. "I guess I don't care how much Gamers look. I'll pullaside, pink, and finger my holes. I pull my keister apart so the Cams can examine my kawazoo. I've done all that before. But I don't want to go back to the Nugget. I really hate the lapdances and all the hands-on."

Molly understands, well, sort of, "I let them touch me last Term and it got me here and now I'm heading back. So I'm fine with it. You need to learn to not be so ticklish." She laughs.

Kimju snorts. "Molly, you know what my goal is," she says. "I need a second Garment and Opt Up so I can keep the Patron's hands off of me. If I don't do anything then I've got one piece at the end of the Term and I'm back to the Nugget again. Perhaps now might be the time to make my play. But I'm also leery and, you know me, I worry about outcomes. I witnessed you defeat Steph. That wasn't supposed to happen!"

"And then Babs impounded my spoils, took my undershirt and converted it into a minidress." Molly provides encouragement: "Listen, Kimju, if you can successfully Flip-Flop with Robyn, you convert Robyn into the topless and bare-assed Pledge she deserves to be. And Robyn's maillot would provide you with more coverage, and you'd like that."

Kimju nods, "Right, but it would not change my Fate."

Molly raises the possibilities. "If you win a Winner-Takes-All, you could wear Robyn's maillot over your g-string and be totally decent. You're a better person than she is. She deserves naked 24x7 and making the streak."

It is Kimju's turn to straddle the Cup that Molly now holds. Kimju separates her private parts and drains her pee. "I hate the Pee-Cam," Kimju grouses to Molly, ignoring the eye. "I especially hate having to pee into a Cup and log my Cups on a Chart. How come I can't Pee-Cam normally."

Molly shrugs, "Kimju, you'll let Gamers measure your pee however they want."

Kimju breaks her flow and Molly adds Kimju's urine into her own, already in the Watering Can. Molly philosophies, "Nothing we can do to stop Gamers measuring us. And not just everything about our body." Molly nods. "Gamers are gonna make us beg enemas, Kimju, they are going to measure how much fluid we can hold, and see how far we can shoot. I feel it coming."

Molly returns the Cup beneath her again and Kimju micturates another Cupful. She again halts her flow as the Cup is removed and poured into the Can. Kimju twitches her lip as she watches the Cam watch her. "One big question remains," she poses. "Would a scrap with Robyn be a fair fight? What if she really does have Charm? If I issue the challenge then Robyn gets to pick the Game, and if Robyn really is protected, then "I'll loose and I'll be stark naked."

"So what?" Molly says, "It doesn't matter for you. If you do nothing or Flip-Flop or lose, the destination is the same as to where you're headed right now. Hands on at the Nugget."

Kimju knows. *The only difference is that I'd have to streak to get there... and probably get jailed on the way.*

Jailed and fucked, Kimju assumes.

Molly brightens, "The good news is that once you've played your Roommate Game, Flip-Flop or Winner-Takes-All, you can Game with any Pledge."

"Like Beka and Elle," Kimju says.

Molly nods. "The way I read it, Beka will give you *both* her pieces in a finger snap."

Kimju smiles. "Maybe I can collect one piece from each newbie and they can both Opt Down.

Molly reacts, "Oh no! Please Kimju, don't put them *both* in my way. There's already too many of us begging to Strip."

Kimju agrees, "Right, but not enough of you are fully-committed."

Molly nods, "Strip Beka stark naked and let her streak. So that whatever happens, you get to Opt Up."

"I like that," Kimju agrees. "That way Tiffany can shed a piece to Steph or to Beka. That would allow four Cosmos—Tiffany, Steph, Beka, and you, Molly—to Opt Strip to the Nugget. Three of you with one Garment, and either Steph or Beka streaking."

"I hope the Gamers make Steph streak," Molly confesses. "I don't like the idea that she secretly watched me lapdance, and that she told me when she had a chance."

"Me either," Kimju says. "Maybe the Gamers want to have Steph get caught and give her a taste of Jail. She never talks about what happened to her at the end of last Term when she was in Lockdown."

Kimju drips the last of her pee into the Cup, Molly pours it into the Watering Can, and Kimju writes her accomplishment on the Logging Chart.

§ Robyn & Beka: Beka begs Pee-Cam for Herself... and Elle

Beka is still counting, chanting, and masturbating her Post when she discovers Robyn in her eyesight. "I love you, Post. Hug 'n' kiss. Rub my tits. Masturbate."

There is spit on the Post because Beka has had to start counting over again more than once. She needs to pee. She wants to climax.

Robyn breaks Beka out of her reverie and almost instantly Beka changes her beg. "Please let me Pledge naked and cum be a Stripper next Term."

Robyn scowls. "Tiffany and Kimju and Moly are all begging too," she says, "except all of them are also Pee-Camers."

Beka doesn't hesitate. "I haven't got to pee this morning and I need to pee badly." Beka pauses, continues. "Ma'am, I'll pee right here on my Post. Please. I'll let the Cam feed me to the Prefecture."

Robyn curls her lip. "You'll *let* the Cam feed you?"

Beka clarifies. "Ma'am, please let the Cam feed me to the Prefecture. I want to be a Pee-Cam Pledge too, like Tiffany and Kimju and Molly."

"And like Steph," Robyn augments.

"Me and my Roommate," Beka begs, "We both need to be Pee-Camers."

Robyn pushes Beka's face forward until she rubs her face in her spit on the Post. "Sequester yourself in the Doghouse," Robyn orders and pushes Beka downward onto all fours. "Crawl! You can pee inside all you want. You won't be the first to make private stock, but you shall save your Pee-Cam debut for an announcement."

"Ma'am, thank you, Ma'am." Beka turns, goes down on all fours, and scrambles for the Doghouse. "Me and Elle both." Robyn doesn't pay much attention that the Cam follows Beka into the squat earth and wood pen under the Back Landing.

§ Kimju & Molly: Complicate Robyn's Bathroom Choices

Beka's micturition catalyzes Robyn's triggers and she heads inside the house and upstairs to pee. *If there are Pledge in the Bathroom I'll simply order them out!*

Robyn arrives in the Bathroom to discover ex-Strippers Kimju and Molly have braided their hair to a pipe. They will not be moving quickly.

Robyn is not amused.

"Very funny," she declares. "The 'Princesses of Piss' secure themselves in their pissadarium. So spread your legs and put you hands behind your heads, Pee-Camers!" Robyn shimmies across the tile floor and addresses Kimju. "You think I forgot who made you a Pee-Camer? Tell me, Kimju Knock Knock Kava Kava, who made you?"

Kimju picks words carefully. "Ma'am, you broke me to the Pee-Cam, Ma'am."

Robyn twitches her nose, draws her head back, and spits in Kimju's face.

The spit splatters the side of Kimju's nose and cheek, and she recoils; she keeps her hands behind her head. Her secured braided hair prevents her from going anywhere.

Robyn advances. "Next stop for you, kippersnapper, is a Piss Mouth, just like your mazed mumping muchwhat ex-Nugget Roommate."

Robyn pivots and spits in Molly's face. Molly doesn't flinch.

Kimju narrows her eyes and looks at Robyn. "You're my Roommate now, Robyn, you rancid rancorous ragazze."

"You know better than to duel a Game with me, you klammy kickshaw kook," Robyn spins and taunts, "right now you can get back to the Nugget without having to streak. Game with me and you be naked. You know that. I know that. Gamers all know that. And if *you* streak, Gamers gonna get ya!"

Robyn leans in, parts Kimju's lips and ovals her mouth. She rears, and spits directly into Kimju's opened lips. She pauses to enjoy Kimju's stern reaction and crossed eyes.

"Swallow!" she commands airily, turns and looks at Molly, and without a word Molly forms oval-mouth. She catches the Cam, they both know, *Kimju's one-up on me now.*

Robyn smiles, turns back to Kimju, and spits into her eye. "Lot of spit going around today," she says to Kimju, who holds an eye closed. Robyn gathers herself and prepares to stomp out of the Bathroom. "You can practice with spit, Stripper wannabes," she decries, "but you gotta make Whores before you can collect jizz."

Molly begs, "Ma'am, Ma'am, please spit on me twice more, Ma'am!"

Robyn ignores the pleading, ignores an oval-mouth violation, and orders, "Unbraid yourselves before you get turned into toilets or I cut you free. And never do this again."

Robyn exits the Bathroom and heads downstairs. *I know that my Roommate and Molly went out of their way to prevent me from using the Bathroom! They and that ex-Whore Tiffany, who lingers applying endless makeup, also limit my access. But two can play this Game.*

Robyn ascertains that the door from the Dining Room to the Living Room is locked, as is the door from the Kitchen to the Parlor, even the side door to the Porch. She walks out the Back Door, observes that the Back Door Cam is not to be seen, and sneeks around the Porch side of the House.

It's a struggle, but Robyn manages to climb up over the Porch railing on the side of the House adjacent to the chimney. She darts past the Parlor windows, slides along the wall carefully, but before she turns the corner and considers what challenge the Front Door Cam might provide, she discovers she can open one of the Parlor windows from the outside.

She slips into the Parlor undetected. The Parlor and Living Room are empty. Robyn pitter-patters to the small Washroom just off the Parlor underneath the master staircase, closes the door behind her, and prepares the toilet seat.

She pauses, confronted with either the noise of a flush or the yellow color of a leave-behind. Robyn reconsiders, then lifts a leg, pulls her maillot to the side, and pees into the sink, quietly running water afterwards to remove all traces.

She retreats back out the Parlor window (forgetting to close it behind her), climbs over the rail on the side of the Porch, and drops to the ground. Back around to the Landing she pauses by the Doghouse door, frees a stuck latch, and hurries past the Bell and up into the Back Door just as an angry Cam buzzes out the Doghouse.

Underneath, in the Doghouse, Beka gulps a breath of fresh air before pulling the hatch closed from the inside again. She hears footsteps pass overhead, lies in her piss, and idly plays with herself.

II-21 Steph: Returns to Henge Post en Route to Nugget (D23)

§ Steph: Returns & Affixes Herself to Her Henge Post

It is not until afternoon that Steph comes enough to her senses to be sent back to the Cosmos House....

As Steph first returns to her senses she inventories herself as a whole personality again. *At least I think there is only one me. Or as many different me's as I always was.*

She touches herself in the darkness as she comes to life, *wherever I am;* she separates her satchel until it is open, and inventories her parts. She rotates her spires, touches her face also, and recoils at the brittleness of her bleached hair. She recounts recent events. *I have never cum so much in my life. Not just all of yesterday, especially whatever Janet did to me last night.*

Steph resolves herself to be in the Corvette House Parlor: shades drawn, duskiness about. The Cam and the Screen have vanished but the oily fiber rug beneath her has not. *I'm grimy and I itch all over.*

She grounds herself more firmly: *a fireplace, steps to upstairs, a Living Room adjacent, a Front Door! The door I came in, although I have a distinct feeling I have not been here the whole time since I arrived last night.*

Steph's former Pledge Janet reappears and speaks down to the naked and untouchable Cosmos. "Listen to me, Pledge Steph Sorostitute, I am going to Opt Up. You are going to Opt Down. I am going to be your House Mom next Term!"

Janet signs Steph onto her feet. "No need to wait, now tell me your dimensions Stripper wannabe."

Steph isn't sure about the providence of this command, but integrates. "I'm 5' 7", 105 pounds, 32A-23-32."

Janet guides. "Start playing with yourself, get yourself into the Chant, and stay pink-wet-and-ready to cum." Janet digs fingernails into Steph's stern, and squeals her out the Front Door of the Corvette House. "Run!" Janet yells after the naked Pledge. "And don't stop masturbating!"

Steph feels too dazed to disobey. The terror of her situation excites her and she freshens immediately. She digs both fingers into her sinkhole while she covers her crotch. *I need to find a way back!*

Steph raises one hand to handbra; a palm clenches one sinusoidal, as the elbow guards the second swell. Steph scans the terrain. *I am on the sidewalk in front of the Corvette House! And I need to chant while I streak.*

Steph turns to look up the walkway to the still curious Front Door Cam, she moves her fingers to her mouth, and recites, "...hole mouth."

Steph forms her arms surrender. *I have no idea if paparazzi lie in wait.* And commences to walk and chant, "Please let me Pledge naked and cum be a Stripper next Term!" Steph scans her event horizon. *Which way do I go if I have to run to escape? I'm going to get captured and gangbanged or jailed.*

Steph doesn't forget to keep chanting; she brings her arms forward with the tease of a pro: she curls her armpits deeper as she draws her hands forward and crisscrosses her hands beneath opposing swells, reaches upward with her fingertips, and pulls full blood into her sweet-tips.

She sees a paparazzo collect her, gives him or her a look, drops her hands and recites, "clitty clitty," and bolts. *My goal is very simple: keep masturbating my strophoid, and find the Cosmos House.*

Somehow Steph is still masturbating when she finds herself, quite out of breath, standing in front of the Cosmos House, looking up at its concrete walkway, front steps, and Front Door. She glances left and right, and quietly tiptoes partway up the walkway, before veering off barefoot through the grass to the narrower walkway around to the back of the House, below the side Porch. If part of Steph could think and not operate solely on instinct, she might assume that the Front Door Cam never gets triggered out of its sleep.

Once in the Backyard Steph also avoids waking up the Back Door Cam; she scurries to her middle Henge Post, wraps it, and commences to masturbate. Steph releases her built-up tension from the streak upon the Post, and it takes her less than a minute to work up a slick. *Safety at last. All I need to do is keep masturbating all the time and stay in some kind of a dream.*

Steph swirls the ball of her clit in her oozing wetness, and Zones herself into a slow ecstasy.

§ Babs Denies Elle Request: No Hairage Shave then Sent Outside

Inside the Cosmos House, the Desktop alerts Monitor Babs to two visitors approaching the Front Door. BB watches them via the Door Cam when Elle enters the Bedroom.

Elle knows better than to look down at the Desktop Screen and presents herself very formal just inside the doorway. She continues to wear a hacked at croptop that ensures she can titter when she moves, and slacks sufficently low-waistlined and skin tight so that her cameltoe details, whilst hairage and rugage erupt above her waistline.

Elle stands at attention with legs open and wrists crossed behind her back. She maintains erectness and keeps her eyes looking forward. *I know that just because my thighs and legs are covered I mustn't touch my legs together, even if they're not bare skin anymore.*

"Ma'am," Elle begs Monitor Babs, "I want to request permission for Tiffany to shave the hairage that's showing above my slacks, Ma'am."

Monitor Babs flashes on her own Dining Room Picture, downstairs on the Dining Room wall. *A Dice Game cost me my hairage.*

BB smiles at her Pledge. "Your hairage pleases Gamers, you should know that."

Elle hesitates. "It embarrasses me," Elle confesses.

"That pleases Gamers double." Boss Babe glances at the Desktop alert, gracefully rises from her chair, stands, and pinches Elle's cheek. "I love whenever a Pledge wants permission for something." BB bows. "But what you really need to do is beg to shave off your entire nest! Center Stage at the Nugget while you climax the Double Dong."

Elle opens her mouth in alarm, but Boss Babe soothes. "Listen and obey, Pledge: Go downstairs at once, exit the Back Door, go around to the Front Door, and escort two visitors to the Backyard." Babs points to the Desktop Screen.

"Ma'am?" Elle questions. "Outside?"

"Obey me," Boss Babe cheers, waves fingers upward and away.

Elle hesistates. "I'll roll my slacks down for you here and masturbate at the same time. I'll stay pink-wet-and-ready."

Boss Babe smiles kindly, "Remember you said that."

Elle panics, "I'll worship the Baseboard Strippers just like I am. I'll let you take my temperature. Hot hot hot, titters and twat, 98.6 in my anus!"

BB laughs, "You'll *let* me take your temperature?"

But before Elle can correct herself Babs augments, "Silly Pledge, don't forget you begged to be here! You're the one begging your next destination! Now scoot, and take these two Camera Club Guys to the Henge Post."

§ Elle & Camera Club Guys: Brazen Exterior Hairage Adventure

Elle steps out the Back Door, off the Landing, and rings the Bell. She spots Steph masturbating on a middle Henge Post. Naked Steph, moaning. Elle pauses momentarily, just long enough to draw the attention of the Back Door Cam, which zips to her and canvasses her reduced croptop & slacks.

Elle hesistates. The enables the Cam to collect titter, hairage, cameltoe. Elle scoots; The Cam collects her rugage as she rounds the house but does not follow. The Prefecture glides the Cam back to monitor naked Steph slicking her Henge Post. Still Zoned, oblivious to Elle's passing.

Elle proceeds around the Porch side of the House. *My new combination showcases my bellage, my overflowing pubic hair, and my butt crack.* Elle re-evaluates herself still another time. *My vulnerabilities are no longer limited to tittering my nips, I'm not just navelage 24x7, I'm tittering, hairage, and rugage 24x7.*

Elle anticipates how she will greet the Camera Club Guys. *What if they're not there any more?* Elle worries. *And what if they demand I drop my pants, part my pink, and arouse myself for them? Will I obey them?*

Elle gives thought to this. *Should I obey them? Well, maybe if it's inside. And especially if BB says I have to.*

And why is that? *Because ever since I presented Babs with my old* Gonzo Videos, *I've known that Babs' demands upon me might escalate. Will escalate. She holds even more power over me now.*

I feel bad Beka doesn't know the fix that I'm in. That we're in.

The Front Door Cam, alert to the visitors, spies Elle immediately and rushes to cam her even before she can beckon the two Camera Club Guys off the Front Porch. They want an immediate portrait with a croptop lift, and Elle obliges them, first single then double nacks. They want a pants-pushed-down and she defrays this request. *They get hairage and rugage already and I give them boobage for free!*

"This way to the Backyard," Elle instructs, "I think what you seek awaits you."

§ Robyn Directs Beka & Elle: Kiss & Make Out & Hickey

What greets Elle is not what she expects. Steph still humps her Post, but now Beka, released from the Doghouse by Robyn, stands spread surrender in the center of a dry Mudpit, with Robyn nearby. Beka's halter remains unbuttoned and hanging boobage, and her jeans' seam digs into her bare lips, separating them and flaring them out.

Beka is filthy.

Robyn wears her maillot cutout and possesses splendid makeup. She knows where the Makeup Case is hidden and uses it to its fullest.

Robyn nods to the Camera Club Guys. She signs Elle forward, stands her spread surrender in front of her Roommate, and asks a question. "So did the Nugget Shooter document you backstage the night you Flip-Flopped?"

Ouch, gulp! Elle blinks her eyes twice, seeks Beka's eyes wait, and answers for both of them. "We don't know. Too much was happening. Overload." *How does Robyn even know to ask that question?*

But the Redacted one remains accusatory, "You both have a memory retention disorder!"

"Really?" Elle responds, "Leave it to the Redacted one to remember too much!"

Robyn twitches a nostril. "Hug each other. Kiss and make out," she commands.

Elle pauses. "Kiss and make out? Here?" She considers contacting her body with Beka's body of filth. *Beka stinks. Right here? Outside?*

"Don't echo my orders," Robyn snaps. "Just for that, be sure to put a hickey on each other's necks."

"A hickey?" Elle asks, astounded.

"More echoes, more hickies," Robyn declares. "Now wrap you arms around each other and make out, Roommates." Robyn steps back and lets the Camera Club Guys collect Beka placing the first hickey.

I find Beka overly willing, Elle realizes, and tries to think. *So if Robyn knows, does Babs know about my secret pee over at the Nugget during our Flip-Flop?* Elle expands her worries. *Maybe Babs also knows about my tinkle in the Doghouse the day I arrived, and the one time I was using the Bathroom when one of the Pee-Camers came in.*

Beka kisses Elle's cheek, kisses her on her lips, carefully rolls her mouth open, and explores with her tongue. Elle resigns.

§ Robyn Directs Steph: Masturbate & Beg for Camera Club Guys

Robyn Redacted scowls to the Camera Club Guys, irritated yet dismissive they do not bother to cam her maillot cutout with its string shoulder straps and the tiniest buttonhole.

"Enough of the newbie trash, Guys," she says and walks them to a position behind where Steph grinds and pants on the Post. Zoned.

The Camera Club Guys photograph, videograph, and make stereometric recordings. They collect the full cycle of Steph's bump and grind. Steph's eyes are open; she looks upward, but sees nothing, sees only hallucinations in her trance. She long ago forgot to Chant.

Robyn watches Steph's reduction with delight but also a latent fear. Gamers know Steph was Robyn Redacted's benefactor last Term, and no matter how much pleasure Robyn gets watching Steph reduced to a naked quivering bag of vibrating ectoplasm, some of her memory cells find the process disconcerting.

Or do they? No matter, this is a fresh opportunity to humiliate Steph.

Confident of Steph's surrender of self, the Camera Club Guys indicate they want Steph brought back into a realm of "a tease," and Robyn obliges them. She digs nails into Steph's naked ribs, dig nails into her shapely dual sterns, the insides of her thighs, and, once Steph breaks with the pole, Robyn pinches her nips—hard—and Steph squeals.

As Steph fringes out of the Zone Robyn spins her to face the Camera Club Guys, directs her to teasy dance, then signs her to part her bleached hair and proffer pink shots.

Steph takes offense at the Signs, takes offense at the signer, looks at the Camera Club Guys, reels as she suddenly observes them, and tries to balance herself leaning back against the Post. *Who are you to come into my Backyard and record me on your pervy little Cams?*

Robyn labels. "Gentlemen, meet Steph Sorostitute, number one on the Stripper-wannabe list." Robyn turns to Steph, "Now spread and pink, and dance like the slithery slippery snapdragon you are!"

Steph obeys. *I'm already wet inside. I've got a hickey on my neck.* Steph directs her window for thought away from humiliation to an opportunity to ponder her predicament. *I got tricked into playing a Greatest House Roar and I got duped.* She glowers directly at the Camera Club Guys. *You two pervs don't deserve looking at me and taking my image away with you.*

Robyn advertises, "This saffronite sex stew won't be limiting herself to showing off her gynecology either, like she made some of her Pledge do last Term."

"Pink-wet-and-ready?" Robyn adds a dirty laugh. "I'd say Steph's ready for some girl-girl and Double Dong work!" Robyn turns on the naked Pledge, "You can beg your Roommate Molly to take you to the Nugget and give you equal treatment: she and Kimju got lingus and ride and climax, now it's your turn, isn't it, Pledge?"

"Ma'am, please, Ma'am!" Steph cries.

"Masturbate," Robyn commands.

"Ma'am, please, Ma'am," Steph begs.

"Rub-a-dub, you slithering surge swag. Faster!" Robyn orders, and Steph squeezes herself with both hands and squeezes a blob out of her surge machine that paints her fingertips. She starts to pant, "Huh. Huh. Huh."

The Camera Club guys find the performance scary and look at each other.

"Beg," Robyn commands.

Steph can't think straight. She looks at the Guys taking her picture, and words spill out balanced somewhere between subservience and pure horny craven Kundalini; Steph steers herself onto proven track: "Please let me Pledge naked and cum be a Stripper next Term," she recites. She considers her sticky fingers, falters, says, "...hole mouth," and draws her fingers to touch her lips and her nostrils.

The effect of her own scent derails her, and she eyes the Camera Cub Guys. "I'll suck your cocks," she tells them. "I'll fuck you. I'll suck and fuck both of you. Right here. Right now."

The Camera Club Guys exchange a glance. No moments to lose. Steph breaks to her knees, crams her sex back against the Post, squeezes with her thighs, and attacks it with a vigorous humping up and down. The Camera Club Guys no longer pay attention to their camming; they stand transfixed as Steph rubs faster, breaks toward a climax. She rubs faster, thrashing as she leans forward and grinds her breasts into the dirt, then rears her head up as she builds her moaning up to a cry, "Uuuuuuhhhhhaaaaaaahhh!"

The Camera Club Guys look at each other and flee. Standing in the albeit dry Mudpit Elle watches aghast until Beka bites onto her lips, turns her face towards her own, connects to her eyes, and concludes with a French kiss that draws Elle's attention away from the motion blurred Camera Guys fleeing past. Steph's howls stimulate Beka's arousal and she drives the kiss deeper, squeezes Elle with her arms, and possesses her tongue.

Robyn, observing the face-and-chest-in-the-dirt Steph, reaches forward with a toenail and with devilish intent ever so gently touches Steph on one cheek, and Steph releases another howl. Then a sob, and into a more muted steady grinding of her sex into the Post, panting and rub-a-dub, with Steph so obsessed with arousing herself that she no longer thinks straight, let alone plans. But sustainably Zoned.

The Camera Club Guys may have fled, but the Back Door Cam remains ever vigilant; Robyn intervenes and commands its eye. "That slippery sleaze skank is not supposed to talk like that! Steph needs to beg an Opt Strip, not beg to suck and fuck like a Whore! She scared them away!"

Robyn wags a finger and lectures the Prefecture. "Yesterday on the Back Landing I forced Steph to pink, cream, and climax herself while lying on her back. Then I forced her to finger her sewer and snatch and climax while on her hands and knees. And just now I forced her to masturbate herself on her Post. I'm good."

Robyn takes pride in climaxing Steph in front of strangers. Again she talks to the Cam. "Gamers, you know I made this smarmy slop-hole slattern beg to Strip next Term," Robyn waves a dismissive hand toward Steph, but not such a broad gesture so as to draw the Cam's attention away from herself. "This screeching scum skank has become a self-climax machine. May she attract attention from the neighbors, paparazzi and any visiting Cams."

Steph, mind and body shaking as one, hears only wind and the flow of Kundalini back and forth between her body and the not-necessarily inanimate Post. Steph's breathing comes in very short bursts, one every second or so, shallow, along with the body's shallow shaking. Zoned, yet self-regulated with the right amount of breath to sustain the climax while not exhausting herself and her orgasm.

Robyn casts her eyes across the houses and backyards adjacent, across the alley, along the hedge line. She purses her lips as she eyes the Mudpit, where Beka and Elle now sit but continue to make out. The Mudpit was dry but now retains traces of their presence. Robyn lifts her nostrils and upper lip, *where is Molly and her Watering Can?* Last seen in the Bathroom with Kimju? Robyn turns to go.

And she doesn't stop Steph from cumming. Doesn't even try.

§ Tiffany & Kimju & Molly: Observe Steph & Robyn in Backyard

Tiffany and Kimju and Molly spill out the Back Door and the old friends observe the Post Henge from the Landing.

Tiffany Transparent glows with her own makeup. Lips reddened. Eraser Heads beneath a clear vinyl longsleeve front-button croptop; thinnish red pubic hair around tush beneath the clear vinyl low-rise miniskirt. Navelage 24x7. *Gamers want me to display my naked body yet still retain two pieces.* Tiffany considers the implications of the miniskirt replacing the slacks. *I have been constrained by my slacks, no matter how much I spread or obeyed the "no thighs touching Rule," all my fans could get was tacky cameltoe stains. Now there is nothing in the way of me spreading, opening my temple, and transuding tapioca for my fans.*

Kimju and Molly flank Tiffany's sides, both of them topless: Kimju's micro g-string hairages all around, Molly's transparent panty hairages both above and through the Garment. Hot stuff.

Some Gamers argue that Kimju and Molly must keep their nipples erect, their areolas bubbled up, and their crotches creamy. Kimju's g-string is klammy and krusty, and Molly's transparent panties have white magma slathered on the inside.

Tiffany speaks in hushed tones to her two confidants, ensuring that their conversation can't be overheard at the Mudpit or at the Post Henge. She tilts her head toward the Post where Steph grinds in slow seething motion. "Maybe someday we will find out what Janet did to her," Tiffany says, "or what Robyn has been making her beg."

"Steph's a naked girl and Bikini Boss wears her dress," Kimju states. "What happens to her next?"

Tiffany says, "Babs has told me that I'll be escorting Steph to the Nugget tonight."

Kimju reads minds, "But you weren't expecting to go totally transparent."

Tiffany joculars, "That kind of bonus shows you how much Gamers love me!"

Kimju nods, "So, what about Steph?"

"Ah!" Tiffany leans back. "As for Steph, I'm going to take her over the top. Zone her center Stage. Watch and see."

"You just want to get to the Nugget to perform your own Audition," Kimju jerks.

Tiffany perks. "Okay, I'll accept that, Steph and I shall both Audition!"

"Robyn says the last time you two played together you washed her feet with your tongues," Molly gurgles. "It's like you two are equals."

"Steph and I are not equals." Tiffany glows. "She will arrive at the Nugget naked; I appear to be naked, but I'm not. I've got Two Garments!"

"Okay, sure, you're Tiffany Transparent," Kimju agrees. "But she's still the new act."

"Maybe I can give her a Garment and we can both Opt Strip," Tiffany proposes.

"Tiffany, not all of us really want to go Strip next Term," Kimju reminds her fellow Pledge. "Besides, right now, with regard to the Garment Count, I'm closer to the Strip than you are. You still have two pieces. I'd rather you gave one to me, rather than to Steph."

"Right," Tiffany expounds, "just as soon as you play a Roommate Game with Robyn, I'll give you my top. Until then you aren't allowed to do any dealing."

Kimju hesistates. She looks at Molly.

Molly shrugs. "I'm fine the way I am, topless and panties, no matter how low or transparent. I've played my Roommate Game." She looks across the Backyard toward naked Steph masturbating on her Henge Post.

Tiffany tries to make it easier for Kimju. "You can have my top *or* my bottom. Your choice."

Kimju contemplates. *Transparency makes Tiffany's top and miniskirt less attractive garments to Game for, so Tiffany's see-through exposure ironically buys her limited protection from predation.* Kimju stabilizes her thoughts. "If I Game with Robyn and lose, I'm naked. If you then give me a top or bottom that only gets me back to where I am now."

"Headed for the Nugget is where you are now," Tiffany states fact, "and it's where you will end up if nothing changes."

Kimju rattles a knocker as she wipes off the top of her nose.

"You'd also be a free agent after you, Even if you Gamed with Robyn you lost," Tiffany reminds, "you'd be a free agent and you could then prey on the newbies.

Yes. Kimju considers the newbies, making out in the Mudpit. Beka has managed to slide one dusty palm up inside Elle's croptop and another downward into the back of her pants. Elle clenches Beka in embrace, grateful for the security she provides. Now Elle kisses Beka back; she kisses Beka on the lips, works her tongue through the French oval, and lets Beka suck her tongue.

Kimju challenges Tiffany. "Are you sure you qualify as a Nugget Alumni? I mean I grant that you were a Porn Star who visited the Nugget last Term. You Feature Danced."

"You Whored in the Champagne Room," Molly recriminates.

Tiffany brushes her hands together. "Excuse me. I shot *Suck Fuck Facials* in the Inner Sanctuary!" Tiffany forswears. "Don't think you know everything."

"That makes you think you're entitled to an Alumni Reprise?" Molly asks Tiffany.

Tiffany rolls her lips outward. "Okay, I'm not last Term's Alumni like you two, but I Stripped there two Terms ago, before I made Whore. So I'm qualified Alumni."

Kimju doesn't struggle. "I want you to Opt to the Nugget, Tiffany," Kimju states. "You deserve it next Term. And as far as I'm concerned, you can do us all a favor and take Steph with you.

"Wait a minute," Molly asserts, "I'm the one who climaxed with her. I've had one piece since I arrived and I'm going to the Nugget next Term, and I'm not going to streak to get there."

Tiffany smiles. "You're already Pledging naked and begging to Strip," she reminds Molly, "and you have no assurances about anything. We're all beggars here." Tiffany nods toward Beka and Elle soaking in the Mudpit, "them too," she says, and then with a different nod, this time toward the naked, masturbating, zoned Steph, and says, "and also that."

Tiffany and Kimju and Molly all know: *Robyn is the only Pledge who has not begged to "Pledge naked and cum be a Stripper next Term."*

§ Tiffany & Robyn: Backyard Confrontation

Tiffany and Kimju and Molly step off the Landing, ring the Bell thrice, and approach the Post Henge. Robyn intercepts them, singles out Tiffany, and again scorns Tiffany's exposure. "The Empress's New Clothes," Robyn laughs.

The Empress's New Clothes is a confusing, but still interesting metaphor because Tiffany's costume is clearly totally transparent but not nude. Two pieces, not zero.

Tiffany bows lightly, "You're a royal princess," she declares.

"I am," Robyn affirms, and backtracks her praise, "You're not really an Empress, you're a lowly Pee-Cam Piss Mouth toe-sucking foot-worshiping Cosmos Pledge. And a used Whore."

This irritates Tiffany. "Get it right," she snaps, "*I* am a Porn Star."

Robyn corrects. "You're a wannabe Porn Star. You'll service me however I want. You may beg me to save all my private pee, so you can drink it in public."

"I'll do your makeup!" Tiffany prides.

"You'll absolutely not!" Robyn corrects. "I don't need to look like one of Cleopatra's Strippers or a tawdry torque twister like you. I make Madam Nurse Beautician do my makeup at the Beauty Salon! But at least you finally earn your name completely, Tiffany Transparent!" Robyn laughs out loud, "Ha, ha, ha!"

"Thank you, Robyn Redacted!" Tiffany rises onto her tiptoe and rolls her eyes to Kimju and Molly. She scans toward the house next door, the alley, and addresses Robyn back, "The best you can offer the Prefecture is headlights and some puffiness in your crotch. My clear vinyl lets me show my Eraser Heads, tapis, and tush. I might as well be topless and bottomless, except I'm not. Always my gorgeous midriff, tidy belly button, and long shaven legs stay bare to the World.

"You wouldn't want to upstage Steph," Robyn snarls.

"Oh no!" Tiffany sings.

Robyn seeks an attack, finds one: "Now that you got bare legs don't forget you're forbidden to touch your thighs together. Just like all the other Cosmos Pledge."

Eyes snap; Tiffany's thighs are not touching.

Tiffany corrects, "You never saw me cross my legs or brush my thighs together, Robyn, even when I wore the slacks and stained my cameltoe. Now the good news is that Gamers get to purview my treasure chest unimpeded." Tiffany dances in place, lifts a knee, and vagflashes the Back Door Cam, which hovers nearby to watch.

Absolutely, the shortness of the clear miniskirt ensures that the Prefecture can now determine not only that Tiffany has red hair, but that the hair on her sex lips grows thin enough so that upskirts always reveal at least the single line entrance to Tiffany's tapestry.

"Boss Bitch is gonna make you spread your legs and pink your pussy in public," Robyn hisses into her ear, "That's why you got Garment-switched with Elle."

Tiffany accepts this hypothesis and firms her posture. "Thank you, Robyn. Finally I get to join the Cosmos vagflashing contingent: photons direct, unencumbered by cloth or plastic, right into the eyes of Gamers.

Robyn runs a mouth attack. "No big deal, you tornillo turning treddle. Everybody has already seen your Pink Pages. And your dancing and prancing and whoring on the Cosmos House Screens. You totally divulged your burgundy-colored vagina last Term and sold it for anything that stuffed it. You pinked and Pee-Cammed since Day One of this Term, but odds are you're gonna cream and cum for everyone, center Stage at the Nugget."

Tiffany perks up. "I hope so. I hope you don't forget to peruse my Porn Star Calendar, it's hanging in the Kitchen you know, and showcases more of my repertoire!"

Robyn's mood darkens. Tiffany's Porn Star Calendar gnaws on Robyn's psyche. She has secretly studied each month's hardcore sex picture. One disturbing image features the centerpiece of a banquet table: Tiffany covered head to toe in honey and food while holding the end of a funnel in her mouth.

So despite her bluster Robyn isn't quite sure of how to appraise Tiffany. In this vacuum Robyn correctly regards Tiffany as dangerous.

Robyn challenges the danger. "Tiffany Transparent, most certainly your tangy twat craves a cock or two, but just because you're an ex-Whore doesn't mean you're allowed to trick for favors any more. So I guess all you're allowed to do is show off your tangy turgescent tenderloin center Stage at the Nugget, whip up some tapioca, and teeter-totter yourself into the Zone."

Tiffany glowers at the haughty one. "My tangy turgescent tenderloin wants one end of the Double Dong inside it, and it wants your rouge ribald receptaculum on the other end. Buried and clit-to-clit. Then we shall have a more meaningful conversation!"

Robyn blinks. *Sometimes Tiffany is not as friendly as she should be.*

§ Robyn & Babs: Take Tiffany & Steph to the Nugget

The Bell announces Babs' descent into the Backyard. BB continues to wear a short-sleeved scoop-neck dress; it's width enables Babs to let her bra straps be visible inside the neckline. The buttonhole is modest yet adequately large so that Babs has no danger of the hole accidentally sliding and covering her button. Navelage 24x7. A hemline just above the knee allows Monitor Babs to control any upskirt! *And even if, there's a nombril underneath!*

Steph, lost in her trance, remains unaware of Babs' presence; she doesn't even register the Bell ring. She's not aware that all the Cosmos are now present in the Backyard, clumped together.

If Steph could think she might excite herself upon the possibility of climaxing on the Dong; the naked and zoned Pledge wraps her thighs wrapped around her Post, her smolder pot rubbing her slick, and one of her fingers probing her stern tunnel. She breathes hard and steady, occasionally kissing and romancing the Post with her lips and tongue. May the Post assist her to maintain a sustained heartbeat.

Boss Babe signs Kimju and Molly to break up Beka and Elle's making out, and help gather them into a huddle of Six Cosmos Pledge around their Monitor. Steph, panting on her Post, is left out of earshot.

Boss Babe details another trip to the Nugget. "House Mom el Capitan has granted Steph's wish to Audition the Nugget." BB pauses to let this sink in. Augments, "So she's on the schedule for tonight!"

Robyn brightens and looks at naked Steph lost in masturbating her Post. But among the other Pledge, unease greets this announcement.

Tiffany trades eyes with Babs. *Only this time Steph won't be a secret witness, she shall be the main act.* BB empowers Tiffany to the circle of Pledge. "MomCap also grants Tiffany's wish to Audition," BB nods, "and to perform with Steph."

Some resolve of unease greats this announcement.

Tiffany feels cut by this decision, yet also understands: *Nothing really changed. I'll still force Steph over the top, and I'll convince the Patrons demand I come Strip next Term.*

Babs looks around the huddle and concludes, "Ergo, Robyn and I shall escort Tiffany and Steph to the Nugget tonight." BB smiles

Some of the milling Cosmos process these implications. Elle, for example, considers, *this set of adventures permits Boss Babe to introduce a different quartet of Cosmos to the Nugget. Last time Kimju and Molly got naked, ate each other, climaxed together on the Double Dong, and got awarded smaller costumes. Then Beka and I Flip-Flopped, and Beka had to flash her boobies and pullaside.*

Perhaps Elle forgets she too flashed her nack-nacks and nookie to the Crowd.

Nonetheless, this time Kimju and Molly, and Beka and Elle, will stay behind. "Upstairs, all four of you," BB directs. "Like on your backs on the Bunkroom floor in a four-leaf Clover position: a circle with your heads together in the middle, arms to the sides holding hands, and with your legs spread and your feet touching. "Stay connected!"

"You two," Babs targets directions to ex-Strippers Kimju and Molly, "combine your power to induce the Bathroom Cam into the Bunkroom, so Gamers can keep an eye on you all."

BB interprets Beka's eagerness to move, and curious stare from Elle. She details to Elle directly, "The Cam will feed your scene to the Nugget, well, to the whole Prefecture actually, and a motion tracker circuit running in Automatron will sound an alarm if you stop holding hands. Should there be any doubt, Gamers will just call up the instant replay."

Elle blinks. *I have that sick feeling in my stomach that I may have stumbled into quicksand and I can't rescue myself.*

Robyn tries to be helpful. "I know where the Makeup Case is; I'll take Steph inside and make her like the scumbucket she aspires to be."

BB smiles, "Excellent, but hurry, the Crowd will be awaiting her. I shall leave with Tiffany at this moment, and House Mom el Capitan will expect you to arrive with her shortly: naked, overdone, and loaded with Obeisance." BB gently waives to Kimju and Molly and Beka and Elle. "Scram," BB orders. "Inside."

And Four Pledge ring the Bell on their way through the Back Door.

§ Beka & Elle: Brodeas & Noble Secretions

Elle confides to her Roommate in hushed tones on the way up to the Bunkroom. "The Game is getting scary, I'm getting more exposed, I have to do more Obeisance, although I still retain my two pieces, and that's a good thing. We both do."

"You're the most-covered Cosmos, Elle," Beka exclaims.

"Yes," Elle agrees, "but I'm also the most vulgar." Elle blinks. "You put hickeys on my neck. That's bad but even worse, I worry I am beginning to believe the Chant."

Beka agrees, "Elle, hello, doesn't everyone believe the Chant? Except Robyn, she doesn't chant. Or maybe Kimju, except Kimju understands that Gamers, not her, will decide if she Opt Strips or not."

Elle has concerns. "Earlier I believed that Babs and the Gamers were just hazing us. But now I think that they really do intend to strip us naked and make us pull pink."

Beka's hanging halter top flows as she climbs the stairs. "Elle," Beka reminds, "you have already shown off full-frontal and pink. On Stage at the Nugget and in the Camera Lounge. Me too! You know I'm always wet, and that you're headed for a creamin' too. So the sooner Robyn lets us masturbate to climax the better. So then we will be just like Kimju and Molly and Steph, and not playing catch-up. That is what we keep chanting, after all. All we have to do is lose one Garment somehow and we'll get to the Nugget."

Elle runs a hand up inside her croptop and scratches one noog. She worries, "Steph Sorostitute has turned into a pretty scary role model. She's stark naked and spread, and masturbates herself all her waking hours. Zoned."

Beka eagerly projects. "I wonder what happened at Janet's Corvette House. I bet Janet made her eat pussy."

Elle blurts, "I hope Janet didn't pee in her mouth. You saw what happened when she and Molly piss-climaxed together."

Beka accepts, "Yeah, sure, Elle, Steph's now a naked pinking, creaming, cumming, Pee-Cam, Piss Mouth Pledge. That's going to happen to us too, Elle, please."

Elle steels herself. *I must consider my own current exposures. My accumulated exposures as well. My unfulfilled begs. The begs I haven't made yet.* Elle checks to see if her croptop covers her nips. *Barely,* she realizes, suddenly conscious of checking herself. *I feel a need to tally up my position if I am to play the Game seriously. I need to update my secret handwritten Manifest.*

Elle casts a glance at her Roommate. Beka's shorts show off her booty cheeks and leak her bush to both sides of the crotch seam, *but these are academic exposures. The leglines where the shorts got cut off have frayed even more since I wore them. Beka aggravates her own exposure; she picks at the horizontal threads and the leglines erode, rising higher.*

Elle observes, *And yes, the pockets have become visible from the outside. My secret notes remained hidden in one pocket and I have not had an opportunity to recover them. I need to do this, preferably without letting Beka in on my secret.*

Beka nudges her Roommate and whispers to her, "Elle, I need Robyn to take my halter or shorts. Please Elle, but you need to come Strip too. Maybe we can beg Robyn to take a piece from both of us, that way she can Double Opt Up and we can both Opt Strip topless."

Elle closes her eyes for a moment, then whispers back, "Unless Robyn games with Kimju she isn't taking a piece from anybody. Sooner or later Kimju has no choice but to challenge Robyn to a Roommate Game. Kimju will lose, Robyn will demand her g-string, and Kimju will streak to the Nugget."

"Elle, listen, everybody streaks," Beka pleads, "Molly's already streaked. Steph has had to streak three times, and you can be sure Robyn will make her streak to the Nugget tonight. So Kimju will streak at the end of the Term, after she turns her thong over to Robyn."

Elle darkens. "Better Kimju than me."

Beka bounces. "Listen, Elle. Even Janet's streaked. I want to streak too, Elle. I want to streak to the Nugget with you."

Beka waits a moment and augments, "Elle, I'm dripping broda again. I can't stop. And knowing you get to taste me excites me a lot."

Tiffany Trains Steph: And Visits the Nugget (D23)

II-22 Babs & Tiffany: Arrive at Nugget (D23)

§ Babs & Tiffany: Journey to the Nugget

Babs and Tiffany receive transport to the Nugget in the back of a limousine, one that picks them up in the front of the Cosmos House. Babs, wearing a minidress over a bra and panties, can pretty much venture anywhere. Tiffany Transparent doesn't qualify for a streak, but her clear vinyl croptop and miniskirt hides nothing. She can titter nipples with an armhole lift, and she has no option but to vagflash when she sits, like now in the limousine.

Tiffany feels alive. *I anticipate a fun evening!*

Babs feels anxious. *Three Days ago when I visited the Nugget, I had to watch Kimju and Molly dance. Well, let's be honest,* Babs details, *I watched Kimju and Molly climax the Double Dong center Stage! And watched Beka and Elle Audition.*

Yes, BB recalls, *Four Cosmos Pledge bared their breasts that night and all of them pinked.*

Has Babs forgotten she also condemned Corvette Louise to strip naked and pink?

Also, BB has yet to learn that two of her Pledge—Kimju and Molly—provided private watersports to the Nugget Shooter, and that they remain indebted to the Shooter for keeping this secret… for a while anyway.

And tonight?

"Steph is on the menu tonight," BB explains, "Sorry. You get to be the ringmaster but she is the headliner."

Tiffany verbally agrees, "Ma'am, I understand, Ma'am"

BB gathers her approach. "Steph secretly watched you and Janet the night of Janet's Alumni Reprise last Term. Janet told me and I told you, but has Steph ever told you she was there?"

Tiffany checks to make sure her thighs aren't touching. "No," she affirms, "I'm sure. I'd remember that. I'd have shared that with you."

"I guess she hasn't told you either," Tiffany ventures.

"Right." BB confirms.

Tiffany ruminates. "You know that during *The Arrivals,* I took a hit for not revealing to you that I Dong-climaxed Janet at her Alumni Reprise last Term. Back when I was a full-fledged Porn Star. You also found out Janet told me about Steph. I'm sorry I wasn't completely forthcoming and anytime you want me to I will beg soap, laxatives in my food, or Castor Oil."

Boss Babe bristles. "I believe you've already begged I possess your entire digestive track, mouth to tailpipe."

Tiffany stammers but straightens, "Ma'am, thank you for possessing me, Ma'am. But perhaps tonight is the time to transfer some of your possessions to Steph."

BB smiles with pursed lips. "Tonight must be degrading to Steph," Boss Babe tells Tiffany as they glide in the limousine. "I'm counting on you to work her over."

Tiffany Transparent centers and affords herself the luxury of touching herself. No cloth in the way. "Okay," Tiffany hesistates, "Only I don't think we should limit her to just eating soap. Just because she's naked doesn't mean we need to be done with her. Let me Dong-cum her for sure, teach her to Pee-Cam in front of the Club, and collect her pee in my mouth!"

Babs laughs. "Silly you. You always want to be the Star. But you are forbidden to upstage her tonight! BB advances. "After you collect her pee in your mouth you can French-kiss it back to her." Babs contemplates Tiffany's bite; she continues, "You've asked for an opportunity to wring Steph out, so your wish has come true. May you afford her the luxury of seeing the Nugget through the eyes of the naked Stripper she so avidly begs to become."

Tiffany squares her shoulders, "Ma'am, thank you, Ma'am! I'll make sure she begs out of control."

A cloud passes across Tiffany's cortex, one side to the other, and now Tiffany dangles what is not really a question. "Ma'am, somehow you prefer having Robyn take Steph to the Nugget," she says.

"Robyn has never been there before," Babs admits, "and she has put the environment out of her mind. So I intend for the experience to unnerve her."

"Part of her doesn't want to go visit," Tiffany observes, "and part of her can't resist dominating naked Steph. Even if she has to enter a place she considers déclassé."

Babs nods, "Things always end up the way Fate determines, but the Fate of the future builds on the now; Karma matters, every flap of a butterfly wing matters, and intent matters, because there are an infinite possible Fates at the next moment."

§ MomCap Welcomes Babs & Tiffany: At the Nugget Front Door

Babs and Tiffany arrive at the Nugget via an open double-door salute through the front; it's mid-evening, and the club has a good swing. Tonight Babs' minidress still shows bra straps and cleavage, leggage mid-thigh, and an especially large circle of bare belly surrounding her olive-skin center-knot navel.

Babs realizes, *when I visited here three days ago I wore only my Black Bikini, now I'm more covered up. No more total bellage, no more thigh, but especially, no more areolage.*

BB doesn't need to follow the thighs-never-touching Rule; may it please her she closes, even crosses her legs. Might a lucky Gamer opportune an upskirt, they will see that Bikini Babe still wears her nombril bikini briefs, just like the straps belie her bra beneath.

Babs gets the VIP treatment; her el Capitan, that is House Mom el Capitan—MomCap—extends power to BB because of Boss Babe's efforts to persuade the Cosmos Pledge to Opt for a Term at the Nugget. BB will persuade the first of them to commit during *The Runup.*

Babs believes that her primary responsibility is Tiffany, her Roommate and occasional accomplice. But not for long.

Make no mistake about it, Tiffany remains totally visible in her clear vinyl see-through. The longsleeve front-button croptop is the very same one she changed into on her day of arrival, when she declined Peacock Monitor William an opportunity to fellate, talked dirty to his Roommate Rodney, and popped the Peacock Lineup. The hip-hanging miniskirt has migrated from Beka to Elle to Tiffany now, and Babs' magic touch allowed the miniskirt to acquire transparency once Tiffany put it on.

The croptop flies above the navel and the miniskirt rides sufficently below the button that Tiffany remains belly-up belly-down. The miniskirt enabled first Beka and then Elle an opportunity to spread and pink, and Gamers have high hopes that Tiffany will seize this opportunity tonight, perhaps even cream and climax. Like she's done in the past, but not this Term.

Tiffany stands politely in the crowded foyer and considers her positioning and goals. *I danced here two Terms ago, broke the Rules, and parlayed myself into a Porn Star. Then last Term I returned occasionally to Feature Dance, suck cock in the Champagne Room, and film twisters in the Inner Sanctuary.*

Tiffany questions her Garments. *Am I even allowed to wear what I'm wearing inside the Nugget? All the waitresses—regardless of their sexual orientation—work topless, and some Strippers hustle their lapdances nude because they are always nude.*

But Patrons? Guests? Coming in dressed like this? Tiffany calculates. *In fact, this is the most I have ever worn in the Nugget! I was always totally naked before and now I'm naked but not. I'm naked through clear vinyl. I'm going to spread, show off the soft fuzz down to my tail tube, open the doors to my treasure chest, ooze tapioca, and, if they let me, climax my brains out.*

Tiffany feels many people crowding the foyer. She casts eyes for Babs, can't find her, and instead makes eyes with the Hat Check Girl, with her overly thick nose ring and crisscrossed double-pierced nipples above an uplifting corset. The counter blocks Hat Check's lower half, *but the little star tattoo below her eye is new.*

Tiffany knows the Game. *I'm in a tricky position. My whorish reputation might precede me—indeed, some Patrons and some of the staff might know about me and some even have known me. But I am not a Nugget Stripper this Term. And I'm not a Whore. I am a Cosmos Pledge.*

And Cosmos Pledge Rules apply to me.

Tiffany turns and encounters House Mom el Capitan—a familiar short and squat figure with three pieces—standing in front of her with her hands on her hips. MomCap wears a front-tie bare-navel shirt, cargo shorts, and flat sneakers.

"Welcome, Pledge Tiffany," MomCap says with a smile, "what can we do for you tonight?"

Tiffany bows to a familiar figure. "House Mom, I return again to the Nugget, this time as a Cosmos Pledge, and I beg you to let me strip naked and cum be a Stripper next Term.

Tiffany knows, *House Mom el Capitan rules. My confidant and Roommate, Monitor Babs, as well as Janet and possibly other Monitors, all report to MomCap, who resides at and runs the Nugget, and gives the Strippers here their directives.*

MomCap teases a multi-Term underling, "Tisk, tisk, Tiffany Titraffle, thinking of yourself first. I heard your mission tonight is to reduce Steph."

Tiffany knows, "House Mom, my mission is to please you. You know I've been reduced to a wannabe Porn Star. Tell me what I need to do to Pledge naked and cum be your Stripper next Term!"

"Perhaps you can please the Crowd and pee into your own mouth," House Mom suggests with a twinkle in her eye. There are only a few persons in the foyer, although a hovering Cam leads her in toward the Club Stage.

Tiffany firms, "House Mom, please give me a workout tonight. I'll spread and pink, scoop tapioca out of my twat, and torque the Double Dong with Steph." Tiffany graces her fingertips across her lower belly. "Steph Sorostitute gets to cum constantly, and Kimju and Molly have cum; but I haven't been allowed to cum at all this Term, so you need to let me go wild with Steph."

"Don't break any Rules," House Mom el Capitan admonishes, and she's gone.

Tiffany glances and catches a Video of herself on a Screen in the foyer. It's from last Term and she's naked, sitting astride a huge cock and bouncing, with two more cocks competing for her mouth, and another cocks in each hand, and still more cocks above her ejaculating onto her face and hair. Tiffany blinks. *I don't dare break any Rules tonight. I know what is legal for Whores and for Strippers here at the Nugget; but I am less clear on what is legal for Pledge. Eating a girl and sharing the Dong isn't allowed for the Strippers, but this is not "sex," so it is not against Cosmos Rules. Kimju and Molly proved that.*

Tiffany purses her lips. *So I will dong, eat pussy, and taste pee.* Tiffany tightens her forehead. *But will the Patrons tempt me to believe that I'm still a Porn Star, and entice me to fuck on Stage to prove it and reestablish myself?*

Then break me to Slavesex for breaking the no-sex-for-Pledge Rule.

§ MomCap Lets Tiffany: Pink & Cream in the Camera Lounge

The bat-like Maître d' sweeps Tiffany into the Camera Lounge. "You are so very chic," it pronounces. "We mustn't confuse you with the literary Fanny Clariet 'impersonating Venus in her transparent skin tights made of woven air and a knitted nothing.'"

Tiffany remembers the vampire from last Term. "I wear clear vinyl," she clarifies, as if that matters. Tiffany ponders. *I was never sure whether the Maître d' possessed a very small cock or a very long clit; I serviced it last Term. Tonight's goth makeup, black eye sockets, and bloodshot eyes are typical.* The Bat smiles its fangs, flaps its cape, and sits Tiffany on a couch so all the camera buggers can purview her upskirt, well, sort of.

"Welcome a Porn Star from last Term!" the Bat projects to the Camera Lounge. "Tiffany got taken to swinger clubs, then biker bars, and was gangbanged photo-fucked everywhere. She snowballed, collected bukkake, and drank gokkun. Didn't you, my tatterdemalion?"

Tiffany inches forward on the couch and opens her legs just past ajar position. "I sucked cock in the Champagne Room. I shot *Suck Fuck Facial Videos* in the Inner Sanctuary."

The Bat flaps in front of Tiffany and she understands completely: in a flash she unbuttons her croptop and throws it back baring both breasts; she spreads her legs wide. "I want you to look up my skirt and at my naked body and lay 1000 facials on me," Tiffany declares.

Tiffany taunts the Camera Lounge. "No panties protecting this twat!"

Applause and even more bytes spooled.

Tiffany raises her own heat; she makes eyes with as many Cams in the Lounge as she can; she give each a smile, an expression, sometimes blows them a kiss.

She stabilizes, looks beyond the lenses and faces and lights and determines that the Camera Lounge remains a familiar hothouse.

Maître d' signs Tiffany to pink, touch her clit, and finger fuck herself. Tiffany obliges and opens her rosy insides. Tiffany looks at the surround of crushing bodies, flashes, hot lights, and smiles. It is a coy look, one of confidence and bemusement.

"All of you looking at her," Maître d' flatters, "excites her."

It does, and Tiffany transudes tapioca.

Maître d' draws out one cape-wing and announces, "Another Cosmos on the broda brigade!" And there is laughter, good-natured, and lots of camera flashes, and a jostling of position for vids. Tiffany's unbuttoned croptop hides not her pert always-erect nipples, and her see-through and upskirted miniskirt hides not the juice running down her inner thighs.

The Eraser Heads come alive, and, as if delayed, Tiffany's scent suddenly fills the Lounge.

Tiffany feels herself tilting her head to the side and breathing in through her mouth and nose, anticipating the Dong, when she suddenly discovers House Mom's presence, who takes her out of it, extends a hand to help her to stand up, and then keeps her hand-in-hand and leads her out the Lounge. "This way my Cosmos Pledge," MomCap says in her kind and firm way, "I will assist you to the Dressing Room."

§ MomCap Takes Tiffany Backstage: Videos & Louise Dancing

Tiffany buttons her clear vinyl croptop as she follows MomCap out of the Camera Lounge and into the main Club. The shooters buzz around as they return to their seats and brag about collecting Tiffany's gyno and cream.

Tiffany's cream is one of those things Elle would add to her secret notes if she were here… and hasn't lost her grip on her folded paper.

Tiffany's arrival creates a swirl of sensation and applause welcomes her. She stands tall as she parades through the Club. *I Stripped two Terms ago on my way to Whoredom—and I know all the moves. Sometimes I Feature Danced here last Term: I stripped, lapdanced, and prostituted my tricks in the Champagne Room. Shot my Tiny Titty Suck Fuck Facial collector videos in the Inner Sanctuary with its bedroom movie set.*

Patrons are conflicted between watching Tiffany on the Screens blowing a cock and getting ass-fucked, or look right through the see-through of a live Cosmos. Tiffany shows off perky 32As with erect tubular nips—her famous Eraser Heads alert to some ultraviolet in the environment and stimulate her. Descending below her 23 waist and 33 hips, Gamers gaze upon a soft red turf completely visible both above and, lower down, through her transparent waistline. Tiffany's able hands keep the miniskirt positioned. Shaven legs, shaven armpits, and long red hair on her head stun the Crowd.

Gamers who want to know if more tattoos become visible in blacklight hope to find out tonight.

Tiffany feels the flashes on her body, "Hello everybody," she waves to a miniscule hovercam leading her entry, and dares claim, "It's good to be back!"

Tiffany glances at a Screen. *I know what happens next in this video,* Tiffany prides, the *penis in my ass comes out and goes into my mouth in one continuous A2M shot!*

Tiffany knows, *I was not a Nugget the last time I danced here, and I am not a Nugget tonight. So maybe I don't need to follow Nugget Rules.* She clenches her front teeth together on that one.

Tiffany looks to find Babs and recollects that *my connection to my Monitor got broken when I was taken into the Camera Lounge. Tiffany sniffs her finger tips. I don't need to worry, MomCap now leads my way, and she wants me here.*

Tiffany spots Babs across the Club, sitting by herself at a prime Stage-side table. Babs is watching a full-figure and very embarrassed dark-haired topless girl dance awkwardly on Stage. The dancer wears only a crochet Spiderweb g-string and closer to naked than anything. She swings 36D hanging horseshoe-arched lactoids, her nipples up like pen tips; she oozes loblolly into an already crosty g-string.

Tiffany processes. The Spiderweb and the dancer are the same as Tiffany witnessed two nights ago at the Greatest House Roar. *Louise. Babs made her rub her nose on the wall. She's part of some deal between Babs and Janet that involves trading Steph for Ginny. Steph spent last night with Janet, but us Cosmos, including Babs, didn't see any Ginny.*

The dancer turns her rear toward Babs, extracts the string from between her lips, pulls it to the side, shows off her lagway, and rolls open her lapland. Applause in the Club draws away from Tiffany to this vulgarity.

Tiffany glowers that a Pledge from a different House be allowed to audition the Nugget. *I deserve to dance on Stage also.* She eyes Babs seated across the Club. *Humph,* Tiffany snorts silently, suddenly uncertain of her own confidence, *Babs seems more interested in the awkward dancer on Stage than on me.*

None-the-less, gentle applause follows Tiffany as House Mom leads her around the far side and toward the backstage Dressing Room; Tiffany doesn't realize the applause honors her until the House Mom turns and gives a wave for the both of them. Tiffany trades eyes at the topless dancer who just got her lactoids and loblolly upstaged. She squints toward Babs.

Tiffany scans the Club but doesn't see Penny and Coco. *Never met, but I have seen their Videos.* Tiffany processes. *I have done everything in their act, plus work cocks. I am a Porn Star!*

Tiffany considers. *Knowing what I know I presume Penny and Coco hate Babs, and Janet, and Robyn, and even Steph. But I have no Karma with them, although with me auditioning tonight, they should have watched my files!*

Tiffany shakes her shoulders. *They better respect that I have not only been a Stripper, but that I am also a Porn Star! The M/C even said so. Once a Porn Star, always a Porn Star!*

Babs feels different anxiety. *Penny and Coco will again dance here tonight. Tiffany has never met them, although she has admired their pussies and clits on the Dining Room wall.*

I'm sure Penny and Coco hate Robyn and Steph.

But Janet and I are the one they are gunning for.

II-23 Robyn & Steph: Arrive Nugget Stage Door (D23)

§ Robyn: Waters Molly & Kimju and Titty Strips Beka & Elle

At the time when Babs and Tiffany left for the Nugget, Robyn had offered to take Steph inside from the Post Henge and "make her ready to go."

Babs had nixed the idea. "That is so unnecessary. Steph Sorostitute has nothing inside." BB considers the naked Pledge rubbing and kissing a Post. And she has nothing here either."

Indeed, Steph has nothing at all. Except love with a Post. "Ahhhaaaahhhaaaa...."

Robyn had shrugged, left Steph to zone on the Post, and returned inside the Cosmos House. She ignores the Bell on her way through the Back Door.

Upstairs and in the Bunkroom Robyn surveys the four Cosmos lying on their backs in the Bunkroom: heads together in the center of a Clover, holding hands, and legs spread outward, but not uniformly touching toes.

Topless Kimju and Molly did indeed collaborate to induce the Cam to venture from the Bathroom; now it hovers above them, looking downward at their g-string and panties.

The Cam pulls back and the Nugget Screens display an exclusive: clockwise from the Cam hovering above: Kimju, Beka, Molly, Elle.

"Newbies interleafed with ex-Strippers," Robyn laughs as she jokes the Clover. Robyn twitches one side of her nose, "Don't forget, you're live on the Nugget screens. That way Babs and I can keep an eye on you. Too bad you all can't return to the Nugget tonight, so you can titter and pink again. Maybe next time you can stay for the next Term." Robyn cackles, then adds in her superior voice, "How does that go, Pledge?"

Elle wonders in a flash, *Does Robyn have authority to order us to beg?*

Robyn details, "All around the room, one after another, don't stop." And prods topless Kimju with her bare foot. "You first."

And so Kimju looks up at the Cam and leads, "Please let me Pledge naked and cum be a Stripper next Term." It doesn't matter if the Patrons at the Nugget can hear her over the din, but they can read her lips.

Beka feels Robyn prods her with a bare foot, and she jumps into the scene, "Please. Please let me Pledge naked and cum, make me a Stripper next Term." Beka squeezes her hands with Kimju and Molly on opposite sides, and advances, "You can Pee-Cam me if you want. I'll play with myself. I'll stay pink-wet-and-ready and cum on cue."

"You'll keep on holding hands and you'll keep the Chant going," Robyn advises the Clover. Then prods Molly.

"Please let me Pledge naked and cum be a Stripper next Term," Molly retorts with enthusiasm. Topless Molly wears but one Garment, transparent panties that qualify her for the Opt Down.

Elle requires a prod to get going, cognizant of both Robyn and the Cam. She grants power to Robyn's authority. "Please let me Pledge naked and cum be a Stripper next Term," she says, and considers, *I have been reciting that beg since my first Day here. I still have two Garments, but I don't like begging when all the Patrons in the Club can watch.*

And possibly the entire Prefecture.

Now topless Kimju is begging again, "Please let me...," and then Beka, then topless Molly and finally Elle again, this time with no hesitation, and ending, "...Stripper next Term." And then Kimju again, and then....

Molly doesn't question Robyn's orders but Kimju wonders why Robyn issues orders in the first place. *I don't like obeying my Roommate, but Babs has ordered this and now is not the moment to test that.*

Kimju looks into the Cam looking at her from the ceiling. "Silly you," Robyn laments, "if you get any applause at the Nugget you won't even know it."

Once again Elle sounds off and Kimju recites in her turn, "Please let me...Stripper next Term." *I resent Robyn's arrogant intrusion into my future, I resent Robyn disdainful grinding the beg into me. I want to see her beg, not me.*

The Chant cycles again and it is Kimju's turn to chant, "Please let me Pledge naked and cum be a Stripper next Term."

If I only knew that Robyn really has Charm! Kimju worries, *Because if we play a Roommate Game and I lose my g-string....* Kimju considers this outcome. *I can handle being naked 24x7, I've already aroused myself and cum on Stage. But if I lose is how do I get two Garments? From Beka and Elle perhaps.*

Robyn steps back and surveys what she has begun. Molly's Watering Can sits in the corner, and so Robyn gets it and gives Molly a watering. "Whatcha gonna do about this, Molly Magnus? Move your hands?" Probably not. Robyn drenches Molly's bunched-in panties, waters her floppy mams, and, just to be rude, splatters her face. Molly sputters but doesn't flub her line when her turn to recite comes around. She can taste the flavor.

Robyn watches them and considers them at their word. Kimju's nipples salute and her skin grows goose bumps. When Beka misses a beat of the Chant Robyn reaches down, unbuttons the halter strap behind the neck, pulls it free, then daintily folds the halter down upon her belly, totally baring both of Beka's conical breasts. Robyn stands, and watches Beka's bare nipples indent. Beka widens her legs that last little bit in response to Robyn probing her inner thighs, and the Crowd at the Nugget can see that the fabric seam through her crotch has become crosty.

"Beka Broda," Robyn points, and directs the Cam for a close-up. Once again, Kimju and Molly must grasp Beka's hands firmly.

Elle doesn't miss her opportunity at the Chant, so there is no misbehavior that warrants Robyn reaching down, pushing her croptop up to bare both breasts. "Boobage the Nugget!" Robyn snarls, and then somewhat violently pushes Elle's legs together and yanks her slacks down. The stroke pulls the slacks down to mid-thigh and completely bares Elle's nether region.

Robyn contemplates her full-frontal Pledge for a moment, and then gives the slacks a second jerk, all the way down to her ankles, and then uses her bare feet to push Elle's knees back wide apart. The result leaves Elle's crotch as widely open as that of her four fellow Cosmos, except she is not reaching with her feet toward her two adjacent Cosmos. And another exception: there is no string, no seam, no fabric protecting Elle's nookie.

Robyn puts her tongue behind her lower teeth and pushes outward; her mouth opens as her upper lip rises. Robyn takes her big toe and uses it to worm Elle's sex lips open. "Congratulations," Robyn tells Elle, "you the only unencumbered nymphaeum in the Clover!" And laughs.

Robyn steps back and addresses the Pledge she has just pantsed, "You're gonna make nectar today," she declares, wipes her toe on Elle's cheek, turns on her heel, and exits. Elle almost misses her turn to beg.

§ Robyn Escorts Steph: Post Henge to the Nugget

Steph had drifted out of reverie and discovers she had been left alone in the Backyard. She becomes very afraid, presses her naked body against the Post, and accidently urinates. The Cam doesn't misses the Cosmos' latest Pee-Camer's contribution, even if it is a short squirt.

While Robyn is away Steph becomes aware of paparazzi—real and imagined—plus there are the hockey players, goalies all—the Rachmaninoffs—who watch her from the alley. Steph imagines they all masturbate to her. Kundalini allows Steph's madness to coalesce upwards from her wet and lubricated inner thighs; once again Steph's scarlet slash rides the Post, and Steph commences to paint the Post with slippery.   .

Robyn returns, not bothering to ring the Bell, and discovers that Steph has auto-Zoned herself. Robyn bites Steph on an ear and spits into her face. This deprecates Steph from the Zone.

Steph wakes up—like the sudden waking up from anesthesia. *I am drenched in my sexual discharge.* Steph's head spins. *I didn't know I had this much soppy in me.* She casts wild eyes about to see if any

Rachmaninoffs still lurk about. *I sensed them feeling me while I hugged the post, but I couldn't see their faces or identify their bodies.*

And for once, Steph is grateful for Robyn's presence. As the Redacted gathers up Steph, her naked former Monitor creams and drips urine for the Cam. Steph no longer appreciates the irony of her former treasonous subordinate dominating her. Robyn feels proud of her power, and rasps sharp fingernails on Steph's ribs.

"Chant," Robyn commands.

And Steph falls into the rhythm.

Robyn walks her across the Backyard to a Van parked in the alley. "Your wish to 'cum be a Stripper' is being granted," Robyn announces, "you get to audition the Nugget. You gonna be a Stripper next turn and the Term after that you're gonna be a money slut."

Robyn ushers the naked Steph into the back of the Van, instructs her to sit herself on the floor, unable to see anything outside. Steph becomes aware she is illuminated—she figures out where a Cam is—and she continues to chant and play with herself.

Now she wants to. "... Titty titty. Clitty clitty. Hole mouth."

Robyn rides shotgun. She curls a lip at the thought of the Nugget Crowd watching Steph in the back.

Steph eventually feels the Van come to a stop and the motor turn off. She hears Robyn descend from the passenger seat, walk along the side the Van and open the back door. Steph looks out into a back alley, a parking lot adjacent, and flat industrial walls. *One of those infrequently populated kind of place that is almost private, but isn't.*

The moment I step out I'm streaking again, Steph concludes. *Stark naked, masturbating, and looking for the Nugget Stage Door.*

True.

"Out, you sloppy stinking sinkhole" Robyn squawks right in her face. "Molly already took Kimju for a ride on the Double Dong, and tonight everyone's gonna watch Tiffany lesbo cum you on the Dong!"

Fear shoots through Steph. "Don't be ridiculous." she halts. "That's out of the question. We're doing solo acts."

Robyn laughs. "Have fun at the Nugget, you sojering screwhole semiwatt! Now Chant for me!"

Twilight fringes Steph's bleached blonde hair. She chants toward Zone level, "Please let me cum be a Stripper next Term. Titty, titty. Clitty clitty. Hole mouth."

Robyn points toward a doorway.

Steph quiets and tries to move quickly on her bare feet; she keeps one hand rubbing her clit and the other pinching her nipples. Fear stimulates more secretions.

Robyn, uncertain, follows Steph hobbling toward the doorway. *My bare feet hurt too. Except I am dressed. I look hot in my maillot cutout, and I am in charge! Steph Sorostitute belongs to me!*

The doorway sits level with a square concrete slab, a small awning atop, and a nameplate next to a buzzer: "Stage Door," nothing else.

Steph stops masturbating. She has fallen sufficently out of the Zone to realize that it is the Stage Door of the Nugget before her. And so she makes a play upon Robyn. "I've been in the Nugget before. Like when I came to pick up the Pink Pages." Steph babbles, she is only slightly coherent, not totally out of the Zone yet. "Except I came in the front door."

"Tonight you're going in the Stage Door, just like all the other acts." Robyn smiles, and queries, "So did you come in the front door last Term when you secretly watched Janet and Tiffany climax the Double Dong and perform Watersports?" Robyn forays.

Steph relinquishes, "I was a Monitor so it was completely allowed. And besides, back then I watched from a veiled booth. But I have never Stripped here. Never Stripped."

Robyn states the obvious, "You're not gonna Strip tonight either. You're already naked. Ha ha ha!"

Steph tries to gather her thoughts and adjust to a changing reality. For Steph the calculus suddenly becomes very simple. *Even though Molly defeated me in the Roommate Game, I still have a chance of not Stripping later—like all next Term—if I beg to Strip and cum now.*

Robyn enjoys the torment, "You have nothing to take off, but you can dance and play with yourself. Now rub yourself. Harder. Stay fresh. You're gonna pink, pee, and cum for the Crowd, you slutty slop skank. You're gonna give up everything you got and make sure this is your next home."

Robyn advises her apprentice. "Ring the buzzer."

Steph looks at her with eyes wild with fear, eyes looking around, stooped over, hands now busy between her legs; Steph expects male bodies might pop out of doorways, throw her down on the ground and forcefully penetrate her. There is no escape. Steph's slush runs down her thighs. Again she leaks pee and this time the Stage Door surveillance Cam collects her. She opens her mouth but no words come out.

Robyn has her own mixed feelings about entering the Nugget, especially via this entrance. On one hand she doesn't want to be associated with "going in with the help" yet she feels proud to be Steph's deliverer. Robyn has never been in the Nugget before, or any place like it.

Steph hesistates, so Robyn pushes the doorbell.

§ MomCap Welcomes Robyn & Steph: At the Nugget Stage Door

The Back Door Man opens the Stage Door and surveys them. The guard already knows they are there, thanks to video surveillance and proximity alarms. Steph backs off rubbing just enough to know she lies on a trajectory of definite reduction. She examines her protector, and winces to herself.

The Back Door Man beckons them in. Robyn goes first, and the guard diverts her in the direction of the backstage Dressing Room. "Dressing room?" Robyn asks, and the guard is curt, "down the hall, first doorway on the left." Robyn obeys him with the attitude of a princess who extends courtesy to a serf.

A shorter, stout woman in a belly-bearing front-tie shirt, cargo shorts, and gym shoes blocks her way, and Robyn immediately complains to this stranger, "I've never been here before, and I'm being separated from my protectorate!"

"Don't worry," the stout woman stabilizes her, "I'm House Mom. I run this place."

"You run the Nugget." Robyn inflects.

House Mom el Capitan smiles. "I hope that wasn't a question. But please don't answer me. The Dressing Room on your left awaits you."

Robyn flaps, dances on toes, swallows. And fakes a smile.

§ Penny & Coco Enable Steph: To Visit the Camera Lounge

The separated and naked Steph finds herself ground onto her hands and knees and pushed through a doorway. She looks up and discovers an equally stark naked Penny and Coco are prodding her down a long narrow twisting turning passageway. One or the other of the Strippers hold a long Double Dong in hand, and as Steph scampers forward she feels the Dong reach for her clit and draw across her wetness. Steph tries to twist around, but the Dong emphasizes that she move forward.

The Dong speaks to me and I obey, Steph accepts.

Penny and Coco have been waiting for Steph to arrive. Their memories of their former Monitor are crisp; both hold Steph responsible for their "promotion."

The humiliation of being walked on all fours by her two former Pledge starts to sink in when a door opens in front of her and Steph finds herself blinded by light. Steph yields as her two former Cosmos have the honor of rotating her onto her back on a couch, spreading her legs, and guiding her to move her hands from her pussy to behind her head, spread surrender position. Steph's bleached scruff parts just enough to reveal a single line and her long bleached blonde hair crinkles.

"Welcome to the Camera Lounge," Penny bows as the pack flashes and clicks and zooms and pans.

"You ever visited the Nugget before?" Coco queries.

"No!" Steph lies.

"You remember forcing us to cum last Term?" Penny queries.

Steph tries to stabelize, "Ma'am, I—"

"Now it's our turn to force you to cum," Coco wrinkles her nose at Steph's pungent scent, and rubs the end of the Double Dong across Steph's slippery sex lips.

"Pull pink for you fans, Steph Sorostitute," Penny orders.

Steph hesistates, hands still behind head.

Coco coaxes, "You can do it, use two hands, one on each side."

Steph surrenders and obeys then moves her arms, hands, and fingers.

Cameras shutter.

Penny and Coco have never worn a stitch of clothing this Term, and relish the opportunity to humiliate their former Monitor and tormentor. Steph quivers; her clit is erected, and her oozing deep pink insides get fervidly documented by the packed room.

Again, they put the Dong into play, extending it within reach of Steph's sexcupidity, and Steph, wanton with desire and beyond shame helplessly yields to her most base carnal desires and arches her pelvis up in order to rub her clit on the Dong. She gathers her breath and lunges her pelvis upward in an attempt to take it into her sloppy sex organ. She abandons pulling pink, thrusts upward for the end of the Dong, and rubs her nipples and clit with her fingers. Many Cams in the Lounge collect Steph's naked pink and wet masturbation.

Is this the full extent that Penny and Coco will get to payback their former Monitor?

"Beg," Penny says.

Steph begs, "Ma'am, please let me Pledge naked and cum be a Stripper next Term, Ma'am."

Coco torments Steph's clit with the Dong. "You, Stripper wannabe, you want this?" she asks.

Steph tremors at the top but manages to ride down a little, to partly come to her senses. Kundalini consolidates her entire pelvis. *The Dong must be dealt with. Or it will deal with me.*

It will deal with me.

Steph, naked and spread on the posing couch finds her voice and addresses Penny and Coco. "Too bad you Strippers aren't allowed to share the Dong. Cause you'd be on opposite ends. Just like when you got to climax together at the end of last Term.

The Camera Lounge quiets; Steph continues, "Be nice to me, I'm not the reason you're here. I was in Lockdown when Babs and Janet beat you in the Mudpit and you know it. If you want to blame Robyn, be my guest, because she denies she was even there.

Penny teases the inside of Steph's pink with the magical tip of the Dong and allows Step to regain her climax.

"Huh, huh, huh, huh, huh..." voices Steph on center Stage.

Penny brings her down just enough so Steph can comprehend her oration. "Strippers can't share the Dong but Pledge can."

Coco predicts. "And you will. Just like you shared the Pee-Cam with Molly earlier today."

"Rub yourself harder."

"Beg for it."

Steph begs, "Please let me fuck the Dong. Give it to me right now! I'll keep it in me and I'll ride it with every Cosmos!

The two Nugget Strippers hold the Dong just out of reach from where Steph can arch up and bury it.

Steph vibrates, rubs her pink harder, grinds three fingers into her slot and slathers slime on her face.

Her clit reaches full height and graces the Dong. Steph, no longer hears words but she feels the press of the Camera Lounge bodies, the hum and click of the Cams, flashes, the smell and taste of herself. She begs, "Penny and Coco please, I'll do whatever you want, and if you Strippers begging to be Dong Whores next Term want me to pee and climax the Dong at the same time, I will."

The Dong intrudes into Steph's mouth, forcing it's way past her tongue, banging her throat, and reinforcing the taste of herself and her craving of violation. The Strippers put Steph into a huffing again, this time Steph widens her mouth, so she may huff around the intruder.

The Lounge has quieted now. Steph opens her eyes and discovers the Dong is gone from her mouth. Steph looks up dewy-eyed from her posing couch and begs her two ex-Pledge, "I'll eat your pussies out. Both of you."

Penny shimmies and looks down at her, "Now that's a prize—"

"—you're gonna work for!" Coco concludes.

The two Nuggets engage Steph to masturbate while she sucks on the Dong, and in moments the pink and wet Pledge is off in the Zone.

II-24 Robyn Gets Tiffany's: Clear Vinyl Outfit (D23)

§ Robyn Greets Tiffany: In the Nugget Dressing Room

Robyn is startled to discover Tiffany in the Dressing Room. *Had not Tiffany come with Babs? So why is she sitting with her tush and feet on a table, legs wide, hands between her legs, playing with herself?*

The table is deep enough for Tiffany to scrunch her torso back, brace her heels on the edge, and balance a good spread.

The room is filled with the smell of Tiffany's freshness.

Tiffany brings her thoughts back to the moment, looks into Robyn's eyes, but doesn't speak. Robyn walks in front of the Cam, momentarily filling the image with a close-up of her torsoed maillot and "the smallest buttonhole," before its view reverts to Tiffany Transparent.

Tiffany wonders, *Did Robyn do that on purpose to me or is she just stupid? She doesn't even know that the Cams feeds Screens out front.*

The Nugget Shooter drifts into the Dressing Room and directs the position and point-of-view of the Cam. Might the Shooter wear headphones to collect feedback from the Patrons out front? Maybe even Gamers out in the Prefecture? The Shooter may. For the moment Shooter augments Tiffany's tangy tart with close-ups. The Shooter next highlights Tiffany's anus.

Tiffany knows, *no hiding my tailpipe.* Tiffany scoops and rubs transuda upon her twiddle twig. *No hiding anything.*

But no cumming. Tiffany purses her lips. *Total revelation not yet.*

Robyn pouts for lack of attention, so the Shooter gathers candids and flatters her. Robyn gestures to Tiffany and reports, "Tiffany Transparent is a Porn Star, and a Whorehouse is her natural habitat."

Tiffany blinks and then considers. *Well, partly true. I need to be a Porn Star again and a Whorehouse is my natural habitat. However, the Nugget is not a Whorehouse and Strippers are not Whores.*

Tiffany stiffens with pride. *Flesh Ranch is a Whorehouse, and that is where I was stabled last Term. I didn't just Feature Dance and work the Champagne Room at the Nugget, I did lots of kinds of sex, in lots of places!*

§ Robyn Acquires from Tiffany: Clear Vinyl Garments

House Mom swoops into the Nugget Dressing Room. Tiffany, still wearing her clear vinyl croptop and miniskirt, looks up from her spread tango; she continues to concentrate on keeping her timbale flowing, her assigned priority for the moment. House Mom gestures to Tiffany and inquires of Robyn, "My dear, do you know why Tiffany is here tonight?"

Robyn looks back to Tiffany, and recalls a month from Tiffany's Porn Star Calendar with Tiffany getting gangbanged in the mud. Robyn should know Tiffany visits the Nugget tonight to work Steph over, but considering Tiffany's pink-wet-and-ready state, Robyn advances a different agenda, "Looks to me like she wants to audition the Nugget because it's her next step to becoming a fuck Whore."

Robyn speaks to House Mom as if she is a peer, but MomCap chooses to ignore Robyn's failure to address her with a salutation of respect.

Robyn gains confidence, turns to Tiffany, and torments her directly, "You deserve to be here you wannabe Whore. You're gonna beg Gamers to rent your money mouth, treasure chest, and tailpipe." Robyn laughs, pleased with herself.

House Mom raises Tiffany's chin with her finger. "You hear that? You hear what she said about you? Stop playing with yourself and put your hands behind your head. Now."

Tiffany complies instantly. If nothing else, she is gorgeously trained.

House Mom speaks again, "Please Tiffany, Robyn thinks you belong in the Nugget next Term. Do you want to beg to cum here?"

Tiffany begs, "House Mom absolutely House Mom. Please let me Pledge naked and cum be a Stripper next Term."

Robyn curls her nose; she fails to consider that all the Cosmos, except herself and Babs, beg to Pledge naked and cum Strip next Term.

House Mom demands more from Tiffany, "Convince me you really do desire to come here."

So Tiffany advances more regimen, "I'll stay pink-wet-and-ready." Tiffany thinks, augments, "I'll pee. I'll pour shots. I'll dildo my trap. I'll double penetrate with dildo and buttplug. I'll eat a girl. I'll let you manage my cum."

"I know. You'll do whatever," House Mom anticipates from experience. She waves an arm. "Tiffany, you may get naked now. Off with your croptop and miniskirt. You don't need them here. In fact you really don't need them at all." MomCap grins, "there's no part of you that isn't public."

Tiffany relaxes, "House Mom, thank you, House Mom. I need to be a Porn Star again. May it please you I'll stay naked and cum be a Stripper next Term." Tiffany might be fully visible wearing clear vinyl, but giving up two Garments does matter.

Robyn can't resist interjecting, and rushes in, "You'll ride the Double Dong!"

Tiffany smiles quietly and trades eyes with House Mom. *Does Robyn pitch way out of her league?* Tiffany focuses her challenge right back to

Robyn. "I already told you, I'll ride the Dong with you; I'll give you a ride you won't forget!"

Robyn blinks. Ouch, not appreciated.

House Mom shushes them like a hen with chicks.

Robyn's head spins. She looks at Tiffany. Tiffany has already slid the miniskirt off, and now she unbuttons the last button of her longsleeve, front-button, clear vinyl croptop. Off the shoulders the shirt comes.

House Mom turns to address Robyn. "You, my darling Cosmos, are so underdressed for the Club out there!"

Robyn's eyes open wide. "Underdressed? Robyn doesn't know what this means. She feel cornered and looks for ways out of the Dressing Room. Except she can't get around House Mom to get out the door, and she can't get past the Back Door Man to get out the Stage Door.

But House Mom doesn't give Robyn time for the panic to build; House Mom immediately quells any uncertainty, points a finger at Robyn and expounds, "why we need to put more clothes on you! They are animals out there. They'll think you are one of the acts!"

House Mom collects Tiffany's shirt with one hand and her miniskirt with the other. And hands them to a startled Robyn.

Suddenly Robyn, like Babs, now possesses three Garments. Super-charged to Double Opt Up so fast she doesn't quite realize it yet.

Tiffany now becomes the second naked Cosmos.

Robyn holds the two see-through vinyl Garments clumsily. Their bequeathment upon her stimulates Robyn to offer Tiffany a suggestions: "Time for you and Steph to piss climax the Double Dong and Opt Down together."

Once again House Mom ignores Robyn's rudeness. "Out on center Stage, no doubt," she laughs, and gestures to someplace out of the Dressing Room.

Robyn feels Tiffany looking back at her strapped maillot cutout. Robyn looks into Tiffany's eyes and finds certainty threatened. Robyn's eyes and lids say it all: *House Mom better not expect me to take my maillot off so I'm only wearing what used to be your clear vinyl croptop and miniskirt.*

Robyn finds her head backed up by Tiffany's stare. But then a toughening of attitude: *Don't mess with me or I am out the Stage Door!*

Then again, wild eyes.

Robyn is not in for a Flip-Flop. "Put them on," House Mom orders Robyn. Disbelief. Then again, "You can do it."

Finally Robyn understands, sorts out what she holds and she steps into the miniskirt. "They will fit you well enough," House Mom adjusts the waist, and Robyn slips her arms into the shirtsleeves of the top. "Now you'll wear as many pieces as Babs!"

Three Garments.

Robyn breaths a sign of relief, *Of course,* she assumes, *Mom Cap can't Flip-Flop Tiffany and me, and besides, I am exempt from any Flip-Flopping.* Robyn gathers her wits and counts her Garments. *Fact: Boss Bitch and I are now equals!*

Robyn further evaluates. *House Mom el Capitan also has three pieces!* Robyn considers House Mom for a moment. *She's kinda dumpy and nowhere near as gorgeous as I am. But because I'm so important, she's made me her equal!*

Tiffany's mind races while she sits naked spread surrender. *Boss Babe never suggested my mission tonight would include reducing myself.* Tiffany frowns. *On the other hand it is House Mom who stripped me naked, and after all, it is I who have begged! I who still beg to Strip here.* Tiffany takes stock of her physical posture: she makes sure her hands intertwine behind her head, ovals her mouth, puts tension into her arms for form deep armpits, and forces her erect and humming Eraser Heads forward. No clear vinyl for them to rub on anymore. Tiffany wiggles her pussy ajar and pumps ooze. *Speak with your body,* Tiffany recites silently; it's a phrase she learned as a Porn Star.

Tiffany considers, *What's next? Naked Steph and I are going to dance Center Stage out front. That's what.*

"And what do you have to say for yourself?" House Mom interrupts Tiffany's silence.

Tiffany replies, "House Mom, please let me Pledge naked and cum be a Stripper next Term. If you arouse me, you will control me."

House Mom puts her thumbs on her belly just between her front-tie shirt and her cargo shorts, and considers Tiffany's request. She turns to Robyn, bows, and solicits, "Do you think we should grant Tiffany's request?"

Robyn offers a creative regimen, only it's directly to Tiffany, and ignores House Mom. "Listen up, trollop. Quietly chant while you hold your hands behind your head, then pinch your nipples and clitty, taste yourself, and then put her hands back behind your head and mouth the Chant again. You keep doing this over and over until your nipples and clitty are black and blue."

Tiffany isn't sure what to do but she obeys. "Please let me Pledge naked and cum be a stripper next Term, titty titty, clitty clitty, hole mouth." *After all,* she adjudicates to herself, *Babs told all of us to obey Robyn 'as if the orders come from my own lips.'* Tiffany tastes herself carefully and confirms, *I'm already erect and wet.*

Tiffany steals eyes with House Mom. *I do know where power resides here at the Nugget.* But House Mom does not choose to correct Robyn nor arrest Tiffany's motion. *I know MomCap,* Tiffany affirms, *and I know MomCap knows that Robyn disrespected her. Twice*

But MomCap needn't deal with Robyn now, Tiffany appreciates. *First, MomCap will put* me *in whatever place she wants* me *in. I am the Gamer of Interest.*

Tiffany runs her tongue around the inside of her lower teeth. *The Chant is getting to me. I can feel it. I'm spread and naked and pink-wet-and-ready to cum. I'm into the Zone soon; I can't control myself under this regimen.*

Tiffany considers the Cam that details her every intimacy. *Been there, done that, can do it again. Toys, Dongs, Watersports. You name it. This is my best Option to get back to Porn Star.*

Robyn primps in her new clothes. "Look at me," she orders, and Tiffany turns her head to look at Robyn. Robyn complains, "Gamers aren't being very nice to me. They give me your two Garments but they stay transparent."

"You got three Garments," Tiffany insists. "You should be grateful and not worry about being opaque."

"I'm not," Robyn says. "Obviously I'm a Double Opt Up and a MomCap next Term. Seems like you, and Steph, shall be Opting Down. Streaking to the Nugget. Wonder if you'll make it?"

"I've fornicated in pubic before, Robyn," Tiffany tests, "And I'd love to take you there."

Robyn shrugs, "Your Opts doesn't matter to me. You're just lucky that House Mom needed to find clothes for me from someone."

"Guess you weren't going to get them from Steph," Tiffany taunts, "and by the way, where is she anyway? Aren't you her guardian or something?"

Robyn startles at the mention of Steph. Neurons trigger. She shifts her feet around. Steph's disappearance into the bowels of the Club earlier gnaws on her.

Robyn doesn't miss a glance from Tiffany to House Mom. She snaps at Tiffany. "How come you stopped chanting?"

Tiffany blinks. She knows how to answer, "You asked me a question. I answered you."

"Chant," Robyn says.

"Ma'am," Tiffany stumbles, then begs, "Please let me Pledge naked and cum be a Stripper next Term." She pauses ever a moment to allow an interrupt. None occurs. She moves her hands from behind her head, touches her fingertips ever so lightly to her Eraser Heads and accelerates their stimulus. "Titty titty," she recites, drops all fingertips to reveal the butterfly head, "clitty clitty," digs into pink to finger dip tapioca, "hole," draw the fingertip upward and sucks her fingers clean, "mouth," and puts her hands to rest behind her head, surrender position. *I am plenty wet now.*

Robyn assumes parity with MomCap. She preens in the clear vinyl croptop and miniskirt worn overtop her maillot. "I guess Tiffany knows she'll be streaking from now on," Robyn declares as she nods toward the now naked and spread Tiffany, sitting a table in the Nugget Dressing Room.

Robyn continues to lecture MomCap, "As for Steph, the only person in denial that Steph will be streaking is Steph." Robyn laughs at her own humor. "Ha ha ha!

MomCap bemuses, "And just where is Steph?"

A strange look overcomes Robyn's face.

MomCap curls her nose. "I hear that Penny and Coco took Steph away."

"Yeah," Robyn agrees, "Right."

Tiffany is still able to think. But the thought processes are getting more difficult now. *Kundalini seeks to take hold of me. If I stay naked, and Steph stays naked, then the two of us and the topless Kimju and Molly will all Opt Strip next Term. That leaves BB and Robyn and newbies Beka and Elle to Opt Monitor.*

Tiffany steadies herself into a steady breathing rhythm as she assesses Robyn's new garb. *The clear vinyl croptop and miniskirt worn overtop her maillot gives Robyn's costume verve,* Tiffany has to admit. *Only it's not my croptop and miniskirt anymore.* The croptop rides high on Robyn's ribcage and the miniskirt hangs low on her belly; however, underneath the vinyl Robyn's stretchy maillot covers all of her belly except for "the smallest buttonhole," where navelage still eyes out the cutout with no vinyl in the way.

Tiffany accepts that House Mom has granted Robyn favoritism, *but why make her a three-piece girl, a Double-Opt Up? Why now?*

Tiffany breathes harder now. I needn't be turned into a Streaker. Topless, bottomless, either will do. A tube belt. A string around my finger.

As House Mom sweeps Robyn out of the Nugget Dressing Room, Robyn gets one final look at Tiffany: Tiffany shakes as she mouths and acts out the Chant, "Please let me Pledge naked and cum be a Stripper next Term. Titty titty, clitty clitty, hole mouth."

Robyn assumes this is easy to do. Most Gamers who try it can't maintain sixty seconds, let alone sixty minutes. But Tiffany knows. *This kind of Chant can make one fried, just like Steph is fried. Fried, conditioned, programmed. Call it whatever you want.* Tiffany feels Kundalini stir and takes a deep breath.

Call it what it is really is girl, Tiffany says as she relinquishes herself to Kundalini, *Hello Zone!*

And purrs.

§ House Mom & Robyn: Complements & Reentry Demands

House Mom halts Robyn in the backstage hallway. She stands in front of her, puts her hands on Robyn's shoulders, looks up at her, beams, and speaks, "You look magnificent!" She breaks the hold and claps her hands together, "And the Crowd demands that you make an appearance!"

Once again a shiver of fear runs up Robyn's spine. She knows that both Tiffany and Steph are here and that both demonstrate commitment to keeping their juices flowing. Naked pudding. Babs should be here also, somewhere, and not seeing her also contributes to Robyn's anxiety. Anxiety? Is that the right word? Concern? Control of the situation? Because Robyn believes, *I have a right to know!*

"You shall make a grand entrance!" House Mom rises onto tiptoes, and leans forward just in front of Robyn's face, and commands, "So you must go around to the front door!"

This declaration leaves Robyn really confused. She starts to speak, but babbles. House Mom knows what to do (that's why she's the House Mom). "Out the Stage Door, turn left and find the space in-between this building and the next, and around front you'll spot the Doorman and he'll let you in."

"But, but…." Robyn doesn't appreciate not getting told the full script in advance. But House Mom has already walked Robyn out the Stage Door, arm around back, and Robyn stands on the concrete in the light of a hanging bulb.

"There is gravel, rusty cans, broken glass," Robyn complains.

"You may rush up the ramp to center Stage, strip yourself naked, and make pink-wet-and-ready." House Mom smiles. "Or you may return via the Front Door as our guest!"

And it's not hard for Robyn to decide.

Robyn steps off the concrete slab, then turns around and asks House Mom. "Where's Babs?"

House Mom waves a finger at her in a cheerful way. She has many responsibilities, "Please don't ask questions, my darling Cosmos." She draws the finger back, "And do ask the Maître d' to show you the Camera Lounge."

"The Camera Lounge?"

"I'm hearing echoes." House Mom speaks sterner now. "Next time I hear you ask a question I'm going to take that maillot of yours away from you, and Robyn Revealing *will* steal the show. Don't forget." She pauses. "Now scram."

Robyn turns away and House Mom speaks again, "And one more thing." Robyn turns to meet Mom's eyes, "Thank me, Pledge."

Robyn stops, unsure of what to say. She opens and closes her mouth. She already discounts her new clothing, the "Empresses' new clothes." Robyn covers some bases, "House Mom, thank you, House Mom!"

Lame, but quite acceptable. House Mom steps inside and the Back Door Man closes the door. Robyn blinks twice and scoots. "I don't feel safe back here."

II-25 Robyn: Entre l'Club (D23)

§ Robyn Observes Coco: Royalty Meets a Baseboard Stripper

The Doorman greets Robyn with a double door salute and defers to her like royalty. *Which I am after all, somewhere in my bloodline.*

Robyn has nothing to contribute to the Hat Check Girl, but a fleeting glance reveals this creature wears a very tight corset that lifts her breasts and ensures double pierced nipples stand out. Hat Check has a star tattooed below her eye.

The Maître d' alights, flaps once, takes Robyn's arm immediately, and inquires, in a French kind of way, "Any requests?"

And luckily Robyn remembers, mostly out of fear, "el Capitan said I should ask you to show me the Camera Lounge."

The vampire gentles a firm response: "Ah, my dear Cosmos, it is House Mom who instructed you! She is only 'el Capitan' to your Monitor, the Bodacious Babs!"

Robyn is frazzled by this reprimand. But before she can get in a question about where Monitor Babs might alight, the Bat sweeps her through a sharply angled black space, and then Robyn finds herself ejected into the back of the Camera Lounge.

Robyn fails to assess the size of the room for her attention is drawn to only one thing. She knows the Stripper posing on the dais at the opposite end of the room. Well, she doesn't know her; officially the amnesic has never met the former Cosmos Pledge, never adjudicated over her demise. But Robyn has seen her picture: *It's Coco, the cunt balling her clit on the Dining Room wall. One of the Baseboard Strippers.*

Now live in the Camera Lounge, naked and pink and encunting the Dong in front of the entire Prefecture. Robyn scowls at the naked spread Stripper. *I've seen all your Dong Videos, you cally-ho cachung cunny. You double dong and shave and climax and you solo your holes, but bottom line is that you and Penny aren't allowed to share the Double Dong this Term, and you are getting horny for it. Too horny, but don't worry, cunt, you will be sharing the Dong next Term, but it won't be at the Cosmos House.*

Robyn remains ignorant of the fact that Penny and Coco brought Steph to freshness in this very Lounge only shortly ago. Or that Tiffany boobaged, pinked herself, and transuded tapioca earlier here tonight.

Is it coincidence that Nugget House Mom has deployed Coco to put some spook into Robyn? Perhaps. House Mom, she's like a witch sometimes, and this small piece of her magic entrances the princess. MomCap knows that *Coco has the potential to trigger recall... and that*

Coco hates *Robyn for the Mudwrestling Contest last Term... and what followed thereafter.*

Stripper Coco does possesses total recall. *I might not know what's in store for the night, but I know a Game's a foot.*

Coco finds it hard to see past the lights; no matter, she pinks and coitals the Dong in front of a Lounge packed with Cams. *I know that spreading naked and keeping pink-wet-and-ready just is.*

Robyn asks a rare question of herself. *Does Coco knows that Boss Bitch should be here tonight? Maybe Penny's here too. And I bet the both of them want to get back at Bikini Bitch for busting them to this place.* Robyn scans the Camera Lounge. *Not here.*

If Robyn's previous Cosmos experience weren't redacted, she might know more about Coco's past than just seeing her Picture, or Pink Page, or watching her *Side-by-Side Videos* with Penny.

Instead of curling her nose Robyn might have channeled the Cam that collects the perpetually naked Coco shaving on Stage every Day, something Coco has done since she arrived at the Nugget, earlier this Term.

Robyn could have discovered that Coco has become a particularly popular lapdancer, and that she is scheduled to get either her nipples or her clithood pierced, and that Gamers are bidding on her tattoo.

Robyn has something more important to consider: *me.*

Robyn silently snorts and purses her lips as she watches Coco plunge one end of a huge Double Dong in and out of her shaven cozy. Even over the din Robyn can hear Coco recites a cantillation, "Please let me share the Double Dong with my Roommate next Term, even if I have to Whore and not Pledge. Please let me...."

The Vampire whispers to Robyn what Robyn may have forgotten, "Coco and her Roommate Penny begged the Double Dong after they lost the Mudwrestling Contest to Bikini Babe and Janet at the end of last Term. They totally climaxed together on it and now they want to play with it more. They fell in love and now they're prepared to Opt either way—Pledge or Whore—to insure they can ride together again."

"Fell in love with each other or fell in love with the Double Dong?" Robyn asks.

The Bat ignores the question and gathers both wings tight against its spindly body so that the forewings cross in front of its chest.

Robyn offers a suggestion to Maître d'. "Too bad Beka and Elle aren't here. Elle could lolly up." Robyn laughs into the back of her hand.

The Bat draws air into its nostrils and Robyn becomes aware that Coco is looking at her. Coco momentary bobbles the Chant, but gets right back into the groove. Robyn hears the beeps and whirs of the cameras, makes out the soft stage lights. *I've been made,* she says to herself. Robyn blinks. *She knows who I am.* Robyn calculates. *But why shouldn't she? I'm famous.*

The two of them struggle to share eyes, neither wanting to break the gaze. At first Robyn dominates the struggle; she looks into eyes of one humiliated. But then Coco's eyes sparkle with the reminder that the one who bent the Rules and then got away with it has been recognized.

Robyn feels heat from the eyes. *I don't' know why Coco looks at me like she does. She looks at me like she thinks I should be in her place.* And Robyn breaks off the gaze.

Robyn again turns to the vampire, "Money-box wannabe."

Maître d' understands that beggars don't always believe what they beg, although sometimes if they repeat themselves over and over again their minds get made up. Coco's plunging reaches a panting, the room quiets, flashes still explode, and Coco goes into a steady rolling climax, the Chant lost to her trills. Hoots in the room.

"Go Coco," Robyn applauds, and louder, " Go Whore."

Robyn finds Coco's eyes coming to meet hers, they contact, and she finds herself looking into pure snake. Coming at her with an out-of-control screaming climax on the wilding Dong.

Robyn takes a step backwards and bumps into the Bat, who helps her step backward further still, toward the exit, and when Robyn looks over her shoulder one last time Coco has relapsed into copulating with her Dong, gurgling and trying to regain her Chant.

Another look at the Hat Check Girl reveals she wears boots with her corset, and displays her butt and bare hatch. Robyn has no way of knowing that since her first Nugget visit (three Days ago) Hat Check acquires the little star under her eye, tattooed live on center Stage.

§ Babs Greets Robyn: M/C Introduces First Timer to Nugget

Maître d' fusses Robyn back through the maze and out and into the Club. Applause in the Club brightens as Robyn immediately catches a spotlight, and applause rises as the Maître d' escorts her to a Stage-side table where the ever-confident Pledge suddenly spots Babs sitting. The vamp threads her thru the tables, and all heads turn toward her as the bat opens its cape, and prepares to seat her at Babs' table, just below the dance stage.

The Master of Ceremonies announces her presence, "Ladies and Gentlemen welcome Robyn, a Pledge from the Cosmos House!" Robyn looks helplessly at Babs, and Babs stands and gestures Robyn to take a bow. Applause ripples.

M/C again, "Ladies and Gentlemen, that's quite an outfit Robyn's wearing tonight!" More scattered applause and one hoot. M/C, "Robyn! Could that be a recent acquisition?"

Laughter ripples through the Club in response to this and Robyn curtsies, touches the sparkling clear vinyl croptop and miniskirt overtop her maillot cutout, and claims full credit in a voice loud enough to be heard throughout the Club, "I took this from Tiffany!"

The Crowd pretends to believe her.

Robyn flits her eyes about. A Screen catches her eye and she recognizes Tiffany, alternatively saying something and then twiddling herself. "See," Robyn observes, "Now Tiffany is totally Transparent!"

Good spirited laughter fills the Club. Another Screen catches Robyn's eye and she recognizes the Bunkroom back at the Cosmos House with its four topless Cosmos. "I titty-stripped Beka and Elle," Robyn brags loudly, "and I brought Steph over tonight. She's here... somewhere." Robyn flusters as she fails to find Steph on any Screen. "And she's stark naked and dripping splooge outta her screwhole."

Soft laughter and mummers fill the Club and Babs motions a smug Robyn to sit down. Robyn curtsies silently to the Crowd, and obeys.

The drummer and the sax riff.

Monitor Babs, clad in her minidress over her black bra and nombril, appraises Robyn's Garment count. *MomCap has elevated Robyn to my status and completely demeaned Tiffany.* Babs hesistates to watch Tiffany on the Screen because Babs suspects, *she's in a trance, Zoned.*

Babs knows, *Robyn never considers the effect of her actions, or considers that some Cosmos might resent her for volunteering them for noxious tasks.* BB considers her Pledge. *Robyn should be at School to learn more about herself. Learning to overcome blind spots. Learning how to cope with smart Gamers. Instead she just damages everyone around her.*

Boss Babe blinks at Robyn's three pieces, *I'm not superstitious, but maybe Robyn really does have Charm.*

§ Robyn Watches Penny: Solo the Double Dong on Stage

A drummer kicks up a rhythm and a sax riffs into the beat; the spotlight focuses back onto the Stage, and a dancer enters and swings around the floor-to-ceiling pole in the center of Stage. Robyn is afraid to look, but out of the corner of her eye can confirm the Stripper is totally naked, poontang shaven, and when she looks back again witnesses that the naked Nugget is poking her poot with the Dong. Amidst hoots. But wait, Robyn recognizes the face of the puddy. *It's Penny! The nasty looking wet poot on the dining room wall. More Baseboard Stripper trash shape-shifted to real-life!*

The Master of Ceremonies focuses Robyn's attention. "That looks like the same Dong that Coco was stroking back in the Camera Lounge," he proclaims. Robyn blanches The long double-header buried in Penny's poontang appears to also twist and vibrate. Penny fucks herself with it in time with the music, breathing harder now, and with the slop coming out of her and running down her thighs.

Robyn tries to get her head screwed on straight. She looks at the Screen from the Cosmos House with Kimju and Molly and Beka and Elle all topless on their backs, leads forward to BB, and declares, "Kimju and Molly must have left the Dong behind after they danced their Alumni Reprise!"

Boss Babe doesn't challenge Robyn's interpretation. *They certainly didn't bring it back with them.* "You're pretty smart," she says.

Was Robyn ever a guest in the Nugget before? If there was a last time it didn't leave much of an imprint.

Drinks arrive. Now Boss Babe leans forward and confides to Robyn, "Enjoy your drink. I guess your appointment for the Camera Lounge will have to wait."

This unsettles Robyn and she blurts, "You probably don't know, but House Mom already sent me there to witnessed Coco cum on the Dong." Robyn gestures toward naked Penny on Stage. "I guess they get to share the Dong one or the other." Robyn laughs. "Not like Kimju and Molly when they climaxed it together, naked and on this very Stage, three days ago."

Babs smiles patiently. "Last Term they even lapdanced naked while they got fondled and finger-fucked. Did you forget about that video somehow?"

Robyn curls her nose and glances at the feed from the Cosmos House once again. "Kimju and Molly belong here next Term. They really are the next Baseboard Stripper trash."

Babs sits up straight and shakes her shoulders.

Robyn's attention returns to Penny, on Stage wagging the Dong in her poot, and watches as Penny and BB's eyes dance fire with each other. Robyn wants to laugh at the naked Nugget, but suddenly Penny looks at her with cold eyes. Yes, Penny had detested Robyn last Term when they were both Cosmos Pledge, but she really came to crave revenge after Robyn "referred" the Mudwrestling Contest. Now Robyn Redacted sits at the side of the stage, transparent crop and mini over the maillot with its itty-bitty buttonhole.

Penny squats, leans back with one end of the Double Dong still in her pooch, licks a fingertip, touches it to the end of her clit, and focus upon

Robyn. The Crowd "awhs," quiets, and watches Penny beckons to Robyn to look while she withdraws the monster, surrounds it with her mouth, and licks her own wetness off the business end, while flapping the other end like a big languid cock. Appreciative laughter and scattered applause.

The snare drum rolls quiet tension as Penny coos to Robyn, "Please let me share the Double Dong with my Roommate next Term, no matter if I have to Whore or Pledge." This unnerves Robyn and she considers the overture most inappropriate. She lifts her nose and fixates on a point across the distance of the Club. Laughter mixes with applause. Then more applause; Robyn looks back toward the dancer, towards Penny, and watches as Penny re-buries the Dong into her sex, and settles herself in a quivering vibration. Robyn refuses to watch, but a rimshot from the drummer, and a hoot from the M/C top off Penny's climax.

Penny arises during the applause, bows, and backs toward the exit ramp still holding the Dong in her privates. She turns, flashes her puckered portnoy to Robyn, and exits. The Club likes her for that also.

Robyn grits her teeth and leans toward Babs. "That puddling purdah poppet is too stupid to know that I've got three Garments now and that I'll soon be running the Nugget! I'll turn Penny into a purring pookie pross before she ever gets to Flesh Ranch."

Babs squints, fiddles a bra strap under her minidress, and makes sure her button stands out.

§ Babs Considers Robyn: Pretentious & Poised to Double Opt Up

Robyn accepts her new reality. *I now wear three pieces. MomCap has ensured I deserve not only an Opt Up, but a Double-Opt Up!* Robyn scans the Screens again and discovers Coco's climax from the Camera Lounge earlier, also a montage of Penny and Coco each soloing the Dong, then with them climaxing split screen. *A poontang and a cunt begging to Dong together, even if they Opt Whores next Term. That's what falling in love gets you.*

Robyn finds herself smiling again. *I became a Pledge knowing that the position came with only one Garment, and I have always been confidant that Gamers would immediately recognize my intrinsic value and ensure that I join their privileged Castes. Now that has happened. My three Garments qualify* me *as a House Mom el Capitan! I'm equal to Bikini Bimbo as long as she wears a minidress over her bikini. More importantly, I am equal to MomCap. I have immunity to all things.*

Robyn spots Tiffany on a different Screen. Tiffany is still naked and spread, still chanting, still in the Dressing Room. Robyn points out the Screen to BB and speaks, "Tiffany gets to be a Stripper next Term, too bad for Tiffany. Just deserts for me."

Once again Robyn fails to consider proper form of address and once again Monitor Babs ignores the slight. Babs does consider Robyn's post-acquisition Garment status: *Robyn arriving wearing Tiffany' croptop and miniskirt provides an unexpected surprise. No matter, what used to be Tiffany's is now Robyn's.*

Robyn's clear vinyl croptop and miniskirt by no means diminish the stretchy curvy contours of the opaque stretch strapped maillot beneath, The croptop and low-riding miniskirt leave exposed a circumference of maillot around the belly and back, including "the tiniest buttonhole" which enables Robyn's navel to always see light.

Robyn feels herself being examined. Not just by Babs, but also by eyes in the Crowd. Handheld amateur Cams as well as hovering Nugget Cams.

Robyn, seated like a queen, delights and preens to Babs. "Tiffany didn't need to get naked to Opt Strip. All I needed was to get myself one of her Garments. But I am so worthy I took both of them. Of course I increase my Caste, but I also extend my coverage. I am now the most-covered Cosmos in fact! Except for you, maybe, but no matter what, you and I are both becoming House Mom el Capitans!

"We are equals now!"

Ah, the audacity of confidence in reporting to a superior what the superior already knows. Oh, the need for correction.

BB raises a finger to stop the babble. It works. Boss Babe sighs and considers her responsibilities.

Robyn opens her mouth again, "Where is Steph? I can't spot her anywhere on the Screens."

Boss Babe leans in and speaks, "Pledge, apologize to me for asking a question."

Robyn startles. "Ma'am," she begins as a hush falls over the Club. The Crowd can't hear the words spoken, but it can interpret body language.

Robyn acquiesces, "Ma'am, I'm sorry I asked you a question, Ma'am." Robyn looks up.

Boss Babe speaks, "Pledge, apologize to me for not addressing me properly."

Robyn hurries, "Ma'am, I apologize for not addressing your properly, Ma'am."

Boss Babe wags a finger, "Next time you don't address me properly I shall assign your maillot to Tiffany, so she needn't streak anymore."

Robyn whines. "Ma'am, please, that would leave me with two Garments, except transparent, like Tiffany was."

"So at least you are not totally stupid." Boss Babe smiles. "Now answer my question, 'what happens to Pledge who ask questions?'"

Robyn rushes her answer, "Ma'am, soap, Ma'am!"

"What happens to you if you fail to address me properly?" Boss Babe inquires.

Robyn hasn't forgotten, at least not yet. "Ma'am, you'll give my maillot to Tiffany, Ma'am."

"Very good, Pledge," Boss Babe breathes in and sits back, more in control, and aware that the eyes of the Club are upon her.

BB leans forward at Robyn again. "I'll give your maillot to Tiffany if you don't obey me anyplace anytime in front of anybody."

Robyn replies, "Ma'am, I run the Lineup for you. I do all your dirty work. I'm gonna make every last Cosmos Pledge beg to pledge naked and cum Strip next Term!"

Boss Babe mellows, "I believe they are all already begging that." BB leans in, "some are even begging Watersports," and orders, "now be quiet, and unless you want to join the beggars, stay quiet. Now."

Robyn hesistates but obeys. *I can feel the Cams upon me. They know Bimbo Bitch dissed me. Gamers know she's all babambas and no brains.*

Robyn sits erect; she casts her eyes around the Club; she sees herself on one of the Screens upward, live. *I'm famous!* She looks for where the Cam might be, but before she can find it, the Screen cuts, a*nd there I am, training Tiffany to pink and masturbate the Post, and training Steph to Zone on the Back Landing.*

Robyn perks. *I am going to be training Tiffany and Steph to climax the Double Dong tonight!*

Robyn sticks her tongue behind her back teeth to help her remember to keep quiet. Robyn takes BB's threat of transferring the maillot to Tiffany seriously, and a shallow haunting fear lingers as she considers this possibility. *Very twisted,* Robyn says to herself, *Because I'd still promote, only I'd be a Monitor and not a MomCap. But taking away my maillot underneath the transparent croptop and miniskirt isn't fair because I needn't play any Game that displays my intimacies!*

Robyn opens her mouth to speak but Boss Babe catches her before breath forms words out of her mouth. BB is kind. "Oval mouth," she directs.

Robyn obeys. She notices a Cam collecting a close-up and scowls at it. *Boss Bitch pretends to haze me because her Caste is supposed to haze Pledge. She imagines a history to prove why she's a Monitor and I'm a Pledge.*

But it wasn't BB who gave me my promotion, MomCap did! Babs might be my Monitor but she doesn't have any power over me anymore. She knows I'm headed beyond Monitor Caste. I have just become a House Mom el Capitan!

Well, haven't you, oval-mouth?

§ Babs & Robyn: Watch Steph on the Nugget Screens

Robyn discovers another Screen and comprehends that she watches a surveillance video. *That's me and Steph entering the Stage Door.* The Master of Ceremonies clarifies spin, "Ladies and Gentlemen, that's Robyn escorting Cosmos Pledge Steph into the Nugget!"

Scattered applause and the action cuts. "That's Monitor Babs climaxing Steph, following her fateful defeat at the Peacock's Greatest House Roar!" Bigger applause, as Steph's climax plays on many Screens throughout the Nugget.

M/C tops, "Congratulations to Monitor Babs!" And the Crowd applauds louder.

The many Screens cut and Babs sees herself live, sitting at her Stage-side table, multiple angles. Babs stands slightly and waves; she wonders. *What am I doing here?*

The Screens cut again, this time feeding a montage of Steph's naked Zoned-out masturbations at the Cosmos House. M/C patters, "That's Steph's Pee-Cam climax with Molly yesterday," another cut, "And here's Robyn keeping Steph in the Zone on the Back Landing. How about a round of applause for Cosmos Pledge Steph, stage-side tonight."

The Crowd "Ooohs." And the spotlight ovals her. Robyn pops up and waves to the steady applause. The spotlight goes dark, and the Screen cuts to video from Steph's visit to Janet at the Corvette House yesterday.

Robyn looks around and Babs signs her to sit down and stay quiet.

Babs concentrates on what plays on the Screens. *This is my first opportunity to see what Janet did to Steph.*

Correct. Babs watches Janet's manipulation. In the scene Steph masturbates in front of a Screen with her own live image, a feed from a Cam above and behind her. Steph masturbates to a voyeur view of her masturbating herself. And she is Zoned.

Now an new Video, a Video made tonight, floods the Screens. It captures Steph in the Camera Lounge, being Dong-vibed by Penny and Coco.

Babs wonders *is the video live or a replay? This explains Steph's whereabouts.*

Robyn assumes the feed is live. She presses her lips together and remains silent, at least for the moment, and squints at Babs. *Okay, so much for Steph Sorostitute's build-up, just send her out to me because I'm here to finish her off.*

§ Tiffany & Steph: Masturbate Together Naked in Dressing Room

Following Steph's humiliation in the Camera Lounge, Penny had escorted her back to the Dressing Room through the hidden passageway, so she does not disrupt the Club. The Dong stayed behind in Coco's cockpit; the cockpit and Coco have come to love it perhaps too much.

Steph enters the Dressing Room to discover a naked and spread Tiffany masturbating the Chant. *Zoned,* Steph correctly deduces.

Penny signs Steph to 'stand spread surrender,' and Steph obeys. Penny with Tiffany sitting on the table before her.

Penny excuses herself. "Stay, form oval mouth," she says, "while I take opportunity to contribute my urine to the Toilet Cam."

Tiffany's presence shocks Steph. Might part of Steph be jealous that another Cosmos joins the naked and zoned? Or coming to grips that romancing the Double Dong lies in the future. Steph ponders telling Tiffany about seeing the instrument, but instead uses the moments to try to figure out *just who controls my arousal. Because it's not me anymore,* she affirms. *Not Babs, either, she wouldn't do this to me. Janet, yeah, sure, except she is not here. Worse, misguided Penny and Coco seek payback, even though I was no longer the Monitor when the Mudwrestling Contest occurred.*

The one behind all of this is MomCap, House Mom el Capitan; she is the one in charge. She controls the Dong. She controls Tiffany too.

Tiffany's scent hits Steph, and Steph's sex cavity gets slippery. She holds her breath before drawing air slowly and carefully into her nostrils.

Steph resists an urge to lower her fingers and open her satchel flaps. *The problem is that I am also driving my arousal. I'm past a point where I can stop myself. Now I want the Dong, and I'll do whatever I need to in order to get it.*

Steph evaluates her surroundings. *When I secretly visited the Nugget last Term and watched Janet's Alumni Reprise I watched the Stage from an upper curtained booth. Nobody told me about any Camera Lounge or Champagne Room or Inner Sanctum or any secret passageway. This must be the Dressing Room where Beka and Elle Flip-Flopped, and where I bet Kimju and Molly shot a Pee Video too.*

Steph tenses her body and makes sure she is balanced and upright and that her hands behind her head cup her armpits tightly. Nipples erect on their own and secretions lubricate Steph's insides. She evaluates Tiffany sitting before her and still chanting. *Tiffany's a Pee-Camer too, so I bet she's going to Pee-Cam here too, just like Penny and Coco do.* Steph recalls her own scene in the Bathroom cross-arching pee with Molly. *I'm a Pee-Camer too, and if Penny and Coco know this, they'll make me use the Toilet Cam.*

And maybe even let Steph pee center Stage.

Steph considers Tiffany again. *Why is she here? Didn't she and Babs leave before Robyn and I? And where are Babs and Robyn anyway?*

Steph twists her neck nervously just as House Mom appears. House Mom turns Steph around, and guides her backward and up onto the table side-by-side with equally naked Tiffany, and spreads her knees until they almost touch the spread and still chanting Tiffany.

House Mom slows down Tiffany's rhythm, turns to Steph and orders, "Sync up. You know the Chant."

Steph does. *It seems like I have been chanting continuously since forever. But never with another Pledge. I'm too special for that.*

No.

Steph watches House Mom gather air into her chest; she gathers air into her own chest, and signals she will begin at the start. She does, and the twosome clasp their hands behind their necks, surrender position, while they recite, "Please let me Pledge naked and cum be a Stripper next Term," followed by the beats to deploy their fingers, "Titty titty, clitty clitty, hole mouth."

The second voice jars Tiffany slightly out of the Zone; she confronts her feelings of ambivalence: now she must share the Dressing Room Cam, however her sugar has arrived. Tiffany loves the attention *but why do I need a co-star? What's not to like? I'm naked and spread, pink-wet-and-ready. I'm horny to the point of craving release. The Gamers play me because I belong to my fans. The Gamers are winding me up, they are going to put me and Steph on Stage, give us the Double Dong, and I am going to fuck both our brains out.*

Steph also tries to gather her thoughts but finds herself lifted into the Zone. Her head spins and the Chant provides safe haven. Once again her sweetness erupts, and her aroma complements Tiffany's airy tapioca. *I'm going to have to touch and taste Tiffany,* she imagines. *And then MomCap is going to make us share the Double Dong.*

Steph's body constricts, and Kundalini's surge runs down to her sternpipe.

"What a beautiful pair of Cosmos Pledge," House Mom exclaims, as the Nugget Shooter collects their stretched armpits, matching A-cups, stood-up nipples, writhing, and dripping valiva. Both of them. "Sweet."

Sweet indeed. Already Steph lies in danger of losing control; MomCap can tell Steph barely has it together, whereas Tiffany can control her let-go. Tiffany rapidly synchronizes Steph, and backs off the rhythm just enough so Steph doesn't tip into uncontrolled, prolonged climax. The Nugget Shooter adjusts the feeds and the Back Door man watches from the Dressing Room door.

Coco enters, ignores House Mom and her two naked spread chanting Pledge, contributes pee for the Toilet Cam, and House Mom shoos her out. If Strippers are not dancing on Stage they should be hustling lapdances.

§ Babs & Robyn: Watch Tiffany & Steph Chant on Screen

Out front Babs and Robyn join the Patrons and watch a new feed on the Screens: a live Dressing Room view. The sound of naked Tiffany and Steph chanting does not accompany the Cam feed, but the Crowd knows the beat, and they can collect the rhythm when the hands "titty titty, clitty clitty, hole mouth." Both spread Pledge drip with excitement; especially Steph, who can't sit still, and is driven by the competition with Tiffany to discharge still more sexual lubricant. Tiffany has more self-control and now breaths in a deep steady rhythm with her eyes half-closed.

The liveliness of the scene percolates into the Club and the Crowd around Robyn starts to holler, "Bring them out. Let's see them go down onstage."

Babs, sitting at the side-table with Robyn, knows full well that Kimju and Molly ate pussy and shared the Dong during their recent Alumni Reprise here at the Nugget. *I was here.* BB looks at Robyn, and without thinking Robyn opens her mouth and opines, "Tonight is Steph and Tiffany's turn to eat each other out and climax the Double Dong."

Robyn checks the neckline of her maillot, feels the straps, tidies her buttonhole. She considers the upcoming contest, and offers, "I'll climax them on the Dong together center Stage."

BB chooses to ignore Robyn's error of decorum. She smiles, and playfully tells her "I guess if you ever had to worry about Kimju demanding a Roommate Game, that's not gonna happen! You've got three pieces now!"

"Right!" Robyn says, "I'm a MomCap next Term!"

Back in the Dressing Room Tiffany and Steph can hear the M/C and the Crowd over their own Chant and masturbation. Tiffany distinguishes Robyn getting introduced; never underestimate a Porn Star for an ability to keep enough rub-a-dub to stay wet but not rise up and cum over the top. Tiffany never forgets when she is on duty, but she is also well able to surrender to climax. Steph possesses less self-control; even the feeling of her stiff bleached blonde pussy hair excites her. Tiffany might decipher the patter of the Master of Ceremonies, but Steph surrenders to the beat of the drum and the sax, and follows the rhythm that Tiffany sets.

Tiffany knows, *we are preparing to dance, but I don't know what awaits us on Stage or what outcomes are planned or what Props might be loose.* The Crowd hollers when they see House Mom touch Steph's cheek on the Screen and cool her down just a fraction of a degree. Steph is no longer able to think into the future.

Tiffany feels a sense of freedom. *If I am directed to climax with Steph, then I will take her with whatever form and beguile is necessary to affect the outcome desired, but I will not likely have to exert overwhelming force. It will not be necessary.*

Tiffany pauses in her thoughts. *The time ahead will require focus and concentration, skills and techniques. A la* Kama Sutra. *And by knowing one's body. A la Tantra. A la channeling Kundalini.*

Will Gaming with Steph be a Winner-Take-All or a Flip-Flop? When there is nothing to take or trade? Tiffany furrows her brow. *I must try to understand what the Game is, because whatever it requires to be winning or loosing, I want to stay here at the Nugget next Term!"*

Tiffany suspects and knows from experience, *There will be a prize and there will be a sacrifice. One of us will make forfeits, and the other will collect useless remains—like the short hairs after they are shaved off the loser's pussy... if not her head as well."*

II-26 Tiffany Leads Steph: Strip & On-Stage Audition (D23)

§ Tiffany & Steph: Chanting, Pink Wet Ready, Into the Zone

House Mom el Capitan looms in front of the two chanting Cosmos. "Stop!" she orders, and both obey, right at the "hole" part of the Chant. Tiffany holds the position and pulls pink. Steph follows.

House Mom speaks. "You two naked Pledge shall be dancing tonight," House Mom appraises the two spread self-revealing Cosmos.

House Mom addresses Steph, "You arrived at the Nugget naked, and you are going to stay naked." House Mom addresses Tiffany, "I stripped you naked and gave your Garments to Robyn, and you are going to say naked."

The Cam collects two wet close-ups.

MomCap continues, "So whatever you play, it won't be your clothes that you win or lose. It will be something else."

Last Term when Tiffany guest danced at the Nugget she had been advertised as a Feature Dancer and worked as a prostitute. House Mom knows Tiffany was a cocksucker, cock fucker, and anal acrobat par excellence. Or, as Tiffany puts it, "A Porn Star!"

Now, in a momentary flash of understanding, Steph realizes, *Gamers will not contesting be contesting Tiffany with Robyn or Beka or Elle, the three Cosmos who claim to be "newbies. They are putting me up against a twisting tail peddler.*

Steph has a very hard time not crossing over into a quivering ectoplasm of cum. "Calm down," House Mom advises her, "or I'm going to give you to Tiffany." This actually helps settle Steph down to a humming vibration. House Mom and Tiffany exchange looks, House Mom shrugs and advises Steph further, "Fact is, I gave you to Tiffany the moment Penny brought you into the Dressing Room."

Tiffany twists some tapioca out of her twat, and watches as the smell hits Steph's nostrils and enchants her. Tiffany synchronizes her own heartbeat and breathing to Steph's. Now that Steph is attached, Tiffany may guide her more precisely.

Tiffany's pink and masturbation tonight at the Nugget provides a rare public forum since Tiffany became a Cosmos. Tiffany also possesses superb self-control, no matter how tightly wound Kundalini coils inside her. *I must be careful to not unwind faster than I can take Steph with me, but I can do this.* Tiffany thinks, *I want to "Opt Strip" and I've committed to bring Steph along with me. Game over.*

And if I can beg to just stay here at the Nugget, and not return to the Cosmos House, I won't have to streak at all.

Steph tries to consider what might happen next, but loses her ability to concentrate. *I crave fucking a real cock!*

Tiffany views cock with professionalism while at the same time can climax on a cock for real. Tiffany likes cock, but cock doesn't control her.

Steph has seen Tiffany cum in her *Suck Fuck Facial Tiny Tit Videos.* She endlessly overhears Tiffany remind everyone, "I am a Porn Star."

Steph wonders, *Might Tiffany be willing to revisit that role here at the Nugget tonight? Twist some dirty cocks, bukkake herself, if only to overpower me?* Steph's cream overflows; she can barely organize her thoughts. *If Tiffany takes a cock I will match her. Not because I have to. Because I need it. I want it first.* Steph goes goners, *I don't care who watches anymore. I want cock in my holes.*

Tiffany feels Kundalini possess Steph and realizes she may be unable to hold Steph back from crossing into the Zone. Knowing this she allows herself to run up to the edge —that place of excitement at the threshold of climax. Make no mistake, Tiffany knows how to make love, and she knows how to Whore. *I am a courtesan, first class, and I fly way ahead of Steph at this Game! Still,* Tiffany suspects, *neither of us will be turning any tricks tonight. It's against the Rules, and besides, I don't need a trick to win.*

But I do expect Steph and I will be turning each other on.

Tiffany runs up the wave, catches Steph, and surfs the two of them right on the cusp of climax, riding the beat of the music. Tiffany calculates, *There is nothing to win; there is only what one can lose. And one can lose a lot of things.*

Steph tries to get her thoughts together, but can't. She doesn't even know she has locked onto Tiffany's vibe, synched to her heartbeat, and been lead into a Zone that Tiffany might, or might not, be able to extract her from.

§ Beka & Elle: Pee-Cam & Cream Back at the Cosmos House

Robyn shifts her eyes to the Screen showing the feed from the Cosmos House. The Chant goes round and round as the four topless Cosmos hold hands in the Clover: Kimju, then Beka, then Molly, then Elle, then all over again, "Please let me Pledge naked and cum be a Stripper next Term.

The sound of four interleaved Cosmos reciting this Chant, one after another, does not come through to the Nugget, but two developments catch Robyn's eye:

The first is that a stream of urine appears to have emerged from between Beka's legs. Robyn, places her hands over her mouth, points, and is about to proclaim Beka's piss debut to Babs when BB's glower suggests she stay shut up. But Robyn knows best, assuming that the significance of her observation overrules any commands of Bimbo Bawd, especially now that both have three Garments. Robyn emotes, "Lookit, Babs, Beka's gonna spend the rest of her time in the Clover lying in her own piddle!" She laughs.

Monitor Babs squints at the Screen. *No disagreement.* No command.

"I watered all four of them up really full," Robyn brags, and augments BB with more enlightenment, "Guess this qualifies Beka as a Pee-Camer, and now leaves Elle the only Cosmos holdout."

"You forget yourself," Boss Babe smiles. "So either remind me to give your maillot to Tiffany, or oval your mouth."

Robyn canvasses the interior of the Nugget: The Stage, the tables and chairs, the two side-stages, the back and entrance and decides here and now is not the moment to argue with Babs, picks option two, and ovals her mouth.

Holding the Clover presents a challenge for the Four Cosmos, but the circle of chanting keeps them alert. *It's a nuisance,* Elle considers, *but it seems like a pretty good deal compared to visiting the Nugget.*

Lying on their backs like the points of a compass and with their heads together the Four Clover Cosmos are able to turn their heads and look at each other, but they are largely unable to view their own bodies, or the bodies of the other three Pledge. One of them, Elle in particular, discovers herself best positioned to view The Minxy Mirror, which has been dark, moody, and non-reflective since their positioning.

Now Elle discovers that the Minxy fades into an incomplete matrix of Screens, and that these Screens replay, from various points in time, events taken place earlier this evening here in the Bunkroom.

Elle imagines that the Minxy breaks into Screens that float around the room in a slow dance. She follows one and watches it replay Robyn yanking Elle's slacks down to her ankles and spreading her knees. *I am the only fully exposed nest,* Elle quantifies. *Kimju and Molly and Beka all wear cloth through their crotch; I don't.*

Elle scans down the timeline and discovers a screen of her legs spread just enough to hint of a double-line vagina. Elle shivers. Maybe Gamers can look at me between my legs; they can verify that I'm ahead of the Game, by not bursting nectar out my inner lips.

Elle is correct, Gamers at the Nugget who watch the Clover feed on some Screens there are well aware that Elle has not produced lubrication. Fear of freshening, even when chanting for climax, needs be overcome, no mater how much Elle frets.

Elle's eyes find a Screen in the Minxy that depicts Roommate Beka. The top of Beka's head might be inches away from the top of Elle's, but her body remains on the opposite side of the Clover. Topless like me, and with only the jeans' seam between her legs. Beka dances her butt on the floor in rhythm as the Chant goes round and round.

Elle startles, and yes, there it is again, *Beka dribbling urine onto the floor. Simple,* Elle concludes, *Beka has just auditioned the Pee-Cam.*

Elle pans down the Minxy Matrix of Screens and finds the last one: real time. *Not just dribbles,* Elle concludes, *Beka lies in her own puddle.*

Back in the Nugget, Robyn surveils Elle via the Screen. Robyn assumes Elle's present; Elle worries about the past, present, and future. *I worry that my own "secret" pee will be brought out from hiding. Then Gamers will demand I turn on the Pee-Cam every time I want to use the Bathroom. Pee in the Measuring Cup and Log every last drop, just like Tiffany and Kimju and Molly, so everyone in the Prefecture can watch.*

Elle considers Steph's plight. *And now Steph's a Pee-Camer too, and she's not some newbie Pledge, she's a fallen Monitor with Karma outstanding.*

Elle contemplates. *I admit, I am afraid of the Pee-Cam. Yes, Beka and I witnessed Kimju and Molly's evolution to Pee-Camers already this Term. Now with Beka begging, am I the only holdout?*

I know, Elle admits as she maintains her full-frontal, hand-holding position in the Clover Chant. *Beka and I aren't exempt from having to watch video replays either.* Elle pauses. *I don't even want to look at them, especially when they depict me. But Beka, she likes to watch, especially our "Audition" three nights ago at the Nugget. At what was supposed to be Kimju and Molly's Alumni Reprise. Now any Gamer can ask Automatron to play me flashing boobage and pulling pink.*

Elle takes a deep breath and lets it out slowly. But *will I pee for the Cam? Or did I already during my short visit to the Nugget? Is my secret really a secret?*

But most importantly, can I persuade Monitor Babe to not screen my Gonzo Videos. And especially to not screen Beka, she doesn't deserve getting outed.

Elle scans the Minxy again for any clips of her own transgressions. None there, she concludes, as the Minxy fades to an oily black, followed by a dim reflection of the four prone Cosmos, still holding hands, chanting carelessly.

Elle remembers Robyn taunting Beka and herself. "You're way or the House way," Robyn had snarled, "but you're gonna pink and get wet, and then you're gonna reveal and offer up your most intimate secrets of body, arousal, and release."

This mouthful from a Pledge who has never cum in her life? So what, Robyn continues, "You two must learn to not only climax, like some ordinary Stripper or Whore, but climax on cue. Performance! That's different than making love or pleasuring oneself. It involves a regimen."

Elle considers, *I know Gamers have wound Beka up tight; Beka stays uncontrollably horny, and her pussy instantly freshens at the most subtle provocation.*

True, just the crotch seam of Beka's jeans shorts rubbing on her clit provides sufficient stimulus to keep the cloth soaked.

And so in the cream department Elle finds herself opposite her Roommate: *The Gamers hold Beka back from release, whereas I know I will not be able to go over the top—certainly not climax in public anyway—on my own, all by myself.*

Unbeknownst to Beka and Elle, Kimju and Molly also share a secret. It happened backstage at the Nugget the night of their Alumni Reprise, three days ago, the same night Beka and Elle auditioned. True, both Kimju and Molly were by then qualified Pee-Camers, but what the Nugget Shooter recorded backstage went beyond that.

For Molly the secret is less precious, given her performance at the Bachelor Party during *The Arrivals*. But for Kimju the secret involves an Obeisance not yet achieved or desired.

And by now, having kept the secret this long, Kimju and Molly remain resigned to keeping the secret, still indebted and beholden may the Nugget Shooter choose to manipulate them.

Of course, the Four Cosmos Clover doesn't hide all its secrets. Ex-Stripper Kimju spots her tanga with kloopings, Molly soaks her panties with mung, and Beka transudes broda. Gamers guide the hovering Cam in the Bunkroom toward a close-up of Elle's spread pussy.

In the Nugget, Robyn can see on the Screen that Elle's nectary now appears to be moist—perhaps for the first time. Perhaps the combination of the intonation and exposure finally brings Elle to wetness.

Robyn snorts; she turns toward BB to proclaim this discovery, but the eyes she meets draw tight and Robyn closes her mouth. Not the oval mouth commanded, but at least not a flapping one. Robyn looks at the Screen clearly now and wrinkles her nose. *Maybe soon Elle will be able to lolly up her own nakodo!"*

Robyn silently watches Elle beg "Please let me Pledge naked and cum be a Stripper next Term." *Elle is starting to believe what she begs for,* Robyn perceives. *Still, she needs to surrender completely.*

Robyn glances at the Screen more carefully, no question at all, Elle's nook oozes. Robyn bounces on her seat, so eager to tell.

§ Tiffany & Steph: Swept Onto Stage

Back in the Dressing Room hydration has caught up with Tiffany and Steph and both now have an urge to use the toilet. This should not be a problem; both are already qualified Pee-Camers. Pee-Camming was Tiffany's first commitment, made on Day One of *The Arrivals.* Steph's commitment is more recent; she is the Cosmos' most recent convert, acquiring this Obeisance only yesterday during a naked, swirling, total-loss-of-control piss climax with Molly in the Cosmos House Bathroom.

Tiffany appreciates that the toilets of the Nugget Dressing Room are definitely Cammed. *No secrets for Strippers... or guests.* Tiffany smiles.

Steph, naked and without a pot to pee in, still ruefully assumes, *I shall retain this last vestige of my privacy, here in this place. Maybe I had to pee in front of the Bathroom Cam with Molly earlier today, although I'm not sure anymore. Besides, that shouldn't matter, because Molly tricked me, just like she tricked me at the Greatest House Roar, took my dress away, and then gave it to Babs.*

For the moment, both Tiffany and Steph shall retain their urine: House Mom el Capitan wants both of them wet—in more ways than one.

"Onto your feet!" House Mom orders with gusto, and sweeps both of them onto their feet. Before either can think twice MomCap propels them out of the Dressing Room and down a dark hallway toward a light. "Keep chanting and masturbating," House Mom orders, and they squat-walk ahead of her, beg together with their hands behind then heads, then each pinches nipples, diddles her intimate spot, dig valiva to feed themselves, and place their hands behind their heads and chant again.

Tiffany knows the way; Steph follows, dizzy with Kundalini running loose inside and barely able to maintain the rhythm of the Chant. *I'm a horny slut and I can do horny slut things,* Steph absorbs. *But I don't want to Double Dong with Tiffany Transparent. I want some real cock.*

Tiffany appreciates cock also, *but I do not teeter on uncontrolled climax.* Tiffany rubs her nipples with damp fingers. *And might Steph decide to go rogue, do I need to try to stop her?*

Nugget Hovercams flying backwards before the two naked masturbators reveal to the Prefecture that Tiffany's tapioca and Steph's slush run down their inner thigh. The applause begins while both waddle forward down the runway to center Stage, still chanting, and at the moment they burst into the Stage circle the Patrons bursts into a rolling cheer. The two Pledge come to a stop in front of the pole.

Tiffany bows and guides Steph to bow with her, stands spread surrender and coaxes Steph to recite in unison, "Please let me Pledge naked and cum be a Stripper next Term," they recite, "Titty titty, clitty clitty, hole mouth!"

"Ladies and gentlemen!" the Master of Ceremonies booms, "Introducing two Pledge from the Cosmos House who are begging to visit and entertain us tonight!" Steph briefly hesitates chanting, casts a look at Tiffany during the applause, and can see that Tiffany isn't breaking rhythm. Steph stumbles and falters—laughter in the Club—and gets synchronized with Tiffany again.

The Club quiets down for a moment so the Crowd can hear them plead.

"Ladies and gentlemen," the Master of Ceremonies builds, "Welcome back a former Whore on her way up, a Pee-Camer, Piss Mouth, and Porn Star. Take a bow and dance for us, Tiffany!"

Tiffany doesn't question the accuracy of M/C's representations. She breaks out of the chant and the repetition, wiggles her naked body in a suggestive fashion and rolls her Eraser Heads in her fingertips. A mummer from the Crowd. Tiffany reaches down and pulls pink, dips two fingers into her twat, and scoops out so much tapioca that it streams from her fingertips as she pulls her hand away. She opens her mouth, closes her lips, and sucks her fingers clean to rising applause.

Tiffany extends her welcome. She grabs the center pole for a 360-degree swing that broadcasts a tangy twat to the entire Club. She jitters on her feet, bows and comes to attention.

Babs watches from the sidelines. *Well done. The former Whore has little to lose by playing it loose.* Robyn watches with a hand over her mouth.

Steph bites her lip. The huge applause that welcomes Tiffany strikes fear. *I have to share the Stage with an ex-Whore and old Nugget favorite. Tiffany's not only danced here, she probably knows every cock in the Club.*

Steph constricts her vagina and feels splurt run down her thigh. She feels the murmur from the Patrons and realizes that *everyone watches me.* Steph takes in a short panting breath, and the M/C booms, "Say hello to Steph, an ex-Monitor tumbling in free fall, live and in-person. A naked Pee-Camming Cosmos Pledge begging to dance here next Term!"

A small ripple of anticipation invites Steph to beg, "Pleeeaase let me Pledge naked and cum be a Stripper next Term," she recites, begging for real, hands behind her head, feet spread wide, yet twisting her body and beyond horny. "Titty titty." Steph squeezes and grabs and rolls nipples in fingertips. "Clitty clitty," and fingerballs, then pulls her pink as wide as is possible "Hooooooole." Digs and consumes slush, "mouth!"

The Patrons roar in approval.

M/C continues, "Steph, take a bow for us!" And cajoles half-heartily. 'Now get down on your hands and knees and show off your pink snapper and puckered sphincter from the backside!"

Steph complies quickly; she drops down onto all fours, pivots her bare butt around to the front of the stage; pulls her butt cheeks wide so that her stern star shines up. Then she brings her hands back around her and in-between her legs and pulls her sex lips apart.

I don't know what I'm doing anymore. Steph studies. *I don't quite know whom to offer my sphincter and snizzle. Somebody here in the Nugget? Okay, except I don't want a cock in my sewer.*

Steph's spread butt cheeks and sex lips gets polite applause, then more as she wiggles sideways around the circumference of the Stage. Steph becomes aware of growing applause and discovers she is rubbing her clitoris. *My strophoid.* The pants. It's *not just the Nugget Patrons watching me pink-wet-and-ready, everyone in the Prefecture watches me.* The applause rises in a crescendo as Steph starts quivering, then suddenly ejects an involuntary blob of splurt from her engorged snatch. Steph moans, and as the applause dies she looks up to discover Tiffany's outreached hand to help draw the out-of-control Pledge up onto to feet.

Tiffany draws Steph to her, wraps arms around her, tit-to-tit, and kisses her on the mouth. Steph has never been kissed by a woman before, but her helpless body shakes with arousal, and Tiffany presses harder, and Steph's mouth opens to French kiss and yield to desire.

The Crowd quiets as Tiffany raises Steph's heat; she rubs their naked bodies together, then breaks off and steps backward. Then, in a single motion, she pivots Steph around facing her forward toward the Crowd. Tiffany moves in closer behind her, bends Steph's head back with her palms, and again possesses her mouth.

Steph yields, moans, and Tiffany reaches to finger Steph's nipples, and then slides them down and into Steph's sex. The Crowd mummers as Steph's sopping slot arches up for satisfaction, and quietly eggs Tiffany on, fascinated, not sure if Tiffany has put Steph into a soft rolling cum or simply rocks her at the top of her tipping point. It doesn't matter; Steph falls into a trance.

A round of solid applause fills the Club as Tiffany lets go of Steph's tongue and lets the helpless Cosmos partly return to her senses. Steph reenters in a dizzying tumble, unprepared, unfiltered, and utters her first words, "please cock-fuck me." The utterance is loud enough for the entire Club can hear, and in the dampening of sound that follows, Steph augments. "You can fuck me all my holes, you can cum on my face, you can spank me."

Tiffany interjects, "You can take on my Piss Mouth."

Steph hesistates, caught between flying high and the sensual. So Tiffany lifts her again, and will leave her hanging on the cusp of the Zone until the Master of Ceremonies again takes charge. So much for the introductions.

§ Tiffany Masturbates Steph: They Taste Each Other

"Enough enough!" the M/C plays the role of an umpire. "Break it up, we have a contest afoot! Pay attention! Listen up!"

Robyn, sitting with Babs, gloats that she has delivered Steph into this contest with Tiffany. Tiffany looks in their direction—she knows where they are sitting—lowers her head so she can make knowing eyes to BB and give her a sly smile. Steph is too Zoned to do anything. Then Tiffany looks at Robyn and makes the smallest of gestures of licking her lips. It is a predatory action directed only to her, and Robyn doesn't like it one bit.

Tiffany looks back into the Club, draws her finger across her nose and smells it. The Club understands the gesture and further approves when Tiffany touches her fingers to the tip of her tongue and tastes the Steph sop she has collected.

Tiffany still stands behind Steph, one arm draped around her, and she shifts her weight to the side so that her full body is visible to the Crowd, reaches down with her opposite, free hand, scoops out two fingers of tacamahac from her own trough, and then lifts her hand to Steph's nose, drags it across to the sound of a surrendering sigh, and works her own tapioca into Steph's mouth.

Meanwhile Tiffany's other hand descends into Steph's sweet spot; her fingers take Steph's body into a soft roll. Steph moans. The Crowd understands that Steph is being initiated into lesbian Zone.

Robyn watches with her hand over her astonished open mouth. She looks up and can see the same multiple angles and views on the overhead Screens that show the feeds routed to Automatron and the entire Prefecture. *No privacy tonight for Tiffany Transparent and Steph Sorostitute! Pinking inner sex lips, oozing twat and screw hole, and begging the Double Dong.* Robyn curls a strand of her long hair around a finger. *And they both still have their pussy hair.*

Steph, alone among them, has had all her hair color bleached out.

Robyn recalls watching Penny and Coco earlier tonight, albeit separately. *Both Strippers are shaven bare, pulled pink, hung out cream, and soloed the Dong.*

The two Cosmos on stage stand side-by-side—forward of the center pole. Steph's head spins. She feels crushed, looks wildly about, she feels totally out of her league, and she becomes even more disoriented when she spots Babs, *still wearing what used to be my cutout minidress. Boss Bitch has abandoned me, I'm becoming a Stripper now and House Mom is my boss.*

Steph registers again; Robyn sits at the side-stage table with Babs. Robyn beams, as she wears Tiffany's transparent shirt and miniskirt overtop her strapped cutout maillot. This explains more things and as if in acknowledgement Steph releases a stream of piss. Right there on stage. Laughter, embarrassment, and extreme humiliation. She catches herself, but she has already spilt.

Steph registers one of the Cams. *Extreme humiliation to follow forever.*

The M/C doesn't miss the beat, "Ladies and gentlemen, put your hands together for Steph, the newest star on the Cosmos Pee-Cam. She qualified earlier with Molly, now she solos!" There are hoots in the room.

Steph squirms. *I'm gonna be peeing a lot, I know it.*

The M/C surges forward. "And what about you Tiffany, how about you pour us a shot!" And to this many hoots follow and almost instantly a pair of shot glasses are thrust up onto center Stage.

Déjà vu? Tiffany tosses her head back, gives the Crowd one of those looks, squats and picks up the two glasses. She slides herself two steps backward while still squatting, pivots the first glass underneath her, and artfully fills it with fresh pee. Big applause and Tiffany positions the second and carefully pours a second shot of golden nectar without spilling a drop. Even bigger applause.

But Tiffany is not only a Pee-Camer and now she wrinkles her brow in thought. *I am also a Piss Mouth. Nugget Patrons watched me down shots from Janet last Term. And once last Term while I was giving this same M/C a blowjob, he not only came in my mouth but also let go a torrent of piss. And you know who cleaned that up.*

She holds the two shot glasses awkwardly, she knows, *I'm going to be drinking pee, but if I'm lucky Steph will down the second shot.*

But M/C has mercy for her, "Ladies and gentlemen, put your hands together for Tiffany! Tiffany the Tinkling Twat, a former Whore, and a Pee-Camming Piss Mouth at the Cosmos House!" What a mouthful.

Tiffany doesn't know what do with the two shot glasses, but she is quick witted. She bows to the Crowd, prances over to the table where Babs and Robyn sit, beckons Robyn to rise, and hands both glasses to her. Ouch. The move catches Robyn by surprise, and earns Tiffany applause and a bow. Robyn sits back down and stupidly puts the warm shot glasses on the table.

Steph watches. *I will never forget that Bikini Bitch forced me to pink, masturbate, finger dip, and freshen.* Steph hesistates, admits, *and cum. And beg to be a Stripper next Term. After the end of the Greatest House Roar BB made sure the Back Door Cam cammed me, pink-wet-and-ready. How low is that.*

Steph shifts her eyes to the Pledge sitting with Babs at the Stage-side table. *About as low as Robyn making Tiffany and me lick her feet and suck her toes; Robyn went beyond Boss Bitch's charter of instruction and abused me.*

Robyn is why I am here in the first place. And as far as sharing the Dong—

Tiffany interrupts. Tiffany sweeps back behind her, grabs her wrists, places her hands on her pussy, and whispers to her, "Next time you're going to drink not just your pee, you'll also drink my pee." The over-responsive Steph moans at this and starts playing with herself again. She can feel her own piss under her feet bottoms, but it doesn't matter anymore.

II-27 Tiffany & Steph: The Double Dong & Depilation (D23)

§ Penny & Coco: Present the Double Dong to Tiffany & Steph

Robyn spots House Mom standing in the shadows of the Club, but lets her attention be drawn to the two side-stages, where the lights come up on Penny and Coco. A grinding beat hits the Club, and the two naked Strippers bob in rhythm on the opposite sides of the Nugget. One waves the Double Dong in the air and the other dances holding a non-descript package high above her head. Beautiful tits and armpits; totally smooth pussy lips. Totally bare and naked, 24x7.

Penny and Coco might be naked according to Garment counts, but in addition to what each waves in the air, both are discretely and secretly plugged: Penny's pooch is filled with large, vibrating ben-wa balls, and Coco wears a long thick procto deep into her colon.

Penny's ben-wa balls vibrate, get hot and cold, and are juiced to give electrical pulses or static stimulation, including directed currents that can reach around and provide clitoral stimulation. Penny licks her lower teeth and bits her tongue and assumes she is possessed by a Demon seeking to control her sex.

Coco's procto rotates and tickles her rectum; it's flexible, more than a foot long, and incorporates a bulb near her anus so she cannot expel it. Coco assumes the procto is practice for real cocks next Term.

Both Penetrators wirelessly connect to Automatron, or in more practical terms, to a cybernetic Running Agent who coordinates all inputs and further synchronizes the Double Penetrators shared by the Stripper Roommates.

The drummer and sax man prepare the Club for an announcement; the riff doesn't last more than a few seconds before the Master of Ceremonies summons Penny and Coco to join Tiffany and Steph center-stage, the spotlights converge and M/C booms, "Ladies and Gentlemen. Say hello to two Nugget favorites, ex-Cosmos and now Nugget Stripers, Penny and Coco!" Applause rises. "A hoot of approval. "Bald, pinking, Dong sharing, wannabe Porn Performers!"

Penny's face tightens, Coco's brightens; both with hang valiva tonight.

M/C targets and a boisterous introduction to the two Cosmos guests: "Tiffany Transparent! Meet two former Cosmos! Steph Sorostitute! Greet two Pledge of yours from last Term!"

Cautious applause ripples through the Crowd; something is afoot, but the Patrons haven't quite figured it out yet. More Payback Time? The two former Cosmos bounce to a stop and share the center Stage. Tiffany two-steps. Steph stops playing with herself. Stops everything. *Is this really happening?* she wonders, albeit standing with her feet spread.

Soft applause ripples through the Nugget in admiration of the four naked Gamers. Steph looks at the Screens and sees *Video* of herself earlier tonight, *when Penny and Coco tormented my pink and wet socket with the Dong in the Camera Lounge.* Steph watches herself climax. *I don't remember that happening!*

The naked Nuggets demand Steph's attention and speak to her in unison, "Hello Cosmos Pledge!" Then they alternate, with Penny first, "It looks like you've found your next home." Then Coco, "Or else you're just another naked slut passing through." Penny adds, "We heard you begging to fuck."

"You're a Whore wannabe," Coco stings.

Steph waits. *That's getting ahead of myself.*

Penny advances, "You require begging correction. You are allowed to beg to cum and you should be grateful your request is so frequently granted!"

Coco augments. "But a request to suck and fuck is totally specious; because for you or any Pledge, fucking is not only strictly forbidden, but has serious consequence... and not just a simple Opt Down.

Steph remains silent.

"So what are you begging, Pledge Steph Sorostitute?" Penny inquires.

Steph looks out at the Patrons, glances stage-side toward Babs, looks back to the Strippers holding the opposite ends of the Dong in adjacent hands. She stammers, "Please let me Pledge naked and cum be a Stripper next Term. Here at the Nugget."

Applause demonstrates that the Patrons are paying attention. "You got it," Coco affirms, "Anything else?"

Again Steph pauses and again she glances at the Screens. Hanging on a giant screen is Molly's image from The Bachelor Party. She watches, losing time, as Molly dips panties into the stein of pee and streams pee out of her mouth. The Crowd hoots. Steph looks outward and realizes. *The hoots are for me.* She glances toward Babs' table at the side of the Stage, and registers that two still-warm shot glasses of Tiffany pee rest affront Robyn.

Steph feels her urethra fill up, but the need to pee is squeezed off at the last moment.

She freshens.

She squints, turns to Penny and Coco, and defends herself, "*I* didn't put you here!" She cants her neck toward a Stage-side table. "Babs and Robyn did this to you."

Penny and Coco glance at the Screen and speak in unison. "You'll drink our pee."

And the Crowd howls.

Steph recoils and seeks firm ground. She gestures to the Double Dong waving in the air. "I'll share the Dong with you! With each of you."

Applause rises but holds back to see what happens.

Penny sucks her mouth inward, "The one thing you are, Steph Sorostitute, is you're not stupid. A slippery schemer like you knows that what you propose is impossible."

Steph knows; she reminds, "That doesn't stop you from begging to share it next Term." Steph charges, "You'll be sharing Dong at Flesh Ranch.

Penny scowls but Coco lays down the practical, "Right now," she concludes, "you, Steph, shall ride the Dong with Tiffany!"

"That's allowed," Penny curls her nose upward and gestures toward Babs and Robyn, sitting Stage-side. "And you can drink Tiffany's pee. That's also allowed."

Steph feels a need to respond but has no opportunity.

Penny turns and addresses Tiffany, "Your reputation here certainly proceeds you!" She continues, "We hear you free fucked all the staff."

Coco augments, "Even ate out the scrub lady and licked the janitor's jizz off the floor."

Tiffany rises up onto tiptoes. "When a Porn Star Feature Dances the Nugget she whores for the Nugget. Every hole every which way. Is there a part of that you don't understand?

Penny and Coco lapse into a uneasy silence. They have seen Tiffany's *Tiny Titter Suck Fuck Facial* videos. Heard her sound tracks. Seen her screensaver, her magazine layouts, Pink Page, and Automatron's archives. They might not have ever witnessed Tiffany collecting a dick live, but one consequence of begging to share the Double Dong next Term could be this lifestyle.

Or it could be Opting Pledge.

Tiffany gets it. *Penny and Coco fear me. They fear me because I show* them *what kind of women* they *could be!*

Tiffany bows to the two naked Strippers. "Ma'am and Ma'am, please let me serve as your Piss Mouth, Ma'am and Ma'am."

Again, Penny and Coco appear flummoxed, they might be Pee-Camers back in the Dressing Room, but live on Stage?

The Master of Ceremonies rescues them. "Ladies. Ladies. Penny and Coco. Why are you here?"

Penny and Coco raise their chins and their arms and declare in unison, "We bring presents for the Cosmos Pledge!"

Penny waves the huge Double Dong by one end while Coco holds the box. Penny speaks first, "Coco and I have been passing this Dong back and forth, one to the other, but once one of us has inserted it, we're not allowed to share it. Not even any hands-on or taking the opposite end in your mouth."

Coco speaks, "But Pledge *are* allowed to share the Dong, aren't you?" Coco nods toward Steph and the Crowd "ooohs."

Robyn watches with riveted attention from the side table with Babs. *I doesn't have a Dong in this fight.* Robyn laughs to herself. *And I love it that Penny and Coco hate Steph, and consider that it was Steph's arrogance that lead to their defeat in the Mudwrestling Contest last Term.*

Steph has come out of the Zone just enough to listen to recent directives, and her feelings connect to her tongue. Her eyes flash and she snaps words: "You Strippers just keep your Double Dong! You begged it at the end of last Term, and since you love it so much, you're begging to Opt Dong next Term."

The Patrons collectively draw air into their lungs. Gasps from every quarter.

It is a rude thing to say, still, it also comes from a Pledge begging to Strip, to an already Stripper; and yes, it also true that Penny and Coco have begged to share the Double Dong next Term, either as Pledge, or as Whores.

Tiffany leans in. "Ma'am," she smarts, "please let Steph and I share the Double Dong, Ma'am." Tiffany holds a hand out. *I am supposed to be the Star tonight! Me playing Steph into the Zone!*

Penny and Coco glance towards Babs. It's the second time during *The Runup* they have traded eyes across the footlights. Babs knows, *Janet and I might be a minor factor that you two Opt Stripped, but we are not the source of your Opt Dong begging.*

Penny and Coco's glances descend upon Robyn, *and yes,* Babs understands, *Penny and Coco especially detest the always-arrogant Robyn Redacted, referee of the Mudwrestling Contest. Penny and Coco believe Robyn chose to not enforce the Rules, rigged their defeat, and afterwards posed them for the Dining Room Pictures.*

Babs glances to see how Robyn absorbs the Nugget's glower and crafts herself. *I shall not be attempting to deflect any Penny and Coco anger.* Babs purses her lips. *Anger could not be directed to a better place.*

Penny lays the Dong into Tiffany's outstretched hand.

Tiffany turns the Dong over in her hands, fingers her twitchet open, slips one half the Dong into her taphole, squeezes on it, lets go with her fingers, and wags her tail. *Kimju and Molly got to ride the Dong on this very Stage three days ago, a first for them, and something forbidden to them when they had been Strippers. Now it's my turn!*

Steph watches, open-mouthed, as scattered applause anticipates what's about to happen.

Yes, ex-Cosmos Penny and Coco's first encounter with Tiffany pales in depth to their relationship with their former Monitor Steph, which goes back to the beginning of last Term.

Penny turns to Steph. "You promised us victory in the Mudwrestling Contest, only you got yourself busted for covering your belly button. You were arrogant and stupid."

Coco augments, "So maybe you pay a little for it by getting broken to Pledge, but we pay every day. Here we are, shaving our pussies bare, pinching and pinking ourselves, and lapdancing naked.

Steph recovers enough to snap, "You two are cheap Pee-Camming Strippers begging to become Dong Whores next Term!"

Penny snarls, "And you are a slush socket skeeze skag begging to Strip! Time for you to share the Double Dong with Tiffany!"

Coco piles on, "You've already made Pee-Cam, and next thing you know you'll be begging to shave your snapper. Just like we do."

Penny snaps. "On your back, you Pee-Camming skank," and Coco completes, "spread that sloppy scraghole." Both naked Strippers say, "Now!"

Steph scrambles onto her back, spreads her legs, and pulls her pink wide. Tiffany pounces upon her in a blur; Tiffany thrusts forward with the Double Dong and penetrates the soppy bleached blonde right up to the halfway point. Steph surrenders to it with a gasp.

The Dong pushes a huge gush of slop out, so Tiffany raises Steph's hips, collects surge from around where the Dong penetrates Steph's vagina, and touches Steph's clit with the end of a finger. And touché, Steph starts cumming immediately.

The Crowd cheers, Penny and Coco step back, Babs and Robyn both watch with their elbows on the table and their hands clasped over their mouth. The hovering Cams detail it all, as Steph rises up to a wail before Tiffany can steady her into a consistent climax. Tiffany makes Steph sing, she plays her pitch up and down, trills her, and runs her to the extent of her breath. The sax plays wild riffs, the drumming pounds, the Crowd climbs up onto chairs, all other activity in the Nugget stops; it is controlled pandemonium.

Tiffany allows herself a few long strokes for her own pleasure and heat, arches back, and pulls the Dong out of Steph's socket, still gripping her end of the Dong with her powerful vaginal muscles.

Slurp.

Tiffany reaches, grabs Steph by the hair, and twists her around onto her hands and knees. Steph doesn't know what is happening until she feels the thick Dong penetrate her sternpipe. Steph screams; it's another first-time experience and the Dong doesn't stop penetrating; it is long, big around and the more Steph slithers across the floor the further it slides into her bowels.

Steph howls. Is it pain? Sexual ecstasy? The shear complexity of being taken completely? All of the above? Steph pants and begs, "I'm cumming. I'm cumming. Fuck me. Fuck me. Fuck me. I'm cumming. I'm cumming. Ohhhhhh. Aaaaahhh. Uuuuggghh. Help me. Help me. I can't stop. I'm a Whore!"

Tiffany tips Steph into a part of the Zone where she has no ability to talk, although she does pants rhythm noises. Tiffany considers, *No, Steph, you are not a Whore, and nor can you be one; you must first become a Stripper, and then you can beg to Whore.* Tiffany bucks. *But you might aspire to be a Porn Star, like me.*

Steph, climaxing out of control center Stage of the Nugget, possesses no ability to think at this moment; she is pure animal sensation. Steph doesn't know "who what when where" she is any more, or even "why." She's simply quivering cum flesh.

Maybe this is why enough.

§ Tiffany Plunders Steph: Dongs Mouth & Shaves Snapper

And it is still not over. Gamers recall that naked Penny and Coco held two presents, and the Dong is only one of them. Now Coco dances forward, opens the small box with both hands, and invites naked Tiffany to extract two items from the inside.

Tiffany extracts a small round bar of soap and a straight razor that is folded closed. She remains on her knees, keeping the Dong penetrating Steph's sternpipe.

Tiffany pushes her tongue against her lower lips. Tiffany knows Nugget lore. *These are two parts from the Shaving Kit.* She casts a glance between Penny and Coco's equally bare pubes. *No razor cuts, no stubble, no hiding any lines.* Tiffany muses. *Surely House Mom makes them pink and shave their bodies on Stage every day—armpits, legs, pussies. I know I did.*

Penny provides details. "You got our Dong, now you get our Shaving Kit."

Coco adds, "Now Steph can beg to shave her pussy like we do!"

Tiffany brightens, "I'll shave my tush too!"

"You'll wait," Penny commands, and the Club quiets.

Coco demurs, "Apparently House Mom now wants us to grow our curlies out."

This produces aaahs from the audience.

Tiffany teases, "Gonna rub your pubbies raw when you grind stubble against each other!"

A rimshot and a "Yeah!" echo the Club.

Penny and Coco scowl. *Not against the Rules. They nod together toward Steph and order Tiffany,* "You can do the honors."

Steph, still kneeling with her face and hands on the floor, continues to climax softly in a shallow Zone while the Dong continues to command her spread rectum. Steph never processes Tiffany's acceptance of the soap and razor from the Shaving Kit. No problem, Tiffany lowers Steph's orgasmic rise just enough so that Steph acquires ears. Tiffany chants, "Please let me shave bare and climax the Dong."

Tiffany repeats, Steph hears, and Steph syncs up on the third or fourth interaction, "Please let me shave bare and climax the Dong!"

Tiffany's fingers reach around to Steph's front and diddle her strophoid; now Steph begs and thrashes even harder. She solos, "Please let me shave bare and climax the Dong!"

Appreciative applause swells in the Club until Steph's crying pleas are drowned out by the cheers.

Again a move: Tiffany tightens her squeeze on the double header, pulls her pelvis back and extracts the wild end from Steph's sternpipe, breaking the pleading and producing a shriek of pleasure, pain, and humiliation.

Tiffany grabs Steph by her long bleached blonde hair, knee-rolls her onto her back, squats over her face, and leans forward to twiddle Steph's clit. And as Steph moans, Tiffany drives the Dong into her mouth.

Past her teeth.

Tiffany's pelvis shoves the Double Dong further in, past Steph's tongue; the Dong bumps on the entrance to Steph's throat and then slides into it.

Steph convulses as she gags, now unable to wiggle backwards, unable to scream, and unable to breath. This produces tears, but Tiffany stops, her hands part Steph's puss, and she buries her entire mouth first around Steph's clit before she dives into her sloppy snatch.

Tiffany pulls the Dong back enough so Steph can gulp air and rise toward climax again.

Enough introductory pleasure: Tiffany levels Steph in medium Zone. She mixes spit with splooge to lather the shaving soap onto Steph's brittle and bleached shag, her inner thighs, even around Steph's stern tunnel.

Steph cums constantly now; she would lose all control were not Tiffany to throttle her back, yet letting her surf on the cheers of the Crowd. Steph continues to cum upon the feel of the hands and the mouth and the soap. She starts to cum harder when she first feels the fear of being cut by the sharp edge of the razor. It removes her short and wavy pubic hair, but Tiffany calms her deep throating, and then extracts the

Dong just enough for Steph goes into a soft pant around the Dong, still filling her mouth. "Huuuuuuuhhh. Huuuuuuuuhhh. Huuuuuuhhh...."

Tiffany possesses confidence. *Every Strippers knows how to shave herself, and every Whore knows how to shave others. I'm no exception, except I've shaved in the Inner Sanctuary while sucking dick!*

The razor misses nothing. Tiffany completely shaves off the hair on the pubes above Steph's slit. She pulls the razor through the hair of Steph's crotch and the inside of her thighs, cleans up the inside of her snapper lips, and depilates her all the way down to and around her stempipe.

Applause approves but doesn't get in the way.

The feel of Tiffany's hands on her now totally bare and exposed pubis advances Steph's crazy climax; she thrashes, tries to push Tiffany off, so Tiffany deepens the Dong into Steph's throat, slowing her oxygen intake, and calming her down. Tiffany's own tasty twang flood into Steph's nose and mouth and her body bucks.

Tiffany finds Steph hard to wind down. When Tiffany again relaxes the Dong, Steph resorts to sucking it hard. Tiffany must squeeze the Dong tightly because her timbale coats it and makes it slippery. She extracts it completely from Steph's mouth and Steph moans.

Tiffany ignores the soap that is ending up smeared on her face and the biting taste of the soap in her mouth. She uses her tongue to flick Steph's stamen, and packs the soap and folded razor into Steph's sex socket. *If you can't quiet them then let them talk in tongues.*

Steph does, and rises into a panting Zoned howl, "Oaaaaaguuh! Oaaaaaguuh! Oaaaaaguuh!"

Steph goes to touch herself, and feels that her pussy hair is not there, and convulses, "Oaaaaaguuh! Oaaaaaguuh! Oaaaaaguuh!"

Tiffany rises to applause and wags the Dong hanging out of her twister. Sidestage, Robyn leans to Monitor Babs and evaluates Steph lying on the Stage floor. "Tiffany's leaves behind a slippery slithering snake dancer. Helpless, useless, and gone. A zoned swaggy shag slut!"

Babs narrows her eyes at her Pledge and imagines Robin doesn't wear the maillot underneath what used to be Tiffany's transparent croptop and miniskirt. *Kimju would appreciate the maillot and is worthy of an Opt Monitor next Term.* BB considers. *And Robyn shouldn't complain about the Empresses' New Clothes might she Opt Monitor next Term.*

Tiffany bows again amidst still louder cheers. Her face is covered in soap; the soap permeates her mouth; the soap tastes awful yet Tiffany's palette also enjoys an under-taste of Steph's saucy secretions. Tiffany loves the vibe. *The Patrons appreciate that they just witnessed a Porn Star performance! Penny and Coco, take that!*

Tiffany steps back, yet keeps a firm grip on the Double Dong that continues to dangle from her toolbox. She reaches and assists Steph to her feet, and guides her into a bow, with the soap and folded razor still stuck in her socket. As Steph descends from the Zone Tiffany gives her a big open-mouth soapy kiss, lets go and backs away, and when Steph yields her head back and casts her mouth open for more air, Tiffany deposits even more soap into her mouth.

Steph gasps, shakes, too drained for the moment to resist. Exhausted. She swallows soap, touches her fingers to own clit, and discovers the soap and folded razor sequestered inside her socket. She surges as she withdraws it, tastes the mixture of soap and her own secretions, moans, and goes after more.

§ Tiffany & Steph: Patrons Award the Dong & Shaving Kit

And is it almost over?

The M/C allows the Crowd to catch its breath, then takes over again, "Ladies and gentlemen, a big round of applause for Cosmos Pledge Tiffany and Steph, begging to shave naked and cum be Nuggets next Term!"

Pink wet and naked Steph rubs herself harder in response to the applause; she surrenders to the Audition and lets the Patrons zone her.

Tiffany watches with hawk eyes and a narrowed mouth. *I am proud of climaxing Steph on the Double Dong and climaxing her shaving her. Still, I remain leery of her latent power.*

I know that just because a Pledge becomes naked doesn't mean there isn't more to forfeit, besides gyno and cum. The Dong was no surprise tonight but shaving? I failed to anticipate that.

No problem, if Gamers want me to forfeit my own thinnish red turf in order to stay at the Nugget, then, turf's gone. Steph shaved bare, I shall beg to shave myself bare bald and naked!

I'll beg them to feed me doing it to the Prefecture.

Tiffany bows, flashes pink, flashes her asshole as she spins around, and tastes her tenderloin off her fingertips.

End of Audition.

Respectful applause.

"Ladies and Gentlemen," the M/C booms again, "Which of these Cosmos deserves to keep the Double Dong?" And the Club responds unanimously and goes into quick syncopation, "Tiffany. Tiffany. Tiffany...."

"And which of these sophisticates deserves to get to keep the Shaving Kit?" And the Crowd answers, "Steph. Steph. Steph...."

Steph's head swims; she looks out at the Crowd and masturbates using the slipperiness of the soap and her own sop. At first, fingers, then Steph presses the folded closed metal straight razor against her hard clit, gasps, and gyrates her satchel. "You can climax me with the Double Dong in my satchel. Climax me with the Dong up my stern tunnel. Climax me with the Dong down my throat. You can climax me with shaving my hair, climax me with any mouth on my smoo, and climax me with cock."

The Patrons all know the last of these offerings, climaxing with cock, is forbidden to Pledge, and forbidden to the Nugget Strippers as well.

Steph goes into a series of pants in synchronization with claps from the Crowd. The synchronization of claps disintegrates into scattered applause and Steph again acquires begging capability. "Please let me Pledge bare and naked and cum be a Stripper next Term! I'm begging in front of you, begging in front of the Nugget Cams, begging to Gamers everywhere throughout the Prefecture. I've just surrendered all self-control; I've lost all my pussy hair. I don't have anything left."

The Patrons know better. So does Tiffany.

Yes you do.

Steph stabilizes above mid-brain; she looks around to try and find Penny and Coco. They are no longer onstage but Steph still feels the sting her two former Pledge dealt upon her: *they are trying to punish me for their failures last Term.*

Steph shakes her bare shoulders. *They tormented me first this evening in the Camera Lounge: they pinked me, showed me Dong, and forced me to beg for it. If they climaxed me I was too gone to remember.* Steph steadies and eyes the Crowd. *And then here on Stage the Patrons get to watch me watch myself on the Screen. How humiliating does that get?*

Steph scans the for Penny and Coco again. No hits. *My former Pledge and pinking Baseboard Strippers gave Tiffany the Double Dong and sicced her upon me. They think I'm responsible for their defeat. I haven't seen the Videos, but from what I've been told, Babs and Janet stripped them naked and held them face down in the Mud. They got beaten.*

Screens in the Club light up with a replay of Tiffany climaxing Steph on the Dong. Steph comes more to her senses. "That's me donging my snatch!" she cries to the Crowd. "That's me," she cries as the action cuts, "donging my chute." Once again, "That me, donging deep throat and my shaving climax!" And then f moment, for the next scene to register, "That's me, live."

Applause!

Tiffany shakes her shoulders square and constricts around the Dong swinging from her treasure chest. She waves the free end like a giant cock and draws her own applause.

Steph normalizes completely and addresses Tiffany, "You look like a naked drag king fit for the Snot House!"

Tiffany looks down her nose. "Talk about the Snot House? You traded for your undershirt on the Snot House front steps and showed yourself publically naked. Except now you have nothing and are naked 24x7."

Steph floats; she lifts the razor into the air. "We each have something. You get the Dong and I get the Shaving Kit."

The Crowd mummers approval of this Game.

Tiffany tips, "There are more components to the Shaving Kit than you might realize, but you are off to a good start." And touches Steph's bare pudenda with a fingertip.

Steph gasps and almost swoons. But she is near enough center to examine herself and for the first time she looks down at her pubis. There is nothing there. She touches herself. There is nothing to touch. She sees a mole that was never uncovered before. Steph looks out at the Crowd and discovers that they quietly watch her. Her skin feels ultra sensitive, and without her pussy hair Steph feels more exposed than ever. She touches herself again, this time gently parting her inner lips, and wetness erupts.

Five rapid gasps, then she moans, moves her head in an arc, and senses the Crowd... with her! Steph raises her eyes, opens her mouth, floats on their applause, and introspects, *I have found my new home!* The spotlight fades to black.

II-28 Tiffany & Steph: The Fat Lady Brings an Option (D23)

§ Babs & Robyn Review Penny & Coco: Naked Insertion Dancers

But, as they say in theater, it's never over until the Fat Lady sings.

The spotlights hit the two side stages; the drummer kicks in: and once again Penny and Coco dance there, naked and bare as always.

Penny and Coco will re-evaluate what they beg for. But they are not empty-bodied. They may no longer share the Double Dong nor the Shaving Kit—naked Tiffany holds the former in her twister, and naked and newly bare Steph holds the latter in her hands—but Penny and Coco do share and shall continue to share the two components of the Double Penetrators.

They exchanged in the Camera Lounge only moments ago; now it is Penny who enjoys the snakelike procto that snuggles into her puckered portnoy, while Coco makes music with ben-wa balls in her cockpit. They have switched, yes, but neither has yet the opportunity to insert both halves of the Double Penetrators at once.

The Double Penetrators measures the Strippers, finds their groove, and interactively stimulates them to spec. Penny lets the procto dance her and displays her rectal portal to the Crowd. Whether Gamers see the bulbous end of the rod, or the shine of Coco's ben-wa balls when she pinks, is unknown. Coco accepts that the two balls desire to live in a slippery environment; no stopping that.

Babs and Robyn watch the two naked Nuggets. BB knows, *Janet and I defeated them and sent them to this place.* She wonders, *can Penny and Coco continue to beg the Dong now that the Dong has been foisted upon Tiffany. Was all their begging to Opt Dong a ruse?*

Babs tucks her front lips together, and with her tongue forward and just behind she bites down on it carefully. *Is MomCap going to let Penny and Coco play more with their former Monitor? They've already Zoned Steph in the Camera Lounge, dispatched Tiffany to Double Dong her three holes, and to kept her Zoned while shaving her snapper bare.*

Naked Penny and Coco watch Boss Babe from their divergent vantage points on the opposite side-stages. Their constantly moving bodies incorporates a wariness of their former nemeses. They worry that BB's hands on the tabletop might control their wireless Double Penetrating insertions. The Double Penetrators tickle their sensitive insides and they dance harder, toss their boobs and their booty, moon Babs and Robyn, pink, and flash their assholes. Penny glares one last look. *You put us here,* the body language communicates, *you and Janet.*

No matter, right now both are designated to get fresh and drip cream in front of the former fellow Pledge who defeated them in the Mudwrestling Contest and is now Monitor: Babs.

And in front of Pledge Robyn Redacted. Another humiliation.

Robyn Redacted curls a nose toward the dancers, leans toward Babs' ear, and lectures her. "You and I both have three Garments and shall be MomCaps next Term. Penny and Coco are naked and bare Strippers who are begging to Dong-Whore."

Nuggets Penny and Coco point their pelvises toward Robyn, pull pink, and pretend to launch pee in her direction.

Penny and Coco have chatted about Robyn since her arrival tonight. "It was Robyn's cheating the Rules that enabled Babs and Janet to defeat us."

"I hate her the most," Coco had agreed, "She made us do things *after* we lost in the Mudpit, but she doesn't remember doing them."

"She did turn us onto the Double Dong," Penny had admitted.

Coco had presented a problem: "Robyn repeats a Term as a Pledge except that's against the Rules. How do you figure that?"

"Okay, so maybe she really does have Charm," Penny had admitted. "And that's how she got Redacted."

Coco had agreed, "Because if she wasn't here she can't be repeating."

Neither Babs nor Robyn know that Penny and Coco each wear one half of the dancing Double Penetrators, however the two naked Nuggets and wannabe Dong Whores fear Babs or Robyn's hands on the controls.

Indeed, Boss Babe's primary concern is Cosmos Pledge (and ex-Cosmos Monitor) Steph. BB looks across the Stage and watches Steph, standing with her eyes at half-mast and singing stretto. BB again looks at Penny and Coco. *Better they take out their revenge on Steph (or even Robyn) than upon Janet or me.*

Robyn interrupts Babs' thoughts. "Hey, I guess about the only thing Steph has left is the bleached hair on her head! Ha ha ha!"

Babs inventories her own Garments. *Cutout minidress over bra and nombril.*

Robyn spouts, "Me and you wear three Garments now. I am like House Mom el Capitan. Just like you."

Boss Babs scrunches up her forehead and makes a most shallow nod.

§ Fat Lady: Offers an Envelope Containing an Option

The Fat Lady wanders onto the center Stage and into the spotlight, un-introduced.

The music stops. Naked Penny and Coco on the side-stages ease into a slower subdued dance rhythm. The Crowd greets Fat Lady with hisses and catcalls. She—he, it, whatever—is a totally naked and disgusting man made-up as a woman, rendered ridiculous with a beauty-parlor permanent, sloppy red lipstick and makeup, rouged nipples and a tiny rouged pecker hidden underneath rolls of fatness.

Fat Lady is a grossly overweight specimen that has also been drenched in perfume. Fat Lady is a missionary from the Snot House; saltpeter in Fat Lady's diet ensures that its smallish penis cannot raise an erection and another modest medication makes sure the puny never stops leaking lube.

The Crowd quiets; the Fat Lady raises an envelope up into the air and, in a repulsive falsetto, singsongs: "I bring an envelope from the Snots for the contestants tonight!"

The Club quiets. Anticipation. Uncertainty. Intrigue. Fat Lady wiggles the envelope with two fingers, drops the other hand to its excuse for a cock, and strokes itself. The Crowd hisses.

The Master of Ceremonies intervenes, "Ladies and gentlemen! That's no way to treat a Lady!" The drummer begins snares; M/C continues, "Patrons, Guests of the Nugget, and especially Tiffany and Steph, don't you want to know what's inside the envelope?"

Curious applause endorses this idea and refreshes the two naked Cosmos. Tiffany still hangs the Dong out her trapdoor; her long red hair sways below her shoulders, and her pussy hair graces her trap line. Steph still holds the soap and razor; the hair on her smoo might be gone, but the long bleached blonde hair on her head remains intact, albeit brittled by being bleached.

Applause and the drummer and sax work up a low beat and set a rhythm for the Club. Steph looks at Tiffany and observes a drag king settle into a slow bump and grind. Steph glances at the two Strippers on the outlying stages and witnesses an equally sexually suggestive slow grind.

Steph flinches. Steph might be smart, but she is not clairvoyant, and cannot tell that Penny wears a procto inside her rectum and does not interpret the glint when Coco pinks her cocoon. Steph looks past the stage, dazzled by the lights, uncertain, and joins the grind.

Fat Lady may not be able to form an erection but its useless cock lubes uncontrollably. Somehow Steph forms the idea in her mind that *I am going to have to suck this excuse for a penis. Right here right now in front of everyone.* This is far from the truth, but not unexpected because Steph hasn't thought straight since the Greatest House Roar, two Days ago.

Whatever the Fat Lady is—man, woman, animal—it now sings falsetto to Tiffany, "This envelope contains an Option for the winner!"

Once again Fat Lady waves the envelope high, fat shaking with small male breasts, armpits shaven, and not a wig, but real permed hair.

Fat Lady prances, collects a palmful of lube in its hand and carelessly transfers the sticky to the envelope. She sings to Tiffany again, "You have first choice to obtain the Option. You've won the Dong!"

Another streamer of lube globs down; this one swings and affixes itself to Fat Lady's thick shaven leg; indeed, her whole body except for the perm on her head is totally shaven.

"Listen carefully," Fat Lady sings, "You can trade the Dong to Steph for the soap and razor, indeed the entire Shaving Kit, shave your *entire* body right hear on Stage, and *then* you may claim whatever Option lies inside the envelope!"

Fat Lady sings downward, "Or you can pass."

Tiffany knows the answer before she can figure it out. *I know that shaving everything includes the hair on my head and my eyebrows, still shaving bare bald and naked is no problem for me.* Tiffany draws one hand up and runs it back through her hair, not realizing what she does until the Patrons provides her a spirited clinking on glasses. She acknowledges the Crowd with a smile.

Tiffany considers, *What I am more concerned about is what is inside the envelope. I have had first-hand experience about prizes inside of envelopes! I might be begging to Pledge naked and cum be Stripper next Term, I might be a Pee-Camer and Piss Mouth, but walking into the inside of an envelope possesses great uncertainty.*

The Club quiets and allows her to think. Tiffany considers what she knows about Options. *A Porn Star I know once got an Option for a branding—she'd never wanted one—but then the brand gnawed on her and she ended up begging for it, "brand me anywhere," she had said. And they did.*

And I saw a Stripper—right here as this very Nugget—sign herself up for enema training. And not just once or twice, but every day thereafter.

The Club audience quiets, curious about Tiffany's reply. The snare drum comes to the end of a roll with a quiet rimshot. Silence.

"Fat Lady, no thank you, Fat Lady." Tiffany replies politely, very formal, but firm. She constricts around the Dong more tightly, reaches down and pops her clit out to the Crowd. "I can think of no greater privilege than staying naked and be-cumming a Nugget next Term."

Approval but reserved applause from the Crowd.

"Your decision," Fat Lady rolls, then turns and addresses Steph using a voice that indicates irritation that Tiffany did not accept the offering. "So what about you?" The Fat Lady digs snot out of its nose and flicks it at Steph. "You've already shaved your snizzle and you still have the Shaving Kit. You don't even have to trade anything."

Steph looks like a deer in headlights. *Yes, I still hold the soap and razor. I don't know what to do; I don't understand what goes on around me.* For a moment Steph pauses playing with herself. She doesn't know what to make of her smooth snatch but it excites her and she wants to touch it more.

Tiffany walks behind her, leans back, and slides the free end of the Double Dong in between Steph's legs. Steph gasps and imbues the room with her scent. Tiffany leans back and arches the Dong (still tightly gripped) upward, and ever so gently touches it to Steph's clit. It doesn't take much.

Steph's mouth goes agape, she takes in three quick breaths of air, and begs, "I want it. I want it. I want the prize." And starts cumming again as momentum in the Club builds.

"I'll shave my head," Steph blurts the words out, stumbling now, "I shave everything. Just please let me be bare bald and naked and cum be a Stripper next Term!"

Steph breaks one hand away from her clit and reaches for the envelope. Freeze frame.

There is silence in the Club for a beat and then a cheer. Banging on chairs, glasses on tables, hand clapping, drum pounding, the sax riffing. The Crowd might love a cum conquistador but they also love brashness.

Steph feels uplifted.

Tiffany twitches her head and suddenly doesn't know quite what to think; she wonders, *Have I just been duped? Did the Gamers plan this for Steph? And why didn't Steph also pass? Because Steph is careless... and craves the Zone.* Tiffany gets a better grip on herself, *Yes, Steph got something I passed over. Who knows what's in the envelope? It doesn't matter. I know I made the right decision for my own psyche. All I really need is to dance at the Nugget next Term.*

Fat Lady lets go of the envelope.

Game changers can take many forms, but as Steph lowers her arm with the envelope in hand a fatalism creeps in. She drifts further away from the Zone. *I know I have lost all my dignity. I am a pink-wet-and-ready bare naked Stripper next Term about to become bald. I no longer can hide my slot machine. I am so out of control I'm begging to fuck cock. I know that's not allowed, whether I'm still a Cosmos Pledge or if I'm a Stripper. But I crave cock. I know that after I Strip I'm headed to Flesh Ranch. I can't stop it. I have hopelessly lost control.*

As Steph takes the envelope she closes her eyes and realizes, *I should have followed Tiffany's direction and taken a pass. I have just made a mistake.* Steph reconsiders. *I'm not going to possess the Option; the Option is going to possess me.*

Steph tries to think. *Except, maybe after Tiffany declined I didn't even have a choice anymore.* Steph touches both her nipples and her clit. *I just don't know anything anymore. I can't care. I really am a cumslop. I belong in the Zone.*

Steph looks wildly at Fat Lady, and Fat Lady points to the hair on Steph's head and sings, "Shave and a haircut. Evvvvvveeeery thing." A rim shot and a blast from the sax.

Steph feels drunk on alcohol except she is not. *It is as if I am walking a plank, except that I am.* Her body spasms, she wavers on the cusp of the Zone. The Dong from behind her butt crack tickles her clit again and Steph starts cumming again. Fat Lady gives Steph a kiss, blobs her with a string of lube, and exits.

Opening the envelope can wait until after Steph gets her bleached head shaved. After she really does become "bare bald and naked."

§ Tiffany: Keeps the Double Dong & Streaks to Cosmos House

Tiffany, dazed for the first time this evening, finds herself on a Stage of shifting identities. She still squeezes—and holds—the Double Dong in her temple; it remains her prize from the conquest a few minutes ago in which Tiffany swept away the thin blonde hair from Steph's satchel flaps.

Tiffany feels sudden irritation. *This Dong is no asset. I bet the Gamers will make me keep one end of it inserted inside me all the time, and find partners for the end that wangles out of me like some wayward erection.*

Tiffany calms herself. *Maybe things aren't so bad. So what if I take the Dong back to the Cosmos House? I'm naked and gonna be Stripping next Term. Hey, I am a Porn Star!* Tiffany thinks beyond her own career. *I'll be able to share this with Kimju and Molly; they're experienced Dongers! Then hey, why not shoot some Videos with the newbies. Some Taut Tandem Trinkums for my fans!*

Babs reads the momentum of the present and projects into the future; but not before Robyn explains it to her. "Tiffany's gonna wring the Dong with every Cosmos Pledge. Then when Janet finds out, she'll make Tiffany wring the Dong with every Corvette."

Babs looks at Robyn. "Janet will wring the Dong with Tiffany herself," she asserts.

"Bet it's not her first time," Robyn giggles, confident of her equality with Boss Babe.

Up on Stage the end of the Double Dong inserted into Tiffany's toyshop expands to fill her more completely; it talks to her. Vibration, temperature, electricity, all wirelessly computer mediated. Tiffany knows. *This dong is totally able to manage my freshness. Yes, like right now!*

Correct, Tiffany does not control the wet twang that runs down the Dong and smears onto her inner thighs. *I don't like being in this situation.* Tiffany finds herself forced to gyrate her pelvis and raises her eyes toward the spotlight, *if you insist on making me shake and if you demand I cum on the Dong, then yes, claim me and you will be able to make me cum uncontrollably.*

The Master of Ceremonies provides clarity over the loudspeakers. "A round of applause for Tiffany! Stroking that Dong and keeping' her torque wrench lubricated." The stage lights suddenly go into black light—ultraviolet—there is a flourish of sax and drum and Tiffany twirls; her always-erected Eraser Heads glow with ultraviolet ink. Above her butt, a tribal pattern of glowing invisible ink romances the contours of her posterior rugage before meeting in the middle to descend down the inside of her butt crack.

A familiar riff hits. Tiffany bends over, lifts her tush up to the Crowd, legs wide now, and reaches around behind her and uses long fingers to pull her tooshy apart.

She side-steps around the outside of the circular center Stage so each Patron can now examine what is visible in the ultraviolet light: A tramp stamp with filigree riding the top of rugage before descending into Tiffany's tail trough, here held wide. After plunging downward the lower portions terminate with ink that encircles her asshole and decorates her with an intricate "second asshole."

"Take a good look at that radial pucker of skin around the end of my tail tube," Tiffany proclaims, "Bet you wish you could push something into my tube." Tiffany straightens and wags a finger, "It's not like I haven't rented my tailpipe at the Nugget before. I am a the best suck, fuck, anal, DP, A2M Porn Star!"

Besides her tattooed titty-tips and tooshy tailpipe, Tiffany does have a third tattoo, albeit still hidden.

The spotlight returns and Tiffany spins and bows to the Crowd, as M/C wraps, "Thank you Tiffany! Now outta here! Go back to your House, stay on the Cams, work up some thick tapioca, and share that other end of that Dong with all those Cosmos Pledge!" Hoots, applause, more sax and rim shots.

The command catches Tiffany by total surprise, but it only takes her about three heartbeats to realize that her impending streak has just been broadcast to every perp, paparazzi, and police in the Prefecture. The Dong extracts more soft tapioca out of her turgescent treasure trap; Tiffany grits her teeth, turns, and flees down the runway with applause to her back.

I'm being played and I know it, Tiffany acknowledges as she moves quickly, *I may never know what's in the envelope. Right now my goal is to steak back to the Cosmos House without getting caught. Because if* I'm *taken a prisoner, they will be really rough on me.*

Robyn watches Tiffany trot toward the backstage holding the Double Dong in her trench; her eyes cut to the feed from the Cosmos House, and the Clover of begging Cosmos. *I figure that once Tiffany gets back to the Cosmos House I'm gonna make sure that the pantless Elle will become the first to share some nookie on the free half of the Dong.*

Tiffany had worried that *I would be drinking the M/C's piss tonight, but that's not happening. Then I worried I would be fucking the Fat Lady up the ass with the other end of the dong, but that's not happening either.*

Tiffany does autograph a picture of herself for the Back Door Man on her way out the Stage Door. She realizes as the door closes behind her that the photo was of her, last Term, sucking the Back Door Man's dick. She looks around her, gets her bearings, and darts into the darkness. "Ah," she concedes to herself, "the tribulations of a Porn Star!"

§ Penny & Coco: Shave Steph's Head Bald

Penny and Coco do get to further reduce Cosmos Pledge Steph. The two bare and naked Strippers dance onto center Stage as Tiffany exits. They flank the bare and naked Cosmos Pledge and face the Crowd. The amps in Penny and Coco's Penetrators increase just enough so that neither Stripper can stop rotating her pelvis.

The Master of Ceremonies takes matters into hand, "Ladies and Gentlemen! Penny and Coco, it's time for you to reward your former Monitor boss!"

Neither Nugget misses a beat: Penny commands Steph, "On your knees. Start masturbating." Coco adds, "Let's see some drip out of you." And the Crowd commences a chant, "Haircut! Haircut! Haircut!"

Penny and Coco might themselves find their own holes manipulated to the point of freshness, and their hips kept in rotation, but these stimulus only magnify their desire to crush down on this particular Cosmos: They both believe Steph's reckless behavior and subsequent Lockdown last Term provided the situation which enabled Robyn to allow Babs and Janet to defeat them in the Mudwrestling Contest, and Opt them Down.

The two naked Nuggets glance at Babs and Robyn before they relish this moment with Steph. They relish getting the opportunity to deprive Steph of self-control, self-esteem, and even the hair on her head. Does the fact that Steph tumbles in free fall change their attitudes toward her? It does indeed; it hardens them.

"We're gonna strip you even more naked," Penny declares, and Coco augments, "We're going to reveal you, mind body and soul."

Penny gestures to the soap and razor that Steph still holds. "Gimme," she instructs, accepts the two components of the Shaving Kit from a befuddled Steph, and augments them with scissors.

Coco instructs, "Now beg, you skeezy, soppy, splurt skank!"

Steph stumbles, pinches her nipples and clit, and states the obvious, "I'm bare and naked," she proclaims, "and pink-wet-and-ready to cum." And this produces laughter and gentle approving applause that reminds Steph that Patrons are watching. *Indeed, the whole Prefecture.* Once again Steph feels the Crowd approve of her, rubs herself harder, and swells with pride, "Please shave my head," she begs of her former Pledge. "Please let me Pledge bare bald and naked and cum be a Stripper next Term."

Penny proclaims, "Your wish shall be granted!" Then from what seems like far away, Steph hears Coco say, "Don't drop the envelope!"

Steph looks and it is still in her hand, where it has acquired her own sticky in addition to Fat Lady's drip. The feel of her smooth slot excites Steph and she dives for her strophoid and snooch, tips herself up to the cusp of the Zone where she still possess enough self to exclaim, "Ma'am, take away everything, Ma'am." Steph moans and then whimpers, "Take my eyebrows. You can even pierce and tat me when I Opt Down." As if Steph must give permission. But still, the applause builds and the still-warm-from-being-climaxed Steph responds with a loud dumbfounded, "Pleeease!"

Steph tries to think to herself, *This is complicated. I'm loosing my ability to think anymore.* But the Crowd applauds her, and she feels their affection; *the Crowd gives me respect! I can feel them with me. I trust them.* Steph looks at Babs with level eyes; she looks at Robyn and sees through her.

Steph's naked former subordinates freshen her, stabilize her into a slow breathing rhythm, and vibrate her back toward the Zone. Polite applause for their efforts. Patience. Penny and Coco set a pace so that Steph will not run out of breath and can maintain a medium climax throughout the few minutes of her hair reduction.

Steph closes her eyes, feels her bleached blonde hair gathered into hands and lifted aloft. Her pelvis gyrates now, not too much but enough to indicate that she joins the program. She plays with her tits; she fingers her clitty. She imagines something long up her ass. It vibrates and she goes into concussions—little shakes of her lower body that she can't quite control. She closes her eyes more deeply now, opens her mouth.

Then scissors separate the hand holding her hair from her head, and her cumming comes out in short bursts of exhalations, "huh, huh, huh, huh, huh" as the Patrons join and clap along with her.

The scissor cuts are close to the skull, and then the hand holding above —and the hair it is holding—separate from her body. Steph opens her eyes, and draws her arms up and her palms across her scalp. She looks up into the spotlight.

"Chant," Penny orders.

Steph interlocks her fingers behind her head and buys time while she recites, "Please let me Pledge bare bald and naked and cum be a Stripper next Term." Now she draws her hands forward across her skull to feel what's left of her butched hair one last time. Her body vibrates, and as she draws her fingertips toward her nipples Steph can feel shaving cream lather onto her scalp.

Steph gasps for air and vigorously masturbates her clit and her vagina with both hands. She cums harder now. She feels hands steady her head and she feels a deft stroke of the razor carve a path across the top of her scalp, from her forehead to the back of her neck. She bursts-cums before the hands steady her head and the another swath of hair and stubble is removed from the scalp. Now Steph sobs and cums at the same time, vibrating in a transcendent climatic oblivion until the butch is totally vanquished.

Penny and Coco step back, Steph reaches up to feel her bald head with two hands, shrieks, and throws herself into a faster rolling cum. She leans back, grinds herself with her hands, and wails beyond shame as she maintains her cum.

Pandemonium erupts in the Club. Automatron must balance loads to feed the Prefecture.

Once again hands steady Steph's head; she feels the soap carefully applied to an eyebrow, followed by the eyebrow coming off with a single long stroke of the razor and a stretto from Steph. Soap on the other eyebrow, and as the razor collects the last brow, Steph emits a wail that starts low and deep in her chest and comes out of the top of her throat as the razor departs from her body. This time she just keeps climaxing through the applause and foot-stopping.

Penny and Coco look at each other, push Steph down into a fetal ball on the Stage, raise adjacent legs, and pee directly on her: body, head, mouth. The wetness and tang damp the climaxing down, and Steph settles into a sobbing cum as she approaches exhaustion. *My head feels totally smooth. It's as totally bald as my pussy is bare; I really am 'bare bald and naked,' and I shall stay this way. And stay pink-wet-and-ready. And I shall love it.*

Penny and Coco retreat during the minutes it takes Steph to get her breathing back under control and her heartbeat back down, closer to normal. While they wait the procto and ben-wa balls remind them of their presence, and eventually encourage the two Strippers forward for a soft bow, and a wiggle connected to an applause meter.

Steph comes more to her senses and the Crowd quiets as the spotlight widens. Steph can see past the footlight now. *Cams everywhere; set pieces, handhelds, hovering Nugget Cams.* She looks around and observes *whatever is left of my hair is now scattered about the Stage.* She touches her bald head and the Crowd ripples. *I wonder who will get my scraps?* She thinks in a moment of confused glee. *They are valuable. They are the last part of my body I have to give. I've given all the hair on my head, my eyebrows, and everything that used to be 'down below.'*

The audience quiets down, uses the calm to refresh their drinks and hors d'oeuvres. As Steph comes to her senses she gets up onto one foot and looks out. *They all have their eyes upon me!* She takes in a sharp breath. *I'm important.* She scans the Patrons; there are many eyes to look back into.

Steph shuffles her feet, closes her eyes and then opens them, throws her hands behind her bald head and recites with more vigor, "Please let me Pledge bare bald and naked and cum be a Stripper next Term!"

The Crowd reacts warmly but holds back.

Steph draws her hands to her breasts, recites, "titty titty," slides her fingers across shaven pubage, "clitty, clitty," pinks and scoops, "hole," and rises to "mouth." She pauses in astonishment because a solid round of applause emerges, and it warms her.

"If you like me you can shave me bare bald and naked, every day center Stage next Term," Steph decrees, and when the Crowd affirms, she adds, "I am pink-wet-and-ready to cum for you. Anytime, anywhere, in front of anybody. Here at the Nugget."

Steph thinks she means it, then turns to exit the Stage.

But a voice in the Crowd yells, "Open your envelope!"

Steph pauses, and turns. *Yes, I totally forgot about it.* She looks and sees that she still holds it in her hand; it's crumpled and damp, but there.

§ Steph: The Proposition Contained in the Envelope

Another voice yells, "Open it! Then another, "Open it! What does it say?"

Bare bald and naked Steph walks forward; she turns the envelope in her hand and looks out into the audience. She looks across to where Babs and Robyn sit. She looks around for Tiffany, but Tiffany isn't around any more. Penny and Coco are not to be seen. No Fat Lady. Not even House Mom. The Patrons are hushed.

Steph recalls, *Tiffany possessed an evil smile when it came to the envelope. I'm trapped,* she realizes, *Tiffany has tricked me.* Steph feels dizzy. She touches her bald head; she touches her bare pussy. She straightens up, takes two steps swaying her hips, and discovers the Patron's approval. Steph flattens the envelope out, lifts it, tears off the side, and extracts a paper note from inside. Scattered applause. She looks out, lifts the note up, and takes a big breath

She reads out loud but has no idea of what she says, "You have an Option to pick a Duel with any Cosmos Pledge. Winner-Takes-All and Opts Monitor next Term; loser collects all Obeisance and Opts Stripper next Term."

Steph isn't sure she understands what she has just read. She takes a big breath, reads it again with her eyes, and looks across to the side of the stage where Babs and Robyn still sit. She sees that Babs has raised her eyebrows, opened her mouth, and has her hand on her forehead. Robyn holds a hand over her mouth. Babs understands right away and slowly Steph understands too, *I can pick a Duel with any Cosmos Pledge. Winner-Takes-All and a guaranteed Opt Up? Yes, I deserve this.*

Again Steph glances to the side-table. She can tell, *Babs is not pleased I have acquired this good fortune!* Babs watches Steph glance at the message again. Babs deduces her own Karma. *I might be a Cosmos but I am not "a Cosmos Pledge!"*

So is Babs really off limits? *Yes.* Steph squints at her, *Oh, but I would so like to reduce you, Boss Bitch. Expand a cylinder rod in your box, ream out your borehole, and make you taste your own asshole. I made you, you're not grateful, and I'd love to teach you a lesson!*

Steph's thoughts swirl and gather and she considers the missing Tiffany again, *If Tiffany had taken the envelope.... Except Tiffany doesn't want to Opt Up. It would be worthless to her, but it is not worthless to me. Which is why Gamers passed me this good fortune.* Steph considers. *I do, after all, want to Opt Up? Or at least I used to, although I haven't felt that desire a while.*

Steph again touches her bald head and then her bare pussy. She feels the Crowd approve of her self-discovery. *I might be bare bald and naked but I holds an Option in hand. So what I had to pink, cream, and climax the Nugget? Probably the entire Prefecture! Next I pick my target, I pick the Game, and I pick Winner-Takes-All. This is the least Gamers can do for me. I've been run out enough.*

Steph looks at Babs again: *Your game with me is over,* the look states, even though Steph, at the moment, remains bare bald and naked and BB wears three Garments, a scoop neck minidress over a bra and nombril.

Monitor Babs smiles. *Guess I am not on your target list,* the look communicates. Yet BB introspects, *If I'm successful and can Hover and be a Monitor again next Term, then Steph and I will be equals.*

Steph casts her eyes across Screens that seemingly float in space around the Stages. Her eyes settle upon the feed from the Cosmos House Bunkroom: Kimju, Beka, Molly, Elle on their backs in the Clover. *I need a Pledge with two pieces. That is my target list. For example, newbies Beka and Elle....*

Steph's eyes pivot toward the table at the side of the Stage. *Or Robyn!* Robyn sits with her elbows on the table and with both hands in front of her mouth, transparent croptop and miniskirt atop a strapped maillot with the smallest buttonhole. They flash eyes. Steph realizes, *the challenge the Option presents is absolute, and yes, I know that I can take Robyn!*

The spotlight follows Steph's eyes and Steph watches as Babs rises, bows to the Crowd, and gestures Robyn onto her feet, amidst a roar.

The Club quiets quickly as Steph reads the Option from the envelope again, only this time she faces Robyn. "You have an Option to pick a Duel with any Cosmos Pledge. Winner-Takes-All and Opts Monitor next Term; loser collects all Obeisance and Opts Stripper next Term."

Robyn lifts her hands to her mouth and Boss Babe sits down.

Steph gives the Patrons a sideways glance and addresses Robyn. "I assume my Obeisance include my shaved head and pubes, my Pee-Cam, and everything else."

Robyn crosses her arms across her chest.

Steph asides to the Crowd, "Such a tantalizing opportunity!"

The Crowd claps for her now. Steph turns and looks out into the Club and smiles at the Patrons. She realizes, *looking at Robyn makes me horny.* A deeper part of Steph realizes, *the Crowd watches how my horniness only further arouses my freshness.* She reaches down, pinks and rolls her clit up, dips two fingers into her smooth slip, very consciously digs out some sweetness, streams it up to her lips, and slurps her fingers clean.

The Crowd roars with approval.

I understand now. Steph smiles to herself, and gives Robyn a dismissive look that suggests Robyn is lunch. *She's about to play a Game she can't win and forfeit her clear vinyl croptop and miniskirt—and her maillot—to me. Winner-Takes-All.*

The Crowd murmurs approval. But Steph is not quite ready to devour her nemesis. *She's the one who set me up to get my navel covered. And I have until the end of the Term to get her. Or whenever I feel I need clothes.*

Steph grabs the pole with one hand and swings around to splay her privates for the entire Club. Steph dances, "Better Cam me while you can, cause I don't expect to be returning anytime soon... unless I'm escorting Pledge."

Inside her head Steph is more restitute: *Got it, Gamers. First you reduce me to a quivering quimquat, then you provide me with a sure pathway to the promotion I deserved in the first place! You're twisting me, forging my sex machine.*

Steph affords herself a large sigh of relief. She feels the Crowd desire her, "Thank you. Thank you. Thank you. You're all wonderful here." *Because if Gamers didn't want me to take the Option, they would not have given it to me in the first place! I'm going to Opt Up!*

Steph feels suddenly calm and prepares to exit. She returns her eyes to the side-table when Robyn still stands and Babs sits. "Sit down," Steph commands Robyn, "You've got more Garments than you need, and when I'm done with you, you'll be naked."

Friendly boos and hisses from the Patrons at this declaration!

Robyn sits down abruptly. Steph steps backward and she waves, gets a big cheer, and runs toward the backstage Dressing Room.

Steph collides with House Mom at the back of the runway, and when she raises her hands to ask House Mom a question, House Mom treats her curtly and spares her a punishment, "Beg and don't stop playing with yourself!" A firm hand on her bare shoulder diverts her not into the Dressing Room and clothes, but on down the back hall. Ahead the Back Door Man opens the door for her.

Steph balks. "Please let me stay. I'll stay bare bald and naked. I'll pink, cream, and climax.

"You'll leave and come back!" MomCap pronounces, and propels her out the Stage Door and into the night air.

And Steph finds herself outside.

Steph turns around to look at the Back Door Man framed in the doorway. "Chant," he admonishes her, and she recites, fingers flying, "Please let me Pledge bare bald and naked and cum be a Stripper next Term. Titty titty, clitty clitty, hole mouth." She watches the door close, and observes that the surveillance Cam watches her. *I'm confused. What just happened?* She takes a step and the gravel and asphalt hurt her bare feet and bring her back to reality.

I'm a streaker now, Steph realizes, *and I need to get back to the Cosmos House before I encounter any cocks.*

§ Robyn Rewards Penny & Coco: Piss Mouth Presentation

Penny and Coco have been given a small encore. Like "house girls" everywhere they get to dance on the evening of the big events, and this evening is one of those times. They reemerge bare and naked, each carrying a metal object. Penny holds a small sphere in her hand and Coco holds a cylinder with rounded ends. This time Penny still wears the procto inside her pucker, *and* she now wears the ben-wa balls inside her bare pooch. Penny pulls herself widely open to verify she wears both components of the Double Penetrators. "I solo Double Penetrators," she declares to the Patrons.

Coco proofs a empty cooze and congo, although she still hold the Shaving Kit. She also provides wide and deep pulls so the Patrons and close-up Cams can determine she really is empty inside.

The Crowd approves with applause and watch the DP pullulate cream from between Penny's legs. The drummer hits a rim shot when the first drop separates and splats on the Stage floor. Penny moves across the Stage toward where Babs and Robyn continue to sit stage-side. The music stops and Penny provokes, "Too bad Elle Lollydor can't join us in person tonight."

Babs double checks: Elle and the Bunkroom Clover remain on a Screen.

Babs stiffens; Coco also advances and addresses Babs, "It seems like your Pledge left all her hair behind, but forgot to take the Shaving Kit."

Babs scowls. *That would be Steph.*

Penny holds up a shiny metal sphere and Coco presents a shiny metal cylindrical rod. Penny speaks first, "The sphere unscrews and provides a place to store soap." Coco continues, "And the scissors and razor fold up inside this cylindrical pod."

Penny leans toward Babs, "You can carry them in your bursa and bugger tube."

"That way they'll be handy when you shave yourself," Coco taunts.

The Crowd enjoys this suggestion and whistles.

Babs scowls, reads the disrespect and spunk, *but there is nothing I can do about it; Nugget Strippers are not in my chain of command.* Still, Boss Babe must react.

BB stands, addresses Penny and Coco, and toughens. Boss Babe does not intend to be intimidated by Strippers, *even if I might have inadvertently helped put them into this place.* BB promotes future conditions. "Listen you two, you're the ones begging to Double Dong Together, so you're going to either Opt-Pledge, which isn't going to happen, or you're going to Opt-Whore and ride the Dong at Flesh Ranch next Term. Which is how I see you ending up."

A low frequency rumbles through the Club as the Patrons endorse this proposal.

Boss Babe sweeps the Club with her eyes, casts her open palm to Robyn and speaks to Penny and Coco, "Pardon me, but you two wannabe

Whores give the Shaving Kit to Robyn; she will carry it to Steph." BB snaps her fingers and gestures Robyn onto her feet. "Robyn!"

Robyn stands awkwardly and takes the metal sphere and cylinder from Coco into her hands. There is polite applause in the Club.

Penny pushes her lips out with her tongue; she turns to Coco and suggests, "Maybe Robyn Redacted should thank us." Coco, now standing at the side of the stage directly above Babs and Robyn, addresses Robyn directly, brazenly, "Yeah, Robyn, give us a tip!"

The Club hushes. The Patrons appreciate Penny and Coco's blend of tease, haze, and malicious intent.

Robyn looks at Babs. BB closes her jet black eyes and her eyelids sparkle. She opens them and waits.

Robyn snarls at Boss Babe. "I've got nothing to give to this poon pumper and coot constrictor, besides, I'm the one doing the favor of taking the Shaving Kit to Steph.

"Make nice to Penny and Coco," BB suggests, and sits down.

Robyn sets the Shaving Kit down on the table and looks around. She has no money, she'd never consider offering her clothes, obviously, and the only other thing on the table is….

Robyn bends and lifts the two shot glasses of pee, one in each hand; and she opens her mouth, "I'd like to offer you these shots for your service!" Robyn proffers the two shot glasses forward and up to Penny and Coco. It is spontaneous, brilliant, and cruel.

The look on Penny and Coco's face demonstrates disaster. Babs laughs. And the Crowd goes wild with approval, and aggresses, "Take it! Take it! Take it!" There is no way out for Penny and Coco; not when they begged their own tip!

There is a sudden lull of expectation and Robyn flows into it, "Why you two little o' Nugget Strippers really did the number on poor Tiffany!" The complement is real and gets applause. "Why you took this little sample of Tiffany right outta her, so… it's yours!" This produces approval applause, laughter directed at Penny and Coco, and again a chant from the Crowd, "Take It! Take It! Take It!" Penny and Coco sense the situation has become risky and each feels compelled to take one of the shot glasses from Robyn and retreat to center Stage.

But retreat doesn't satisfy the Patrons. Now the Crowd chants at them, "Down it! Down it! Down it!" And they look at each other and try to out bluff the other and then in rapid succession both throw down the shots. Big applause. The yellow nectar tastes awful and will dry their tongues and smell in their nostrils for hours. Hello Piss Mouths!

Penny and Coco will not forget Robyn. Or the taste of Tiffany! Or the danger of Boss Babe.

II-29 Tiffany & The Cosmos: Double Dong Adventures (D23)

§ Tiffany: Streaks with the Dong to the Cosmos House

Gamers know that Tiffany leaves the Nugget just before Steph comes backstage for the last time. Tiffany remains naked; she still has her long red hair on her head and her thin tapis. She still holds half of the Double Dong in her twat. Some prize.

Tiffany moves quietly but also carefully; she does not wait for Steph and starts her own bold streak toward the Cosmos House. "I can hurt myself," she realizes. Tiffany imagines rupturing her insides and the Dong coming up her throat and out her mouth. "Reality please," she settles herself, and wraps the Dong in one fist pressing tight up against her pussy, so she can jog reliably and not puncture herself. *I can take them thick and deep,* Tiffany brags to herself, *but this Dong is still a Double and needs another Cosmos on the other end!*

Tiffany settles herself into motion. There is also another part to the streak: *I must avoid taking the Dong out of my body. That is forbidden to me. There may be surveillance Cams. Paparazzi or spotters that I never see. I don't want to know about the consequences of cheating or even letting the Dong slip out.*

Tiffany does not worry about getting spotted. *I'll be gone before any police arrive, and besides, I'm lithe and can outrun them.*

Her instructions upon arriving back at the Cosmos have been very explicit. "You are to ring the Bell, proceed inside to the Bunkroom, and position yourself leaning back and facing the Mirror, oval-mouth, legs spread, and pussy lips pulled wide open. Then stroke herself with the long Double Dong, twist your nipples, and juice. But no Zone."

Tiffany had forgotten about the Clover of four Pledge in the Bunkroom and her entrance startles them. Tiffany sits to the side where there are no pools of water or urine on the floor. She observes that all four Cosmos—Kim and Molly and Beka and Elle—are in one way or another bare-breasted. Elle dangles cream from her intimate parts. *Hey,* Tiffany nods to herself, *that's progress.* Tiffany looks at Beka lying in her own pee, *maybe that's progress too.*

As the Clover Cosmos continue to recite their begs, they lift their heads up to gaze at the now-naked Tiffany. Tiffany follows her instructions and doesn't volunteer explanation; that's impossible when one "holds oval mouth." Tiffany doesn't tell them that Robyn wears her vinyl, or that Steph…. *Well, I know Steph volunteered to shave all her hair, and took an envelope that contains an Option. But what it contains and the implications for me are unknown.*

Tiffany watches herself in the mirror, keeps one end of the Double Dong rotating in her tenderloin, and keeps herself breathing firmly but hard. Yes, the Dong has a mind of its own. It monitors me, wirelessly connects to Automatron, and.... Yes, talks to Tiffany's twat. Tiffany gasps, tremors, and transudes tacamahac.

The four pleading Cosmos recognize that a naked Tiffany is a Game changer; and that the prize Tiffany twists has consequences. Kimju and Molly already rode the Dong together this Term, but that was inside the Nugget.

Now the Dong has arrived inside the Cosmos House.

§ Tiffany Invites Kimju: Share the Double Dong

Babs and Robyn return to the Cosmos House. Upstairs in the Bunkroom the tall Monitor, still in her tight minidress overtop bra and panties, examines the chanting, bare-breasted, and spread Cosmos Clover quartet lying on the Bunkroom floor.

Robyn's accoutrement of the clear vinyl shirt and miniskirt over her maillot balances an equation, but a further explanation must wait. Tiffany, now absent the transparencies, continues to sit naked and spread. She twiddles her Eraser Heads and rotates the Dong firmly ensconced in her twat.

BB and Robyn know Steph was last seen fleeing the Nugget—totally bare bald and naked—but they do not share this knowledge with the Clover quartet or with Tiffany.

Monitor Babs signs the Clover quartet onto its feet. Kimju and Molly stand up, topless as always; Beka leaves her halter untied in order to hang boobage, Elle's hacked croptop falls back down her nack-nacks and she pulls her slacks back up.

Robyn points to a small spot on the floor. "Elle's naughty secretions," she informs Babs.

"I'll lollydor myself," Elle puts in.

"You will," Robyn confirms. She directs a question to Kimju and Molly. "Which of you wants to clean up this mess?" Robyn taps a toe near Beka's piss discharge gracing the Bunkroom floor.

Kimju and Molly look at each other. Molly volunteers, "I'll do it."

Babs intercedes and approves. "Good," She trades a look with Tiffany and taps her big toe to Kimju, "That means you can share the other end of the Double Dong."

Kimju stammers at this one. "But but...."

"Butt butt pussy pussy." Boss Babe teases her Pledge. "We all saw Pledge Kimju and Molly wring the Dong at the Nugget. And saw Tiffany dong Steph. Now Tiffany's brought the Dong to the Cosmos House, so you can share the Dong here! Later Molly, you can dong Steph, but right now it's Tiffany and Kimju Donging. So climb aboard! Now!"

Kimju obeys. She pushes her micro g-string to the side, sits and faces Tiffany, and notices how bruised Tiffany's feet are. She grabs the free end of the Dong with her fingers, fits the end into her keyhole, and humps herself forward. Tiffany allows her gaze to move from the mirror to Kimju's eyes; yet she manages to continue to hold her mouth ovaled and open as her breathing accelerates. *I know what Boss Babe gives me,* Tiffany appreciates, *BB gives me live koot to climax the Dong!*

Kimju watches Tiffany play one hand on her nipples and the other rub on her clit and she smells Tiffany's treasure box transude tapioca. Kimju feels herself freshen as she wiggles forward. Her kunny swallows the long firm instrument until the two pussies rub their clitties together, the Double Dong buried in both insides. Babs prods them closer together, "stay connected, wrap your arms around each other, kiss, stare into each other's eyes, arouse each other."

Tiffany obeys; she moves her attention from her mirror image to her newest Dong companion. She leans forward and kisses Kimju lightly on her forehead.

Kimju feels Tiffany want more of her, tenses, and feels the Dong conspire to motivate her arousal. She intakes air quickly and doesn't know what to do.

Tiffany does, and draws her fingers through Kimju's hair, "Easy does it," she coos, "We have nothing to do except let Kundalini guide us to pleasure each other.

Kimju looks back at Tiffany and Tiffany draws her into a kiss.

Time to make love now.

§ Robyn & Cosmos: Explains Dong, Shaving Kit, & Steph's Option

Tiffany and Kimju continue to occupy the Double Dong as they sit on the Bunkroom floor. Or perhaps the Double Dong occupies the two Cosmos Pledge. Besides a lot of local artificial intelligence, the Dong does have a wireless handshake with a Running Agent inside Automatron. The embedded Double Dong measures Tiffany and Kimju's heat, moisture, vibration, pulse rate, blood pressure, and more. The Running Agent localizes the analysis and with the assistance of Automatron's histories, determines that the Dong be warm or cool, vibrate fast or slow, swell or contract, slither, or tingle or shock electrically.

Babs departs to her Bedroom and leaves the Six Cosmos Pledge. Pledge Seven, Steph, was last observed leaving the Nugget, bare bald and naked, and streaking toward the Cosmos House.

Robyn watches the Dong duo kiss and hug and arouse themselves, and Robyn feels empowerment, "I am the chosen Pledge," she announces to the now-standing Beka and Elle, the piss licking Molly, the sitting and spared Piss-Mouth Tiffany, who faces Kimju and shares the Dong with her.

The Cam, brought into the Bunkroom by Kimju and Molly earlier tonight, remains in the Bunkroom, and upon Robyn's proclamations moves away from the Double Donging Cosmos to square off upon Robyn's words, "It was Nugget House Mom el Capitan!—Babs' superior!—who awarded me this transparent longsleeve shirt and miniskirt!" Robyn pirouettes; her acquisition lies overtop her string strap maillot cutout, "This signifies my promotion, and my elevation of Caste."

The only parts of Robyn's body that are not covered with something are her head, hands, legs, and outie belly button. Robyn spies the Cam and teases it, "I've got the smallest buttonhole!"

Navelage 24x7.

Double Donging Tiffany and Kimju hold themselves just outside the Zone so they may follow the proceedings. Kimju considers her Roommate, *Robyn. If Robyn had brains she might understand that her "promotion" is not without its problems. Does her acquiring the croptop and mini (however transparent) circumvent a Roommate Game with me?* Kimju wants to whisper to Tiffany but resists the impulse. *Robyn's three pieces do make her an even bigger Steph target. But instead Robyn feels more secure and Steph is not here. Mostly I need a second Garment somehow!*

The Redacted one remembers an item and she lectures newbies Beka and Elle. "Steph forgot about navelage last Term, or she wouldn't be a Pledge now." Robyn qualifies, "At least, that's what I've heard."

"You took Steph to the Nugget tonight but you didn't bring her back." Elle states a question to Robyn.

"I escorted her to the Stage Door," Robyn affirms, "I came in the front. Tiffany donged her socket, shaved her slit, and Zoned the skank.

Tiffany interpolates, *I declined the Fat Lady's Option and streaked back here, holding the Dong.*

Robyn makes a wave and the Bunkroom Minxy Mirror flicks into Screen mode; it reprises highlights from tonight's Nugget extravaganza.

Tiffany locates the scenes that followed her departure, however the Dong she and Kimju currently share asserts itself more vigorously and Kimju find themselves swimming in each others eyes and suddenly mingling their cream. Tiffany breaths out softly between parted lips, and murmurs "cum with me" in between soft kisses placed all over Kimju's face. It is not until the Screen replays Penny and Coco hacking off Steph's head of hair, and then shaving her bald, do their kisses waver.

"They Zoned the scallywag too," Robyn says. "Then MomCap chased her out of the Nugget. You'll all see." Robyn considers uncertainty, "Or hey, maybe she's gotten herself into the streaker slammer."

Tiffany braces herself to discover what Option the envelope she passed up contains but finds no answer among the Screens.

Robyn remembers a role and signs the Minxy to black. She announces, "I have returned with the Shaving Kit!" She manifests it in her hand and waves a sphere and cylinder in the air. "And it's not just for Steph." She says with a sadistic glee, "Our former Porn Star also begged to shave *all* her hair off. Just like Steph already has."

This produces a ripple of anticipation. Robyn walks over to the Dong-sharing duo, looks down, demands, "Didn't you, you trap tart!"

Tiffany gathers her senses. *I don't remember any such commitment, and I resent Robyn for injecting a promise into my mouth.* She looks up at the Pledge who now wears what was her clear vinyl croptop and miniskirt overtop a maillot. And begs, "Please let me Pledge bare bald and naked and cum be a Stripper next Term."

Robyn gloats at Tiffany and Kimju wringing the Dong, then turns back to Beka and Elle. She makes a rolling motion with her hands as she addresses them, "You're both gonna be Dong socketed!"

Elle blinks just as Boss Babe returns to the Bunkroom. But before BB can get a word in Robyn leads. "Beka and Elle want to share the Dong too. And the Shaving Kit!"

Boss Babe bows to her, "Excellent suggestion, Robyn! But technically the Shaving Kit belongs to Steph, because the soap and razor and scissors was awarded to her as part of her Option."

"However," Boss Babe leans into the newbies. "You can always use to razor in the Makeup Case."

Elle opens and closes her mouth.

Again Robyn advances. She bounces on her feet and wags a finger to up over her head, "The most important thing is Steph's Option."

Tiffany's mind screams. *So what's in the envelope?*

Robyn relishes recounting what happened, "First this envelope was offered to Tiffany because she won the Dong. But Tiffany chose not to accept. But then Steph did, even though she had to forfeit all of her body hair to get it."

"Steph has an Option to pick a Duel with any Cosmos Pledge. Winner-Takes-All and Opts Monitor next Term; loser collects all Obeisance and Opts Stripper next Term."

The Bunkroom rustles. Tiffany feels her heart skips a beat as she considers to herself, *Okay, so I made the right choice. I'm where I want to be.* Tiffany considers wider. *However, this is a Game changer for Steph!*

Tiffany feels Kimju react, tightens her arms around her, and leads her into a kiss. Molly, custodian of the nearby Watering Can and still licking pee up off the floor, pauses for a moment. Beka gets suddenly wet, and Elle startles, *It's me she'll come looking for.*

Outside the Back Landing, the Bell continues to await Steph.

§ Robyn Torments Tiffany & Kimju: Dong and Spit Together

It is later in the evening, just before bedtime, when Robyn inspects Kimju and Tiffany again and suggests that the Dong lovers continue their embrace, "You two shall spend the night together," Robyn announces to any who can hear, "The Dong should always stay occupied!"

Occupiers enjoy occupation! The Double Dong responds to Robyn's suggestions, tingles deep inside both vaginas, and Tiffany and Kimju freshen afresh… and rub their tits and clits together.

Robyn looks down upon them. "Just so you know," she pronounces, but focuses her haughtiness toward Tiffany, "I'm not just 'any Cosmos' anymore. I've replaced your naked teats and twat as BB's trusted assistant. You're finished. I'll be sleeping in her Bedroom tonight. And let me be more precise, Boss Bitch and I are getting promoted together."

Robyn pauses, leans over, spits into Tiffany's face, spins on her heels, and exits.

Kimju overcomes her resistance to lesbianism, draws Tiffany's face to her own, kisses the spit, and commences to clean Tiffany's cheeks, "Hey, I don't hold you responsible for the Dong, even though when it vibrates against my clithood ring I convulse. But Robyn…." Kimju's voice trails off.

Tiffany draws Kimju's mouth to her own and they share Robyn's spit. Kimju looks into Tiffany's eyes, and feels Tiffany take her knockers into hand and rotate her nose cones erect. Kimju puts passion into her kiss, Whatever suspicions I have about Robyn possessing Charm, her acquisition of Tiffany's transparencies make her even more untouchable. For me especially."

Once again Tiffany draws her in, and Kimju surrenders, "Damn you," she whispers to Tiffany under her breath in between kisses, "Your gonna take me into the Zone."

And Tiffany graces Kimju's body, "Not at all," she whispers back, "We're going make love together," and leads them onto a cusp that is by no means out of control, but also hard to escape from until they drift into sleep.

II-30 Steph & Rachmaninoffs: Streaking & Climaxing (D23)

§ Steph & Rachmaninoffs: Out-of-Body Climax

Steph steps out of the Stage Door of the Nugget into the chill and dampness of the night air. Tiffany is nowhere to be seen; she has long since taken her separate route back from the Nugget, and Steph quickly discovers that she shall streak solo. "Bare bald and naked."

The streak is a long one, well over a mile, and Steph considers her route. *It is my first since my run back from the Peacock's Greatest House Roar, when I got stripped naked.* Going from the Van to the Stage Door hardly counts. This does, and Gamers have had plenty of time to stake me out.

Steph gives the surveillance Cam at the Stage Door a final look and disappears into the night. She takes a stealthy but slower route, moving in shadow, but even with the night air she glistens. She scratches herself going through bushes, runs into a fence in a backyard, backtracks, bruises her feet on gravel. But speed is not the Game here; not getting caught is what it is all about. Getting caught means getting jailed, with all of those complications....

Suddenly, Steph finds herself trapped by a hockey team wearing goalie masks. *The Rachmaninoffs.* The Rachmaninoffs carry sticks and force Steph down onto the ground on her belly. She arches her body up and feels a stick on her butt. She presses her belly and bald puss down and feels mud. What is this? What is going on? She feels the end of a second hockey stick on the edge her anus, panics and feels too scared to struggle against it. She grovels forward as a third stick ascends her inner thighs, she instinctively spreads her legs wider, now a fourth stick presses her face down into more mud. She tastes mud. She brings her hand to her head to brush her hair back but there is no hair. Steph feels her baldness; the sticks push her arms up so she is face-down spread eagle.

A Rachmaninoff Cam collects a surge of Steph secretions. She pants. Exactly what combination brings Steph to wet? It matters not. A stick under Steph's pelvis lifts her buttocks and she wiggles her spheroids in a most shameless way and rubs her other cheek in the mud.

It takes but the subtlest of touches against Steph's ribs to roll her over, and the smallest of nudges to spread-eagle on her back. Steph looks up at hockey masks and uniforms. And sticks. "Please let me Pledge bare bald and naked and cum be a Stripper next Term," she blurts out, too disorganized to come up with anything else.

Steph braves to bring her hands to her nipples, tweaks them, recites, "titty titty." She passes her hands into her muddy pussy, "clitty clitty."

And pulls her pink wide, "Now fuck my hole with your sticks," and masturbates harder.

The Rachmaninoffs step backward and fade away into darkness, like Indians vanishing into shadows.

Steph breaks out of the Chant. She fantasizes that the finger touching herself is the end of a Rachmaninoff stick, and she fucks on it, gets fucked by it, feels it circumnavigate her clit, feels the end dip into her slop. The stick penetrates and flushes her wetness up and out of her, her slippery slash lubricates her inner thighs with creaminess, and she looses control and starts cumming.

Steph climaxes with a scream heard for two blocks. And she stays out of control. Floating and suspended: Her entire being becomes alive and vibrating, and her spirit shakes loose from her body. The body supplies blood to her brain, her breathing holds solid and steady, and she passes into a..., *a spirit world, a space of different consciousness, a lateral view?*

The images flood past and Steph discovers *I am transported to a Taj Mahal, a palace of immense beauty. Wherever I look all the details are there.* Steph drills down to the beauty of the cut marble, the beauty of water and plants, of the designs and motifs of the structures, the layout. She starts to come down and her breathing slows. A lion approaches walking along the side of a reflecting pool, and she looks into its eyes and becomes one with it; she becomes a cat in heat and she howls. She rolls over onto her knees and rubs herself in frenzy; she scoops cream out, thrashes her bare pelvis as her body arches and sways. Steph has never felt anything like this before in her life.

Hands and knees. The lion mounts her from behind and drives her into her smoothness, her heartbeat quickens, and animalistic caterwauling awakens and terrifies a neighborhood. She starts to run out of breath and the lion and the world spin. As she comes down during the next minute or so, she opens her eyes, and sees the world with the eyes of a lioness.

I am on my hands and knees; my head is level with the lioness. Steph looks out and sees the trees and bushes and backyard. She twitches her tail but discovers *I don't have a tail, but I am pulling the muscles around the base of my spine.* She gathers more sense to herself. *I should move,* she realizes, *and quickly.* She has announced her presence by her caterwauls, although few listeners would recognize the creature as human.

Steph rises up with her arms and pushes off with her legs, she drives herself forward, crouching, and moves again. She fugitively takes stock of her situation. *I appear to be all by myself. I know how to get home, get to the Cosmos House. I want to be there. It is a safer place. A safe place. The only safe place.*

Steph wipes her lips and looks at her muddy hand. She looks down at her own muddy body. It is dark out. She touches and feels herself. *I am bare, bald and naked. And I need a bath.*

Like her cat-self, Steph sneaks her way back; the thinner mud dries to dirt and sticks to her naked torso and butt and belly and crotch and boobs and yes, face. Steph brushes herself off as best she can, detours through a back yard nearby the Cosmos House and cleans herself partially by rolling in grass. She doesn't consider she may have made a cameo appearance on someone else's Cam and broken a Rule.

Steph wonders, *Did I cum in the Club? Before or after I became bare bald and naked? Both? I can't remember and it doesn't matter any more. I'm pink-wet-and-ready to cum anyplace anytime in front of anybody.*

Steph introspects; she can't quite forget the encounter with the hockey team and the lion and wonders if it was real. *Did I really masturbate a hockey stick? Fuck? Eat my muddied cream off the end?*

Steph wonders many things. Rolling in the grass doesn't get all the dirt off; Steph itches. She reminds herself, *running water in the Cosmos House Backyard.*

And what to do about the hockey team? *I know the Rachmaninoffs are one of the eight Houses, but tonight, did they go rogue? Should I report them to Babs?* Steph brushes dirt off her slit. *If I've been bartered does BB know about it? Or maybe the Rachmaninoffs are a tease Gamers put on me? Any angle, I don't like it. I've seen what happens to streakers.*

Steph sneaks into the Backyard from the back alley, a choke point for sure, but with multiple approaches. She works her way in between the hedge and the Garage and scratches herself from her upper arms to her calves. It's dark out.

It takes a few minutes for her adrenalin to subside and the breathing to catch up. Steph reluctantly considers, *Maybe it's not just Babs, maybe Babs and Janet intend to break me in at the Nugget? No thank you. I've seen some of the acts at the Nuggets with my own eyes. I've seen all the media.*

Now that she is on firmer ground in the Backyard, Steph acquires confidence. *Wait. I just headlined the Nugget! I am the new act.*

Steph considers. *Okay, maybe I will Strip next Term. But there is no way I will lapdance.*

Except, *I begged the Dong tonight and Tiffany climaxed me in front of the Patrons. Shamelessly. So yes, I am begging toys, begging to cum, begging to stay bare bald and naked and begging to be a Stripper next Term.* Steph regains herself, *But it's not real.* She puts her hands between her legs, and the bareness of her pussy excites her. She finds her clit with her fingertip, feels herself freshen, and she masturbates again. *No one tells me to do this,* she declares. *I'm the one who wants to be aroused all the time.*

Not far from the Back Landing, Steph tries the hose, but the water is turned off. And the Watering Can is gone; *Roommate Molly hauled it off before I left for the Nugget. So I'm going to say filthy with streaks on dirt on me.*

Steph moves one hand away from her shaven snizz, reaches up, and pulls the Bell clapper soundly. She sits down on the Back Landing facing the Backyard, positions her legs wide, and begs the hovering Back Door Cam looking at her in infrared, "Please let me Pledge bare bald and naked and cum be a Stripper next Term. She pinches her nipples, "titty titty," fingerballs "clitty clitty," digs fingers into her soggy swamp, and eats herself off her fingertips, "hole mouth."

Steph chants while she waits for what's next. She feels paparazzi creep her skin. The night air tingles her naked body and the Zone beckons. The Back Door Cam transmits her images to the inside of the Cosmos House... and to the Prefecture.

She has no idea of how much time has gone by when someone finally appears.

And she has completely forgotten she holds an Option.

§ Beka & Elle: Consider their Possible Fates

The Cosmos upstairs in the Bunkroom hear the Bell ring and Babs dispatches Beka and Elle down to the Back Door to deal with the arrival of the ever-horny Steph Sorostitute. Beka lets her halter continue to hang down so both her boobs are exposed and the remains of her shorts fail to completely cover her brush and her behind. Elle can no long avoid flashing her nack-nacks, and her low waistline ensures she displays hairage and rugage above it, and details cameltoe in the tight-fitting crotch.

Elle understands, *Beka and I have just become prime Steph targets.* Maybe Beka goes with the flow, but Elle thinks about things. *The Double Dong, the Shaving Kit, and Steph's Option are now loose in the Cosmos House.*

Beka assumes Elle wants to Opt Strip as much as she does, and she confides to her Roommate as they patter down the back staircase together, "Seems like Tiffany and Steph are going to be staying naked now. I wonder when we will get to strip naked? I hope we don't have to wait until the Beach Day."

Elle closes her eyes briefly. She pulls her pants tighter into her crotch and tries to ensure that her hacked croptop covers her naturals. "Like is it a nude beach?" Elle wonders out loud.

Beka shrugs, "Elle, no big deal. We've been to nude beaches before. We've even skinny dipped."

Elle surges, "Yeah, and we fucked our boyfriends out in the middle of the woods during a camping trip!"

Oops.

Beka shrugs, "I wonder when *we* will get to shave ourselves bare bald and naked, and climax the Dong together?"

This makes Elle's head snap; her eyes dart, "Huh?" She steadies herself. "This is different, Beka. First of all, Robyn will cam us, so we have no deny-ability. Pink wet and cumming in public, no secrets."

Beka scratches her sparsely covered body. "Hey Elle, don't talk to me about secrets. "You're the one who gave BB our Measurement Nudes. You didn't have to do that. And you especially didn't have to include me."

Elle backtracks, "You don't know what I had to do to get *my* Measurement Nudes."

Beka raises her palms. "Our Measurement Nudes. Listen, Elle, no offense. I forgive you, I don't hold you responsible, and I don't care who looks at me naked. Or memorizes my measurements."

"I don't think Babs is so cruel that she was behind that order," Elle theorizes. "Maybe MomCap made her make me fetch them."

"Call her House Mom, please, Elle," Beka pleads, "because that's what she'll be to us when we are Strippers next Term."

Elle flinches and inventories her two Garments: *my hacked croptop that keeps me a-titter and slacks so tight that my nachas are separated. But still, two Garments.*

"I liked when we danced the Nugget, Elle," Beka reminisces. "It makes me hot we both tittered and pinked the Camera Lounge. I want to go back, Elle. I want to eat you out and climax the Dong with you center Stage."

"I know." Elle takes a deep breath.

"I love you, Elle," Beka bubbles, "you know I'd never do anything to hurt you."

"I know." Elle gathers a thought. *But I'm not sure I'm able to protect you from yourself.*

§ Beka & Elle: Muddy Up & Masturbate Steph into the Doghouse

It is one thing to hear Robyn's descriptions and watch video; it is a raw shock to encounter a filthy Steph in the flesh—her bare bald and naked flesh.

The appearance of the two newbies disturbs Steph's reverie. Beka still wears what used to be Elle's halter and jean shorts, although the shorts seem to be ripped almost up to the waistline. Elle wears what used to be Tiffany's low-ride slacks and Beka's croptop, only with the neckline and armholes cut out, the rib-line ragged and titter, and the hip-hugging slacks flaring pussy hair and a pronounced butt crack.

Steph feels dismay. *I am being given to the newbies!*

But it is going to get far worse; Beka and Elle have been given unambiguous orders:

Elle begins, "On your knees."

Beka escalates, "On your belly."

Elle delivers the punch line, "Slither into the Mudpit."

Steph obeys. Somehow the hose now works and the newbies spray water onto Steph and onto the earth. "Spread your legs wide apart. Pull your lips wide. Masturbate. Now." Steph scrambles and obeys. She already has dirt on her spooters and belly; now Steph feels wet mud squish between her legs and cover her satchel flaps. A bright light hurts her eyes and she detects the hovering Back Door Cam documenting her exploits. Steph understands, *I might be a live feed.* Might be? Hah!

"On your belly," Elle commands.

"Spread 'em!" Beka augments.

The cold water from the hose hits Steph right between her legs. She impulsively goes to squeeze her thighs together but constrains herself to a twitch. She surrenders her hairless screwhole wide open and sloppy inside. She feels for her clitoris and rolls her full spike outward. Her brown nipples harden and her puckered beige areolas lift them upward like fruit offering to be plucked. Once again touching the bare skin excites her to freshen herself, and when she reaches a hand to her head to confirm her baldness, she surrenders more, moans, and discharges a gush of her thick creamy pheromonic announcement of arousal, memorialized on the video feed. Steph cringes and pushes the front of her tongue hard against her lower front teeth, rolling the center of her tongue and opening the lips ever so slightly. She licks her lips.

Steph wonders, *I already had to grovel in the Mudpit, when I had to strip off my undershirt and offer it to Molly. But now I have nothing to offer, not even the hair on my head.*

Nor is it fair that the newbies manipulate me. Aren't they both begging to be Strippers? Aside from flashing their tits and pinking, they are pale imitations to my *reduction.*

It turns out that even the newbies know how to return Steph into the Zone. "Masturbate yourself," the newbies dictate, "Grovel. Rub your face side to side in the mud."

Steph sighs as the mud coats her face. She feels the wet mud on the front of her legs, her belly, her tits, her pelvis. Do Beka and Elle know what happened at the Nugget tonight? Well, yes, sort of. But do they really understand the psychological trauma? Not really.

But they do know how to use the hose! Instead of getting sprayed clean from the encounter with the Rachmaninoffs, Steph discovers that the earth around her turning into a thick mud; mud that splatters up onto her skin and makes her more dirty. This arouses her further.

And her treatment intensifies. "On your back, spread your legs apart, masturbate yourself!" And Steph obeys. She feels the mud on her back and issues a soft moan. The light spray of water only makes the mud thicker and deeper.

Beka orders, "Take one hand and scoop up handfuls of mud and rub it all over your head."

"Don't stop masturbating!" voices Elle.

Steph obeys this instruction as well, and covers herself with more wet earth.

The feeling of the soft thick mud on her bare scalp escalates Steph's arousal.

"Smear it all over you. Cover yourself. Every last inch."

Again Steph obeys; she scoops up huge handfuls of mud and smears the sloppy wet earth onto her tits, her belly, her arms, her pelvis, her feet. When she feels her bare snatch she can't stop herself from attacking her clit and her satchel, and enters into a shallow cumming. Beka and Elle's must make sure she doesn't take herself totally over the top.

"Pay attention. Smear it on. Really, really thick."

"More. Don't stop."

"Wallow in the mud, you slippery slithering scumbucket!"

Steph breaths harder now, rubs her hands all over her body, she talks to the Cam, robotically, "I'm a skeezy skank slut. I'm a skeezy skank slut. I'm a skeezy skank slut...."

But not yet. Beka and Elle sense Steph drift into the Zone and they need something to bring her back. Steph's body now wallows in mire inches deep, but Steph doesn't question; she forgets humiliation, she abandons concern about getting worked over by newbies. Steph's only concern is arousal.

"Scoop up two big handfuls of mud and dash over to the Doghouse."

Steph doesn't quite know what Beka and Elle are telling her. "The Doghouse?"

The Doghouse. The cramped space under the Back Door Landing.

Elle knows all about the Doghouse; she spent her first night at the Cosmos House there. "Except Elle wasn't dripping in mud.

Beka prods her, "Move!"

Elle curls the hairs overhanging her pants in her fingers. "Now!" she demands.

Steph, dazed, obeys. One of the newbies already hoses down the inside of the box with its dirt floor. Steph just darts to the box.

Elle dictates again, "Rub the mud all over the ceiling and walls."

Steph ducks inside, throws mud against the wall and reemerges.

Beka sustains pressure, "Keep masturbating."

Steph obeys. She returns her hands to her sex cavity and again discovers her strange bare snatch. The mud coats her so thickly now she can't tell if she discharges slush between her legs or not.

Beka and Elle push her harder, "More! Move it!"

Steph skedaddles, claws up a huge helping of mud and runs back to the Doghouse, ducks inside and slathers.

"Keep masturbating! Faster!"

Steph does, back and forth and back and forth, muddier and muddier and hornier and hornier until inches of mud cover every wall, floor, and the ceiling of the narrow little box.

"Get in," they yell at her together.

Thick mud covers Steph totally. Her entire body. She lies down in mud. And mud covers every surface of her environment. She knows she has lost it, but Beka and Elle finally let her have what she craves.

Beka issues their final instruction, "Cum for us!"

Yes, somewhere down inside Steph knows, *I reduce myself not simply for Beka and Elle, I polish myself off for Gamers everywhere!* Steph puts on quite a show. She detects only dark shadows in the box, and cannot escape from the mud. Its texture covers her bare bald and naked body. She lies in mud and mud drips from the ceiling. She masturbates harder now, on her back, legs wide apart, totally surrenders to her reduced position, and drives herself higher again. The cumming begins, different than the last climax, this time about helplessness and textures and imprisonment and her fate now and next Term. Her sounds penetrate the Doghouse walls, fill the backyard, and flows out into the neighborhood. Even Robyn, in the Bunkroom upstairs, can hear Steph's shrieks; Robyn smiles.

Steph's Zoned vocalization come out from somewhere deep inside her, she howls and she keeps cumming until finally she becomes too exhausted to cum any more and drifts into a deep sleep.

The Cosmos: Beauty & The Mermaid Parade (D24-D25)

II-31 Tiffany & Kimju & Molly & Steph: Pass Dong (D24)

§ Tiffany & Kimju: Discuss Steph & Robyn while Donging

At some point deep in the morning and before sunrise of Day 24, the Double Dong reminds Tiffany and Kimju of its presence. Like a puppy dog wanting attention it vibrates just enough to bring Kimju to squirm and pussy rub Tiffany; and then to thrust her chest forward and rub her knockers up against the Porn Star's Eraser Heads.

Tiffany responds with a kiss and wraps her arms around Kimju's back, draws them tighter together, legs up and over the other, pussy-to-pussy, clit-to-clit, with the Double Dong all the way double buried, resting, but by no means extractable.

Neither Cosmos Pledge quite wants to wake up completely. Tiffany takes a finger and wipes sleepy dust out of Kimju's eyelids. Tiffany remains naked; Kimju has rolled her g-string down her hips; it still slides tangent to the Dong, but it doesn't dig into her crotch. Both adjust cramped muscles, look each other in the eye, and spill urine onto the Bunkroom floor, and, by default, each other. It has been a hard night and unlike the still-sleeping other Cosmos, they didn't get to visit the Bathroom before going to sleep.

The hovering Cam, never put back away into the Bathroom, flags both Pee-Camers. Automatron logs they fail to use the Measuring Cup and Logging Chart.

Tiffany draws Kimju's face up again with a kiss, this time one that rolls Kimju's lips apart and takes her breath. Tiffany leans forward so she can whisper into Kimju's ear. "Can you hear me?"

Kimju whispers back into Tiffany's opposite ear. "Yes." And Kimju asks a question: "Robyn took your croptop and miniskirt and let you streak naked? She's moved into BB's Bedroom and is sleeping underneath her. She thinks she's BB's equal."

Tiffany responds. "If I get caught streaking I'm in Lockdown and will get triple penetrated, and maybe more than one at once."

Tiffany whispers softly, "On one hand my fans would love to watch me get gangbanged again. My problem is I could get charged with seduction and sent to the Dungeon. I don't want to become Slavesex, so I ran out the Stage Door and vanished before they could think twice about me."

"It was easy for Steph on her way to the Nugget," Kimju observes. "Robyn says all Steph had to do was present herself naked at the Stage

Door. But after you left naked with the Dong, Gamers had to know Steph would have to run for it,"

"Well, not her first streak and it won't be her last," Tiffany appraises. "But from what I can overhear she's been wallowed in the Mudpit and moved into the Doghouse. Welcome to the Game."

Tiffany and Kimju share a glance. They know they have also done time in the Doghouse, as has Beka and Elle—minus the mud bath and mud coat environment.

Kimju twists a lip. "Steph is still dangerous, especially if what Robyn says about the Option is true.

Tiffany considers, "Steph holding the Option does change the calculus for some Pledge, except I am already naked, so there is nothing for Steph to take from me."

Kimju frowns. "I don't have a chance in a Duel with Steph, especially if she gets to pick the Game."

Tiffany consoles, "Steph won't pick a Duel with you either, because even if she wins, one g-string doesn't provide her with two pieces. Same for Molly, who also has insufficient assets for Steph, and besides, who needs wet panties. As for Babs, well Babs is not a Pledge."

Kimju speaks, "I had been wondering about calling a Winner-Takes-All Roommate Game with Robyn, but now that she wears three Garments, that changes things too."

Tiffany agrees, "If Robyn's sleeping in the Babs' Bedroom then maybe she's not even your Roommate anymore."

Kimju grunts. "Maybe you're my Roommate now," she says, "I guess that's okay. Maybe even better."

Tiffany runs her hands up the center of Kimju's back and feels the bumps of her vertebrae, "If you are indeed now a free agent it still doesn't make sense to Game with any Pledge at this moment. If you win another Garment you just become a viable Steph target. Sometimes less is more."

Kimju nods. *I must make a timing decision.* She shifts, "If gaining two pieces has also made Robyn a free agent, then she should be concerned about Dueling with Steph. But such possibilities never enter Robyn Redacted's mind. She believes she has become a House Mom el Capitan."

"Boss Babe has commanded we obey Robyn," Tiffany reminds.

"Except Steph has nothing to lose," Kimju argues. "Because if Robyn isn't Charmed then Steph will strip her naked and send her round rump off to runt at the Nugget. And not just for an Audition. Steph hates her for outing her last Term."

Tiffany draws her opposite fingers around the outsides of Kimju's shoulder blades, then follows each shoulder curve around to the front of the ball socket. "I don't think Steph will attack Robyn; it's too complicated," Tiffany opines, "even though Steph doesn't think Robyn has Charm."

Tiffany draws Kimju's head forward and gives her an honest kiss. She looks into Kimju's eyes, "If Robyn is Charmed, then Steph will say 'hello' to the Nugget no matter how beneficial her Option might be!"

Kimju returns a kiss on the lips with an ever so open mouth. "The 'old Steph' could turn Robyn into a wet pinker in about three bats of Robyn's eyelashes."

Tiffany's tongue tips Kimju, "But the 'new Steph' is Zoned!"

§ Tiffany & Kimju: Quietly Climax the Double Dong

Morning vibrations and somewhere between Tiffany's kisses and the Dong, Kimju quietly looses herself into Tiffany's lips before losing her body into Tiffany's flesh.

Tiffany draws her fingers upward until she touches Kimju's neck then graces Kimju's cheek with a light kiss.

Kimju drifts on the sensation of Tiffany's naked body. She smells Tiffany; she smells the pee on the floor. She looks. *Our pee is all over us.*

Am I a Pee-Camer by now? Kimju wonders in a rare moment of panic. She knows. *I am. I Pee-Cammed on the Yacht, and after we got back I begged to Measure and Log officially. My world is spinning too fast. I can't even remember if I Pee-Cammed during my Alumni Reprise.*

The Dong speaks to both of them; each get different vibrations but achieve the same results. They squeeze the Dong tighter, and Kimju tightens her hug upon Tiffany. They rub their nipples together, then reach out and touch each other with their fingers. An inch of Dong is visible in between them so they snuggle forward until their clitties mesh and the visibility of the Dong reduces to zero.

Kimju tries to anticipate. *Maybe I'll never get a second Garment and I really am headed for the Nugget next Term.*

Tiffany whispers advice. "Take it from a Porn Star. Everyone has already seen your knock-knocks and your kypsey. Seen both our wet insides, watched us pee, watched us climax. This Term Gamers watched you with Molly eat pussy and cum on the Double Dong for the first time. You're making progress!"

Kimju speaks louder than a whisper. "I never donged anyone when I was a Stripper last Term! I never ate pussy before at the Nugget! I always followed the Rules. I still do. Four Days ago on Stage with Molly *was* my first time. Strippers aren't allowed to, you know that. I've danced at the Nugget before, and I don't want to go back. I'm not like you, Tiffany. Really, not every Pledge wants to be a Porn Star."

Tiffany again whispers, "Ride with me, Kimju. We'll keep it quiet like, because we don't want to wake up any sleeping Cosmos."

They touch tongues together. Kimju wonders, *Am I still able to process and not succumb to total passion? Is it the Dong or Tiffany bringing me to climax and taking me into the Zone?*

Kimju sighs and fondles Tiffany's cheek, neck and armpits. *Tiffany loves to get into me,* Kimju understands as she squeezes the Dong, rubs her chest against Tiffany, and shares tongue. *I know that coupled with the Dong I have little alternative but to kiss and fondle her back. What better to do?*

The Dongers reach and squeeze each other's breasts and excite each other's nipples. Kimju knows, *I am about to go under again. But can I escape climaxing the Dong? Should I even want to?*

Kimju vibrates and deepens the passion into her kissing. *I'm losing control to my new Roommate, and I'm gonna get Zoned again and climax the Dong with Tiffany. I can do that, but I can't let Tiffany take me with her to the Nugget.*

Now Tiffany and Kimju somehow grasp opposing parts of Kimju's g-string, and, carefully and with precision, they play the string across their burbling clitorises atop the buried Double Dong. They share their lips, synchronize heartbeats, and breath together as they fall into controlled but sustained climaxes that surf the Zone with a singular heartbeat.

And they don't wake up any Cosmos.

§ Tiffany & Molly: Share Double Dong & a Piss Mouth Kiss

Robyn summons Reveille. "Stand spread surrender," she orders the three bunked Pledge. Robyn wears the clear vinyl croptop and miniskirt overtop her strapped cutout maillot: three pieces.

Her call bristles Tiffany and Kimju out of the Dong Zone. The Dongers remain embraced in the corner, still impaled on their shared Double Dong. The naked and nearly so still sit in a pool of their own urine. It has been a long night, but since the Cam never left the Bunkroom, it's easy to query Automatron for downloads.

Molly and Beka and Elle form a Three Cosmos Lineup in front of their bunks. Robyn makes a sign and Elle lifts her croptop, rolls it, and takes it into her teeth. Now all breasts in the Lineup display fully exposed. The Cam, still loose from the Bathroom, collects the trio: Molly topless wears only see-through nombril panties, Beka dangles her halter full boobage and hangs ripped jean shorts on her hips, and Elle holds the croptop in her teeth, her hairaged and rugaged skin-tight stretch slacks depict cameltoe stains.

All Pledge presume, correctly, that Steph still lives in the Doghouse.

Boss Babe now wears a knee-length minidress over a lacy brassiere and nombril. Matching lingerie, with the waistline of the culotte kissing the bottom of the dress's buttonhole. Three Garments, always barefoot.

Boss Babe appreciates the squeeze play. She sidles to the spot where the Bunkroom meets the hallway and stairs, and watches quietly. Whereas the Minxy delivers Babs a full reflection of her Lineup, were any eyes in the Lineup to scan the Mirror for Babs, they would see nothing of her.

Robyn prances in front of the Lineup. "Steph's raised the bar here at the Cosmos House. You're all in motion, because Gamers will allow you to advance your Chant. How about, 'Please let me Pledge bare bald and naked, eat pussy and juice the Dong, and cum be a Stripper next Term?' Think you can remember that? Because I'm sure Steph will teach you." Robyn laughs, "Ha ha ha ha!"

Babs smiles, *Robyn is even better than me at escalating tension. But I'm better than her at knowing how to sculpt.*

Robyn, confident that the transparent croptop and miniskirt overtop her maillot embellish her MomCap status, shakes her shoulders and stands tall on her bare feet.

She approaches Tiffany and Kimju and sneers at Kimju. "I am going to store the Shaving kit in your kunt and your anal kram," Robyn twitches her nose and continues. "So you need to remove the Double Dong outta your kunt and bury it in your mouth—and quickly before I decide you will penetrate your kram on the way."

Kimju scrambles. Much to her surprise the Dong in her koozy slips out easily, and once in her mouth and in the oral space behind her teeth it inflates and makes itself at home. Kimju now resides with her nose rubbing Tiffany's trembling clit and her open-mouth kissing Tiffany's trench around where the other end of the Dong remains firmly embedded. *Does Robyn know I'm now cleaning my own kloop off the Dong?*

No problem. The Dong tickles the back of Kimju's throat and Kimju reminds herself about legends: *The Dong can extend a thin finger all the way down my throat and into my stomach. It's not coming out.* Tiffany's pelvis constitutes most of Kimju's frame of vision, and the taste of Tiffany's pee lingers with her tang.

Kimju feels, but can't see, what slides into her kunny.

Tiffany can see just fine.

Kimju feels a foot kick her. She moves and Tiffany moves with her, helping her into a new position. Kimju knows. *Gordian Submissive, well sort of.* She keeps her mouth and nose buried against Tiffany's treasury, draws her knees forward and wide, elevates her keister into the air, and awaits the long cylinder.

It arrives. Robyn steps back. "You hold onto that for me, you understand?"

Kimju grunts, "Auhhh auhhh!" This is how one talks with a Dong in their mouth. Kimju feel her vocal vibrations against the stainless steel ball in her kootch.

Robyn appraises Kimju, "Tiffany here can switch the Dong around to her different holes," Robyn lifts a shoulder, "but now that you got the Shaving Kit in your kunt and crude pipe, it seems to me that you'll be sharing the Dong in your mouth for a long time.

Robyn spins and signs topless Molly onto her hands and knees. "Clean up the mess, Piss Mouth," she says.

Molly obeys. She uses her long black hair and pendulant mammies to quickly swab the floor; she casts her eyes toward Boss Babe. *Am I supposed to clean up all by myself? After all, I'm not the only Piss Mouth here.*

Robyn kicks one of Kimju's hanging knocks. "Lucky you," she says, "You've already got a full mouth." Robyn laughs. "Ha ha ha ha!"

But not for long.

Robyn, impatient, drives a sharp toenail into Molly's butt. "Stop licking. It's time for different wannabe Stripper to ride the Dong with a wannabe Porn Star!"

"Move," Robyn kicks Kimju and the Dong deflates and falls out of her mouth. And its no sooner free and waving in the air extending from Tiffany's twat that Robyn urges Molly on. "Slide that Dong into your meatlocker, you massive mazed mandragorite."

Molly obeys. She splatters into whatever pee remains on the floor as she settles her moonatonentot maximus onto the floor. She pulls her panties to the side and slides the end of the dong, still wet with Kimju's phlegm, into her own mutton. She carefully advances on the Dong until she and Tiffany are clit-to-clit. The Cosmos House's newest Double Dongers wrap their arms around each other and kiss. The Dong settles into its new home.

Molly knows, *the hair on my head still stinks from mopping up Beka's piss yesterday, and now it drips with Tiffany and Kimju's piss from the floor. I've even got pee on my lips.*

Molly needn't worry. Tiffany's kisses Molly on her face and lips and allays Molly's fears *that Tiffany will find me unclean.* Molly lets out a sigh and arches her body forward on the Dong, pressing it into her mainspring. Molly looks: Tiffany's clit sits framed in its hood atop the Dong, her inner lips arch sideways around it, and her outer lips mark the beginning of her wispy red pubic hair. Molly looks harder. *By contrast I am a black muff, but I still show color around the Dong and I'm already oozing muscovado.*

Robyn points a foot at the Double Dongers. "You two French kiss."

And so they do, and Tiffany collects her first taste of Kimju's urine, as well as her own. *Kimju and me on the lips of Molly. What not to like!*

Robyn advises Molly, "I'm important. You get to share the Dong with Tiffany, just like Kimju did. And you get to sit in Tiffany and Kimju's piddle, just like Kimju did. What's missing from this picture, you miserable melting mellonpot?"

Molly knows, but Robyn harkens first, "That's right Molly Mammoth, soon you're gonna augment the piddle on the floor. You're gonna share your warm wetness with Tiffany's tail skin on the floor!" Robyn laughs, "Ha ha ha ha!"

Kimju feels relieved heading toward the Bathroom. The Cam follows her, observes her strip off her pee-soaked g-string before entering the Bathroom, and trails her back inside the Bathroom to watch her wash the g-string out. *That's not against the Rules, is it?*

Robyn leaves Beka and Elle standing spread surrender with boobs and nacks displayed. Robyn, after spending the night in what used to be Tiffany's bunk in Babs' private Bedroom, returns there now and affords herself the privilege of using Babs' private shower, conveniently avoiding the issue of confronting a Bathroom with its lit-up Cam.

Maybe three pieces means something after all.

§ Babs Invites Beka: Fifth Cosmos Begs the Pee-Cam

Tiffany and Molly continue to share the Double Dong throughout the morning of Day 24. Do they occasionally talk in whispers about Watersport Games—peeing and getting peed on? They do, for after all, they are both Pee-Camers and Piss Mouths and they sit in a puddle of pee. Some Gamers hope Robyn will splash them.

Tiffany and Molly might be zoned dongers, but the issue of yesterday's puddle—contributed by Beka during Clover time—still requires Boss Babe's attention. Beka and Elle stand side by side, backs to their bunks, hands behind heads in surrender position, legs spread wide, and they look at their visages in the Minxy Mirror.

Beka's halter, unbuttoned at the neck, hangs boobage. Elle hold up her hacked croptop with her teeth, more boobage. Beka's ripped jean shorts display hairage in the front and a cheeky back. Elle's skin-tight stretch slacks hairage in the front, rugage the back, and cameltoe dampness.

Boss Babe walks behind them but her reflection in the Minxy Mirror does not appear to Beka and Elle, and this unnerves them. Boss Babe asks a question. "Which of you peed on the floor during the Clover yesterday?"

There is a pause and a stumble. "Ma'am I didn't mean to pee on the floor," Beka confesses,"and I should not have freshened myself. But everyone creamed, Ma'am, even Elle!" Beka tries to rationalize.

BB elects to ignore the Elle bait. "But not everyone voided their bladders," BB observes, "only you did."

"Ma'am, I know, Ma'am," Beka replies, "I lost control of myself."

"May it please Automatron to serve your little pissy bit to the Prefecture." Babs speaks in a very matter-of-fact manner. "I gather you want to volunteer to join the Pee-Cam posse?"

Beka can't hide. "Ma'am, I guess I can do that."

But BB isn't with guessing, "You guess or you want to?"

Beka understands, "Ma'am yes, please let me use the Bathroom naked and become a Pee-Cam Pledge."

Boss Babe exhales.

Beka hustles, "I'll pee for whomever whenever wherever you want, Ma'am."

Boss Babe pinches Beka's cheek and speaks more, "Remind me to let you drink lots of fluids, pee only occasionally, and train you to pee on command. You'll also keep track of your input and output. You'll do that for me, yes?"

"Oh yes Ma'am, I'll use the Measuring Cup and Logging Chart, like all the others." Beka resigns herself to what she must do. Her broda pushes out and the smell of her freshness hits the Bunkroom. She surrenders further, "Maybe Tiffany can teach me to pour shots."

"Maybe later," Boss Babe says to Beka. And smiles at Elle.

Elle, standing next to Beka, convulses. Elle knows, *Beka can learn to pour shots. But there is no way she has the self-discipline to keep track of her inputs and outputs. Surely Babs knows this too. Babs knows I'll have to keep track, most probably for the both of us.*

§ Robyn Hazes Beka & Elle: Orders Beka Pee on Back Landing

Beka has just laid her halter and ripped jeans shorts on her bunk in preparation of her initial Bathroom Pee-Camming when Robyn appears. Robyn remains attired in what was once Tiffany's transparent croptop and miniskirt, overtop her own maillot cutout. She has availed herself of the privacy of Babs' private loo this morning and made herself fresh and sparkly by utilizing the Makeup Case.

"You need to honor your commitment to 'pee wherever and whenever,'" Robyn preaches to the naked Pledge. "So go out to the Back Door, squat on the Landing, and release your yellow stream in full Backyard view!"

Beka looks to Babs in horror.

But Boss Babe only shrugs. "What are you waiting for?" she says to her still-naked Pledge, so Beka scoots downstairs, out the Back Door, and comes to a stop on the Back Landing.

Beka knows what she does is not something a polite Pledge would do, and of course the Back Door Cam purviews her as she stands with her legs spread, her pelvis pushed forward, and bravissimo! *I am a naughty girl!* Does Beka know that the wooden Landing also demarcates the ceiling of the Doghouse?

Yes, Beka knows. *I spent time down there. Not as much as Elle or Tiffany, or for that matter, its ongoing occupant, Steph. Except it never rained when I was inside, although I peed on myself and then had to lie in it.*

Elle waits upstairs in "stand spread surrender" position.

Robyn examines her; she runs the back of her hand from Elle's exposed and cupped armpit across to Elle's nipple. There is no Cam witness. Robyn pivots her hand, cups Elle's breast, and then draws back and pinches Elle's nipple.

The croptop abruptly falls down. It floats such that the swell of Elle's under-breasts is fully visible, and the lower line of the croptop tickles her areolas and nipples.

"Did I say 'Open mouth'?" Robyn queries the Pledge.

"Ma'am, no, Ma'am," Elle hurries.

"You opened your mouth without permission?" Robyn queries.

"Ma'am, yes, Ma'am." Elle begs, "I'll put my croptop back in my mouth. I'll take it off completely. I'll shave. I want to please you, Ma'am."

"Please yourself, Pledge." Robyn snaps. "You opened your mouth, now keep it open. Oval mouth."

Elle obeys. She quietly inventories her status. *Areolage to boobage, hairage and rugage above the waistline, cameltoe. I've auditioned the Nugget, tittered and pinked, and I think I've shined by nadir aperture. But I know I am unable to climax all by myself, or in front of people. And I know I can't handle any Dong, even if it were just Beka and me in private.*

Robyn affords herself the luxury of spitting into Elle's opened oval mouth. Elle holds still, gathers the spit with her tongue, and swallows.

Elle overcomes her shock and continues to think. *My problem is that Monitor Babs holds Karma over me; she has my Gonzo Videos. And then there is Steph, because with her Option she can send any Pledge to the Nugget.* Elle considers Robyn. *Robyn seems to exert more power than the rest of us Pledge. Special treatment, like Babs putting her in charge of us.*

Robyn graces the back of her hand down Elle's belly until she encounters the helter-skelter hairage that spills overtop Elle's low-rise slacks. Robyn curls strands of Elle's hairage between two fingers; Elle holds her erect position, tenses her body.

Now Robyn slides opposite fingers around the waistband to the sides, then around to the back until they meet in the crack of Elle's naches.

Robyn. Robyn hooks them into the rear of Elle's slacks and as she draws her fingers downward Elle's hips roll into view: total buttage. Robyn takes a breath and worms her fingers around to the front of Elle's slacks, rolling them down until Elle's pubic hair comes into full view. Elle knows, *I'm full-frontal right now.*

Robyn steps back to admire her handiwork. She signs Elle to stand with her legs apart, "Roll the slacks down far enough so there is daylight in your naked crotch. But no further!"

Elle tightens her face, quizzical. Then moves her arms and obeys. *Is this the last time I will display hairage above my slacks?* She wonders.

"You're been staining your slacks," Robyn admonishes. "So Gamers want to know if you're excited or if your peeing yourself? Now they may witness both your pudenda and the stains inside your slack's crotch!"

Elle trembles, "Please, Ma'am, please."

"Lift your shirt up, Pledge," Robyn commands.

Elle obeys; she uses two hands to lift the croptop up under her chin, putting her nackers on display. *I'm full-frontal now,* Elle accepts. *At least there is no Cam here in the Bunkroom!*

Robyn lightens. "Do you know you are the only Pee-Cam hold-out?" Robyn's assertion conveniently omits herself from any Cosmos Pledge commitments.

"Ma'am!" Elle says. She considers, *Perhaps Robyn really has promoted? Really has Charm?* Elle feels a surge in her bladder and her pee pushes its way into her urethra. She holds tight, *but I will not be able to hold for very long.* Elle wonders, *Has my turn come too?*

Babs interlocutes. "Off to the shower!" she tells Elle. Elle flinches. *Kimju's presence in the Bathroom ensures that the Cam remains lit, so I might get cammed full frontal.* But nature calls and Elle moves; she walks carefully, with the tightly rolled-down fabric *feeling like a rubber band around my thighs. I got my nipples and nappy and naches on full display. And the Bathroom Cam is about to benefit from my total exposure.*

§ Kimju & Elle: Bathroom Discussion Re Steph Option Targets

The Bathroom Cam collects Elle as she pulls the croptop off over head and rolls the slacks down and off. She dashes into the shower; the water is sufficently chilly to raise goosebumps and nipples; Elle doesn't want to linger, yet she must stay long enough to disguise her urine release while the water streams over her naked body. *I fear that Babs deliberately reduces my modesty,* Elle worries, but reconciles. *I shouldn't forget that I pulled my shirt up and parted my pink at the Nugget, so showering naked here in the Cosmos House should seem pretty benign.*

Elle blushes when the Cam collects her naked body getting out of the shower, but adopts a wry smiles when the Cam can't decide to look at her or at Kimju, lounging in the bathtub and using the soap and razor from the Shaving Kit to shave her armpits and legs and carefully trim around her kohlrabi.

Kimju asks a question, "Say, Elle, are you begging to shave? Because then Robyn could stash the Shaving Kit in your nook and nedash."

Elle looks at her own nappy in one of the mirrors. *My growth extends from well above my notch to the insides of my thighs.* "Steph's a bad influence because I just begged Babs to shave." Elle gestures toward her pelvis, "All of it, not just the part above my slacks."

"Steph's Option changes the Game," Kimju reminds, "You and Beka are her prime targets."

Elle squints. "That's a theory, but what about Robyn? Steph hates her for slamming her last Term."

"Ah, Robyn. Robyn presents a special challenge for Steph." Kimju reaches deep into the tub and rinses her inner lips. "Steph desires to crush her, but Steph has also succumbed to the Zone. And if Robyn can keep Steph tuned into the Zone—and she's done it before—then Game over."

"And if she doesn't?" Elle asks a little too quickly.

"Kimju calculates, "Well, if Robyn has Charm she will defeat Steph, no matter what Game Steph choses. Why will Steph take the chance, especially when you and Beka are already flashing your tits and asses, learning to part puddy and cream, and begging to 'Pledge naked and cum Strip.' Steph shall make that wish come true for one of you."

Automatron logs Elle's pulling her croptop back on and stepping into her slacks. *Beka and I both still do possess two Garments,* Elle considers. *So Steph could Option either of us if she doesn't Option Robyn.*

Elle compounds her thoughts. *First Steph has to get out of the Zone long enough to remember she has the Option. This means Robyn must keep her in the Zone all the time, because if Steph gets out she will option Robyn and if she doesn't option Robyn she'll come for Beka or me. For Beka, actually, because that's not so hard.*

Kimju wipes away the last of her soap and water, gathers her g-string in hand, and exits. And the Cams on Elle turn off.

§ Steph: Morning in the Doghouse

Steph awakes in the morning with the feeling of wet urine dripping down on her head, startled, she attempts to rise up. She bangs her head.

She remembers where she is. *I reside in the Doghouse, the shallow box underneath the Back Landing of the Cosmos House.* Some of the mud has hardened and inside the confined space she finds her flat tits rubbing the dirt. She crawls. She wiggle-rolls over onto her back. There is enough space to do that. She tries to scrape some of the dried mud off her body, but the ceiling and walls still retain moisture and the dirt floor remains muddy with new urine moisture.

Steph suddenly feels afraid. She feels her head—it's bald—and she checks her pussy. It's bare also—and it itches.

Steph oscillates between touching herself and getting her wits back. She worries about her health but imagines, *I've been inoculated*! She tries to remember the events that led her here. *I need to pee.* Except Steph can't move around in the small space, so she drains her bladder right in the middle. *It doesn't make much difference, one way or the other, I got pee all over me now.* Drip drip drip.

Steph remembers, *I am begging to Pledge bare bald and naked and cum be a Stripper next Term. Tiffany dildo fucked and shaved me bare at the Nugget, Penny and Coco shaved my head bald and climaxed me, the Rachmaninoffs captured me and took me to the Taj Mahal, and the newbies muddied me up. Payback from Boss Bitch for last Term.*

Steph feels trapped. *I stink. I am exhausted. But if I leave this box where could I go? I am safe here. Filthy and shamed. Bare bald and naked, begging to eat pussy, twist a dildo, and cum Strip next Term. But it is not safe outside. Not safe at all. I'd have to streak and I have no place to streak to. I am safe here.*

Steph carelessly touches her sex. She parts and rubs her strophoid, draws in a deep breath, and suddenly remembers, *I hold an Option!*

Steph stops playing with herself. *I've not had a chance to think about that while I've been cumming. Been kept cumming. Kept cumming before I got the Option and kept cumming afterwards.*

Except now. Maybe shortly I will have to start stroking myself again but now I can think.

A very valuable commodity.

Let's see now, Steph remembers, *just what do I have an Option to do?*

Steph reconstructs in her mind her naked on-Stage appearance at the Nugget last night. The Fat Lady singing it out, "You have an Option to pick a Duel with any Cosmos Pledge. Winner-Takes-All and Opts Monitor next Term; loser Opts Stripper next Term."

Steph ponders, *A Duel. I know the Winner-Takes-All includes all Garments, and the loser will collect all my Obeisance, which includes my bald head, bare snapper, and Pee-Cam. I'm home free with my Monitor promotion.*

So the Option offers a serious opportunity.

Steph considers the flip side, *Should I exercise the Option but lose, I am guaranteed to be a Stripper next Term.* She rolls over onto her side, purses her lips, and brushes a mixture of caked-on dried mud, and newer wetter material, away from her lips. *Yes, I could lose, but if I don't call the Duel I'm going to stay bare, bald, and naked and Strip anyway.* Steph tries to examine her body. *The Crowd at the Nugget loves me, but Boss Bitch puts me down. I'd make a great dancer, but once I Opt Up I become equal to BB, and after that I become a House Mom el Capitan, and the Strippers dance for me.*

Steph ponders. *The only question is which Pledge do I take and with what Game do I crush them?*

She hears footsteps above. *I have little time left to think,* her mind darts, *How will I escape from the Zone long enough to exercise my Option to Duel? And when? I don't trust BB on this one. I think Boss Bitch intended that Tiffany get the envelope, and will try to get in the way of my Duel.*

§ Molly Tends Steph: Passes Her the Dong in the Doghouse

The ground-level door of the Doghouse opens and sunlight floods in. Steph sees Molly leaning over and looking in at her. Molly her Roommate. Steph quickly considers, *Might I want to Option Molly?*

Steph studies Molly's swinging her pendulous bare mammary glands, sees her very low totally see-through panties with the big muff of hair above the top. She see that Molly still makes sure to keep them tightly bunched and rolled into the crack of her ass and narrowed in the front so that her muff splashes not just over the top but also out the sides. Molly can't make the panties any smaller.

There is one other thing: Molly's bundled up panties are pushed to the side, so that the Double Dong snakes out of her pussy, one half of it gripped inside her meatlocker, while she holds the other half in her hand, like a long cock waiting for a pussy to penetrate. Steph's pussy perhaps?

Steph assesses that besides the Double Dong sticking out like a penis waiting to penetrate her, that Molly's skin glistens—indeed, Molly holds her Watering Can next to her. Droplets of fluid run down Molly's mams, drip off a clit ring clearly visible above the inserted Double Dong, and soak the long black hair on her head. Molly seems pretty much wet all over; and if filthy Steph has much distinction of smell she could smell that Molly stinks of urine just as much as she does, probably more so.

Steph wonders if Molly intends to climb into the muddy Doghouse with her; Molly's wet body will just make everything more slippery. Of course she will, it's dirty work, but somebody's got to transfer the Dong to the mud-humper in the Doghouse and force her to start cumming again.

In the last of her own thoughts, Steph concludes that *Molly is not my Duel opponent; Molly's panties are of no use to me. In order to secure a Monitor slot I need to challenge a Cosmos who has two costume pieces, not one. A Pledge whom I can take for sure.* This is Steph's last thought of her own.

Stinking-wet Molly crawls into the Doghouse. "Point your slit at me," Molly tells the bare bald and naked filthy one, "Spread your legs. You very well know how to take this."

Steph does; she obeys a Pledge she failed to defeat at the Peacock House; all the intimidation comes back. "Yes, Ma'am," Steph respectfully addresses her Roommate. To whatever extent Molly contributed to putting Steph into this hell-hole, Steph acquiesces and offers up her smooth socket. Molly cringes when Steph's muddy hands pull her forward and help to fit the dong into her snatch, but accepts she's gonna get muddying up sooner than later. Steph takes a big breath as she gentles the Dong into her totally shaven stash, lubricating herself the moment Molly and the Dong make contact with her body. Molly wonders if wringing the Dong in the mud is healthy. Steph, no longer considering anything, allows herself to be lead by sensation; Steph will not be considering anything very long.

The Dong comes alive inside Steph's socket, her body responds, and Steph accepts, *The dong possesses me once again.*

"You're a lucky Cosmos," Molly whispers to Steph. "You get an intelligent Dong. It's got electricity, vibrators, thermal stimulation, sensors, and a wireless connection to Automatron. It will stay stuck in your snapper and keep you on remote homeostasis. Slow drip. From now on, you're just a horny Cosmos wanting to fuck."

Steph can feel the dildo inside her vibrating. Molly's correct. Steph goes horny again.

But Molly is not quite finished. There is barely room inside the box but she passes the Watering Can to Steph. Roommates share, remember? "Sprinkle." Molly instructs her. Steph tries, but mostly she just spills the water all over herself and makes fresh mud out of dried dirt.

Steph gets some in her mouth, and imagines she tastes caster oil, or urine, or worse. Big imagination, small know.

The combination of the oral stimulation and feeling the Dong inside her body excites a primitive urge in Steph, and Gamers may rest assured that Automatron will build a circuit in Steph's brain that associates losing control of her mouth with arousing herself. Steph starts to cum again and readies her chant.

Molly, initially reluctant to share the Watering Can and the Double Dong with her Roommate out of fear that Steph might come to her senses and exercise her Option again her, finds herself feeling sorry for Steph.

Steph sucks very hard on the bottle as she settles into a quiet cum. And it's very unbecoming for Steph to beg her Roommate, "Please Molly, let me cum on the Dong with you."

But Steph's pleadings are more personal than Molly wants to hear. She extracts herself from her end of the Dong, leaving it behind in Steph's slippery slash. She places her empty Watering Can outside, backs out of the Doghouse on her hands and knees, closes the door behind her, and leaves Steph to drift into bliss. "Maybe getting around to calling an Duel will be too far from Steph's brain to recall," Molly considers, "But if I need to twist Dong with her again to get to the Nugget next Term, I will."

Molly rises; she's covered with mud, but rinses herself and the Watering Can with cold water from the hose. She rings the Bell, and retires through the Back Door to the upstairs. A shower and makeup await her. All the Cosmos, except the mudpie in the Doghouse, are getting cleaned up. They have an appointment in the Village today.

II-32 Beautician Preps Cosmos: For Mermaid Parade (D24)

§ Madam Nurse Beautician: Hair Dyes Six Cosmos Pledge

For reasons not yet revealed to them, the Cosmos make a trip to the Beauty Salon. All the Cosmos except Steph that is, who remains in the Doghouse, bare bald and naked, caked in wet and dry mud, living in mud, and with the Dong humming in her snatch. Steph tries to resist the Zone but the Dong insists on Gamers having their way.

Babs herds the six Pledge into the back of the Van. Naked Tiffany leads the way and is eager to avoid any streak. Topless and buttage Kimju and Molly follow, and Beka and Elle climb in last, the hickeys on their necks still fresh.

Robyn takes a final look before she closes the Van door. Four of the Pledge already sit on bare butts: Tiffany, Kimju and Molly, but also Beka, whose jeans backside is sufficently raveled she has no choice but to add her booty to the gritty floor.

"You too," Robyn tells Elle, so Elle pulls her slacks down her butt so she may sit her nachas directly in the grime. "Teeth," Robyn adds, so Elle gathers her croptop up into her teeth. Now all Five Cosmos display tits. Robyn closes the door and walks around to the side of the Van to ride shotgun. Monitor Babs drives.

None of the Five Cosmos Pledge are afforded any opportunities for public exposure upon their arrival at the Beauty Salon, a downstairs shop in a house in the Village. They arrive topless or boobage and display butts gritty with Van floor dirt.

Madam Nurse Beautician greets Babs and Robyn and the Five Cosmos Pledge.

Beautician is a stocky Hispanic in her thirties whom statuesque Babs bows to as she says, "Madam Nurse Beautician, thank you, Madam Beautician." Forms of address have meaning in the Game.

Beautician wears four Garments: A frock dress over two undergarments, and shoes. Beautician was last seen wearing a rubber dress, gloves, hose, and boots.

Babs retains her cleavaged cutout minidress over a lingerie bra and nombril; the neckline teases the bra strap and the cutout teases the sexy waistband of the nombril lingerie briefs. Babs, like Robyn and the Five Cosmos Pledge, stands on bare feet.

Babs tries to not look Beautician in the eye. BB enjoyed Beautician's presence last Term, when as a Cosmos Pledge, Bikini Babe volunteered to visit the Beauty Salon and service Madam's feet with her tongue. She practiced manicure, foot massage, and nail painting, yet never once did Babs allow her eyes to stray above Madam's ankle.

Now, for the first time, BB sees a full figure, even a face.

"Relax, Bikini Babe," Beautician orders Babs, and lifts her chin with her finger. "It's okay to read my eyes."

Robyn retains her transparent croptop and miniskirt overtop her strapped maillot cutout; she assumes her new role as Babs' Roommate and equivalent, and radiates royalty.

Robyn actually visited the Beauty Salon earlier this Term after she demanded Beautician do her hair and makeup, but she's forgotten Nurse Beautician sent her back to the Cosmos House with a Measuring Cup and a Logging Chart, so the Pee-Camers could quantify their productions.

The Pee-Camers have not forgotten.

Tiffany knows Beautician *because I tricked for her last Term.* Tiffany knows that Madams (and Pimps) are a Caste above MomCaps (and DadCaps). Madams run Whores, MomCaps run Strippers, and Monitors, like Monitor Babs, run Pledge. *Madam Beautician resides two Castes above Monitor Babs; she is three Castes above us Cosmos Pledge.*

Tiffany recalls. *Beautician was five Castes above me last Term, when Pink Cowboy sent me out from Flesh Ranch to work her Medical Room. She knows I'm a natural-born Porn Star, and that I begged Piss Mouth to avoid Slavesex. Big deal, so I'm a Watersports Whore.*

Molly remembers Beautician from *The Arrivals,* when in the Medical Room, *Beautician presented an oral spreader into my mouth, a speculum opening my muliebre, and an anoscope deep into my mawk port. I was totally revealed, and all while my Roommate Steph watched.*

Now, my Roommate Steph is beyond totally revealed: she is bare bald and naked, filthy with mud, and pissing herself in the Doghouse.

So I guess I wasn't totally revealed after all. Right now I am topless panties buttage, and I need to get back to the Cosmos House with just that one piece.

For Kimju, and for Beka and Elle, this is a first opportunity to meet Babs' boss's boss. MomCap's boss. All three Pldge present topless or boobage, all present hairage, and all present rugage or cheeky buttage. Two have crost in their crotch seams; one has spotted cameltoe.

Beautician surveys her three new acquaintances. "Strip naked," she orders them curtly, "Drop you clothes into that basket."

Kimju and Beka go into motion and Elle slowly follows.

"You too," Beautician orders Molly, who obeys. Tiffany trades eyes with Beautician but orders are unnecessary: Tiffany is already naked and has been so ever since MomCap gave her Garments to Robyn. *So I would also be naked when I shaved and dong-climaxed Steph at the Nugget.*

Madam Nurse Beautician surveys five now-naked Cosmos Pledge. "Good!" She gestures them forward. "Now sit your naked selves into that row of side-by-side beauty chairs. You know your order: Tiffany, Kimju and Molly, Beka and Elle."

The five Cosmos move deliberately. For all practical purposes the chairs are no different than gynecological examination chairs, with foot stirrups that raise and spread the legs. And why not, since one of Madam Beautician tasks involves making their pubes (if not their pink) beautiful.

And what a pretty sight they are: Tiffany, Kimju, Molly, Beka, and Elle all sit back in their chairs: naked and with their legs parted just as wide as possible, pussies inching toward agape.

They see themselves in a mirror in front of their chairs; they see Robyn standing next to Monitor Babs.

Robyn signs their arms to surrender position and the Five Naked Cosmos sit spread surrender, finding extensions of the chair left and right of the headrest a comfortable place to reside arms. Now not only are their legs parted and crotches on display, but also their armpits.

Elle tremors. *At least no men are here and no Cams.*

Tiffany competes with Beka and adds the smell of her tang into the air, already quick with Beka's scent. Babs and Robyn stand behind Beautician and watch her reign.

Kimju and Molly assume Madam Nurse Beautician with examine all orifices. Neither makes any assumptions that they will be getting back the Garments deposited into the basket.

A figure arrives, and the Cosmos all recognize the Nugget Shooter.

Shooter brushes a pocket and a hive of hovercams fly out. Miniatures. Shooter waves a hand toward the five naked, sitting spread surrender Pledge. "Patrons want to evaluate each of you more closely, so they allocated a mini Cam for each of you!"

Shooter gestures and the hive collects Tiffany, Kimju and Molly, and Beka and Elle in their naked and explicit positions. Few physical secrets remain to be revealed, although some of their souls still need turned out.

Elle cringes. *I consider this treatment inappropriate. I deserve my two Garments and not having them get mixed up in a basket. Maybe I did go topless in the Backyard, or titter and pink at the Nugget, but that was not like here, just sitting back in this chair stark naked with my hands behind my head, my legs spread wide, and my feet in stirrups. This is really embarrassing that Gamers to see me like this.*

This is my first nude spread for the Game. And I know what's coming next.

Elle checks that her armpits well cupped, her mouth is closed, and her thighs aren't touching. *Of course not, not siting spread like this.*

Beautician casts an eye at Elle's squirm as a hovercam lingers on Elle's naked nookie, and inquires, "Haven't you been begging to Pledge naked and cum be a Stripper next Term?"

Elle stutters, "Madam, ah Madam, Yes," Elle has.

Beautician demands full chorus of commitment, "All five of you, recite," she commands.

All Five Cosmos Pledge chant together, "Please let me Pledge naked and cum be a Stripper next Term."

Beautician beams, "Now that you have part of your wish come true, may your whole wish be fulfilled."

Tiffany acts on the opportunity and catches Shooter's eyes. Did not a Feature Dancer/Whore/Porn Star service everyone at the Nugget during her visits? On Cam or off, their choice. Tiffany rotates her body, lifts her pelvis up, Gorean Fuck-Offering. She settles down. Shooter remembers.

Kimju absorbs that the Nugget Shooter *concentrates the hive upon my opened crotch.* Shooter's nose twitches. The presence of the Nugget Shooter unnerves Kimju. *Molly may not care if Shooter broadcasts the Private Backstage Video of us dunking to retrieve our thong and panties,* Kimju acknowledges, *but I need to back off sharing a Piss Mouth.*

Kimju catches a sly and knowing grin on Shooter's face; she had refused to fuck when she was a Stripper last Term, correctly so. *Letting Shooter fondle my knockers and finger my koot already bent the Rules.*

Kimju tries to catch Babs' eye. *I don't know what Babs knows about the Shooter's Backstage Video, and I worry about what I might have to do keep that Video secret.*

Molly knows Shooter. *Last Term when I was a Stripper at the Nugget he demanded I stream muscovado out my mooe and collect it in a jar. Shooter put me on all the Screens.* Molly twists her pelvis, augments the vapors in the Salon, with a streamer of her own muscovado, and watches Shooter's nose twitch. They trade eyes. *I'll do it again for you.*

Beka and Elle fleetingly remember Shooter from their Nugget Audition, four days ago. The brightness of the lights and the tumble of events mazed out impressions of the Crowd.

Beka doesn't forget. *Shooter called out my pink at the Nugget. And now that I'm spread surrender and wet, Shooter's going to climax me on the Nugget Cams!*

Elle reconciles, Maybe *I tittered and pinked for the Nugget Shooter before, so maybe I'm doing it again. Except I'm not tittering anymore, this time I'm naked and spread surrender. I am not flashing any nookie or making nectar, Maybe Beka can climax, but for me it's impossible.*

Madam Nurse Beautician claps her hands. "Time has come to get you ready for the Mermaid Parade!" Madam engages Robyn to squirt a large helping of bleach into the hands of the five naked Cosmos.

Beautician commands, "Rub that bleach into the hair on your heads." The five naked Cosmos obey and ensure saturation. All of them are canvassed by Shooter's hive.

Robyn assists, "Rub a little bit into your eyebrows."

Beautician signals Robyn to dish out another round of bleach; and Robyn again fills palms with a second helping. Robyn can't resist sniping to her fellow Cosmos. "You rub *this* handful into your pussy hair. You know what's happening. You saw Steph beg the bleach and lose all her natural color. That was before she lost all her hair!" Robyn laughs. "Ha ha ha ha!"

Beautician smiles and assures, "Don't worry, Pledge, we are not bleaching you out to shave you. At least not today."

The gyno chairs make it easy for the naked and spread Cosmos to slathers the bleach into their pussy hair. All watch themselves in the mirror opposite.

Robyn gives Molly an extra handful, "All over, mollywog, and especially your hairy armpits!"

As they come to a finish Robyn signs all five to pull open their pussies. "Butterfly! All of you," she commands. "Pink-wet-and-ready!"

And they obey. Tiffany, Kimju and Molly advance pink immediately, and all touch their clits with a free finger to stimulate cream. Beka Broda never stops brimming.

Elle laggards but finally offers her intimate parts. *My first naked and spread, pink, but I'm not wet and ready....*

"Beg to Audition the Nugget!" Robyn snaps. And five Cosmos Pledge recite in unison, "Please let me Pledge naked and cum be a Stripper next Term."

No rush. The butterfly command occupies both hands and keeps all five pussies wide open while the bleach sets in and they quietly chant.

Once again the Shooter's hive of micro-hovercams record them with stills and video. Five of Five Naked Cosmos pull pink. And right now, Tiffany, Kimju, Molly, and Beka transude wetness; Elle's pink stays dry.

The totally nude pinking is a first for Beka and Elle. Beka relishes in the exhibitionism of her brodeas. "Come along with me," Beka whispers to Elle, "I need you. I need you to be pink-wet-and-ready too."

Elle catches Beka's scent, looks at her own pinking in the Beauty Salon mirror, and looks at the Cam hovering in front of her examining her between her legs. The explicitness of the exposure causes her to flush with humiliation: first a blush coloring her cheeks, then spreading downward into her chest. Her body twitches and a ring of bubbles rise around the circumference of her areolas.

Elle looks at her pink in the mirror and feels her pubes glow warm an blood flushes her in this spot and betrays her sexual excitement. Elle gasps as she watches her nacelle come out from under its hood. She tries to draw her head back but it already lies on the chair's headrest. *I am stuck in this place, this position, right now,* Elle accepts, *and I can't stop them from revealing me.*

Elle feels a sudden surge of nectar inside her vaginal canal. *I've gone slippery, next they are going to make me push it out, and reveal I am sexually aroused.*

Elle needn't wait. She watches in the mirror as white viscous nectar escapes out of her pulled-wide pink nookie and run down to her nadir gate. Thus Elle adds her scent to the Salon; she watches in the mirror to see when it hits Beka's nose.

Robyn offers more direction, "Masturbate for Nugget Shooter. The Patrons want to review you. So many beggars, so few slots at the Club!"

Robyn hurls this statement toward Elle, but all Five Pledge respond in unison, keeping the butterfly and balling the clit with a finger. Tiffany, Kimju, and Molly finger-fuck themselves, and once Beka sees what's going on, she follows.

"Masturbate!"

Elle rubs her clit with a finger and worries. *I am losing control of my body!* She examines her open nook and oozing nectar in the mirror, and realizes *I can even see my peehole pointing out.* Elle looks into her own eyes, rubs harder, and confesses, *I have lost control of my body.*

Beka releases a gush of broda and rubs herself in an attempt to climax; Elle sort-of maintains cream, and Tiffany, Kimju, and Molly freshen and take themselves toward the Zone. Madam Beautician quickly corrals them, "Pink-wet-and-ready! No cumming! If any of you cum, all of you will be punished! You can surf on the edge of the Zone, but never forget that your purpose in life is to let the bleach react."

After about an hour of self-discipline, Beautician allows the Five Naked Cosmos to rinse the bleach out, and reposition themselves back in the chairs with their legs spread and their ankles in the stirrups.

"Surprise," Beautician announces, "you're being colorized with vibrant hair dyes, first the hair on your heads, your eyebrows, and then the hair on your pussies." This time Robyn passes out thick colored gels; and each Cosmos' bleached-out hair absorbs the color each rubs in. The colors in the gels bond with the hair and will last for days.

Tiffany's long hair on her head, her soft pubic hair, and her eyebrows are dyed with a deep purple; Kimju is struck with a vibrant orange; Molly, including her underarm and body hair, a scarlet red; Beka a bright green; and Elle a vivid royal blue.

Robyn, never one to let another Cosmos get something she doesn't, also demands a styling. Madam Beautician honors her with a formula that does little to bleach out her natural blonde but which augments it with streaks of gold. (Of course only the hair on Robyn's head gets streaked.)

Once again the Five Naked Cosmos sit, spread, pink and cream, and chant while the dye sets in. They recite "Please let me Pledge naked and cum be a Stripper next Term" over and over again.

Madam Beautician repeats the dying process a second time, and then a third, so that the color in the hair on their heads and pudenda sets deeply and permanently. It will not wash out.

Madam Beautician encourages the always-ornery Robyn to use the waiting time to add a final touch and paint all the Cosmos finger and toe nails to match their dyed hair. Robyn easily paints the five Cosmos' toenails. But she must more carefully paint their fingernails, which continue to hold five now-colorful pussies wide open.

Elle experiences the most torment. *What if someone finds my Manifest, still hidden in Beka's jeans pocket? In a basket somewhere, mixed with everyone else's Garments. What if I don't get my clothes back at all?*

Robyn snarls as Elle looks at herself in the mirror. "Love your bright blue pussy hair and blue fingernails yanking open your rosy red nautch." Robyn cackles. "You nazy nigmenog nincompoop!"

Robyn indulges herself to add a golden yellow polish to her own nails; Babs bright red nails are already immaculate.

A final fixing and rinse completes the hair coloring process.

And what a sight the Cosmos are: Babs at the height of her glamour, with sleek black hair and vibrant red finger and toenails, proud Robyn with dashing golden yellow hair freshly matching nails, and then the Five Naked Cosmos, all sitting spread in their chairs:

Tiffany, with a head full of purple hair, a thinner purple bush, and purple fingernails, holds open a wet, burgundy-colored twister.

Kimju, orange as a carrot on her head, and with a trimmed, inverse triangle orange bush around her natural deeply pigmented inner lips and rosy pink vagina, fingers her clithood ring with orange fingernails.

Molly, now with crimson red hair, red fingernails, and a huge flaming red muff around her brown insides, accumulates a powdery white dry crust around her clithood ring.

Beka sports a green crop of hair, bright green nails, and a vibrant green bush surrounding her glistening inner lips and darker brown interior.

In the last chair, Elle, her thoughts spinning wildly, hair bright blue, finger and toenails sky blue, and a full bright blue bush surrounding a very deep violet vaginal canal, shamefully lubricates her delightfully creamy flushed interior. Has Elle ever posed pink-wet-and-ready before? Well, certainly not since she signed up for the Cosmos House!

Madam Beautician takes pride in her work and encourages the five naked and spread Cosmos to finger their clits and heighten their arousal. She allows them to raise their fever but also demands they synchronize their breathing and moans until they lose their individual identities and become a single melded mind of horny arousal.

But no cumming!

Babs feels proud too, and learns as she observes Madam's skill at not just the beauty of the five brightly colored Pledge, but at the beauty of their psychological synchronization.

Babs also marvels at how Madam brings them down slowly, never lets them cum, but slows their breathing, keeps their moans in synch, keeps them as one, until she snaps them out of it, almost like a hypnotist bringing her subject back to the real world, only doing it with all five together, silencing them together, quieting all rubbing of clits, and melding them into a row of colorful naked Cosmos, softly shaking their hands that hold their hatches wide open. Then all hands at their sides and standing on their feet again.

Tiffany remembers, *I am a Porn Star! I need to suck and fuck on Cam!*

Kimju and Molly anticipate that their brightly-dyed pubic hair will soon surround the Double Dong, now making its rounds through the Cosmos House. Kimju assumes, *Just because the Double Dong currently pleasures Steph, it doesn't mean the other end will be idle very long,*

Beka's thoughts jumble in confusion. Elle senses something has changed but can't quite put a finger on it.

But Robyn can. Covered up, proud of her bright golden hair, Robyn never passes up the chance to offer a suggestion. She pokes Elle in her belly. "Looks like the last newbie has finally learned how to make herself slippery!" Robyn laughs at her own observation. "Maybe Steph wants to make you her Option! You can return to the Doghouse and maybe if you eat her snatch good she'll cum you good on the Double Dong!" Robyn snorts. "Ha ha ha ha."

Harsh predictions, and Elle feels not just embarrassment, but fear. She casts her eyes toward the basket where all of the Garments lie in a jumble, and estimates what might be involved if she were to dash across the room to rescue her own. Or rescue her secret and forbidden notes from Beka's jeans shorts.

Elle eyes the Cam between her and the mirror. She adjusts her hands so she holds pink with one hand while she uses the other to gather up her noble secretions that have run down past her nadir way. She brings the hand to her mouth, cleans it with her tongue, sucks on her fingers, and leaves her nakodo all around her mouth and under her nose. Elle watches the Cam follow her every move, and she watches it follow her hand down to brush on erected nipples, and come to a rest at her nautch, so she can double-hand the butterfly.

But what about Steph, the only Cosmos not here? Fact: Steph doesn't need to be here. Steph doesn't have any hair to dye, and given that she is head-to-toe muddy and confined to the Doghouse it serves no purpose to make Steph beautiful. Were Robyn to see Steph at this very moment she might watch the bare bald and naked Cosmos struggle about whether she will ever have a chance to exercise her Option.

One thing Steph does not struggle about is the location of the Double Dong: one half has secured itself inside her vagina. Sometimes it vibrates up by her clit, sometimes it twists to find her g-spot, and sometimes it provides electrified excitement. Steph possesses no way to remove it. Steph drifts between the Zone of intense arousal and simply being in heat. The Dong consulting with the wirelessly connected Running Agent deep inside Automatron, keep Steph on a tight reign, yet occasionally, somehow, *I manage to find some mental space to plan how I might exercise my Option.*

If Robyn understood this she might not be laughing.

§ Madam Nurse Beautician: Realigns Kimju & Beka's Costumes

As the Cosmos prepare to leave, Madam Beautician recovers the basket of Garments the Cosmos shed upon their arrival, earlier tonight here at the Beauty Salon. Beautician holds the Garments in a bunch in front of five naked Cosmos Pledge.

Tiffany, obviously, is offered no Garments: the former Whore will present her purple hair on her head and her taco naked to the world.

Kimju finds herself handed Beka's shorts; Beka appears distracted, so Kimju puts on what Beautician has put into her hand. The shorts don't completely hide her orange pussy hair, but they do obscure much of it.

Molly, never one to bend the rules, points out her panties so Madam may sort them out; Molly puts them on without rolling them into mooe or moonshadow; her red hair spills over the top of the nombril panties and is brightly visible through the see-through material.

Beka watches as Beautician returns Elle her croptop and slacks. Elle slides into the croptop before tugging the slacks up; but yes, even with tight cameltoe and parting the nake-nake, Elle definitely presents a flush of blue hair and some naughty gorge above the low waistline.

Finally Beautician offers Beka the two pieces left, her own triangle halter and the micro g-string last worn by Kimju.

"Wait a minute," Beka complains as she holds the halter and g-string in hand, "This is not mine."

Madam Beautician gives her a quizzical look, "Put them on my dear, before they become abandoned property." Beka stammers, still naked and holding the halter in her hand, and positions the micro g-string in front of her. Her green hair surrounds it on all sides. Robyn laughs. Some hive Cam plays back to the Nugget.

"This isn't funny," Beka protests. "This makes me look vulgar." She grasps for straws, "It's one thing when you are natural, but it's quite another with this stupid green hair."

Oooh! Babs forms her lips but doesn't utter a sound. *Beka should not insult Madam Nurse Beautician's art!* BB raises her eyes, but Madam Beautician handles Beka with grace as she addresses the Cosmos. "Why don't the rest of you run along and while I fix up Beka right now," she announces magnanimously. She turns to Beka, "I'll makes them cum in their pants at their first look of you!"

Babs takes the cue, "We really want to thank you for all the beautiful colors!" BB makes a sign and the Cosmos chorus, "Madam, thank you, Madam Nurse Beautian." All the Cosmos except Beka depart.

§ Madam Nurse Beautician Awards Beka: A Mohawk & Hitler

Beka finds herself back in the beauty chair, still naked and spread, again with feet in stirrups and her bolus popped up. Beautician makes quick work about it, first with lather and a razor and then with shears.

But Beka's reduction is not quite total: Beautician reduces the flaming green hair on Beka's head to a Mohawk running down the center of her scalp, and depilates all the green hair on her pussy except for a little horizontal green mustache above her slit that will soon float *above* the micro g-string. "We call that a 'Hitler,'" Beautician advises.

Madam affords herself an extra moment with a sewing machine to narrow what began as Elle's halter down to two tiny triangles that barely cover Beka's nipples. No liner in these cups.

Beka dresses and examines her near-naked body in Beautician's mirror. Beka touches her booty. *It's there!* She touches to the side of the g-string. *Well, I have no pubic hair to leak any more. The Hitler rides completely above my g-string and the Mohawk make me look wild.*

The micro g-string consists of little more than a tiny inverted triangle, which barely covers her now-smooth, slit and wants to fiddle itself into her breech. The halter cups are particularly slippery and one immediately slides off a breast.

The hive of Cams that never went away feeds Beka's recovery back to Nugget Patrons. Beka squirms and the other boob pops out. "I'm not so sure I can stay covered wearing this halter," she grouses to Madam Beautician. "It's really slippery."

Beautician opines. "Maybe Gamers are tired of you keeping you neck strap untied so you can hang boobage. Your new challenge will be to keep what remains of the halter covering your areola and nipples. Now thank me for making you an more playful Stripper wannabe!"

So Beka thanks Beautician, "Thank you, Madam Nurse Beautician, for making my halter smaller, and trading Kimju for the micro g-string." Then asks a question. "Why don't you just let me go topless? I only need one piece to get to the Nugget. I'm already begging to Pledge naked, stay pink-wet-and-ready, and cum be a Stripper next Term!"

"Patience, Pledge," Beautician cheers, "You may beg to let Gamers see you totally topless at the Mermaid Parade tomorrow."

Beka considers this. "I'll wear this micro g-string and nothing else, totally topless in public. And I don't want my top back afterwards," she insists. "Just one piece for me, please. I want to be a Stripper next Term. Really. Me and Elle both."

"No problem." Beautician sighs and nods of her head. Beka feels a rush of excitement, freshens, and transudes brodeas onto her g-string.

"No secrets for you, Beka Broda!" Beautician says merrily. "Now lean over, run your finger down the string between you booty, pull your cheeks to the side, and give the Cam a good view of your bogey. The Crowd at the Nugget wants to examine you: mind, body, and soul. They'll decide if you deserve to Strip at the Nugget next Term."

"Madam Beautician thank you for being so kind!" Beka stumbles the words out of her mouth, "Madam."

Beka's solo journey back to the Cosmos House is uneventful. Just before she rings the Bell near the Back Landing, Beka puts her ear to the Doghouse. Yes, naked Steph still lies inside, reeking, caked with dirt, slippery with mud, still impaled on the Dong, and still off in the Zone."

The Back Door grants Beka access. Once into the Kitchen, she pauses to study the Screen in the Kitchen as it cycles the Pink Pages of Five Colorful Cosmos Pledge. *I'm hot the hottest of the colors,* Beka says to herself. As she heads up the spiral staircase, she reaches below her green Hitler, slides fingers inside her g-string, and touches herself.

§ Steph: Struggles with Dong & Considers Who to Option

While the Cosmos are made colorful at the Beauty Salon, Steph tries to regain some of her senses. Steph's problem isn't her bare bald and naked body, the mud and dirt that covers her body and the interior of the Doghouse, or the stink of pee. After a while Steph can't even smell herself any more.

Yes, it is soloing the Double Dong that provides Steph with the double-edged sword of pleasure and predation. Yes, Steph keeps the Dong firmly planted inside her; more correctly, the Dong possesses Steph. It arouses her, ensures her sex cavity stays sodden, and, might she struggle to resist it, the Double Dong, at least the half of it that's embedded inside her, doesn't willing disengage. Pulling on the stuck-out half makes it swell inside, vibrate and electrify. When Steph relaxes and squeezes on it, the Dong finds her vibe, ensures that she yield to her sexuality, and returns her to the Zone.

Except occasionally for Steph the Dong becomes only a nuisance, an irritation; the instrument imperfectly dominates her, and Steph is able to consider her predicament. *And plan what to do next.*

I know that the entire House departed en masse today, but I have no idea of where or why. The Dong strikes a vibe that tickles Steph's clit and she touches herself. She gasps, and looks out a crack in the door toward the Backyard. *One thing I am sure of is that I don't dare break out. I haves no place to run to. And it's not like I'd be streaking, I'd be a runaway, and if I get caught, I'd be Slavesex.*

Steph struggles as the Dong advances and her thoughts run wild, *I don't know why I got shaved bare bald and naked while I climaxed the Dong, center Stage at the Nugget. I don't know who dispatched the newbies to coat me in mud, or why I am living in a box with one end of the Double Dong sunk in my snizz.*

The Dong aggresses. When Steph comes to again she discovers she is rubbing smelly mud on both nipples. Steph's self-arousal seems to have causes the Dong to back off and Steph finds herself able to think again. *Something happened to me at the Nugget. Penny and Coco think I'm responsible for them becoming Strippers this Term. Somehow they want the Dong, except I have it. They gave it to me.*

Steph runs her fingers across her bald head and bare pubis and starts to vibrate again. *Except no, that's not what happened. Tiffany took the Dong and I took the Option.*

The Option!

Steph puffs air out of an ovaled mouth as her body quivers with a new sense of excitement. *So who do I Option?*

Steph starts at the top. *Babs? No. Babs is not an ally; She's a Cosmos but not one of us Pledge.*

Tiffany? Before last night Tiffany was Babs' confidant. Today Tiffany is a naked Cosmos, a cummy Pee-Camer Piss Mouth who owns nothing, wears nothing. Tiffany stays as naked as I do, although she is not bare or bald—although she begs to be.

Steph conjectures, "Tiffany screwed me with the Double Dong at the Nugget, brought it back to the Cosmos House, passed it to Molly, and now I'm being screwed with it again."

But still, Steph senses something different about competing against a self-proclaimed Porn Star and Whore. *Excuse me, a former Whore. How do I know if Tiffany really plays fair? Did she pass out any hand jobs, blowjobs, or fucks during her final moments at the Nugget last night? I had to listen to the Back Door Man tell me what a great cocksucker she is, how when she Feature Danced she blew all the help, fucked the clientele, and licked House Mom's feet clean with her tongue.*

Steph's thoughts drift to an interracial image in Tiffany's Porn Star Calendar in which Tiffany gets fucked with an eight-inch schlong rammed up her tailpipe. *I too would like to suck and fuck cock,* Steph confesses to herself, *more so every day. But I don't want to take it up the ass like Tiffany did. Or clean up afterwards.*

The Dong reminds Steph of her adventures with Tiffany last night and she rolls onto her belly, reaches around behind herself, runs a finger down her stern split and fingers her stern star. Steph gasps and pops out of the Zone, and finds her thoughts again, *while I have the chance.*

Tiffany screwed me so hard last night I was not even been able to pack away memories. Suck cock or not, Double Dong or not, no matter what, in a Duel with Tiffany, I'll lose. If I Option someone else I can win. Once I'm a Monitor, then cock will be mine for the taking.

But the crux of the decision comes easy. *Naked Tiffany has no Garments to donate to my cause!*

The Dong, sensing a lack of attention, vibrates back to action. Steph arches her semiglobes upward, grinds both boobs into the mud floor, sucks in her breath, and mouths words out loud. "Fuck me!" She fingers her stern tunnel up to the knuckle, wiggles her full finger inside, and relinquishes herself to the Zone. The Dong shall maintains Steph in a soft gentle climax for an indeterminate time, until she has utility again.

It is later in the afternoon when Steph drifts back to her harsh reality. *I am in control!* Steph assures herself. *I have the Option! I am simply relinquishing to pleasure.*

Steph considers her next prospect: Kimju.

This one is easy to dismiss, Steph concludes quickly. *Yes, Kimju is another Pee-Camer, yes Babs is increasingly bringing Kimju to climax, yes I know that Kimju has moxie and every intent to promote to a Monitor next Term. She could be a very tough competitor, no matter what the Game. But the bottom line is that Kimju parades topless; and her single garment will not provide me with the requisite two Garments to lock in a promotion.*

Steph does not know that Kimju has swapped her kunny kover for Beka's ripped shorts, but what Steph doesn't know wouldn't change her conclusion.

Steph can feel the Dildo beckon her but she resists it to consider the other former Stripper at the Cosmos House: Molly.

Molly and I traded panties back and forth before I got badly stung by her in the Winner-Takes-All. The Gamers deceived me and I got rendered naked and put on the trajectory that has brought me to this current miserable position, naked and filthy and a prisoner of sex. I don't even have my eyebrows. But like Kimju, Molly's only got panties and I need two Garments.

Once again the Dong senses Steph's rhythms and arouses her again, and she yields to it, her body juicing now, legs wide, now on her back lifting her pelvis up and pushing her hard clit up. Steph squeezes the Dong as it talks to her with motion and electricity and she imagines a kind of robot fucking her and she goes into bliss again, this time into a faster heartbeat, deeper breathing, and sustained shallow cumming.

She doesn't really remember coming out of the Zone; it is not unlike coming back from an anesthesia, and simply being back, not quite the same thing as waking up. Steph remains aware of the snake coiled inside her, fully conscious that it's alive, but wonders if it might be sensitive to the fact she has been comatose. She realizes, *I may have only moments to think before it possesses me again.*

Steph imagines the snake wraps around her body and squeezes into her pelvis from the front side; she sharply inhales and discovers it is she who is pressing herself with her hands. She reacts sharply, takes bearings, and touches her pubes and the top of her head—*just to be sure they are indeed bare and bald. Verified. And I'm naked, dusty, and dirty with mud.*

Robyn. *I want nothing more than to crush Robyn, but Robyn appears by all induction to be off limits; she now wears three pieces and behaves like the anointed one. Babs never stops her. Does Robyn have an angel somewhere? Kimju thinks she possesses Charm. I don't, but what if Kimju is right?*

Steph feels the Dong compete for her attention again and she processes quickly. *Beka and Elle. When all is said and done my choices come down to the newbies. Both have two pieces. Teasers, but I needn't be picky, and once I win, the Opt Up is guaranteed. Either will do.*

The Double Dong wags in Steph's socket; Steph imagines that Beka or Elle ride the other end and she starts floating again, finds a steady heartbeat, touches her nipples and clit in a constant rhythm, rotates her pelvis, and squeezes. *But will the Dong lets me free long enough to exercise the Option?* She wonders, but she can't stop, doesn't want to stop, and won't be stopping anytime soon. The idea of screwing with one of the newbies excites Steph, and this time it is Steph who leads the Dong into the Zone.

II-33 Steph: Dongs & Options & the Mermaid Parade (D25)

§ Robyn Extracts Steph: Shows Five Cosmos Backyard Lineup

A new morning arrives and Day 25 begins. If *The Runup* lasts through Day 27 and *The Beach Day* happens Day 28, then the Cosmos are nearing the end. They sense it, well, sort of.

Robyn, who slept again in Babs' Bedroom, herds the Five Pledge from the Bunkroom out the Back Door. Robyn still wears her maillot with its spaghetti shoulder straps underneath the clear vinyl croptop and miniskirt, and her belly button still gazes out of "the smallest buttonhole." But unlike Tiffany, Kimju and Molly, and Beka and Elle, who proceed her, Robyn ignores ringing the Bell.

"Lineup," she orders once they are all in the Backyard. "Side-by-side. Stand spread surrender."

The Five Cosmos Pledge complete forming their Lineup just as Monitor Babs exits the Back Door to survey them from the Landing. One naked Pledge, two topless buttage Pledge, and two titter newbie Pledge. Babs, like Robyn, continues to wear three Garments, but since she continues to stand on the Landing and not step into the Backyard, she does not ring the Bell.

It is not a secret that the Cosmos shall participate in the Mermaid Parade, an annual beach-side event with much gaiety, home-made costumes, and limited public nudity. Each has already been awarded an individual hair color. Except for one Cosmos: Steph. Steph remains donged in the Doghouse this morning and Steph doesn't have any hair.

The bare bald and naked Steph Sorostitute will not participate in the Mermaid Parade today, and nor will another Cosmos Pledge, the naked Tiffany Transparent. Mermaids can be topless, of course, but nudity is a sufficently rare exception that no naked Cosmos shall participate today.

Boss Babe signs Robyn to roust Steph from the Doghouse, and Robyn gleefully follows instructions. She bangs on the small door, unlatches it, and demands Steph crawl out on her hands and knees.

Steph obeys. Her head spins, her eyes reel from the daylight. She is bare bald and naked, dusty in some places, muddy in others, and filthy all over. Overnight more than just Beka peed on the Back Landing; today stale urine mixes with the more fresh. Gamers might say Steph looks bedraggled, but that image usually connotes someone with hair.

The Double Dong holds itself in Steph's satchel and tingles to encourage her to inch forward. *I belong to the Dong,* Steph accepts. She keeps her knees and feet spread wide and crawls forward until she comes to a stop in front of Robyn, who stands in front of the Five Cosmos Lineup.

Steph steals a glance toward Boss Babe and finds bemusement looking back. Steph's still pretty jazzed, but she out of the danger Zone at this moment. She licks her lips and updates. *Boss Bitch has the audacity to upgraded my undershirt to a full minidress and then wear it herself! Over either her Black Bikini or her bikini swapped for lingerie underwear.*

Steph struggles against the will of the Dong and casts thoughts wildly. *I am not fooled by any Molly diddle-daddle about Garment Exchanges with Boss Bitch. Fuck BB. Fuck her for making me lick piss off her feet in the Bathroom, getting pissed on and pissing all over the place. For making a streak outta me. Pinking me. Forcing me wet. Taking my cum and demanding that Tiffany dong and shave me.*

Steph wrinkles her nose and steals another glance toward the Landing. *May a gorilla spread you on your back and fuck you, you Babbeljaz Baudetrot!*

Robyn used the top of one foot to guide Steph's eyes back down to the ground. The foot presses Steph's head to a horizontal position. Robyn lectures the newbies, "When someone tells you to assume Gorean Table Position, this is the position you form: Hand and knees, head level and forward, eyes looking down."

Steph shifts her thoughts to Robyn. *Something is not right about my former Pledge dominating me.*

Robyn lifts one side of her lips and brushes her nostril. "Your face got my foot dirty."

Steph keeps her cool. "Ma'am, Beka and Elle wallowed me in the Mudpit before they put me in the Doghouse."

An understatement.

Robyn lifts Steph's chin with a big toe and presents her insole to Steph's mouth.

"If I say your face got my foot dirty," Robyn advances, "You say, 'Ma'am may I lick your foot clean, Ma'am.' Now clean it up, you wannabe sperm-mouth!"

Steph grimaces, makes an attempt, but her dirty face only makes Robyn's foot dirtier.

"Stop!" Robyn commands, then leans over, lifts Steph's head, and spits down across her bald head and missing eyebrows. Steph recoils and Robyn charms, "Thank me for giving you a bath, you piss stinking scum slut."

"Ma'am, thank you, 'Ma'am,'" Steph gurgles. A surge of vengeance runs up through her body. *You're the one who betrayed me!* Steph remembers, *and you pretend to not remember.*

The Dong intervenes; somewhere among its temperature, vibration, electrical circuits it arouses Steph sufficently to seize upon a foot-worship opportunity and kiss Robyn's foot.

Robyn turns ever so slightly, lifts her other bare foot, and presents Steph with the bottom of this sole. "I think I tracked through some pee today," she says.

The Dong adjusts its stimulation between Steph's legs to enable Steph to stay with her foot-worshiping opportunity. Steph blinks, sobers up, and licks the sole of Robyn's dirty foot more carefully. During a moment of reflection, she senses Robyn is not paying attention and the Cam is focused elsewhere. She sneaks a look at the Back Landing. Monitor Babs is not there anymore. *So where are you when I need you, Bimbo Bitch?*

Paparazzi don't miss that Steph's eyes go astray.

Steph twitches, becomes aware that Robyn's spit runs down her cheek. She artfully stems its flow with Robyn's toes, and licks the spit from in between them. The Dong relaxes it's stimulation and suddenly Steph's mind grasps. *I hold the Option right now!*

Steph scans the Lineup. *I'm going to Option one of you: Naked Tiffany, topless Kimju or Molly, or newbie Beka or Elle. I decide!*

Even Pledge Robyn is fair game. Steph considers the Redacted Pledge. *She for whom the past doesn't exist. You act like you're equal to Boss Bitch,* Steph processes, *and not just BB's haughty aide-de-camp.* Steph snorts. *I am your worse nightmare, even if you might be exempt from Dueling with me!*

Robyn aggresses Steph. "You still able to pee with that Dong stuck inside your summersault?"

Steph calculates. "Ma'am, absolutely, in the Doghouse, Ma'am."

"Show me," Robyn demands.

And Steph processes and gathers up a few seconds of stream, followed by three drips. Steph twitches her nose. *Robyn doesn't like me upstaging her!*

So you got that, Steph concedes, but continues to consider Robyn. *Last Term you betrayed me. I got broken yet you, Robyn Redacted, remained a Pledge, something that is supposed to be against Game Rules.*

Steph frowns. *So did you arrange for Molly to win the Greatest House Roar, so she could turn my minidress over to Boss Bitch? And what did you promise MomCap to take Tiffany's transparent croptop and miniskirt, so that Tiffany could force-cum me naked on the Double Dong. Did you arrange for Penny and Coco to have the Shaving Kit, so I could get made bare bald and naked?*

Robyn moves a foot from licking position, places it upon Steph's head and pushes downward. Steph allows the palms of her hands to slide forward until her face lies in the dirt next to them. She positions her knees wide, so that she more easily balances on the triad of support. *I have my snooch and sternway lifted upward, so that everyone can see the Dong in me.*

"Gorean Submission Position," Robyn points and informs the newbies as she steps in front of them; Robyn toys with Beka's micro halter so that one nipple may escape, and lifts Elle's croptop and offers it to Elle's teeth. The Cam and paparazzi collect boobage.

Steph unobtrusively rubs her face on the ground; the ground is dirty *but I am more dirty still.* The Dong stimulates, and Steph seeps. *The Cam had better hover back and collects me.* It does, and so do paparazzi. *I'm too important to be just another Pledge, because Gamers want me.*

And because the Fat Lady brought me the Option!

I'm not tongue tied. I just need to know when to call out the Pledge and call out the Game

Steph suddenly feels a hand on the end of the Double Dong that is waging out of her snatch. Steph recoils but recovers, and feels the Dong relax its expansive grip and slide out.

A voice accompanies the hand; Robyn says, "Time for something different," and Steph feels the Dong touch her stern star. Again she tries to jump, except that her face and hands are already braced in the dirt, and her knees are already spread wide apart.

Steph braces, the Dong pops through the sphincter; it's in and slowly and steadily and relentlessly penetrates until it reaches the middle. Steph gasps, and squeezes sauce out her now-empty socket.

Robyn points to a bead of sex secretions that now swings between Steph's thighs. "Now you can sluice your satchel slop out your sallyport without the Dong in the way," Robyn laughs. "Ha ha ha ha!"

Right, Steph admits, and feels the Dong settle itself it. *No getting it out by myself,* Steph realizes, *no way at all. And no way to get off the Back Door Cam. I'm famous.*

The Dong measures Steph's sensitivity to its presence and settles in. Steph realizes, *The Dong will put me flat on my face and screaming if I need that.*

Robyn casts an upheld hand across the Five Cosmos' view of Steph's Gorean Submission. "Observe your future, Pledge. Now beg for me. Over and over again."

Six Cosmos beg. Five Pledge stand spread surrender, one Pledge presents the Dong upward while chanting in Gorean Submissive Position. "Please let me Pledge naked and cum be a Stripper next Term."

And Robyn heads toward the Landing and through the Back Door.

§ Steph Considers Five Cosmos: Morning of Mermaid Parade

Four half-naked and one naked Cosmos continue to stand spread surrender in the Backyard. Steph presents in front of them, face and knees on the ground, stern held high, with the Dong wagging out of her small bore.

Steph accepts that the Dong occupies her rectum, *and rotating my upheld stern section seems to keep it happy.*

A bead of sexual secretions now swings downward between Steph's spread thighs. Might Steph swing her spheroids too far and stick the bead to her inner thigh, no problem, the Dong will make sure surge keeps flowing.

Steph tries to stabelize herself. *I've been naked for five straight days— ever since the Greatest House Roar—and now I am bare bald and naked. I'm filthy and stink of urine, I'm stiff from cramped quarters, I lack sleep.*

Steph tries to think again but the Dong demands more secretions. Steph submits to its arousal and casts her thoughts aside for a moment, presses her face harder into the dirt as she grinds. The Lineup, the newbies especially, contemplate Steph's taking of pleasure and inviting vaginal penetration.

"Fuck me," Steph utters under her breath. The Dong relaxes its grip and Steph rotates her ass and transudes a stalactite of swag. She can think again:

Getting stripped bare bald and naked, muddied, and force Donged in the Doghouse has been a testing experience, and coming back into this reality requires effort and adjustment.

But I can't forget that I hold the Option.

Steph casts wider thoughts. *If my sex secretions string all the way down to the ground will Elle be required to lolly them up?* Steph tries to focus her thinking. *In some respects the Game is more difficult now, I am able to think yes, but I'm still a prisoner to the Dong, whereas in the Doghouse, the Dong Zoned me and I was totally helpless. It even forced me use my own fingertips to hold onto the climax.*

Steph uses these moments to sharpen theories about what might have happened while she was sequestered and it's relevance going forward. *How did Robyn acquire golden yellow dyed hair and get exquisitely permed? And is her roughage dyed yellow as well?* Steph smiles and savors this idea, true or not. She wants to raise her head and scan the colored Lineup, but controls herself.

The Five Cosmos, who stand side-by-side in a row, feet spread wide and fingers interlocked behind their heads, watch Steph maintain her stern rotation. Might Steph babble, the Dong will provide correction.

Steph keeps her face on the ground and her stern risen; she forms a mental picture of the Lineup: *I can remember in my mind: Armpits, bare bellies and buttons, bare arms and legs, bare faces. One naked, two topless, two newbies still with two pieces.*

And what stands out? *Colors: purple, orange, red, green, blue. New hair dyes, and for Beka, a haircut! Boss Bitch keeps her black hair.*

Steph feels fresh air on her skin. *I am bare bald and naked, ergo colorless.* She rolls her face in the dirt so she rests on her other cheek. Once again she analyzes the Lineup for Option possibilities:

Tiffany is still naked but now with purple dyed hair—long on the head and thin on her mons. Steph incorrectly assumes Tiffany spent last night under Babs' bunk, but she correctly assumes, *no Garments to Duel for.*

Orange-haired Kimju remains topless and wears what I last saw as Beka's ripped jean shorts with its belly button notch. This is a change-around, Steph updates herself. *Her shorts have become so badly frayed that most of Kimju's kaboose hangs out astern, and most of her brightly dyed orange kerf leaks out in front.*

Correct, Kimju's inguinal had been completely visible in her g-string, and ironically it remains visible in the frayed shorts. *So Kimju has also been dyed on her pussy as well as her head.* Steph images Kimju in more detail. *Eyebrows too.*

Steph blinks. *Maybe the shorts represent a switch in the right direction for Kimju,* Steph accepts, *but I need to acquire two Garments!*

Steph refreshes her image of Molly. *Dyed eyebrows as well, bright red, with bright red hair on her head and bright red hairage that shows right through her see-through panties, and sprouts above her waistline.* A feature snaps into Steph's brain. *Big tuffs of underarm hair also dyed bright red, and ably presented in the standing surrender position.*

I know something happened but I don't know what it was, Steph deduces, *because I can see the difference: Beka looks to be wearing Kimju's micro g-string, and it looks like her triangle top has been reduced to a matching micro minimum.*

Steph's tries to frame the glance she got of Beka's hair a few moments ago. For a moment she ceases to rotate her semiglobes but the corrective stimulus by the Dong is gentle and guiding, and provides adequate thought space for Pledge Steph. No problem, Steph's visual memory is photographic: *Beka is almost as bare and bald as I am—she's got a shaven head except for a bright green stiff Mohawk down the middle, and the very neat and tidy bright green Hitler an inch above what used to be Kimju's micro g-string! No other hair on that pudenda!*

Steph evaluates. *Two pieces, but not quite what I'm questing for.*

Finally there is Elle, standing at the end of the Lineup. *Elle retains her croptop and low-ride slacks, with her bright blue hairage radiating upward above her waistline.*

All five Cosmos got all of their hair and eyebrows dyed, and that didn't come from Babs' hand. Something happened while I was in the Zone, but it doesn't matter, I now know who to Option.

§ Steph Passes the Dong to Tiffany's Tailpipe: Travel Time

Boss Babe and Robyn return to the Backyard. One of them rings the Bell on the way and one does not. BB twinkles her eyes toward her recent Roommate, Tiffany. "Get on your hands and knees, and back the free end of that Double Dong up your tailpipe," she commands.

Naked Tiffany scrambles onto her knees, and her face contorts as she presses herself backward against Steph's stern; she feels the Dong penetrate, attempts instinctively to squeeze it, but then accepts its intrusion, until it comes to a stop, as she and Steph press butt-to-butt. Tiffany anticipates what happens next: the swelling bulb just inside her anal sphincter. *No pushing it out, a*nd a very full feeling that suggests *little room for negotiation.*

The Dong disengages from Steph, Steph crawls forward, and Tiffany discovers she now solos the Dong in her tailpipe.

Robyn attacks Steph. "No one told you to lift your head up! You want your head up so much? Okay, so turn around, crawl, and get the loose end of the Dong in your mouth. Now! Suck it clean you filthy stinking sleaze skank!"

Steph obeys. *This is vulgar and disgusting. Has Robyn Redacted forgotten I hold the Option? Or does she just think she can make her own Rules?*

Steph licks around the Dong, resigns her mouth to it, and sucks. Sucks down until it touches her throat. Tiffany crawls forward so that that the Dong slides out of Steph's mouth, before it can embed there and tease Steph's throat. It leaves behind her own residue. Steph seethes, ungrateful that Tiffany has helped her out of a jam.

Tiffany rises onto her feet. She touches the wagging end of the Double Dong with one hand but realizes, *I don't need to hold this because the Dong is totally able to keep itself inserted.*

Correct.

Babs nods approval to Tiffany, "Nice to see you possess the Dong again. Now take your purple hair and scamper over to the Corvette House. Keep that," Babs gestures to the Double Dong, "up your tailpipe. When you get there, do whatever Monitor Janet tells you to do." Babs smiles. "Go. Now."

Tiffany hesitates. *I don't have any problem kowtowing to Janet; we were Stripper Roommates two Terms ago. She Opted Pledge, I Opted Porn Star and that was a Win-Win for both of us. Now she's a Monitor and I'm a Pledge. So she can act upon me now.*

Tiffany reflects, *One never knows how one will Opt in this Game. Or who ones' friends are.*

But Tiffany's fear is not Janet, it is something else. She addresses Babs carefully. "Ma'am," Tiffany frames. "May I remind you that even though I carry the Dong in me, that the Dong doesn't count as a Garment. I'd still be streaking, Ma'am. And if I get caught I won't just get chained to the flagpole and get gangbanged overnight. Then Gamers keep me Lockdown until the end of the Term. And because I was already once a Porn Star, Gamers will demand, that I become Slavesex. You'd lose me forever, Ma'am."

Monitor Babs understands the potential legitimacy of this argument. She considers the Lineup of five nude and semi-nude Cosmos. She casts her gaze at Beka, with her green Mohawk and Hitler standing spread surrender. Both triangles of Beka's micro halter have slid off her nipples, and the inverted triangle micro g-string has wormed itself into her breech, verifying her shaven lips.

Babs contemplates Beka's escaped boobies, shallow cones with nipples atop that indent when excited, like right now. Beka could tuck her buds back into her halter, certainly, but first she must regain the use of her hands, which she currently clasps behind her head.

"Looks like you don't need your halter very much," Boss Babe says. She points. "Off."

Beka pulls the knots and doffs her halter top. She hands it to Monitor Babs and returns her hands to surrender position.

BB hands the halter to Tiffany. "Here, you can borrow this, so you won't have to streaking anymore. Now go. Move it."

Robyn adds a kicker, "And keep your tail wagging!"

"Ma'am, thank you, Ma'am," Tiffany retorts and scoots, haltered and bottomless. She feels her Eraser Heads sensitize, and then synchronize with the Dong.

I am your full-frontal, Pee-Camming, Piss Mouth, Double Dong Cosmos Pledge begging to cum be a Stripper next Term.

§ Steph Selects Elle: A Dueling Companion

With Tiffany gone, Four Cosmos Pledge hold the stand spread surrender Lineup: Kimju, Molly, Beka, Elle. Robyn detects an opening while Babs considers what to do next, and pushes Steph, still on her hands and knees, with her foot. "Roll over," she commands as she digs toenails, so the bare bald and naked Pledge rolls onto her back.

"Point your snatch toward the Lineup," Robyn orders, "and pull your pink wide."

Steph obeys and arches her pelvis up. *I am indeed bare bald and naked. I'm messy with dirt, mud, and pee. And I'm still sloppy down there. But I don't care; I can't care! The Dong doesn't have a hold on me anymore. Tiffany's taking it to the Corvette House.*

The time has come for me to pick a Game and a Pledge to Duel with. I shall Opt Monitor next Term, and they shall Opt Strip.

Robyn points to Steph, now on her back, knees up and feet wide, hands pulling inner lips from opposite sites and with her stamen popped out. Robyn crows to the Lineup, "This sex glutton earned herself the Shaving Kit at the Nugget." She turns to Steph, "You forgot it and left it behind. Do you know where it is now?"

Steph has not a clue. "Ma'am, no, Ma'am!" she responds.

Robyn leans over and queries, "And do you wish to share it with the Lineup?

Steph casts an eye down the Lineup: Kimju, Molly, Beka, Elle. *I'm not sure.* But puts sense into a response. "Ma'am, yes, Ma'am. Please let me stay bare bald and naked. I'll shave all the Cosmos so we can all pink bare pussies together, Ma'am."

Some Pledge in the Lineup purse lips.

Robyn snarls. "You're not just gonna pink that shaven snatch of yours," Robyn twitches. "You're gonna eat pussy and juice the Dong with every single Cosmos Pledge," Robyn leans forward and again spits onto Steph's face. "You're a sizzle splurt smug. That's what you are. After you Strip for a while you'll be begging to Whore in no time. You got the itch in you."

Steph blinks but keeps holding her sex machine open with both hands. Steph finds the spit invasive but calms herself. *It is the action of the aggression, and not the danger of spit, which violates me. Fear not. There is more spit in a French kiss, more slop eating pussy, more disgust getting pissed on.* Steph eyes her nemesis and balls her clit with her thumbs. *Robyn, I shall destroy you! You deserve Slavesex!*

Enough. Steph holds pink, turns, and speaks directly to Monitor Babs: "Ma'am, I acquired an envelope! At the Nugget! Last night!"

The Lineup rustles and four pairs of displayed boobs bob.

Boss Babe corrects her Pledge, "Steph Sorostitute, that was two nights ago. Now get up on your feet!"

"Keep pulling your pink, you seeping scum slut!" Robyn interjects.

Steph does, as she stands with her legs apart.

Babs enables. "So tell us what is in the envelope, Pledge."

Steph takes in a breath. *I know the answer.* "Ahhh," she bides herself time. "Ahhh, the envelope contained an Option. Ma'am."

Robyn tries to talk but Boss Babe talks overtop of her, "An Option for what, Steph dear?"

Steph nods and appeals to Monitor Babs' authority. "Ma'am, I possess the Option to challenge any Cosmos Pledge to a Duel of my choice. Winner-Takes-All and becomes a Monitor next Term."

The Cosmos Lineup reacts to this claim with a ripple of motion.

"And what becomes of the loser?" BB probes.

Steph knows this answer too, "Ahhh, Ma'am, the loser shall take all my Obeisance and Props. They take my pink-wet-and-ready and my Pee-Cam. They take the Shaving Kit, shave bare and bald, and stay naked. They Opt Down and become a Stripper next Term."

Steph wants a lock. "Final solution."

"Final solution." Boss Babe confirms, "no way out for the loser."

The Four Cosmos in the Lineup react uneasily while they wait. Steph's claim confirms Robyn's eyewitness recounting, and adds credence to a source considered unreliable and less than forthcoming.

Elle releases a droplet of pee into her cameltoe and resists an urge to touch the blue nappy that erupts above her waistline. *I know who the target is. But getting shaven bare and bald represents an escalation on Steph's part beyond stripping me naked. Steph wants to foist her Obeisance upon the loser. She just added that.*

Elle steels a glance at the four other Pledge in the Lineup. *I'm the only Pledge with two pieces.* Elle studies just how filthy Steph is. *Perhaps the loser shall also be condemned to the Doghouse? No thank you, been there, done that!*

But Elle is not the only Pledge in the Lineup to feel nervous. Bodies move about. Armpits bead sweat. Eight nipples shine out, several erected. Hips move, shoulders gyrate, torsos twitch, and toes bounce heels off the ground, if only for a moment.

But Elle knows, *the result of the Option is clear: One Cosmos will Opt Up to Monitor Caste; one Cosmos will Opt Down to the Strip. Steph will the one Cosmos to Opt Up, and until recently Beka and I were the odds-on favorite to be the other. Except now, at this moment, Beka only wears her micro g-string. Lucky her.*

Elle glances at Steph and detects that Steph masturbates her scarlet, not only that, a string of languid sloss hangs down between her legs. Elle can tell that Steph's head is still spinning.

Monitor Babs speaks to Steph again. "You may pick your Dueling companion now, but you shall pick your Game later."

Steph breaths through her open mouth.

BB continues to lead, "Have you selected a companion, Pledge Steph?"

Steph constricts her vagina but instead of the Dong *I have a finger in there!* She rubs her sensitive spot, makes a gurgling noise, and even more sweetness springs forth. *It's now or never!*

It's not the Dong trying to possess me! I am masturbating myself toward the Zone.

"Tisk, tisk," Babs chides her merrily, "You could lose too, you know. You didn't tells us what would happen then. Piss Mouth and the Doghouse, I presume? Until it's your turn to streak to the Nugget?"

Steph blinks. *Getting captured between Terms is particularly dangerous because there is not supposed to be a gap in between.* Steph regains composure. *I control my own hands and I want to Opt Monitor next Term!*

Steph opens her mouth and answers BB's first question, "Ma'am, I have made my selection, Ma'am!"

Some Cosmos in the Lineup conclude Boss Babe makes it easy for Steph, although they are uncertain why.

Certainly BB finds Steph's luck disgusting. *It makes me paranoid that Gamers and Automatron manipulate the Game. Like, where did the envelope with the Option come from?* Babs considers. *Not me. Steph now possesses a huge opportunity. I certainly can't stop her.*

So Babs pops the question. "And who shall it be my dear Pledge?"

Steph answers carefully, "Ma'am, I Option to Duel with Elle in her croptop and slacks, Ma'am!"

"So a Duel shall be scheduled!" Boss Babe affirms and turns to study Elle. Elle holds her position stoically: blue hair on the head, croptop held in teeth, hands behind head, armpits concave, bare belly flat, legs wide, and low rise slacks embracing a burst of blue hairage frontside, and sweeping rugage posterior. Elle's coffee-colored nipples bubble-up like volcanoes, and her body hair rises.

Elle soaks a bit more pee into her cameltoe. *How come Babs doesn't stop Steph? Dial her back? Cagey Steph just locked both my Garments into her Game.*

Elle fidgets; her eyes dart. *I have been feeling myself losing. I tittered and vagflashed at the Nugget, I get shot naked and spread, pink-wet-and-ready, in the Beauty Salon. Now this. I goners. Game over for me.*

Or maybe not. Boss Babe addresses Steph, "Very well. You have identified your combatant. Unfortunately Elle and the other Cosmos are going to the Mermaid Parade today. You shall get your Duel before the end of *The Runup,* but not before we come back today."

Robyn butts in. "But until BB permits you to identify your Game, you shall continue to stay shaven bare bald and naked, and masturbate pink-wet-and-ready. You'll cum on cue and Zone when told to. Is that clear?"

"Really now?" Steph challenges, and looks at Babs.

"Not quite," BB corrects. "You're a Pledge until Midnight, and even if you win your Duel, and you shall continue to obey Robyn. Am I clear on that?"

Steph relents, "Ma'am, thank you, Ma'am." Steph gushes, and adds, "I intend to pick a Game that's a sure win!"

§ Kimju Gives Beka Shaving Kit: Elle Gives Steph Croptop

"Tell me Steph Sorostitute, who qualifies for the Shaving Kit," Robyn taunts.

Anger starts to boil in Steph's blood. "I do," she clips.

"You said you don't know where it is, Steph Sorostitute, but you know where it belongs, don't you?" Robyn queries.

Steph formalizes, "Ma'am, yes, Ma'am."

"Tell me, you slippery stink socket," Robyn demands.

"The Shaving Kit belongs in my snatch and sewer, Ma'am," Steph says.

Robyn turns to the Lineup and orders Kimju, "Get it out and give it to her!"

The Cam pivots, and eyes follow Kimju as she pulls her jeans shorts to the side and extracts the stainless steel sphere from her koot. It has soap inside. Then a different pullaside, and Kimju extracts the long hollow stainless rod from her kawazoo. It has scissors and razor inside.

Kimju bounces, "I've been storing them for you!"

Steph takes the sphere and rod gingerly into her hands. This action causes her to let go of her pink.

Robyn snaps, "Wash them off in your mouth, you stupid slush slot."

Steph eyes Babs and finds only firmness. She obeys. As the second piece comes out of her mouth Babs directs. "Give them to Beka, Pledge. She will store them for you. You shall burnish your stubble and beg to shave."

Robyn rushes to augment, "You'll want to shave soon enough. But you need to grown out some stubble so you really itch. You need to grovel and beg for it!"

Steph bristles. Babs ignores Robyn and nods to Beka to take the sphere and rod and to "Hold onto that."

Babs offers Steph advice, and she points with her chin. "Feel free to use the Watering Can and wash yourself. After you finish wait for us here in the Backyard. We'll be back by evening."

Robyn interjects, "Too bad you won't be zoning yourself on the Back Door Cam, because I'm taking the Cam with us to the Mermaid Parade."

Steph avoids asking a question, "Ma'am, a towel would be useful to advance your directive, Ma'am."

Babs nods agreement and addresses Elle, "You. Give Steph your croptop."

Elle balks; she reaches up with both hands to take the croptop out of her mouth. "Wait a minute. We haven't had any Duel. Who is Steph to make me topless today? This isn't fair."

Monitor Babs gentles her Pledge. "Silence. You disrespect me using an improper form of address, asking a question, and offering unsolicited opinions. You and your fellow newbie will be parading topless today. But then, so will Kimju and Molly. All four of you: hair dyed, body painted, very public exposures."

Elle horridly pulls the croptop tighter into her teeth, clamps down and hurries her hands to surrender position. This avoids apology, but is also avoids BB's order.

Robyn jives Elle, "Beka loans her halter, you loan your croptop; this way your Roommate can't complain about unequal treatment." She laughs, "ha ha ha ha."

Babs adds a serious note to Elle, "And Steph can't complain you and she don't start her Duel with an unequal number of Garments." Babs smiles, "In the Game, stay the Game."

Robyn signs Beka to unscrew the Shaving Kit cylinder rod and hand her the scissors from inside. She accepts them, walks behind Elle, and cuts upward at the center back of the already reduced croptop. It parts and falls forward, still hanging by the straps. Robyn cuts through these one-by-one, so that the croptop is only held in Elle's teeth.

"Take your rag," Robyn tells Steph, and Elle lets it got into Steph's hand.

Steph appears to have acquired one Garment, albeit un-wearable. Elle firms her hands behind her head. Elle understands, *Ok, so I've loaned my croptop to Steph. Well, no, I've relinquished it forever. I really am topless now. My croptop is now a Steph rag. And once Steph finishes Optioning me, I won't have my stretch slacks either. I won't have anything, and I will beg to shave bare bald and stay naked.*

Elle squints toward Kimju and the jeans shorts that Kimju now wears. *I need to rescue my secret Manifest notes. Maybe if Kimju finds them she won't turn me in. But if Robyn does, I'm a bare bald and naked Stripper next Term.*

Elle blinks. *I could be a bare bald and naked Stripper no matter what.*

Robyn tells Beka, "Put the Shaving Kit away."

So Beka, unquestioning, works the micro g-string out of her bene and to the side, so that she can pop the sphere with the soap inside into her breech, and then settle the slightly curved tube containing the folding scissors and razor into her bowel. She settles the g-string as best as possible back atop her now packed boneroo, although its micro size hardly hides the slit.

The question both Beka and Elle want to ask, but don't, is whether either will be getting her top back anytime soon, no matter how reduced to a rag. But why should they ask such a question? After all, "all together now," BB insists, and the four topless Pledge recite, "Please let me Pledge naked and cum be a Stripper next Term."

So many beggars, so few openings at the Nugget.

II-34 Tiffany Visits Ginny & Trixi: Shares Double Dong (D25)

§ Tiffany: Carries Dong to Corvette House & Janet Greets

Tiffany finds holding the halter in her hand awkward, so she ties it around her neck as she races otherwise naked from the Cosmos to the Corvette House. Yes, Tiffany holds onto the half the Double Dong that is outside her to minimize its wagging the end inside her. The unpleasant feeling goes way up into her rectum and Tiffany can feel her bowel trying to reject the intrusion. But the fat bulb that the Dong has grown inside her sphincter ensures *I can't accidentally expel it. Thank you Dong.*

Tiffany finds the run uneventful, except when she rings the chime at the front door of the Corvette House. Paparazzi must have been tipped off and lie in wait to record her purple hair and penetrated position.

Worse, the Corvette House Front Door Cam speaks to her. "Bend over, pull your butt checks apart, and stretch your pink out."

Tiffany obliges Paparazzi and Prefecture alike with choice views of the snake penetrating her tailpipe. She squeezes and hangs a bead of tapioca out of her tangle.

The Front Door opens and Monitor Janet welcomes an old confidant. "Greetings Porn Star," she flatters. "Enter."

Tiffany escapes inside. She evaluates her host. The sultry heavyweight continues to tightly pack herself into a stunning T-front maillot with a high-riding legline and bare rump overtop a tight-fitting bandeau. Gamers recall Janet acquired the bandeau and T-maillot after her Pledge Louise stripped naked at the Nugget, five Days ago, and part of a deal with Babs to acquire Steph overnight.

Tiffany observes details. *When Janet wore these Garments at the Greatest House Roar she wore the bandeau overtop the T-front; today she wears the T-front overtop the bandeau. It's more secure this way.*

"Ma'am, hello, Ma'am," Tiffany offers respect, "My orders are to obey you."

"Looks like you are getting your wish to Pledge naked and Opt Down," Janet observes. "Except—"

"Ma'am, Monitor Babs saw fit that Beka loan me her halter today. I've turned it into a collar and made sure it covers nothing."

Janet smiles. "But it covers your neck dear."

"Ma'am, I'll wear it inside me: In my twat, in my tailpipe, in my mouth. You know I'll do that."

"You just want an excuse to be quiet." Janet twinkles.

"BB doesn't want me to get caught streaking," Tiffany sombers. "But you know I really mean it when I say I'll stay pink-wet-and-ready, lick pussy and share the Dong, and cum be a Stripper next Term."

"You're getting very accomplished at licking up pee," Janet commends. "I love the way you always clean out the Measuring Cup with your tongue."

"Thank you. Kundalini is in the details. You know I'm a Pee-Camer and Piss Mouth because you have used me before and you will use me again. You're the one who made me."

"Don't hold me responsible for everything that happens to you in the Game," Janet retorts. "You became a Piss Mouth to avoid Slavesex. And you're the one who keeps begging me to use you."

"Ma'am—" Tiffany starts, but Janet signs her to silence.

Janet shifts, "By the way, I like how you mauled Steph."

"Ma'am, thank you, Ma'am," Tiffany politely acknowledges.

Janet squints. "But why did you give her the Option?"

Tiffany doesn't quite remember it that way. "Ma'am, if I may—"

Janet cuts her off, "Nobody cares if *you* Opt Down. But to provide that slut an opportunity to Opt Up! That's inexcusable!"

Tiffany offers, "Ma'am, I'll eat your pussy. I'll swallow your juices."

"You'll eat any pussy assigned to you," Janet corrects.

"And you will open your mouth to collect piss from anybody!" Darleen speaks.

Tiffany had not heard the bare footsteps come up behind her; she squeezes the Dong inside her rectal tube.

Darleen joins Janet in front of Tiffany and Tiffany evaluates Janet's Roommate and sidekick: *Darleen was a Monitor last Term who pretends to have been promoted to MomCap and be training Janet. But I think she's just a Pledge.*

A lucky Pledge somehow.

Tiffany evaluates further, *Darleen still wears a shortsleeve front-button shirt that kisses the top of her slacks near her button, just like on the Yacht and at the Greatest House Roar. And despite perpetually flashing bellage with the slightest rise of an arm, Darleen remains far away the most-covered Corvette, even including the more-dressed Janet.*

Darleen sucks in a cheek on one side of her face and tilts her head to the full-frontal Cosmos Pledge bearing the Dong in her tailpipe. "Ah, Tiffany *really* Transparent!" Darleen advances, "Last time I saw you you were licking Molly's pee up at the Peacocks' after the Greatest House Roar. Before that you cleaned Kimju off the Yacht Deck. Rumor has it you've been practicing with man streams?"

"That would be Steph," Tiffany corrects. "Although I've been a Piss Mouth ever since I became a Porn Star."

Nothing prevents Tiffany from sassing Darleen, "Hey Darleen, you didn't tell me on the Yacht that you're a broken Monitor. Just like Steph Sorostitute."

"I can't speak for Steph, but I'm Opting Up next Term." Darleen gestures down to her two Garments and augments, "Unlike you, Eraser Heads." Darleen curls her nose. "I saw you dong Steph Sorostitute on the feed. I saw you pass up the Option. You provided that skeeze with a path up. You're the one who deserve to be a Slavesex!"

Janet takes charge. "Enough, both of you! Proceed me into the Living Room!"

§ Tiffany: Watches Trixi Tubes Watch Naked Ginny Suck Cock

The Corvette House layout is the same as the Cosmos House, but it still takes long seconds for Tiffany to digest the scene that confronts her. In addition to Janet and Darleen the Room contains six Corvette Pledge and one unidentified naked hooded man. Four Corvettes stand spread surrender in a Lineup, all topless. A fifth Corvette, wearing two stretch fabric tubes, kneels and rivets her eyes upon a kneeling and naked sixth Corvette cocksucking the naked hooded man.

Tiffany processes the view. *I know the naked blowjob artist.*

Janet performs introductions, "Tiffany Transparent, once a Porn Star always a Porn Star, I believe you already know Pledge Ginny, Whore-For-Life, Stripper last Term at the Nugget?

"Ma'am," Tiffany advances, "Ginny and I shot cumswap and felching videos when I was on active duty."

Darleen bends a knee and flashes a side of bellage toward Tiffany. "I recall you licked up Ginny's pee on the Yacht and at the Greatest House Roar?" Darleen looks at Ginny's naked and exposed backside. "Looks like Ginny's gonna need to pee sooner or later, you know?"

"Ma'am, no problem, Ma'am," Tiffany answers deliberately. "I will lick up any pee on the floor. She can pee directly into my mouth. I can swallow and keep up. I am a Porn Star!" Tiffany rustles. *I wanna be a Porn Star again but I don't wannabe a Whore for Life like Ginny.*

Naked Ginny Whore-For-Life casts her eyes upward toward Janet and Tiffany. She knows not to take the cock out of her mouth. But trading eyes is not forbidden.

Tiffany scans the Living Room another time: *So if the Garments match Ginny's watcher then Ginny's watcher is Trixi Tubes, Ginny's Roommate. But I can't identify the hooded man.*

Tiffany scans the Lineup and deduces, *Four topless Pledge about to be transported to the Mermaid Parade. One of them I've met before: Lee Lollydor, who was Ginny's Roommate at the Nugget last Term.*

Darleen sidles toward Tiffany again, "I bet you want to know just how many times Ginny has had a dick in her mouth this Term. Don't you, tamtart?"

"I'm so jealous!" Tiffany mocks.

"A Whore-For-Life befits a Porn Star!" Janet needles Tiffany.

"Right now you just get to crave getting fucked," Darleen quips. She looks at Tiffany, naked except for the halter tied as a collar.

True. I'm hanging tacky outta my trap. Tiffany recalls Beka and Elle's descriptions of Ginny Cravat, bound, plugged, and mouth fucked. *I've seen the videos. Ginny climaxed out of control. Karma for her Roommate Trixi's indiscretion! Today Ginny is not in bondage; although she does have a cock in her mouth. And that cock is in bondage.*

Well, to be fair, the cock of the naked hooded man is not in bondage other than firmly inside of Ginny's mouth, however his wrists are cuffed behind his back and his mouth is tightly gagged.

Janet points toward the naked hooded gagged handcuffed man. "We call that Boy Toy," Janet amuses. "It's Slavesex on loan from the Dungeon. Body shaven, well behaved, doesn't say much."

Janet points to Ginny again. "I gather she'd be the first to want to share the Dong with you!"

Ginny quivers but she keeps the cock in her mouth. She began drooling a long time ago.

"That's Trixi Tubes," Janet explains, gesturing to the Corvette with her gaze fixed on Ginny's oral duty, and wearing two Cams mounted on the sides of her head. "You've probably heard about her. She's Ginny's Roommate and has been... selfish. Again."

Unlike Ginny, Trixi does not look up. Like Ginny, Trixi kneels, but at right angles to the fellation, knees apart, hands clasped behind her head and eyes obediently fixed on the cock in Ginny's mouth.

Tiffany experiments with lightness. "I gather Trixi Tubes is keeping her eyes on oral stimulation today."

"Indeed!" Janet augments. "It's very simple, really. Gamers see what she sees inside their virtual reality goggles. And if Automatron catches her looking astray? Well, then, she and Ginny trade places. Everything. Garments, Obeisance, Whore-for-Life. Last time Trixi made a mistake she didn't have to do anything to atone. This time she has to prove herself. I'd say that if Trixi wants to go to the Dungeon, right now she's got an easy shot at it."

"But what would Ginny say?" Tiffany teases Janet, and looks at Ginny's mouth surrounding the cock. "That's pretty extreme," she adds. "Ginny might hate you for taking her Whore-for-Life away!"

Janet shares a laugh. And Ginny knows this is true.

Trixi feels both nipples go hard. The one stretch fabric Tube that Trixi wears as a bandeau will let one nipple peak out soon. The Tube she wears as a miniskirt already upskirts.

Janet advances, "Trixi deserves whatever she does to herself. Right now she's catching a break; she should be naked and streaking already, pinking and begging Dong in *her* asshole."

The Dong in Tiffany's asshole pulses.

Janet lifts a finger and adds a caveat, "Trixi arrived with five tubes—five different colors and five different widths—but she may only wear two at a time."

Tiffany glances. *Yes, Trixi wears two tubes—one as a bandeau the other as an excuse for a miniskirt.*

Janet sing-songs, "Trixi Tubes needs to learn to share with her Roommate, and today she must study the consequence for not wanting to share."

Trixi wriggles her body but continues her stare.

Tiffany understands. *We're going to be here a while.*

Janet lectures Tiffany. "You are honored to be the first Cosmos to witness Trixi Tubes, and you are correct to read her as conservative and scared.

"You, of all Gamers, Tiffany," Janet bemuses, "must know that 'Trixi' is a particularly insulting name to grant to a newbie. It might be the name of a Stripper, and of course it is a perfect name for a Whore."

Trixi's eyes threaten to waver, but she holds true.

Tiffany evaluates Trixi's potential to Opt Stripper next Term. *Her two Tubes don't let her hide much. Maybe her titties will sneak out, but no matter how much Trixi wants to hide, I can see that her tackle will flash.*

Tiffany wants to study the man with his cock in Ginny's mouth, but Janet demands Tiffany turn and study the four topless Corvette standing spread surrender side-by-side in a Lineup.

The Back Door Cam looks in through the windows.

The four topless Corvettes have matching white bodypainted nipples with red outlines, and bright red painted lips.

Two of the Pledge wear the remnants of Janet's crochet bikini as g-strings; their nearly bare pubes are also bodypainted with a thick matching white, also with a red outline. Janet introduces them. "Tiffany, you know Lee Lollydor from when you Feature Danced at the Nugget last Term." Janet fans a hand. "What you don't know is that after Steph popped the Peacocks at the Greatest House Roar, it was Lee who cleaned up afterward."

Janet shifts her gaze. "And that's Lee's Roommate, Louise. She's a big-busted sensuous full-blooded Portuguese, them's real 38Ds, and she's a fallen Monitor, just like Steph."

Janet feigns concern, "Last week Louise *begged* to trade her swimsuit for my crochet bikini."

Janet sweeps her hands across her own body and showcases her recently acquired bandeau and T-front maillot, "I was unable to resist her pleadings. So BB took it away from her at the Nugget and gave it to me. So, no more hairage, no more areolage for me, although you'll notice that that I can tug the butt line right down into my jutcrease, so I can wear this maillot bare-assed."

"I guess we all have our commitments," Tiffany amuses, and looks at Lee and Louise again, who share what used to be Janet's Spiderweb Bikini.

"I am a very nice person," Janet asserts. "It was good for Babs that she directed Louise to strip naked and pink at the Nugget, retain the bandeau and maillot for me, and give Louise the Spiderweb. A slightly smaller Spiderweb, but then, I got slightly larger Garments."

"Very thoughtful of you," Tiffany commends, and studies Louise with her horseshoe-shaped lactoids. Tiffany connects, *I saw her dance topless at the Nugget two Days ago. I bet she knows she's a pawn to Opt Down because of some deal Babs and Janet made, and she doesn't like it.*

Too bad. Everyone in the Prefecture can tell that Louise isn't shaven at all. Her bush grows as thick and lush as Molly's, and her every-more public exposure deeply humiliates her. Gamers hope so.

Louise often leaks milk from her full breasts and the careful eye can see it mix into her bodypainted nipples and areolas.

Janet commands Tiffany's attention again. "After Louse got my Spiderweb halter and g-string, she *insisted* on sharing the crochet bikini with her naked Roommate! Very magnanimous but Roommates should share, yes?"

Yes. Tiffany squints. *I guess Louise shall Opt Down, not Opt Up.*

Janet states the obvious. "After Louise give the spider halter to Lee, Lee re-tied it like a g-string today! Now they can both go naked at the Nugget next Term but they won't have to streak to get there!

"And today? I've let them put a layer of thick white bodypaint over their pubes in the event anyone thinks their g-strings are too revealing."

For Lee, half a bikini beats none, and she details a topless 36C-24-35, conics and curves, strings, white bodypainted pubes.

Lee and Louise are not entirely Parade legal. For example, everyone can tell Lee shaves except for a racing stripe."

Indeed. Tiffany casts Lee a look and can see the sparkle of metal from a clithood ring inside her spiderweb. *I also took on Stripper freight two Terms ago, but when I made Porn Star my Eraser Heads got tattooed and implanted with stims.*

Tiffany feels the thick snake up her ass talk to her and she rotates her hips in response. The Dong swings in the Living room air. "Ma'am, it would be my pleasure to share the Dong with any Corvette."

Tiffany grins, "Including you, Monitor Janet."

Janet introduces the two remaining Corvette Pledge to Tiffany. Both present topless, also with whitened areolae with red outlines and red lips; both and wear lingerie panties and heels, although one of the panties is more correctly a thong.

Janet tells Tiffany, "I'm not sure you've met. Say hello to the Lingerie Twins, newbies and Roommates, Caroline and Wendy." Janet pauses, "Each brought five Garments with them when they Pledged this Term: a bra, panties or a thong, hose, a full slip, and heels; but like Tiffany Tubes, they have Pledged to wear only two pieces at any one time."

Tiffany squints. Janet again, "Okay, so Games can be complicated. Any Game worth playing is never simple."

Tiffany pays respects. "Ma'am, you are wise, Ma'am."

Janet explains, "Caroline's a 33B-22-34 and usually wears a full slip and heels; Wendy, at 34B-24-34, usually presents herself as a 'bra and panty girl.'"

Darleen invites herself into the discussion. "And neither are required to navelage, like you and the Cosmos. Today I made sure they both wore their most revealing combinations. Once they put on their heels, I decided that their panties and thong were their wisest choice for today."

The Lingerie Twins ripple, anticipating their upcoming topless humiliation during their public exposure in the Mermaid Parade. In fact, like Lee and Louise, the twins have a small respite: Caroline's crimson areolas lie beneath the white areola makeup, and Wendy's ruddy areolas also lie underneath the white paste.

"Caroline and Windy will probably get their pasties hosed off and end up truly topless today," Janet says succinctly, "but they shan't complain; they still have two Garments each!"

Tiffany glances at Lee and Louise again. They share the Spiderweb. One Garment each.

Darleen preens. "Janet and I are escorting Four Topless Corvettes to the Mermaid Parade."

Janet directs her comments to Tiffany. "Ginny and Boy Toy, along with Trixi Tubes, shall be staying behind today. And you shall join them to keep an eye on things until we get back."

"Ma'am, yes, Ma'am," Tiffany replies, "and please let me share the Dong once again!"

§ Tiffany & Ginny: Share the Dong at the Corvette House

Janet surveys her centerpiece, and carefully addresses not only Tiffany, but also Ginny, Trixi Tubes, and Boy Toy, the hooded naked man. "What I want is very simple," she says, "you four make yourself comfortable, take any position, except, you, Ginny, keep that cock in your mouth, and you, Tiffany, slip the other end of that dong into Ginny's asshole."

Janet looks at Trixi Tubes. "And you, don't take your eyes off that dick in Ginny's mouth!"

Janet gives pause. "You understand?" Tiffany and Trixi answer in unison, "Ma'am yes Ma'am," while Ginny grunts affirmingly. The male says nothing; he's hooded, gagged, cuffed with his hands behind his back, and erected.

The male bends his knees, drops and rolls back, and Ginny follows, keeping her mouth around her object of attention as they work their way onto the floor. Besides curly hair on her head, the only hair Ginny has "down there" is a racing stripe above her gap. Her clithood ring sparkles.

Ginny offers a clean and accessible gut pipe for Tiffany to penetrate. A tattoo surrounds it, a circle of dollar signs interspersed with a filigree of words, "Whore For Life."

Most rude, Tiffany considers, *however I too have a tattoo that circumnavigates my tail pipe, except mine's only visible in ultraviolet light.* Yes, and the Cam documents that Tiffany's tattoo does become visible in normal light as it ascends her rugage.

Tiffany settles her buttocks tight up against Ginny, and while the cock in Ginny's mouth holds Ginny firmly in place, Tiffany presses the Double Dong way up into Ginny's rectum. Tiffany feels the Dong inflate into Ginny's rectum and hold firm. She relaxes.

Ginny feels the Dong grow a ball inside her sphincter. *Yes, the Double Dong shall hold us butt-to-butt secure.*

May it please Gamers, the Dong shall dance with Tiffany and Ginny.

Gamers in the Prefecture, and most certainly the Nugget Patrons, have seen Tiffany and Ginny perform before: the Crowd has cheered them naked and pinking center Stage, watched them roll around DPed, seen the Calendar month photo when they suck dick together.

But Gamers have never seen Tiffany and Ginny share the Double Dong before. Tiffany knows *the Dong, even up our tailpipes, is a risky proposition, it can vibrate, get hot or cold, electrocute, wiggle, embowel me. Us. It can make the two of us work together or make us work apart. Only one thing is certain, the swell inside the base ensures neither of us will push it out our rectum. It's in for the duration of the Mermaid Parade, and that will last for hours.*

Trixi moves and lies down on the floor to the side so she can observe the oral penetration unobstructed. Some say Trixi has the easy task. All she has to do is never let the sucked cock out of her Cams' view. But in reality that's not easy at all. Trixi's downside is that if Gamers discover that the view of the Cam has wandered elsewhere, then Trixi will no longer just be trading places with Ginny to suck cock; changing places with Ginny now includes taking in the Dong as well.

So may Trixi Tubes reveal herself?

§ Tiffany: Observes Ginny's Blowjob & Trixi's Dilemma

Janet and Darleen and four topless Corvettes depart and Tiffany settles in for a long day. The Dong up her tailpipe talks to her…and to Ginny…and the former Whore and Whore-For-Life rub their asses together. May they both drip.

Tiffany considers Ginny again. *I'm happy to share the Dong with her, but I'm jealous she gets a cock in her mouth and I don't.*

Ginny and the gagged hooded naked man both have their mouths full, but nothing prevents Tiffany and Trixi from conversing.

Tiffany breaks the ice, "I'm Tiffany. How long has she been like this?"

Trixi almost takes her eyes off her subject, "Jeez, Tiffany, we've all heard about you. Seen your Videos. I don't know. Hours and hours we've been here. He donated cum. He pissed in her mouth. He throated her."

Trixi struggles to keep her eyes fixed on the erection filling Ginny's mouth; questions flood her mind.

"Hey Tiffany," Trixi inquires, "Are you gonna suck cock and fuck like Ginny?"

"Goodness knows we've worked cocks together!" Tiffany explains, "Do I want to suck cock? Always! But am I allowed to? No. So I will not. Whores suck cock, but I am a Pledge, now and until the end of the Term. Babs tries to deny that I'm still a Porn Star, but a Porn Star is a Porn Star forever. Gamers are making me and my fans sexually frustrated. Because I need to return to sucking and fucking on Cam."

Trixi accepts that the Cam canvasses one escaped nipple and an open upskirt. She tests Tiffany, "So when you were a Porn Star did you do tricks like Ginny here does? Sucking a bound hooded man?"

"Honey, we all do tricks," Tiffany firms, "although some people don't even know they do them."

Tiffany feels Ginny react and squeezes her asshole tighter around the Double Dong. They communicate back and forth... and arouse each other.

Tiffany considers, *Apparently the Dong is going to let us feel ourselves out before it tries to do whatever contortions it might demand upon us. They can't be too extreme if the Dong expects Ginny to keep that cock in her mouth.*

Trixi has the determination to keep her eye and her Cams trained on Ginny's cocksucking. Ginny never takes the cock out of her mouth; she keeps her lips around its deep penetration and breathes around it.

Trixi abstracts to Tiffany, "The Gamers deny you and prime you."

"Thank you." Tiffany is careful to not create any alarm that might cause Trixi to look away from her target; she elaborates, "Pledge can volunteer Dongs and they can explore girls, but sex with guys remains forbidden, no matter what. I might cum on my fingers or cum on the Dong, but cumming on a cock I have to wait past Stripper Term for."

Tiffany feels Ginny's fingers reach between her legs and play with her clit. Shameless, but Tiffany stays put, and contributes her own fingers to Ginny's ringed clit and the twosome freshen immediately. Ginny doesn't have much else to do with her time, and goes into a soft Zone.

Trixi wants to cast her gaze about but knows Automatron will record any wandering eyes and that Janet replace Ginny's mouth with her own. However Trixi can talk just as long as her eyes stay focused. She props her head in her hands so she can stay pointed at her target.

Trixi confesses. "Janet wants me to share the Tubes with Ginny, but if I do I'll only have one piece and I'll be Stripping next Term." A second tit now threatens to escape Trixi Tubes' bandeau.

Tiffany fails to provide comfort to Trixi Tubes' plight. "Lucky you. Share the Tubes and you get to accompany Ginny to the Nugget. She's a pro in more ways than one.

Trixi holds her eyes steady but obliques the question. "I hear that inside the Nugget that the Strippers possess nothing. So do you stay naked all the time?

Tiffany answers, "Once you get to the Nugget you and Ginny can turn in your Tubes to the Stage Door Man. But at least you won't have to streak to get there.

Trixi repeats her question. "So do you stay naked all the time?"

"You stay naked unless you are given something to wear for the purpose of taking it off," Tiffany retorts. "Although some Strippers are kept naked 24x7."

Trixi flinches but asks another question, "I don't quite understand why you volunteer to share the Dong with Ginny."

Tiffany realizes that she may have a reason. "I'm a Porn Star," she tells Trixi, "I do sex on camera. The Dong isn't sex but it's as close as I can get right now. I like Ginny just fine, but I'd love to share the Dong with you too."

Trixi wilts. Ginny's accepts that the cock in her own mouth rises. She pounds it on the back of her mouth, swallows, and throats the cock all the way down to the testicles. Ginny and Tiffany cum together in unison. And ignore Trixi Tubes' silly talk. Or whether she can stay on target.

II-35 Six Cosmos: Colorful Mermaid Parade (D25)

§ Six Cosmos: Van Ride to the Mermaid Parade

Yes, the Cosmos Pledge are being taken out to be paraded in the very public Mermaid Parade, only one block from the beach.

Yellow-haired Robyn rides shotgun with Babs in the Van on the way to the Parade, and everything about the trip promotes Robyn's confidence. "I am no longer just second-in-command," she tells the four topless Cosmos Pledge during a moment when BB is out of earshot, "I'm Boss Bitch's equal! After all, both of us have three garments: BB with her minidress over her lingerie, and I with my clear vinyl shirt and miniskirt over my maillot cutout. Me MomCap now!"

But Kimju, always a reader of tea leaves, oscillates her thoughts, *Maybe Robyn's yellow hair dye marks a turning point for the anointed one. Except Robyn does not have her bush dyed like the rest of us. And Robyn does have three pieces, whereas all I have are ripped jeans shorts and orange hairage. She's gonna Double Opt Up, while I'm Opting Down."*

Kimju steals a glance as a blue-hairaged Elle crawls into the back of the Van, topless and wearing just her low-riding slacks. *I had hoped Steph would Duel with Robyn instead of Elle, because Robyn needs to be taken down.*

Indeed, even Robyn seems bearish on Elle, telling her, "I doubt if you will ever get your shirt back to cover up your bouncing nubs." Robyn laughs at Elle with a hand to her mouth, "And your hairage and butt crack will be moot once Steph takes your pants away, followed by a shave and a haircut. Two bits, inevitable"

Elle releases enough urine to lubricate her urethra but to not drip or shoot out. *I'm going to be a bare bald and naked Stripper next Term no matter what! I can't defeat Steph if she picks the Game.* Elle glances at her Roommate again. *I really do need to make sure Beka comes with me. Even if I have to become a Pee-Cam Pledge like her.*

But if Beka wants me to climax the Double Dong with her on Stage at the Nugget? That's impossible!

The four topless Cosmos array themselves on the floor in the back of the Van. Orange Kimju retains the remains of ripped shorts and leaks fuzzy orange hair to the sides of her ripped crotch. Red Molly hides little in see-through panties; like Elle, Molly spills colored hairage and makes cracks her moonshadow. Aside from the green Mohawk and Hitler, Beka's micro g-string exposes most of her nearly bald and nearly bare body. And all Four Cosmos Pledge sport finger and toe nails to match!

I am the barest Cosmos, Beka accepts, *and I am also the most wet.*

Yes. Elle Lollydor observes, *My Roommate already hangs a streamer down from her blossom. My Roommate will leave a puddle behind.*

The topless Cosmos who bounce around in the back of the Van during the ride do not all share Robyn's sense of entitlement and optimism. Gamers observe that neither Steph nor Tiffany have been invited; both remain far too naked for this environment, and besides, both have other assignments. Steph, back in the Backyard washing herself up, contemplates how to take Elle down, and Tiffany, sharing the Dong up her ass with Ginny at the Corvette House, worries about Elle. *Poor Elle,* Tiffany thinks, *Elle could lose, and she still has so much to learn about Stripping next Term!*

Perhaps the vibrations of Cosmos thoughts catalyze Robyn in the front seat. She double checks her own "smallest buttonhole" and makes sure she positions it correctly. She double checks Babs. All is well. Robyn turns in her seat and addresses the four topless Cosmos sitting on the Van floor, "You're about to meet the Bodypaint Artist, and you are going to parade topless." Kimju and Molly know they will do what they have to, Beka gushes so much cream that she creates a spot on the floor. Elle accepts, *I'm fine to lick up valiva, I just don't want to lick up Van floor.*

But Elle correctly senses doom beyond licking cream off the floor. Beyond licking the entire floor of the Van. Or licking the Van all over. *Once Steph gets her hands on me, I will be lucky to be a bare bald and naked Stripper at the Nugget next Term. For sure I will have to streak to get there, and if I'm caught, there will be no escape.*

Because I won't exist any more. They will just make me vanish.

§ Four Cosmos: Topless & Hair Dyed & Hairage & Brodeas

It is a camera zoo from the moment the Cosmos tumble out of the Van and stand up by a building on a side street; there is no way they can count the shutters, the camcorders, the handhelds. There is no way the Four Pledge can hide.

The paparazzi love the bare tits and colorful hair: Kimju, wearing only the ripped jeans shorts, leaks colored hairage and cheeky buttage, but the paparazzi demand more, so BB signs her up onto a fender, legs opened.

Topless Elle is already blushing and holds her hands across her chest, handbra style, when BB signs her to sit on the opposite fender. The paparazzi collect a few nipple peeks as she adjusts position, and they collect blue hairage above her tight and low waistlined, skin-tight slacks. And, for any shooter who walks around behind her, a prolific butt crack above stretch slacks molding Elle's naka-naka gorge. Elle feels the fabric cross her nadir gate and rise up forward and part her cameltoe.

I know the paparazzi can tell I've stained myself there. Elle blushes and decorates her slacks with a dark spot of fresh pee. Graffiti on a steel grate behind the Van makes a great background.

"You're gonna be everywhere!" Robyn chides Elle. "Apps and sites, photo sharing, downloads from Automatron, books, magazines, video tapes. You aspire to Strip naked, pull pink center Stage at the Nugget, and lick cumshots off your photograph in front of the Crowd? How do you like that idea, Pledge Elle Lollydor?"

Robyn cackles.

The Bodypaint Artist takes his time to prepare. Robyn signs Molly to roll her see-through panties into a bundle and pull them tight into the crack of her ass, baring her big butt. Molly feels very exposed. *My tight panties split my mooe and spill my red minge to both sides. I would be vulgar were it not for my hair dye.* She uses the Van as a background and lets the mass of amateur paparazzi collect her. She raises her arms, dances her bright red hairy armpits, and cradles her mammae in her hands. *It doesn't matter where I dance, and if I can keep one piece I won't have to streak to the Nugget.*

Kimju and Elle are still fender art. Beka poses for shots: handbra with titty tease, micro g-string buried in her beneficent; she lifts a foot onto a bumper and shows the string cross her bogey. Babs shuts her down, so Beka seeks out her Roommate.

Elle feels relieved Beka comes and talks to her. Beka also holds a handbra. *Somebody's orders,* Elle surmises.

"You're gonna be a Stripper next Term," Beka affirms. "No doubt about it, you won't have a chance once Steph picks the Game."

"She could make us each guess at what she has written on the inside of an envelope," Elle crabs. "I don't want to be a Stripper next Term. That wasn't our plan."

Beka consoles, "Shucks, Elle, that doesn't matter anymore. We both need to Strip. It's the safest way to get to be a Porn Star!"

"You've lost control of your sex!" Elle firms. "I don't need to dong with you. I don't need to parade topless. I don't need to strip and pink all next Term."

"*We* need to!" Beka insists. "We get to lapdance too! Please Elle, after Steph strips you naked, and if I still have two pieces, promise me you'll take one of them so I can go Strip with you next Term.

"Strippers aren't allowed to eat out or share the Dong," Elle defends.

"Yeah, but Pledge are!" Beka reminds. "And we will, while we have the chance. Please, Elle!"

A worry flashes into Elle's consciousness. *Beka already knows I gave Monitor Babs our Measurement Nudes. But Beka doesn't know I gave BB the* Gonzo Videos. *And maybe Janet and Tiffany know, because Robyn said Babs streamed them.*

§ Elle: Hair Cut & Dividing Line & Stains & Bodypaint

Beka and Elle assume Kimju and Molly will get painted first and it off-balances them when Robyn takes Elle's hand and leads her off the fender. Half a handbra remains and one tit outputs. "Your Game has changed," Robyn whispers into Elle's ear, "if your *Gonzo Videos* get out they will follow you to the Nugget and prequalify you as a Whore. Every Patron who wants to see how you fuck will get a preview."

Robyn position Elle nearby the side of the Van. "Stand spread surrender," she commands.

Elle obeys. The shooters jostle for position, and Elle poses with her legs wide and her hands behind her head. Armpits, and yes, a fully topless lass.

"I'm the Bodypaint Artist," the painter introduces, "And congratulations," he teases, "I hear Steph's gonna confirm you as a Stripper next Term."

Elle expands the dark spot in her cameltoe. The Bodypaint Artist bows to a TV documentary crew that joins the onlookers and documents the Bodypaint Artist at work. The Artist walks behind Elle.

And surprise! From behind so Elle doesn't see it coming, a battery-powered shears enters into her blue-dyed hair just above the neck and moves steadily up and forward and over and down her forehead. Elle gasps, breaks a rule and touches her head; the sheers cut *extremely* close, a band of hair one inch wide is gone, and she feels bare scalp in its place. She holds her mouth opens in surprise. The TV crew loves it.

The Bodypaint Artists explains, "You are now like your Roommate, only an 'inverse Mohawk.'" Elle gets the idea, but doesn't anticipate step two: The Bodypaint Artist pulls the front of her slacks away from her body and pushes the sheers downward from below the navel to the top of her sex lips; this downward push that makes another one-inch wide strip of bare skin.

The shaver lets the slacks go with a "snap" against her lower belly. Now the hairage showing above the slacks erupts as a left patch and a right patch.

I've just been vagflashed! Elle mouths to herself. The TV crew and paparazzi all get me.

"You can shave your nest later," Bodypaint Artist advises. "And then you can pink and cream smooth. Have you cum yet?"

Elle babbles, "Sir, no, Sir."

"Beg him to butch you and stain your nipples," Robyn commands.

Elle obeys. "Sir, please bodypaint me. I've already got blue hair." Elle halts, augments, "blue eyebrows too."

Bodypaint Artist helps along. "Blue nails and a blue nest too. You're sweet, and I'll make you special. So let's stain your lips and nipples blue and give you a coat of blue bodypaint. Yes?"

Elle nods uncertainly. "Yes, please stain and bodypaint me." She widens the dark spot in her cameltoe.

Elle hears a different cutter click into place, and feels the rest of her curly blue hair on her head get butched. She sneaks feels with her finger tips and discovers *a one-inch tall pelt. With an inch wide notch down the middle, from my neck up across the top of my head to my forehead, separating me left and right.*

And my nest has also been divided. Elle looks around. *I know I'm being taken. Collected. I can't stop it. It's not as if someone pulled my halter string today; I gave my entire top away. I had no choice. I'm being—*

Elle's thoughts interrupt when the Bodypaint Artist again pulls her slacks down and away from her body and butches her nest. Another one-inch tall carpet, another snap of the waistband as the Artist lets go, and leaves the itchy nidus inside her cameltoe.

Elle whinnies. *I am slipping away, spinning.* "I'll pull my pants down, I'll cream for you," she offers Bodypaint Artist

"Silly Pledge, not here!" Bodypaint Artist laughs at Elle and waves a brush in her direction. "But maybe if you behave I'll paint your nates too."

Elle presses her lips between her teeth.

The Bodypaint Artist studies his blue-haired beauty, and then speaks into Elle's ear. "Before you only stained your cameltoe with urine. Now you mix in some nectar."

Elle tries to steady herself. *My noogies aren't mine any more. Anyone can look at them.* Elle feels herself flush. *Okay. So now I can't stop transuding my noble secretions. I'm not just scared, I'm becoming aroused by the fear. Blue hair and topless is just the beginning. I'm going to beg to dance topless.*

Bodypaint Artist, this time with brush in hand, again pulls the front of Elle's slacks away from her pelvis, extends the tip of his brush down to her clit, and draws upward, leaving a indelible indigo stripe. The brush rises upward through the tranche of bare skin between Elle's bisected and butched pussy hair, up her pelvis and belly, and comes to rest in her belly button.

Artist again lets the slacks go with a snap.

"Indigo blue stain," Bodypaint Artist informs, "Indelible. Doesn't wash off, not water, not alcohol; fades in a week or two. I recommend you beg for reapplication before it fades away."

Artist swirls his brush full of the deep blue into Elle's belly button and then draws up her belly to her ribs, in-between her bare breasts and stained nipples and then up her neck. Elle senses what's next as he reloads his brush. *Yes, up my chin, across my lips, up my nose, carefully in-between my eyes, up my forehead, through the inch-wide trough of bare scalp on my head, down to the back of my neck, and on down in-between my shoulder blades, down my back, and toward the crack of my ass.*

This garners applause from the circle of assembled voyeurs, paparazzi, and the TV crew.

Elle wonders, *Is the Bodypaint Artist done with his brush?*

Bodypaint Artist bows to the admirers, signs Elle to bow also, and to stay bowed and moon her backside.

Elle blinks, considers her *Gonzo Videos*, and bows. She reaches her hands around behind her back, and pulls her slacks down and away from her nachas.

Elle feels the brush swab stain into her nadir gate, and then draw upwards, between two parted butt cheeks until it joins up with the line bisecting the back.

"Stand up." Bodypaint Artist commands.

Elle does and rolls her slacks up. She looks at the hoard of Cams, goofy looking guys, a hot gal with a bare midriff, a dumpy overweight man in a silver jumpsuit. With her thumbs now in her waistband, the Prefecture sees a more relaxed pose, a pose in-between action.

Elle hunts for Babs' eyes but doesn't find them. Molly appears to have taken Elle's place and joins Kimju on the opposite fender. Cams transverse Elle's stained dividing line in close-up, and watch Bodypaint Artist uses the brush to swab the dark blue, deep purple stain again into Elle's button, soak Elle's nipples up to erection, and bade Elle hold Open Mouth while painting her lips.

Elle stains her cameltoe with nectar.

Now Bodypaint Artist switches from a stain to a blue paint and a wider brush. Elle holds stand spread surrender position, Artist shoos the paparazzi back, and commences to envelope Elle's surface in earnest. Artist coats her breasts and torso with blue paint, then her belly below her button, her sides, shoulders, arms, and ankles and feet. Artist paints her hands completely, and even demands Elle lift each bare foot so that they too may be painted completely.

Lastly, Bodypaint Artist paints Elle's face, ears, and neck.

Bodypaint Artist steps forward and rolls Elle's already low-rise slacks down another two inches. The slacks in the front still ride above slitage, but the rugage is deepened precariously. Bodypaint Artist paints blue over this circumference of belly as well. Now, no skin on Elle's body, except for that inside her slacks, is not totally bodypainted.

Bodypaint Artist adds a second coat and while it is drying, Elle finds Beka in her face. Beka no longer holds handbra and waves arms in Elle's stoic face. She jumps up and down and glees, "We're headed for the Nugget, Elle, just please, please make sure I get to go with you. We're Roommates Together. You can't leave me behind!"

Elle's head spins. "You've lost control of your sex and I'm being exposed and humiliated," she says.

"You got a lot of Gamers looking at you!" Beka enthuses. "They love you topless. They love when we tittered and pinked at the Nugget. And we're gonna get our own Pink Pages with us nude, hair dyed, and pulling pink in the Beauty Salon. Did you see how the hover Cams squealed about us? We're going get made even more explicit. Especially you, because you can't win Steph's Duel. Please Elle, I'll shave bare and bald too, I don't have much left anyway. And I'll pink with you anywhere anytime in front of anybody."

Elle trembles. *Beka scares me. She wants me to lose and she wants me to take her with me to the Nugget next Term.* Elle looks outward at the TV Crew, the paparazzi, and sees Robyn, *camming me now. They are stocking up on me because they all assume I'm a Stripper next Term. Naked, pink-wet-and-ready, climax on cue.*

Bodypaint Artist shoos Beka away, and carefully pulls Elle's waistline back up. The slacks will never rise enough to cover the left and right patches of blue hairage above the anterior waistline, nor the swells left and right of the rugage posterior. *And yes, they will be able to tell, that my cameltoe stays visibly damp, and with two kinds of stains.*

"See, you like this," Bodypaint Artist admires his subject. "You can't help yourself. The shooters adore you. May your cameltoe cream spread." Artist delights Elle with a dab of bodypaint to strengthen her clownish nose.

"You can give your slacks to Steph after you lose the Duel," Robyn chimes. "She's already got your worthless croptop."

Bodypaint Artist dismisses Elle, and Robyn shepherds her to a point in front of a wall where she can strike poses for a passing swarm of shooters, cam crews, and paparazzi.

Robyn hazes, "Tell me you like it; tell me you don't like it. I don't care."

§ Beka: Bodypaint & Brodeas

Bodypaint Artist loads Beka's green Mohawk and Hitler with a stiffening gel, but instead of being totally painted over like Elle, Bodypaint Artist paints green spots all over Beka's skin, including her navel and nips, which harden and indent immediately. Darker green lips, eyebrows, ears, and painted hands all are icing on the cake.

Beka's upside-down isosceles triangle micro g-string hides in Beka's boneroo and every telephoto and video Cam captures every pore of Beka's barren mons to the sides of her g-string. Hopefully aptly placed spots will obscure any clit trying to act out.

Robyn signs Beka to scratch her big toe, so Beka leans over, bends her knees, and shoves her bare booty up and invites Bodypaint Artist for one big brushful spot on each bonbon. Robyn signs Beka to spread her butt cheeks and shine sunlight onto where the g-string bifurcates her bronzo, and, further forward, where it digs into her slippery bare lips. Beka feels the brush swab into her anus before spotting her with green bodypaint up between her bonbons.

The attention excites Beka. She doesn't realize that her hands, like Elle's, are a darker shade and will leave traces of color wherever she touches herself. She checks out the only Garment she wears, and smoothes bodypaint mixed with her own brodeas over the micro g-string. Already the very bottom of the apex of the triangle shows finger paint marks.

Beka acquires confidence. *Elle has slacks over her crotch, but I've got a buried g-string! My overexposure overshadows my Roommate, and even though Elle's cameltoe appears sopping, I can hang broda down between my legs. I'm more popular, I'm more exposed, I'm more hot.*

The only reason Steph picked Elle instead of me is because she knows I'm part of the package.

Next thing Beka knows she's posing with Elle while Bodypaint Artist charts the next Cosmos Pledge. Both newbies have been warned to not touch themselves, least they mar Artist's craftwork. Beka compares herself to Elle, "I'm hairless except for my Mohawk and Hitler, and you got a trough and a butch, upstairs and down."

Elle appears distraught, "At least when I wore the croptop and ripped jeans shorts, or even the halter with the miniskirt, I had the illusion of modesty. Even if I had to titter and vagflash."

Beka affords comfort, "Yeah, okay, so now you really are totally topless in public. Steph's not gonna give you your top back. Your noogies are gonna stay uncovered and your areolas and nips are gonna stay publicly exposed. How come I didn't get stained?"

Elle oozes fresh wet into her cameltoe, "Beka, I don't have a chance. Steph's going to strip me stark naked and send me to the Nugget next Term."

Beka shrugs, "Yeah, well, look at me Elle. Two square inches of g-string. A micro is all I got, and I'm begging the one square inch nano size. And you can see my broda leak into my bodypaint. Just because we never really restricted our exposures doesn't mean we controlled our tease. Just please let me come to the Nugget with you, Elle! Roommates Together!"

"I haven't lost yet!" Elle snaps. "I'm only down one piece."

"You've been begging to Opt Strip since the first day we arrived," Beka argues. "Maybe you didn't mean it, but I did."

Paparazzi press in upon the two of them. Telephotos, flashes, cameras on sticks. This time Boss Babe backs the hoard off.

§ Kimju & Molly: Bodypainted & Stained & Greased

Molly finds herself being covered completely with a thick layer of red bodypaint. Special details are applied to her eyes and lips, her nipples and navel, and the Bodypaint Artist draws multiple circles of black paint around her pendulant breasts, her neck, legs, torsos, and arms. Bodypaint Artist insists Molly rub a thick grease, possibly Vaseline, into her red hair, armpit hair, and splayed muff. This especially thick layer helps matte down Molly's vulgarities but doesn't completely disguise them.

"Ugh," Molly completes, holding up her red greasy hands, and having no way to wipe them off. And then, as if to top off a cake, Bodypaint Artist sprinkles her with a coat of gaudy sparkles.

Unbeknownst to Molly, the bodypaint contains a red stain, so that long after her greasy bodypaint scrapes off the red stain will remain. It sets in as she stands.

Kimju gets a similar treatment, a thick coating of orange bodypaint over her entire body...*except* her areola and nipples. Kimju also gets her hands and feet covered, and like Molly, the bodypaint is followed with fistfuls of Vaseline Kimju must rub into her hair on her head, and then another two fistfuls to rub down inside her shorts. She too receives a lively coating of sparkles.

Kimju smiles for the shooters, but inside she worries. *I've been topless in public before, I've been naked in public before, I've been wallowed in the Mudpit; I don't care how much the paparazzi and Gamers masturbate me. But somehow or another I need a second piece in order to Opt Up next Term!*

Babs, much to the Pledge's astonishment, allows the Bodypaint Artist to draw a tribal pattern between her shoulder blades on her back.

§ Robyn: Gets Bodypainted Too...and Loses Her Straps

Suddenly the Bodypaint Artist decides to paint Robyn! Unexpected for sure, lured in by Babs, so that now Robyn finds herself in an impossible situation.

The Bodypaint Artist makes a suggestion, "Perhaps you might remove the shirt and miniskirt."

Robyn doesn't like what is coming. She rises up and gathers her thoughts, draws in air, prepares to speak.

Babs interjects before she can start to breath out, "Give them to me, my dear. I'll hold them."

"But but," Robyn tries to slow things down.

"Now!" Boss Babe speaks firmly. "Or you'll be giving me *everything*."

And so Robyn gives the vinyl croptop and miniskirt to BB to hold.

"Perhaps also the shoulder straps?" the Body Paint Artist advocates.

Robyn is not quite sure who she gives them to.

"Surrender position," BB commands firmly. Robyn does know how to form this.

Bodypaint Artist paints her yellow. Face, neck, arms and hands, chest and back above the maillot, feet, and all the legs up to the leglines of the maillot.

Robyn never learns just who pulls the back of her maillot up into the crack of her ass but she keeps her composure, which is a good thing. She can feel the body paint brushing on, getting swirled by a hand on her butt. "Yes," Robyn grits, "The Gamers choose to show off my bare ass; except it is not bare; it is covered with paint." Robyn farts.

The Bodypaint Artist steps back and surveys Robyn from an oblique, swabs a very thick blob of something into Robyn's navel, and turns to Babs, "Perhaps she wants to de roulè?" Experienced Gamers understand this question: should the top of the thin Spandex, now strapless, maillot be rolled down to render Robyn topless?

Babs does understand the question and elects to gently torment Robyn, "She can roll her maillot down into a tanga later on," she directs the words to the Bodypaint Artist, and then addresses all of her Pledge, "Right now we need to climb up onto the float. We're still all barefoot, remember. You get used to it, but this is still a street."

A policeman hurries over to where they are standing about to alight on the float; he hands a camera to a friend and the Cosmos crowd around him for a picture. It's good. Two more pictures with just him and Robyn follow, one front and one backside. They're good also. He splits. Robyn feels important again.

Robyn finds herself holding her clear vinyl. Awkward. She doesn't know whether to put it on over the body paint and muss it up, or to hold it, or put it down. But the bodypaint has pretty much dried, so she slips back into the clear vinyl shirt and miniskirt. And besides, it provides one more layer of protection for a more-or-less bare ass. And should discourage Bodypaint Artist from making any more suggestions that she roll down her maillot and bare her chest. *No thank you.*

Robyn regains her composure. Her shoulder straps seem to have become lost.

And she will never see them again.

§ Six Cosmos Ride Float: Rodney Bosses Peacock Mermen

And so parade they do. The six bodypainted Cosmos ascend a small float. The four dyed, bodypainted, and topless Pledge sit at the four corners. No handbra, no titty tease, legs ajar with thighs not touching. They shall wave to the Crowd with one arm or the other. Monitor Babs sits in the center of the float, two steps up from the corner positions. Robyn sits nearby BB, but one step below her. Robyn regains her composure. Her shoulder straps seem to have disappeared.

The float is pulled and pushed by a pod of six bare-chested mermen and a pod boss, whom the Cosmos recognize as the Peacock Pledge Rodney. It is the pod boss's task to command the Peacock Pledge float forward and maintain pace with the float. Rodney is dressed for the task: he wears a black muscle maillot tanga and boots.

The six bare-chested mermen have been stained dark purple, they cascade flowing phosphorescent hair, and wear cache'sex that contain their genitals but leaves their buttocks exposed. If indeed the mermen have sprayed-on rubber feet to protect their otherwise bare soles, Elle is still correct when she deduces, *one Garment each.*

Babs remembers the Peacocks from their naked, masturbating performance during the Greatest House Roar. Tiffany, were she to be here, would remember she popped the mermen on the very first day of *The Arrivals* while changing her shirt. Robyn proscribes them no importance and might she have observed them before she remembers it not. Steph, left behind in the Backyard, would certainly remember the Peacocks masturbating for her during the Greatest House Roar. Molly, perched on one corner of the float, and the winner at the Roar, also recognizes Rodney and the Peacock Pledge. Kimju recognizes Rodney from the Yacht and assumes that the mermen are Peacock Pledge. Like Molly, Kimju processes that Monitor William appears absent.

Beka and Elle have had their own encounters with Rodney, but fail to conject that the six bare-chested mermen are Peacocks.

Beka is instantly aroused by Rodney whereas Elle is disturbed by his appearance: Beka identifies Rodney as *the Pledge who cammed me and Steph sitting spread on the Front Steps, cammed me at the Corvettes, and cammed me collecting the thermoprobe in the Dining Room.*

Elle suspects, m*aybe I shined my asshole for Rodney when Beka and I worshiped the Baseboard Strippers at the Corvette House and maybe I didn't; I can live with that. But Beka is rushing headlong toward the Nugget, and I have to separate from her.*

Elle blinks. *Except that Steph has singled me out for her Duel. And she gets to pick the Game.*

If I lose, I do need to bring her along with me. So her rushing headlong might not be so bad. She can be like a buffer with the Nugget.

Beka and Elle drink in the spectacle not entirely cognizant of their surroundings. Three mermen pull the float with thick ropes; three mermen push from behind. Beka loves the attention and waves at block after block of spectators. Nobody tells her to open her legs so that the g-string buried in her sex lips pans past the Crowd; she just seizes the opportunity to display herself. The green dye, gessoed Mohawk and Hitler draw cheers from her side of the street; bodypaint obscures the liquidity between Beka's legs, and makes any hang ambiguous.

Elle bites her lip, waves, and when Robyn signs her to open her legs wider, Elle obeys, so that every passing angle now displays cameltoe. Elle looks around; Kimju and Molly now sit open-legged too, each with their own treats of hairage, buttage, and vagflash.

The Crowd feasts upon them. The telephotos detail their every pore.

Elle watches as cell phones catch her blue nubs, and her long now-blue belly button; Cams record her blue face, butched hair, and indelible indigo central dividing line.

As the float rolls forward many Cams document her cameltoe: contours of discolorment and crost around a wet spot tightly wedged into the bare nook beneath; the stretch fabric is so tight that it outlines the edge of the bright blue butched bush which erupts out of the top of her stretch slacks' waistband. Elle turns and looks behind and yes, *they collect the line coming up from the crack of my ass.* Elle looks out at the faces gliding by. *They all know. They know before I pass by. They know the dividing line has a break, and that my goal in life is to complete this line, whatever it takes. Didn't Robyn say so?*

Molly accepts her perch on the float corner. It provides her an opportunity to advance her concept of "the empowerment of body," while at the same time doing little more than holding a pose and waving. Still, one should not diminish the importance of empowerment: Molly's heavy and drooping milk sacks, her rolls of belly fat, maximum magnus, thick thighs are a romance of roundness. And to top it all off? Shaggy body hair everywhere that is dyed red: long red hair on the head, red pubic hair spilt both sides of the gashed panties, red armpit hair, red hair on the arms and legs and torso. Molly understands, *I'm getting cheers from everybody.*

Topless and orange Kimju also knows her power. *I can do this,* Kimju asserts. *I just don't want them to love me so much that I go back to the Nugget.*

§ Beka & Rodney: Flirt during the Mermaid Parade

Beka examines Rodney as he paces astride the float and keeps his six Peacock mermen pulling and pushing in stride. She contemplates how his body fits exceptionally well into his black muscle maillot tanga and boots.

Beka freshens. *This is the guy who cammed my pink boneroo on the Front Porch during* The Arrivals. *He cammed me hanging a bead at the Corvette House, and then cammed Elle lollying it up. He cammed my bunghole getting probed in the Dining Room with Steph.*

He's hot, he's already seen me naked and turned out, and today I want him to ooze for me!

Indeed, Rodney diverts attention from his crew and looks at Beka. Looks at her face. Now he falls into pace with the float so he can look directly into her open crotch.

Beka nervously adjusts the g-string so it lays atop her boneroo and not enfolded into it. Actually the patch, bodypaint, and brodeas are all one smear, with the patch slipping and sliding back into her bourse and stimulated her clit in new ways.

Beka makes eyes with Rodney, then looks for a wet spot on his maillot tanga. *My spot.* She glories in his appraisement. *He likes what he sees.*

There is a lot that Beka doesn't know about this attractive young man: This is Rodney's third Term in the Game: he has gone from Pledge to Stripper and returned to Pledge again, much wiser, but still jostled by the Game.

As a Stripper he had not only been required to work the "Chippendales Circuit," where he danced for the ladies, but also had been required to wag his wanker for men.

Beka's fascination with *this man who has Cammed me multiple times* overwhelms her and she squeezes enough fresh brodeas to hang a drip.

Rodney observes but controls himself.

Even although fraternizing is forbidden, Beka leans forward and down and yells a question to Rodney, "Where's your Cam today?"

Rodney shrugs. "I left it back at the Peacock House." He waves his arms at this crew. "I've got an entire pod to keep moving.

Beka nods and touches her nipples. The darker color on her hands and fingers leave a spot behind. Beka smiles. *Rodney likes what he sees!*

The din of the passing spectators fades into distant white noise.

Rodney's attraction excites Beka Broda. She has seen stills of him naked and bearing an immense erection, and secretly watched a masturbation video, in which Rodney strokes his meaty tool and ejaculates a big load. It had made her very, very horny, and at the time she had masturbated imagining sex with him.

Beka collects her spot. She smiles, leans back, and nods toward the fresh seep in Rodney's stretch fabric. Rodney inhales, touches his wetness, collects it on the outside of the fabric, and offers it upward so that Beka may kiss his fingertip.

Robyn, perched above, breaks it up.

Rodney breaks his pace and surveys his pod again; they continue to push and pull.

Beka casts eyes outward to see who else might have been watching. Spectators pan by, and for a moment Janet and Darleen crystalizes out of the mix, along with four delightful, delectably topless Corvettes with their nipples all painted white. *Just like us, us except for Kimju that is, because everything about her is painted orange except her areolas and nipples. Not much embarrasses Kimju, but this does.*

Kimju catches Beka looking at her totally exposed kronors and watching her knobs knurl up.

Beka glances at Elle, riding equally topless, catches her bare shoulder with her eyes, glides upward, meets Elle's eyes, and lip-shouts to her across the din, "Please Elle, ride the Dong with me, Elle, let's climax together while we can, because next Term we won't be allowed to. Now, Elle, before it's too late!"

The Parade comes to its end somewhere near where it started. Amidst the confusion of disembarking the float and the pod gathering its ropes, Beka finds herself bumping into Rodney. They make eyes and touch each other's torsos. The space around them collapses.

Like Beka, Rodney wears a costume that bares the ass: Beka's micro g-string barely covers her boneroo, Rodney's stretch maillot tanga tightly packs his equipment. And the both of them have shaven chests, shaven armpits, shaven legs, shaven pubes.

The sight of Rodney's freshly shaven body excites Beka, and when the opportunity to surreptitiously flirt with him presents itself, Beka transudes a blob of brodeas that spins down between her separated thighs. Rodney leaves a handprint on Beka's booty and Beka casually rubs her bare nipples against Rodney's arm, leaving marks. She gathers her hanging béchamel and deposits a blob just under his nose. The smell of her intoxicates him, and as she rubs her thigh against him she can feel him rock hard and obvious.

Beka doesn't consider if the Monitors might keep Rodney on an erector drug, so she thinks she deserves full credit for the hard bulge in his Spandex. He encourages her to touch him, and she gingerly traces his hardness, first with the back of her hand, and then pinches him through the cloth with a thumb and two fingers, then watches as a new spot of lube appears. Beka wants to touch Rodney's erected cock for real, and not just feel it through cloth. She presses a fingertip against the wet spot, swirls its scent into her nostrils, and licks her finger.

"We'll hook up," Rodney states. They disengage before anyone detects their engagement.

§ Babs Demands Beka & Elle: Beg Topless Roommates Together

Boss Babe herds the Cosmos Pledge into the Van.

Elle has reverted to a handbra; she asks, "Will I be getting my croptop back when we return to the Cosmos House?"

For a Monitor who has had a busy day BB responds politely, "Pledge are not supposed to ask questions."

Elle whines, "So am I allowed to hold handbra?"

"Question me twice, so you shall stay topless." Boss Babe speaks firmly now, "Ask me thrice and you shall be a Piss Mouth. Capisce?"

Elle doesn't quite know what to do with her hands. She lifts one then the other off her breasts then bounces up and down on her feet. She attempts compromise. "Ma'am forgive me Ma'am for asking about getting my top back, Ma'am."

"Thank me," Boss Babe orders.

"Ma'am, thank you for allowing me to run topless to the Nugget next Term," Elle pleads, somewhat ahead of herself.

Beka chimes in. "Me too. I'll cum on the Dong with Elle."

Boss Babe steps back and considers both newbies. "Both of you, stand spread surrender next to the Van. Face out."

Beka and Elle almost touch elbows. Elle feels the press of paparazzi held back by an invisible space delineated by BB and the three other Cosmos.

Maybe neither of us are getting our tops back, Elle realizes. *If we have one Garment each, we're both Strippers next Term. Except Steph still gets to play for my slacks. And she'll take them off of me.*

Robyn invites herself into the conversation and pokes Beka. "You've been touching yourselves," she laughs, "you've been touching your nipples!"

Indeed, the darker painted fingers have left marks. But not only are Beka's nipples indeed marked, so too is her neck, her belly, her booty.

Robyn looks at the palm prints on Elle's nick-nacks and mocks the newbie. "You're gonna be dancing at the Nugget for real. Your Fate is sealed. That vulturous Steph is gonna strip you, then shave you bare bald and naked! Ha ha ha ha."

Babs trades eyes with her Pledge, but says nothing.

Beka breaks in. "Robyn, please let me Pledge naked and cum be a Stripper next Term! I'll give my g-string to Elle and streak. I'll eat her out. I'll climax the Dong with her."

"Maybe you should share the Pee-Cam with her." Robyn advises.

Elle gasps.

Beka pulls her micro g-string taut, fingers her bare beaver, and rubs the g-string on her aroused clit. Beka casts her eyes past Robyn into the Cam of a TV crew. "I've seen the inside of the Nugget," she announces, "I've seen the Videos. I belong there! I want everyone to look. I want everyone to watch me!"

Elle keeps her hands behind her head, her armpits concave, and her legs open. *I know that my cameltoe contains several rings of stains. I'm topless from now on. And when Steph is done with me, I'm naked.*

Robyn signs the newbies to crawl into the back of the Van.

Outside the Van door Beka and Elle watch Robyn complain to Babs that her shoulder straps have gone missing. But when Robyn questions Babs about it, even addressing BB by her first name, Babs ignores her transgressions.

"Why," Beka whispers to Elle, "is the yellow-haired Redacted one totally inoculated from Pledge Rules?"

Elle realizes she may know the answer. "Maybe Robyn really does possess Charm, so she gets whatever she wants."

Topless orange Kimju and red Molly climb into the Van, sit, and spread their legs like Beka and Elle. One much-frayed jeans shorts, and one panties buried somewhere. Greasy orange and red hairage everywhere. The Vaseline swabbed into their hair and on their hands has migrated all over their bodies, and as they sit on the grimy floor the grease attracts still more grit, grime, and grout.

"I still need one piece," Kimju complains to Molly and points to the newbies, "whereas these two are down to one Garment each."

Molly looks at Beka and Elle. "Lucky you two; you've each still got once piece, so you won't have to streak to the Nugget.

Kimju nudges Elle, "Except, Steph will be taking your slacks before the end of the Term."

Kimju gestures to Beka in her topless g-string, "And you, Beka Broda you're going to join her. Roommates Together. You're both going to streak. Because you won't be giving Elle your g-string, you'll be giving *me* this last possession of yours. Game over for you two."

All their bodies accumulate grit from the Van floor during the ride home.

§ Elle: Worries Ahead

Elle worries during the ride back to the Cosmos House. Sand and grit work their way into the crack of her ass. *Beka and I are now both topless. I'm the blue mermaid. I'm not at all sure I will ever get my croptop back, and even if I do I suspect it will be little more than a ripped rag that gets discarded in the mud-lined Doghouse.*

Elle clenches her teeth. *But my shirt and bare tits are the least of my problems.* Elle sighs. *What if I have to climb into the Doghouse with Steph and ride the Double Dong together with her? I do not even get to pick the Duel. Steph does; her Option contains more power that picking a Flip-flop or a Winner-Takes-All. I helped put her in the Doghouse and if I loose...?*

Elle casts her eyes about the other Cosmos in the back of the Van. Beka plays with her nipples and appears Zoned.

Lose? Of course I'm going to lose. Elle reconciles. *I spent a night in the Doghouse once before, except it was mostly dry and I had not been slathered in thick mud before. Or pissed on. Steph will take me, force me to climax, and when that happens, I'm not going to just be shaven bare bald and naked and Opted to the Nugget. I'm going to be Zoned.*

II-36 Steph & William: Sneaks Out and Whoring (D25)

§ Steph Calls William: Plans a Risky Rendezvous

Steph, left alone in the Backyard, relishes her newfound freedom. Tiffany has gone to the Corvettes wagging the Dong in her tailpipe, and Babs and Robyn have taken the gussied-up gaggle of Four Topless Cosmos to the Mermaid Parade.

Steph washes up quickly. The water in the Watering Can is cold, and the rag-remnant of Elle's croptop combines as washcloth and towel. Steph considers how the Back Door Cam might be roaming the Backyard and camming her, and while scanning for it remembers, *Robyn took it with her to the Mermaid Parade.*

She sits on the back Landing, runs her fingers through stubble, and examines her pink insides. *It is nice to be alone without the Cam hovering all the time.*

Steph fails to consider the possibility that paparazzi still stalk.

She suspects that *leaving the Backyard is a no-no,* but with the Cam absent *my movements are not traceable by the Cosmos House.* She eyes the Back Door, decides to go inside, and considers whether to ring the Bell or not. She solves the latter problem by holding onto it while she rings, and thus dampens the sound. She slides through the Back Door, confident that *if someone were to discover this later I can come up with a good excuse for coming inside.* She takes the rag with her.

She bounds up the spiral case, quickly eyes the Bunkroom and Bathroom to assure they are empty, and pauses in front of Babs' Bedroom Door.

She enters, walks around behind BB's Desktop, and considers it from above, without touching. Yes, it is a touch sensitive Screen, and Steph knows that when logging in the Desktop sniffs the DNA of the toucher, and either allows access, or sound an alarm. Most certainly Automatron would record just who attempts to jump security.

However. *I was the Monitor last Term and I found out that once logged in, that the Desktop doesn't check the DNA again; it executes the click and will not sound an alarm.*

Steph does have something she wants enough to break the Rules.

Steph pushes a button or two and connects on the first ring: William, the handsome young man and the Monitor of the Peacock House, answers. She looks at him on the Desktop Screen, head and shoulders. William sees Steph bald and topless.

William was a Monitor last Term, just like Steph had been, and given the extra liberties that Monitors are afforded—like being able to travel outside—William and Steph had "gotten to know each other a bit."

William had chosen to Hover, which is why he is a Monitor again, whereas Steph had.... Well, Gamers know much of her story, her overconfidence and downward fall.

Steph had flirted with William on her way to the Bachelor Party during *The Arrivals*, teasing him with a strapoff and titter while wearing panties under her minidress. But the power had been very different on the last day of *The Arrivals*, when Steph and Beka offered up their assholes to a thermoprobe and a melting egg. Steph thinks about William being the one to cam her privates, and although she was not able to see him at the time, *the fact that he feasted upon me pleases me.*

William can't resist me. He watched me at the Greatest House Roar, four Days ago. He watched me get stripped naked. He watched me pink, cream, and climax. He watched me get rushed out the Front Door stark naked.

Steph tightens her confidence. *All his Pledge ejaculated watching me, and I'm sure he did too. I know he watches me because he knows how good I am. He wants his dick in me badly. I can feel it. He might be a Monitor but he knows he is not* my *Monitor, so he won't be launching me into the Zone. And besides:*

I have the power, the proxy, the Option to Duel. I'm Opting Monitor next Term. I shall control William.

"Nice tits," William greets Steph via the Screen. "Nice of you to call, even if you're not supposed to. I've been following your exploits."

"You're breaking the Rules talking to me. You should turn me in." Steph tweaks both nipples. She teases, "You're probably already masturbating to me with your hidden hand."

William rolls his lips. "You wish. So I gather you're bare bald and naked right now. Back off from the Desktop so I can see all of you. Hike your leg up and show *me* your snatch. Just like you do for the Prefecture."

Steph lifts a leg and pulls wide pink.

"The last time I saw you," the handsome man continues, "Molly stripped you naked at the Greatest House Roar. Then BB pinked, creamed, and climaxed you."

Bikini Bitch force-came me." Steph asserts, and flatters William, "I should have broken her to Stripper last Term."

"You are like an animal when you have sex," William observes.

"I imagined it was you fucking me," Steph flatters.

William advances, "I watched the feed of you and Molly piss climax in the Bathroom. I love the Nugget Stage when Tiffany lesbo-piss-climaxed you on the Double Dong. Then you got shaven bald by Penny and Coco and peed on by them. You're were hot, let me tell you. Talk about payback."

"I bet you masturbated to me!" Steph insists.

"You were so hot I a print made from one of the frames and ordered all my Pledge jerk off on it. They piled a lot of cum on that print of you. It's hanging somewhere."

Steph pauses, unsure if she is being complimented; she steels a reply. "I'm flattered," she says. She catches her breath and seeks to establish: "Okay, so at the Nugget, MomCap gave Tiffany's croptop and miniskirt to Robyn so that Tiffany could Game with me on Stage, and with both of us equally totally naked. Then Tiffany lezzes me and forces me to cum on the Dong. In the end, Tiffany won the Dong, although I won the Shaving Kit, except that Beka's carrying it now."

William smiles, "You got to shave bare bald and naked. Everyone watched your feeds. You're gonna be a Porn Star before you know it."

Steph snaps back. "No way. Because I got an Option to Duel! Any Pledge, any Game, my pick. I can't lose, and besides, it's my just due."

"Have you decided who to Duel with yet?" William asks.

"I have: Elle."

William affirms, "Good choice. You can take her."

"I know." Steph assures him, "BB let me pick her this morning, but I have to wait to pick the Duel."

"Hardly a contest," William smoothes. But then adds, "but I guess we all thought the same thing about your Winner-Take-All with Molly."

Steph straightens, "I guess the Gamers want me all the way down before they finally convey me my Opt Up. Robyn especially."

"So where is your Monitor Boss?" William inquires. He knows the correct answer.

No need to lie. "BB and Robyn took Kimju and Molly and Beka and Elle to the Mermaid Parade. They all left topless. Yesterday Madam Nurse Beautician dyed all the hair on their heads and their pussies rainbow colors. Eyebrows too."

"The last time I saw Beka and Elle they had tops," William recounts.

"Not since this morning. BB sent Tiffany over to the Corvettes today with the Dong wagging out her tailpipe and Beka loaned Tiffany her string micro halter so Tiffany would not have to streak. Janet's going to hook Tiffany up with that other former Whore. I know it." Steph talks fast.

"Ginny I suspect," William analyzes. "And she's not just a former Whore, she's a Whore-For-Life."

William curls, "So they left you all by yourself."

Steph agrees, "I just have to wait around until they show up. They'll be gone all day." Steph pauses.

"That's very interesting." William pauses to see if Steph is more forthcoming.

She is. "We could hook up," she says.

"You'll come visit me." It is a statement of fact, and almost a question, but it contains no inflection. William bides his position.

Steph stammers, "Well, okay, but yes, I can do that. Besides, there is a reason Elle is topless, because Babs made Elle leave her croptop with me."

"So you can go into combat as equals, one Garment each!" William declares.

"I might be bottomless but I'll be wearing something to get there. Robyn cut the croptop in half and cut the shoulder straps, but I'll tie it around me when come over," Steph offers.

William evaluates and dismisses Steph's coverage. "I think not. I want you to streak over and arrive naked. That turns me on. I'm worth taking the chance for. You do want a good fucking, yes?"

"I don't want to end up in Lockdown," Steph proclaims. "Been there, done that."

"You want to see me, you streak to me. No other option." William shifts. "Besides you have it easy, most everyone is at the Parade. Leave now."

"Well. Okay. Yes." Steph resigns and commits herself. "I leave soon."

William soothes. "Go pee in the Bathroom first, you qualify for the Cam," William orders, "besides, it justifies you coming upstairs."

Steph blinks. "You know I'm supposed to pee into the Watering Can, except there is no Cam in the Backyard.

William steers. "I'll be watching. Drain off one Measuring Cup of pee for the Pee-Cam, and save the rest for the Watering Can in the Backyard." William orders. "You know that making everything private about you public, arouses me."

Steph retorts, "You probably liked the feed of Molly and I cumming together and arching pee all over each other."

"I like the way you licked BB's feet off afterwards," William says. "That I did masturbate to, Piss Mouth."

"You don't deserve to fuck me," Steph snarls.

"You shall deposit your rag into the Watering Can while you visit me," William decrees.

Steph curls her nose, yet plays the Game. "Robyn took the Back Door Cam to the Mermaid Parade. So there isn't any way for you to watch."

"I'll dispatch a paparazzo to collect you!"

Steph cringes. She is not at all cool about having to streak to see William and dunking her rag into piss adds insult to injury. She attempts to deflect William, "Boss Bitch didn't tell me to pee."

William doesn't care. "Time to get creative. Besides, you are a Pee-Camer, yes?"

"It gets you aroused to mind-fuck me," Steph sasses.

"I shall fuck you every way possible!" William asserts, and disconnects.

So Steph has a date, and she has her Option. She exits the Desktop, draws her body up full, and tosses the rag aside as she marches into the Bathroom and she lights up the Bathroom Cam, bare bald and naked, of course.

Steph squats, gives the Cam a look meant for William, pinks and rolls her clit out for him, points her pee spigot toward the Measuring Cup, and haltingly fills the Cup. She empties the cup and writes "1" on the Logging Chart.

The prospect of surreptitiously sexing with William arouses Steph, so in a moment of passion she raises one leg to the Cam, pinks herself and scoops surge out of her socket box and mouths words to William, viewing her on the Cam feed. "Take that, motherfucker, I'm coming to get you!"

She bows, hurries out the Bathroom, gathers the rag in her hand, heads down the back stairs, and out the Back Door. Again she holds the Bell with one hand, and pulls the clapper to produce a most silent of rings.

Steph scans the outside, doesn't detect any telephoto lens, pees into the Watering Can, pauses and remembers William's directions, then tosses her rag into the Can, completes her urination, and stashes the Can in the Doghouse.

Steph considers the best way to streak to the Peacock House.

§ Steph: Streaks from Backyard to Peacock House

Steph makes her way to the Peacock House, despite the fact that she has an Option, and if she plays it wisely, a ticket to Opt Up. Or perhaps it is the Option that provides Steph the confidence to break a Rule.

Steph rationalizes, *I seek to raise the security of my position in this regard. I am anxious to get William's input on how to play my Option, and if this involves a little goodwill, so be it!* Steph streaks with stealth, it's not her first time, but she does not desire another encounter with the Rachmaninoffs... nor anyone else.

As a Monitor, William surely participates in what the Monitors think and what they decide. Steph remains bare bald and naked; she touches herself and discovers that her slash is slippery. Steph does not think of herself as secretly whoring herself up the ladder, but knows that others might be offended by her behavior should they find out.

But Steph's motives are not limited to whoring either. *I'm gonna fuck cock!* Steph anticipates. *I deserve some real cock, and William better please me and give my horny screwhole a satisfaction that Tiffany, the Dong, and my own fingers cannot.*

William will do nothing to correct her mythology that sucking his cock will somehow get her ahead. But does he thoughtfully consider the consequences in joining her conspiracy.

Steph keeps her thoughts to herself during her uneventful, sneaky streak to the far side of the School. *I know leaving the Cosmos House and Backyard is forbidden, especially with carnal intent, but since I have my Option I can get out of any complications.*

This may not be a correct assumption; an Option is not a Get-Out-Of-Jail-Free card, and might Steph gets caught she is will be in Lockdown. Not just bare bald and naked, but bound spread-eagle and sexed.

And not just a Stripper next Term.

§ Steph & William: Blowjob and Fucking and Anal

Prior to Steph's arrival William appropriates the Cam that Rodney has used to video various events: Tiffany popping the Peacock Pledge at the Peacock House at the beginning of the Term, Steph and Beka's probed assholes the last day of *The Arrivals*, the Pledge on the Yacht, and Molly and Steph's Greatest House Roar.

William had appropriated the Cam on the Yacht to record Ginny sucking his cock below decks, and now he secretes this Cam in his bedroom prior to Steph's arrival, so that its unblinking eye may quietly record all that transpires there. William figures that *if Steph tries to lean on me that I'll use the video to take her down.* William actually relishes the idea of blackmailing Steph into more sex.

Steph, seeking to augment her advancements never considers that the handsome William might be foolish enough to video an encounter that would incriminate him. She also assumes, *William won't tell anybody about my secret visit. He'd be confessing his own guilt; he's not allowed to screw Pledge! I got him!*

Steph arrives at the Peacock House before noon for her rendezvous. She arrives via the Front Door, ascends the stairs, and crosses through a secret passageway that leads through to William's private bath and then into his Bedroom. Steph senses William is the only Peacock present; indeed his seven Pledge have all gone to the Mermaid Parade where they push and pull a float decorated with the painted Cosmos.

William listens to the bare bald and naked Pledge's strategies for defeating Elle before pacifying her with his cock in her mouth. Steph sucks, and then William heaves her over onto her back, opens her smooth sloppy sex lips with his fingers, and fucks her snatch until Steph's body heaves in a prolonged climax.

Steph lavishes the feeling of a real cock in her pussy, and controlling her own lovemaking, rather than have BB decide how to force the cum out of her via her fingers or the Double Dong. But not all the lovemaking follows Steph's design. William lays her out onto her belly, presses her spooters into the mattress below, parts her butt checks, and penetrates her stern star from the backside. Steph screams as William wraps his hands around her bald head and pumps her. William ejaculates.

"Squeeze," he commands her, and Steph squeezes the creampie into William's fingers.

"Lick," he commands, and Steph cleans William's creampie off his fingers.

She opens her mouth to complain, and William shoves his dick all the way into her mouth. "Clean," he commands, and Steph cleans herself off William's dick.

Now he dumps a second, albeit smaller load, into her mouth. "Swallow," he orders, and Steph swallows.

"I told you I picked Elle, but how should I take her down?" A naked Steph tries to get a word in edgewise as she sits on William's bed afterwards.

The Peacock Monitor gives her a kiss of encouragement, but doesn't seem concerned enough to even bother to answer that question, "Beat it, outta here, streak back to your House. Here's a secret for you to not share: You've seen Elle's Measurement Nudes? Well rumor has it she gave Boss Bimbo a *Gonzo Video* as well. Toodaloo. I'd go the long way if I were you. That way no one will see you. You're gonna win. I'm sure of it. You come back afterwards, and I'll fuck you good again."

"Promise me." Steph demands.

And William promises, "You'll fuck me whenever I give you a chance."

Steph flees. She has to dodge a delivery truck on the way home, but it is no matter, she gets back safe and sound long before Tiffany or the others arrive.

§ William & Rodney: Share A Secret about Steph

But late that night, long after all the Peacocks have returned from the Mermaid Parade, and after they all have been put to bed, Rodney discovers the Cam in the Bedroom he shares with William. William reluctantly lets him in on his dirty little secret, and the Roommates screen the Steph and William *Suck Fuck Anal Video*.

Rodney watches with shock and awe as Steph reveals herself in a noisy coitus. Watching Steph get soundly fucked seriously arouses him, and makes him deeply jealous of his Roommate, especially after his flirtatious encounter with Beka at the Mermaid Parade. He can still smell Beka's scent under his nostrils.

But Rodney contains his feelings. "The one who really doesn't know about this—this video—is Steph herself," Rodney jockeys his Roommate and superior, and they both laugh.

"We can't show this to anybody!" William assures himself. They both laugh again.

"Except there is one person we can show it to," Rodney's thinks slyly.

"No way!" William's reaction is fast.

"We can show it to Steph." Rodney grabs his Monitor's arm, and they suddenly both guffaw together.

"She'll suck both our cocks after that," William agrees, but is circumspect, "but we'll just have to find the right time."

Ah, finding the right time to reveal a secret is always tricky.

II-37 The Cosmos: Evening After the Mermaid Parade (D25)

§ Tiffany Helps Steph: Coverts Rag to Bib Bottomless

Tiffany returns from the Corvette House to the Cosmos Backyard. The halter has been transmogrified into a bra, and like a halter, a bra bottomless counts for one Garment.

Tiffany discovers Steph_hunched on the Landing, resting her head on her rag. Steph may have washed her muddy body clean this afternoon, but her bare bald and naked figure still has streaks.

Tiffany does not consider that Steph made a bold excursion inside to Pee-Cam and log Measuring Cups, or that William had demanded that the paparazzi have a shot at her contributing to the Watering Can in the Backyard. Or a shot at her streaking to the Peacock House and back.

Steph assays Tiffany's costume. "You left wearing Beka's micro halter and you come back wearing a bra?" Steph queries.

Tiffany breezes, "I gained an edge, but a bra bottomless is still counts as one Garment, just like the halter."

Steph frowns and interrogates. "So where is the Double Dong?"

"Ah!" Tiffany takes a deep breath. "I regret to inform you that I had to leave it behind. Last seen wagging in Ginny's asshole, at the Corvette House."

"I've had enough of the Dong," Steph states. "I need to keep my senses and crush Elle." Steph squeezes her rag. "This still counts as one piece and her pants will make two."

Tiffany purses her lips. "Maybe a rag isn't a Garment anymore. It's not something you're wearing. Maybe it's a prop and you're naked right now?"

Steph scowls. "Be nice to me, you tawdry tailpipe peddler, because I ended up with the Duel and I'm a Monitor next Term."

Steph adjust the rag so it hangs in front of her. "Tie it behind my neck," she orders, and Tiffany deftly fits the rag and ties a knot behind Steph's neck.

A rag tied around the neck is not much of a Garment, except, "Let's call that a bib," Tiffany suggests, "maybe you can trade it for a collar, but you are right, Ma'am, that this way you definitely are *wearing* a Garment."

Tiffany gathers, "Now we are both bottomless! And although we can't dong together right now, any time you want to go oral, I'm pink wet and ready to rock."

Steph frowns and talks, "Upstairs, Tiffany Transparent. Settle yourself in your bunk. You don't live in Bimbo Bitch's Bedroom any more.

And with this Tiffany bows, rings the Bell, and disappears in the Back Door.

§ Robyn, Kimju & Molly, Beka & Elle: Greet Steph after Parade

Robyn returns from the Mermaid Parade with Four Topless Cosmos and the Back Door Cam in tow. Kimju and Molly and Beka and Elle remain topless, filthy with streaked bodypaint, with sand and grit in their hair and butt cracks, and with stale sweat from being in sunlight too long. Even Monitor Babs seems fatigued.

Robyn continues to wear her clear vinyl atop yellow bodypaint and her maillot cutout that still remains strapless. Greasy orange Kimju wears the remnants of the jeans shorts, now little more than a waistband, zipper, a seam through the crotch, and pockets hanging out. Greasy red Molly's panties bury themselves in her mutton, splay her red-dyed muff and hide nothing. Caked green Beka's micro-g can't hide shaven pussy lips and her Hitler; and caked blue Elle, with her deep blue dividing line remains topless with divided hairage and a crackin' above her low-riders.

They encounter a bare bald and bottomless Steph sitting under the Bell.

"Look at you!" Robyn hoots, "Bib bottomless. Who did this to you?"

Steph squints. "You did, Robyn Redacted. You cut the croptop off Elle and gave it to me as a rag. Tiffany figured out how to turn it into a bib."

"Can't say it covers your spooters or slit, slut," Robyn opines. "So are you boobage or topless? Cause you are way past a titter or two."

Steph retorts. "I'm full-frontal, rag face. It's too bad I already Optioned Elle, because next time I'll Option you."

Robyn points to Kimju, Molly and Beka. "Upstairs! Go directly to your bunks! No Bathroom! No showers!"

So Three Topless Cosmos ring the Bell and pass through the Back Door. It will be a crumbly night for them upstairs in the Bunkroom.

Robyn points to Elle and Steph. "You two stay. One of you is going to ring the Bell and head inside, and the other shall move into the Doghouse.

But only after I'm done with you two!"

§ Tiffany Gives to Kimju: Beka's Halter Turned into a Bra

Upstairs the three Cosmos Pledge—Kimju, Molly, and Beka—discover Tiffany ensconced in her bunk. Tiffany is naked, her hair will continue to remain dyed purple, but she is not crumbly with dried bodypaint.

Kimju climbs into her bunk to discover a bra tossed there.

"What's this?" Kimju rolls on her side and holds the bra up.

Tiffany acknowledges. "Don't ask me why but Janet converted the halter into a bra. I borrowed it, so I'm returning it."

Beka chimes in. "Wait a minute. I'm the one who loaned you the halter. So *I* should get the bra back!"

"I guess I left it on the wrong bunk," Tiffany acknowledges.

"I'm keeping it," Kimju says.

Beka looks for Elle, but Elle is still in the Backyard. *Or someplace.*

Kimju leans out of her bunk. "Besides, Beka, you don't even want this. You want to Opt Stripper with Elle, remember. You need to have only one piece."

Beka hesistates. "Well, okay, I guess." She settles down in her bunk.

No regrets. Greasy orange Kimju dons the bra; it complements her ripped jeans shorts. *Two pieces, she thinks, sort of like what Beka once wore.*

§ Robyn Torments Steph & Elle: About the Upcoming Duel

Robyn still wears the transparent croptop and miniskirt over her now-strapless maillot cutout, still with golden hair and a vestige of yellow bodypaint.

"Stand spread surrender," she commands two remaining Pledge in the Backyard. "Face each other. Stay."

Steph and Elle obey, somewhat uncertainly. *I thought Steph was supposed to pick a Duel with me?* Elle considers. *Except Robyn's in charge.*

Patience please. After all, it takes days for Elle's hickeys to fade.

Robyn disappears in the Back Door; she doesn't bother to ring the Bell. Steph stands bare bald and naked; Elle stands topless in low-rise slacks. *Hairage, rugage, I can't stop it.*

Elle takes stock of her situation. *I was outted at the Mermaid Parade. Shucks, I was outted at the Nugget, and here I am facing Steph.* Elle purses her lips. *This is the moment that Steph is going to pull a Game on me. She does not intend to return my croptop, and until and unless I win it back from her in the Duel I will remain totally topless from now on. 24x7.*

Except I'm not going to win it back. I'm going to lose, give Steph my slacks, masturbate in the Mudpit naked, and she is going to zone me.

Then move me into the Doghouse for the rest of this Term and
Then streak me to the Nugget so I can become a Stripper next Term.

Elle releases a tiny drop of pee into her cameltoe.

And yes, I really need Beka with me this time.

Robyn's "standing spread surrender" command had not included an "oval mouth," so Steph seizes upon this opportunity to give the butched blue-haired competitor she faces some haze. Steph does not whisper, and the Cam incorporates the sound with the picture.

"I've seen your nude spreads from the Beauty Salon," Steph drawls and slightly lifts her chin. "Everyone has. Nice nest, creamy nakodo flowing out of your nockandro." Steph surveys her victim, and practices voodoo, "Gamers love how you brought in your Measurement Nudes. And not just for yourself, for your Roommate too!"

Elle does not appreciate an old sore being reopened. She gawks.

"Did you bring Babs anything else of your past work?" Steph needles.

Elle startles and lies, "Absolutely not!"

Steph asks Elle another leading question in that friendly but pushy manner of hers, "So when are you going to become a Pee-Cam Pledge?"

Elle recoils. She pivots around her waist, leans back, and opens her mouth to talk….

But Steph get words in first, "I've already done my naked squirts. All the other Cosmos Pledge have drained on the Cam. All but you… and Robyn, of course." Steph nods toward the Back Door.

Elle offers diplomacy, "Of course. And except Babs."

"Babs isn't a Pledge," Steph says.

Elle peddles. "It is one thing to be observed while peeing in the privacy of the Bathroom, it's a sacrifice to pee for the Bathroom Cam, but it's capitalistic to pee on Stage at the Nugget."

Steph enriches, "And it's public domain to pee in the Backyard where any stranger can watch. Isn't it Elle?"

Elle counters, "Just because you're a Pee-Camer, Steph, doesn't mean that everyone wants to pee anywhere, anytime, in front of anybody. I'm surprised you're not a Piss Mouth already!"

Steph agrees, "Be careful what you wish for, Elle Lollydor, because when I am done with you you won't be just naked, you'll be taking on all my Obeisance. You'll be filling the Measuring Cup for the Bathroom Pee Cam, and pointing your nozzle into the Watering Can in the Backyard."

Elle scowls. *Yes, unless I defeat Steph in the forthcoming Option Duel, I will for sure be a Pee-Camer. I won't just be peeing for the Back Door Cam, every Cam is going to want me.*

Steph augments torment. "One more thing, Elle Lollydor. Just before I crush you for good, I'm going to taste my pee on the tip of my tongue. Since you're taking my Obeisances with you to the Nugget, you will be able to toss shots center Stage all next Term."

Elle begs, "Really, Steph, you don't need to do that." She rolls her tongue against the inside of her lower lip. *No. There is no way I will take on a Piss Mouth!*

A pang of fear strikes Elle and she deposits a spot of pee to complement the other stains in her cameltoe.

Steph spots the transgression immediately and looks downward. "Oooh, Pledge Elle adds pee-pee into her pants. You're already a Pee-Camer, and the only person who doesn't know it is you!"

Robyn returns, stealthily and absent ringing the Bell.

Elle squirms in a body that shape-shifts. The bodypaint has dried on her skin and is crumbling. She carefully runs her fingers, held behind her head in surrender position, into the back of the notch running through her hair. Elle finds the notch especially disconcerting; she fiddles with it and runs her finger up and down over the strip of bare scalp. *A trench between butched halves.* She looks down at her body and sees the indelible dividing line, the stained nipples and navel, the divided blue hairage.

Robyn observes. "You need to beg your Roommate to share the Shaving Kit with you, Elle Lollydor. Then you can shave *all* your hair, just like Steph Sorostitute here.

"Ma'am, if you please—" Elle begins.

"Beg for it, you needy nizzy notch girl," Robyn commands.

Elle sees a ray of hope to avoid Stripping next Term. She begs, "Ma'am, please let me shave myself bare and bald and naked...," She pauses, eyes bore into her and she advances, "...and cum be a Stripper next Term."

It's hopeless.

Robyn rides a wave, "Both of you beg."

Maybe not after all, and so Elle stares into Steph's eyes and reads the hesitation. Catches the twitch of Steph's lips, and so Elle begins anyway, "Please let me Pledge..." and Steph joins in and their lips form the words together "bare bald and naked and cum be a Stripper next Term."

Elle watches Steph fidget but holds position. She holds position too, becomes aware of the Cam surveying her topless chest, and her nipples erect. Once again she dampens her cameltoe, although absent a sensor, Automatron can't make a definitive determination if it is pee or noble secretions.

Elle watches the Cam collect Steph's nipples; they are hard too.

Elle has yet to grasp that the deep blue stripe that bifurcates her body uses indelible ink. When, if, she ever gets permission to wash the crumbling bodypaint off, she will discover that her hair stays dyed, that the indigo stripe remains, and that the dark purple-blue stain continues to sink deep into her lips, nipples, and belly button. *Steph's going to make me roll my pants down and stain me inside my nookie.*

"Want your shirt back?" Robyn asks Elle.

"Ma'am, yes, Ma'am," Elle brightens. Elle considers. *Recovering the repaired rag that bottomless Steph wears would confirm me with two Garments!*

"Pink the Cam," Robyn commands, "both of you Stripper wannabes."

Steph obeys instantly. Bib bottomless qualifies as full-frontal; Steph draws her hands down to sex, stays standing and spread, and opens her inner lips with opposing fingers and thumbs.

Elle, topless with slacks, becomes confused.

"If you roll your pants down you can pink too, you newbie numskull nitwit," Robyn advises.

Elle looks at Steph, then closes her eyes as she gathers her legs together, and works the slacks down below her pubis and buttocks.

Robyn gloats, "Roll 'em down to your ankles, you neophyte niche nockandro!"

Elle obeys. She rolls her pants down and hobbles her ankles, parks her knees as wide as she can, and pinks the Back Door Cam. They stand side by side at this moment. *We are pinking the entire Prefecture.*

"Turn around, bend over, pink, and show off your assholes," Robyn orders.

They do. Naked Steph shoots fire out of her eyes but obeys cautiously. Elle discovers she must keep her knees apart, reach around and part her naches, and pulls shallow pink.

"On your knees and put your faces in the dirt, you worthless Cosmos Pledge," Robyn directs, "but keep your hands between your legs a-pullin' your pink!"

Steph and Elle adjust their postures; Elle closes one eye as she rests one cheek on the ground. *I know what this is. Gorean Submission Position.*

Robyn needles Elle in particular. "You should be delighted you're allowed to spread and show off all your bottom blue butch and that blue dividing line through your trough. You can air dry your nookie."

Robyn fingers Elle's private parts, "But look at you! Your dividing line between your nitro button and your nadir needs completion. So beg me to stain across your naughty parts. Talk dirty, you noxious naïve nabob."

Elle begs, "Ma'am, please complete the indigo line across my nookie. You can paint my nib and pee-hole, swab inside my nockandro. You can paint me wherever you want, Ma'am."

"Freshen up," Robyn commands.

Steph, stark naked but not Zoned at the moment, remains balanced between reality and a state of high sexual excitement. She obeys Robyn's orders and drift fingers to touch her stamen, then fingers inside her satchel. Plenty wet. The physical smoothness of her satchel flaps arouses her, and slippery surge slides from her smooth slit. Indeed, Elle nearby can smell the fragrance of Steph's white secretion, and they trade eyes.

Steph surges again, but this time the arousal comes not from the feel of her smooth skin, but from a conclusion: *I am going to be shaving Elle very soon. She's going to be bare bald and naked, and she will service me with her mouth.*

The eyes of the victim and the predator meet again and Elle flinches.

Steph might have picked her victim, and she might be out of the Zone, but she remains insatiably horny, still bathing in afterglow. *My fucking with William today leaves a sensation inside my snitz that stays with me still.*

But Steph also feels ambivalent about her tryst. *William abused my asshole today,* she confides to herself. *Then he put himself in my mouth. That was just a power play, but it also demonstrates that I'm hot.*

Like Steph, Elle continues to rub a cheek in the dirt and arch a butt up in the air. Elle doesn't know what to do. *I'm loosing control. If Steph challenges me to ooze nectar, I'm going to lose. She's going to force-cream me masturbating my Post.* Elle blinks. *I'm going to lose a lot more than the Duel.*

I need to beg Robyn to finish my dividing line across my nookie. I need to get wet and hang a streamer out of me!

Robyn turns her attention to Steph. "Thank me for training Elle so you can control her," Robyn snides at Steph.

Steph grits her teeth. "Ma'am, thank you for preparing Elle for me, Ma'am." She curls, "I'll be giving her a thrill just as soon as Monitor Babs permits it."

§ Babs Returns & Greets Robyn: Steph & Elle's Assignments

Indeed, that could be right now, as Babs returns, done with putting the Van away, and still wearing her minidress over a bra and nombril lingerie.

"My, my," Robyn says, and surveys the two Submission Position Cosmos Pledge. She kicks Steph, "Look who has arrived. Time to pick a Game, any Game."

"Time to be still," BB orders and lifts Steph's chin with the top of her foot. "I see you visited the Bathroom and peed today. I don't recall suggesting you come inside to. Was it I who suggested for you pee into the Watering Can?"

Steph nods her head. "Ma'am, Robyn took the Cam today, so there was no way to document me in the Backyard. So I drained one Cup in the Bathroom, and logged my commitment to the Pee-Cam. Then I returned to the Backyard and peed in the Watering Can. You can see."

"If you drink it you can confirm a Piss Mouth!" Robyn snides.

"Are the others safely upstairs?" Monitor Babs inquires of Robyn.

"All present and accounted for!" Robyn declares. "I sent them to their bunks without a shower. They will have a crunchy night of it as the bodypaint flakes off.

"And these two both want to spend more time in the Doghouse," Robyn proposes.

"Lucky Pledge." Boss Babe considers, and asks them a question, "But if I had to look it up, which of you has spent *more* time there?"

Steph and Elle look at each other. They both know the correct answer.

"Steph."

"Me."

Boss Babe nods to Steph, "Since you want to play a Game you don't want to lose may I suggest you return to the Doghouse. That way you can increase your lead.

Steph starts to speak, "But even if Elle—"

Boss Babe snaps, "Shut up. Obey. Crawl, squirm on your belly. Into the Doghouse. Now!"

Steph finds no contradiction in BB's command, she knows the Cam watches, so she lifts her face out of the dirt, pulls her elbows back, and crawls to the Doghouse. *Tonight will be my third night in a row. Will I be forced into the Zone, and cruise there until exhausted? My challenge will be in the morning. I'll need to come out of the Zone, and collect my Option. Or will I be too lost to know the difference?*

Elle rises but questions. "Wait. Don't I get my croptop back?"

Robyn snaps, "Shut up. Upstairs and into your bunk. Now!

Elle hesistates about what to do with her slacks, rolled down to her ankles at the moment and hobbling her. She catches a wry smile on BB's lips, rolls the slacks up just above the knee, yanks the Bell cord and displays gorgeous nachas as she ascends to the Landing, and swirls her butt as she disappears through the door, unintentionally, unavoidably, and soon unnaively.

Babs rings the Bell and Robyn follows her and Elle in the Back Door. BB really doesn't know the whole truth about Steph's adventures today.

Not even Steph knows the whole story!

§ Beka & Elle: Consequences of the Upcoming Duel

After dark Beka and Elle whisper between over-and-under bunks. They discuss the events of the Parade and the consequence of Elle's upcoming Duel. Beka constantly masturbates herself. Elle frets nervously.

"I got exposed topless today," Elle understates. "In public. I didn't sign up for this." Elle whispers to Beka. "Everyone looked at me. Everyone cammed. I don't think I can go on like this. Next Steph intends to strip me naked and streak me off to the Nugget."

Beka flaps a wrist, "Relax, will you. This is nothing. Hey' haven't we both been to a topless beach before? Gone skinny-dipping at night? Worn transparent tops at a Fashion Show?"

Elle chagrins, "You wore the transparent top. I was totally topless." \

Beka defends. "Yeah, Elle, except my skirt was also transparent. You wore slacks."

"I'm not sure I'm getting my top back from Steph," Elle worries.

Beka waves her arms, "It's gone Elle, just like Tiffany took my halter. We're both topless 24x7 from now on.

"So we're both wearing one Garment now," Elle tests. "So we are like equals right now."

Beka shrugs, "Well, if you say so. Because today all I got is a micro g-string." Beka offers optimism, "I got my picture taken a whole lot. A lot Gamers watched me."

"Tomorrow I'm supposed to shave myself except for my Mohawk and Hitler," Beka whispers, "but after Steph shaves you bare bald and naked I want to be just like you! We can sit and rub our bare pussies together and cum on the Dong."

Elle retreats.

"I should never have let you talk me into playing the Game," Elle declares.

Beka confesses, "I know. But you gotta admit you kinda like it."

Elle scowls, "You like it more than I do. I thought we'd have a lot more control over things."

Beka sort of agrees, "Well, I did think I would be allowed to cum."

Elle voices an opinion, "You and I don't cum for the opposite reasons: You don't cum because the Gamers won't let you. You're horny all the time and the Gamers control you by holding you back. I don't cum... well you know I can't get off by myself. So they expose me even more; I'm shamed to the point where they've got me horny and wet."

Beka kisses Elle's cheek, touches her neck, and sympathizes, "I know Elle, you've always needed someone to take you over the top. Please don't worry, Elle, I'll ride the Dong with you. I promise."

Steph Denudes Elle: Mansion Open House (D26-D27)

II-38 The Cosmos: The Day After the Mermaid Parade (D26)

§ Robyn Hazes Five Cosmos: And Babs Inspects to Bunkroom

Morning of Day 26 arrives and Robyn rousts Five Cosmos from their bunks. "Lineup!" she commands, so Tiffany and Kimju and Molly and Beka and Elle put their hands behind their heads, spread their legs wide, and set themselves into a formal stand-spread-surrender position facing the Minxy Mirror. All without being instructed to.

The Five Cosmos see themselves reflected in the Minxy, and they see each other. But they do not see Robyn, although they can hear her walking behind them.

Some assume Robyn still wears a clear vinyl croptop and miniskirt over top her now strapless maillot cutout, with golden hair, golden painted nails, and golden lipstick.

All Cosmos know exactly who "has the smallest buttonhole." They surmise Babs remains in her Bedroom, although she might have glided down the stairs. And have not heard from Steph since was ordered, bare bald and bibbed, into the filthy, cramped, stinky, muddy Doghouse last night.

"Good little girls," Robyn praises. "Beg for me."

And they do. "Please let me Pledge naked and cum be a Stripper next Term!"

Robyn, having moved into the bunk underneath Babs' bed, has availed herself of Babs' private shower. She has taken it upon herself to use the Makeup Case without Tiffany's guidance and do her own makeup. Besides, it's mine now.

Now that she wears three Garments, Robyn assures herself of a Double Opt Up promotion and a Caste of House Mom el Capitan next Term.

Robyn assumes, *Me MomCap now!*

Robyn surveys the Lineup from behind it. She can see the Pledge in the Minxy, feels cheated she can't see herself in the Mirror. Still, she twists a lip as she digests that the Pledge can't see her either. *They don't deserve to see me,* Robyn projects.

Only Tiffany stands naked. Aside from an interlude when she delivered the Dong to the Corvette House, Tiffany has been naked 24x7 ever since she gave her transparencies to Robyn, two days ago at the Nugget.

Now that Tiffany is Kimju's Roommate, and with Robyn absent in the Lineup, Tiffany still stands at the head end of the Lineup, with Kimju next to her. Tiffany, having spend yesterday double donging with Ginny at Janet's Corvette House, did not participate in the Mermaid Parade. She still has purple hair on her head and her pussy, but she never got any crumbly bodypaint.

Elle stands at the other end of the Lineup, and next to her, Beka. Beka presents topless and micro g-stringed, and Elle presents topless with low-riding stretch pants, hairaged, rugaged, and cameltoed. The hair on their heads and their pussies remain bright green and blue. Both still possess traces of bodypaint; they slept its crumble overnight and ground bits of crumble into every inch of exposed skin, from their faces to the soles of their feet. Both relish a shower.

But Beka and Elle know they have it easy. Molly stands between Beka and Kimju, Steph being absent from the Lineup. Orange Kimju appears to be respectably attired in a bra and shorts; red Molly stays topless with her panties yanked into her mooe and moonshadow.

Like Beka and Elle, the two ex-Strippers are also dusty with crumbling bodypaint, except both retain an overlay of grease that saturates their hair and hands. Grease that has spread, and which packs larger crumble into it. Very uncomfortable.

Elle knows there is one Pledge missing: *Steph, who before the Mermaid Parade yesterday morning declared that I would be the one who would Duel with her. I loaned my croptop only to have it reduced to a bib, and not even offered back. Once I lose her Game, I'll have to give her my slacks and it's over.*

Correct. Right now Elle's nemesis resides in the Doghouse. *I spent a night in the Doghouse once,* Elle recalls. *But Steph has already spent too many nights for me to catch up before the end of the Term at Midnight, because it's the day after tomorrow.*

Boss Babe did define a Game, and right at this moment she emerges from her Bedroom, sidles into the Bunkroom, and surveys the Lineup, first via the Minxy Mirror and then directly. BB's shortsleeve dress covers all her cleavage and extends down to her kneecaps. Of course Babs bares her button, and Gamers adore her for it!

Babs signs Tiffany to the Bathroom; Tiffany, appreciative of the gesture, hustles. Being already naked she need not doff anything to enter the Bathroom and activate the Cam. She will shower, shave her armpits and legs, and measure her urine for the Pee-Cam.

Kimju considers registering an appeal about having to sleep in her grime and grease, but recalls visions of Steph in the muddy Doghouse. *Life can get a* lot *worse. I might be dirty and itch, but I have the two pieces I need to Opt Up.* Kimju bites her tongue. Physically.

Molly finds the grit in her panties especially annoying; like Kimju she has spent a fitful night, and now, standing spread surrender in the Lineup, the bedraggled Cosmos, itchy with dirt, begs her Monitor, "Ma'am please may I wash my panties out. Health reasons, Ma'am."

Boss Babe examines the red Cosmos who presents herself. Hairy arms, hairy legs, hairy red armpits. Red hair, red muff spilling out, red eyebrows.

"If I can wash my panties out I won't leave a mark when I sit down," Molly proposes.

" Nice of you to consider the furniture," BB finally retorts. "So just stay on your feet." Babs doesn't want to hear more, but Molly whines, compounded by a long night. "Ma'am, please I don't need to get germs!"

BB responds with cool consideration, "Okay. Have it your own way. Strip naked, like you beg to."

Molly grimaces, closes her eyes, gathers her legs together, and rolls the wet panties off. They are stained with bodypaint, grease, dirt and crosting. Molly stands and holds them stupidly. *I asked for this,* she admits to herself. *But staying clean is very important. But if I have to give my panties away, I'll be streaking to the Nugget next Term, instead of going there topless.*

Robyn interrupts and issues a directive, "Now stuff 'em in your mouth so we don't have to listen to your suggestions, you wannabe meatwagon moneybox moll."

Molly steps aback, looks at Boss Babe… and obeys. She feels relief as she pushes the panties into her mouth. *At least I am keeping them!*

"Keep yourself stuffed," Robyn adds. "If you get hungry you can beg a feeding tube through your nose." Robyn laughs. "Ha ha ha ha!"

And cackles, "Or you can beg for rectal feeding." And cackles again.

Molly consoles herself. *However long I keep in the panty gag I won't be begging to give it away. Nor getting my mooe infected!* Molly looks at herself in the full-wall mirror. She sees a fat Cosmos with saggy mammies, greasy red hair and muff, stained red skin, and her cheeks bulging out. *Just me and my panties now,* Molly examines herself, *even if I just added sand, grit, and panty pudding into my diet.*

Robyn commands Molly: "Go down to Post Henge in the Backyard, embrace your Post, and masturbate yourself into the Zone."

Molly moves. Before she waddles down the back stairs she is reciting inside her head, *Please let me Pledge bare bald and naked, stay pink-wet-and-ready and zoned, eat pussy and juice the Dong, and cum be a Stripper next Term!* The panty gag will sop and swell, but no matter how much it hurts her jaw and irritates, Molly holds onto her goal. *It doesn't matter if they think I am naked when they watch me from over the fence. I'm heading to the Nugget next Term, and I won't have to streak to get there.*

An apparently naked Molly masturbates her Post and Zones. Publically, Molly admits, publically.

Monitor Babs retreats to her Bedroom.

In the Bunkroom, Robyn addresses Kimju. "Finally you acquire two Garments, and you have no one to give them to! How sad. Too bad, Roommate, I have no use for you. So haul your keister down to the Doghouse, tell Steph to report up here at once, and wait inside."

Kimju takes her hands off the back of her head for a moment, then returns them. "I'm to wait for you in the Doghouse?" she asks.

"Ah, questioning details!" Robyn preens. "So wallow around in the Mudpit real good, empty the Watering Can into the Doghouse, climb in, and make yourself at home."

"Ma'am, thank you, "Ma'am," Kimju steadies.

"Thank you, MomCap," Robyn directs.

"MomCap, thank you, MomCap," Kimju balances.

"Might you decide to toss your clothes out, you can thank me when it comes time to streak to the Nugget."

Kimju responds. "Ma'am, may I please emerge from the Doghouse as a Monitor next Term. I will serve your every need. I will eat your pussy. You can pee on me. Please let me serve you, MomCap."

"You shall drink my piss!" Robyn projects and waves a hand, and Kimju heads down the back stairs.

Beka and Elle still stand spread surrender facing the Bunkroom Mirror, except that the Minxy reflects Elle's body in oily blacks and her dividing line with an electric glow that splits her face and body left and right. *Am I radioactive?*

Elle scans herself downward in the Mirror, starting at the top of her head where the strip descends from the trough of missing hair. *Down my forehead, my nose, across my lips, chin, down my neck, xiphoid and sternum, down my breast bone in between my bare noogs, down my belly and in and out of my button, down the shaved path notched out of my pussy hair, and then (inside my pants) across my nib, then jumping to my nadir gate, up my crack, erupting up from the center of my posterior rugage and across the lozenge of Michaelis up in between my sacral dimples, up my spine, in between my shoulder blades and then up my neck again, and then through the trench coming forward over the top of my head.*

No, the indelible indigo stripe that divides Elle left and right won't wash off. Somehow the Minxy knows how to make it radiate.

Robyn singles out Elle to haze: "In case you don't know, you nutty nuzzy nimwit, an Option Duel is Winner-Takes-All with a lock-in on the outcome; it is not a Roommate Game, it is not a Flip-Flop, it a final solution."

Elle spots urine into her cameltoe. *I know that.*

"Too bad for Elle Lollydor," Robyn mocks, and flits Elle under her nose. "You don't have a chance! Your every private moment shall be cammed. You're gonna lose and once you lose you're going to stay lost. Maybe after your Term at the Nugget, you can convince the Gamers to let you work a notch house for a Term or two, maybe then you'll start rising. Or maybe you just can't wait to become Slavesex."

Elle shudders. *This is not how I want to think about things.*

"You'll be all in, just like Steph. No second chances for you!"

Beka interjects, "Please Robyn, I need to Opt with Elle next Term. We'll climax the Dong, we'll Pee-Cam, we'll streak together!"

Robyn rolls a shoulder. "Sounds like a plan."

§ Robyn & Steph Haze Beka & Elle: Beg Bare Bald & Naked

Beka and Elle do not see or hear Steph approach from behind them, and, like Robyn who stands behind them, they do not see her reflected in the Minxy Mirror. Elle jumps when she suddenly hears Steph's voice in her ear. "Good morning, Stripper wannabe."

Steph saunters in front of the newbies and leans into Elle. "Aren't you special! You're going to learn how to pull your slacks down and show off your naka-nake trench and your nasty puckered nadir. You're going to learn to take off your clothes one at a time, then play with your nips and nookie at the same time."

Both newbies study Steph. Elle in particular considers *this is the Pledge I shall succumb to, Steph.* Steph remains bare bald and would be naked were it not be for a slender but round metal collar curving around her neck. Full-frontal? Absolutely, with three days of stubble on her otherwise bald head, eyebrows, armpits, satchel, and legs. Also totally dusty, dirty, and covered with grime from her stint in the Doghouse.

Steph's focus retracts to include Beka as well as Elle. "Once you two become Strippers next Term you both shall beg to Opt Whore. Dong when you're Strippers and you'll Whore for sure. Dong now while you have the chance."

Robyn signs Steph to silence and addresses the newbies. "Don't think you're going to be Porn Stars like Tiffany. You're going to be entry-level massage Parlor handjob girls popping dicks as well as streetwalking blowjob tunnel Whores. Don't think you're going to work as an escort for sports stars. No indeed, Pledge, you're going to start at the bottom, suck off some smelly, awful-tasting, malformed, uncircumcised, jiz-drenching cocks. Then you can consider dance, acting, and courtesan classes."

Robyn straightens up, leans back, and cackles. "You cunts are headed to the bang house and notch joint. The Nugget's a way stop. Ha ha ha ha!"

Steph disobeys Robyn's directive and directs fresh intimidation Elle's way. "Listen to me, Stripper wannabe," she says. Steph folds her hands together and speaks in a matter-of-fact tone to her Dueling companion. "I've got more hours in the Doghouse than you can ever get. Even if you move in right now and stay till Midnight. So you're going to lose, Elle Lollydor."

Steph wipes mud off her face as she addresses her Dueling Companion. "You might have butched blue hair with a stripe down the middle of your face and your body. And thank goodness you still have your stretch slacks. You will be wearing them to the Mansion Open House tomorrow but you won't be wearing them back. Because when I'm done with you, you're not going to just be bare bald and naked, you're going to orgasm your brains into the Zone!"

Robyn intercedes, "Betcha Elle can't wait to take on Steph's Obeisances! Bare bald and naked, pink-wet-and-ready, force-cummed, forced to eat pussy and cum on the Double Dong. Toe sucker. Pee-Camer. Piss Mouth. Everything."

Steph glowers at Robyn, "I don't have any Piss Mouth, Robyn Rembrain. And Gamers don't need you making stuff up. But since you are—"

Robyn cuts her off. "Betcha *you* can't wait to recover your Shaving Kit and trim all your stubble off."

Steph snaps upright. *My stubble* is *starting to itch. In fact I need a soap, shower, and shave.* Babs is not present, only Robyn and the two newbie Pledge.

Steph chooses to challenge the newbies. "Tell me where the Shaving Kit is, Pledge," she commands.

Elle frowns and Beka answers, "I have it. It's in my bonker and borehole.

Robyn consolidates control over the newbies. "Beka Broda, loosen the knots of that g-string, spread your legs, and extract the Shaving Kit! Now froth up some cream, lather your skin, and use the razor to trim your pubes and asshole."

Beka hurriedly performs the extraction.

Robyn details. "Don't hack away your Mohawk and Hitler, because after you forfeit the g-string, they will be all you got. When you do finally beg all your hair off, you will match Steph here."

"Right," Beka responds, quickly masturbating herself.

Elle blanches at Beka's eagerness to plunge ahead. And she blanches at her own inability to run away from the Game.

§ Beka Gives Steph: The Shaving Kit Acquires a New Home

Robyn holds her hands out as Beka completes tidying her stubble up, and Beka lays the components of the Shaving Kit into Robyn's hands. Beka adjusts her g-string, returns her hands to her breech, and continues to masturbate herself. Elle, still standing spread surrender, witness Beka in the Mirror, and suppresses the urge to correct her Roommate's behavior.

Robyn ignores any Beka obsession and lets Beka accumulate broda onto her fingers and the palm of her hands. Robyn collects the shaving implements from Beka and hands them to Steph. "Put the soap back into the stainless steel ball, put the razor and scissors back into their cylinder, and stuff your snatch and sewer pipe. No shaving until I say so. It pleases me that you shall continue to itch!"

Steph casts eyes about the Bunkroom, grits her teeth, and obeys. *I am a Monitor next Term.* She eyes Robyn. *And maybe you really will be a MomCap.*

"Now go affix yourself to the Mirror and kiss yourself," Robyn orders her former Monitor. "And never forget that you're still a Pledge!"

Steph obeys. She looks at Elle and suspects that the newbie fails to understand the threat of the Minxy Mirror. When she presses her naked body against the Mirror it grabs her, immediately and tightly, breasts and lips compressed, belly pressed, arms and legs pressed. She squeezes the sphere as the ball and cylinder of the Shaving Kit come alive, she grinds her pelvis, and in seconds Steph is gone, out of control, Zoned.

Elle tries to understand. *Might the Gamers accelerate Steph so she dances deeper into the Zone?* Elle wonders. *So deep in fact she will never come out of the Zone enough to Option me Down!*

But then a different panic attacks. *Maybe Gamers will put me in the Zone next to Steph. And then leave me in the Zone. No other outcome anymore.*

Yet as Elle watches Steph grind her body on the Minxy, Elle reflects, *Except, I am not Zoned. I am free and playing the Game. I am not a Stripper or a Whore or a Slavesex, I am in control of my body. Like now.*

Elle straightens and squares her stand spread surrender topless posture. Elle looks at Beka who continues to masturbate herself. *I need Beka now, so whatever she wants, I'll do.* Elle's body cinches. *No! What I must do is control Beka's needs.*

Beka floats and volunteers. "Robyn, Elle and I want to be bare bald and naked Strippers next Term. We'll do whatever it takes! We'll both Pee-Cam. We'll both Piss in our own Mouths."

Elle cringes and spots her cameltoe again.

Robyn examines the newbies. "You may piss into *each other's* mouths, but right now, go to the Bathroom, both of you."

Pee-Camer Beka knows to shuck her g-string and leave it on her bunk before heading into the Bathroom and lighting up the Cam.

Robyn nods to Elle, "You too shall be naked in the Bathroom from now on." Elle doesn't question this logic or rationale. She rolls her slacks down and off, deposits them on her bunk, and assumes, *I will never wear these again.*

Beka hurriedly advances, "And please, we want to climax the Dong!"

Robyn ignores this beg, "Move it." And Beka and Elle rush to the Bathroom, both naked now.

§ Beka Urges Elle: Let's Piss Climax the Double Dong Together

The two naked Roommates sit on the edge of the bathtub and talk in hushed tones least the Cam overhears them. It overhears them anyway and after a while they forget their world is anything but private.

Naked Elle sits her nachas on the side of the tub and double checks that she keeps her thighs wide open for the Cam. *Not apart, not spread either, just open. No taking chances. Exposed nookie for vagcam from now on.*

Elle worries to her Roommate, "Steph will do anything to win, and gets to pick the contest! When it actually occurs I am sure to lose."

"Yeah. Okay." Beka scratches her berries, "But didn't Bikini Babe already allow that whoever had the most time in the Doghouse could be the victor? So Game over." Beka opens her legs wider and masturbates an opened vagina. "Besides Elle, aren't we already begging to Pledge naked and cum be Strippers next Term?"

Elle rolls her eyes, "If Babs lets Steph have her way I will get tossed completely." Elle asserts, "The last of my clothes, shaven bare bald and naked, made pink wet ready, and force-climaxed."

Beka augments, "It will make your spreading naked in the Beauty Salon and creaming your nook seem tame."

Elle begs, "Please Beka, stop it." Elle closes her eyes, reaches down, and verifies her butched pubic hair with the shaven trough down the center. She cringes. "You know I hate showing off my shaven trench."

Beka touches her green Mohawk, parts her pink, and continues to masturbate. "You do and you don't, Elle. Your juice was running down to your asshole at the Beauty Salon! They took our picture like that, Elle, me and you, and we're gonna beg that we have Pink Pages made up and pass them out."

Elle tests to see if she is wet at this moment. *Not wet. But I do need to pee.*

Elle blocks out Beka's observations.

Beka persists, "Elle, we're gonna stay topless from now on, until we get naked that is." Beka brushes her Hitler, "You're gonna take on all of Steph's Obeisance too, don't forget, and I want to be there with you, bare bald and naked, Pee-Cam and Piss Mouth."

Elle starts to object.

Beka persists, "And don't forget the Double Dong either, we need to dong like everybody else."

"The Dong is not one of Steph's Obeisance!" Elle firms.

"Steph has Donged more than once," Beka argues, "With Tiffany at the Nugget, then Molly then Tiffany again."

Elle touches her head and feels the bare trough through her blue-dyed butched hair. She wonders, *Do I even have eyebrows any more?*

She carefully fingers her nether parts. "I anticipate Steph is going to make me ride the Dong with her as part of her Duel," Elle confesses, "but I will ride with you if it comes to that. I've considered attempting escape but I've discarded the idea. No chance of making it."

"Jeez, Elle, don't try to run away!" Beka looks astonished, "Dong or not, we worked hard to be here!"

"I really am just an inexperienced first-Term newbie," Elle wags her head. "You and me both. And we're going to pay for it."

Beka agrees, "Yeah, Elle, we're just Pledge in the Game. And we're gonna be Strippers next Term! What you need to do is get the Dong back from the Corvette House and bring it here. I'll eat your pussy and juice the Dong with you. We'll piss climax on the Dong together!"

Elle has a hard time hearing this.

Beka helps with excitement, "We'll kiss and hug and rub-a-dub the Dong and piss climax and Zone center Stage at the Nugget!"

"It seems like every day I get more reduced," Elle admits to her Roommate. Elle runs her fingers down and feels the inch-wide smooth trough where her pubic hair has been shaven away. Tiffany, not long ago, had razored the trough smooth.

"You shall learn to cream at the touch of a razor," Tiffany had prophesied, then touched to razor to Elle's clit, used the surge of nectar to lubricate the razor, and shaved the front-to back channel on her head equally smooth: a trough of scalp with butched hair on each side.

Elle parts her lips just enough to finger-ball her clitoris. *My nitro button, my nugogo, my nugget, just like where I am headed next Term.*

Beka should be a friend, but Elle's indelible ink centerline stripe and general predicament excites Beka and she feels her own bare breech make broda. Beka adds more touché, "Just don't forget the Double Dong, Elle. Steph's gonna make you ride the Dong with Molly and Kimju you're probably even gonna make videos with the 'Porn Star.'"

"Dong Tiffany!" Elle realizes with a shock, and raises her hand to her mouth. "She'd wring me out. Please don't suggest I'm going to have to eat her out too." Elle huffs, and puts her top front teeth over her lower lip and bites softly.

Beka is sanguine, "I know Elle. I'm sorry. I can't help it. I wanna ride the Dong with you while we both have a chance. We ate each other out once before. We can do it again. We're both gonna Opt Down, and you know that once we are Strippers we aren't allowed to. This might be our only chance!"

Elle takes a big sigh, "We might have to eat out everybody. I have a lot of unanswered questions." Elle scratches an armpit, "How come Cosmos *volunteer* to share Double Dong when Strippers aren't allowed to?"

"How come we have to beg the Pee-Cam, whereas at the Nugget the Cams are always lit up?" Beka asks back.

Elle knows the cynical answer to that question, "Well, not all Pledge become Strippers. So if a Pledge wants to get ahead in the Game they can volunteer to pee *before* they Opt Up. Or Opt Down, where 'volunteering' isn't an option."

Beka presents rare sarcasm, "I wonder if Babs or Janet ever Pee-Cammed? I bet not. Except that Janet was a Stripper two Terms ago."

Elle silently recalls. *I've already made a debut sitting on the Nugget glass toilet; it's an appearance which seems to have been overlooked... but that does not mean unseen. Or forgotten about.*

Beka suddenly realizes that she has committed to the Pee-Cam while her Roommate has not. More to the point, "So Elle, are you gonna beg the Pee-Cam?"

Elle ponders how to answer this question and Beka concludes, "You might as well, because once we Opt Strip next Term, it won't matter any more."

Elle looks at her Roommate with a look of total submission. Beka cheers her up, "It's okay. I'm ahead of you Elle; all I've got is my green Mohawk, green stain in my nips, and my Hitler above my shaven bonker. And a micro g-string back on my bunk."

Elle considers, *I wonder if my slacks are still on my bunk?*

Beka shakes Elle on the arm, "Elle, so do you know where you want to get pieced and tattooed?" Beka wants to know. "Cause we're gonna be Strippers soon!"

"Jeez Beka, we're not Strippers till next Term." Elle adjusts her utterance, "I've already been naked and pinked, I am learning to cream. And if I have to let the rest of my hair go, well, it will grow out sometime. I'm willing to cum, you know, well maybe, although I can't do it solo. You know that. But getting Zoned? There I'd be trapped."

Beka agrees, "Yeah Steph lost herself completely. I know that once I'm zoned, I just want to stay there. Both of us, Elle."

§ Beka & Elle: Distribute Pink Pages of Themselves

Robyn stomps into the Bathroom just as Elle exits the shower and Beka logs the last of her Measuring Cups. "Listen up, Stripper wannbes," she commands, "get dressed, go to the Beauty Salon and pick up your Pink Pages, and then drop one off at every House!"

Beka rise slowly and Elle calculates. "This could take a while," she complains to Robyn.

"It will take until it is done and you make it back here," Robyn snaps. "So get moving and it will get done sooner rather than later."

The newbies sprint. Getting dressed for Beka means tying on her micro g-string; Elle slips feet and legs into her low-ride stretch slacks. They race out the Back Door, pull the Bell, form handbras to conceal their otherwise bare breasts, and finds the shortest distance to the Beauty Salon that bruises their feet the least.

Madam Nurse Beautician greets them in the doorway and hands them each eight freshly-minted Pink Pages. Glossy stock, full figure, full-frontal nudity. "Eight copies of yourself for each of you. Give one to each House and beg them to support your Opt Strip."

Beautician draws in a breath. "The sequence of Houses is different for each of you, so follow it exactly."

Elle speaks, "You gave out our path to the paparazzi."

Nurse Beautician furrows her brow. "Tisk, tisk, Pledge. You're street legal, even if you are extreme. Enough with the handbras. When you visit a House, ring the doorbell on the Front Porch and you may be sure their Cam will collect you. Be sure to titter and topless them without them asking, and if they request you pink, oblige them.

Beka advances, "I'll dance naked and collect tips in a garter!"

Beautician firms upon Beka. "Pledge, you shall pass out your Pink Sheets. Tell the creeps they can purchases glossies of you dripping brodeas outta your box just as soon as you start Stripping at the Nugget next Term. And as soon as you make Whore they can finger and fuck you."

Beautician turns to Elle, "Be sure to remind everyone you'll be begging 'bare bald and naked' at the Monitor Open House tomorrow."

Beautician closes the door. "Go now," she says.

And they separate and scoot. Boobies and bellage, one butt completely exposed and the other cracked, and both of them hairage.

Once again they must move carefully, barefoot, and slow enough *so that sometimes one has no choice but to let the paparazzi collect you.*

And fast enough so the Rachmaninoffs can't catch you.

Beka drops off her flyer at the first House before she realizes that one side features a full color picture of her sitting in Beautician's chair, stark naked with bright green hair, spreading, pulling pink, and oozing juice. Beka touches her own head, but the only green hair still there is the center brush of the Mohawk. Then she looks at her pelvis. The only green hair still there is the Hitler that sits in full view, flying above the micro g-string, again completely buried into a gash already awash in cream. The bodypaint and crost got washed away in the shower so that now the strings bare shaven skin to all sides.

The bare box always shows, the strings meet at and irritate the clithood, and yes, Beka will beg to flash pink at every Front Door... if not drip on the Porch.

Elle, travelling a different route, observes that the back side of the Pink Page contains her dimensions and cup size, height, weight, astrological sign and blood type. Elle feels embarrassed to have her intimate statistics revealed, and avoids turning the Page over to confront her own blue dyed hair, and naked spread and pinking position. She wets her cameltoe with fresh pee.

Elle always remember to remind whoever answers the Front Door to "Please come and watch me beg 'bare bald and naked' at the Monitor Open House tomorrow." Elle is relieved no one demands she beg pink. When a speaking cam demands that she get on her hands and knees to display her nadir hole to the Prefecture, she blushes from the humiliation.

Elle more scared as she becomes even more aroused by the hazing.

The Peacock House is her last stop on the route back to the Cosmos House. The hands that open the Front Door slides a plate out onto the porch and a voice commands, "Lolly!"

Elle kneels and lollys. *Except the Peacock lolly doesn't taste like valiva.*

§ Steph: Quiet Time in the Bathroom

Robyn steps behind Steph, performs a manipulation on the collar that surrounds her neck and removes it. She waves and the Minxy gives Steph a tingle that bounces her off the Mirror and out of the Zone. Robyn hands Steph the collar. "Bathroom," she commands. "Go make Pee-Cam."

Hairless Steph is smart enough to leave the opened collar on her bunk before entering an otherwise empty Bathroom. She lights the Cam, of course, squats her bare buttocks in front of the Cam, and streams into the Measuring Cup. She Logs. Steph recalls practicing watersports with Molly... and confronting Robyn's golden feet afterwards. She rises, dabs, wipes her ass, and takes a long awaited, *and much deserved,* shower.

Steph uses her time alone—for the Pee-Cam can't record her thinking—to organize her thoughts. *Elle easy-pickings aside, I must also be careful! When I tussled with Molly, somebody schemed against me and enabled Molly to come out on top, and for me to end up bare bald and naked! And then Zoned.*

I'd be a Stripper right now if Tiffany hadn't bailed on the Duel. I think Boss Bitch and probably Janet Jintoe are behind all of this, but Tiffany failed to take the Duel they so aptly laid down in her path. Now I got it!

Steph considers how to process her former Pledge and current Monitor: *Boss Bitch. When I get my hands on her again I will break her completely. Right now all BB needs to do is stay out of my way. I'm about to lock my Duel Option in. I can't have her or Robyn taking me into the Zone any more.*

Steph ponders the secret that William shared with her about Elle. *After he pounded my ass and I cleaned up afterwards I'm no longer sure I really believe William watches my back. Nor have I forgotten that he and Janet suggested the Greatest House Roar and set me up.*

But what he revealed to me about Elle is priceless.

II-39 Beka & Rodney: Secret Fuck During an Errand (D26)

§ Elle: Returns to the Back Landing

Topless Elle is the first to arrive back after passing out her Pink Pages. After Seven Houses, she rings the Front Doorbell of the Cosmos House, and after no answer, Elle retreats to the Backyard and rings that Bell. Still no answer. She sits in her slacks with one Pink Page in hand. *I know what it contains. Me. All my statistics, all my begs. And on the other side of the Page? Naked me with dyed blue hair lying back spread and pulling my pink. Unless something drastic happens, I'm a Nugget next Term.*
There is a reason it takes Beka longer to distribute her Pink Pages:

§ Beka & Rodney: Secret Sex During Pink Page Handouts

Beka's flirtations with Rodney acquired momentum at the Mermaid Parade, where Beka's freshly topless micro g-string, green painted body, and green Mohawk and Hitler stood out and captured Rodney's attention.
Alone among the Gamers, only Rodney has learned that while he and the others cavorted at the Mermaid Parade, that back at the Peacock House Monitor William had drilled Steph and secretly recorded the private fuck using the House Cam usually handled by Rodney. After the Parade, when Rodney made this discovery, he and William had shared the visual and aural delight of Steph sucking William's cock, getting fucked, and even taking it up the ass. The Roommates had laughed at Steph being made to clean up after herself. Rodney, jealous if not horny, considers his own possibility of a sexual encounter: the Beka possibility.
He shall not be disappointed.
Rodney intercepts Beka during her drop-off of Pink Pages and signs her into the side door of the garage behind the Peacock House. Beka follows; it's dusky inside, and she clenches her shallow conical tits, 33Bs, with beige areolas outlined in dark brown, and nips that indent when they get excited. Like right now.
Beka still wears only one piece, her two square inch micro g-string, complemented with a green greased Mohawk and Hitler. Rodney embraces Beka. Beka runs a hand down Rodney's back and discovers that Monitor William has him wearing thin tight stretch shorts that cover his butt. When Rodney reaches around and runs his hands down her spine he makes contact with Beka's bare buttocks; he spots the front of his shorts. He reaches upward, fondles both of Beka bare boobs, and discovers her nips' indented "erections." Beka springs wet.
"What about breaking the no-sex-for-Pledge Rule!" Beka whispers.

"Don't worry," Rodney smooth-talks her, "No one knows about us."

"I can't afford to be caught," Beka retorts, "The Gamers would make a Whore outta me. Outta both of us."

"Everybody fucks around," Rodney argues, "It's okay. Even your fellow Cosmos sleeps around."

"Elle?" Beka questions. "No way!"

"How about Steph?" Rodney states.

Beka, surprised, queries, "Steph? Who's Steph fucking?"

"Try William." Rodney leads now, "They've been screwing since they were both Monitors last Term."

Beka wrinkles her brow. Rodney's hand slides inside her g-string, twiddles her clit, and broda erupts and fills the garage with her scent. She concedes Rodney might be telling the truth, and starts, "Maybe last Term...."

Rodney interrupts, "This Term too. I know. William secretly made videos of them having sex together."

Beka hesitates while Rodney's fingers enter her vagina. She offers a theory, "Maybe the slut is whoring to gain an edge."

"It's real," Rodney assures her, "I've seen the video. Top secret!"

"Maybe William got her the Option," Beka speculates. Beka looks into Rodney's eyes and he leads her into a kiss.

She tests Rodney through the shorts. *Hard.*

Each Pledge pulls their opposite's Garment down. Rodney's hard penis rises in between Beka's thighs. Beka feels it rub her inner thighs. Feels it rub against her clit. Beka tries to process Rodney's romantic attraction while at the same time rotating her hips. She touches Rodney's nipples, reaches downward and for the first time, touches the base of his dick, at first wrapping both hands around it to position it to firmly rub in between her thighs. *Hard and lubing.*

Rodney collects three fingers of Beka's broda and feeds it to her. She swoons and as Rodney's swabs brodeas from one cheek to the other across her nostrils. She shakes, and jerks the cock in her hand.

They neutralize, and Rodney anticipates how Steph will affect Beka's future. "I know your Fate," he whispers as they hug and body rub. "Once Steph exercises her Option and 'plays for keeps' with Elle, Elle will lose. So unless something changes, it will be Tiffany, Molly, Elle and you who will be Stripping next Term. Not begging to 'Pledge naked and cum be a Stripper next Term,' but the real deal."

"I'm going there!" Beka asserts. "For sure. I need to. I want to."

"You are," Rodney confirms.

Beka feels Rodney's hands on her behind, leans backward, reaches down, and tips Rodney's cock up into her vagina. It's a bit rough finding the hole in her box, but once aligned it slides in and the experience of cock and pussy engaging feels very good. Beka wraps her legs around Rodney's body, holds onto his shoulders with her hands, and finds herself rolled back onto something as the cock buries itself up to the hilt. Suddenly a Kundalini surge engulfs them and they conjoin into a quick passionate, wild zip fuck culminating with Rodney ejaculating inside Beka's soaked pussy.

They disengage and align themselves horizontally. Beka cleans herself off Rodney's cock with her mouth while he eats his own mess out from between her legs. They both reek of sex, and quickly redress: Beka secures her g-string and Rodney pulls up his shorts.

"Our secret!" Beka reminds Rodney.

"Top secret!" Rodney affirms.

Beka sneaks back out into the daylight, and runs to the next House to make up time so she is not detected as being overly late or even missing.

§ Beka & Elle: Reunite on the Back Landing

Beka makes no attempt to hold her arms or hands over her breasts and nipples while she completes her rounds and returns to the Cosmos House. *Let the Cams and Paparazzi collect me because once I'm a Stripper next Term, all this media will be valuable.*

Beka is less sure how to evaluate the secret she learned from Rodney. She blinks three times in rapid succession with her new knowledge. *I am not sure I believe Rodney, but if what he says about Steph and William is true I am in on a privileged secret which...? What? Explains how Steph got the Option? It doesn't matter, Elle's going to Opt Strip and I'm going to Opt Strip Roommates Together with her!*

Beka finds Elle sitting on the Back Landing waiting for her. She rings the Bell and sits next to her Roommate. Elle holds her remaining Pink Page so as to block her toplessness from the hovering and prying Back Door Cam, and she still wears her low-riding cameltoe-stained slacks. Beka sits, ensures that her thighs aren't touching, and fiddles the g-string in an effort to cover her brim. Topless Beka opens her legs more widely then necessary, adjusts a soaking micro g-string to cover her bourse and ensures the Cam documents her Hitler and Mohawk.

Elle furrows her brow. "Did you drop off your last Pink Page at the Front Door?" Elle inquires, observant that Beka is absent her last copy.

"Huh, oh, no, Elle," Beka exudes. "Listen, everybody loved my Pink Pages and wanted more, so I signed the last one away. Crazy how much they want us."

Before Elle can answer Steph steps out the Back Door.

II-40 Beka & Elle: Gonzo Suck & Fuck Videos (D26)

§ Steph Separates Beka & Elle: Prepares to Win her Duel

At first glance Steph appears on the Back Landing bare bald and naked, but Elle is quick to observe Steph continues to wear the metal ring collar *the transmogrification of my croptop!* Beka, less of a Garment-counter, subliminally concludes that collared Steph is controlled. Elle wets her cameltoe, while Beka soaks her g-string with brodeas.

Steph looks down at sitting Elle and smiles. "I'll take that," she directs, and Elle delivers her Pink Page to the Cosmos House. Elle scans the Backyard. *No hiding topless from the Cam any more.*

Steph turns to sitting Beka. "Give me *your* Pink Page," she commands.

Beka looks up, "Hey Steph, I gave mine away. Autographed copy."

Steph draws her pelvis closer to Beka's face. Steph might be bare and bald, but when close-up, Beka detects Steph is starting to stubble.

"Do you know the meaning of 'every', Pledge Beka Broda?" Steph inquires.

"Ma'am, I thought Babs would already have one," Beka defends.

"You think too much, don't you Pledge," Steph states.

"Ma'am, please, I just want to Pledge bare bald and naked, make pink and stay wet and climax the Dong with Elle, Ma'am!"

Steph tilts a shoulder. "Pullaside your g-string and pink for the Cam, Pledge. I'm sure Automatron and the Gamers want to analyze your béchamel."

Beka squints, digs out the g-string and pulls it to the side, constricts, and hangs broda out of her bare breech. Hitler salutes.

"Enough," Steph decides and orders Beka, "into the Kitchen! Now! Bury you g-string in your bang box, then stand spread surrender and face your future, Tiffany's Porn Star Calendar."

Beka scrambles inside the Back Door.

Steph returns her gaze to Elle.

Elle fidgets. "Please, Steph. You don't need to hurt me on my way down."

"You wait here," Steph commands. "You shall beg total reduction later today, and prove it tomorrow at the Mansion Open House. Meanwhile, pee in your pants while you wait. Kapish?"

Elle rushes, "Ma'am, thank you, "Ma'am."

And Steph is gone.

§ Steph Demands Beka: Tell her about the *Gonzo Videos*

Steph considers Beka standing spread surrender in the Kitchen, studying Tiffany's Porn Star Calendar. It shows the month where Tiffany and Ginny's mouths share a cock, while both point their asses to the Cam, and use a free hand to pull pink.

Beka fidgets and the small movements cause her g-string to ascend into her bonnet, and a blend of Rodney jiz and brodeas brims out. The cocktail transudes around the buried g-string and dangles down in between standing spread thighs.

Beka watches out of the corner of her eye with fish lips as Steph tacks Elle's Pink Page to the wall next to Tiffany's Calendar.

Steph points to the opposite side of the Calendar. "What goes there?" she asks Beka.

Beka knows. "My Pink Page!" She removes her hand from her head for a moment and offers. "I'll go back to the Beauty Salon and get another one. I'll get more too. I'll autograph and hand them out. I'll pink and cream and masturbate and cum center Stage at the Nugget. I'll piss climax the Double Dong with Elle! You know I will."

Steph speaks. "You're leaving your Mohawk and Hitler unattended?"

Beka opens her mouth, closes it, and returns her hands to her head in surrender position, and scans bare bald and naked Steph. "I'll shave bare and bald and stay naked if you let me Opt Down with Elle."

Steph arches her eyes toward Tiffany's totally hardcore performance. "That's you, a cocksucking Whore after next Term!"

Beka flinches.

"Tell me about Elle's camping trip video." Steph orders.

Beka's head snaps. "Say that again."

Steph repeats. "Tell me what you know about Elle's Gonzo Sex Video."

Beka reels, "Well, if they are of a camping trip then they are not only of Elle!"

Steph admires. "Nice! So you two blew a couple of guys."

"More like we fucked five guys and did each other," Beka says, and then questions, "Hey, how do you know about this?"

Steph appraises, "Maybe your Roommate bartered it to Boss Bitch for a favor, like a guaranteed Opt Up."

"Babs has the *Gonzo Videos*?" Beka asks. "Elle gave them to her to Opt Up? I thought you are busting her, so she and I will Strip next Term?"

"Videos?" Steph narrows.

Beka core dumps. "Yeah, Videos. Everybody took turns shooting during the camping trip. Then when we went to get the files afterward we ended up shooting another Video, and then we left without either the Gonzo camping trip Video or the pick-up. We've never had them. Neither of us."

"Maybe Elle got them when she procured the Measurement Nudes and never told you," Steph seeks to confirm.

Beka defends, "No way. I doubt she even knows Babs has them; she'd have told me." She takes her eyes off the Calendar and looks at Steph. "Maybe some Gamer leaked them to Babs."

"Sounds like it's gonna be pretty hard to edit you out," Steph speculates. She grinds, "Gonna be fun for all the Nugget Patrons to watch you and Elle suck and fuck cocks on the Lobby Screen. Might put ideas into the Patron's heads about where you go next."

Beka grimaces but advances a goal. "Yeah, whatever. Elle and I are already pink-wet-and-ready Pledge, and after you take Elle in the Duel, I just want to go be a Stripper with her."

"You'll do anything to climax the Dong together," Steph advances.

"Yeah, well," Beka hedges. "Hey, if you want me to find out if Elle knows about any *Gonzo Videos*, I'll do that for you. But you gotta let us climax the Dong together. *And* it has to be before the Term ends!"

Steph muses, "You'd probably even take on her Stripper piercing and tattoo. Cause you're a greedy little blowzabella wannabe Whore."

Beka falls into silence as she sops her sunken micro g-string.

"Fetch your Roommate in and wait here," Steph orders, and heads upstairs.

§ Beka Asks Elle: Elle Admits She Gave *Gonzo Videos* to Babs

Beka waits for Steph's footsteps to vanish up the angular back staircase and gathers her thoughts. Steph's collar stimulates Beka's wetness, and a long drop of brodeas and Rodney cum detaches itself from her bourse and drops on the floor. She swells with pleasure. *I fucked Rodney! He likes being in me. Pleasure that no one knows!*

Beka continues to feel the glow from Rodney's dick inside her. She glances at the puddle of brodeas and jiz, and suppresses worry from her mind! *Rodney would never break the Rules unless he was sure we couldn't get caught. So I'm sure he'll keep us a secret!*

Another thought arcs across Beka's lobes: *My secret tryst has increased my sense of security! Maybe Steph is trying to spook me with the Gonzo Videos. They were just a fun thing, even if we did have sex, we're not Whores.*

Beka feels very satisfied. *As for Rodney, I seduced a man who prizes my affection!*

I satisfied my itch and got away with it!

And I can make sure Steph will make sure I get to Opt Strip next Term.

Beka waves Elle in the Back Door. Elle stands awkwardly, still topless, and unable to hide the fact that her pants are soaked with pee. Beka shrugs. "I had to stand spread surrender and look at the Calendar," she reminds Elle, points her chin, and eyes the Kitchen floor. Elle understands, kneels, and lollys Beka's puddle. *Tastes different than last time.*

The sit down at the Kitchen table together. The Kitchen is without a Cam, and quiet.

"What happened about your Pink Page?" Elle asks, concerned.

Beka waves off the question and advances to a more pressing agenda. "Listen, Elle, have you heard anything about Babs having our gangbang *Gonzo Videos*?

Elle turns and looks at her Roommate. Beka catches her eye-to-eye, and sees shame, hopelessness, and agony there. Elle mopes, "I'm sorry Beka."

Beka straightens. "Elle, tell me you didn't give our Videos to Babs. Like you did our selfie Measurement Nudes."

"I'm sorry, Beka. I had to do it."

"You had to do it?" Beka stomps. "You're not the only one that sucks cock. Or fucks either."

Elle confesses, "I know. We even suck cock together and go down on each other."

Beka complains with her hands and whole body. "Maybe you had to fetch our Measurement Nudes. But you didn't have to give Babs something she had no idea about."

"I was required to present the Videos to Babs in order to get the Measurement Nudes. Trust me, it wasn't simple. I had to make some 'insurance,' if you know what I mean, to guarantee I actually delivered the Gonzos to Babs."

"You did that without telling me," Beka states.

Elle continues, "I'm sorry. I'll make it up to you. I'll do whatever I need to do to make sure Babs doesn't show the Videos."

"Doesn't show the Videos?" Beka seems astonished, "Jeez Elle, Babs is going to give them to Steph and Steph is going to use them to control you and crush you in the Duel."

Elle licks her lips, "Okay. I mean, really, it's all about Steph and me. It's only a matter of time before she strips me naked, blushes me, creams me, and tries to climax my brains out. Except you know I need cock in order to climax. So Steph doesn't need to screen the *Gonzo Videos*."

Beka shrugs. "She's sadistically privileged, and intends to mar you on your way to the Nugget.

"All she needs is for me to lose and it's her Game. She has more hours in the Doghouse than I do. I can't win."

"I'm in the Videos too, Elle," Beka states.

"It's not about you. I let Steph take me and break me." Elle pauses. "And I'll let her do to me whatever she requires so she doesn't screen the Videos... or give them to House Mom el Capitan."

Beka rolls her lips into her teeth. "You really mean that?"

"I do." Elle's head spins. "I was forced to harm you. I didn't do it deliberately. I care for you. So tell me what I need to do to make it up to you."

"You know you're going to beg to screen them, no matter what," Beka resigns, "and I agree you owe me." Beka cocks her head back and offers a solution. "All I want is for you to beg to fetch the Double Dong and then climax it with me, while there is still time this Term. And then you must make sure I Opt Strip together with you!"

Elle visualizes a movie *of Beka and me climaxing the Double Dong playing in the Nugget Lobby, while inside....*

Beka leans forward. "Elle, I cream all the time. But nobody lets me cum. And you haven't cum either. I want to cream and cum with you, Elle. Please, on the Double Dong. Kimju and Molly got to. Tiffany took Steph over the top. But you and I haven't gotten to ride and we both need to beg to climax."

Elle tries to collect her thoughts and looks around wildly. *How have I managed to get to this place? That I owe Beka begging to climax the Dong with her? Thank goodness the Dong isn't even here.*

Elle reconnoiters. "Beka, how did you find out about the *Gonzo Videos*?"

"Steph asked me about them," Beka says.

"Steph?" Elle startles. "And how did she find out?"

Beka shakes her head. "I don't know. I asked but she didn't say."

"Steph controls me," Elle admits, "and now she holds the *Gonzo Videos* over my head. I worry that the *Gonzo Videos* playing in the Nugget will make a difference about how the Crowd treats us once we become Strippers there—they will demand we Opt Whore and head to Flesh Ranch! Me or you, but I will go solo if I have to."

Beka pines, "Gosh Elle, don't say that. You know I love you and if you have to go Whore I will go with you. We could be lesbians and do cuckolding scenes."

Elle takes a deep breath, "I love you too, and if I have to eat you to make it up, or let you climax me on the Double Dong, then, well...."

"We will take on the *Gonzo Videos* together, Elle," Beka says. "Maybe we are destined to become Porn Stars!"

Something snaps in Elle's brain. *Wait! I don't owe Beka any protection! She got me into this!* Elle skips through a series of flashbacks. *I'm unsure if my begging to Opt Strip is for real.* Or that it makes a difference. Elle slowly turns her head to her Roommate and poses a question: "What happened to 'we want to Opt Up next Term? Two pieces and all.'"

"That was then, Elle!" Beka agrees. "Now we got one piece each and we're beggin' to Opt Strip. Plus you got Steph comin' at you. You're gonna lose the Duel. You can't help it. I understand. She's gonna take your pants, shave you bare bald and naked, and put *you* in the Zone. You need to beg her to streak over to visit Ginny Corvette and snag the Double Dong in *your* notch, then bring it back here! So you and I can ride it together! Please, Elle, I need to cum be a Stripper with you!"

Elle blinks.

"You promised, Elle," Beka affirms, "You owe me. Pay attention. We're both begging to Pledge naked and cum Strip next Term. You're going to the Nugget for sure and you need to take me along. And before we go you need to cum together with me so we can be one. So beg Steph to fetch the Dong and we'll fondle and kiss and eat and dong-cum together. I'll even zone outta body with you."

Elle closes her eyes again. "Maybe Babs wants me to defeat Steph." Elle circumspects. "Like, look how Molly came out ahead. Nobody expected that."

Beka retorts, "Right now Molly hangs out naked with her panties stuffed her mouth, her hair and body dyed and stained red. She's another Stripper next Term."

"Steph is wearing thin on Babs' nerves," Elle opines.

Beka furrows her brow and wags a finger. "Babs might be pulling for you, Elle, but fact is that Steph has the Option, and Steph's gonna spread you, pink you, and force-cum you. You're a Stripper next Term. Me and you both! We're headed for the Nugget, Elle, you can't stop it." Beka gathers her points, "I want to go with you, Roommates Together! We're already topless and slit shaven, pink-wet-and-ready, and begging."

Elle evaluates their Garments. *Me in slacks and Beka in a g-string.*

She tries to be optimistic. "Beka, I guess if we can keep what we got we won't have to streak to get there."

Beka clarifies, "Except Steph will be stripping you naked because she needs two Garments."

Elle retreats, "I need to beg her to not screen the Gonzos, and if she does, to leave you out of it."

"Whatever," Beka waves her arms, "Tell Steph you'll shave bare and bald and eat pussy. Tell her you'll fetch the Dong and ride it with me. Tell her you concede."

"But Babs doesn't want me to loose!" Elle repeats the conundrum.

"Babs doesn't decide!" Beka argues, "You get in front. You go to Steph and beg her for total surrender. You belong to her. You do whatever she says as long as it's legal. You beg to Opt Strip! Give her your pants! Duel over. Beg to fetch the Double Dong so we can cum on the Dong together!"

Beka pauses. "I'm still your friend Elle. We're gonna be friends at the Nugget. Hey, face it, we're gonna be great Strippers!"

Elle squints. "Yeah, great Strippers maybe. I might like sex but I have *no* desire to be a 'Porn Star!' Because the *Gonzo Videos* suggest that we are cocksuckers and easy fucks! We were just out on a camping trip and having a good time."

Beka seeks to calm her Roommate. "Yeah, except the second time was not so innocent. We traded sex for a video, except we got so cock drunk we forgot to take either video with us. But don't worry," Beka begs, "I'm coming with you Elle, I promise. Even if Steph makes me a Piss Mouth."

Elle sighs. "Maybe I can't win. It's Steph's Game. If the Pledge with the most hours in the Doghouse wins, then I'm gonna loose."

"If you have to make yourself cum you're gonna loose!" Beka declares, emphatically. "You have to surrender to Steph and beg her to force the cum out of you. On Cam. That's how it will end. So you might as well make it easy for yourself."

"And I'll do whatever I can to keep our gangbang *Gonzo Videos* secret." Elle acknowledges.

"It's okay, Elle, I know you got conned into bringing me into it," Beka touches Elle's shoulder, gracious, forgiving.

"I turned over the Videos on my own," Elle confesses. "Hold me responsible. Besides, I figure Steph's gonna climax us on the Dong one way or another."

"Elle I love you. And I know you will try your best." Beka leans forward, kisses her friend on the mouth. "It's okay Elle. I really liked it when we made out that once. Just so you know, that while we have this chance before we become Strippers, I don't care who else you eat or joy stick with, I just want to make sure that *we* eat out and dong and rub bare clitties together until we both rock."

"I love you too." Elle confesses. "I'm trying to protect you from Gamers, but I may not be able to protect you from yourself."

II-41 Steph & Elle: Components of Total Surrender (D27)

§ Steph Listens to Elle: Surrender & Beg to Not Screen Videos

Morning of Day 27 arrives, and after a Lineup and Bathroom experience Elle seeks out a quiet moment with Steph. She locates her downstairs, sitting at the Kitchen table. Steph is bare bald and naked except for an seemingly continuous ring of metal around her neck. *One Garment,* Elle assumes, *and my slacks will be her second.*

It is an awkward moment. Elle glances around, momentarily rests her eyes on Tiffany's Porn Star Calendar, and digests Tiffany on her back; Elle doesn't approve, *The tramp thinks that inserting a huge cucumber into her twat is sexy.*

Elle considers herself. *Topless just is, just like my nappy and nates erupting above my low-rise slacks. I've got blue hair and hairage.* Elle looks at Steph. *Steph doesn't have any color in her because she doesn't have any hair.*

Not even eyebrows.

However, Steph has picked me for her Option Duel and Steph will pick the Game. She's going to be a Monitor next Term and I'm going to be a Stripper. I'm done. It's over. I'm about to be a naked pinker from now on.

Yet there is more. So Elle presents herself smartly and begins, "Steph, Ma'am, I know I'm doomed to lose to you. You picked me, you pick the Game, you take me. So I'm prepared to surrender. But I need your help beyond the call of duty and I'll do whatever you require to obtain it."

"You'll do whatever I want, period." Steph admonishes, "I don't make deals. Now put your hands behind your head and beg me to roll your slacks down your crotch. Right here, right now, in front of me."

Elle obeys. Steph reaches forward, yanks Elle's slacks down the rest of her pubic hair, down her curving behind and naughty gorge, and then all the way down her slit. Steph gathers the slacks level with Elle's crotch, considers, then yanks them just a tad lower so that Elle's full crotch lies in view.

Elle knows, *I'm topless bottomless which means I'm full-frontal.*

"Seems like you got some wetness in your cameltoe," Steph suggests.

Elle stutters. "Ma'am, thank you, Ma'am."

"Is it your nectar or piss, Elle Lollydor?" Steph inquires.

Elle stumbles, "Ma'am, some of both, probably, Ma'am."

"Beg me to make nectar and pee, Pledge," Steph commands.

Elle sighs. No choice. "Ma'am please make me pink-wet-and-ready. Ma'am, thank you for letting me pee in my pants yesterday. I want to freshen my nookie and climax in front of *everyone*. Please."

Elle casts her eyes around the Kitchen to ensure that there are no Cams present.

Steph stretches the fabric in the crotch of Elle's rolled down slacks and squints at the newbie Pledge. "Looks like you want to be on the Pee-Cam."

Elle gasps. "Steph, please, Steph."

"Beg me to take on my Pee-Cam," Steph orders.

Elle closes her eyes, open them and hang-faces. "Please, Steph, let me take on your Pee-Cam." Elle falters and babbles, "Ma'am," and augments, "I'll do more for you too, if you hear me out, Ma'am."

"I know," Steph narrows her nostrils. "You're gonna beg a Piss Mouth."

Elle opens her mouth to respond but Steph catches her in motion and signs her to oval-mouth.

Elle obeys. Upstairs and earlier Tiffany had ensured that the notch across Elle's head and down her pubes got freshly shaven, right down to smooth bare skin. Then Tiffany had strengthened the indelible line dividing Elle into left and right sides; now Steph traces a fingernail from the trough of Elle's bare scalp, down her face, between her breasts and down and through the shaven trench in her nappy.

Elle moans, "Please, Steph," whatever that means.

Steph wonders. *Does the dividing line inside Elle's crotch now span from her clit to her asshole so as to totally circumnavigate her body? And might such a line ride atop shaven lips or dip into her nookie?*

Steph will answer these questions whenever she wishes to. She reaches forward to twist both of Elle's stained nipples; like Elle's lips and navel they are stained blue and match the blue hair on her head and nymphaeum. Tiffany had also deepened all of this blue.

"Seems like Tiffany has lavished makeup and perfume upon you fitting of a Whore. So are you begging to Whore or are you begging to Strip?"

Elle rushes, "Strip please. Steph! Please let me Pledge naked and cum be a Stripper next Term. Ma'am!"

"You'll beg what I tell you to beg," Steph states. "Do you understand me?"

"Ma'am, yes, Ma'am," Elle grits. *I'm doomed. Steph's got my* Gonzo Videos *and she going to demand I beg to Whore.* She tries, "Steph, I'll follow the Rules."

"You don't know any Rules," Steph advises. "You obey me."

Elle accepts, "Ma'am, I will beg what you tell me to beg."

Steph runs the palm of a hand across the butched blue hair on Elle's head, then the back of her hand against the butch on her nook. She detects that a stiffener has been worked in.

Steph stands. She turns a faces Elle, still standing thighs-not-touching surrender, and backs Elle up two steps. She dances her arms upward and rubs first one concave armpit cross Elle's face followed by the other, carefully romancing Elle's nose.

Steph steps backward, reaches down with her hands touches her smurfs, considers the full-frontal blue newbie before her, and her saucers bubble up. Steph slides her hands down her ribs, rests them on her pelvic bone and measures the psyche of her prey.

Steph touches her neck ring, own bald head, and then her bare, always-legs-apart pussy, with a wettened clit hanging free.

Steph reaches forward and wiggles a finger into the very top of Elle's nautch, finger balls Elle's newel, and Elle squirms.

"Thank me," Steph commands. "Then beg me for more."

"Ma'am, thank you for touching my clit, Ma'am," Elle says and adds, "Please more, Ma'am."

"Very well," Steph begins, "you belong to me now. But before you seek dispensations, expand me your beg."

So Elle recites, "Ma'am, please let me Pledge bare bald and naked, stay pink-wet-and-ready, and cum be a Stripper next Term." Elle wonders, *Do I really mean it after all? Maybe I do. I feel myself slipping into free fall; Beka's already gone, controlled and held back from eruption. My problem is just the opposite. Now Steph intends to control me to climax.*

Steph again slides a finger into Elle's nook; this time her middle finger slides into a creamy vagina. Steph withdraws her finger, and standing now, she draws the back of it across Elle's nostrils and then presents it to Elle's ovaled mouth where it is dutifully sucked clean.

Steph waves Elle two steps backwards and Elle wiggles back, her slacks still down just below crotch. Steph challenges: "I guess we've all seen you make yourself pink-wet-and-ready, but nobody has seen you cum. Not only that, but the scuttlebutt is that you can't climax yourself. Is that true?"

Elle shifts her weight uneasily, ever more conscious of her indelible dividing line, stained nipples and navel, blue hairage. She tries to hold back but squirts pee into her rolled-down slacks. Clearly visible.

Elle begs, "I'll pee outside in front of the Back Door Cam."

"You'll pee anywhere anytime in front of anybody." Steph declares. "My question concerned climaxing. Kimju and Molly came. Tiffany too. They've all gone over the top."

Elle shrugs her shoulders, "You came too. You were Zoned for days on end."

Steph winches but lets it go. She walks behind Elle, presses her naked body up against Elle's back, reaches around to cup Elle's breasts and hisses into Elle's ear, "Are you sure you're able to cum at all?"

Elle rushes, "Oh sure. I've cum before. But only on cock. Many times."

Steph glides, "I hear you have proof of that."

Elle falters. "Steph, please, Beka told me Babs shared them with you. That's what I need to talk to you about. The *Gonzo Videos*. Especially if you control them now."

"I do. You shall obey me, now, no matter what." Steph curls, "Do you understand that?"

Elle formalizes, "Ma'am, yes, Ma'am."

"Tell me you brought Babs these Gonzos to guarantee yourself an Opt Up."

Elle's eyes dart, "Ma'am, no, please, that's not true! Babs ordered me to fetch my Measurement Nudes. But in order to get *them* I had to fetch the *Gonzo Videos* as well."

Steph flashes eyes. "I told you 'tell me.' Now obey me."

Elle obeys. "I brought the *Gonzo Videos* to Babs to guarantee me an Opt Up."

"Nice present for Beka," Steph drolls. "I guess surprising her with the Measurement Nudes wasn't enough.

"Steph, please, Beka doesn't deserve it. I told her I'd make it up to her. I told her I—" Elle pauses.

"—deserve it," Steph concludes. "Just what have you promised your horny Roommate?" Steph probes.

"I promised her I'd ride the Dong with her before the end of *The Runup*. I told her I'd beg you to—" Elle quiets.

"—let you go streak and get it," Steph concludes.

Elle gasps.

Steph advances, "Did you tell her you'd beg me to take on *all* my Obeisance?"

"I'm doing that." Elle gathers her thoughts. "I told her I beg you to not screen the *Gonzo Videos*!"

"Because it wouldn't be fair to Beka," Steph projects sympathy.

"My point exactly," Elle says. Elle keeps her hands behind her head, and her pants rolled down below crotch. Blue hair and indelible dividing line through the notch. Another trickle of urine.

"Guess Beka's feelings were of less importance when you fetched this saving grace for yourself," Steph observes.

"Ma'am, please, I'd never think Babs would let you have them." Elle backpedals. "What Babs showed you was Beka and me messing around during a camping trip. These videos are private and personal videos, made long before Beka and I Pledged into the Game! They have no purpose here!"

Steph stretches and dances the ring around her neck. "That's not what the second Video shows," she taunts.

"Steph, please," Elle says, and loses control of another squirt of urine across the gap between her peehole and the rolled-down slacks.

"Remind me why you gave these *Videos* to Babs," Steph orders.

Elle huffs and rolls her eyes. "I gave the *Gonzo Videos* to Babs to guarantee me an Opt Up."

Steph sleazes. "Your *Gonzos* not only reveal you as a Whore, they reveal your Roommate as one also."

Elle snorts. "Yeah, well, Beka can take it. She got me into this! This was her idea. But I'm the one who had to deal with fetching the *Gonzos* and Measurement Nudes.

Steph chuckles, "You really are a vulgar cocksucking nockandro after all. Tell me, Whore, do you swallow?"

Elle squeezes fresh nectar out her nookie and steadies herself, "I know the Rules. Only Whores and Slavesex fuck and suck cock, and I am not a Whore! Nor about to be!"

Steph shrugs. "The only thing you know is to beg what I tell you. Beg me to Double Opt Down and Whore next Term. Do it nicely."

Elle proceeds carefully. "Ma'am, please let me Double Opt Down and be a Whore next Term, Madam."

"Except you know that's not possible, don't you Pledge?" Steph queries.

Elle rolls her tongue behind her front teeth.

Steph continues, "Except here's how it can work. You take your Opt Down and make Stripper and you add to that your Roommate's Opt Down. So you get a Double Opt Down and make Whore next Term."

"I can't leave Beka behind," Elle protests.

Steph firms. "Obey me, Pledge, and beg for real."

Elle begs, "Ma'am, please let me Double Opt Down and be a Whore next Term, Madam. And leave Beka behind."

"You deserve it," Steph says.

"I deserve it," Elle agrees.

Steph waves Elle to silence. "Right now you're just a wannabe Stripper who can only climax on cock. Lucky for you, your Gonzos provide evidence you're not just another frigid nikey, and that you really are able to climax after all!"

Elle again opens her mouth and sounds come out, "Ba ba ba...."

Steph dominates, "Maybe you should beg to screen these *Gonzo Videos* of yours." Steph smiles, "That way the entire Prefecture can critique your technique. I bet you're a hot little suck artist. You any good at eating pussy?"

Elle pleads, "Ma'am, help me, Ma'am."

Steph shrugs. "How about I help you lesbo climax at the Mansion Open House tonight."

"Ma'am please," Elle begs. "You know I'll do anything for you to make sure they stay secure."

"You'll break the Rules." Steph states. "You'll beg what I tell you to beg. You don't know about Rules, so you needn't know if you break them or not."

Elle says, "Ma'am!"

Steph crosses her arms in front of her, lifts her chin, and torments, "beg for a woman to climax you. You ever done that before?"

"Please, Steph," Elle begs. "I'm ready, willing, and maybe Beka wants to try. I've just never been able to cum by myself!"

Steph again slips a finger into Elle's exposed nook, audits wetness, and feeds Elle a fingertip. She leans in and offers advice. "Listen to me, you wannabe Whore, you'll have to be patient to fuck here at School. But here's the good news: Now that you're making it to Stripper, a cock 'n' pussy Whore lies only one more Term away!"

Elle babbles, "Ma'am, please the Gonzos, they're private, Ma'am. Even if I have to Double Opt Down Ma'am. Better you make me a Whore then reveal me to have been one."

Elle goes tactical; she begs, "Steph, please, Ma'am. Please take my slacks. Please let me shave bare bald and naked, make pink-wet-and-ready to climax. I'll streak to the Corvette House, fetch the Dong, and ride it with Beka. At the Mansion Open House, center Stage at the Nugget, anywhere, anytime in front of anybody."

"You beg me to take on my Pee-Cam!" Steph states.

"Ma'am, please let me take on our Pee-Cam. All of your Obeisance," Elle claims.

"You'll piss into your own mouth."

"Please, Steph, you know if the *Gonzo Videos* get played at the Nugget that the Patrons will insist that I beg Whore. They would condemn me. Beka too; Gamers would condemn the both of us. Maybe I deserve to be turned into a nutcracker, but Beka, she's totally innocent."

"Totally innocent?" Steph laughs, "But let's focus on you. You're improving, Pledge Elle Lollydor, and soon I will train you to cum—and in front of everyone!"

Elle rustles but holds position. *I think my armpits have sweat, my nookie is wet, and I keep spilling pee down onto my pants and the floor. I might still be standing upright but I have lost control.*

Steph mulls the recent developments. *Maybe William gave me a good tip,* she concedes. *He certainly pleasured me and made me cum. But he also fucked my asshole and made me clean up the mess. I'm not sure I like him anymore.*

But when I get my hands on Boss Bitch and Robyn I'm going to hogtie them on their backs, hole gag them, and pour piss and laxative into their mouths.

§ Steph Takes Elle's Slacks: And Promises to Climax Her

Elle holds her position: She stands topless, hands behind head and shaven armpits, with her slacks down just enough so that her notch shows. Daylight shines between the crotch and the top of the rolled-down slacks.

Elle's lifted pear breasts no longer have sag.

"Eyes forward and oval mouth," Steph commands.

Steph walks behind Elle, presses up against her body, and places three fingers into Elle's exposed crotch and forces upward with the middle finger. Wetness saturates Elle's vagina. "Hello nectar notch," Steph whispers into Elle's ear, then presses her own bare pussy against Elle's buttocks.

Elle ripples. Aside from the two of them the Kitchen remains empty. No sounds of footsteps approaching, no voices, no Cams.

"Stay," Steph commands, and reaches her arms around to Elle's face, feels inside her teeth, then slides her hands down Elle's chin and neck. She cups Elle's breasts and tests a nipple tweak. Continuing on, Steph lingers a moment on the ticklish part of Elle's goosebumped belly, then draws her hands around to Elle's lower back and press against kidneys. Elle, always loose with her urine, dribbles.

Elle comes to her senses. *Is being fondled part of the deal?* She flusters and blinks three times in rapid succession, *Of course. So is maybe sharing the Dong.*

Elle looks ahead and upward, observes Tiffany's Porn Star Calendar, and loses her breath.

"Legs together," Steph commands, and as Elle adjusts her posture she feels the back of Steph's hands work the waistline of her pants down to hobble her ankles. *I been naked before, but never handled,* Elle balances dizzily, *and I have never been handled by a woman!*

"Let's examine your indelible dividing line," exuberates Steph and she pushes Elle's knees apart. Elle feels Steph's fingers part her sex lips and verify that her indelible line crosses her clit, dips into her vagina, and bisects her asshole. *So when did this happen?* Steph wonders.

Elle doesn't dare look down but feels Steph step on the bunched slacks about her ankles, so that Elle is able to lift one leg then the other upward, extract her feet, and be nudged into a standing spread surrender position.

Elle feels Steph's fingers open her flaps, feels Steph's finger roll her own fresh nectar around on her erect nib, then dip a finger deeper into her nookie. Elle arches her pelvis forward and yields to the sensation and sacrifice. Not quite a moan, just the way she takes in air.

Steph controls her and swabs her finger across Elle's upper lip so she may whiff her own scent. Steph brushes her finger across Elle lips, then wipes it dry on her cheek, leaving a streak in Elle's makeup.

"Thank me," Steph commands.

Elle obeys. "Ma'am, thank you for finger-fucking me. My nookie belongs to you. Please finger my nookie whenever you want."

"Beg me to finger your asshole," Steph commands.

Elle gasps. "Ma'am," she stumbles, starts anew, Ma'am, please finger my nether aperture. Finger me whenever you want."

Steph walks behind the Pledge. "Bend over," she orders, and this time dips a finger into Elle's nadir gate. Steph returns to stand in front of her now, lifts Elle's chin, and offers the finger to Elle to clean off.

"Beg nicely," Steph commands. "Just remember, I don't make deals."

Elle blinks, "Ma'am, please let me clean me off your finger, Ma'am."

Steph accepts her beg, and Elle leans forward. Her head spins. *Steph wants to turn me into a Whore. The* Gonzo Videos *confirm me. Beka wants to be a Porn Star. And climax with me on the Double Dong. I need to be a Stripper next Term!*

Steph advances, "Hand me your pants."

Elle looks down at her rolled slacks lying on the floor. She bend over, adjusts her bare feet, picks them up with one hand, hesitates, and hands them to Steph. *Gone forever,* Elle accepts, and volunteers. "Please let me stay naked from now on," Elle offers, "24x7."

"You shall." Steph bows to her.

Elle doesn't quite know what to do. She wants to put her hands over her blue pussy hair and her colored nipples, but knows better. She moves her feet apart and retreats to a standing spread surrender position. *I'm stark naked now.*

Steph carefully works the slacks up her own body. The slacks ride five inches below her navel and together with the collar radiate power. Elle considers, *unlike when Tiffany or I wore the low-riders, Steph doesn't leak hair overtop.* Elle smiles. *Steph has nothing to hairage, although she is beginning to grow shadow.*

Steph runs a finger around what is now her waistline, then rotates her upper torso so she can look down her backside. *Posterior rugage,* Elle observes, *lot of it, just like I used to be.*

Some things don't go away even when advantage is gained.

Steph scourges now naked Elle. She reaches forward with both hands and pinches two nipple tips. Hard. The pressure increases until Elle flinches and wants to break position.

Steph appraises, "I might crack butt, flash stubble, and appear topless," Steph rotates her shoulders, "I might be boobage, but I've got two pieces and a guaranteed Opt Up!"

"I am the first Cosmos to actually Opt Up, and you are the first Cosmos to actually Opt Down.

"I'm going to take my time with you," Steph says.

Elle demurs, "Ma'am, I belong to you. Ma'am. I will shave bare bald and naked."

Steph appears unimpressed, "For a Pledge who owes her Roommate some Karma, surely you can expand your beg better than that. Beg, you needy nectar notch!"

Elle takes a breath and tries harder, "Ma'am, please let me Pledge bare bald and naked, stay pink-wet-and-ready, eat pussy and juice the Dong with Beka." Elle catches her breath, "Please let both of us cum be Strippers next Term, Ma'am!"

Steph augments details. "You are gonna take on my Pee-Cam, although it won't matter much, because once you get to the Nugget, you're Pee-Camer 24x7."

Elle must surrender, "Ma'am, thank you, Ma'am."

Steph acquires confidence that comes with wearing pants along with her collar. "You shall beg to acquire a Piss Mouth."

Elle shirks at this verbal assault and realizes that *events may not always play out like I anticipate; nor do I necessarily have control over them.* Still, Steph's pitch unnerves Elle and she doesn't know what to say, so she gurgles, "Ma'am, you've don't have a Piss Mouth to give me!"

Steph steps backward then forward again. "Then you shall make a preemptive acquisition!" Steph cracks and fine-tunes her control, "You shall obey my commands. Make your nipples erect and keep yourself pink-wet-and-ready."

Elle's mind whirls. *I have seen the videos of Steph with Molly from the Peacock House. I have witnessed first hand Steph Zoned for hours on end. Correction, days on end. Now the possibility of my own reduction looms ahead of me.*

Elle rolls her nipples in her fingers, fingers her pussy, and follows Steph's dictum.

"Beg to use the Shaving Kit at the Mansion Open House," Steph commands, unthinkingly, and coincidently squeezes her sex canal, feels something, and realizes *it—the Shaving Kit—occupies* my *socket and sternpipe!*

Elle knows to beg. "Please let me shave bare and shave bald at the Mansion Open House."

"You Naked 24x7," Steph affirms. "You need to fetch Double Dong now."

Elle considers. *Steph possesses the* Gonzo Videos *and I'm a Stripper next Term.* "Ma'am," she ventures, "I'll streak bare bald and naked to the Corvette House, bring the Double Dong back."

Elle pauses, then worms in a question. "Who else knows about the *Gonzo Videos*?" she asks.

Steph squints, and completes Elle's commitment, " and climax it."

Elle agrees. "And climax the Dong with Beka, Ma'am."

"You'll whore for me so I do not screen your *Gonzo Videos*," Steph advances.

Elle recoils, "Please, Steph, that's against the Rules, and you know it, Ma'am."

"No reason not to screen them," Steph says. "I bet you whored yourself so you could acquire your *Gonzos* for Boss Bitch," Steph asserts.

"Steph please," Elle begs, "You're not supposed to know what I did. Every time I go to get a *Gonzo* I make a new one."

"You shall beg me to Screen them when I require that," Steph says.

Elle sighs, "I get it, Steph, cause you want to make a Whore out of me. But don't me Double Opt Down and Opt Beka up. Please. "

"Maybe you should beg to take on Beka's marks," Steph suggests.

That would be Beka's first tattoo and piercing on top of my own, Elle calculates. A blob of nakodo that has been gaining volume on the end of Elle's clit detaches itself from her body and drops to the floor. Steph casts her eyes toward it, "Lick it up, Lollydor," she commands, and Elle descends to her hands and knees, and obeys.

Steph, empowered by the renewed decency of two pieces and the assurance of the Opt Up, does not doubt her possession of Elle. *Screw Boss Bitch,* Steph growls to herself. *Me Opting-Up is not her desired outcome for me. She's snookered me before. Maybe she's been coaching Elle or protecting Elle's secrets, but that's now over. Elle's Fate has been determined. She is mine to twist now.*

§ The Cosmos: Last Morning Before Beach Day

Boss Babe seeks Janet's advice about tonight's Mansion Open House. She leaves Robyn in charge of a naked quartet confined to the Bathroom, composed of Tiffany, Kimju, Molly, and Beka. All are surveyed by the Pee-Cam. All are showered, and their legs and armpits shaven.

May it please Robyn, this Cosmos Quartet will insist they spread and pink themselves, finger their assholes, and pee into the Measuring Cup. May Robyn be persuasive, share pee in their mouths. Only Beka, despite her begging remains virgin.

If the Quartet are lucky, Robyn will let them pose pink-wet-and-ready, and then slide them into the Zone so they can breath and cum as one unit.

Downstairs, and before exiting the Kitchen, Boss Babe moves Steph and Elle to the Dining Room so they may kneel with faces on the floor before the Baseboard Strippers. "Don't ever forget that until Midnight, you both remain Cosmos Pledge. So put some soak in that cameltoe and hang some nectar for me. Kapish?"

"Ma'am, yes, Ma'am," they respond in unison.

Steph seethes. She still wears the metal collar with her newly acquired, low-riding slacks. The collar ensures she continues to display her spooters, and the slacks guarantee Steph cracks her stern swale. Two Garments.

Elle, now totally naked, can't begin to hide the indelible line down her back and through her naka-nake trench, across her puckered nadir portal, and coming forward to highlight her nymphae and ascend toward her button. Elle still has some butched blue hair to remove. *I know, Steph's going to take that away from me too.*

BB opens a back Dining Room window so that the Back Door Cam can look in, even come inside to the to keep an eye on the two Pledge. Elle studies the portraits of Baseboard Strippers Penny and Coco, observes that both of them pull pink. She accepts her future and reaches between her legs to pull pink herself for the Cam.

I'm surrendering, Elle realizes, *maybe Steph will cream in her pants, but I've been commanded to arouse myself and hang out my nautch secretions.*

I think I'd rather be commanded to pee on the floor and beg to be a Pee-Cam Pledge. I'm going to take on all of Steph's Obeisance, I know that.

§ Babs & Janet: Strategy re Steph & Elle and Penny & Coco

A topless full-breasted Pledge Louise, now wearing only the lower half of what devolved from Janet's Spiderweb Bikini, greets BB at the Corvette House Front Door.

Devolved indeed, except the size pico Spiderweb has no size smaller. It's crochet, all right, but only strings. One string ascents up lateral divide, cresting at the top of her butt, parting and flashing forward over her hip and descending to meet two strings ascending up the insides of Louise's inner lips so as to part just below her clithood, and ball her clit out.

Louise rolls a shoulder at Babs and snides, "Thank you for forcing me to cum be a Stripper next Term." Louise knows she's on Cam, points her crotch to the Cam, and uses the string to roll her lips open. Louise straightens, bows, and commends, "Ma'am, may you too get to pink the Cam soon, Ma'am!"

Babs blinks; she follows Louise into the Parlor where Janet rises from a chair. Louise bows and walks backward through the door to the Kitchen. Janet smiles. Babs surveys: same layout as the Cosmos House.

The ex-Cosmos Roommates and now House Monitors exchange pleasantries. Janet continues to wear what was once Louise's bandeau and T-front maillot, only today Janet wears the bandeau overtop the maillot. Janet might be plump but she always looks hot, and her Monitor powers have enabled her to better tailor the Garments to her own special frame.

Janet takes the lead in costume complements. "Congratulation on three Garments, Babs!" she says. Janet gestures to her own fleshy figure sculpted into the bandeau and t-front. "As for little o' me? I've upgraded! If I don't want to Hover I intend to acquire a third piece from someone."

Babs furrows her brow. "So Louise and Lee Lollydor now share what used to be your Crochet Bikini."

Janet prides. "Strippers next Term, both of them. Lee will get to take her Lollydor back to the Nugget. As for ex-Monitor Louise, she shall enjoy her second consecutive bump down: A naked pinking Nugget next Term, masturbating and begging toys in her holes. Just like the rest of us."

Janet looks Babs in the eye, "Well, not all of us, actually."

Babs considers her own three pieces: a black stretchy shortsleeve cutout minidress over a bra and nombril. Straps showing, button hole centered on an oval of flowing skin that kisses the top of the nombril beneath. "I'm going to Hover, Janet," BB states, "I'll give a piece away at the last moment, I'll give it to you if that would be allowed."

Babs references Louise. Guilt abounds. "You made me audition Louise at the Nugget. Make her strip naked, then trade her your Spider Bikini for her bandeau and maillot." Babs looks Janet in the eye. "That's okay, because you're my friend and I owe you. I turned Louise into a Stripper and let you play with Steph."

Janet holds steady. "I accept that. But don't forget MomCap seized an opportunity to monetize Ginny, who got loaned for Steph. Collateral. Maybe you didn't get to use her, but MomCap got to work our Whore-for-Life at the Nugget."

Some of Babs' guilt is assuaged. She adds, "You got to use Steph."

"I force-climaxed her out of her body!" Janet pitches for her own. "Besides, I made sure Steph got to watch Ginny up so close she could smell her sweat, smell her gyno glop, and watch her collect cum."

"Some good it did," Babs retorts, "Steph somehow collected a Duel, and Elle is the first confirmed Opt Stripper next Term. Steph intends to take her to the Mansion Open House, shave her bare and bald in front of the Guests, climax her naked, and make her piss on herself."

Janet snarls, "Maybe Robyn made Steph taste pee this Term, but she is hardly a confirmed Piss Mouth. For Steph to think she can foist Piss Mouth off upon Elle is mean!" Janet shakes a fist, "Steph needs to swallow a good dose of what she's proposing to dish out! While we still have time!"

"I'm not so sure," Babs says, "it would have to be this afternoon, before the Mansion Open House. Because if Steph turns Elle into a Piss Mouth, she can claim any Obeisance she had, will have been transferred."

"I think that if Steph wants to foist watersports upon Elle, that Steph had better understand her gift," Janet states firmly. "

"We can't do this, Janet," Babs complains. "Steph's a Monitor next Term no matter what. I'm going to be a Monitor too. We'd be equals. She'll get back at us."

"We outnumber her, even if I Hover and don't Opt Up," Monitor Janet states. "Steph already thinks she's a hot-shot humiliating Elle. Suddenly kaboom! Piss Mouth!"

Babs hesitates and recalls Steph's decision to cover her button last Term. "Last Term Steph's own arrogance broke her."

They speak in unison, "Steph helped us get ahead!" They both laugh.

Janet opines, "Steph wants to make Elle the slut that she was proving herself to be, before she got lucky with the taking a Duel."

Babs feels sympathy for Elle. "Steph doesn't just want to defeat Elle, she has already done that. Steph wants to grind her. Get this, somehow Steph found out about the *Gonzo Videos*. I didn't tell her. But I don't think I can go to the Open House and watch whatever Steph does to her."

"Come," Janet says, and leads Babs out the Corvette House Back Door. A sturdy wooden platform sits waist-level above the ground in the Backyard, and upon it, sit Corvette Pledge Ginny and Trixi Tubes.

"The insights your lovely Tiffany provided during her visit are a lesson they have learned." Janet gestures toward the two sitting Corvette

Pledge. "Today each of them wears a tube over their bosom. Ginny wears the two inch wide orange tube and Trixi the eight inch wide blue tube.

"It's wonderful that Tiffany taught them to share!" Janet proclaims.

Share they do, as they sit face-to-face, they not only share the pair of tubes, they also share both ends the Double Dong in their works.

Janet commands Ginny and Trixi Tubes demonstrate "The Nine Dong Combinations." Babs finds herself repelled when the Corvette Roommates rapidly share the Dong in nine different pussy-anus-mouth combinations, ending with mouth-to-mouth.

"Well, congratulations," Babs hesitates, awed at the precision of the drill and the presence of a Cam feeding the drill.

Janet catches Babs' look. "I'll advise Automatron to make sure your Cosmos Pledge can watch the Dong put to such good use. Some of them beg for it, yes?"

Babs sighs.

The twosome walk around the side of the Corvette House and out to the front as Babs prepares to depart. BB worries to her colleague. "We must both be careful. Steph has it out for us and she's for sure a Monitor next Term.

"That's one reason I'm considering to Opt MomCap," Janet states.

Babs worries more. "Penny and Coco still have it out for us too. For Opt-Downing them last Term."

Janet assures, "Don't worry about them, they're already begging to ho-Dong. And we shall help them achieve their begs! Just like last time."

II-42 William & Rodney: Steph Piss Mouth & Elle Lolly (D27)

§ William & Rodney Visit: Elle Begs Dong & Lollys Lube

Bringing males into the Cosmos House rarely occurs and violates any expectations of Cosmos privacy.

Janet had encouraged Monitor Babs to let Robyn perform Steph's final crush, least she escape the Term unscathed before becoming a Monitor next Term. With this goal in mind, and upon her return to the Cosmos House, Babs gathers up naked Steph and Elle from worshiping the Baseboard Strippers in the Dining Room, and herds them upstairs into the Bathroom where Robyn continues to supervise four other naked Pledge, who sit spread surrender in a row on the tile floor: Tiffany, Kimju, Molly, and Beka.

Babs wears a shortsleeve black cutout minidress or'top a bra and nombril; the oversize cutout hole kisses the top of the nombril, inches below Babs' belly button. Robyn still wears her transparent croptop and miniskirt overtop her golden maillot cutout, with "the smallest buttonhole."

Robyn looks at Steph and Elle and orders, "Sit spread surrender. "Join your fellow Pledge, look at yourself in the mirror opposite until you are transfixed with yourself, then hang some cream for the Cam.

Elle steels a glance at the Four Cosmos, sits and settling herself at the end of the Lineup next to Beka, and contemplates her nose, nipples, navel and notch in the mirror. Elle wavers. *This mirror isn't supposed to be Minxy, so maybe it's just me.*

Five of them—Tiffany, Kimju, Molly, Steph, and Beka—are naked because they are committed Pee-Cam Pledge who always activate the Bathroom Cam and always use the Bathroom naked, all but Tiffany have Garments back on their bunks. One of them—Elle—is not naked because she is a Pee-Camer; Elle is naked because she no longer possesses any Garments.

Elle understands, *I am naked now, 24x7 and I'm Stripping next Term. No one can help me, except Beka, and only then by being with me.*

Beka's g-string lies back in her Bunk, and yes, provided that she doesn't get another Garment, she will accompany Elle to the Nugget next Term.

Steph chaffs at being forced to join the other Pledge, but Robyn insists, finds fortitude in Boss Babe's eyes, and so Steph sits with the others, spreads her legs, exposes her bare crotch, and clasps her hands behind her bald head. *Boss Bitch and Robyn Redacted intend to keep me bare bald and naked until Midnight. They think they can do this, but I won't forget.*

Six naked Cosmos sitting spread surrender in front of the Bathroom Cam is a treat. Robyn augments, "pink."

They all do. Hesitantly at first, and rippling down the line from Tiffany, through Kimju and Molly, Steph with hesitation, Beka ahead of Steph actually, and finally Elle on the end. Elle moves her arms slowly and gracefully, reaches between her spread thighs, grabs opposing flaps, and opens. Her body shakes, she pants. She pines to the live Cam, consoles herself. *I've already had to audition the Nugget, pass out my Pink Page, and next Steph is going to climax me at the Mansion Open House.*

"Freshen!" Robyn commands, and they all diddle, even Elle, who watches herself in the mirror and finds the synchronization and excitement overwhelming. *After the Mansion Open House, Gamers are going to streak me to the Nugget. But I'll never make it. I'm going to be captured—*

All ears capture the sound of feet climbing the back stairs and then walking down the hall—multiple footsteps—but it is still a shock to the Six Cosmos Lineup when William and Rodney walk into the Bathroom.

To whatever extent the Six Masturbating Cosmos break form, Robyn quickly takes charge. "Gentlemen," she prims, "May I present Six Cosmos Pledge, all of them 'pink-wet-and-ready' to cum!"

William glances at a silent Babs and then squints at the Lineup. He wears a black long-sleeve shirt and slacks with black moccasins. His Roommate, the over-testosteroned Rodney, remains bare-chested, body shaven, and wears only a jockstrap. The narrow straps around Rodney's waist and around to the sides of his butt ensure that his butt crack stays uncovered and his asshole opens to the wind.

Babs completes the introductions, "Pledge, some of you may have met William and Rodney, the Monitor of the Peacock House and his Roommate."

"Three Garments, one Garment," Robyn edges in.

William bows; Rodney looks uncertain.

BB addresses Steph and Elle. "I'm considering not going to the Mansion Open House tonight, and that being the case perhaps you two can induce William to assist in your transport."

Steph blinks but squares her posture: *I'm sitting spread, pink-wet-and-ready, bare bald and naked. Except I've exercised my Option to Opt Monitor next Term. This is not fair.*

Steph studies the power dynamics with caution. *I have a collar and slacks on my Bunk: Two Garments. I am a Monitor next Term. So I hold power, despite having to present myself naked right now.*

Robyn charms, "Steph might be a guaranteed Opt Monitor next Term but she's still a Pee-Camming Cosmos Pledge until Midnight tomorrow."

Robyn cackles. "Elle's naked 24x7 until Midnight and begging to be a naked Nugget next Term. She's anticipated at the Mansion Open House and will need to streak to get there, and to the Nugget afterwards."

Steph trades unrevealing eyes with William. *Nobody here has any reason to suspect William and I are fuck buddies. And William isn't about to tell.*

Besides after he analed me and then made me clean myself off, he's on my shit list. Even though he owes me Karma.

Robyn charms Elle. "Elle Lollydor, you're gonna take all of your Obeisance to the Nugget next Term, so I betcha you wants to lolly up lube that comes out of a man. Cause there will be a lot of them there and you won't want to miss out."

Elle considers Rodney stationed in front of Steph. *Blowjobs and facial is Whore work, Elle believes, but lube, pre-cum, is not cum, is it.* Elle feels an urge to pee. The blue hair on her head and her nook remain shaven down the middle, her engorged nugogo comes out from its hood, and goose bumps form along the indelible line that divides her left and right sides. She blushes, first her cheeks, and then a V down into her bare chest. *I shouldn't touch myself,* she admits as she pulls her rosy pink, but does it anyway, and her areolas and nipples bubble up and erect.

Beka, with her gessoed green Mohawk and Hitler but absent the g-string for the moment, looks sideways at Elle and then Steph. "Elle will take on not just her own Obeisance, she'll take Steph's Obeisance to the Nugget too." Beka blurts. "She and I both!"

Rodney scans the sitting spread pink and masturbating Lineup, passes eyes with Beka, and they both spot. More correctly Rodney lubes into his stretch fabric jockstrap, and naked Beka extends an already hanging bead.

Molly, naked with dyed red hair and stained skin, is grateful for the Bathroom's costume restrictions *because they provides relief from holding panties in my mouth or pussy or asshole.*

Besides, I prefer it when the Cam canvasses me. Molly eyes study William and Rodney. *They watched me pee into my own mouth while climaxing at the Greatest House Roar, and may want to top me.*

Orange hair and orange body stain cover Kimju's temporarily naked body. She worries, *what if William or Rodney steal my halter and shorts back in the Bunkroom?* She reminds herself that *Rodney cammed my pink and piss on the Yacht, and insisted it was my Pee-Cam audition.*

Tiffany, naked 24x7 and with purple hair, shares disaffection for Rodney. *Rodney abused me when I changed my shirt and popped the Peacocks during* The Arrivals, *he tried to fuck me on the Yacht, and he's the one who made me lick up piss at the Greatest House Roar.*

Tiffany evaluates more, *Still, Rodney has never had more than one Garment, so likely he's a Stripper next Term. I like that. I'd like even better that he becomes a rimjob and anal Whore if the turn after that. I'd fuck him.*

Robyn sweeps a hand before the Lineup. "Beg once," she orders.

And Six Cosmos do. "Please let me Pledge naked and cum be a Stripper next Term."

Robyn turns to William and Rodney. "Four of these Pledge are gonna be Strippers next Term. Some have already passed out their Pink Pages, and some have shared the Double Dong. Only Steph is for sure an Opt Up and only Elle is for sure an Opt Down. That leaves Tiffany, Kimju and Molly, and Beka vying for the opportunity. So many wannabes, so few beds at the Nugget."

Beka blurts, "Me please, Ma'am, I want to Opt Down with Elle. I'll shave bare bald and naked. I'll streak to the Nugget. We both will!"

Robyn spins on her heel. "You may be sure that your most explicit *Videos* will pay in the Nugget Lobby next Term. Every bit of pink and pee and Dong media from now on. And everything from ever before." Robyn snarls at Beka. "You and your Roommate both."

Steph observes Rodney staring at her opened pink and wet snapdragon. As she catches him he averts his eyes and casts them upon Molly's crimson wet meat.

William chooses to speak, "So nice to visit with you again. He bows to Molly and Steph. "Last time in the Backyard I was with Janet, and you two proposed the Greatest House Roar. It was such an honor to have you come perform."

Rodney chimes in, "And it was so much fun to watch one of your lose, Steph Sorostitute!"

Molly tunes up her mainspring and freshens crosty meringue. Now William stares at Steph's pink, with a renewed diddle and wetness. Spurge out. Camming to the Prefecture.

William offers Steph his condolence, "You've been pretty Zoned, Pledge."

Steph takes in a sharp breath, and Rodney rudely rubs it in, "We've seen all your feeds. My favorite is when you and Molly piss climaxed all over each other."

Robyn interjects and bloviates, "Steph licked the pee off my feet." She bows to Steph, "Nice work, Piss Mouth."

Steph scowls. *That's not how I remember it.*

Tiffany and Molly trade a look via the mirror. *Sure, but we cleaned up the floor.*

Steph holds calm and feels confident that she and William can stay out of a fight. *All I have to do is crush Elle tonight at the Mansion Open House. And then I'm Opt free.*

Rodney piles history upon Steph, "Kimju jammed you into the Zone and Janet took you out of your body. You juiced Tiffany's Dong, shaved bare and bald, kowtowed to the newbies, and moved into the Doghouse." Rodney bounces on his feet, "Too bad you missed the Mermaid Parade."

Steph glowers and sneaks a glance at William. *I am not entirely sure William contributes to my good fortune.* Steph mulls. *Throating me after using my ass is an act reserved for Whores and Slavesex. Not me.*

Steph may have forgotten that sucking and fucking and facials are also acts reserved for Whores and Slavesex.

"Too bad you're not a Whore-for-Life like Ginny Corvette," William drawls.

Steph narrows her focus, maintains her cool, and diddles her clit to make sure her shaven slit stays slippery. The Cam collects every intimate detail, including her stern hole pucker.

Steph worries. *William did give me a valuable tip about Elle's* Gonzo Videos. *But right now I just need to get Elle to the Mansion Open House without any complications.*

William looks down at Elle and asks a question. "So, Cosmos Pledge, do you want to streak to the Mansion Open House or do you want to beg for a ride?"

Elle finds herself speechless. "Mister," she begins, baubles, tries again. Mister, please may I beg you to transport me to the Mansion Open House." Elle casts a wild glance, "I'll do what you want. Provided that Steph approves, Mister."

Robyn interjects, "You'll lolly that spot of lube out of Rodney's jockstrap." And signs Elle onto her hands and knees. Now she is in front of Rodney.

Elle looks toward the Bathroom doorway. *No way out.*

Boss Babe interrupts just as Elle's head approaches the jock. "Pull the fabric away from his body, Elle, so that when you lolly the stretch fabric it is free of his skin.

Elle obeys, and vacuums Rodney's lube out of the fabric. She can not avoid observing an erect penis inside.

Beka tenses up, suddenly jealous that *Elle services my guy!*

William applauds Elle. "You're special. Strippers never volunteer to Lolly, but once a Pledge does, they never give up the habit. Whores lolly, obviously, but unlike Pledge, they can't take it with them to the Strip."

This time the Cam documents Elle releasing a dribble of pee onto the floor. Elle blinks. *Thank goodness I'm not a piss mouth!*

§ Robyn & Rodney: Ensure Steph Qualifies as Piss Mouth

Robyn signs Steph onto her hands and knees and to crawl into formation with Elle.

Steph worries. *Yes, I might have a guaranteed Opt Up, but for now I remain a Cosmos Pledge. Worse, my former Roommate and traitor, Robyn Redacted, continues to possess the power of Boss Bitch's voice. I hate her.*

Politics is frequently tricky.

Robyn gesticulates to William. "Steph insists she never licked pee off my feet yet she also insists she intends to bestow a Piss Mouth upon Elle. A contradiction of conditions, it would seem to me," Robyn says.

"I said—" Steph begins.

"Shut up!" Robyn interrupts.

Several Cosmos hear a facet drip; most know what drips are about.

"Fetch the Measuring Cup," Robyn points, and the Cam watches Steph's blood boil as she obeys. *I've been pouring pee into the Measuring Cup since Molly and I piss climaxed in this very Bathroom five Days ago. And now I have to pee live in front of men?*

The Cam follows Steph as she crawls, returns with the Cup, and watches as Robyn kneels her in front of Rodney. Steph turns to look for Elle, but Elle is no longer by her side but is behind her. *Somewhere. Now what?*

Steph scowls. *She examines the bare-chested chiseled male before and above her.* Directly in front of her face, Rodney's taut Spandex jockstrap lacks any ability to disguise a massive hardon inside. Furthermore, the bubble of lube that Elle lollyed out of the jockstrap only moments ago has reconstituted itself, indeed, it has grown larger.

"Pull the jock down," Robyn commands.

Steph pauses. *Blowjobs are forbidden to Cosmos Pledge.*

But pulling a jock down and looking a cock in the eye isn't a blowjob. It's not even sex.

Steph considers. And uses two hands to work the jock up and over Rodney's erection and down level with the crotch, then below his balls, and backside down the butt.

Indeed, Rodney's massive hardon stands upward. William adds narration. "Fact is Rodney's uncut, but you can't tell when he's erect because his foreskin stretches back."

Yes, Steph observes, *the skin is so tight that the head displays fully!* But also this: *More lube hangs out the end!*

Naked Elle, back a step and not kneeling, watches naked Steph as Rodney eyes Steph's mouth and dares her to beg for his drip. Elle's entire pelvis goes into a twitch, because Elle knows *I just got that taste in my mouth! Rodney's lube.* And this triggers her to transude fresh nectar, now seeping toward the insides of her thighs.

Beka, back in the Lineup, feels a flush coming on; *I'm the one who has fucked Rodney, and I don't like him using Steph to arouse himself!*

Beka drops a globule of her own brodeas onto the floor.

Something deep in Robyn's Redacted psyche enables her to once again take opportunity with her Monitor from last Term. She commands Steph. "Oval mouth, you bare bald and naked shallow sloss scallop."

Steph purses her lips before she opens her mouth but keeps the oval open. *No other Pledge made an issue about my button getting covered. Only you.*

Robyn explains to Steph. "Rodney is making a guest appearance on the Cosmos House Pee-Cam today. You shall hold the Measuring Cup."

Steph frowns. *I thought the Duel guaranteed me an Opt Up.*

Next Term. Next Term starts after Midnight of the Beach Day, tomorrow.

And I have already stripped Elle naked. I have a guaranteed Opt Up.

True, but it doesn't start until Midnight, end of day tomorrow.

Robyn addresses Rodney, "Bend your pecker down and shoot a stream of pee into Steph's mouth."

Steph makes to talk but Robyn waggles a finger. Steph looks to the side, sees the Cam monitoring her, and adjusts full oval mouth.

Robyn addresses Steph, "Hold the Cup below your mouth. Let the pee drain out of your mouth into the Cup."

Robyn addresses Rodney, "Turn the pee off when the Cup fills up. Steph will beg to drink the pee, and collect more. Rodney, after you've drained, we shall log your Cups on the Measuring Chart. Guest of Honor!"

Steph closes her mouth and prepares a question.

"Oval mouth!" Robyn reminds. "No swallowing! No depriving Rodney of his full measure!"

The shot of hot piss arrives sooner than expected. It hits Steph on the top of her bald head, wham, and as she tilts her head upward the stream slices across her face and catches her mouth.

The pee runs off Steph's head and torso onto the floor, and out of her mouth and into the Measuring Cup. The cup fills and Steph closes her mouth before Rodney shuts his stream off.

Robyn signs Tiffany to take and drink the Cup and Tiffany plays to the Cam shot.

Again Steph poses Open Mouth and holds the Cup to collect her overflowing mouth. Rodney sharpens his aim and again streams yellow into Steph's reopened mouth.

Once again there is reaction: Steph bends backward but recovers enough to tilt forward and spill the stream back out of her mouth, and again fill the Measuring Cup. By the time Rodney shuts down this time the Cup overflows and Steph blows pee out of her nose. She swallows. Still more pee runs off her head and down her body.

This time Molly gets to drink the Cup. No smiles; down the hatch.

Babs watches as Steph sluices and collects a third Cup, one not quite full but draining Rodney completely.

"Your turn, Piss Mouth," Robyn tells Steph. Here in the Bathroom Robyn still wears three Garments: the transparent croptop and miniskirt over the maillot cutout. Steph is naked. *Except I have two pieces sitting on my bunk. I better have.*

Steph carefully brings the Cup to her lips, sips, chokes, spills much of the Cup, and in desperation gulps the balance.

The man-piss dripping off of Steph's body, the smell in her nostrils, and the taste in her mouth suddenly overwhelms her, and she voids a burst of her own urine. She catches herself, but not in time to avoid puddling the floor.

Robyn snaps. "You are supposed to use the Measuring Cup, you slithering splurt scumbucket."

Steph suppresses a sob at her humiliation and looks up to catch Babs' eye. *Bimbo Bitch needs to put a stop to this.*

BB just watches.

The sound of tinkle hitting the tile floor occurs behind Steph and Elle, and they turn to watch Tiffany arch pee forward from her spread legs, purple thatch and opened twat.

Tiffany now commands the Cam. Tiffany fears not the consequence, "I'm a Pee-Camer and Piss Mouth just like you are," she declares to Steph, "and I am a Porn Star! The more co-stars I shoot scenes with, the more my fans love me!"

Steph sputters, still with the sting of pee in her mouth and eyes. Elle catches Tiffany give Babs a wry smile; Elle grits her teeth, and considers that *besides already begging to Pee-Cam, Am I now going to inherit Steph's Piss Mouth?*

And I need to pee. Now.

So does Steph.

Suddenly Elle hears another stream of urine release. She looks, and watches her Roommate arch a stream. And then to her horror, watches Kimju and Molly join the quartet.

Elle's eyes widen as she tries to control her own urge.

Monitor Babs calms her. "Wait!" Boss Babe commands. "You may commence using the Pee-Cam and Measuring Cup tomorrow, because tonight you shall donate your pee at the Mansion Open House."

Elle gasps, squeezes her pelvis tight, but Robyn already commands Steph. "You, Steph Sorostitute," Robyn snarls, "hold the Measuring Cup in your teeth, curl yourself on your back with your spout held high, and pee into your Cup."

The Bathroom Pee-Cam feeds Steph's Piss Mouth to the Prefecture.

Steph takes a deeper look into the Pee-Cam, licks her lips, and Steph ends up writing "1" on the Logging Chart, but that is only because she already spilt and decides to hold back the rest.

Steph constricts her vagina to feel the stainless steel sphere in her snatch, and constricts her anal snake around the Shaving Kit rod.

She glowers at Robyn. *I am going to break you to Slavesex some day!*

II-43 Steph Invites Elle: Shave Pee Cum at Mansion (D27)

§ Steph & Elle: Transported to Mansion Open House

Did the Professor forget to notate that on the way out of the Bathroom that Tiffany rouged Elle's cheeks; added stain and then gloss to her lips, nipples, navel, and clit; touched up her finger and toenail polish, and strengthened her eyes? Tiffany had pronounced, "You're ravishing and irresistible!"

Indeed, Elle admits to herself, *and somehow I know it. I'm caught between retaining my modesty and showing my holes. I'm showing my holes. I can't stop leaking nectar. I'm going to beg the Dong tonight and climax somehow.*

If Steph shows my Gonzo Videos *that prequalifies me to Whore.*

Plus there's what I had to do to get them to give me the Gonzos in the first place, so I could present them to Babs.

So I could turn myself in and become a Slavesex.

Elle had traded vanishing glances with Beka on her way out the Bathroom. *Fear and anguish.*

Elle had read Beka's lips, "Don't get tattooed and pierced without me!" Elle trades wide eyes. *I had forgotten ink and steel were a part of becoming a Stripper! Except I'm not a Stripper until the clock strikes Midnight of the Beach Day tomorrow!*

And then? *I'm naked and spreading and pinking on Stage.*

Steph gritted and followed Elle out of the Bathroom, with Rodney's fresh urine still sparkling on her naked body. Steph had gritted with the man-smell, had stood upright, and taken charge of Elle. "Come along Elle Lollydor. You're gonna go for the ride of your life tonight!"

William had followed them out of the Bathroom. Rodney, the last to leave and with his jock back in place, had looked back as he existed the door, somewhat proud of his mess.

Gamers may decide how to manage the cleanup.

§ Steph & Elle: Arrive at the Mansion Open House

Darkness has set upon the planet when Steph and Elle find themselves discharged from William's Van onto a curving driveway in front of the Chancellor's Manson on a hilltop overlooking the School. Rodney opens the door for them.

Upon leaving the Bathroom and picking up her clothes from her bunk, Steph had discovered that her metal collar, that Garment which was once Elle's croptop, have been magically restored to an open-armhole, scoop-neck croptop, and as if to counterbalance her gains, that her low-riding slacks have become crotchless, with an oval of fabric missing, so that her stubbled slit (and sternpipe might she bend over) are now completely visible. Steph grimaces as she pulls them tightly up; they continue to ride low on her pelvis, and completely mold her stern semiglobes above the absent crotch fabric and butt crack.

The lithe Steph is hardly respectable: bald, titters if she leans over or lifts, and with four days of stubble displaying on her pouted pussy lips.

Steph acquires confidence and poise as she walks, yet she still worries. *I still have the Shaving Kit stainless ball in my socket and the long cylinder up my shitter. Will the Visitors demand I spread my slit, extract the Shaving Kit, and masturbate to climax for them?*

Steph squares up. They can jerk off to me as much as they want, because the bottom line is I'm a guaranteed Opt Up.

Steph takes a deep breath. *Besides, Gamers are done hazing me. Because we all know that has to happen next: I have a job to do.*

"The job" departs from the Van stark naked. Elle's butched hair on her head and her nookie still have a shaven trench down the center; her lips, nipples and navels are stained blue; and the narrow, indelible line divides her body into left and right sides. The line rises vertically up across the belly button, in between her noogies, up her chin and face and nose, through the trench across the top of her head, down her spine between her shoulder blades, fully inside her naka-naka trench, across her nadir gate, and into the narrows and darkening the nib, and up to her button again.

"Hands and knees," Steph orders, and as Elle drops down Steph prods her with a sharp toenail to crawl forward. "Bark for me," Steph commands, "and keep barking."

Elle obeys. It hurts to crawl on hands and knees on the concrete, but Steph's sharp toenails keep Elle in motion. Steph exchanges words at the front door, it opens before her, and she leads Elle in. Steph's curving bellage lies framed between her scoop neck croptop and low-rise stretch slacks, and her stubbled bare snooch attracts eyes as she glides through the house... but the eyes drop to the colorful naked creature that crawls at her heels. "Arf! Arf! Arf!"

Elle follows Steph out another door and onto a patio at the backside of the Mansion. Elle finds her forward motion arrested. "Arf! Arf! Arf!" Elle find it hard to remember to keep barking, but she knows where the dog lives. Steph's voice speaks from above her. "Silence. Stand up. Recline back on this pool chair. Open up; legs to the side. Hand above your head. Folks want to look you over—before they freshen you up."

The dog becomes human again.

§ Steph Demands Elle: Beg to Shave Bare Bald and Naked

Elle discovers herself lying back in a patch of light surrounded by faces. She looks up and detects Steph's crotchless slash directly above her, and then, higher still, Elle looks up inside Steph's croptop and sees both of Steph's flattish breasts and nipples.

Above that Elle looks into Steph's eyes, for an instant, and then panning down and away Elle detects a swimming pool not far away.

A blur of bodies and faces and Cams surrounded Elle's pool recliner. Elle, with her spread legs and nook on display, is stunned for an instant. It is a long instant before she can spin the blur of faces and voices into her consciousness. She stabilizes, connects moving lips with a command: "Look this way," and she does, And then to another cry, "run your tongue around your lips," now casting her eyes and wetting her lips.

"Roll over," a voice commands, and she obeys, "lift your ass in the air," and she obeys and convulses, and "pull your cheeks apart and show us your asshole," and Elle gives up all self-respect.

"Pink!" she hears in the night air, so she lowers her fingers, digs into the skin, and pulls outward with opposite hands.

Elle hears murmurs from the Visitors milling about and discovers herself rolled on her back again, again with her legs spread and her center line showing between her butched blue nest. With its indelible centerline.

Elle watches her own hands move to perform a two-hand butterfly. As wide as possible, pink inner flaps laid flat to the sides, clit balled out of its hood, pee hole showing, anal puckering, pink vaginal canal vanishing to darkness.

Elle knows, *I'm being Cammed. Should I be starting to like it?*

It doesn't matter. Elle lifts her index fingers upward, pushes her clit from opposite sides, and wells nectar from inside her hole.

Elle more carefully surveys the throng around her. Handheld Cams everywhere, hovering Cams too, micro Cams embedded into the lounger itself, made from a transparent rubberlike fabric, supported on a sturdy frame.

Future Stripper Elle casts eyes further afield from future Monitor Steph: Visitors of the Chancellor populate the Open House, and include many from School. *My driver, William is here.* Elle spots Janet and Darleen, House Mom with a bare and naked Penny and Coco in tow, and Madam Nurse Beautician, tonight wearing white nurse rubber with red crosses. *Once I take on Steph's Obeisance they will all piss in my mouth.*

Further back Elle spies Game Mistress, wearing a black rubber bodysuit with a zipper crotch, and accompanied by a wonderful bare and naked China Doll, with the backs of her buttocks and thighs striped with vicious mulberry-red welts. Elle feels faint when it sinks in that the blisters result from a fresh caning. *They hurt! No way China Doll wants to sit down!*

Besides, Elle recollects, *Tiffany told me Game Mistress had unzipped her crotch at the Greatest House Roar and affixed China Doll's mouth to her privates. I first assumed China Doll serviced Game Mistress's clit, but Tiffany said she also collects pee.*

Elle draws her eyes away from Game Mistress and China Doll, then back to Steph, who looks her in the eye and speaks. "You lucky naked wannabe Stripper right now. You'll beg to cum whenever I want you to!"

Elle rubs her clit harder and gasps. "Ma'am, yes, Ma'am," she says, and squeezes out more nectar.

But most of the faces are strangers. *I don't see Beka or Babs or Robyn anywhere, so I have to do this alone, I don't see Ginny, nor any other Pledge who might share the spotlight with me.*

Of course not, Elle accepts, *I am the star of tonight's show.*

True.

But climax for the Cosmos' first Opt Down shall wait for a while; Steph steers the agenda and announces, "You're going to shave tonight, you notch nug!" Elle looks up and sees stubble framed from the crotchless oval in Steph's slacks, and stubble on Steph's bald head. Steph looks down at Elle, "Everybody knows you were begging to shave off the hair *above* your slacks, but now that you're not wearing slacks anymore, maybe you got a different beg?"

Elle stumbles but agrees. "Ma'am, yes, Ma'am," Elle states. "Please let me shave bare bald and naked and cum be a Stripper next Term!"

§ Steph lets Penny & Coco: Shave Elle's Head & Pussy Right

The Crowd ripples as Strippers Penny and Coco emerge out of the background a holding a bowl of warm water and a tray. The two naked Nuggets trade uneasy eyes with their once-upon-a-time Monitor Steph: Penny and Coco had used the Shaving Kit to keep themselves bare prior to deftly removing Steph's long hair while climaxing her senseless at the Nugget, four Days ago.

But after Steph's Nugget depilation the Shaving Kit had traveled to the Cosmos House, where it migrated from Kimju to Beka and eventually to Steph, only yesterday, and where it currently resides and whose possessor has had no chance to utilize.

A hush falls over the crowd as, the two naked long-haired Strippers, Penny and Coco, face Steph.

Steph makes the next move: She lifts one leg up and places her foot down upon Elle's face. Cams cluster as her crotchless snatch splays wide to the Prefecture.

"Step and fetch it," Steph orders, and Penny and Coco comply. One of them finger scoops the metal ball out of Steph's sex cavity while the other extracts the curved cylinder from Steph's stern tube.

Elle again looks up to see nipples inside Steph's croptop. Elle looks at Steph's stubbled pubes framed by her crotchless slacks, only now the slit is expanded so that Steph's inner lips hang free, her clithood doesn't completely hide the clit, her peehole shows, and the way into her socket is clear.

Steph puts her foot back down, and stands with her legs ajar, so that her crotchless slacks display her shaven slash.

The sphere and cylinder are laid on the tray; soap, scissors, and a straight razor are extracted.

Elle feels the Visitors push in around her. She detects many Cams. One, two, three, …she abandons counting, accepts *I'm being captured in full figure and close-up. Full resolution. Every pore, mole, and clit freckle. They look inside me, scan my noble secretions, evaluate my nail polish. They all watch me, take me down, collect me!* Elle makes a big gush, and receives a warm murmur. *I'm going to lose control of myself if I'm not careful,* she concedes. Elle reconsiders. *Correction. I am going to loose control of myself completely.*

Elle creams. *I know what's coming next.*

She barely hears Steph pronouncement, "Listen up nuzzle notch. *You* get to decide. You can shave either your left side, or your right side."

Elle looks at her naked body. Penny and Coco, holding soap and a razor, press closer.

Steph taunts, "And you already have a dividing line, don't you, Stripper wannabe?"

I do. Elle accepts. *I've got butched hair, butched nidus and a trough down my middle. But not for long.*

Elle feels urine trying to release. She traps it.

"Beg, you naked nichey!" Steph says.

Elle looks up at Penny and Coco and gurgles, "Please shave me one side then the other side and I'll cum for you bare bald and naked." Images from the *Gonzo Videos* well up. *Steph knows!*

Elle begs, "I'll eat pussy and juice the Dong with Beka. Please let us cum together and be Strippers together next Term."

Steph makes a nod and Penny and Coco go to work on Elle's nappy.

Penny lathers up the right side of Elle's pussy hair and Coco puts the razor to dexterous work. The butched blue nidus has brunette roots and all the fluffy tops were long ago butched. Coco pulls the razor through easily, but total depilation of the right side requires a second, cleanup pass.

Elle's cream keeps flowing with only the occasional clit flick, and this helps keep the razor slick.

The Visitors hush as Penny fingers Elle's intimates. Elle's dividing line is already smooth, but Coco tidies it up anyway; she runs her fingers along the long deep blue puffy ridge of Elle's outer lips, feeling for stubble as she strokes with the razor. Then she carefully parts Elle's flaps and examines her brown inner lips and violet vaginal canal, filled with a pond of white loveliness. Elle moans. Penny carefully pushes back any prepuce around Elle's erected clitoris, and Coco cleans up any stubble thereabout, making sure not to nick Elle's hot-button. Finally Coco makes sure no loose hairs grow out in between Elle's nook and her nadir way.

Elle floats, and now her own valiva plus thin soap provide all the necessary lubrication for her detailing. The nectar erupts faster now and drips onto the chaise lounger with a delightful fragrance that hangs in the moist night air. The Visitors ooh and awh and Elle feels the appreciation. Feels proud of herself. *I wish Beka could see me now,* Elle projects, *she'd be proud of me!*

Elle reconsiders. *She'd be jealous!* Elle makes eyes directly into one of the Cams. *She's probably watching me now.*

Elle reaches her hands up to her head and rubs her palm on her butched hair. *Sometimes I don't anticipate what awaits me. Curve balls. I should have anticipated my final framing: I'm next Term's Cosmos House Dining Room Baseboard Stripper. Only bare bald and naked.*

Elle pauses her thoughts long enough to reach two fingers of each hand down to her pubes. One hand feels butched pubic hair, the other feels bare skin. She descends a finger into her notch and presses her clit out with her opposing thumbs. She bounces on her buttocks, and casts away her thought, *I used to be smart enough to anticipate the future, but now I'm just flying in real time. 100 per cent!*

Steph coaxes Elle, "You're getting to masturbate and get shaven at the same time. Thank me."

Elle tilts her head to look up with heavy eyelids and her slowly panting mouth hangs open. Inside her spread nave she touches her nitro button, constricts, and gathers a gush of nakodo onto her fingers. She raises her fingers to her nipples, and rotates fresh nectar onto them. She pinches, arches her body upward, and utters, "Please."

Steph smiles and naked Penny leans in and lathers the side of Elle's head to the right of her centerline. Elle vibrates as she feels Coco cut her hair away with the straight razor, feels Penny rub more soap onto her scalp and Coco strokes the scalp a second time, a finishing cut. With Elle shaking softly and surfing the fringe of the Zone. Trying to climax.

Hands remove Elle's hands from her nookie, place them above and behind her head, and Elle looks up into faces and can tell in an instant. *The Visitors approve of me!* Again she constricts, and again a gush of nectar erupts from her nook. Elle shakes.

Elle touches her head and the sensation of bare skin sinks in, as Steph proclaims, "Half butched, half bald!"

Elle looks down and touches the left and right side of her nest.

"Half butched, half bare!" Steph proclaims, then reaches down to spread Elle's vagina, scoop two fingertips of nectar out, and deposits them on Elle's upper lip, so the scent can best penetrate Elle's nostrils. More applause.

Steph leans over—she doesn't care that she titters—and reminds all concerned, "Eyebrow." Elle puts a hand to her mouth; she looks out, escape is impossible. So Penny carefully lathers and Coco shaves. Right eyebrow dispatched.

Bare and naked Penny and Coco collect the soap and razor and dirty water basin, and when they take a bow, Elle catches a glimpse of a ball chain hanging from Coco's rectum. *Might the two Naked Nuggets still share the accoutrements of Double Penetrators?*

But Elle loses the thought as Steph squares her up on the lounger: arms above head and each Elle foot firmly on each side of the lounger, gyno gaped. A half-shaven Opt Down. A sloppy wet photo-op breathing hard wannabe Stripper.

This time Steph leans over, reaches out with a finger and rolls Elle's clit with her fingertip. Elle convulses, gasps, and looks up into Steph's eyes.

"Correct me if I'm wrong," Steph advances, "but you did beg to ride the Double Dong?"

Elle affirms, "Ma'am, yes, Ma'am. I'll even climax the Dong with you, Steph."

Steph laughs, "Maybe not. You'll dong with whomever I say."

Elle corrects, "Ma'am yes, I'll ride the Dong with anybody anywhere anytime. Especially Beka, I promised her."

"Chant for the Open House," Steph commands. "I'll be back for the rest of your hair."

So Elle abandons herself and chants.

§ Steph lets Penny & Coco: Shave Elle's Head & Pussy Left

Elle looks up and out at the people packed around her; she licks her lips, and proceeds with caution. "Please let me shave bare bald and naked, stay pink-wet-and-ready, eat pussy and climax the Dong and cum be a Stripper next Term." Elle hesistates but augments, "And Please let Beka and I climax the Dong together!"

She pauses, senses the faces demand she repeat herself; she suddenly glances wildly around the patio and pool. *Looking for Screens!* No big ones. *Except everyone has one in his or her hand. And everyone is camming me.* Elle squeezes nectar and breathes a sigh of relief. *If they had seen my suck and fuck* Gonzo Videos *they'd tease and haze me. Steph still owns my secret, so she owns me. Maybe Babs and Beka know about the Videos too, but Beka just wants to drop with me, and Babs couldn't care.*

Of course Elle doesn't know that William, who now feasts his eyes upon Elle's naked and half bare vagina, also knows about the *Gonzo Video* where she has dicks inside it.

Elle takes a careful sigh and calms herself. *I know what it's like to lose it in a climax, and if I let myself go here and now, I will beg to not just prance naked and pink the Nugget, but to screen my Gonzos and reveal myself totally.*

"Lounge Dance!" Elle hears a voice and a ripple of approving applause. Fear causes her to present a small tinkle (much to the delight of some Cams) and to writhe into action immediately. The order is an excuse for the naked and spread, half-shaven Cosmos Pledge to draw her hands down and grab at her now-gyrating body.

Kundalini nudges and Elle dances her torso up by her shoulders and hips, she slides her hands downward, squeezes her nubs, and rolls her nips in her fingertips. She opens her legs wide, and finger-fucks her pinked nookie. Elle's slop runneth over and runs down to her nadir way before detaching from her body, and dripping onto the lounger. Elle imagines *naked Gamers with hardons masturbating while they watch me. Now I want them to masturbate to me. Spot their pants, make cum fly through the air.*

So much imagination, and now Elle masturbates, but still Elle can't cum.

Elle slows her breathing down, catches a slower pace, and confesses hard truths to herself. *No one forces me to do this. This is me! I perform this way because I am chosen to. But I am also horrified at my situation. What has become of me? I'm shaving and I'm trying to cum in public. Why am I here?*

Because I want to cum be a Stripper next Term!

Elle shudders, oozes nectar, but still doesn't cum. Rational process again: *Steph is going to take the rest of my hair, then what happens?*

I know what happens. Somebody I don't even know will ride me to climax on the Dong and I'll beg the Gonzos out.

Because they prove I got Whore in my blood.

Elle's thoughts are interrupted as Steph pushes through the circle of admirers, Penny and Coco in toe. Do naked Penny and Coco resent their former Monitor bossing them? They do, but choose not to show it.

Penny and Coco carry a bowl of clean warm water and a tray with the soap, straight razor, and scissors from the Shaving Kit. Both halves of the metal sphere, and the cylinder, also lie on the tray.

Elle hears the ringing chimes of big and heavy ben-wa balls.

Steph reads her mind, "Elle Lollydor, surely by now you know that Penny and Coco share Double Penetrators; tonight Penny carries her holes empty, whereas Coco gets to wear a long procto up her colon *and* the ben-wa balls in her cunt!"

Coco opens her mouth to respond but Penny touches her quiet. Steph snarls at the empty Stripper. "You're not gonna stay empty very long, are you, Penny Practitioner."

Penny squints at her former Monitor, "I have room for the Shaving Kit, Pledge, but so do you in your scrag and shit chute, Ms. Steph Sorostitute!"

"Pledge Elle Lollydor also has free space," Steph spins, "so maybe she should take the Shaving Kit to the Doghouse on her way to the Nugget." Steph scowls at her two former Pledge. Except you won't be stripping at the Nugget next Term, will you, Penny and Coco. You're going to be sharing Dongs and whoring cocks at Flesh Ranch."

Penny and Coco stiffen up.

Steph tightens Elle's hands in their surrender position and asks a kindly question, "So are you gonna DP at the Nugget next Term?"

Elle looks around at the throng of watchers, feels a rush of panic, and gives the Cams a long squirt of urine that spans the length of the lounger and the onlookers beyond.

She hurries an answer out. "I'll Double Penetrate right now. I'll carry the Shaving Kit. I'm wet. I'm as good as a Stripper right now. I'll do anything a Stripper will do.

"I'll cum on the Dong with Beka!" Elle concludes. And silently? *I'll beg you to play my Gonzo Sex Videos. In front of everyone. I'm a Whore.*

Steph returns Elle to the path she must travel. "Time for Penny and Coco to finish shaving you."

This time Penny and Coco stand erect; Coco holds the water and tray. Penny turns the soap into lather, unfolds the razor, and depilates the sinister half of Elle's nestie. Coco follows, and depilates the left side of Elle's head. Elle touches her body and she feels smooth all over.

Steph points to Elle's left eyebrow, and in a breath it too is gone. *They are finished with me,* Elle accepts, *it is done, I am bare bald and naked now. I have nothing more to give.*

Well, that's hardly correct.

She feels Steph's hands on her body and Steph rolls her onto her side for an odalisque pose—first with her thighs almost touching and then with her foot drawn in so that her thighs spread wide. Elle rolls her shoulders and proudly presents herself, "I'll stay bare bald and naked, pink-wet-and-ready, eat pussy and juice Dong and cum be a Stripper next Term."

"You just really need to ride the Dong with Beka right now," Steph observes

Elle scans the onlookers and pauses for shots.

"Pink!" And she does, her cream now flows continuously.

"Masturbate!" Elle tosses her bald head and laughs, then rolls her clit with one fingertip, and pinches a nipple with the other.

Elle has the bug in her, and maybe for the first time in public she wants to let go.

§ Steph Force-Cums Elle: Loses Pee Riding Glass Bull

Steph reappears before her and helps a bare bald and naked Elle onto her feet. "Your nookie can't stop making nectar," Steph observes, and the Visitors around the pool murmurs approvingly.

Steph might be bare and bald but she is not nude, even if her croptop ensure she titters and her low-rise slacks display rugage and stubble above the waistline. What is most rude is the crotchless cutout that bares her slit from above her clit to her shitter. Four days of stubble show there too.

Elle knows, *I am the barest baldest most naked Cosmos of all.*

Elle now thinks she knows what's coming, but she only knows to beg the easy part, "Please, please, please, Steph, force me to cum!"

Steph presses Elle's hands into her smooth nookie, pushes her palms, an commences to walk her backwards. Steph steers her with a sharp fingernail on Elle's windpipe and Elle surrenders to Steph's steering. Visitors make way for her as she walks backward around the pool, and Elle senses darkness out past the Visitors sitting nearby who pause to look up at her. Steph pulls her finger back and says, "Stop."

Elle feels hardness in the small of her back. Steph takes a step back away from her and the Visitors settle into a circle. Elle looks around her, sees faces, but can't see what's directly behind.

Elle feels all eyes are upon her and realizes *I am still masturbating. I can't stop.*

Steph preaches, "Game over loser!"

Elle feels as if she is bout to tumble out of control. Her fingers have become sticky with her thick cream of arousal, she smells her scent, she volunteers, "Ma'am please force me to cum Ma'am."

Why should Steph rush? "Cum?" Steph inquires, "Why you're just mastering how to make cream. I saw your images from the Beauty Salon. Pretty colorful."

"Ma'am, thank you, Ma'am"

"And you creamed at the Nugget?"

"Ma'am no. But I pulled pink in the Camera Lounge." Elle pauses, "And I peed in the Dressing Room toilet." *Didn't have to say that.*

Doesn't matter. "Now that you're a Pee-Camer all your secrets can come out," Steph affirms.

"You're the only Pledge that hasn't cum so far this Term!" Steph advances. "Rumor has it there is something wrong with you! Can't let go?"

"I can only cum getting fucked with cock," Elle confesses. "You know that's true."

"Too bad Pledge are not allow to fuck cock," Steph amuses.

Elle retorts, "I know the Rules, Steph."

"Maybe you have proof you can cum on cock from before you entered the Game," Steph suggests. "That wouldn't be against the Rules."

"Please, Steph," Elle begs, her hands between her legs now, masturbating faster, slop inside her thighs running down as she pleads, "You can make me cum, Steph, I'll streak and get the Double Dong and bring it back and cum on it with you. Right now, in front of everybody. I'll get Beka and we'll both streak and get the Dong, bring it back here, and climax in front of everybody. I belong to you, Steph. I am your Piss Mouth, I am—"

"Silence," Steph commands, and cuts a bare bald and naked masturbating Elle short of climax.

The Open House has a final treat for Elle and her admirers tonight. Elle hears the splashing in the water in the pool go quiet, and feels all eyes settle upon her during this moment. Elle's memory of what happens next grays into the vague, and will remain so until Gamers at some time in the future will enable her to watch herself on Screens, reconstruct her memories, and masturbate in unison with them.

Elle discovers what presses into her bare back. Steph turns her around and helps a dazed Pledge swing her leg over the back of a kneeling clear Glass Bull. Elle feels her bare netherlands ease into the saddle of a near life-size Bull. She looks out into a surround of Open House Visitors and hovering Mansion Cams.

Elle looks down and around her. *I'm on a replica bull complete with, hoofs, bent knees, and a saddle horn.* Elle rubs her nook in the saddle. *I straddle a clear glass molded western-style saddle, no secrets for me.*

Now the Glass Bull rises upward, so naked Elle grasps the horn of the saddle for stabilization. Good idea, since Elle's feet now swing free of the ground.

The Open House Visitors hush, and Elle feels something arise out of the center of the saddle, a very smart probe that slides up out of the saddle, and feels its way upward, separates her nymphae, and penetrate her naos. Elle attempts to rise into a standing position but the saddle lacks stirrups, so that the full weight of her body bears down on the saddle.

As Elle feels the very special dildo rise up out of its saddle, she surges nectar, and as she feels the curved plunger penetrate her, she gasps. Once established Elle feels the protuberance get bigger around, and penetrate deeper.

Steph smiles as Elle reaches the tipping point, "You're going for a ride tonight!"

Elle nods, constricts around the plunger, and her eyes flutters back. "Please make me cum. Please make me cum now."

The Glass Bull embodies an extremely advanced fucking machine. Of course it can buck around but tonight its pivots are subtle compared to the strokes that stimulate Elle's nautch, and the electrical stims and vibrators that bare upon her clitoris and sex lips, her shaven inner thighs, and her nadir way.

The guests quiet as Steph removes a wireless control panel from the Bull's nose ring. Steph is a sight for the ages: tight bare midriff, rounded rugage squeezed into her slacks, and anything from a single line to a pink triplet inside the triangular patch of crotchless sexcupidity.

But Steph knows *I am the director, not the act.* She uses the controls and stabilizes, one might say possesses, Elle, via the electro-mechanical Glass Bull. One set of controls operates the plunger stroking Elle's vagina: speed, rotation, vibration, heat, electrical tickle, diameter, shape. The thick warm fluid that oozes out the plunger's head lubricates Elle's nectary.

Besides Steph's ministrations, the Bull has its own AI that seeks to dominate the vagina completely, find the g-spot, and accelerate nectar secretions.

Another cluster of dials control the region of the clear glass saddle that supports Elle's bare clit and sex lips—and here too a combination of vibration, heat, and electricity permit Steph and/or the AI to fine tune Elle's orgasmic release.

A third cluster of dials control the part of the saddle that Elle grips with her inner thighs, and which engage with the two round globes of her bare butt that rest on the saddle's back curve.

But being impaled on the saddle is but one of Elle's humiliations. Elle has difficulty accepting her new bare and baldness; *I've been naked in public before, but without my hair I feel horribly exposed.*

Elle's feet can't find any stirrups, so she can't lift herself upward, and the Gamers watch as Steph takes Elle into a trot. Steph knows how to work the controls and pace the Bull skillfully; and Steph knows how to listen to Elle. She brings Elle up to a level pant. More? Steph lifts Elle up, and then ever so gently pushes her to the brink of sexual release.

Elle has been fucked before, but never by a Glass Bull and never in front of a group of people. The Bull does not compromise or relent, Elle touches her hands to her bald head, opens her mouth wide, and as Steph tips her that last little bit, Elle gathers in air, thrashes, and pitches into a rolling cum. Guests watch in amazement as Elle starts panting, grabs the horn of the saddle, and shrieks.

Steph backs off a bit as Elle runs out of breath, lets her regain her breath but not her wits, and dials the Bull to leap into life, stroking and vibrating and pumping and electrifying—a forced climax that raises Elle's arms into the air and produces what can only be described as a prolonged banshee wailing climax.

Elle looses her senses, and her fucking and cumming and screaming break into a scary loss of control. Steph reigns in the Bull, steading Elle's heartbeat into a steady refrain of "aha aha aha" that brings the guests into a clapping rhythm; this lifts and stabilizes Elle until her own faltering breath slows the rhythm until the applause fades away and Elle comes to rest leaning slightly forward in the saddle, totally penetrated, in a daze now, relaxing again into a valley of serenity.

Elle tremors, and voids her urine, which runs down the outsides of the clear glass saddle.

Elle casts eyes across the Open House Visitors, looks past their Cams and the grounds and up past the trees to the sky and the stars, takes a deep breath and allows herself to come down. *Applause surrounds me,* Elle realizes. It does.

The Glass Bull kneels down, and Steph helps a dazed Elle off the Glass Bull's saddle. Whistles. Elle looks up, whimpers, bare bald and naked, all secrets gone, yet the Open House Visitors murmur in appreciation. Elle looks out into lights too bright for her to process correctly. She feels warm yellow fluid on her feet. She feels Steph turn her around, bare butt to the guests, push her feet apart, bend her belly over the Bull, part her ass cheeks, open her pink, roll her finger on her clit, and Elle starts cumming again. Elle feels two fingers penetrate, scoop out her white cream, and she cums even harder as Steph reaches around and feeds ambrosia into her mouth. Elle Lollydor knows *I get to lolly myself.* She again feels that the guests support her. She voids more urine, splattering her bare-footed tormenter. No secrets for Elle anymore.

Steph doesn't know what to say.

"I'll lick your feet clean," Elle babbles.

"Of course you will," Steph snides, "You're a Piss Mouth now, but you'll have to let it age first."

Again Elle looks out at the faces that press in, and it dawns on her that the Gamers adore her. Elle smiles, resigns herself to her new position in life, and waves demurely. More applause; Elle gathers her thoughts, *I am going to be taking more dance classes. I'm going to learn new signs, work toys in all of my holes, and masturbate, make wet, pee in public, and cum all of the time.*

Well, some of the time, certainly.

§ Elle: Penny & Coco Give Elle the Shaving Kit

As the applause and goodwill quiets the guests watch respectfully as naked Penny and Coco reemerge, and guide the drained Cosmos back to the lounger. Elle feels Penny and Coco wash her face and feet with fresh water, and slowly Elle recovers her wits.

"Hold still," Elle hears Penny's voice overhead to her side. Elle feels her legs parted and a ball pop into her vagina. "Keep that in your nookie," Penny commands, "It's stainless and watertight, and has your shaving soap inside."

"Hold still," Elle recognizes Coco speak from behind. And feels a thick and then thicker plug enter her nadir way. It reaches maximum width, and then slides forward and home, and expands to hold itself into place. "It's stainless and watertight and has your scissors and razor inside."

I know that, Elle admits to herself, *because I've already watched Kimju and Beka and even Steph carry the Shaving Kit. Now I'm going to carry it all the way to the Nugget.*

Elle, still semi-dazed and powerless, doesn't know what to do. She opens her mouth.

Penny pats Elle's bald head, "Don't worry, Elle Lollydor, Gamers will find a way to fill your mouth soon enough!"

Coco consoles the Opting-Down Pledge, "Don't worry, Stripper wannabe, the Shaving Kit has got a micro-AI inside. So if it wants you to beg shaving then you better start begging."

Elle touches her bald head and bare pubis. *For right now, I'm done with shaving.*

Elle squeezes with her rectum; it is an involuntary attempt to eject the cylindrical buttplug. Nothing happens.

"Lucky you," Penny mocks, "you still have one hole left."

Coco augments, "You can move your sphere to your mouth and fuck the Double Dong with your nockandro."

Elle blurts, "Please let me Pledge bare bald and naked, stay pink-wet-and-ready, and cum be a Stripper next Term." Elle pauses, then proclaims, "I'll streak to the Nugget right now!"

"You shall wait until Midnight tomorrow before you move," Penny informs. "You're still a wannabe one of us."

"I'll streak to the Corvettes and get the Double Dong!" Elle interjects.

Coco orders, "You shall streak to the Doghouse."

"The Doghouse?" Elle wonders. *I know that place.*

"Now!" Penny commands.

"On all fours!" Coco orders.

Elle's eyes get wider and she drops to her hands and knees. Again she feels a toenail startle her nook. Steph's bare slit hovers above. "Move it," Steph says, "and bark!"

Elle moves her bare bald and naked body onto all fours and barks, "Arf. Arf. Arf." And Elle's bruised hands and knees find the way through the Mansion and then exits out the front door.

§ Elle: Streaks Bare-Bald-Naked to Doghouse

The streak back to the Cosmos House provides Elle another new experience. She is not just naked, but bare bald and naked. She squats and pees again while still in the Manson's driveway, again getting more on herself. A security Cam delightfully records this latest addition to Elle's watersports collection.

She gets spotted during the streak back, abandons the dog and the bark, and runs for her freedom. Her pursuers only abandon the chase once she makes the Cosmos House Backyard.

Elle crawls inside the Doghouse with welcome relief. Needless to say, *From now on I will keep myself bare bald and naked, pink-wet-and-ready, and pee on command. I am the first Cosmos to Opt Down and become a Stripper next Term.*

"I am the first Cosmos to Opt Up!" Steph announces to Open House Visitors back at the Mansion; Monitor-to-be Steph stands for a bow, then raises both arms up and stretches her bare midriff in victory.

Steph does not witness Penny and Coco depositing the Shaving Kit inside Elle's nook and nadir, and assumes, incorrectly, that the two Nuggets have pocketed the Shaving Kit themselves. Steph is chagrinned that *neither returns the Shaving Kit to me,* but doesn't raise the issue. *It doesn't matter, once I turn Monitor after Midnight tomorrow I can either shave myself or let my hair grow out.*

Steph does have a final humiliation for Penny and Coco however. She leads them to the Glass Bull, orders them to mop up Elle's pee with their hair, and then lick the saddle clean. Penny and Coco hesitate, but when Steph reminds them that Robyn committed them to downing shots of pee on stage at the Nugget, they reluctantly capitulate.

Steph, aware of the swirling crowd around the three of them and the Bull, and aware of her own crotchless exposure, is suddenly overcome with disgust for her two former Pledge. She lifts a leg, parts her satchel flaps, pees directly onto the two licking Strippers, turns on her heel, and exits.

When Step finally returns to the Cosmos House she rings the Bell by the Back Landing but decides she doesn't need to await permission before entering. Not any more. *The Runup (Book II)* is over. Tomorrow, *The Beach Day (Book III)* begins, the Fates of the six remaining Cosmos will finalize when the Clock strikes Midnight. Some of the Cosmos look well positioned to Opt Up or Opt Down, but a lot can happen in the next 24 hours.

Steph pauses on the Landing. She knows the Cams light it up. She doesn't care. She pushes her butt-cracking slacks down to her calves, squats, and completely empties her bladder. Did she do the right thing? Do Gamers hear the squeals of joy from the Doghouse beneath?

II-44 The Cosmos: What Happens Next? (After D27)

§ The Cosmos: *The Runup* Come to an End

And so *The Runup* draws to a close. One Cosmos, Steph with two Garments, has a guaranteed Opt Up; another Cosmos, naked Elle, has a guaranteed Opt Down. Two Cosmos, Babs and Robyn, wear three Garments and has the potential to Opt to MomCap. Kimju wears two Garments and has the potential to Opt Up to Monitor. One naked Cosmos with no Garments, Tiffany, and two topless Cosmos with only one Garment, Molly and Beka, all have the potential to Opt Down and work as Nugget Strippers next Term.

Things could change during *The Beach Day*, Day 28, the final day of the Term that ends at Midnight tomorrow, the events of which are detailed in the next volume. But might actions during *The Beach Day* precipitate the fourth Book, *The Runout?* Or require a fifth and final Book, *The Play Party,* to fully detail and resolve their outcomes?

Can every Pledge get what they want?

Perhaps. Perhaps not.

May Kundalini smile.

Gamers' Reference Materials: Introduction

Description of the Various References Materials

§ Cosmos Front Pages: Preface, Table of Contents, Diagrams

This section details the various front and end materials that are part of *The Cosmos Book II: The Runup.*

The **Preface** contains a story from the *1001 Arabian Nights*.

The **Table of Contents** includes the Chapters, as well as the Scenes, symbolized this: (§). Scene names are frequently in "GamerName & GamerName: Actions that Take Place" format.

Gamers of all ilk are reminded that **Diagrams** at the front of the book detail floor plans of the Cosmos House and surrounding front and Backyard; the plans include the Cosmos House's first and second floors, and reaching further away, a floor plan of the Nugget.

§ Cosmos Back Pages: The Appendices

Appendices are near the back of the book, following this last Chapter. They include:

The Frame of the Eight Castes compares each Caste versus its properties (e.g., number of Garments, Hover Options, applicable Rules, etc.).

The List of Positions and Hand Signs recommends a minimum visual vocabulary that every Cosmos should know.

The List of Capital Words details words that are capitalized; these include most if not all of the Props, Locations, and Events, especially those beginning with a Capital Letter. All Capital Words are also found in the Index. Many specialized words, words with precise meanings, are not capitalized. These include most Obeisances (e.g., 'coitus' or 'lapdancing'), Exposures (e.g., 'areolage' or 'hairage'), and Garments ('bra' and 'panties.'

The Location List provides a hierarchical list of all Locations with capital letters. All Locations are also found in the Index in the form *Location: GamerName* and *GamerName: Location.*

The Props List provides a list of all Props with capital letters, as well as a few objects included in the Index that do not have capital letters. Note: Props starting with capital letters are indexed thus: *Prop: GamerName,* whereas props that are lowercase are indexed *GamerName: prop.*

The Event and Time List provides a list of all Events and time-related words with capital letters. All of these are indexed thus: *Event: GamerName*. This list also includes a few specialty words, including 'Clock,' which is an important index term that tracks day-by-day action, and the word 'Midnight,' which defines the end of the last Day of the Term.

A Summary of Garment Exchanges logs all costume exchanges between the individual costumes during Days one through 14 of The Arrivals, as well as Exchanges that occur during The Runup. This is a rare situation where information from the Arrivals is detailed out in these end materials.

An Inventory of Chants (lest Gamers need reference for training) is also found in the Appendix.

§ Cosmos Back Pages: Two Manifests

Two Manifests detail the Cosmos' physical bodies and Garments.

Manifest II: Beginning of *The Runup* first details each Cosmos physical features; other Gamers are more thinly inventoried. Next four stats are inventoried: the Garments they wear at the beginning of The Runup, Props and Obeisance they carry, and their Exposure commitments. These four stats are the same, of course, a their Garments, Props, Obeisance, and Exposures at the end of *The Arrivals.*

"Manifest II: Changes During *The Runup*," details the ebb and flow of each Pledge's Garments, Props, Obeisances, and Exposures throughout *The Runup.* Each Cosmos status at the end of Day 27 posits them for the final Opt decisions tomorrow, and their status as they begin *The Beach Day*, which will end the Term at Midnight tomorrow.

§ Cosmos Back Pages: The Glossary

A **Glossary** defines many Capital Words, as well as some of the specialized language used throughout. Most of these terms are also Indexed, and the Glossary will occasionally provide examples that contain italics for where a Cosmos name would go (e.g., *GamerName*: body & exposures: figure).

§ Cosmos Back Pages: The Index

Finally, an **Index** provides ways for Gamers to search out individual Cosmos, Locations, Props, Obeisance, and Exposures (body parts), as well as other themes germane to our Game of Kundalini forces.

Individual plot lines, and the back and forth dynamic between Cosmos may also indexed.

§ Acknowledgments

The Professor wishes to thank a small cadre of readers and editors for their invaluable contributions to this book. These include Louis Peluso, whose insight into character relationships and wordplay has been unrivaled; Victoria Wolf, whose reading of the manuscript incorporates her knowledge of costume and fetish, Riley MacLeod, whose editorial reviews contributed much to strengthening the plot, lightening the touch; and finally the management and line editing staff at All Ivy Writing Services, who have provided consultation and clarity throughout the project.

Appendices

The Frame of Eight Castes

Caste	Residence	Proper Address	Garment Count	Tasks, Requirements, Restrictions	Movement Potential
Game Mistress / Master	Mansion	Mistress Master	5	Owns Slavesex, manages Madams	Hover, Opt Slavesex
Madam Pimp	Whorehouse (e.g., Flesh Ranch)	Madam Sir	4	Leases Whores, manages MomCaps	Hover, Opt Up, Opt Down
MomCap DadCap	Strip club (e.g., the Nugget)	House Mom, el Capitan	3	Bosses Strippers, manages Monitors	Hover, Opt Up, Opt Down
Monitor	House (e.g., Cosmos House)	Ma'am Mister	2	Manages Pledge	Hover, Opt Up, Opt Down
Pledge	House (e.g. Cosmos House)	Pledge	0, 1, or 2 (total 8 in House)	Beg pink, cream, climax, solo toys, lesbian acts, share Double Dong	Opt Up, Opt Down
Stripper	Strip Club (e.g., the Nugget)	Stripper	0	Nude dancing, lapdancing, solo toys, pinking, cream, climax, ALL sex acts forbidden, Double Dong forbidden	Opt Up, Opt Down
Whore	Whorehouse (e.g., Flesh Ranch)	Whore	0	All Pledge tasks, all Stripper tasks, all sex acts, Double Dong	Hover, Opt Up, Opt Down
Slavesex	Dungeon	Slave, Slavesex	0	All Pledge, Stripper, and Whore tasks, plus bondage and pain	Hover, Opt Up

Rules of Engagement by Caste

Inner-contact means within a Caste, e.g., Pledge-to-Pledge.
Fondling is defined as physical contact outside of one's Caste.
Sex is defined as lesbian, homosexual, or heterosexual oral-genital or genital-genital contact.
Bondage is defined as restraint, possibly coupled with physical punishment.

Pledge: inner-contact allowed, fondling forbidden, sex forbidden, bondage forbidden.
Strippers: inner-contact forbidden, fondling allowed, sex forbidden, bondage forbidden.
Whores: inner-contact allowed, fondling allowed, sex allowed, bondage forbidden.
Slavesex: inner-contact allowed, fondling allowed, sex allowed, bondage allowed.

Capital & Lower Case Words

Capital Words are used in the Cosmos to denote a series of proper nouns relevant to the Game. A comprehensive list of them will be found in the following four sections, which detail capital words for Gamers, Locations, Props, and Events. Also detailed are other classes of words that tend to not be capitalized (e.g., individual exposures such as 'areolage' or 'hairage').

Gamer Words List

All names of Gamers
All names of Houses; e.g., Cosmos House

Pledge, Stripper, Whore, Slavesex
Monitor, House Mom el Capitan a.k.a. MomCap
Madam or Pimp, Game Master or Mistress, GM
Roommate, Roommates
Crowd
Revelers
Gamer(s)
Prefecture
Matron
Manifest
Baseboard Strippers
Automatron
Kundalini
Cam

Locations List

Cosmos House
  Downstairs
    Kitchen
      Tiffany Porn Star Calendar
      Screen
    Dining Room
      Dining Room Pictures
      Screen
    Parlor
      Washroom
    Living Room
      Screen
  Upstairs
    Bunkroom
      Mirror / Screen
    Bathroom
    Bedroom
      Desktop
      Private bathroom
  Backyard
    Bell
    Doghouse
    Garage
    Mudpit
    Post Henge
  Transition
    Front Door & Porch
    Back Door & Landing
  Cams
    Front Door Cam
    Back Door Cam
    Bathroom, a.k.a. Pee-Cam

School
  Quad
  Library
  Lecture Hall
  Laboratory
  Gymnasium
  Amphitheater
Village
  Beauty Salon
  Figure Drawing Studio
  Medical Room
  Bachelor Party Place
Nugget
  Camera Lounge
  Champagne Room
  Dressing Room
  Inner Sanctuary
  Stage
  Stage-side
Mansion
Jail

Not Capitals
  alley
  flagpole
  stocks
  hitching post

Props List

See Index. Prop: *PropName* for more complete list. Only Props with upper case are listed here.

Alabaster Flask
Cravat
Dice (two different colors)
Dining Room Pictures
Double Dong
Double Penetrator, a.k.a., DP
Makeup Case
Measurement Nudes
Pink Pages
Shaving Kit (scissors, razor, soap)
Skeleton Keys (2)
Tiffany Porn Star Calendar
Watering Can

Events & Time Words List

Alumni Reprise (at Nugget)
Auditions (at Nugget)
Bachelor Party
Figure Drawing Class
Greatest House Roar (at Peacock House)
Medical Exam
Mudwrestling Contest (in Mudpit)
Mansion Open House

Day
Term
Clock
Midnight

Obeisance and Opts List

The following words are capitalized in the Cosmos and may be found in the index:

Option, Options, Opt Up, Opt Down,
Opt Strip, Opt Monitor, Double Opt Up, etc.
Garment(s)
Obeisance
Exposure
Redacted
Charm
Duel
Fate
Karma

See Index Obeisance: *ObeisanceName* for full list of Obeisances. These include solo body activities (e.g., pinking, streaking), as well as activities performed by couples and groups (e.g., handjob, coitus). Most Obeisances are not capitalized), but two are:

Pee-Cam
Piss Mouth

Further definition of an Obeisance is found in the Index Introduction.

Exposures & Codes

A list of Exposures is also found in the Index as Exposures: *ExposureName*. No exposures are capitalized (e.g., hairage, navelage).

Exposure codes for exposed parts of the body are used in the Manifests. Here is their meaning:

T = Top (cleavage)
M = Midriff
L = legs
B = breasts
A = ass
P = pubis
C = male chest.

The order is always in sequence, TMLBAP (full nude). For example, TML is the exposure produced by a bikini, or a bra and panties. L usually flags as above the knee. Obviously the world is more complicated than this, so consider this a first approximation.

The N- code is the inches of waistline below the navel.

Exposures relate to flashings, a word used herein which indicates that an Exposure is intermittent and is not logged as an Exposure Code, which implies some permanence.

Many of these tactical exposures have Glossary definitions, Cleavage is the partial exposure of breasts, nippage is flashing of nipples, hairage is the exposure of pubic hair, posterior rugage (or just rugage) is the exposure of butt crack, pubage is the exposure of the pubis, slitage advances the top of a (shaven) vagina, lipage leaks out the sides of a thong, and buttage is the exposure of the butt cheeks. All these terms and many more are found in the Glossary.

List of Positions & Hand Signs

§ Standard Body Postures

Stand
Sit
Kneel
Belly
Back

§ Standard Arm Positions

Surrender > Hands behind head
Present > Wrists crossed behind back
Attention > Hands at sides
Horizontal > Held wide away, horizontal
Veed > Hands held away and upward
Handbra > Hands crossing breasts (3 ways)

§ Signs for Mouth & Eyes

Oval mouth > Thumb and 2nd finger
Close eyes > Thumb and 2 fingers together
Open eyes > Double snap
Present tongue > Two adjacent fingers extended
Lick tongue around mouth > circle in air w/finger

§ Hand Signs for Legs

Legs Crossed > Cross fingers
Legs Together (Touching) > Close fingers
Legs Apart (No touching) > Two fingers open
Legs Open > Two fingers midway
Legs Spread > Two fingers held wide
Kneel – two fingers bend at knuckle

§ Hand Signs for Movements

Walk > two fingers walking
Crawl > palm rubbing horizontal
Grovel > palm up with active fingers
Stop > steady hand

At ease > circle in the air and drop

§ Hand Signs for Arousal

Leanover > Two fingers waving downward
Nipple play > Roll thumb & 2nd finger
Pullaside > Thumb & 2 fingers, sweep
Pull pink (butterfly) > Thumb & 2 fingers apart
Clit play > Roll thumb & finger
Finger Fuck > Wiggle middle finger
Rub Masturbation > Rub thumb atop 1st knuckle

Inventory of Chants

§ Gamer Chants

In the Game stay the Game.

§ Pledge Chants

Please let me Pledge naked and cum be a Stripper next Term.

Please let me Pledge naked and cum be a Stripper next Term. Titty titty, clitty clitty, hole mouth.

Hot hot hot. Titters and twat. 98.6 in my anus.

I love you, Post. Hug 'n' kiss. Rub my tits. Masturbate.

Please let me shave bare, bald, and naked.

§ Stripper Chants

Please let me pullaside, pink, and finger my holes.

Please keep me pink-wet-and-ready. I'll cum on cue.

§ Whore Chants

I've done everything explicit, all holes, all sexes!

I'm a cocksucking, cunt fucking, anal Whore.

Inventory of Garments

Garment inventory is not included in these Appendices, however all Garments are indexed at Garments: *garmentName*, and by individual Cosmos, *GamerName:* Garments: *garmentName*.

Garment Exchanges

§ Exchange Equations

< indicates single costume trade to the party on the left.

> indicates single costume trade to the party on the right.

<< or >> indicates two pieces

§ The Garment Exchanges

From *Book I: The Arrivals:*

Molly > Steph. Topless Molly gives Steph her panties, which Steph dons under minidress.

Steph > Molly. Steph gives naked Molly panties back and wears minidress sanpan.

Tiffany <> Kimju. Voluntarily nude Tiffany borrows Kimju's tanga during Post Henge; returns them afterwards.

From *Book II: The Runup:*

Beka <> Elle. Flip-Flop. Beka's croptop & miniskirt are exchanged for Elle's halter & shorts. Beka now titter and hairage; Elle titter and vagflash (Nugget D20).

Janet <> Louise. Louise strips off maillot and bandeau, which Janet acquires in exchange for Spiderweb Bikini (Nugget D20)

Steph > Molly. Steph, wearing an undershirt, forfeits same to Molly at Greatest House Roar. Molly dons over panties. Steph shall remain naked (Peacock House D22).

Molly > Babs. Molly, wearing undershirt and panties gives Babs her undershirt in exchange for the Watering Can; when Babs dons the undershirt it transforms to a minidress, which Babs now wears over her bra and nombril Black Bikini; Molly again topless with panties (Bedroom D22).

Tiffany <> Elle. Tiffany, wearing a transparent croptop & slacks, and Elle, who wears a croptop and minidress, trade the slacks for the minidress. When Tiffany dons the minidress it becomes transparent. The skintight slacks on Elle guarantee hairage, rugage, and cameltoe (Bunkroom D23).

Tiffany > Robyn. Tiffany, wearing a transparent croptop & miniskirt, gives both to Robyn, who dons them overtop her strapped maillot. This leaves Tiffany naked (Nugget D23).

Kimju <> Beka. Beautician gives Beka's shorts to topless Kimju, and Kimju's g-string to haltered Beka. (Beauty Salon D24)

Beka > Tiffany. Babs orders Beka loan halter to naked Tiffany, leaving Beka topless, and Tiffany bottomless. Tiffany returns wearing a bra bottomless instead of the halter (Backyard D25)

Elle > Steph. Babs orders Elle give croptop to Steph, leaving Elle topless w/miniskirt sanpan; Robyn hacks the croptop to a bib rendering Steph bib bottomless (Backyard D25). The bib will become a collar.

Tiffany > Kimju. Tiffany gives her what used to be Beka's halter to Kimju as a bra, leaving Tiffany naked; Kimju now wears the bra & shorts (Bunkroom D25).

Elle > Steph. Topless Elle forfeits her slacks to Steph, Elle is now nude, Steph wears the collar & slacks, which become crotchless (Kitchen D27).

Infrequently Asked Questions

Where is the School? Cyberspace?

What is the purpose of School? To gain knowledge, to learn about oneself, to discover Kundalini, to explore power exchange, to achieve harmony with romance, power, and pain. *See The Cosmos: The Arrivals,* for more details.

What are the Rules of the Game? There are many of them, some secret. Start your search in the Index under Game Rules.

What are some of the Games? The Roommate Games will be played during The Runup, and they pit pairs of Roommates together against another pair of Roommates (Roommates Together) or they pit Roommates against each other (Roommates Apart). Other Games alluded to include: Dice Games, the Mudwrestling Contest, performances such as Tiffany's visit to the Peacock House upon her arrival, and the backstory behind Babs and Janet's Bikinis. Steph's Game with Elle is "who clocks the most time in the Doghouse?"

Is Kundalini real? Gods are expressions of Forces in Nature. The Forces of Nature give rise to existence, to space and time and momentum, and the structures forged throughout the Universe, from the subatomic to planets to Gamers. So of course Kundalini is real, and if welcomed, will speak.

Which Pledge have danced at the Nugget in the past? Tiffany (two Terms ago), Kimju and Molly (last Term), Janet, Monitor of the Corvette House (two Terms ago), and Corvette Pledge Ginny and Lee (last Term).

Which Pledge were Monitors last Term? At the Cosmos House, only Steph. At the Corvette House, both Darleen and Louise were Monitors last Term.

How do Redactions take place? Is it induced by drugs? Brainwashing? Trauma? Self-inflicted? Amnesia? Delusion?—Sorry, but that's six questions.

What is navelage? Areolage? Each 'age' corresponds to an exposure of a body part, like cleavage, leggage, bellage, buttage, areolage, hairage. Index directs you to *GamerName: -age,* since their control and abandonment matters across culture and time.

What are the sizes of halters?

Assume triangle halter, the area of a triangle is equal to one-half the width times the height (Area = ½ width x height).

Mini soutien-gorge: two triangles plus string 2.83 x 2.83 inches = 4 square inches each.

Micro soutien-gorge: two triangles plus string, 2 x 2 inches = 2 square inches each.

Nano soutien-gorge: two triangles plus string 1.41 x 1.42 inches = 1 square inch each, or pasties 1 square inch each.

Pico soutien-gorge: neck and torso strings to tie together using knots. Can be tied as halter or bra, but is never more than the torso string (bow tied front or back) and the two strings ties to it, and which either rise upward to tie being the neck, or ride over the shoulders to tie back again to the string around the torso.

What are the sizes of G-strings? A g-string always has three edges: a waistline, and two leglines that expose the buttocks arising up the posterior rugage before parting in order to cross the hip, descend down the inguinal to meet in the crotch again.

Table of sizes available to the Cosmos and other Pledge follows. (Similar sizings may also be applied to tanga.) Alternate sizings work by stitch count.

The area of a triangle is equal to one-half the width times the height (Area = ½ width x height).

Mini g-string: 2.83 x 2.83 inches = 4 square inches.

Micro g-string: 2 x 2 inches = 2 square inches.

Nano g-string: 1.41 x 1.42 inches = 1 square inch

Pico g-string: .22 x .22 inches = ½ square inch (or, one knot near the anus and two cords up through the vagina up both sides of the clit, with the three strings joined at the top.).

The Manifests

Overview and How to Use

§ Overview

This reference harbors the Garment Descriptions, Exposures, and Garment Counts of each Cosmos at various points throughout the Runup. These Manifests are probably more useful after a Gamer is deep into the Game and needs to recall the status of a Cosmos at a particular point in time.

Two Manifests are included in *Book I: The Arrivals*. The first of these Manifests details each Cosmo and her Garments at the beginning of *The Arrivals* and the second Manifest details Garment exchanges during those first 14 days of the Term. Neither of those Manifests are included in this Book.

Two Manifests detail this book, *Cosmos Book II: The Runup*. Like the Manifests in *Book I*, the first of these Manifests details each Cosmo and her Garments at the beginning of *The Runup* (simultaneous with the ending of *The Arrivals*), whereas the second details changings which occur during *The Runup*, from Day 15 through and including Day 27 and the Mansion Open House.

The Beginning of The Runup
Changes During The Runup

Two Manifests are also anticipated in the three future Books, which will describe events until the end of the Term. *The Beach Day*, Day 28, decides all the Fates and is supposed to end at Midnight.

Book III: The Beach Day
Book IV: The Runout
Book V: The Play Party

§ A Note on Style

Style Rules do exist for composing this reference, but their rule is not always rigorous. There is an attempt to describe costumes from the outside layer working down layers, and to describe Garments, and the body, from the top to the bottom.

The Beginning Manifest includes also body measurements and physical description of each Cosmos in addition to their opening costume.

Manifest: Beginning of Runup

The Garment and body descriptions may be complemented with: Props, Obeisance (skills and forfeits), body hair and shaving details, Exposures (which part of the body is visible), as well as the critical Garment Count.

The Changes Manifest contain a concise overview of Garment changes, Props and Obeisance gain or loss, body hair styling, and occasional media Events; that is those that occur during *The Cosmos Book II: The Runup*, Days 15 through 27.

If there is no change in the costume then the Garment description will not contain a doff or a don, and Gamers may assume the Garment remained unchanged throughout *The Runup*. The first costume listed is the costume at the beginning of The Runup, and the last costume listed is the costume at the end of The Runup.

The order of the individual Cosmos Gamers (and other Houses) is that of paired Roommates: Monitor Babs begins The Runup with Pledge Tiffany. Pledge Roommates Robyn and Kimju, Molly and Steph, and newbies Beka and Elle sequence in bunks, Henge Posts, and any Lineup. This order is consistent through the Manifests, and it might or might not imply an internal hierarchy, if only because multiple internal hierarchies exist.

Unless noted, all Cosmos have hair on their heads, shaven armpits and legs, hair on their pubic region, and bare feet. Molly is totally unshaven. All Cosmos must expose their navels 24x7. They have no Garments other than the Garments described.

These descriptions include Exposure Codes (e.g., TML, TMLB); these are described in the Appendix at "Exposures & Codes." Help for the many exposure and teaser terms might be found in the Glossary.

Occasional copy in curly brackets ("{}") is provided for reference only. It includes information not currently visible to Gamers in the Cosmos House. Examples include physical descriptions of Cosmos body parts where that body part remains covered, secrets withheld from the Cosmos, and changings that are not yet deduced.

The use of the vertical bar character "|" connotes the end of a Gamers (e.g. a Cosmos) opening position at the beginning of *The Runup*, and the beginning of changes which transpire thereafter. It is unneeded in Beginning Manifest, and delineates in the Changes Manifest. The Beginning Manifest contains a full description of each Cosmos' physical body, and in the Changing Manifest this is abridged.

§ The Cosmos: Garments & Props & Obeisance & Exposures

Cosmos Monitor Babs (BB, Bikini Babe, Boss Babe, Boss Bitch): Long black hair, olive skin, eyes black as pearls, 5' 11", 140 pounds, 37D-24-36, hourglass figure, full bust, {deep maroon areolas with milk glands and puffy nipples}, cratered remains of a center-knot navel, {full black bush}, full butt, shaven legs and armpits, {deep purple vagina}. No tattoos or bodyart. Monitor of the Cosmos House. Arrives wearing bra and culotte nombril bikini a.k.a. the Black Bikini; TML; N-4; cleavage, areolage (crescents d'areolage). Was newbie Pledge last Term. Roommate is Tiffany.

Tiffany Transparent: Longhaired redhead, milk-white skin, blue eyes, 5' 10", 105 pounds, 32A-23-33, flat chest, a deep curvy concave belly, small butt, round carnation-colored areolas with cylindrical nipples. Navel is a vertical slit set inside a harder, firmer rim, and with a question-mark dot at the bottom. Thinnish red bush, shaven legs and armpits, burgundy-colored vagina. Three tattoos: {Tattoo of words "Porn Star" on inside of lower lip, reversed so she can read in mirror.} Second, an invisible ultraviolet ink tramp stamp that descends from rugage into her trough and becomes visible as the ink surrounds her anus. Third, deeply set ultraviolet ink tattooed nipples. No piercings, but Eraser Head nipple implants count for three piercings and are linked to a Cybernetician. Naked Pee-Camer. Commences *Runup* wearing longsleeve clear vinyl front-button croptop & low-rise stretch slacks; M; N-7; headlights; hairage, rugage, cameltoe stained with valiva; TMB in see-through. Stripper two Terms ago, Whore last Term, and a Double Opt Up this Term. Roommate is Babs. During *Arrivals*, 1st to beg Opt Strip next Term. 1st Pee-Camer and Piss Mouth. Masturbated to climax in Backyard.

Robyn Redacted: Big hair streaked blonde, skin that tans easily, green eyes, 5' 6", 108 pounds, 34C-25-34, curvaceous figure, modest butt, {rose-colored areolas}, outie navel, {trimmed blonde bush}, shaven legs and underarms, {raspberry colored vagina}. No tattoos or bodyart. Begins *Runup* wearing Spandex strapped maillot with navel cutout; TML (M is cutout navelage). Acquired straps during *Arrivals*. Pledge last Term, but Redacted and is Pledge again. Roommate is Kimju.

Kimju: Not quite shoulder-length brunette hair, polyglot mixture of Hispanic, Asian, African, and indigenous Indian, brown eyes, 5' 8", 117 pounds, 35C-24-35, stacked figure, taut butt, beige silver-dollar sized areolas with puckered and knob-like nipples with lines in

them. Navel is vertical oval with a custard swirl inside. Shaven armpits and legs, trimmed brunette bush, deeply pigmented inner lips surrounding a rosy pink vagina. 14 gauge clithood ring hidden beneath pubic hair, and an astrological sign tattoo (Pallas) secreted in navel. Was Stripper last Term. During *Arrivals* pullaside, naked in Backyard, spread, masturbate, pink, cream; 2nd Cosmos to climax. Arrived topless and solid color Spandex tanga; TMLBA; N-1; inguinal, which she continues to wear, sometimes gathered into the crotch, hairage. Stripper & Molly's Nugget Roommate last Term. Current Roommate is Robyn.

Molly: Long black hair, Irish-Spanish skin, gray eyes, 5' 3", 140 pounds, 38DD-30-37, a square face, a fleshy Rubenesque figure, large splotchy sepia areolas, deeply set navel, {a full black bush}, big butt, unshaven armpits and legs, copious body hair, and a deep brown vagina with purple deep inside. Hidden 14 gauge clithood ring and small alchemy sign tattoo (phosphorus) hidden on her body. Was Stripper last Term when Roommate was Kimju. During *Arrivals* streaks, spreads, gapes anus, pinks, creams; 1st Cosmos to cum. 2nd Cosmos to beg to Opt Strip, 2nd Cosmos to beg Pee-Cam and Piss Mouth. Arrives topless with soiled pale-rose cotton panties underwear; TMLB; N-3, sometimes gathered into moonshadow or crotch or both; TMLBA, hairage. Current Roommate is Steph.

Steph: Long blonde hair, white skin, blue eyes, thin lips, 5' 7", 105 pounds, 32A-23-32, slender figure, brown nipple stalks with areolas that burst forth like fruit. A small puckered navel features a round crater with a fleshy rim, and a hard outie bulb in the middle. Medium butt, thin blonde pussy hair, shaven armpits and legs, scarlet vagina with distended clitoris. Was Monitor last Term, but broken to Pledge for covering her navel. During *Arrivals* wears a variety of minidresses (always sanpan of course). She titters, upskirts, and extends vagflash, but never pinks. Demonstrates rectal thermoprobe, produces one drop cream (D14). Arrives wearing a strapless cutout minidress; TML (M is cutout navelage); that ensures she flashes nippage and upskirts vagflash. Roommate is Molly.

Beka: Longhaired brunette, half-Asian, brown eyes, 5' 7", 105 pounds, 33B-25-33. Shallow conical breasts, beige areolas have a dark brown circumference and pigmented dots, and nipples that indent when excited. A flat belly, a long and narrow vertical ovaled navel that suggests a lightning bolt, smallish butt, shaven legs and underarms, trimmed pubic hair, a vagina with inner lips tinted dark brown and darker pigment around her anus. Newbie; 1st Term in the Game. Arrived wearing and continues to wear sleeveless cotton open-armhole croptop and miniskirt; TML; N-6; able to flash nippage, titter, upskirt hairage, and vagflash. Also practices rectal thermoprobe and suppository. Forbidden masturbation, creams constantly. 4th Pledge to Beg to Opt Strip. Roommate is Elle.

Elle: Curly-haired brunette, olive Middle Eastern skin, brown eyes, 5' 10", 115 pounds, 34B-24-34, small bone frame. Nipples and coffee-colored areolas resemble a weathered volcano, with crevices that run from the tip of the nipple down to the very edge of the pigment. The navel is a horizontal oval with an overhang, buttocks of medium proportion, legs and underarms shaven, however a full growth of bush extends into her inner thighs and is partly visible inside her shorts, {with a darker brown vagina and inner lips and a violet-hued vaginal canal}. Newbie; 1st Term in the Game. Arrived wearing and continues to wear front and neck-buttoned halter and ripped jeans shorts; TML; N-1. During Arrivals nippage, titter, hairage, buttage. 3rd Cosmos to beg Opt Strip. Begs Flip-Flop. Lollydors Beka. Roommate is Beka.

§ Others: Garments & Props & Obeisance & Exposures

From the Corvette House:

Corvette Monitor Janet (Janet Jintoe): Dark hair, beige skin, dark brown eyes, 5' 7", 180 pounds, 40EE-34-46, plump figure, heavy bust, large brown areolas with bubbly milk glands, very full pubic bush, large buttocks, shaven legs and armpits, long outer sex lip. {One hidden tattoo, the name "Janet Jintoe" on the inside of lower lip, which reads reversed so it can be read in a mirror.} Pierced inner labia, consisting of three holes on each side worn with whatever stainless Gamers might let Janet wear, including rings currently, and a chastity if needed. Was Cosmos Pledge last Term (was Babs' Roommate), Nugget Stripper two Terms ago (was Tiffany's Roommate). During Arrivals wears crochet Spiderweb micro halter and g-string, a.k.a. the Spiderweb Bikini; technically TMLA; N-7; nippage, areolage, cleavage, hairage, buttage; although in practice the open-mesh qualifies as full-frontal and is essentially TMLBAP. Commences Runup unchanged, with her nipples frequently erected into the Spiderweb, the string crusty through her crotch, and her clit frequently sticking out with her rings jangling. Roommate is Pledge Darleen.

Corvette Pledge Darleen: Sender brunette. 33A-25-32. Monitor last Term. During Arrivals

and starting Runup continues to wear longsleeve pullover top & tight slacks, flashing bellage, no navel requirement, but always flashing M. Roommate is Monitor Janet.

Corvette Pledge Ginny: Slender brunette, 33B-26-34. Nude; TMLBAP; racing stripe, clithood ring. Whore-for-Life. Was Nugget Stripper last Term (and Roommate of Lee Lollydor), and Whore two Terms ago. During Arrivals streaks, spreads, pinks. Practices Cravat, buttplug, dildo; performs blowjob, coitus, anal. Pees, peed on. Gamers have rights to two additional piercings, and (unless hidden), three unique tattoos. Roommate is Trixi Tubes.

Corvette Pledge Trixi Tubes: Slender brunette, 34A-26-35. Newbie; 1st Term in the Game. Any two of the Six Tubes; the bands around the body ranging from one inch to 32 inches wide, worn any two at any one time, such as a green bandeau and red miniskirt. (The widths and colors are: 1" magenta, 2" orange, 4" green, 8" blue, 16" violet, 32" red). During Arrivals when Trixi wore the violet and red Tubes together she lauded a conservative TM, she demoed many combinations to TML, and with just the magenta and orange she accepted a double belt and confess full-frontal, TMLBAP. Roommate of Ginny, who has been punished in the Cravat after Trixi put her legs together.

Corvette Pledge Lee Lollydor: Black-haired Italian with full figure. 36C-24-35. Nude; TMLBAP; racing stripe. Possibly one tattoo; clithood ring. A Lollydor. Was Nugget Stripper last Term (and Roommate of Ginny). No details from Arrivals. Roommate is Louise.

Corvette Pledge Louise: Curvy black-haired Portuguese, 36D-28-36. No piercings or tattoos, {purple areolas}, {full bush}. Bandeau and T-front maillot. Was Monitor last Term. No details from Arrivals. Roommate is Lee Lollydor.

Corvette Pledge Caroline: Petite blonde, 33B-22-34; crimson areolas. Newbie; 1st Term in the Game. Shares Lingerie Kit w/Roommate Wendy; each shall wear any two of six Garments (bra, panties, slip, thong, hose, heels), e.g., a bra and panties, a slip and panties, a thong and heels, hose and heels.

Corvette Pledge Wendy: A very randy brunette, 34B-24-34; ruddy areolas. Newbie; 1st Term in the Game. Shares Lingerie Kit w/Roommate Caroline; each shall wear any two Garments at one time.

From the Peacock House:

Peacock Monitor William: Dark brunette, an all over light coverage of body hair, brown eyes, 5' 10", 160 pounds. Shirt and slacks. Was Monitor last Term, Hover this Term. During

Arrivals demanded Tiffany titty strip and excite his Peacock Pledge to climax. She declined to break the rules and blow William. William and Steph free-fucked last Term and continue to flirt. Roommate is Pledge Rodney.

Peacock Pledge Rodney: Blonde, blue-eyed, wiry, 5' 10" 140 pounds. A totally shaven body, chest, back, arms, armpits, legs, buttocks, privates. Was Stripper last Term. During *Arrivals* wears jockstrap or thong; TMLCA. Spots jockstrap, ejaculates. Status unchanged as *Runup* commences. Roommate is Monitor William.

Six Peacock Pledge: Nude, TMLCAP. Names, Roommates, bodies not detailed. During *Arrivals* all Lineup, form erections, masturbate, ejaculate. Why the Peacock House is short on Garments is not explained to them, and they should not be asking questions.

From the Rachmaninoff House:

The Eight Rachmaninoffs: Hockey masks and sticks.

From the Nugget:

MomCap (House Mom el Capitan): Body details redacted. Front-button shirt tied bare-midriff and cargo pants plus casual shoes. Navelage; M, 24x7.

Nugget Stripper Penny: Full-breasted brunette. 36C-24-36. Always naked. Freckles on her inner lip. See "Both" just below.

Nugget Stripper Coco: Full-breasted brunette, 36C-25-35. Always naked. Keloid adjacent to anus. See "Both" just below.

Both: Nude; TMLBAP; heart-shaped pubic hair trim. Cosmos Pledge last Term, defeated by Babs and Janet in a Mudwrestling Contest. Penny and Coco, Roommates then and now. Following their defeat, they shared the Double Dong and during *Arrivals* they take it with them when they streak to the Nugget. There they stay naked 24x7, and spread, pink, work toys, cream, and climax center Stage. They shave themselves in public. Videos of them lapdancing and soloing the Dong circulate the Cosmos House. Both are scheduled for one piercing and one tattoo.

From the Beauty Salon:

Madam Nurse Beautician: Body details redacted, although believed to be 36C-25-36 5' 10". Her Caste permits four Garments: Low-cut white nurse minidress over panties, rubber hose, shoes; TL; cleavage. History unknown. Has access to large collection of medical instruments.

From the Dungeon:

Game Mistress (GM): Body details redacted and often veiled, sometimes stealth. History redacted. Owns Slavesex. Five Garments include black full or décolletage leather or rubber bodysuit with many zippers and cutout holes around navel, nipples and clit. Clithood ring. Navelage 24x7, so always M, sometimes MB, sometimes MP, sometimes MBP.

Slavesex China Doll: Long black hair, slender Asian; 5' 8", 100 pounds, 31A-24-32. Nude; TMLBAP; vulva shaven bare. {Spreads, pinks, gapes; creams, cums, dildos, dongs. All sexes all holes.} Heavily pierced and tattooed. Total surrender includes Mind, Body, and Soul, including but not limited to all skin and holes, all body functions, all control over eyes, ears, mouth, nostrils, rectum, vagina, urethra, skin, movement of muscles and limbs, and the mind inside. Slavesex has been owned by Game Mistress for many Terms.

Fat Lady: Nude; feminized; TMLCAP. Lubes. Believed to belong to the Snot House.

It: Male, no body details. Nude. TMLCAP. Totally shaved, totally violated, totally immoblized.

§ Cosmos: Garment Counts

Babs: 2.
Tiffany: 2.
Robyn: 1.
Kimju: 1.
Molly: 1.
Steph: 1.
Beka: 2.
Elle: 2.

Total Garments for Eight Cosmos: 12. At the beginning of *The Runup* four Cosmos have two Garments and four Cosmos have one Garment.

§ Corvettes: Garment Counts

Corvette Monitor Janet: 2.
Corvette Ginny: 0.
Corvette Trixi Tubes: 2.
Corvette Lee: 0.
Corvette Louise: 2.
Corvette Caroline: 2.
Corvette Wendy: 2.

Total Garments for Eight Corvettes: 12. At the beginning of *The Runup* six Corvettes have two Garments and two Corvettes are naked.

§ Peacocks: Garment Counts

Peacock Monitor William: $2 + 1 = 3$.
Peacock Rodney: 1.
Six other Peacocks: 0 {or 8}.

Total Garments for Eight Peacocks: 4 {12}.
At the end of *The Runup* there is no evidence that
any Peacock Pledge except Rodney possesses
any Garments.

§ Others: Garment Counts

Nugget House Mom el Capitan (MomCap): 3
Nugget Stripper Penny: 0.
Nugget Stripper Coco: 0.
Five Nugget Strippers: 0.

Total Garments for Eight Nuggets: 3.

Madam Nurse Beautician: 4.
Game Mistress: 5.
Slavesex China Doll: 0.
Fat Lady: 0.
It: 0.

Manifest: Runup Changes

§ The Cosmos: Costumes & Props, Obeisance & Exposures

Babs: Body as previously described. Underwire bra and culotte nombril; TML; N-4; cleavage, areolage. | Dons navel cutout minidress (from Molly D22) over bra and nombril. Freedom of silhouette of the dress enables M (cutout navelage), ML, TM, or even TML exposures. Occasional cleavage; upskirt but nombril underneath.

Tiffany: Body as previously described. Keeps thighs apart, Pee-Camer, Piss Mouth, Begs Opt Strip. Longsleeve clear vinyl front-button croptop and low-rise stretch slacks; M; N-7; headlights; hairage, rugage, cameltoe stained with valiva; TMB in see-through. | Pants exchanged (with Elle) for miniskirt which becomes clear vinyl (D23); ML; N-4; full-frontal TMLBAP in see-through; parted red pubic hair. Upskirt, spreads, displays burgundy-colored vagina; creams. Doffs croptop and miniskirt (and gives to Robyn at Nugget) to become nude (D23); TMLBAP; hairy; spreads, pinks, creams. cums; pees. Naked 24x7 now. Cunnilingus and shares Double Dong with Steph (Nugget D23); shares Double Dong with Kimju, Molly. Spreads, pinks, creams at Beautician's; purple dyed hair (D24). Shares Double Dong with Steph (again). Borrows micro string halter from Beka and wears as collar bottomless to share Dong with Ginny Corvette, in anus (D25). Returns gives halter to Kimju as bra, and retains naked (D25). 3rd Cosmos to climax during *Runup*.

Robyn Redacted: Body as previously described. Spandex strapped maillot with navel cutout; TML (M is cutout navelage). | Dons clear vinyl longsleeve front-button see-through croptop and see-through miniskirt (from Tiffany at Nugget) over strapped maillot cutout (D23); M (skin in cutout); TML in see-through. Acquires Shaving Kit at Nugget from Penny and Coco on behalf of Steph, (D23), and gives it to Kimju (D24). Yellow dyed hair at Beauty Salon (D24). Maillot straps lost, now clear vinyl longsleeve front-button see-through croptop and see-through miniskirt over strapless maillot cutout (D25); M. Maillot also worn as a tanga under clear vinyl; TMLA in see-through. Yellow bodypaint (D25). Flashing buttage. Faded yellow bodypaint.

Kimju: Body as previously described; keeps thighs apart. Has spread, pinked, creamed, climaxed. Topless and solid color Spandex tanga; TMLBA; N-1; inguinal, crotch; butched pubic hair cut so lip of hairage follows the contour of the thong. During *Arrivals* flashed and pinked

her vagina. 14 gauge clithood ring hidden inside lips, and an tattooed astrological sign (Pallas) secreted in her navel. | Occasionally handbra and tanga TMLA, and occasionally with tanga gathered front side to splay hairage and outer lips. Temporarily nude on Yacht; TMLBAP; trimmed, spreads, pinks, pees. 3rd Cosmos to begs Pee-Cam (D17). 5th Cosmos beg Stripper (on the way to her Alumni Reprise at Nugget D20). Temporarily nude again at Nugget; kisses, mutually masturbates, cunnilingus, creams, borrows and shares Double Dong with Molly to be 2ed Cosmos to climax; TMLBAP; pees. Secretly shares Piss Mouth with Molly. Tanga reduced to micro g-string (Nugget D20); TMLBA; but N-7; hairage, and sometimes with handbra TMLA. Robyn returns with the Shaving Kit on behalf of Steph, stores it inside Kimju (D23) who gives it to Beka (D25). Besides Molly, Kimju shares Double Dong with Tiffany. Acquires Piss Mouth. Temporarily naked, spreads, gynos, creams at Beautician's; orange dyed head and pussy hair. G-string exchanged (with Beka) for ripped shorts, still always worn topless (D23); TMLB; hairage, buttage. Orange body paint with heavy grease (Mermaid Parade D25). Followed by acquisition of bra (Beka's halter transmogrified by Tiffany), so at the end of *The Runup* she wears a bra and ripped shorts (D25); TML; N-4; cleavage, flashing hairage, faded orange bodypaint and Vaseline remnants.

Molly: Body as previously described; keeps thighs apart; Pee-Camer, Piss Mouth. Has spread, gynoed, creamed, climaxed. Topless and soiled, pale-rose, cotton panties underwear; TMLB; N-3; Hidden 14 gauge clithood ring and small alchemy sign (phosphorus) tattoo hidden deep in navel. | Topless and panties also yanked into tanga (D15) and gathered into vagina from front; TMLBA; N-3; hairage; totally unshaven; and see-through-when-wet TMLBAP. Occasional handbra and panties, TML, TMLA. 4th Cosmos beg to Opt Strip. Brief nude interlude while at Nugget (D20); kisses, mutually masturbates, cunnilingus, and shares Double Dong with Kimju; and climaxes TMLBAP; hairy, spreads, pinks; creams, cums; pees. Acquires smaller, see-through panties, also gather back-side tanga style (Nugget D20); TMLBA; N-6. Also frequently yanked, in the front, essentially TMLBAP. Acquires undershirt cutout minidress (from Steph at Greatest House Roar D21) with panties; TML; but doffs it (to Babs D22) and becomes topless with see-through panties (again); TMLBA; N-6; TMBAP in see-through. Reacquires Watering Can; wet. Besides Kimju also shares Double Dong with Tiffany, Steph. Temporarily naked, spreads, pinks, creams at Beautician's; eyebrows, arms, armpits and legs shaven; red dyed head and pussy hair with red body stain (D24). Red bodypaint with heavy grease (D25). Moves panties to mouth (D26); TMLBAP; hairy everywhere. Faded red bodypaint, red body stain, and grease remnants. Leaves panties on bunk for nude Bathroom Cam (D27).

Steph: Body as previously described; keeps thighs apart. Has spread. Strapless then single-shoulder-strap minidress with navel cutout; TML (M is cutout navelage); nippage, upskirt hairage, vagflash. | Under Janet's and later Robyn's direction, she temporarily rolls minidress downward and upward into wide belt, effectively full-frontal, TMLBAP (D15). Exchanges for undershirt cutout (D16), also rolled into tube belt (D21). Spreads, gynos, creams, cums (3rd Cosmos to do so); 6th Cosmos begs to be Stripper next Term. Doffs dress (Loses Roommate Game (Greatest House Roar)to Molly), and becomes nude (D21); TMLBAP; spreads, gynos; creams, cums. Pees. 4th Cosmos begs Pee-Cam. Begs Piss Mouth. All Cosmos participate in an extended forced climax (4th Cosmos). Zoned. Pees. Muddy messy and wet. Taken to the Nugget for an Audition with Tiffany (D23), naked Steph shares the Double Dong with her, becomes the 1st Cosmos shaven bare, 1st shaven bald, and acquires Duel Option (D23)! Streaks. Also acquires Shaving Kit (conveyed by Robyn to Kimju (D24), cleaned using Steph's mouth before being transferred to Beka (D25), who gives to Steph (D26), who gives to Elle (D27). Besides Tiffany, Molly passes the Double Dong so Steph may solo it and succumb to an extended forced climax in the Doghouse (D24), before surrendering it to Tiffany (D25). On the morning of the Mermaid Parade, Steph announces shall Duel with Elle (D25). Elle "loans" Steph her croptop, reduced to a rag, then bib (D25), then collar (D26). Steph avoids Mermaid Parade, secretly sexes William; oral 69, vaginal, anal, oral; creams, climaxes, collects cum (D25). Retains collar full frontal; TMLBAP; bare, bald). Elle surrenders prior to the Duel and Steph acquires Elle's stretch slacks (D27), and secures the Opt Up Monitor promotion. She re-balances the collar and slacks to an open-armhole scoop-neck croptop and low-rise but now crotchless slacks; TMLP; N-5; stubble. Retains Pee-Cam and Piss Mouth.

Beka: Body as previously described; keeps thighs apart; begging to Strip next Term. Has spread, gynoed; creamed. Sleeveless and open-armhole croptop and miniskirt; TML; N-6; nippage, hairy upskirt. | Spreads, gynos; creams (Nugget Camera Lounge D20). Exchanges croptop and miniskirt (with Elle) for halter and ripped jeans shorts (Nugget D20); TML; N-1; nippage, hairage, buttage. Temporarily titty and pussy stripped; TMLB (by Robyn); pees. 5th Cosmos begs Pee-Cam (D19-24). Pees nude in Backyard; TMLBAP. Temporarily naked, spreads, gynos, creams at Beauty Salon; green dyed head and pussy hair ; exchanges shorts (with Kimju) for micro g-string; Beautician reduces halter to size micro matching micro g-string; green hair to Mohawk and Hitler pussy hair styling, visible above the g-string (D24). On Morning of Mermaid Parade, donates halter to Tiffany, leaving Beka topless with a micro g-string (D25), TMLBA; crotch; trimmed, spreads, gynos; creams. Green bodypaint (D25); Faded green bodypaint remnants. Acquires Shaving Kit from Kimju (D25), gives to Steph (D26). Secretly sexes Rodney; BJ, oral 69, coital, creams, climax together (D26).

Elle: Body as previously described; keeps thighs apart; begging to Strip next Term. Has flashed only. Front and neck button halter and ripped jeans shorts; TML; N-1; nippage, hairage. Lollydor. | Unbuttons halter, boobage TMLB (D15-D17). Exchanges halter and shorts for croptop and miniskirt (with Beka at Nugget D20); TML; N-4; nippage, upskirt hairy, spreads, pinks (in Camera Lounge), reveals dark brown vagina with a violet vaginal canal (D20). Croptop reduced to enable titter, boobage (D21). Exchanges miniskirt (with Tiffany) for low-rise slacks (D23); ML; N-7 titter, hairage, cameltoe. Temporarily titty and pussy stripped; TMLBAP (by Kimju & Molly D19); hairy; spreads; creams. Temporarily naked, spreads, pinks, creams at Beauty Salon (6th Cosmos to cream); inverse Mohawk and hair butched, inverse Mohawk of pussy hair, blue dyed haircut and pussy hair (D24). "Loans" croptop to Steph and is topless w/slacks (before Mermaid Parade D25); indigo blue-black stripe divides body, blue bodypaint; TMLB; N-7; hairage; rugage. Gives slacks to Steph (Kitchen D27)) and stays nude from now on; awarded Opt Stripper next Term; TMLBAP; hairy, spread, gyno; creams; pees. Begs Steph to not play Gonzo Sex Videos. Licks cum and pussy cream off the floor (Lollydor). Shaven bare, shaven bald; climaxes on Glass Bull (5th Cosmos to officially climax), pees (but not officially 6th Cosmos to become Pee-Camer). Faded blue bodypaint remnants. Acquires Shaving Kit from Steph (Mansion Open House D27), and carries naked to Doghouse.

§ A Players: Garments & Props, Obeisance & Exposures

From the Corvette House:

The Corvettes are only seen occasionally so their Garment details are more sparse. Monitor Janet is seen the most.

Corvette Monitor Janet: Body as previously described. Crochet Spiderweb was size mini during *Arrivals* but as *The Runup* begins appears reduced to a size micro halter and g-string in a different color; TMLA; N-7; nippage, hairage, slitage, lipage; full-frontal TMLBAP in open mesh. Ring in long labia lips. | Exchanges for size nano Spiderweb halter and g-string (Yacht D17). Exchanges (with Louise) for bandeau and t-front maillot (D20), sometimes tangà; TML, TMLA; cleavage. Roommate is former Monitor Darleen.

Corvette Pledge Darleen: Body as previously described. Longsleeve pullover top & tight slacks. | Flashing M. Roommate is Janet.

Corvette Pledge Ginny: Body as previously described. Whore-for-Life. Has spread, gynoed, creamed, cum. Nude; TMLBAP; racing stripe. | Reveals clithood ring. Spreads, gynos; creams, cums; pees. Sexes (William) BJ, coitus, facial (Yacht D17). Shares Double Dong with Tiffany (D25). Roommate Trixi Tubes loans her the smallest Tube, the 2" orange, which Ginny hangs on her hips, TMLBAP. They share the Dong (D27).

Corvette Pledge Trixi Tubes: Body as previously described. Tube bandeau and miniskirt (two of the Five Tubes). TML; N-4; headlights; flashing hairage. | Two tubes, but shares one with Roommate Ginny, and wears the 8" blue Tube bottomless; TMLAP (D27).

Corvette Pledge Lee Lollydor: Body as previously described. Nude; TMLBAP; racing stripe. | Spreads. Reveals clithood ring. Lollydor. Nude at Greatest House Roar (D21). Receives crochet spider halter (from Louise) and wears as topless g-string (Corvette House D25); TMLBA; N-7; hairage; TMLBAP in open mesh. White painted nipples (D25). Roommate is Louise.

Corvette Pledge Louise: Body as previously described. Bandeau and T-front maillot; TML. | Babs requires she strips naked on Nugget Stage, then given smaller Spiderweb Bikini size pico halter and g-string. (Nugget D20), TMLBAP, in exchange (with Janet) for bandeau & t-front maillot (D20); TMLA; N-7; areolage; hairage; TMLBAP in open mesh. Donates halter top to Lee; becomes topless g-string (after D23, before D25); TMLBA; N-7; hairage; TMLBAP in open mesh. White bodypaint (D25). Roommate is Lee Lollydor.

Corvette Pledge Caroline: Body as previously described. Shares Lingerie Kit with Roommate Wendy; each may wear any two pieces. | Topless and lingerie panties with heels (part of a bag of five items); TMLB; N-3, with white bodypaint w/red lips & nipples (D25).

Corvette Pledge Wendy: Body as previously described. Shares Lingerie Kit with Roommate Caroline; each may wear any two pieces. | Topless & lingerie thong and heels (part of a bag of five items); TMLB; N-3, with white bodypaint, red lips and nipples (D25).

From the Peacock House:

Peacock Monitor William: Body as previously described. Black t-shirt and slacks. | Same on Yacht, sexes (Ginny Whore-for-Life); BJ, coitus; lubes, cums (D17). Together with Janet advocates the Greatest House Roar between Molly and Steph (Backyard D18), Greatest House Roar (Peacock House D21). Secretly sexes (Steph); oral 69, vaginal, anal; oral; lubes, cums (D25). Next seen in three Garments, a long-sleeve shirt, slacks and moccasins (D27). Roommate is Pledge Rodney.

Peacock Pledge Rodney: Body as previously described. Bare-chested and jockstrap; TMLCA. | Bare-chested and thong (D21); TMLCA. Black muscle maillot tanga & boots (D25); TLA. Bare-chested & shorts (D26). Secretly sexes (Beka); BJ; oral 69, coitus; lubes, climax together (D26). Bare-chested & jockstrap (D27); TMLCA. Masturbates and ejaculates at Cosmos. Pees.

Six Peacock Pledge: No body descriptions provided. Nude, often with erections; TMLCAP. | Nude, lube, climax (D21).

From the Rachmaninoff House:

The Rachmaninoffs: Hockey masks and sticks.

From the Nugget:

Nugget MomCap (House Mom el Capitan): Body as previously described. Front-button shirt, tied bare-midriff, cargo pants and gym shoes; M; N-2. | No changes.

Nugget Stripper Penny: Body as previously described. Nude; TMLBAP; shaven bare. Roommate is Coco. See Both below.

Nugget Stripper Coco: Body as previously described. Nude; TMLBAP; shaven bare. Roommate is Penny. See Both below.

Both: Scheduled for one piercing and tattoo. Has spread, pinked, creamed, climaxed, peed, shaved on Stage. Their last act as Cosmos last Term was to climax the Dong together, but this Term sharing is forbidden. | Videos of Penny and Coco soloing the Double Dong play for the Cosmos. Both Roommates beg to share the Dong next Term, knowing that Whoring is a likely outcome. They loan the Dong to Kimju and Molly to ride on Stage (D20), again to Tiffany who shares in pussy and ass with Steph (D23). They give it to Tiffany who takes it to the Cosmos House (D23). In return they get to share Double Penetrators: a very intelligent dildo and buttplug. They also give the Shaving Kit to Robyn for Steph (D23). Acquire Piss Mouth from Tiffany (courtesy Robyn D23). Briefly acquires the Shaving Kit from Steph, and use it to shave Elle bare bald and naked (Mansion Open House D27).

Nugget Stripper Odee: Racing stripe. Nude; TMLBAP; shaven bare. Roommate is Hottie

Nugget Stripper Hottie: Tattoo around anus. Nude; TMLBAP; shaven bare. Roommate is Odee

Three Other Nuggets: Bodies not described Nude by default;; TMLBAP.

From the Beauty Salon:

Madam Nurse Beautician: Body as previously described. White low-cut dress over bra and panties, shoes; T; cleavage. | Same.

From the Dungeon:

Game Mistress: Body as previously described. Redacted or veiled. | Black full or décolleté leather or rubber bodysuit with many zippers and cutout holes around navel and clit. Clithood ring.

Slavesex China Doll: Body as previously described. Heavily pierced and tattooed. Nude; TMLBAP; bare. Assume spreads, pinks, gapes; creams, cums, dildos, dongs, and all sexes all holes. | Same, with braided ponytail. Also with cane welts on buttocks, later cane welts on thighs.

Fat Lady: Body as previously described. | Nude; feminized male; TMLCAP. Lubes.

It: Body not described .Unseen.

§ Cosmos: Garment Counts

Babs: 2 + 1 = 3.
Tiffany: 2 ± 1 - 2 = 0.
Robyn: 1 + 2 = 3.
Kimju: 1 + 1 = 2.
Molly: 1.
Steph: 1 - 1 = 0 + 2 = 2.
Beka: 2 ± 2 - 1 = 1.
Elle: 2 ± 2 ± 1 - 2 = 0.

Total Garments for Eight Cosmos: 12.

The Cosmos costume count remains unchanged at 12. At the beginning of the Runup four Cosmos have two pieces and four Cosmos have one piece. At the end of the Runup four Cosmos have two or pieces, and four Cosmos have one piece or are naked.

§ Corvettes: Garment Counts

Corvette Monitor Janet: 2.
Corvette Darleen: 2.
Corvette Trixi Tubes: 2 – 1 = 1.
Corvette Ginny: 0 +1 = 1.
Corvette Lee: 0 + 1 = 1.
Corvette Louise: 2 - 1 = 1.
Corvette Caroline: 2.
Corvette Wendy: 2.

Total Garments for Eight Corvettes: 12. At the end of the Runup four Corvettes have two pieces and four Corvettes have one piece.

§ Peacocks: Garment Counts

Peacock Monitor William: 2 + 1 =3.
Peacock Rodney: 1.
Six other Peacocks: 0 {or 8}.

Total Garments for Eight Peacocks: 4 (12). At the end of *The Runup* there is no evidence that any Peacock Pledge except Rodney possesses any Garments.

§ Others: Garment Counts

Nugget MomCap (House Mom el Capitan): 3
Nugget Penny: 0.
Nugget Coco: 0.
Nugget Odee: 0.
Nugget Hottie: 0.
Three other Nuggets: 0.

Total Garments for Eight Nuggets: 3.

Madam Nurse Beautician: 4.
Game Mistress: 5.
Slavesex China Doll: 0.
Fat Lady: 0
It: 0.

Glossary

Alabaster Flask—A **Prop.** Babs keeps in the Bedroom desk drawer. Contains **diuretic.**
Alumni Reprise—An **Event,** last **Term** with Tiffany & Janet, this **Term** with Kimju & Molly.
anal—An **Obeisance,** penetration of the **anus** and **rectum** by a **penis,** also by **strapon, dildo, dong.**
anus—The rear entrance to the **rectum,** a.k.a. asshole.
ass-to-mouth (A2M)—The relocation of a **penis** from the **rectum** into the **mouth.**
areola, areolage—An **Exposure** or partial exposure of the areola of the **breast.**
Auditions—**Events, Pledge** including **Cosmos** beg to **dance** the **Nugget,** beg **Opt Strip** next **Term.**
Automatron—A giant Artificial Intelligence (AI) data storage and analysis system somewhere.
bandeau—**Species** of **soutien-gorge,** which covers the **breasts** but lacks straps. Has two edges.
Baseboard Strippers—Two of the **Dining Room Pictures,** of Penny and Coco, both **naked & pink.**
begs, begging—Usually lower Caste Gamer requesting privileges or punishments from higher Caste.
bellage—An **Exposure** of the belly, not necessarily including the **navel.**
belly-up belly-down—**Bellage** above and below the **navel,** and certainly exposing it.
ben-wa balls—Spherical balls worn inside the **vagina;** may be hollow or heavy, with hot/cold, vibration, electricity; AI; wireless to **Automatron.** Comboed with **procto** for **Double Penetrator.**
bikini—A two-piece **Garment** consisting of a **soutien-gorge** and a **culotte,** maximally a **nombril.**
bodyart—An **Exposure,** any piercing, tattoo, or other permanent adornment of body or skin.
bra, brassiere—A **Garment** and **species** of **soutien-gorge** that covers the **breasts** and has two shoulder straps. A brassiere has four edges.
blowjob—An **Obeisance.** The gratification of a **penis** using the **mouth** and tongue.
blush—An **Exposure,** reddening of the face and/or chest with blood, of a sign of sexual arousal.
body & exposures, an Exposure—A part of the body that is uncovered (e.g., breast, leg), also teases (e.g., titter, vagflash). A full list of **body & exposures** is found in the Index: body & exposures. Almost all are lower case words and indexed as: *GamerName:* body & exposures: *bodyPart.*
boobage—An **Exposure** of one or both entire **breasts,** barebreasted and wearing a **Garment** above the waist, so *not* **topless.** Boobage may involve a single-bare-breasted maillot, an evening gown uplifting bare **breasts,** a bib, a cutout bra, etc. *See* **cleavage, areolage, nippage, titter.**
bottomless—A "**Garment**" which is the absent case of itself. The baring of the body below the waist. **Count** = zero. Presumes **pubage, buttage, leggage.** A **topless + bottomless = nude.**
breast(s)—Female anatomy **Exposure,** crowned by **areola & nipples.** *See* **boobage, breastplay.**
breastplay—An **Obeisance.** Arousal of **breasts** and **nipples,** especially self-arousal.
bukkake—An **Obeisance.** Discharges of multiple male ejaculate onto a subject's face and body.
butt, buttage—An **Exposure** of all or most of the buttocks. A **g-string** or **thong** is always buttage. Compare to **cheekage.** A buttage is not a **bottomless,** but a bottomless contains buttage.
buttplug—A **Prop,** including a **procto,** which is inserted into the **rectum** via the **anus.**
Cam—A still or video camera, able to hover & transmit wirelessly; some have specific **Locations.**
Caste—One of eight ranks in the **Game.** The Castes are: **Game Mistresses or Masters (GMs),** who manage **Slavesex; Madams** or **Pimps,** who manage **Whores; House Mom (or Dad) el Capitans (MomCaps or DadCaps),** who manage **Strippers;** and **Monitors** who manage **Pledge.**
Chant—A series of words, sometimes with an accompanying action, designed to train endurance, inculcate ideas, or produce arousal.
Charm—Possibly a magical property, which some Gamers think protects them and provides good fortune, and which some Gamers don't believe exists.
cheekage, cheeky line—An **Exposure** of the bottom, or cheek, of the **buttocks** out the bottom of briefs or shorts; the line where the **buttocks** meet the **leg** in a crease. The opposite of **rugage.**
clit—An **Exposure,** the sensitive ball of erectile tissue in a female above the **vagina,** inside a hood.
cleavage—The partial **Exposure** of breasts. *See* **décolletage, downblouse, leanover, lift-up.**
climax—An **Obeisance.** A male or female sexual release, possibly accompanied by fluids.
Clock—A timepiece that keeps track of **Days.** Index references Days (Dnn), nn range 15 > 27.
coitus—An **Obeisance.** The sexual joining of the **penis** into the **vagina.**
concerns—Anxieties and fears of **Pledge,** be they irrational or the result of careful evaluation.
conflicts—Situations between two **Gamers** that involve clashes of personality, style, and contests.
Corvette—One of eight **Houses** at the **School,** as well as a resident thereof.
Cosmos—One of eight **Houses** at the **School,** as well as a resident thereof (singular and plural).
costume—*See* **Garment.**
Count—*See* **Garment Count.**
Cravat—A **Prop;** an bondage frame for holding a **Gamer** in a fixed position for a prolonged time.

cream—**Valiva**, female **vaginal** secretions produced during arousal. The transuding of secretions.

culotte—A **Garment**; the generic term for a **bikini** or underwear bottom regardless of its **species**. Examples include **g-string**, panties, **tanga**, shorts, and a *bikini* **nombril**.

cum—Verb, meaning to **climax**, both for a male and a female. Noun, **semen**, produced at climax.

cum drinking—*See* **gokkun**.

cum sharing—*See* **snowballing**.

cunnilingus—Oral pleasure to the sex organs of a woman, by either a man or a woman.

dance—Movement of the body in a rhythm, often with music; may be sexually suggestive.

Day—One Day of the **Term**. Spans: *Arrivals* (D01>D14). *Runup*, (D15>D27). *Beach Day*, (D28).

décolletage—An **Exposure** of the **cleavage** of the **breasts** resulting from wearing a low-cut neckline. Also a low-cut neckline that exposes the neck, shoulders, and parts of the **breasts**.

Dice—A **Prop** located below the Desktop, in the Bedroom; Games of Dice are under Babs' control.

dildo—A **Prop** designed to be inserted into the **vagina**. A **Dong** presents two simultaneous dildos.

Dining Room Pictures—Four Pledge last Term: Babs, Janet, **Baseboard Strippers** Penny & Coco.

dishabille—A state of partial, careless undress, often intentionally careless.

diuretics—Substances that induce the bladder in one's body to void urine.

double cock penetration—An **Obeisance**. Penetration of any two of the **mouth**, **vagina**, **anus** by two penises; three combinations, and three possible double insertions into the same orifice.

Double Dong, Dong, DD—A **Prop** with special Rules and powers, seen at the Nugget as well as the Cosmos House. For those who are permitted the experience, the Double Dong enables two **Pledge** to share the Dong in their **vaginas**, **rectums**, and **mouths**, or any combination thereof. **Pledge** and **Whores** are allowed to Double Dong; **Strippers** may not, but may solo one-half as if a long **dildo**.

double penetration—*See* **double cock penetration** for penises; *see* **Double Penetrator** for **Props**.

Double Penetrator, Double Penetration, DP—A **Prop**; two toys that together penetrate both the **vagina** and **anus**. A single **Gamer** may simultaneous enjoy both toys, or two Gamers may each enjoy a single half of the DP. DPs include the **ben-wa balls** and the **procto**, and the **Shaving Kit**.

downblouse—An exposure of the **breasts** and/or **nipples** created by leaning forward.

DP—*See* **double cock penetration** for real penises; *see* **Double Penetrator** for **Props**.

Duel—An opportunity to pick any **Game**, and play it with any Cosmos Pledge. A sure win.

el Capitan—*See* **Caste**.

enema—An **Obeisance**, insertion of fluids into the **rectum** via the **anus**, often by a syringe or tube.

Exposure—*See* **body & exposures**.

Event—A performance or contest, e.g., the **Mudwrestling Contest**, the **Alumni Reprise**.

face and eyes—An **Exposure**, the front part of the **head** below the hairline, extending to the ears.

facial—An **Obeisance**. **Semen** ejaculated onto partner's face, often into the **mouth** for a **swallow**.

Fate—Each **Cosmos'** outcome at the end of the **Term** (at **Midnight**).

feet and toes—An **Exposure**, the extremity of the **leg** and connected to it at the ankle.

fellatee—The recipient of a **blowjob**.

fellator—The provider of a **blowjob**.

figure—An **Exposure**, and repository of details, indexed *GamerName:* body & exposures: figure.

finger-fucking—An **Obeisance**. The insertion of one or more fingers into the **vagina**, either by one's self or another individual(s). This behavior can also be applied to the **rectum**.

force-cumming—The providing of a **climax** to a recipient.

fresh, freshen—The exudation of **valiva**, a.k.a. **cream**, by a female.

full-frontal—An **Obeisance**. The baring of the **breasts** and the **pubis** (hairy or shaven). Not all **nudes** are full-frontal, and not all full-frontal exposures involve total nudity (e.g., hose and heels).

g-string—A **Garment**; a **culotte** that covers the **pubis** but not the **buttocks**, and ties with strings.

gangbang—An **Obeisance**. Sex by many individuals upon a single one; presume all holes taken.

Game—The practice at **School**.

Game Mistress or Master (GM)—the highest Caste in the **Game**; *see* **Caste**.

Game Rules—The Rules of the **Game**. *See* the Index, Game Rules, for details.

Gamer—One who plays the **Game**, both those who play in the **Cosmos** and **voyeurs** who look in.

Garment—A single costume piece that a **Cosmos** might wear. *See* **Garment Count**.

Garment Count—The number of **Garments** that a **Gamer** wears; determines Opt Up, Opt Down.

GM—*See* **Game Mistress or Master**.

gokkun—An **Obeisance**. Drinking semen, often from a glass, off a dish, out of a pan. **Swallowing.**

gokuraku-ojo—Sexual orgasm resulting in death, caused by hyper-stimulation.

goal—Something a **Cosmos** seeks to achieve. Indexed by *GamerName:* goals

hair—An **Exposure**; used here only for hair on the **head** and sometimes the body, but to be distinguished from **pubic hair** and its partial exposure, **hairage**.

hairage—An **Exposure**. The partial exposure of **pubic hair**; including **pubic hair** that leaks out, be it above the top or to the sides of a **culotte**, be it an accidental or a deliberate **pullaside**, or, in relaxed usage, pubic hair viewed **upskirt** (via a **vagflash** or an extended spread).

halter—A **Garment** and **species** of **soutien-gorge** that covers the **breasts** and has a neck strap and a back strap. A halter has three edges and at least fastening possibilities (neck, front, back).

handbra—Hands covering **breasts**. Included in "**Garments;**" **species** of **soutien-gorge**; **Count** = 0.

handjob—An **Obeisance**. The **masturbation** of the penis by the hand of a partner. May lead to **climax** and ejaculation of **semen**. Does not include oral-genital contact (a **blowjob**).

Hand Signs—Commands made with hands and fingers to indicate body **positions** and actions.

hands and fingers—An **Exposure**, the extremity of the arm and connected to it at the wrist.

headlights—An **Exposure**. Aroused nipples that form shapes in clothing.

head—An **Exposure**, top skull connects by the neck to the body, includes **face and eyes**, **mouth**, nose, ears, **hair**.

House—One of eight **Locations** where students who attend **School** reside.

House Dad el Capitan—Masculine. The third highest Caste in the **Game**; *see* **Caste**.

House Mom el Capitan—Feminine. The third highest Caste in the **Game**; *see* **Caste**.

Hover—Situation where a **Gamer** doesn't change **Caste** at end of the **Term**. Only available to certain Castes, including but not limited to **Monitors** and **MomCaps**. Hover is not available for **Pledge** or **Strippers**, who must either **Opt Up** or **Opt Down**.

inguinal, inguinal line, inguinalage—An **Exposure**, this body landmark delineates **pubis** from **leg**.

Jail—A place of detention maintained by the **Game** at which **Game Rules** applying to a **Caste** member may be violated. One quick way to Jail is to be apprehended while **streaking**.

Karma—Good and bad will disbursed into the **Game**, accumulated and traded by **Gamers**.

kissing—An **Obeisance**. Mouth upon the body of another individual; sometimes mouth-to-mouth and augmented with the tongue, a variation called French kissing.

Kundalini—The sex force in the Universe, present in the **Game**, The **Cosmos**, the **Locations**.

Lady-Part Words—Words tactical to individual **Cosmos'** body parts. These are not included in this Glossary nor the Index; there exists many Lady Part Words, e.g., for **breasts**, **areolas**, **nipples**, **pubic hair**, **vaginas**, **valiva**, **buttocks**, **anus**, and various proposed sex acts and characterizations.

lapdancing—An **Obeisance**; a **dance** by a **Stripper** performed in the lap of a Patron.

laxatives—Substances that induce a body to void bowels.

leanover—A body movement that permits a voyeur to look **downblouse**. The resultant **Exposure**.

legs, leggage—An **Exposure**, a **body part** which joins to the torso and **butt** at the **inguinal** and **cheeky line**, and which includes the thighs, knees, calves, ankles, and feet, with toes.

lift-up—An action that enables a shirt to ride upward and reveal the **breasts** if not **nipples**.

Lineup—The assembly of the **Cosmos Pledge** into a side-by-side line, often for morning **Reveille**.

lipage—An **Exposure**. The exposure of the labial lips to the sides of the **vagina**. If opened, *see* **pink**.

Location—A place where **Events** take place, e.g., the **Cosmos House**, the **Nugget**, the Backyard.

Lockdown—A destination for select Gamers where space & time don't exist & Rules needn't apply

lollydor—An **Obeisance**. One who licks up semen or **valiva**. Verb is "to lolly."

Madam—The second highest **Caste** in the **Game**, equivalent to a **Pimp**; detailed at **Caste**.

Makeup Case—A **Prop**, controlled by the **Monitor**. Contains makeup and beautification products and tools. As an upper case **Prop**, it is a primary Index item, e.g., Makeup Case: *GamerName*.

masturbation—An **Obeisance**. Sexually arousing one's self, often by touching one's sex organs, or rubbing them on an external object. Sometimes helped by a partner, e.g., a **handjob**.

Measurement Nude—A **Prop**; full-frontal shots provided by newbies showing body & dimensions.

media—Records of Events, sometimes served by **Automatron**, indexed by *GamerName:* media

messy—An **Obeisance**. Coverage of the body by substances such as cum, food, paint, mud, ...

Midnight—The end of the last **Day** of the **Term**. Currently scheduled end of *The Beach Day* (D28).

Mirror—A.k.a. the Minxy Mirror. A special mirror, located in the Bunkroom, which can simply reflect, serve as a **Screen**, and interactively manipulate who and what reflect on its surface.

Monitor—The fourth highest **Caste** in the **Game**; *see* **Caste**.

montante—A **Garment**, a high-waisted **species** of **culotte**, with a waistline above the **navel**.

mouth—A **body part**. The oral entrance to the body; surrounded by the lips, includes the tongue, and exits to the throat. Uses for **kissing**, **cunnilingus**, **blowjobs**, and **throating**, and **swallowing**.

Mudwrestling Contest—**Event** last **Term**; determined Ops this **Term** for Babs, Janet; Penny, Coco.

Mudpit—A **Location** in the Backyard, a pit of dry earth or wet mud; **Cosmos** grovel here.

navel—A body landmark. A scar resulting from the detachment of the umbilical cord during birth.

navelage—The **Exposure** of the **navel**. Cosmos must be navelage 24x7.

newbie—A **Pledge** attending their first **Term** in **School**; their first **Term** in the **Game**.

nombril—A **Garment**, a **species** of **culotte** with a waistline below the **navel** and wide sides.

nipples, nippage—An **Exposure** of the nipple. This infrequent term is dominated by **titter**. Do not confuse nippage (or **titter**) with **boobage**, the exposure of the entire bare **breast**, or **topless**, which is a "**Garment**" (not an Exposure), and the complete absence of a Garment above the waist.

nepenthe —An ancient drug to induce forgetfulness. Possibly employed in **redaction**?

Nude, naked—A "**Garment**" and absence of clothes. **Topless + bottomless = nude. Count** = zero.

Nugget —A **Strip** club near the **Village**. Some current **Pledge danced** at the **Nugget** last **Term**; some last-**Term Cosmos dance** there now; some current-**Term Cosmos** will **dance** there next **Term**.

Obeisance—A merit gained or a forfeit made; examples include **shaving, pinking**, and **Pee-Camming**. Most Obeisance are found in this Glossary; *see* a full list at Index, obeisance.

Opt Up, Opt Down —Expansion or reduction of responsibilities by one **Caste** for next **Term**.

orders—Commands issued, usually by a **Gamer** of a higher **Caste** to a lower, to be obeyed.

paparazzi —Unauthorized gatherers of images and video outside official **Game** channels.

pasties—plural, sing. **pasty. Garment, species** of **soutien-gorge**, glued over **areolas** & **nipples**.

pee—An **Exposure**. The discharge of liquid body waste via the urethra. *See also* **Pee-Cam**.

Pee-Cam—An **Obeisance**. A Pee-Camer urinates on camera and in public, in front of anybody.

penis—An **Exposure**, a body part of the male what can become erect, discharge **semen**, urinate.

phlegm—Liquids produced in the back of the mouth, nasal passages, and throat. *See* **throating**.

pink, pinking—An **Obeisance**. The display of the inside of the **vagina**, also the action thereof, regardless of the actual color of the inside. An invitation to cunnilingus and sexual penetration; an element of **masturbation, finger-fucking**. Indexed as *GamerName:* pinking.

Pink Pages— Data sheet prepared for a **Stripper**, includes stats, explicit naked **pink** & toy images.

Pimp—The second highest **Caste** in the **Game**, equivalent to a **Madam**; *see* **Caste**.

Piss Mouth—An **Obeisance** that involves getting pissed on, possibly in the mouth.

Pledge—The fourth lowest **Caste** in the **Game**; *see* **Caste**. Pledge are both singular and plural. Is not capitalized when used as a verb.

position—An **Obeisance**. A formal body arrangement, often in three parts indicating stance, leg, and arm positions, e.g., stand spread surrender. *See* Appendix, List Of Positions & **Hand Signs**.

Post Henge—A **Location** in the Backyard containing seven Posts, two rows of three, plus end Post .

posterior rugage—An **Exposure**. *See* **rugage**.

Prefecture—The **Gamers** who view the **Events** of the **Cosmos** through **Screens** or read this book.

procto—A specialized **buttplug** with hot/cold, vibration, electricity; has AI, wireless to **Automatron**. Comboed with **ben-wa balls** for **Double Penetrator**.

Props—An object that may migrate among **Gamers**, especially **Cosmos**. Not to be confused with an **Obeisance**, which each individual **Cosmos** may take on, or a **Garment**, which has a **Count** value.

pubic hair—A **Exposure,** the growth of hair on the **pubis** or **penis**. Often trimmed or **shaven bare**.

pubis, pubage—An **Exposure** of the **vulva**, with or without **pubic hair**. Achieved with a **pullaside, upskirt, bottomless**. Indexed, for example, as *GamerName:* body & exposures: pubis.

pullaside—An **Obeisance**. The drawing of fabric in the crotch to the side so that the sex organs and/or **anus** may be displayed. One way to **vagflash**.

rectum—The execratory tube terminating the intestines and GI tract at the **anus**. Penetrated by **anal**.

redaction—Various processes of removing memories and records of the past.

Reveille—The morning **Lineup** of **Pledge** for inspection by their **Monitor** Boss.

Roommates—Pairs of **Cosmos**, defined by who shares over and under bunks in the Bunkroom and Bedroom. There are four pairs of Roommates in the **Cosmos House**.

Roommate Game —A **Game** played between **Roommates**; the first Game of the **Term**.

rugage—**A.k.a. posterior rugage**. An **Exposure**, the top of the **butt** crack. Opposite of **cheekage**.

Rules—*See* **Game Rules**.

sanpan—Without panties, possibly **bottomless**, or a discovery upon **upskirt**.

School—The place where the **Cosmos** study and the **Game** is played.

Screen—An area where images and videos are displayed. Monitor Babs controls Cosmos Screens.

semen—Male discharge, ejaculate, cum.

shave bald—An **Obeisance**. Removing all the hair from the **head**, including the eyebrows.

shave bare—An **Obeisance**. Removing all the **pubic hair** from the **pubis** or around the **penis**.

Shaving Kit—A **Prop** including scissors, soap, and a razor; carried in a hollow stainless steel ball and a cylinder, intended to be carried inside the **vagina** and **rectum**.

sixty-nining—An **Obeisance**. Simultanous oral sex by two partners. *See* **blowjob, cunnilingus**.

Skeleton Keys—A **Prop**; two keys. The 1st locks a door between the Kitchen & Parlor, the 2ed between the Dining & Living Rooms. Both together open the door between the Kitchen & Porch.

Slavesex—The lowest Caste in the **Game**; *see* **Caste**.

slitage—An **Exposure** descending from the top of the (often shaven) **vulva**; *see* **lipage**.

snowballing—An **Obeisance** practiced by **Whores & Slavesex** trading cum between mouths.

soutien-gorge—A **Garment** worn to cover the **breasts** but which may leave the arms and midriff bare. *See* **bandeau, brassiere, halter**, also **pasties**, which are also **species** of **soutien-gorge**.

species—of a **Garment**, a variation of a **soutien-gorge, culotte**, etc., created by the **Garment** style.

spit, spits—An **Obeisance**, rather than an **Exposure**, connoting action, rather than body fluid.

strapon—A **Prop** permitted for **Strippers, Whores, & Slavesex**, which permits **dildo** insertion.

streaking—An **Obeisance**. The transport of one's self while naked from one **Location** to another. May be volunteered, required, punitive. Capture may involve **Jail, Lockdown**.

Strip, Strip Club—A **Location** where **Strippers** work. The **Nugget** is our most familiar Strip Club.

Stripper—The third lowest Caste in the **Game**; *see* **Caste**. Repertoire includes undressing, **nudity, shaving, pinking, cream, dildos, buttplugs, Double Penetrators, climax**, and **pee**.

swallowing—An **Obeisance**. Swallowing semen. Either following **facial, snowballing, gokkun**.

Switch— A **Gamer** who vacillates between dominance and submission, wittingly changing **Castes**.

tan lines—A.k.a. **edge lines**. The edges of a **Garment** such that if exposed to sunlight or ultraviolet the part of the skin not covered will tan.

tanga—A.k.a., **a thong**. A **Garment**, **species** of **culotte** that covers the **pubis** but not the **buttocks**. It must have fabric sides, and fabric above **rugage**. Not to be confused with a **g-string**.

Term—A collection of **Days** that entails a passage of learning at **School**. Projected 28 **Days**.

thermoprobe—A **Prop** and variety of **buttplug**; a long rectal probe that collects temperature and vital statistics. Can vibrate, electrically stimulate; communicates wirelessly with **Automatron**.

thong—*See* **tanga**.

throating—An **Obeisance**. The insertion of a **penis** into a throat. Presumes a **blowjob**; the superior throater knows how to relax the gag reflex and allow the **penis** to pass down into the throat.

Tiffany Porn Star Calendar—A **Prop** in the Kitchen featuring Tiffany photographed when she was a Porn Star and **Whore**, containing twelve explicit images/virtual reality spaces.

titter—An **Exposure**. The flashing of the **breasts** and **nipples**. Often accomplished by a **leanover, downblouse**, sideboob, or **lift-up**. The transitory titter differs from consistent **boobage** or **topless**.

topless— A "**Garment**" which doesn't exist; the absent of a top, the baring of the body above the waist. Whereas **boobage** may still involve a **Garment** above the waist, **topless** may not. Not to be confused with a **titter**. A **topless** plus a **bottomless** equals a **nude**. **Garment Count** = 0.

transude—Verb; the process of excreting **valiva**.

triple cock penetration—An **Obeisance**. Penetration of **mouth, vagina, anus**; many combinations.

upskirt—An **Obeisance**. The purview of the crotch up a skirted **Garment**. If **legs** are apart, open, or spread, upskirt may reveal undergarments or **pubage, slitage, lipage**, also **anus**, also **vagflash**.

vagflash—An **Exposure** of the **vulva** (with or without **pubic hair**), often fleetingly, but sometimes a position held for a prolonged period. Achieved by **upskirt** or **pullaside**. A vagflash does not entail the opening of the sex lips to expose the interior of the **vagina**, which is called **pinking**.

vagina—The interior of the female sex organ. The **Exposure** of the **vagina** is called **pinking**.

valiva—Female lubrication transuded from **vagina**; Index *GamerName*: body & exposures: **cream**.

Village—The town where the **School** is located and the **Game** is played.

vomit—An **Obeisance**. The offering of stomach contents. Produced by throating, gagging, drugs.

voyeue—The individual watched or looked at, possibly surreptitiously.

voyeur—The individual looking at another individual, possibly surreptitiously.

vulva—The external parts of the female sex organ. *See* **pubage, vagflash**.

Watering Can—A **Prop**. Filled with water of other fluid, can help moisten **Mudpit**, a **Cosmos**.

Whore—The second lowest **Caste** in the **Game**; *see* **Caste**. Porn Stars are of this **Caste**.

Zone, the; also zone (verb)— Sexual ecstasy by an Gamer climaxing for a sustained period of time; involves steady rapid heartbeat and breathing rate, self or assisted stimulation, penetration or not.

Index Introduction

Tips on Using the Index

§ Overall Comments and Guidance

The major topics in this Index, that is, topics that are listed at the **topmost level**, include:

Gamers
Locations
For Each *GamerName*
 Garments
 Body & Exposures
 Obeisance (including Positions)
 Other keywords (including media)
Props
Events

We will briefly explain each; followed by a short section on each:

The first and foremost Gamers are the Cosmos themselves. Indeed, all the Gamers who appear in *The Runup* get topmost level Index entries. This includes the Manifests.

Each Gamer in the Index is cross-referenced to interactions with other Gamer.

Locations ground all interactions. Interaction between two Cosmos occurs at a Location. Also, many Locations carry latent agenda; they may be public or private, cammed or not, crowded or sparse.

Three major sections are found in the index beneath each Gamer, especially for each Cosmos, since they are the main Gamers we observe.

Garments and Body & Exposures are duels in our Game and critical components of Cosmos Fate. They detail what a Gamer wears and what parts of her (or his) body is exposed.

Obeisances are also attached to individual Cosmos. Obeisances tend to be invisible; include actions, behaviors, commitments; Obeisance can include solo aspirations and activities, as well as interactions with other Cosmos/Gamers. Solo Obeisance include upskirt, pinking, masturbation; partnered Obeisance range from kissing to sexual penetrations. Many Obeisance are forbidden to Pledge Caste. The section below addresses their indexing issues.

Props tend to be physical objects; Props are not attached to Gamers, Gamers are attached to Props. This is also explained in a section below.

Events fall into roughly two categories: there are a series of specific events, e.g., the Yacht Party, the Alumni Reprise at the Nugget, The Greatest House Roar, Steph's Nugget, the Mermaid Parade, and the Mansion Open House. And then there are a series of temporally related words. These are listed in the Appendix and include Clock, Day, Term, and especially Midnight, which marks the end of the Term.

In conclusion, if we use the old Who-What-When-Where-Why model, then The Cosmos are the Gamers and the who in the equation. The Garments compliment Body Parts & Exposures and are a what. Events are when, Locations are where, Obeisance and Props mold the why—the action dynamics.

§ Indexing Gamers, Locations, and Interactions

Gamers include all the **Cosmos**, as well as Gamers who reside at the Corvette and Peacock Houses, certain Strippers at the Nugget, a few other players in other Castes. Sometimes virtual Gamers as well.

Any Gamer detailed in the Manifests also appears in the Index at the topmost level.

The general index format for a Gamer is:

GamerName: *selectWord:* Description (Location Day)

where *selectWord* might be another GamerName, a Location, Prop, Event, Obeisance, Garment, or "body & exposure" (e.g., Tiffany: dildo).

If the *selectWord* is a Gamer then there are most likely two index entries so that each Cosmos is indexed by the other Cosmos:

"*GamerName1: GamerName2:* Description (Location Day)"

"*GamerName2: GamerName1:* Description (Location Day)"

e.g.

"Babs: Molly: Description (Location Day)"

"Molly: Babs: Description (Location Day)"

Sometimes *GamerName2* is eluded and the index compressed, so bi-directionality is not always present. Threesomes and more complex relationships may also have incomplete networks.

Reciprocal index references are included for all Gamers of equal Caste, and also for convenience between the Castes of Pledge and Monitor, and Pledge and Stripper. But Gamers of higher Caste, especially Mistresses, Madams, and MomCaps (and their male equivalents, Masters, Pimps, DadCaps) do not index bi-laterally with lower Castes, so indexing is consolidated with them, and not subordinates. Examples of this are found in the "Unilateral Indexing Decisions" section below.

In a situation where a number of Cosmos are in the same Location but one or two are relevant, the Index may or may not identify all Cosmos present. This can be a judgment call, and given that in a situation where all Cosmos are present that indexing each of them by each other demands many entries; here less is often more.

In addition to being indexed with each other, Gamers (Cosmos) are also indexed by their Locations, Garments, Body & Exposures, Props, Obeisance, and Events.

Locations. Each Location identified in the Location List in the Appendix that starts with a capital letter is included in this Index. All such Locations are indexed at the topmost level, as well as relative to a Gamer, so that each Cosmos is indexed by Location, and visa-versa, in other words, bidirectionally (e.g., this form: Locations are all double indexed by both Player and Location.

"*Location: GamerName*: Description (Day)"

"*GamerName*: *Location*: Description (Day)"

e.g.

"Backyard: Babs: Description (Day)"

"Babs: Backyard: Description (Day)"

Sometimes the *Location* is transposed adjacent to the Day:

"*GamerName*: Description (*Location* Day)"

"Babs: Description (Backyard Day)"

Note that the Location may be the present time reference to an event that occurred somewhere else in the past.

Interactions involve two Gamers at a Location. A solo scene involves a Gamers at a Location, but an interaction requires two (or more) Gamers at a Location. All Scenes that involve two or more Cosmos are indexed by the two players and a single location.

Subsets of this have been presented above, the full basic format is:

GamerName1: GamerName2: Location: Description (Day)

GamerName1: Location: Description (Day)

Location: GamerName1: Description (Day)

GamerName2: GamerName1: Location: Description (Day)

GamerName2: Location: Description (Day)

Location: GamerName2: Description (Day)

e.g.

"Babs: Molly: Backyard: Description (Day)"

"Babs: Backyard: Description (Day)"

"Backyard: Babs: Description (Day)"

"Molly: Babs: Backyard: Description (Day)"

"Molly: Backyard: Description (Day)"

"Backyard: Molly: Description (Day)"

Within the Index some of these references may be abbreviated, condensed, and transposed. For example, removing one level from some of the entries and placing it next to the day:

GamerName1: GamerName2: Description (*Location* Day)
GamerName: Description (*Location* Day)
Location: GamerName1: Description (Day) --unchanged
GamerName2: GamerName1: Description (*Location* Day)
GamerName2: Description (*Location* Day)
Location: GamerName2: Description (Day) --unchanged

e.g.

"Babs: Molly: Description (Backyard Day)"
"Babs: Description (Backyard Day)"
"Backyard: Babs: Description (Day)" —no change
"Molly: Babs: Description (Backyard Day)"
"Molly: Description (Backyard Day)"
"Backyard: Molly: Description (Day)" —no change

Indexing **Locations within Locations**, in the event they begin with a capital letter, are indexed at the top Index level, same as the environment that physically contains them.

Thus the Mirror in the Bunkroom is found at the topmost level; likewise, the parts of the Backyard, including the Back Landing, Doghouse, Bell, Mudpit, Post Henge, and Garage, are all topmost level index items, and not indexed within the Backyard. Among the locations in the Nugget, The Camera Lounge, Champagne Room, and Inner Sanctuary are all primary entries in the Index, although the Dressing Room is not.

§ Indexing Garments, Body & Exposures, Obeisances, Positions

Garments, the official term for all costumes and articles of clothing, are listed in a roll call beneath topmost level "Garments". This provides an overview of the costume landscape as well as clues about actions, trades, and forfeits and acquisitions. Advances Gamers can search for Garment details such as edge counts and tan lines. Garments include croptops, halters, bras, slacks, miniskirts, g-strings.

By definition topless and bottomless and nude are also indexed in the Garment department, although unlike all other Garments, they count for zero.

Garments are primarily indexed by who wears what, in the format (e.g., *GamerName:* Garments: *garment)*. Note that any reverse transcription of this ("Garments: *garment*: *GamerName*") points right back to "*GamerName*: Garments: *garment*".

Body and Exposures. Each Cosmos is indexed by their Body and Exposures. A full list of body parts and their corresponding exposures is found in the index entry "body & exposures" at the topmost level of the index. This list includes parts of the body (e.g., face, belly, legs), body marginals (e.g., hair, cream, pee), and exposures (e.g., titter, vagflash).

The index entry for an body part / exposure for an individual Gamer takes the format:

"*GamerName:* body & exposures: *bodypart:* Descr. (Location Day)"

e.g.,

"Babs: body & exposures: areolage: Description (Location Day)"

Note that "body & exposures" and "Garments" together comprise two large slugs of each Cosmos' index world; together they occupy about ¼ to 1/3 of each Cosmos index. The distinction between a "body & exposures" and an "obeisance," both of which are local to each Cosmos, may sometime be blurry, and is discussed more at the end of the Obeisance description.

Obeisance. Each individual Cosmos index may also carry one or more Obeisances; an Obeisance implies some kind of action or commitment on behalf of the Gamer. A full list of around 50 is found at "Obeisance" in the top level of the Index. Obeisances include solo teases as well as partnered sexual actions (the latter being largely forbidden to Pledge and Strippers). Solo Obeisances include breastplay, pinking, masturbation, climax, streaking, positions, and others. Partnered Obeisances include handjobs, blowjobs, vaginal sex, anal sex, creampies, facials, etc.

Again, as with Garments, note that an Obeisance is always subservient to a Gamer and are not indexed directly and are always **a** secondary index to GamerName (e.g., *GamerName*: pinking).

There exist structural difference between "body & exposures" and "Obeisance" as well as conceptual ones. Bodyparts are three levels down (e.g., *GamerName:* body & exposures*: bodypart*) whereas Obeisances are two levels down (e.g., *GamerName: obeisance*). A Body & Exposure typically identifies which part of a Pledge's body is exposed (including fleeting moments) whereas an Obeisance entails a Pledge behavior, that is, an individual (solo) action, or an interaction with another Gamer.

All Body & Exposures" are lower case; all Obeisances are lower case also, except for Pee-Cam and Piss Mouth.

Sometimes a sharp and obvious distinction exists between a Body & Exposure and an Obeisance within the Index. Sometimes the language is subtle but the distinctions are clear: the "anus" is a Body Part, whereas "anal" is an Obeisance, the act of inserting a penis into the rectum. It is less clear if "spit" is a body part or an obeisance; perhaps it is both, as it is both a noun and a verb.

It is correct that many of the Obeisance listed in the Index are behaviors forbidden for the Cosmos Pledge as well as to Strippers. One rare exception concerns sixty-nine behavior, which is forbidden to Strippers but permitted by Pledge. Likewise sharing the Double Dong is forbidden to Strippers but encouraged for Pledge. In practice Double Donging is most likely an Obeisance, however it is indexed as a Prop with its own Rules.

Positions are an Obeisance but they have indexing peculiarities.

Cosmos are required to respond to positions triads describing a body posture, e.g., "stand spread surrender" or "sit spread hands-behind-back."

The first element of the position denotes the orientation of the body (e.g., stand, sit, kneel, back, belly), the middle term the position of the legs (e.g., crossed, touching, ajar, open, spread), and the third element the deployment of the arms and hands (e.g., at sides, handbra, hands-behind-back, surrender, pinking"). See the Appendix for more details.

Unlike most Obeisance, positions are indexed two ways. The richest is beneath the Gamer (e.g., *GamerName*: positions: *positionName*) but positions are also indexed generically (e.g., positions: *positionName*).

Gamers who follow Pledge often want to compare them at different Locations and Days.

§ Themes Index Per Cosmos: E.g. Media, Conflicts, Begs, Chants

Each Cosmos index includes (in addition to the aforementioned Gamers, Locations, Garments, body & exposures, and Obeisance) additional themes for each Gamer.. These additional entries include: the Cams each Cosmos appears upon; their Front and Back Door passages, Bell soundings; and a selection of themes including "assumptions, begs, commitments, compromises, concerns, conflicts, consequences, goals, media, memories, momentum, motivation, name, and orders."

Some of these are obvious, "goals" are indeed a Gamer's goals (e.g., Kimju: goals: acquire two Garments & Opt Up).

Media includes live as well as recorded documentation, movies, pictures, stories. Titled media is cross-referenced (e.g., Tiffany: media: *Suck Fuck Facial Video*) and also media: *Suck Fuck Facial Video*: Tiffany). Indexing media is complex because there is the who-what-where-where-why at the time of the media's creation, and a different who-what-when-where-why when the media is displayed.

Conflicts between pairs of Gamers are indexed bidirectionally. During The Runup these struggles will acquire power points. Conflicts are where the power struggles and power alliances of Gamers are indexed.

There does exist a correlation between Scene names in the Index and the Scene Titles (§) in The Chapters, but the match is not a lock step. Scenes typically change when one or more Gamer(s) enters or exits, or when the Location changes.

Begs and Chants: A distinction is made between begs and Chants. Generally speaking, a beg is a spoken statement, often predicated "Ma'am, please may I..." and ending with "Ma'am" (or whatever appropriate title). The request may be stoic ("Ma'am, please let me sleep naked in the Mudpit tonight, Ma'am."), to the plaintive ("Ma'am, may it please you to shower me may I never dirty your presence, Ma'am."), even self-indulgent ("Ma'am, please may I strip naked and masturbate my Post, Ma'am."). Hornyness has risk.

A Chant often also involves spoken language, frequently it incorporates a beg, but by contrast, a Chant is often impersonal, institutionalized, and may also involve body movement."

An example of a Chant is "Please let me Pledge naked & cum be a Stripper next Term" where its extension incorporates corresponding hand movements, "titty titty, clitty clitty, hole mouth."

Another Pledge Chant is "Hot hot hot. Titters and twat. 98.6 up my anus."

In general both begs and Chants should be in quotes, since they are spoken dialog.

Chants are indexed under each Gamer (e.g., *GamerName*: Chants: 'Chant text here'), and by the Chant (e.g., Chants: 'Chant text here').

Begs are only indexed under each Gamer (e.g., *GamerName*: begs: 'Beg text here').

§ Indexing Props and Events

Props. A list in the Index at "Props" includes all the Props listed using Capital Letters on the Prop Words List in the Appendix, as well as many lower case props. In general an Upper-Case Prop is an object that may be shared among Gamers; a Pledge belong to a Prop, not the other way around.

Upper case Props include the Alabaster Flask, Cravat, Dice, Dining Room Pictures, Double Dong and Double Penetrators, Shaving Kit, Makeup Case, Pink Pages, Skeleton Keys, Tiffany Porn Star Calendar, and the Watering Can.

Because a Pledge belongs to a Prop, Upper Case Props are indexed as primary references (e.g., Watering Can: Molly).

Lower case props include many pieces of medical equipment, also buttplugs, dildos, feeding tubes, gags, and other items. They may come and go in the Game, and are earned or bestowed upon a Gamer, thus lower case props are always indexed by GamerName first (e.g., Tiffany: buttplug).

Events include roughly two categories: a) specific events such as The Greatest House Roar or the Mansion Open House, and b) time-related words and moments, including Clock, Day, Term, and Midnight.

See the "Events and Time List" in the Appendix for a list of Events, and see "Events" in the Index.

Some Events in the Index occurred in the past Term (e.g.,; the Bikini and Mudwrestling Contests). Some Events occurred in present Term during *The Arrivals*, e.g., the Figure Drawing Class and Medical Exam (D08), the Bachelor Party (D09). Events during *The Runoff* include the Yacht Party (D17), an Alumni Reprise and an Audition at the Nugget (D20), The Greatest House Roar (D21), Steph's Nugget Seduction (D23), the Mermaid Parade (D25), and the Mansion Open House (D27).

The temporally related words can provide useful searches might one need to look by "Day" or "1 Term ago." The top-level index entry to examine is "Clock" which contains a short morning and afternoon entry for each Day during *The Runup*. Midnight, one of these terms, marks the end of the Term and is scheduled on Day 28, the subject of the next book, *The Beach Day*.

Events and time-related words are also indexed unilaterally (like Props), because Events often involve multiple Gamers, so they are also the primary index (e.g., Bachelor Party: Molly). Again, the reciprocal index is not supported.

§ Unilateral Indexing & Other Index Style Decisions

Unilateral Indexing concerning Gamer Castes:
There exist a number of Gamer-Gamer relationships that, for space and other reasons, are not bi-laterally indexed. In these cases a single pointer to the primary reference may be included.

Of as matter of Index style:

While Monitors and Pledge are indexed reciprocally with themselves and all lower Castes, including Strippers, Whores and Slavesex.

Gamers of the three highest Castes—Mistresses, Madams, and MomCaps (and their male equivalents, Masters, Pimps, DadCaps)—do not index bi-laterally with lower Castes (e.g., always Game Mistress:

GamerName), never (*GamerName*: Game Mistress). In this example *GamerName* includes any Madam, MomCap, Monitor, Pledge, Stripper, or Slavesex.

Likewise, and by example one Caste lower (e.g., Madam Nurse Beautician: *GamerName*), where *GamerName* includes any MomCap, Monitor, Pledge, Stripper, or Slavesex, but never Mistress Caste. (Here understand the feminine stands in for the masculine also.)

For the House Mom el Capitan Caste (e.g., MomCap: *GamerName*), where *GamerName* includes any Monitor, Pledge, Stripper, or Slavesex, but never a Mistress nor Madam.

Indexing style for Nugget Gamers does not follow the rule that every Gamer in *The Runup* is fully indexed at the top level. The Hat Check Girl does command a topmost entry, however the Master of Ceremonies (M/C), the Maître d', the Nugget Shooter, and the Back Door Man are detailed subservient the Nugget (e.g., Nugget: Back Door Man).

However, if the any of these Nugget characters are referenced by a Gamer, they are not indexed subservient to the Nugget (e.g., Janet: Master of Ceremonies).

Finally reminding Gamers that locations inside the Nugget, including the Camera Lounge, Champagne Room, and Inner Sanctuary are all indexed top level and backpointed by *GamerName*.

Alphabetical vs. Cosmos Lineup Sequence: Gamers are reminded that the Index follow alphabetical and *not* temporal sequence. Use the Day numbers (e.g., D14) and page numbers to help sequence. Also, the alphabetical order of the Cosmos is not their Lineup order, nor reflective of the Roommate pairings.

Also note that in the names of Scenes (§ Titles), the name always begins with Gamers. And the order of the Cosmos' names always follow their "position in the Lineup" and not their alphabetical sequence. In the Cosmos House, the "position in the Lineup" sequence is: Babs, Tiffany, Robyn, Kimju, Molly, Steph, Beka, and Elle. Roommates are Babs & Tiffany, Robyn & Kimju, Molly & Steph, and Beka & Elle. In other words, a scene with Robyn & Kimju & Elle is always indexed with these three Cosmos listed in this order. And to repeat what one might expect to find in the Index, each of these three Cosmos plus the Location should all be indexed to each other.

Janet shares rank with Babs but since the Cosmos is Babs' House, Janet extends Babs the courtesy of going first, so always Babs & Janet. However, Game Mistress, Madam Nurse Beautician, and MomCap always precede Babs in a sequenced list.

Other Unilateral Indexing Decisions: The following are some of the unilateral indices; some of these are Props, some are not.

Auditions: *GamerName*
Automatron: *GamerName*
Double Dong: *GamerName(s)*
Double Penetrators: *GamerName(s)*
Hand Signs: *GamerName*
Kundalini: *GamerName*
paparazzi: *GamerName*
Zone: *GamerName*

§ The Lady-Part Words

Neither the Glossary nor the Index records Lady-Part Words.

Lady-Part Words are terms used by Cosmos to refer to their own, as well as each other's intimate body parts, including the breasts, areola and nipples, pubic hair, vulva, clitoris, anus, valiva (a.k.a. cream). They are also used to refer to sex acts including fellatio, coitus, anal, facials, etc.

Lady-Part Words are unique to each Cosmos; they range from the benign and fanciful to the vulgar and gross.

In general Lady-Part Words share the same initial letter or sound as the name of the Cosmos Pledge, except for Elle, whose Words begins with "n.". Astute Gamers recognize that although both Babs and Beka share a "B" that they have mutually exclusively Lady-Part Words: Babs begin with "ba, bd, bg, bl, bu," and Beka begins with "be, bi, bo, br".

Gamers recognize that Lady-Part Words are not always equal. Space and time are elastic. Sometimes it matters from whose mouth the terms emit, sometimes not. Some Lady-Part Words are self-referential, some are generic and professional, some flatter, and some intend to debase and vulgarize the referent. Robyn especially favors insulting talk.

The Index continues in Part 2

Due to page limitations the Index is is in a second printed volume.

The volume is title *The Cosmos: The Runup: Book II Index*

Page numbering continues unbroken from this "Part 1 of 2" volumes, as to all rules of syntax and design described above. There does exist an interstial title and copyright page before prodeeding to index.

The Runup Backstory

The *Cosmos* is a virtual reality cyber Game played at a BDSM Fantasy School. Here one finds the two-story Cosmos House, home of the Eight Cosmos gals: Monitor Babs plus Seven Pledge, Gamers all, as are you, reader-participant, in this story of power exchanges, disagreeable options, yet romance, mystery, and of course sexual tease, congress, and control.

Cosmos II: The Runup follows *The Arrivals* and details the next two weeks of the Game. Now competitions among the Cosmos begin in earnest. At the end of this Term all Pledge must acquire a new Caste: three Cosmos Pledge will Opt Up and become Monitors next Term, and four will Opt Down and become Strippers. Monitor Babs, a caste above her Pledge, has additional options.

The Eight Cosmos are the primary personalities in the Game, but they are not the only Gamers inside this rich virtual world. Gamers like you who probe from the outside will meet Mistresses and Masters, Madams and Sirs, MomCaps, Pledge from other Houses, Strippers, Whores, and only rarely a Slavesex, the lowest of the seven Castes.

Opting for the Cosmos Pledge involves a movement between Castes. It occurs when a Pledge accumulates Garments, Exposures, Props, Obeisance, and other factors. Automatron (that giant AI consuming the end of every sensor) and the Prefecture (all the watchers including you) create and enforce (or not) the Game Rules. But follow the Rules or not, the goal of the Cosmos is to play the Game. So feel your way in.

And Beware! The Cosmos House is full of tricksters like the Minxy Mirror, half screen, half reflection, sensorially interactive, and an anathema to Pledge. The School is a most unusual theme park, a destination for Gamers in quest of high-stakes sexual stimulation. Here at School, Gamers explore the arts of Kundalini, the sex force in Nature. Gamers study ways to exchange power and make love at the same time!

Yes, the story arc of *The Cosmos* borrows from the sorority initiation, a Stanton or Willie environment, Sade, love camp movies, *O,* S&M parties, ecteras. Our VR Game has its own Rules and Castes. The Cosmos Pledge play and get to know themselves. Gamers in the real world grow and experience also. Kundalini exists in all of us, and can float into consciousness not just for the Cosmos, but for any Gamers.

Some Cosmos Pledge want to Opt Up next Term; some *want* to Opt Down. Play the Game, win or lose. Some Cosmos will get what they want, some will change their minds, and some will get their Opt wrong.

Please. These Eight Cosmos struggled to be here! Begged to attend! And now that they're here? Remember, for the Eight Cosmos, there is no turning back. "In the Game stay the Game," is one of the Chants.

The Runup Backstory

www.ingramcontent.com/pod-product-compliance
Lightning Source LLC
Chambersburg PA
CBHW070534030726
47505CB00001B/40